Jerusalem falls

Also by Jack Dixon:

The Pict

Jerusalem Falls

Jack Dixon

Standing Stone Press
USA

Jerusalem Falls

Standing Stone Press is an imprint of Ridley Park Books

Standing Stone Press books may be ordered
through booksellers, or by contacting:

Standing Stone Press
www.standingstonepress.com

Because of the dynamic nature of the Internet, any
Web addresses or links contained in this book
may have changed since publication and
may no longer be valid.

This is a work of fiction. All of the characters, names, incidents, organizations, and dialogue in this novel are either the products of the author's imagination or are used fictitiously.

ISBN: 978-0-981-76713-0 (pbk)
ISBN 978-0-981-76714-7 (cloth)
ISBN 978-0-981-76715-4 (ebk)

First Edition, 2012

Ridley Park, PA
United States of America

For Karen

MY DEEPEST GRATITUDE to Rachelle Chaykin, my friend and my editor, whose valuable time and unswerving dedication made this a far better book than it otherwise would have been; to those who took the time to read the manuscript and provide me with honest criticism; to Arlene Oakley, for her thoughtful suggestions for the story line; and most of all, for Karen, whose faith in me encouraged me in ways she never knew.

"[A Templar Knight] is truly a fearless knight, and secure on every side, for his soul is protected by the armor of faith, just as his body is protected by the armor of steel. He is thus doubly-armed, and need fear neither demons nor men."

— Bernard de Clairvaux, c. 1135, *De Laude Novae Militae - In Praise of the New Knighthood*

✠ ✠ ✠

Part I

Chapter 1

The sun blazed intensely, relentlessly. Its shimmering waves turned the undulating desert dunes into a merciless furnace of glass. Thundering hooves pounded the sand as twelve hundred Templars drove their destriers into a ferocious mass of charging Mamluks, eight thousand strong. Louis spurred his stallion, brandished his sword, and clenched his jaw in anticipation of the impending impact.

The Templars fanned out as they sped toward the Mamluk army, forming an arrow that would penetrate deep into its heart, driving a wedge to split the Mamluk forces in two. The Mamluks knew it was coming, but as always, there was little they could do to defend against the brute force of the Templar charge.

Lances snapped as they found their targets, and maces wrought devastation upon the bewildered horde.

Templar sergeants and foot soldiers, two thousand in all, followed closely behind the knights. They descended upon the divided Mamluks, who had fallen into frenzied disarray under the onslaught. Their first charge successful, the knights dismounted and brought their lethal swordsmanship to bear.

The Mamluks, once the warrior slaves of Egypt, had seized power when their military strength grew to eclipse that of their Egyptian rulers. When their masters collapsed before the advance of King Louis IX's Crusade, the Mamluks had rallied and captured the French king, and ransomed him for twice the annual revenue of his kingdom. Their victory assured their dominance, and now they were the masters and guardians of Islam.

The Templars paid the ransom for the king, and the Mamluks' newfound wealth magnified their power considerably. Now the Mamluks roamed these deserts with swelling ranks, and a fierce and intractable determination to annihilate the Christian crusaders.

These Mamluks would not submit easily; their resolve was matched only by that of the Templars they faced. This battle, like all the others, would be to the death.

The din of steel on steel was deafening, and the blinding sun flashed harshly across a teeming sea of flailing, polished weaponry. Louis's scalp baked beneath the steel of his flat-topped helm and chain mail coif. He swung his sword with precision. With his battered shield, he deftly deflected the blows of long, curved Mamluk blades.

Young Louis de Garonne, the new Templar Knight, struck hard and with conviction. He dealt a fatal blow with nearly every stroke of his sword. He had long ago mastered the patience to await the superior strike, not wasting precious energy on futile strokes. He fought mostly with his shield, dodging and parrying and allowing his enemy to expend precious energy on a maddeningly fruitless offense.

The Mamluk horde had come into view suddenly, unexpectedly, as the Templar detachment topped a mountainous dune on their southward march. Scouts had reported no sign of the enemy here; these Mamluks had crept into position in the ink black darkness of the desert night's new moon. The battle-weary knights had halted momentarily at the sight and summoned the determination to launch against the waiting army. The Templar charge had prompted the Mamluks to follow suit, and the resulting collision of massive force had made the earth tremble.

Louis growled at the ache in his muscles as he hoisted and swung his razor–sharp sword. He was a fearsome, powerful knight, ferocious in battle and merciless toward his foes. Although they were far outnumbered from the start of the attack, he was pleased to see that his Templar brethren fought undaunted, with vicious, relentless fury. They were gaining slow but significant ground.

He dispatched an attacker and shifted his focus to a new opponent. The swarthy Mamluk that faced him was older than he, but bigger, and stronger. The scars that marred his bearded face, and the practiced movements of his hulking frame told of years of grueling battle. Louis held steady, evading and studying his opponent's movements. He deflected a dozen blows, all the while learning their rhythm and style. Suddenly, just as the Mamluk raised his long crescent blade to strike, Louis swung hard. His sword found its mark an inch below the Mamluk's left ear. He grimaced as he always did, involuntarily, at the feel of the rending of his enemy's flesh. The sudden and furious elation of his triumph mingled with agony over the brutal destruction of life. He felt it every time, and it fixed his features into a ghastly mask.

He stood back as the Mamluk's body crashed to the scorching sand, the severed head rolling awkwardly down the sandy slope, its turban flapping angrily.

He reached up under his faceplate to wipe sweat from his gritty eyes, and he cursed the scorching sun. He would give anything to be free of his helm, lying in the shade, and gulping cool, clear water drawn from the stream that ran through his family's estate. He shook the image from his mind. With a quick and final glance at the Mamluk's headless body, he wheeled and leapt over fallen comrades and foes, searching the bloodstained battlefield for another attacker to engage.

He had been trained for battle in the Templar tradition by some of the fiercest fighting men the world had known. He wielded his sword with unmatched deftness and skill, as if it were but an extension of his muscular body. The sword that felt so natural in his armored fist was now drenched in the blood of his enemies.

From the corner of his eye, Louis spotted another Mamluk bearing down on him from behind. He turned and crouched instinctively to meet the attack, his sword and shield to the ready. His thighs burned, and his forearms felt weighted in lead. He had lost count of the Mamluks he had felled, and fatigue was creeping slowly through his body. He shook off the strain and tensed in anticipation of the clash.

He quickly evaluated the manner of this Mamluk's advance. The Mamluk was angry. His attack was emotionally driven, reckless and imprecise. Louis was encouraged by the advantage that presented to him.

This Mamluk, like the last, was a practiced veteran of desert warfare. A jagged scar ran from his narrowed, deep-set left eye, across his thickly stubbled cheek, to just below the corner of his rigid scowl. As they engaged, despite the Mamluk's careless approach, Louis felt that he was evenly matched. He fought with all of his will, thrusting and blocking and slashing as though he were demon–possessed. The raging Mamluk gained ground.

Louis found himself backing away, increasingly on the defense. The Mamluk was relentless. Louis was nearing the edge of his ability to battle, and the very real danger of defeat. He prayed in silent desperation for strength from his God to vanquish this heathen beast. He felt panic creeping into his gut, threatening to overwhelm him.

As he felt nearest to defeat, a sudden and inexplicable calm came upon him. He sensed a strengthening presence. In the distance, in the shimmering desert heat, a beautiful and wondrous apparition took shape, beckoning for his attention. He retreated from the Mamluk's raging advance, gaining time to observe the mystical image.

The apparition spoke softly, as if it were but a breeze. Louis recognized the gentle voice and the azure eyes of the woman he most loved. She whispered to him her prayer that he would summon the strength to prevail over his enemy.

He drew desperately upon a deeply hidden reserve. He filled his lungs and drew himself up, and he abruptly halted his retreat. A flicker of surprise flashed in the Mamluk's eyes as Louis blocked a rapid succession of skilled and forceful blows. The Mamluk was caught off guard, having thought wrongly that he had won the advantage, and he faltered. For a brief moment, his focus was broken. He shifted his weight to regain his balance, and Louis reacted instantly, seizing the fleeting opportunity.

He sprang to his right and swung his blade in a blinding arc toward the Mamluk, whose black eyes widened in alarm. His blade struck deeply, mortally, into the Mamluk's side. He felt the blade cut through chain mail, and then deep into flesh, with a slight and brief resistance as ribs gave way.

The Mamluk fell, his face contorted in bewildered agony. Louis watched him fall heavily to the sand before he let his own throbbing arms drop limply to his sides. He turned to find no new attackers.

He scanned the battlefield. Sporadic flashes of a rapidly diminishing battle were scattered across the desert sand. Struggling warriors, mostly Templars, and fallen bodies, mostly Muslim, shimmered in the heat that rose from the burning sand. The clanging of steel on steel rang less loudly in his ears. He was pleased to see that his Templar brethren had weathered yet another overmatched battle, and that they would realize yet one more extraordinary triumph over the Mamluk tide that pushed relentlessly from the south.

A short distance away, a group of Templars had gathered around a kneeling Saracen, who was richly armored and of obviously high rank. The Templars had captured the Saracen general. Several of the general's men knelt around him in a hopeless effort to shield him. The Templars were about to kill them all.

As Louis watched, inspiration seized him. He shouted and ran to stop the execution. The Templars turned to him in annoyance, but as they recognized him, they lowered their swords and stepped away from their captives.

"Wait," Louis said. "Let me speak to him." He faced the general, who looked up at him in wary surprise. "What is your name," he said to the general.

"I am General Tarik 'Adin," the Saracen replied.

"General Tarik, you have a choice to make," Louis said. Tarik nodded uncertainly. "You will renounce Muhammad, the false prophet, and accept the Lord Jesus Christ as the Savior of the world. If you do so, you will go free."

The thread of hopefulness that had crept into Tarik's expression faded. "And my other option?" he said dryly.

"Is to die," Louis said.

Tarik turned his gaze to the expanse of sand, littered with carnage and drenched in blood, that stretched away to the undulating horizon. "That is no choice," he said softly. *"La alaha ila Allah. Muhammad rusulla Allah."* Louis looked to one of the Templars who understood the Saracen tongue.

"There is no god but Allah," the knight translated. "Muhammad is the messenger of Allah."

Louis nodded slowly. He studied General Tarik for a moment, wondering if it was faith or foolishness that sealed his fate. "Then die," Louis said, turning his back on the Saracen. He took a few steps, and then he turned back just as one of the Templars raised his sword. "There's another option," he said. The Templar lowered his sword for the second time with obvious exasperation.

Tarik stared blankly at Louis. It was clear that he felt mocked. "And what would that be?" he asked.

"There's something I want," Louis said. "I believe you know what it is, and I believe you can bring it to me."

"What is it that you want?"

"You know what I want. And when your men bring it to me, you will go free."

The gathered Templars beamed admiration of Louis's ingenuity.

"The True Cross," one of them whispered with deep reverence. Tarik's face clouded.

The actual cross upon which Jesus Christ was crucified had been retrieved nine centuries earlier from a cave near Golgotha, in the city of Jerusalem. The most highly venerated of all Christian relics, it was carried into the First Crusade, which it inspired to spectacular victory.

Early in the Crusades, when the Templars distinguished themselves as the most formidable of the Christian forces, they were given charge of the relic, which they carried into every battle. The True Cross became the driving inspiration for the Crusades, and it was protected in battle by the best of the Templar knights.

But tragedy struck. A hundred years earlier, in 1187, the Templars lost possession of the cross. At the Horns of Hattin, an entire crusading army was lost to the sultan Saladin, among them the bulk of the Templar force along with the cherished True Cross.

"The True Cross," Louis said to Tarik. "Bring it to me. When your men return with it, you will go free."

"*I* don't have it," Tarik said, "and I don't know where it is."

"I think you do," Louis said. He shook his head. "But if you don't, then you have only the first two options. I'm sorry to have troubled you." Louis turned again and waved to the Templars. "Carry on."

One of Tarik's men lurched forward. "Wait!" he cried. Louis turned back once more. He motioned for the man to speak. "I will bring it to you," he said. The man met Tarik's fierce glare with humble apology.

Louis nodded with satisfaction. He may well have finally recaptured that most venerated of relics. It would be an accomplishment beyond belief, for which he would be remembered for all time.

"Bring it to me," Louis said, barely restraining his excitement. "You have three days, and then your general dies." The man nodded quickly and scrambled to his feet. He grabbed another of the Saracens by the collar and pulled him to his feet, looking to Louis for permission to take him along. Louis waved them away, and they ran off across the scorching sand.

"Unbelievable," one of the Templars said.

"Do you think they'll bring it?" another asked.

"I don't know," Louis said. "He seemed loyal to Tarik. I'm hoping it was genuine, and that he's not merely stealing his own freedom."

"We'll find out soon enough," another said as they moved to bind the Saracen captives.

Louis's sword was heavy in his hand as he walked painfully away. But he smiled with warm satisfaction. The loss of the True Cross had been a heavy blow to the Templars. Its recovery would breathe new life into both the Order and the Crusade. He was going to be the one to get it back.

He scanned the endless horizon across a vast sea of reddish-gold sand, squinting against the intensity of the mid-morning sun. He closed his eyes and let the image fade.

Chapter 2

THE IMAGE FADED, and Louis allowed his mind to drift away from the sweltering battlefield, and back to the sunlit pasture in which he stood, a twelve–year–old clutching a wooden sword, panting from exertion and savoring a cooling breeze. He stood among gently swaying grass not far from the edge of a pleasant, gurgling stream.

He was satisfied with the outcome of his latest battle. He gazed into the cloudless sky and inhaled deeply; he so loved the familiar smell of the springtime Languedoc air.

He raised his arm to the sky, holding his worn wooden sword aloft in a triumphant salutation to God. Its form was a silhouette against the brilliant summer sky. The sight of it stoked his burning passion and nurtured his pious pride, and fed his unceasing yearning for the future.

The sword was fashioned in the Templar style. Its splintered blade and polished pommel told of countless imaginary battles against the beeches, the junipers, and the massive stones that stood as Muslim warriors. These infidels, mute and resolute, had fallen to that sword time and again.

Louis grinned at the skill with which he fought his private battles among the undulating waves of thick, green meadow grass. He knew that one day his victories would be real, once he had fulfilled his Templar destiny, once he had become an invincible crusading Knight of the Temple, a Poor Fellow-Soldier of Christ and of the Temple of Solomon. And, oh, how he loved the sound of that glorious name.

He lowered his sword and walked to a spot in the shade of a towering oak. The branches of the majestic tree hung protectively over the water that rushed toward the Aude River. He sat on a rock at the edge of the stream and dangled his feet into the water's coolness, stroking the blade of his cherished sword. It was a gift from his uncle, a distinguished Templar, who had carved the sword himself from a cypress slab somewhere in the Kingdom of Jerusalem.

He cast his gaze into the cool, clear water. He willed the reflection to remain his favorite image: that of the fervent, battle-hardened warrior of God, in chain mail coif, his eyes afire with the passion of his unyielding convictions.

How he longed to be that Templar Knight, fighting so bravely and so well for the Church he adored, defending the Kingdom of Jerusalem for his God. But alas, here he remained in spite of his yearning, a twelve-year-old boy among the rolling hills of the verdant Languedoc, dreaming of the glory of Crusade.

He sighed and placed his hand on the head of a small, black, shorthaired terrier that had trotted over to sit beside him at the stream. The terrier watched him now with curious, attentive eyes. Louis gazed into the stream at the battle-worn face that reflected back at him from the rippling surface. He wondered if his face would look like that when he'd grown into a battle-hardened Templar.

"It's done, Max," he muttered, exhausted. "Another battle won. Another heathen horde vanquished for the glory of God's Kingdom." He smoothed a wrinkle on his doeskin breeches and straightened his linen shirt across his slender, developing shoulders.

"Yet one more victory over the Muslims, Max. One more blow for Jerusalem!" Maximilian tilted his head to one side with an affectionate look of approval. "One day, the entire Holy Land will be Christian once again. We'll build God's Kingdom there yet, no matter how long it takes. There will be no more conflict, no more fighting – only peace...God's peace." Louis gave his attentive companion a determined look. "I'll be a part of that," he proclaimed, "unless Uncle Willem finishes the fight before I have the chance to join him! I'll fight beside him to the death for Jerusalem, if I must!"

Max looked suddenly into the distance as a startled hare sprang from its camouflaged hole and raced across the field. Its path blurred as it moved through the gently swaying grass. Max wagged his tail at the sight, but he knew well the futility of chasing the fleeing hare. Louis watched the hare too, and he wondered what had stirred it from its nest.

"Father thinks I'm idealistic," he said idly, still gazing after the rabbit, now long gone. "He's always said that, as if it were a bad thing. Mother says I'm young and naïve. But I'm not! I'm smart for my age," he said defiantly, "and I think I've learned a thing or two by now!" He looked closely into Max's eyes. "You don't think I'm idealistic or naïve, do you Max?"

Max placed a reassuring paw on Louis's knee and nuzzled his hand.

"I didn't think so," Louis said, reassured. "You're my best friend in the world, Max. You know me better than anyone does."

He thought quietly to himself, and then he reconsidered.

"Well, I have to admit...I do like Colette quite a lot, too. I hope you don't mind that, Max."

Max wagged his tail at the sound of Colette's name.

"You like her quite a lot too, don't you, boy?" he said. He scratched the hollow behind Max's ear. Max closed his eyes, enjoying the affection.

Colette's father, Jacques Marti, was Louis's mother's older brother. Colette was a year younger than Louis, and his favorite companion. They were as close as brother and sister.

Almost as much as he longed to be a Templar, Louis cherished his cousin's love, and the time they spent together. His love for his family rivaled his dreams. A Templar life would take him away from them, of course. It was a price he was willing to pay. But in moments that shamed him, he wondered if he might forsake his dream, his commitment to God, to remain among them, to revel in the warmth of all he knew.

He winced at the sharp and familiar twinge of guilt. He cursed himself silently, and he forced the whimsy out of his mind. He instinctively traced a small cross at his forehead with his right thumb, and then he repeated the sign against his lips and over his heart. He accompanied the gesture with a silently mouthed prayer.

May Christ be ever in my mind, on my lips, and in my heart. God give me strength, he prayed. Louis shuddered at his single source of self-reproach. Such selfishness was unbecoming a Templar knight, and he would entertain it no more, he told himself yet again.

Max stood and shook his head hard, his ears flapping loudly. It was his signal to Louis that it was time to play. Max glanced around, searching for a suitable fetching stick.

"All right, boy," Louis sighed, "get the stick." Louis took the stick from Max's grip and threw it hard to give Max a distance to run. He turned back and gazed into the rippling stream.

A movement far across the field caught Louis's attention, from the corner of his eye. He turned toward it and squinted in the sunlight. He caught a glimpse of wavy reddish-blond hair as it disappeared into the privet and scrub oak that lined the forest's edge.

Max veered from his track toward the stick and headed toward the movement. He slowed, and then stopped, a front paw raised mid-step, his eyes fixed intently on the brush.

After a moment, Max turned from the disturbance and headed back toward his stick. Louis turned back to the stream. He shook his head and muttered to himself.

Tenants, he thought. They should be working, and not skulking around in the woods. That thought made him wonder for a moment what it must be like to be a serf or a tenant, who had little free time and no possible dreams of seeking the glory and the honor he would realize. He shook his head and gave brief thanks to God.

He tossed the stick idly until Max grew slower on his returns, and they finally headed toward the de Garonne house just beyond the nearest hill. The sun cast his shadow longer to the east, and it rippled across the green and golden grain as he bounded toward home, his faithful hound at his heels.

Chapter 3

THE SOUND OF COMMOTION echoed through the trees just as Louis approached a familiar sharp bend in the road that would take him to the dusty, rutted drive of his family's estate. He strained to hear. Strident voices mingled in discord, and the loudest of them was his father's.

Raimon de Garonne was not in the habit of raising his voice, but he was doing so now, in a tone of adamant defiance. The tone alarmed Louis. He wondered what had inspired his father to such distress.

He peered over the stone wall that bordered the estate, through the branches and the brush, to the clearing between the stables and the solid stone house. Beyond the clearing was the kitchen, but Louis could not see it for the crowd.

Half a dozen men of the Church, and more than twenty soldiers of the French king filled the clearing. Raimon stood before them, flanked by two powerful men-at-arms, waving his hands in the air and protesting the clearly unwelcome intrusion. Servants had gathered to watch from the shadows of the undercroft of the house.

Louis veered from the road and hopped over the stone wall. He raced through the brush toward the edge of the clearing on the back side of the wooden stables, until he was out of sight of the gathering. Max bounded after him, his tail wagging wildly. When Louis got to the clearing, he ran to the stable. He crouched behind it, peering around the corner at the disturbance.

He heard more clearly now the exchange between his father and the churchmen. He squinted his eyes, listening intently.

"It's only an inquiry," said the ranking churchman. He was a Dominican, wearing a heavy black cloak over the pure white habit of the order. "I don't understand your defensiveness; it only raises my curiosity further. I should think you'd be more welcoming to men of God."

"I'm offended by the implication of the reason for your visit," Raimon said. "What have I to do with men of your particular vocation? My standing in the Church is pure."

"I have no doubt," the Dominican said deferentially. "I'm simply here to ascertain facts and clear up misunderstandings, and not to find fault or dispense punishment. We're not here to pass judgment; we merely have questions that quite clearly warrant answers."

Raimon lowered his head and glared at the Dominican. "I'm familiar with the nature of your inquiries," he said. "Speak your questions now, for all to hear. I'll answer what I can, and then see you off."

It astonished Louis to hear his father speak in such a manner to a friar of the Dominican Order. It was clear that the Dominican was equally astounded. His mouth had dropped in disbelief, but he quickly regained his composure.

"Sir Raimon," he said, "you well know that I could have you arrested, and that we could discuss this in a...less bucolic setting. I'm curious about the source of your enmity toward me, and I'm wondering if it isn't cause enough to do just that. Perhaps you might enlighten me, and rather quickly." The Dominican's posture had grown more menacing, as had his tone.

Raimon visibly quelled his emotions. He relaxed a bit. He regarded the friar coolly, and then he nodded and pointed toward the soldiers.

"A Black Friar traveling about this country under escort of the French king's men," Raimon said, "cannot fail to inspire misgivings and invite scorn. You are aware of that. I am an honest man, Friar. I'll not mislead you with false admiration or feigned acquiescence, and I don't think that should offend you if you are humble. The inquisitor's reputation precedes him. Surely, my wariness of you would not be deemed heresy."

"Your contempt toward men of the Church could be interpreted so," the friar said.

Raimon nodded thoughtfully. As if in response to Louis's silent will, he suddenly relaxed his shoulders and adopted a more amiable tone. He waved a dismissive hand and shook his head quickly, as if he'd just recovered his senses.

"Forgive me, brother," he said, suddenly conciliatory. "I've forgotten my manners. You are welcome in my home, of course, and I'll gladly answer your questions. I've had a great deal on my mind, and my worries seem to have gotten the best of me. I pray you might overlook my rudeness."

The friar stared at Raimon intently, as if he were weighing his destiny. He did not seem inclined to weigh in his favor.

"Very well," the Dominican finally said, dryly. "Where is your wife?"

"My wife? What have you to do with her?"

"I have questions specifically for her."

Raimon stiffened again. "*I* will answer anything you like," he said. "You'll leave my wife well enough alone. I will speak for her."

"That will not suffice," the Dominican said. He motioned for the French captain to locate Louis's mother. "My questions have to do with her."

"No," Raimon said. His voice was guttural and growling, and it stopped the captain in his tracks.

Louis became aware of the distant pounding of horses' hooves coming from the north, from Carcassonne. The others had heard it too; they turned to look toward the sound, the soldiers hesitating in their assignment. The Dominican started almost imperceptibly, but he did not lose track of his purpose; he waved impatiently for the captain and his men to proceed.

Raimon peered into the distance to identify the approaching troop. As it came into view, his expression changed from one of heightened alarm to quiet satisfaction. Louis looked hard for the source of his gladness.

He gasped. Templars! There were at least eight knights on powerful warhorses, their brilliant white surcoats with embroidered crimson crosses unmistakable even from the distance, and as many as twenty sergeants, whose black surcoats starkly contrasted those of their brethren knights.

In Louis's excitement, he bounded from behind the stables, his mouth slack and his eyes fixed on the approaching Templars. Raimon turned, startled by his son's sudden appearance.

"Louis!" Raimon's voice rang out across the clearing, but Louis was only vaguely aware of it, and he did not acknowledge it. "Louis!" Raimon shouted again, more stridently. Louis looked at his father then, blankly. "Where were you? Come to me!" Louis realized that his father was distressed that he had witnessed the scene with the churchmen, but he was too enthralled by the Templars to pay it proper mind. He drifted toward his father, still gazing across the fields.

Could it be? Louis wondered. He did not dare assume that Uncle Willem was among the Templars. If he did, and Willem turned out not to be among them, he would be terribly disappointed. Maybe they will have news of him, he thought. It was all he would allow himself.

His heart leapt when he spied the powerful mahogany bay stallion, his Uncle Willem's favorite courser, trotting proudly among the other Templar horses toward the house. He broke into a run to meet them.

The Templar contingent slowed as it approached the rutted drive. As it reined into the drive at a leisurely pace, every knight focused on the gathering at the house.

The appearance of the Templars transformed the demeanor of the French soldiers. They backed their mounts a few steps farther from Raimon and the friar, and gave ground to the Templars, who drew to a halt between Raimon and the Dominican.

Willem gazed calmly into the Dominican's eyes. "Brother," he said, with a terse nod. He turned to Raimon. "My brother!" he exclaimed. He dismounted and rushed eagerly to Raimon and embraced him. "How have you been? Everyone's health is good, I trust." He hesitated then, looking troubled. "But I suppose we haven't time for greetings just yet." He turned once more to the friar.

"Hello, good friar!" he exclaimed. "What brings the honor of your visit this fine day?" He sounded almost playful. "It's a social call, is it? A Black Friar come to see to the welfare of a good Christian family? That's a blessing, to be sure, but as you can see, they're all quite well." Willem gave the Dominican no opportunity to answer. "But...you have the look of an inquisitor. What purpose would an inquisitor have here, with the family of a Knight of the Temple, a sworn servant to His Holiness the Pope? Perhaps you are a legate from His Holiness, conveying thanks for the many offerings my brother-in-law has made to his parish?"

Louis wanted badly to run to Willem and embrace him, as he normally did upon his arrival. He understood, though, that now was not the time for that.

The monk regarded Willem coolly, and he glanced at the Templars with barely concealed disdain. "I'm pursuing questions raised in a hearing several months ago at Toulouse," he said. "I am Fra Diego Vañez de Mondragón. I am a protector of the Church, a friend to faithful Christians, and a threat only to the enemies of God's good work. And yet, I am made to feel unwelcome here." Mondragón looked quizzically at Willem and jerked his head toward Raimon.

Willem nodded thoughtfully. "Yes," he said. "That's to be expected, is it not? But never mind that; how can we be of service?"

"As you know," Mondragón said icily, "our work of returning

stray sheep to the fold is far from finished here in the Languedoc. Of course, I must pursue every lead toward the conclusion of that mission, or I should not have assumed it in the first place. That often means disturbing the local nobility, as much as I am loath to do so." He said the last part with mock deference.

Willem matched the friar's discourtesy. He raked the estate with searching eyes. "Well…I don't see any sheep wandering about here, Brother Mondragón. Are you certain you're on the right trail?"

Mondragón shook his head with impatience. He turned to Raimon. "May we retire to the hall, so that we may speak more constructively?" His demeanor, though forced, had turned conciliatory, almost pleading. Raimon gazed back at him, appearing hesitant to concede. Willem nodded almost imperceptibly, and Raimon turned on his heel, motioning to the friar to follow him. The soldiers moved to dismount, but Willem held up a hand to stop them.

"Only the friar," Willem snapped. The captain looked uncertain, but the friar nodded his reassurance as he followed Raimon to the house. The friar's secretary fell in behind the friar, as his attendance was a matter of course. Willem did nothing to stop him; he turned to follow them, beckoning to one of the Templars to join him.

Louis could contain himself no longer.

"Uncle Willem!" he cried, breaking into a run. Willem turned to face him, and the dismounted Templar stopped to wait. With a broad smile, Willem knelt and held his arms out to receive Louis, who threw his trembling arms about his uncle's neck.

"Louis! How has my valiant young knight been keeping himself in my absence? It seems ages since I saw you last."

"Ages, Uncle, yes! I'm just fine, thank you…but so much happier now that you're here. I was thrilled to see Apollonius among the knights' chargers." Willem was beaming, but he seemed anxious to get to the hall. Louis glanced to the top of the stairway as the last of the friar's cloak disappeared into the doorway. "I'll see you after, then," he said, backing away and nodding toward the stair.

Willem stood and extended his right hand toward Louis, palm upward and fingers relaxed, and then he brought the hand swiftly to the hilt of his sword, with a slight bow. Louis returned the Templar salute, as his uncle had taught him long ago, and he watched proudly as Willem turned to mount the stair. A stable hand came out of the undercroft to tend to the visitors' horses, beckoning to another of the servants to assist him.

Louis stood staring after his uncle. He wanted desperately to follow him, to slip into the hall unnoticed and hear whatever discussion would take place there. He knew it had to be important, and if it were important enough he'd be learning of it soon enough. But he wanted to know now. On the other hand, his father would surely be vexed to discover him eavesdropping.

"Louis!" his mother called from the direction of the kitchen. His heart sank. He looked longingly at the door at the top of the stair. He had briefly decided to follow, but now he was thwarted. He turned toward his mother, who beckoned him.

"Yes, mother," he said, trying to hide his disappointment.

"Go and tell the steward to fetch refreshments for our guests," she said. Now his heart leapt; the steward was in the hall, and now he had a reason to go there, too. He could take his time with the errand, and perhaps get a glimpse of the unfolding drama. He nodded to his mother and bounded toward the stair.

A chilling thought gripped him, and he halted and turned back to Marie. "You must stay here, mother," he said in a voice hushed by grave concern. "Stay here until they've left."

Marie nodded, and Louis knew that was what she had intended. He gave her a grim smile and resumed his mission.

He pushed into the hall as quietly as he could. He didn't want to interrupt too abruptly, but more than that his aim was to enter undetected and take his time drawing the steward's attention, and satisfy his curiosity. He stood for a moment in the shadows by the door.

The steward knelt by the fireplace, stoking the smoldering coals to revive the fire for the guests. Raimon, Willem, and the churchmen were taking places about the heavy oak dining table, a massive board fastened by wooden pegs to a pair of sturdy oak trestles.

"And so, Fra Mondragón," Willem said cordially, "what is it exactly that brings you to my family's humble estate?"

Mondragón regarded Willem quietly for a moment, then glanced at Raimon before he answered. He spoke curtly, but with a casual tone. "Your sister," he said. Willem exaggerated a dubious expression in response. He gave Raimon a skeptical look and shook his head.

"My wife," Raimon said firmly, "is a devout woman, loyal to the Church."

"Which is why I need to speak with her," Mondragón said, "to clear up confusion that has come out of an inquiry at Carcassonne. There are questions, and that is all."

"What questions?" Willem asked.

"They are questions for your sister."

"Asked in the name of the pope," Willem replied. "As an ordained protector of the Church like yourself, I'm entitled to a response."

Mondragón's eyes narrowed, and he reluctantly conceded. "Very well," he said. "As you know, during an inquiry, an accused heretic will often implicate associates in the process of their repudiation. Often, the elucidation of their descent into heresy alone will bring to our attention others who may have shared their lapse."

Raimon opened his mouth as if to protest, but Willem waved impatiently and spoke first.

"Yes, yes, of course," he said. "Again, what has that to do with us?"

"It has to do with François Marti and his wife," the Black Friar said, "and therefore, also with their daughter..." Mondragón paused and gave Raimon a meaningful look. "...Madame de Garonne...and also, of course, with you, Sir Willem."

Willem appeared to pale almost imperceptibly. He showed no fear; Louis had never seen the smallest evidence of fear in his uncle, and to see it would have shocked Louis. But Louis sensed foreboding, if not fear, in his uncle now.

Raimon seemed only immensely irritated with the friar's implication, whatever it was. Louis wondered what it was. Suddenly, though, Louis turned to a movement to his left. He hadn't noticed the steward, Hervé, moving toward him, but here he was next to Louis, looking at him expectantly.

"Master?" Hervé whispered to Louis.

"You'll be fetching provisions?" Louis whispered back.

"Of course," the steward said. "I'm about that now." The steward seemed chagrined that his tending to his duties was not presumed. Hervé was meticulous, almost to a fault, and he took pride in his work. Louis didn't know anything about Hervé's life prior to his employment with Raimon de Garonne, but his impression was that Hervé had suffered, and was grateful for his station. Hervé was tall and gaunt, dark-skinned and balding, with a ready smile that was both warm and vaguely sad. While Hervé was unlikely to adequately defend himself in an armed confrontation, he was fiercely loyal to the de Garonne family, and he would likely die for them if necessary.

Louis smiled apologetically. "Of course," he said. He leaned toward Hervé with a conspiratorial look. "I think Mother's just a bit nervous about our visitors." He nodded toward the table. Hervé nodded, but he still seemed faintly pained.

Louis realized that his father was looking directly at him with disapproval. Willem followed Raimon's eyes and gave a start when he saw Louis. He moved around the table toward Louis.

"Sir Nephew," he said playfully, using a pet name he'd used for as long as Louis could remember, "I thought you stayed outside. What are you doing here?"

"Mother sent me," Louis said, a little defensively. Willem placed a firm hand on Louis's shoulder and steered him toward the door.

"I'm anxious to see you," Willem said earnestly, "but we must be patient." They went through the door and down the stair to where the Templars and the king's men were waiting. Louis noted that one of the Templars shot Willem an anxious glance, but it was fleeting, and Louis wondered if he had imagined it. When they got to the bottom of the stair, Willem guided Louis toward the kitchen until they were out of earshot. "There's a matter to which your father and I must attend before we can visit in peace."

"What matter?" Louis asked. He glanced anxiously back toward the house. "Why is Father unhappy with that monk?"

Willem knelt in front of Louis, his sword clanging against his mailed leggings as he stooped.

"The friar has questions," Willem said. "That's all. He's looking into some things that worry the Church, and he thinks your father is the one who can best help him with that."

"Why?"

"Because your father is a powerful man, and people talk to him, and he is aware of almost everything that ever happens in this county. He knows he can trust your father's integrity. He knows your father won't lie to him."

"But Father is angry with him, and he spoke to him as if he hates him. Does Father hate a man of the Church?"

"Your father doesn't hate anyone. It's a complicated thing to explain, Louis, but just now I have to go back to your father and talk to the monk with him, so the monk can be on his way. I'll find you when we're through." Louis smiled nervously, and Willem patted the top of his head, ruffling his wild, tawny hair. Willem stood and went back into the house.

Louis remained perplexed. His father had always demanded absolute reverence for the Church, and respect for anything connected to it. His father's demeanor toward the visiting monk had violated his own principles, and that bewildered Louis. He tried to imagine a rationale for what he'd witnessed. He'd rarely seen his father so angry; he'd never seen him cross with a man of the Church. He sensed danger in that. All the same, he'd have to wait until they were through to learn more.

He turned his attention to the Templars, whose presence had transformed the demeanor of the king's men, who had grown uncharacteristically subdued. He gazed longingly at the Templars' tunics, brilliant white with their finely embroidered crimson crosses, and the gleaming pommels of their heavy-bladed swords. Each knight cut an imposing figure in his own right, but the group of them, poised motionless and watchful astride powerful warhorses, was a formidable sight.

The knights watched casually as the king's men sat muttering nervously among themselves. It seemed to Louis that the king's men would rather be off to other errands, rather than here facing a Templar detachment and waiting for the monk to carry out his mission. Louis watched the king's men, too, wondering how it must feel when one's mere presence rendered even the king's finest soldiers timorous. The thought of it filled him with an odd satisfaction.

✠ ✠ ✠

Willem entered the great hall noiselessly. He saw that Raimon sat listening impassively as Mondragón plodded through his monologue, uninterrupted by Willem's return. Willem moved to stand behind Mondragón.

"As I have learned," the monk was saying, "François Marti had a broad reputation for geniality, even toward the basest of characters. When he showed empathy toward all, equally, even to those who were at odds with the Church, everyone apparently saw that as Christian compassion. But in light of recent allegations, I'm not so certain that's what it was. I'm wondering about his sympathies for the Cathars in particular, and his apparent ambivalence towards heresy."

Raimon paled slightly, and he closed his eyes in a silent groan.

Willem fumed, but he checked his anger with a deftness he had mastered long ago. He knew that the accusation extended to him, and toward his sister, Marie, who was clearly the reason they were here. He also knew that Mondragón had not expected him, and he wondered if his presence would restrain or encourage the monk. That would depend upon the monk's predisposition and the weight of the evidence he possessed. He sensed no malevolence, but inquisitors were typically skilled in the art of masking their malice.

"My father is dead," Willem said. His sudden voice startled Mondragón, who turned abruptly to face him. "He can obviously not answer your charge. Why would you bother to make it, unless your charge is really against me, and based on the flawed notion that soundness of faith is hereditary?" Raimon glanced appreciatively at his brother-in-law; Willem had placed himself at the center of the matter, in Marie's stead.

Mondragón's response was immediate. "Are you admitting, then, that François Marti's faith may not have been entirely sound?"

"No," Willem shot back. "I said that my father is dead, and that you should address your concerns with him in chapel. He'll no doubt be represented by the Highest Judge, at whose feet he surely sits in worship." Willem moved around to stand at the table, next to Raimon and facing Mondragón. "If some poor soul, broken beneath your hand, implicated a dead man to save his own skin, then your evidence itself is suspect, and your accusations misplaced."

Mondragón sat back and regarded Willem with placid appraisal. "I have angered you," he said.

Willem smiled widely despite his ire. He would not make this monk's job so easy. He leaned toward Mondragón with a conspiratorial air. "Heresy angers me," he said, winking. "The talk of it inspires passion in any man who has pledged his life to God, and to God's pope. It's an anger I share with you, Brother Mondragón – or so one should hope."

Raimon muffled a smile, looking away into the fireplace.

"This is really quite simple, brother knight," Mondragón said. "We can conclude my visit here with satisfactory answers to my simple questions, or we can remove ourselves to Carcassonne for a formal hearing. I had hoped to make this quick and move on."

"You're threatening to take me into custody?"

"You would resist if I did so?" Mondragón did not wait for

an answer. "You know I have that authority. But I'm here to speak with your sister. I expect compliance, and I think I'm reasonable in that. If there's no guilt, there's no reason to resist. If there's guilt, we should be doing this at Carcassonne after all." He turned to Raimon. "I encourage you to summon Lady de Garonne so that I may conclude my business here."

Willem and Raimon exchanged glances, and both men shrugged in resignation.

"Very well," Raimon said.

"You won't further your cause by questioning her," Willem said. "She has nothing to offer you but her innocence." Mondragón gave a skeptical nod, and Raimon motioned to Hervé, who left to check on the search for Marie and to see to her well-being. "It's interesting to me," Willem continued, "that men like you really believe that you're advancing the cause of the Church, coming to places like this with a heavy hand, casting suspicion and fear among faithful Christians. It's hard enough to gain support for the real battle, the one where good men risk life and limb fighting heathens in defense of Jerusalem. Your inquisition, in its zealousness, only erodes what little support remains. Do you not see that?"

"I'm saving souls," Mondragón said.

"And here, you think you see a soul that needs saving, based on no evidence but the false witness of a desperate man. And this, in spite of years of heartfelt, indisputable support for the Church and its clergy, on the part of my sister and her husband, as well as my own personal sacrifice defending Jerusalem from the Saracens. Do you not see why your presence inspires distrust?"

The monk sat quietly for a long moment, considering Willem's argument. Finally, he raised his wine goblet as if he were inspecting it in the shaft of sunlight that pierced the room through a window on the southern wall. He nodded slowly.

"Very well," he said. "Your point is taken. But you must be aware of the allegations, and take appropriate measures to assure the Church of the purity of your faith. If we took this to trial, you'd surely serve a penance; it would help to dissipate suspicion were you to take that upon yourself without a trial. Be sure that Marie Marti de Garonne also takes heed, for she has raised suspicion in her own right."

"How?" Raimon snapped. Mondragón seemed startled by his tone.

"Her manner with the clergy is aloof," he said, "to the degree that some consider the charges entirely plausible. She will want to remedy that."

"Let me understand this," Raimon said. He was visibly annoyed. "You suspect my wife of heresy because she's demure in her behavior in the presence of clergy? How would you have her behave, friar?"

"You underestimate me, Lord de Garonne," Mondragón said. "Let me be clear: François Marti associated with people who have since confessed the Cathar heresy. Each of the heretics acknowledged their accomplices, and Lord Marti was implicated. As you well know, not even the family of a heretic is exempt from the obligation to expose the heresy. Failure to do so invites suspicion." He paused and glared meaningfully at Raimon, and then shrugged with an air of finality. "You have *all* invited suspicion. Lady Marie was closest to her father, and so she, most of all, should have known about his heresy and brought it to the attention of Church authorities." He paused again, as if considering his next words. "This is not my doing."

The door burst open, and the king's captain pushed into the hall, guiding Marie ahead of him with her arm gripped firmly in his chain-mailed fist.

Raimon lurched from his seat. "Take your hand off her!" he bellowed. The man released his grip and faltered in his steps. He averted his eyes from Raimon's rage.

Willem stood and walked around the table to the captain, fixing him with a piercing glare. He stood before the captain with his hand on the pommel of his dagger, and their faces inches apart.

"By the wounds of Our Savior," Willem said, seething, "if you ever again lay a hand on my family, it will be the last mistake of your life."

The captain paled before the imposing, infuriated Templar. He looked as though he might collapse. He bowed weakly and turned to leave.

"Stay," Willem growled. He waved angrily toward a bench by the wall. "Stay and take heed."

Marie stared at Willem, horrified, as though he had cursed God Himself. The friar watched calmly, noting every detail. Willem set his jaw and gently guided Marie to a seat between Raimon and himself, where he motioned her to sit. Willem and Raimon stood looking at the friar with an intensity that he had clearly not expected. He shifted uncomfortably, though his face retained its mask of authority.

"Is this soldier's coarseness the manner in which you will conduct your affairs for the duration of your assignment to this region?" Willem asked. "For if it is, I assure you, your tenure will not be long."

Mondragón cast a glance at the captain and gave a perfunctory wave. "The king's men," he said with feigned exasperation. "They're trained for violence. It's distasteful, I agree. Try as I might, I cannot seem to make them understand that those we mean to save are not the enemy, but rather innocent sheep trapped in the snare of the enemy. Unlike the Saracen devils, our heretics are but fallen Christians, who may yet be returned to God's graces."

"Mind yourself, friar," Willem said evenly. "And know that while you tarry here among good people of God, barking up empty trees and casting lanterns into sunlit meadows, your lost sheep roam ever farther from your zealous grasp."

Mondragón stared quietly into Willem's eyes. Willem knew that he was calculating, assessing, and taking note of all that transpired. Tension made the moment seem like hours before the Dominican friar finally resumed a practiced sneer and broke his steady gaze.

"What is this about?" Marie asked. She looked anxiously from one man to the other.

"It's nothing, Marie," Raimon said.

Mondragón gave Marie an appraising look, his eyes narrowed. "What can you tell me, Lady Marie, of the rumors I have heard regarding you and your brother? And about your parents?" He said the word *parents* with meaningful inflection.

"Since I'm not aware of the rumors," Marie said calmly, "I can hardly have anything to say about them."

"There are rumors about your parentage."

"Friar, I'm surprised that you'd trouble yourself with idle talk," Marie said. "What would gossip about my parentage have to do with you? If we are to go chasing after gossip and rumors, many monks might find themselves answering indelicate questions about such things as celibacy among the clergy, and other vexing scandal."

Mondragón blanched. He pursed his lips in restraint. Willem noted that he was shrewd enough to keep his emotion from distracting him.

"I suspect that even there," Mondragón said coolly, "there may lie cause for suspicion. Be assured that in the face of such cause, I would investigate it with equal thoroughness." He cast a reptilian gaze upon Marie, and his voice turned icy. "Your irreverence toward the clergy, Lady Garonne, is noted."

"Oh, it's not irreverence, Friar..." She looked to Raimon for an introduction.

"Diego," Raimon said.

"Friar Diego," Marie said, smiling. "It's not irreverence. To the contrary. It's just that I should think that our efforts to serve God would rise above the pursuit of idle gossip—"

"You're telling me how to serve God?"

"I'm telling you that I give little credence to disparaging conjecture, about the clergy or anyone else, especially from questionable sources. I should think you would do the same. If there are rumors about me, they were conceived by people who have not the courage to speak plainly in my presence, and who are therefore unreliable at best."

"I have to ask," Mondragón said. "I'd be remiss to ignore an allegation of heresy."

"Heresy!" Marie exclaimed. "That's what this is about?" She laughed in nervous disbelief.

"Yes," Mondragón said. "Your father's heresy. You have knowledge of this?"

"Surely, he has not been accused," Marie said in disbelief.

"Were your parents heretics, Marie?" Mondragón pressed.

"That's enough!" Willem snapped. "You've asked her, and she answered."

Mondragón was about to protest when Raimon cut him off.

"As I was saying, Marie," Raimon said, "it's nothing. Our *guests* are about to take their leave." He made no effort to veil his contempt.

"You've overstayed your welcome," Willem said. He was tempted to eject the friar forcibly from the hall.

"My apologies," Mondragón said, raising his hands in a conciliatory gesture. "I truly mean no offense. As a man of God yourself, Sir Willem, you understand that we must do what we can, to the extent that we can, and leave no stone unturned in our pursuit of God's perfect will. I'm following my convictions, and nothing more. If I am wrong, then so be it. Time will make that clear." He drained his goblet and stood from the table. "If, as you say, we serve the same God, then you cannot be offended by my zeal. By my ignorance, perhaps, or my unfamiliarity with the facts of this matter, but not by my intentions or my zeal. You'll not hold that against me, I trust."

Willem stared stolidly at Mondragón. He wanted desperately for the infuriating monk to leave, and he would do just about anything to make him do so. Raimon made an ominous sound that moved him to a quick response.

"Of course not," he said. "It's nothing more than an unfortunate misunderstanding." Raimon stared incredulously at him. "On my honor, Fra Mondragón, I assure you that neither I, nor my sister, have ever had reason to doubt our father's piousness. He was a good man, and a devout Christian, as is everyone in this room. I trust that as you spend more time in this country and learn more of my family's reputation, you'll come to share in the respect to which we are accustomed. In the meantime, we understand your intentions, and we thank you for your efforts on the part of all pious Christians."

Raimon looked at his brother-in-law with an expression of perplexed admiration, as if he did not know whether to protest or to concur. He kept his thoughts to himself and bowed curtly to the friar. Together, Willem and Raimon escorted the friar and his secretary to the door. The captain stood from the bench by the wall, stubbornly avoiding Willem's glare.

As the door closed and the inquisitor's steps receded, Willem and Raimon exchanged an anxious glance.

Chapter 4

The visiting knights sat around the main refectory table on the east side of the great hall, closest to the fireplace, in which a roaring fire blazed. Louis sat proudly next to his uncle, their backs to the fire. His father and mother sat on the other side of Willem, and the knights took up the remaining space at the table.

The sergeants crowded a much larger table on the west side of the hall, closest to the door. They drank their ale and laughed among themselves, quietly, so as not to disturb the peace.

The knights shifted in their places on the long wooden benches to gaze appreciatively as Hervé and two servants came into the hall bearing plates of bread and ham, and jugs of warm spiced wine. Satisfied murmurs greeted the delicious aromas that filled the room as dinner arrived.

Louis stared in wide-eye admiration at the solemn, powerful men. As Hervé served dinner, Willem and Raimon talked among themselves, and the knights listened quietly. Louis mimicked the refinement of Willem's bearing and expression.

"The Dominican is casting a wide net," Willem was saying.

"It's the Inquisitors' way. He'll want to show that he is needed here, that his assignment is important, and not in vain. It's the enthusiasm of an ambitious neophyte, and not much more than that. In time, his judgment will find balance, and his aspirations will grow less fervent. He'll realize the practicality of more amiable relations with the populace."

Raimon seemed doubtful. "I do understand his mission," he said. "He was out of place here."

"He'll come to understand that," Willem insisted.

Louis saw that the friar's visit troubled his mother deeply. Her distress, in turn, troubled him, as did his father's inhospitality toward the Dominican. It was contrary to the teaching of the monks at the abbey, that the Dominicans were defenders of the faith, and due infinite reverence. He could not understand why this Dominican troubled his parents. He knew instinctively, though, not to voice his thoughts. In any event, he wanted the talk of the monk to end, and Willem's tales of Templar battles to begin. He awaited an opportunity to nudge the conversation in that direction.

His mother did it for him; she seemed equally anxious to shift the conversation.

"This is a pleasant surprise," she said, interrupting. She smiled warmly. "I didn't expect you, my brother. You didn't send word." Her expression was faintly quizzical. Willem turned to smile at her.

"No one expected my visit," he said. "It was a surprise to all of us...myself included. I hadn't expected to be back in Europe for at least another year."

"What brought you back?" she asked.

Willem's eyebrows bunched up as if he were working out an answer. It took him a moment. "The situation in Jerusalem is... intriguing at the moment. It's sometimes difficult to entirely understand, and even more so to explain." He paused and glanced at the other knights. "We're troubling over our future course with regards to the Mongols and the Mamluks."

"We're still at peace with the Mamluks, are we not?" Raimon

asked.

"Yes, for now," Willem said. "The treaty ends next year. It's hard to say what will happen after that. Muslim attacks on pilgrims have increased dramatically, especially over the last two years. It's unacceptable, but we deal with it delicately so as not to shatter the truce; we're not prepared to resume open hostilities, and we won't be, without increased support from Europe."

"You don't get enough support from the pope?" Marie asked.

"We get *no* support from the pope, as of late." There was an unpleasant edge to Willem's voice, and it amplified Louis's uneasiness. "It seems that Nicholas's attention has been dominated by arbitrating Franciscan rifts, renovating palaces, strengthening his own political position, and building his nest at Soriano. He gave not the slightest response to yet another overture from the Mongols. Jerusalem seems at times to be the least of his concerns."

"The Mongols?" Marie said. "What have the Mongols to do with anything?"

"It's complicated, Marie," Willem said. "The Mongols have wanted for years to join forces with us against the Mamluks. The bulk of Mongol strength is engaged in Asia, where Kublai Khan is consolidating his hold. Their western armies are not quite evenly matched with the Sultan Kala'un's Mamluk forces. Our presence in Jerusalem is the only thing keeping the Mamluks from driving the Mongols back into Persia. The Mongols are the only thing keeping Kala'un from turning his entire Mamluk force against us and driving us into the sea."

Louis watched as Uncle Willem's Templar brethren quietly ate their food and drank their wine. They betrayed no tension, no anger, no disconsolation – not the slightest indication that Willem's dire tale caused them any anxiety. Louis marveled at their composure. They took grave danger in stride. *I'm going to be like that,* he resolved. *Stoic and brave.* He was struggling, though, with the idea of peace with the Saracens.

"What do you do when there's a peace treaty?" he interjected. Raimon shot him an admonishing look, and even Willem seemed taken aback by the interruption. Louis's face reddened, but he persisted. "How does that help us to keep Jerusalem?" The idea of peace with the Saracens made little sense to him. The Templars were in Jerusalem, after all, to free it from infidels, not to make peace with them. They were there to defend God's kingdom against the non-believers, not share it with them. He didn't understand how a peace treaty with God's enemies could accomplish that. He also didn't like the idea of the Crusaders depending on the cooperation of the Mongols for success in their mission.

Willem considered the question for a moment. He looked thoughtfully at Louis, and smiled. "That's a good question," he said. "An effective strategy has both offensive and defensive elements. In the long run, a good army uses both." Louis nodded his understanding. "The Crusading forces have been weakened by protracted hostilities, and punishing battles. Even those we've won have been costly. At the moment, it's in our best interests to avoid battle, at least for a time, and focus on recruiting and training, and reinforcing our positions. There's a time to rush into battle, and a time to hold back and plan, or recover, or build strength. A good warrior recognizes the appropriate time for each."

"But the Saracens reinforce, too, don't they?" Louis said. The other Templars exchanged anxious glances with Willem. "Aren't they growing stronger, too?" he added.

"Not necessarily," Willem said. "There's turmoil among the Mamluks; they fight among themselves for power, and at the same time they face a major threat from the Mongols. They need this peace even more than we do."

"Then why don't we attack them now?"

"You think deeply about this, don't you?" Willem said. "That's exactly the reason I'm here now. If we joined with the Mongols now, while Mamluk leadership is in contention and the Mongols are pressing them from the east, we could push the Mamluks back to Egypt for at least a decade, perhaps for good. But if we don't, and the Mongols turn back, we'll face the brunt of the Mamluks' strength, fierce after successfully repelling the Mongols. Kala'un appears to be the leading contender for the sultanate; he seized it from Baibars' sons, and he's battling the

Governor of Damascus to keep it. Their internal strife is distracting them both from us and from the Mongols, but not for long. The Grand Master, William de Beaujeu, believes that now is the time to strike." He paused for a moment and looked thoughtfully at the other knights. "Not everyone agrees with him."

While Louis understood that there were complicated issues surrounding the Templar mission, he didn't think they should allow that mission to be muddled by them. It seemed to him that the Crusaders had lost their way. It was clearly the right timing for an offensive.

"It just seems to me that you're not doing what you went there to do," he said in a sulky tone. "I remember your stories of your first days as a Templar." He brightened a bit at the memory. "You fought great battles and laid fierce sieges alongside great kings and generals. I loved those stories. Would you tell them to me again, Uncle? Tell me more about those days?" He realized that he had stood from his seat in his excitement.

"Louis," his mother said, "sit, dear. Catch your breath. Give your uncle a moment to relax before you press him into tales of battle."

Louis looked sideways at his mother, and then nodded in reluctant compliance. He looked at Willem's handsome, travel-weary face. It occurred to him that Willem looked much older since he'd seen him last, though it had only been just over a year.

Marie said, "Uncle Willem was telling me that they've nearly finished the new transept and choir at the cathedral of Saint-Nazaire. He'll be going there from here, to meet with archbishops on his way to see King Philip. I'd like to hear more about that – both the cathedral, and the mission to see the king."

The king! Louis looked at Willem with yet greater awe. That was quite something, he thought, but he also knew that his mother was avoiding the inevitable tales of battles among the desert dunes, Saracens converting or dying in the sun, and pilgrims escorted safely to the holiest of sites to seek penance and holy relics, the prizes of their spiritual quest. It annoyed him that she was unimpressed by such things, and he found talk of cathedrals and choirs quite dull in comparison.

"New transepts!" he said, in mock astonishment, as if it were the best news he'd heard in a very long time. He turned to Willem. "They must be grand," he said, solemnly, as though he cared tremendously. A smile tugged at the corners of his mouth, and Willem visibly repressed a grin.

"Yes, quite grand, I'm sure," Willem said. "Saint-Nazaire's cathedral is the grandest in all the land, and now more so with its new transept and choir. Bishops and abbots will come from all over Europe just to see them. The master builder has introduced some dramatic innovations in his design. I'm anxious to see it myself. I'm sure I could talk about that cathedral until nightfall, and never grow weary of it."

Marie caught Willem's mischievous grin. She shook her head indignantly and glared at him.

Louis couldn't help himself. "And will there be battles with Saracens there at the cathedral, and sieges, and blowing sand, and fearless Templars?"

At that, all the Templars laughed, and Marie shook her head in exaggerated consternation. For the first time in hours, Louis was relieved to see his father's face relax into a congenial smile. He liked Willem's tales almost as much as Louis did, even if it was often only because he knew how much Louis enjoyed them.

"Not now," Marie said with a scolding look. "I don't want to take my dinner over tales of conflict and carnage. I'm sure that can wait until after. At least then I'll not be sitting through it."

The knights ate in silence while Father and Uncle Willem discussed the politics of the local nobility, recent developments in the Diocese of Carcassonne, and in particular, the visit of the somewhat threatening Black Friar earlier in the day. Louis was not interested in local politics, he didn't appreciate the significance of church developments, and they spoke of the Black Friar in infuriatingly veiled terms. Louis grew anxious for dinner to be finished.

As the guests began to show signs of having had their fill, Hervé and two servants cleared the remnants of the meal, replenishing flagons of ale and goblets of spiced wine. An exceptionally pretty servant girl named Marguerite, who Louis loved to watch, brought a tray of custard tarts, which the knights eyed with interest. Mother rose from the table and took her leave, bowing to the guests before she disappeared up the stairway to her private quarters.

Hervé stoked the fire and added fresh logs as the guests drank heartily. Louis devoured a tart before diving into the opportunity for which he'd patiently waited.

"Tell me more about Louis's Crusade, the siege at Tunis," he pleaded, leaning eagerly toward Uncle Willem. Louis knew more about that campaign than most boys his age, but he never tired of hearing more, especially from Willem. Willem added spice and vigor to the tale, so it was always as exciting as the first time he'd heard it.

Willem gazed intently at the ceiling, revisiting the campaign that was his first as a Templar initiate. As usual, he formulated a telling that would captivate and inspire his audience, and in particular, his idealistic nephew.

"King Louis," he began, nodding to Louis, "your virtuous namesake, launched a noble effort in the same year you were born. Sadly, it was to be his last campaign in the name of the Holy Church. Had he lived, I suspect we'd be telling a different tale, of a Kingdom of God resurrected and fashioned into the most breathtaking kingdom on earth. But, alas, heaven is not yet at hand, and so we must yet fight on with the resolve to make it so, as he commanded from his death bed."

Louis nodded excitedly. Willem's voice turned musical when he embarked upon tales of Templar valor, as if he were a jongleur retelling the timeless classics of the ancients. Louis wished his mother had stayed. He knew that while she disliked the battle stories, it made her proud to hear Uncle Willem tell them, his voice rich with the pride and satisfaction of having achieved his lifelong dream, and the joy of nurturing that same dream in the heart of a hopeful apprentice.

"It was a great siege," Willem was saying, "a glorious assault.

Thousands of Christians descended on the Mamluk stronghold, pressing into it with a vengeance, intent on winning back all that we had lost to the Saracens. King Louis rode at the head of the army, his banner fluttering in a stiff sea breeze that barely cooled the burning sand. The mood was optimistic in spite of the blazing heat, and I think the enemy felt our optimism, even from within the city walls."

"They felt our optimism *and* our heat," one of the Templars said, laughing. His laugh was hearty, but also touched with irony. Louis knew it was because of the outcome of that noble undertaking, so masterfully planned, yet gone so terribly wrong. Willem and the rest of the knights joined in the laughter, but all with a similar inflection. Willem took a long drink from his goblet and smiled with satisfaction before he continued.

"Certainty filled the air," he said, "and our fierce resolve marched before us like a vanguard. My good friend David of Atholl, may God rest his noble soul, rode beside me." Each of the Templars crossed themselves at the mention of David's name. "We both felt as though we'd live forever, and survive whatever came, to ride into the glory of the restored Kingdom of God, triumphant at long last."

Louis's eyes sparkled as he imagined the sight of that fierce, magnificent army, a teeming sea of gleaming knights in pure white tunics emblazoned with crosses of red, flowing inexorably toward the edifice of the Mamluk stronghold. Louis, of course, rode proudly among them, tall and fearless at Willem's side.

He imagined David of Atholl, a giant of a man with powerful shoulders and the countenance of a king, whose fearless strength had so profoundly impressed his uncle and these fervent knights.

Another knight, Geoffroi de Neuilly, continued the story.

"The plan was to weaken Mamluk resolve before moving east into Egypt. In truth, King Louis believed that the Khalif of Tunis might be won to Christ, and in turn his armies would join with ours in an assault on Baibars in Egypt."

"We arrived well-stocked," Willem said. "Although we thought it would be a relatively short siege, as King Louis truly did believe that the Khalif was predisposed to convert to Christianity, we nevertheless planned for a long season.

"We landed on what must have been the hottest day of the year. My sword was searing to the touch, and the mail beneath my tunic felt as though it would blister my skin. I feared that my brain would bake inside my helmet before any Mamluk projectile could harm me. It wasn't long before our fresh water was in short supply."

"What it must be like to feel such heat," Louis said, marveling at the harshness his uncle had survived.

"Indeed. It's as if the Evil One himself was there, defending the Saracens and breathing down our necks."

Willem told of the placement of the siege engines and the earth works to undermine the Saracen defenses, and how the Crusaders laid siege for nearly a month against the fortified city.

Sickness and thirst from the lack of clean water weakened King Louis's Crusaders, and in short order killed his son John. The king himself grew violently ill, and within weeks he lay feeble upon his own death bed. He heaved and retched and gasped for water until he finally accepted his fate. He pointed a trembling finger to the east and raised his raspy voice in one last, desperate exhortation.

"Jerusalem!" he said, and then he fell lifeless to his pillow.

In less than a month, King Louis had given his life to the fight, without ever wielding a sword. The Crusaders fought in his honor, as if he were still beside them.

"His death convinced us," Willem said, "that Satan himself was there against us, with all his scorching hatred. We could not let the king die in vain, nor the devil win the day."

"How many Saracens were there?" Louis asked.

"There were easily four thousand warriors within the city walls," Willem replied, "one for every ten inhabitants. We were less than twelve hundred Templars: knights, sergeants, turcopoles, and archers combined. The king's men and bands of mercenaries made up the rest."

"So few for a crusade..."

"More were expected. The king was anxious to launch, and he acted more quickly than may have been advisable. He was optimistic, and held tremendous faith in God's protection. Besides, siege takes time and equipment, more than numbers. The numbers would be more critical at the end of the siege. We were certain the numbers would arrive before that; Prince Edward was close on our heels with an army of his own."

"It was your first real battle with the Templars," Louis said.

"I'd been a Templar for almost five years, and I'd spent all that time training, studying, and praying. I was anxious for action in the Holy Land, and we'd heard that it was coming for nearly three years. It thrilled me to be along with King Louis, and finally on the march. I expected the experience of a lifetime, a victorious march from Tunis to Egypt, and on to victory at Jerusalem."

Louis gazed dreamily through the window to the rolling fields and the sky streaked with wispy clouds. He imagined such a march, and the joy of fighting for his faith against infidels, against terrible odds. He longed to experience such a display of God's greatness, and reap the eternal rewards for his part in it. His reverie was momentary, though, dashed by the troubling truth of the outcome at Tunis.

"Why did it fail, Uncle?" he asked. He had never wanted to accept his uncle's explanation.

Two months after the king's death, the Crusaders had yet to prevail, and sickness decimated them long before reinforcements arrived. By the time Prince Edward got there, an agreement had been reached with the Khalif, and the siege was brought to an end.

"We didn't fail at Tunis, Louis," Willem said firmly, "any more than the blessed Saint Euphemia failed beneath the claws of the wild bear in Diocletian's pagan arena. She went to her death with purity, and with the strength of God's love, and her courage attested to the resilience of her faith. So it is, on occasion, when we face the armies of the Wicked One: sometimes we are handed defeats that strengthen our resilience, deepen our faith, and steel our resolve to work harder toward our final victory over evil. Our resolve in battle is a testament of our faith before the unbelievers. Even in our defeat, we often win converts for our Lord. When the Evil One overpowers, and we die, we die gladly, knowing why we die, and secure in the rewards that await us in heaven. Our faith in the face of death is as indispensable as our sword, our mace, and our lance. Our faithfulness brings us victory even in death."

"You didn't feel defeated, then?" Louis said. He struggled with the concept of victory in the clutches of defeat. He felt that nothing short of triumph was worthy of God.

"It was a military setback, but a strategic success," Willem said. "King Louis's crusade ended in a peace agreement with the Khalif that allowed our priests and monks safe haven in Tunis, and access to an entire population of potential converts, the Khalif himself chief among them. The increased Christian presence at Tunis drew forces from Jerusalem, as Baibars saw them as a threat, however modest, and deduced that Christendom had shifted its focus to Africa. As a result, Jerusalem was more vulnerable when Edward joined his forces with ours, and we sailed there straight away."

"It must have been disheartening, though, to lose King Louis, and to go no farther than Tunis with him."

"Only in the momentary despair of faltering faith. Tunis inspired us, as it did Edward, to push directly to Acre to break the siege of Tripoli…to continue what King Louis had started. Prince Edward and Charles of Anjou secured once more the foothold of our Outremer kingdom. If not for that, I'd be living in Europe now, tending a commandery farm, or fighting Saracens on the Aragon frontier instead of in Jerusalem."

"So," Louis said, "Tunis was a sort of martyrdom for the cause, because it drew more support to Jerusalem."

Uncle Willem nodded. "Just as Euphemia's martyrdom, to this day, draws warriors to the fight for God's Kingdom."

"To honor Saint Euphemia alone, I would fight and die," Louis affirmed.

Willem smiled broadly, but with a hint of sadness. "As would I," he said. He waved his hand toward his brethren knights. "As we all would, and often *do*." He paused and looked meaningfully at Louis. "We should endeavor, though, not to become martyrs too soon, that we may fight yet one more day, and triumph in yet one more battle for our Holy Savior."

Louis nodded. He liked the sound of that.

Chapter 5

As THE YEARS PASSED, Louis grew to look more like his father. At fifteen, he was nearly as tall. Though not nearly as stout, his shoulders were equally broad. His hair had grown darker until it was almost as dark as Raimon's, framing an angular face and the same bright hazel eyes. Louis wondered what his father had looked like at fifteen, and if the years would see his girth match his father's as well.

"Lord Jacquette will take you on as squire," Raimon said to his son. They rode side by side along a narrow trail that bounded the northern woods, touring the estate to monitor the early spring plowing and seeding.

Louis rode an old rouncey he'd named Soranus, which he'd inherited from one of his father's men–at–arms when the knight was awarded a new warhorse. Raimon cut a powerful figure astride his great dun charger.

"You'll finish your schooling at the abbey, of course," he continued, "but you'll spend most of your time with Jacquette from now on."

Louis nodded. He was pleased. He'd looked forward to this day since he was a boy. But he was also apprehensive; Lord Jacquette was stern and formidable. His tutelage would be arduous, but potent. Jacquette's knights were among the most capable, and highly regarded. Many had received titles and land from both Aragon and France for their accomplishments in war. Several had joined the Templars and risen to positions of trust and responsibility. Jacquette himself was closely tied to the leadership of the Templars, and in particular to the order's Grand Master, William de Beaujeu.

"Thank you, father," Louis said. "I'm looking forward to my training." Louis had worked hard at the Abbey of Saint-Hilaire, in his studies of theology and language. He had learned to read and write both Latin and English, and one of the younger monks had tutored him in the fundamentals of mathematics, enthusiastically explaining its relationship to the music the monks so loved. The intricacies of mathematics intrigued Louis, and he suspected that its usefulness extended well beyond the appreciation of musical composition. He reasoned that while squiring for Lord Jacquette would be more physically demanding, it probably wouldn't be more challenging than the rigors of his academic training.

Still, he thought, it was time he mastered the combat skills that would make him a successful knight. He longed to learn how to fight like the best of the Templars. He longed to rival his Uncle Willem and the champions of his spectacular tales.

"You'll train at Jacquette's manor house at Villar–Saint–Anselme," Raimon said. "It's closer to the Marti estate than it is to here. You'll spend more time at the Martis, I expect, than here at home."

"I know," Louis said matter–of–factly, hiding his delight. "I'll have to get used to being away some day, anyway. It'll be good to be around Uncle Jacques."

Jacques Marti was Louis's mother's older brother. Although Louis had always heard much about him, he had not met Jacques until the Martis returned to the Languedoc seven years earlier from traveling abroad. They had gone to Scotland when Louis was too young to remember, and they had stayed there until the day they suddenly – and quietly – returned to their old Limoux estate.

Louis liked the Martis immensely. He had stayed at their home for long summer stretches when he was not away for schooling at Saint-Hilaire. His memories of those visits were among his most pleasant. His respect for his Uncle Jacques had grown until it rivaled that which he held for his father. But Louis's deepest affection was for his witty, vibrant, and beautiful cousin, Colette.

Colette was two years younger than Louis. He feigned indifference to her angelic beauty, preferring to think of her as an accomplice and a kindred soul. Her tomboyish ways had always reinforced that image, but he was not oblivious to her femininity. Her soft, symmetrical features, her chestnut hair, and her bright azure eyes drew endless – and often unwelcome – attention.

It annoyed Colette when strangers stared at her. It made her self-conscious, as if her movements were awkward, or her appearance grotesque. Louis knew, though, that it was because her beauty was like the finest art. Indeed, he thought to himself, she was the unparalleled work of the Master Artist Himself, a porcelain sculpture of angelic brilliance. He knew that one day she would make a fortunate man tremendously happy, if that man possessed the tiniest shred of good sense.

"The Martis will come calling later," Raimon said. Louis smiled widely at the pleasant surprise. "We'll discuss with Uncle Jacques then our arrangement with Lord Jacquette. He'll be pleased. I know he'll look forward to seeing you more."

Louis thought of a conversation he had had with Uncle Jacques the previous summer, which suddenly had deeper personal meaning for him. "I was wondering," he said, "about Lord Jacquette and the question of France and Aragon."

Raimon nodded dolefully. "Ah," he said, "that's complicated." The nobles of Toulouse had long been caught between the opposing forces of the kings of France and Aragon. Most of the them had pledged loyalty to each king at one time or another through the years, depending on the circumstances. But recent developments had bound them firmly to France. Philip III of France, King Louis's son, had formally annexed the entire Languedoc region into his kingdom fourteen years earlier. He demanded the unquestioned fealty of the Toulouse nobles. Many of them, though, had ancient ties to Aragon, and their loyalties were not so easily changed.

"King Philip is still at war with Aragon," Louis said.

"Yes," Raimon said briskly. "It's not going well for him."

"I imagine Lord Jacquette would be loath to go against Aragon. Should he be pulled into it, I wonder what that would mean for me."

"You'll follow your lord," Raimon said plainly. He looked thoughtfully at Louis. Clearly, he was equally uncertain of what that meant. "You'll have an obligation, and you'll meet it. Then you'll deal with the consequences honorably." Raimon's logic was typical for a knight. Military training and battlefield experience dispelled philosophical uncertainties in favor of simpler and more concrete choices. The Chivalric Code transformed shades of gray into sharply focused lines of black and white, so that in any given situation the knight's options were clear, and reliably predictable. In battle, all lives depended on such discipline. Raimon's character was founded upon it. Louis had yet to attain such clarity.

He turned his thoughts to the Martis, and the prospect of their visit lifted his spirits immediately. "Will they be here for dinner?" he said.

"Yes. Probably within the hour."

Louis couldn't wait.

✠ ✠ ✠

The carriage slowed as it approached from the south. It lumbered off of the Carcassonne road and onto the drive, bouncing on the ruts as it made its way toward the manor house. The carriage was old, but solid and well–maintained. It's wood was carefully polished, and its wheels amply greased. Otherwise, its construction was plain, and its adornments few. Louis smiled. Jacques Marti could easily afford a more ostentatious carriage with gilded metalwork and decorative pommels. But he was far from ostentatious; he preferred elegant simplicity. "Why would one require a garishly gilded carriage," he would say, "when one such as mine, old and plain as it might be, and bound with simple iron, works just as well or better? The wheels and the axles, and the grease between them are all that matter." Jacques exemplified modesty that was rare, and some would say inappropriate for a nobleman. It inspired in Louis yet greater esteem for him.

The carriage came to a halt in front of Louis and Raimon. As the dust settled, a servant hurried to open the carriage door and help the passengers out. Jacques climbed out, waving off the servant's assistance and carrying his short, stout frame with surprising agility. He turned to face his welcoming party with a generous grin.

Raimon shook Jacques' hand vigorously, then embraced him. "It's good to see you," he said. "How was the trip?"

"Perfect," Jacques said. "But I'm glad to be here." He turned to Louis. "Ah, Louis! You've grown, even in the short time since I saw you last." Louis grinned. "And you'll begin your squiring soon! How wonderful." He embraced Louis.

"Very wonderful," Louis said. "It seems as though I've waited forever."

The servant stepped aside from the carriage, extending his hand to Colette as she emerged. She was as beautiful as ever, Louis thought. She wore a pale yellow dress of Venetian linen, and a light cloak the color of the cloudless summer sky. The combination highlighted the stunning azure of her eyes. She curtsied gently and took Raimon's kiss on her cheek, and then she warmly embraced Louis's mother, Marie. Finally, she turned to Louis and bowed with a cheery smile and a mischievous wink.

"How have you been, dear cousin?" she said. Louis bowed in return. He took her hand in his and kissed it lightly.

"I've been well," he said. "And somewhat improved at the

moment," he added, with a grin. "I've missed you."

"I know. And I you. It's been too long. I understand though, that we'll be seeing much more of you now."

Louis laughed. "I'm not so sure of that. Lord Jacquette is a stern master. His demands will likely leave little time for leisure. But of course I'll visit as often as possible."

Colette smiled. "Of course you will," she said. She batted her eyes playfully, saying, "How could you not?"

The hostler drove the carriage toward the stables to unhitch and water the horses, and the servants led the way into the great hall, where dinner was already being served. Colette walked beside Louis with her arm in his.

"Tell me how happy you are," she said. She looked at him with admiration, and then with practiced patience listened as his animated reply extended well into the midday meal. "You should eat," she said, indicating the trencher he'd barely touched.

Louis realized that he had allowed his enthusiasm to dominate the conversation yet again. He caught himself and bowed apologetically. "I'm sorry," he said. "I suppose I've gotten carried away." Marie smiled knowingly at Colette.

"It's all right, Louis," Colette said. "I can't blame you. I'd be the same if I were on the verge of realizing a lifelong dream." She said it with a hint of melancholy, and it occurred to Louis that while the two of them had often discussed their hopes and dreams for their lives, he held his with sanguinity and a sway that Colette would never know. While Jacques Marti doted on his daughter, her fate would ultimately be determined by the political and economic maneuverings of her extended family. While they both understood that it was the way of things, he tried to imagine the emptiness of dreams that might never be sought.

Louis turned to his trencher and began to eat. As he did so, Uncle Jacques' voice rang out as he lifted his cup of wine.

"To our new squire!" he said. "May his service be valiant, his name marked by honor, his journeys blessed, and his returns to us often and lengthy." An exuberant cheer went up, not only from the family and the nobles in attendance, but from all the servants as well. Louis's heart swelled with pride, and it quickened when Colette leaned into him and kissed his cheek. He turned to her, and saw that she was beaming.

"You'll receive the best of training," said one of his father's knights. André was in his forties. He had been with Raimon since before Louis was born, first as his squire, then as a man–at–arms, and then as his most trusted knight. "Lord Jacques is one of the most accomplished fighting men I've ever known. One could not find a better mentor."

Louis smiled. André had always been watchful over him, and he could see that he was pleased now.

"When do you leave?" Colette asked.

"In a few weeks, as soon as the spring planting is done and I'm sure father no longer needs me."

"So soon! What about your schooling?"

"I'll divide my time," Louis said. "I've excelled, and I'm close to completing most of my subjects. I've more work on Latin and music – Latin because I love it so, and I want to master it completely, and music because it bores me, so I dally."

"Music bores you?" Colette said with surprise. "How could one be bored by something as beautiful as music?"

"It does nothing to prepare me for God's service," Louis retorted. "It's tedious, and a waste of time."

Colette raised her eyebrows. "I disagree," she said. "To the contrary, I fail to see how one could serve God without music in their heart. Music is the highest expression of God's beauty. I think if you'd pay it more mind, you'd find that it quite complements true service to God."

Louis shrugged and rolled his eyes.

"So," Uncle Jacques interjected, "you'll spend a few days a week at Saint-Hilaire, and the rest with Lord Jacquette?"

"Yes," Louis said. "One or two days at the abbey, but the rest of the time in training."

"I'm sure you can't wait for your training," Jacques said with a wink.

Louis smiled. After a brief pause, he nodded toward Colette

and said, "Perhaps after dinner, we could walk for a while." He turned to Colette and added, "But only if we can agree to no more talk of God's music."

Colette snickered. "I'd like that," she said. "I'm so glad that you'll be closer to us now."

The servant girl, Marguerite, stood across the table from them clearing the remnants of the main course. Louis noted that she had grown more feminine and attractive with each passing year. She had always been especially attentive toward Louis, and while it often embarrassed him, in truth he didn't mind. He wondered if there was someone she hoped to marry. Her eyes met Louis's gaze, and she shyly averted her eyes. Colette caught the look that had passed between them.

"She's pretty," she said after Marguerite had moved away from them.

"She's an excellent servant," Louis replied.

Colette smiled and gave him a knowing glance. "She likes you," she whispered. "I'm sure of it."

Louis shook his head and dismissed the comment with a wave.

As the meal was cleared, the servants brought a variety of tarts and custards, cakes with raisins and apples and honey, and spiced wine and ale. Louis's appetite was diminished by the excitement of the day, and he wished for the meal to end so he could walk with Colette to their favorite place in the clearing by the stream.

In that peaceful glen, they had shared wondrous dreams, fantastic conjecture, secret conspiracies, and heated debates; they had formed an alliance that both would treasure and neither would betray for as long as they lived. It was appropriate that they should go there today, to celebrate the crossroads that Louis had reached, and to contemplate the places it would take him. In his boyish exuberance, he had always imagined this moment not only as one they would share, but as one that would impart to both of them the same measure of meaning and opportunity.

It was dawning on him that this was his day alone, and that his dear cousin would forever remain a spectator to his life's adventures.

"Are you finished?" Colette asked. He started at the sound of her voice, then nodded. "Let's walk," she whispered. Louis nodded again and rose to his feet.

"Are you finished, Louis?" Marie asked in surprise.

"Yes, mother."

"I thought you'd stay and visit with Uncle Jacques."

"I will," he said. "I want to walk a bit." He nodded to Colette. "May we?"

"Of course." Marie smiled warmly. "We'll visit later, when you return." Louis wondered if every mother bathed her children in the warmth and affection to which he had always been accustomed. Marie nodded mindfully to indicate the guests who had gathered in his honor.

Louis turned towards Jacques. "Monsieur Marti...," he said with exaggerated formality, bowing deeply and indicating Colette, "may we?"

Jacques turned stiffly toward Louis with an aristocratic air, and he gave him a hard, appraising look. He held it for a moment, which was all he could manage before his face broke into a wide smile.

"Of course, sir knight," he said, bowing his head ceremoniously. "See to her safety, and have her back soon, or I'll have you in the stocks for a week."

"Of course, my liege," Louis said. Marie shook her head at their silly routine, repeated every time the Martis came to visit. Colette curtsied to her father and the pair took their leave.

They walked to the stables, where a groom disappeared inside to ready horses. The groom reappeared leading Soranus, followed by a stable boy leading a palfrey for Colette. They mounted and reined the horses toward the fields to the west, and as they cleared the stable grounds, they spurred the horses and raced toward the stream at a full gallop.

"It's wonderful to ride," Colette exclaimed exuberantly. She rode as well as any man, and better than some. She could probably fight as well if necessary, too, Louis thought. He loved the race, even though Soranus could easily outrun Colette's youthful horse, which was better suited to longer, more casual rides.

They crested a hill and slowed as the stream came into view. As much as they loved to run the horses, they didn't want the ride to end so soon, so they pulled back into a lazy walk.

"So, tell me all about your duties as a squire," Colette said as they dismounted.

Louis nodded solemnly. "It will be grueling," he said. "My days of leisure are over. I'll work ceaselessly to prove myself to Lord Jacquette."

"He's a severe man," Colette said. "He's seen terrible things, unspeakable things done to people he loved." Louis looked questioningly at Colette, but she disregarded the look and continued. "I imagine that from his perspective life is cruel and unforgiving. His demeanor reflects that. He'll no doubt want to prepare you for the kind of things he has seen. I'm not sure that's possible, though. I hope that at some level he realizes that."

"What has he seen?"

Colette was quiet for a long moment, contemplating what she knew. She spoke reluctantly: "Like most of the nobility of Toulouse, he sided with his Count, Raymond of Toulouse, in his conflict with France and the pope. In fact, as a young man, Bertrand Jacquette served as squire to Raymond, and then as his knight. Raymond offered protection to Bertrand's family, many of whom were Cathars. But King Louis's brother, Alphonse, married Raymond's daughter in accordance with the Treaty of Meaux. That marriage sealed the fate of Toulouse, as Alphonse became heir to Raymond's title and land. The treaty was supposed to end the crusade against the Cathars, but their persecution had only begun."

"And there were Cathars in Lord Jacquette's family..."

"Lord Jacquette himself was Cathar."

Louis's jaw dropped. After a stunned silence, he said, "But he recanted." Colette raised her eyebrows slightly, as if in negation. "He *did* recant," Louis persisted. Colette said nothing. Louis was perplexed. "Are you saying that Lord Jacquette is still a heretic?"

"I did not say that."

"You didn't deny it."

"It's not for me to judge."

"Did he *recant*?"

"I wasn't there."

Louis shook his head in frustration. "I need to know," he said.

"Why? What has it to do with you?"

Louis looked at Colette with incredulity. "I won't serve a heretic!" he said. "I plan to serve the Church. How can I take my training from an enemy of the Church?"

"Louis!" she said sharply. "You should mind your words. That man has served God all of his life. He's a pious man, whose family was tortured by men of the Church. I won't speak against the Church, but I also won't speak badly of a man who has been hurt more than I can understand. You should be mindful of that, too."

Louis felt ashamed. He'd spoken ill of the man who had offered him the opportunity of his life, who held the respect of all who knew him, as well as most who only knew *of* him. He had to admit that he didn't fully understand the tortuous political loyalties that shifted like desert sands across the landscape of this ancient land, or the religious intrigue that for nearly a century had pitted friend against friend, father against son, and priests against people whose piety put the clergy to shame. Louis regretted his judgment of Bertrand Jacquette.

But still, Jacquette was a Cathar, and Louis had been taught that they were a loathsome lot. They worshipped Lucifer and reviled the pope. They called the God of the Old Testament Satan, and all of his creation evil. They held that the true God, the God of heaven, was Lucifer, and that he could not coexist with man in the physical world, as it was the domain of the false and evil God of Abraham. The blasphemy of the Cathars was twisted and sick. They burned the children of their incest and consumed their remains. How could a man like Jacquette, who Louis knew to be faithful and righteous, embrace such heresy? Surely he had recanted and been reconciled to God.

But then, to Colette's point, who was Louis to judge? Lord Jacquette had turned out fine knights who fought heroically for

Christ. He had contributed large portions of his own wealth in support of the Crusades. Perhaps that was his penance. Moreover, he avidly supported Louis's commitment to the fight for Jerusalem. If Louis was to judge, his judgment should be founded on the evidence of Lord Jacquette's life, and not on tales of bygone battles with the Church. Jacquette was a good man, soon to become his mentor, and he deserved far better from Louis.

"You're right," he finally said, nodding softly. He looked hard at Colette and repeated, more decisively, "You're right. I have no place judging anyone, least of all Bertrand Jacquette."

Her smile was pleasantly forgiving. But he knew that his struggle with this profound contradiction was not over. He decided to put it out of his mind for now.

"My life is about to change dramatically," he said. "I find myself wondering what it will be like. I've always imagined the battles, and killing Saracens by the score. But now that it's a less distant reality, I feel trepidation. They weren't real men that I was killing in my daydreams, and there was never a chance that I'd lose, or be killed."

"Did you really never imagine that possibility?"

"I suppose I did, but only with a sort of detachment that made it unreal. I've never truly examined the reality. I find myself doing that now. My dream has a different feel to it now."

"It's not a boy's dream anymore."

"I'm also coming to terms with the reality of leaving Verzeille, of going away from my family, of not seeing them – or you – very often anymore. That's difficult to contemplate. It was never part of my dreams. I see now that it's a central part of them." His voice choked. "I'm...struggling with that."

"I'm glad," Colette said with a mordant smile. "You should be."

"The killing will be real," he said after a moment.

"Yes, it will be."

"It's hard to imagine killing someone. I know that it's inevitable. I know it's the way of things. But it's a hard thing to contemplate."

They sat quietly watching the stream rush by, listening to the sounds of the leaves in the breeze and the fauna in the field. Louis shifted his gaze to the hawks that circled slowly, their eyes fixed on the movements of rabbits and field mice.

"What will you do?" Louis asked.

"What do you mean?"

"Do you have plans?"

"What plans could I have?" She shrugged simply.

That was the truth that had been troubling Louis most deeply. Colette had shared his fancies, walking with him, riding with him, hunting heathens with drawn swords and ready shields. She was his unspoken partner, squire to his knight, and the wings that gave his aspirations flight. In his mind she was his constant, eternal companion; she would be with him to the end. But he knew that wasn't true, and it broke his heart.

He thought of her future, and he loathed it.

"There's a noble at Fanjeaux who has a nephew," she said, as if she were reading his mind.

"Henri of Fanjeaux," Louis said.

"Yes. He has a nephew, a young knight. My father has mentioned him to me. No doubt he would like me to take an interest in him if he's suitable." Louis felt a hollowness in his gut that grew so that it pressed into his lungs and made it hard to breathe. "I can't imagine it, though. I can't seem to imagine myself married."

"Why not?" Louis glanced at her sideways. "What else would you do?"

"Yes. That's it, exactly," she said caustically. "What else would I do?"

"What *would* you do, if you could do anything you chose?"

She smiled then, and thought for a moment. "I'd be a jongleur," she said. "I'd wander and explore and tell tall tales for lodging. I'd eat when I could and sleep where I chose, and I'd make my way to Scotland, where I'd live happily among the people there."

"Scotland? Why Scotland?"

"When we lived there, until I was eight and we returned to

Limoux, I loved it with all my heart. I didn't want to leave. The people are rough, but they're honest and simple and you know where they stand. They laugh when they're happy, and they can be happy in the worst of times. When they're not happy, you know it, and they don't much care if you do. Most of all, they don't fear their nobles or the Church. My father always said that he'd rather be in a pub full of Scots than a court full of nobles if he had to choose one place to spend the rest of his days. He said that, if nothing else, he would always know where he stood. They treated my father like he was one of them, a commoner. He liked that, and so did I."

"I've heard that it's dreary there."

"If all you notice is the weather, I suppose that's true."

"I'm not sure I'd like it there."

"If you got to know the people, you would. They have their troubles, but they have an indomitable spirit that I think you'd admire. The troubles they have are political, and in that respect they're not much different from anyone else. But I believe that Scotland will one day stand as one of the greatest kingdoms of Europe."

Louis nodded thoughtfully. "And you don't see the nephew of Fanjeaux going along with you, then."

"If I could do anything I chose, then no. But that's not very likely, is it?"

Louis wished with all his heart that Colette could have the freedom to follow her dreams. But he knew that their fates were predestined. It mattered not whether Colette wanted to marry, or who she did or did not want to marry. It mattered not that he would prefer, in the depths of his heart, that she not marry. His time with her was drawing to a close; he had no real future with her. It mattered not whether he wished to ride into battle in the deserts of Outremer. It was the destiny his God had reserved for him. Neither of them had a choice in the matter, and so their wishes were futile and irrelevant. Perhaps those wishes were nothing more than the work of the devil, after all.

Colette would marry, and he would serve God. He would do

his part to defeat that scurrilous author of their deepest desires. Any other choice was the path to perdition. He knew this with all of his heart.

In this life, that is our lot, he thought. *Perhaps in the halls of the Kingdom of God, such things will be different.*

Chapter 6

Louis and Colette wandered aimlessly through orchards, vineyards, and fields of lavender and barley, admiring the vibrant vitality of the well–tended Garonne estates. They roamed with no regard for the distance, or the time they spent lost in the pleasure of their friendship.

They came to the edge of a field and pushed through the brush and the brambles that separated it from the road to Carcassonne. They emerged onto the road and turned north, toward the city. The bright sun was at their backs, and muggy heat rose from the dusty road.

Carcassonne was nearly a three-hour walk, or an hour on horseback at a moderate trot. They had no intention of going to Carcassonne, of course, or they would have taken horses and one or two of his father's men–at–arms.

Their conversation lulled, and Louis gazed idly at his cousin. He wondered at the beauty of her features, and the grace with which she carried herself. Her back was straight, and her head held high, as if she were a lady of the court, but her eyes shone with compassionate humility and clarity of thought. He never tired of admiring her elegance.

"Colette," he said softly.

"Yes?"

"You're picturesque." He felt awkward the moment he said it.

She whirled to face him, her eyebrows raised in mock disdain.

"And you're a lunatic," she said, shaking her head. "Don't say such things." Her expression turned demure. "I may grow to be too full of myself, and dispense with my modesty altogether."

He laughed. He knew that to be most unlikely. "But you know it's true," he said. "You're always so...splendid." She shook her head again, ever so slightly. "I'm glad I have you to talk to," he continued, "and to walk with me. I can speak to you of things I don't discuss with anyone else, and you make me think of things in ways I never did."

"I enjoy your company, too, Louis," she said. She stepped gracefully around a deep puddle in the rutted road.

"I'm glad," he said, smiling broadly.

"There's something in particular you'd like to discuss, then?" she asked. He wondered how she always seemed to know such things. It was as if she could read his mind. "Perhaps," she said with a frown, "something other than Templar Knights crusading in the desert sands, and Saracens dying under a blazing sun."

He looked sheepishly down at the ground.

"No," he said. "I'm simply enjoying the day, and walking with you. I just wanted you to know that."

He was lying. His Templar dreams were exactly what he wanted to discuss. He felt it was time they started preparing for the inevitable. He was fifteen now, and preparing to sign on as squire to a local noble, the fiercely intimidating Lord Bertrand Jacquette. He was honing his riding and fighting skills, and by all accounts excelling at those things. He fully intended to petition for his acceptance into the Order of the Knights of the Temple at his first opportunity, and if all went well, he would be joining them in three short years. He wondered how often he would see her in those three years. "Because the day *will* come," he said, "when I'll be far from here, chasing my destiny, and I'll want you to know then that I'll be missing you badly, and that I'll always be thinking of you."

She slowed a bit and started to roll her eyes, but she caught herself. She stopped and turned toward him. "That's so sweet, Louis," she said. "But I already knew that. I always know that."

"It doesn't hurt to make sure," he said with an affectionate smile.

"But that won't be for a long time now, and no, I still don't want to discuss it. I'll probably never want to discuss it."

He felt growing frustration with Colette's recent, unyielding disinterest in his greatest passion. He wished desperately that she would share in his enthusiasm the way she did when they were younger. He started walking again, trying to think of an effective protest to her indifference.

Just then, he saw three young men approaching from Carcassonne. He did not recognize them. Their clothes were shabby, and he guessed them to be stable boys, or migrant farm hands. They could also be outlaws; there were not many of those in the vicinity of the Garonne estates, but there were some. These were not city boys, nor judging by their clothing, native to the local towns.

Louis moved to pull Colette from the road and into the brush, but it occurred to him that if they were outlaws, they had accomplices in the brush moving toward them, just off the road. His heart pounded at the thought of confrontation. He moved ahead of Colette and placed himself between them and her. The larger of the lads moved into Louis's path. He lowered his head and glared through his eyebrows, like a bull about to charge. He was calculating Louis's reaction.

Louis slowed.

"Where do you think you're going, boy," the biggest of them, a thuggish lad, said with a snarl, "and with such a tender piece of flesh as that one?" His eyes were dull and gray, and vacant in a way that conveyed lethal malevolence.

"Where we please," Louis said defiantly. He tried to sidestep the bully with Colette securely in tow.

"Where you please?" the ruffian taunted. He held out his arm to block Louis, and he shook his head. "I think not." He stood squarely in front of Louis, his arms crossed and his feet firmly planted. Louis tried again to move around him, guiding Colette by the elbow, but he shifted to block their way.

"Step back," Louis demanded. "Leave us alone. This is no place for outlaws, and I'd suggest you be on your way."

"Or what?" the ruffian said, laughing. Louis tasted bitterness at the back of his tongue. He knew that if the confrontation turned physical, the other two would not stand by if he gained the upper hand. He worried for Colette's well-being, and he thought it best to avoid trouble at all costs.

The stranger suddenly shoved Louis backward into Colette, who cried out. He threw back his shoulders in defiance and let out a hearty, bullying laugh.

Louis regained his balance quickly. He spread his feet and squared off, pushing his sleeves up his forearms. He tensed for a thrashing, but he determined to make it costly for his foes.

"Well, that's hardly fair now, is it?" a voice called out from the distance, somewhere off the road.

Louis, Colette, and the thugs turned toward the voice. A sandy-haired peasant boy, slightly older than Louis, emerged from the brush. He was shorter than Louis, but more stout. He carried a walking stick, and he looked as though he had been herding sheep.

"That's quite brave," the shepherd boy said to Louis, "the two of you picking a fight with these poor, defenseless lads." He glared menacingly at them. He moved to stand beside the larger ruffian with the soulless eyes, who crossed his arms in defiance. The peasant boy crossed his arms, too, almost as if he were mocking the thug. "We'll have to even this up a bit, now, won't we?"

The ruffian turned to stare at the shepherd boy, perplexed. Louis and Colette exchanged nervous glances. The newcomer gave the ruffian a toothy grin, and then he glared back at Louis and Colette. Colette clutched Louis's arm.

Louis was fascinated by the newcomer, and bewildered by the

turn of events. He knew that if the boy was a shepherd, he was in the employ of Louis's father, who owned all the sheep from here to Verzeille. The shepherd did not appear to know the ruffians, but he had inexplicably sided with them. Louis thought for a moment that he recognized the boy, but he couldn't place him.

Suddenly, the shepherd boy swung the tip of his walking stick from the ground and into the groin of one of the assailants who stood behind him. As that thug crumpled in pain, he swung around and brought the other end of the stick squarely across the second thug's jaw. The blow spun the thug around, and the peasant boy shoved him with his foot, pitching him face first into the dusty road.

Before the larger thug could grasp what was happening, the peasant boy had squared off in front of him, his walking stick at the ready.

Louis stood amazed. Colette released his arm and backed away.

"Victor," the boy said amiably, nodding toward Louis. "At your service." Victor raised his stick menacingly toward the bully.

"I'm Louis."

"I know."

"It's good to meet you."

"Yes, I bet it is," Victor said, laughing. To the ruffian, he said, "And what's your name, pretty boy?" The lad stared dully at Victor. It occurred to Louis that if the boy were capable of expressing anxiety, he would be doing so now, but he betrayed no hint of it. He seemed only to be mildly confused.

"Gilles," the thug said in a voice as thick and dull as his stare.

"Gilles," Victor repeated, rolling the name off his tongue. "Three against one, Gilles. And a girl present. Have you no couth?" Victor moved sideways, sparring, as Gilles backed away. The other two boys were recovering, and Louis advanced to keep them in check.

"We didn't mean any harm," Gilles said, raising his hands in innocence.

"Oh, no, of course you didn't," Louis mocked.

"So, then, Gilles," Victor said, "how did you end up here, dancing in the road with me?" He lunged playfully, laughing as Gilles flinched. Gilles held his hands in front of him and continued to back away. Noting that the other two had fully recovered, Gilles grunted a command, and the three of them rushed Louis and Victor.

As Colette watched in distress, Victor whirled with his stick, swinging and striking with practiced accuracy, focusing his efforts on Gilles and one of the other lads.

Louis squared off with the third boy, advancing aggressively with the fluid movements of a well-trained fighter. Raimon had taught him early, before Louis knew it had anything to do with fighting, to move quickly, silently, and with precise balance. Louis knew that battles were won first with a combination of wits, skill, and fearlessness, and only secondarily through strength of arms. He jabbed deftly, connecting solidly but with moderate force, and he moved in a way that his opponent felt relentlessly pressed into defensive dodging and weaving. Before long, his opponent was gasping for breath and struggling to keep his arms raised in front of him. When the boy lowered his weary arms for the third time, Louis struck full on, his fist crashing solidly into the boy's face. The boy's nose flattened with a sickening crunch and gushed blood. It was the first time Louis had ever felt the breaking of bone, and it startled him. The boy reeled backward, covering his face with his hands.

Gilles extracted himself, with difficulty, from his conflict with Victor. He retreated, raising his hands in surrender. Colette gasped in relief when the other thug followed suit. Louis sprang to Victor's side, and they stood ready to finish their foes. The thugs' clothes were more tattered than they had been, and their faces were bruised and bloodied.

Victor moved menacingly toward Gilles.

"Enough," Gilles gasped. The welts on the boys' faces would proclaim their defeat for some time to come, and the nose Louis broke would probably never be the same.

"Don't threaten my friends again," Victor said firmly. Gilles nodded his head wearily.

"Nor anyone else around here," Louis added, "particularly when you outnumber them, or are in the presence of a lady!"

Victor looked sideways at Louis, as if he thought him odd.

"Well, aren't you the gallant knight!" Victor mocked.

Louis grinned with pride. "I am," he said. "Or at least I will be one day."

Victor shook his head. "Your knighthood is going to be eventful, if this is how you get on with strangers."

Louis beamed. His opponent had struggled to his feet, and the vagrants circled warily around them, moving to the opposite side of the road to get past. They appeared ready to run.

Victor gave them a threatening look. "Keep moving, pigs," he said. "No need to stop any time soon. Off with you, now." He shooed them away, as if they were misbehaving children.

Louis stared hard at Victor, remembering him. He'd seen him around, working on local farms and estates, including those owned by Louis's father, Raimon.

"Does that happen often?" Victor asked, nodding toward the retreating ruffians.

"Hardly," Louis said, laughing. "Apparently, only when you're around...fortunately."

Victor smiled broadly. He appeared to be restraining laughter at some private joke.

"Thank you," Louis said. He extended his hand. Victor grasped it enthusiastically.

"And who's the fine lady?" Victor asked. He leaned toward Colette, a little more closely than Louis would have liked.

"This is Colette," Louis said. "My..." He faltered. Victor looked at him expectantly.

"Your...?"

Louis answered with reluctance. "My cousin," he said quietly. Colette shot him a quizzical look.

Victor's eyes grew wide.

"Your cousin!" he exclaimed. "Well, that's just grand! What an exquisite cousin you have there, Louis." Victor bowed deeply, with comical exaggeration.

Louis glared a subtle warning, but Victor did not notice.

"You've quite a gallant cousin here, milady," Victor said. "He's strong and brave."

Colette smiled weakly and barely curtseyed. "Thank you," she said. "And thank you for coming to our aid."

"How could I not?" Victor replied.

"It was noble of you," Louis said, raising his voice. "May I repay you before we're on our way?"

Victor was clearly insulted. "Repay me?" he asked. "You think I stepped in for reward? I did what was right, and nothing more."

Louis could tell that Victor was sincerely offended. He was aware that his protectiveness of Colette was getting the better of him, inspiring undue skepticism. He should be more grateful, and more gracious. He quelled his growing resentment.

"I'm sorry," Louis said. "You're right. That was rude of me." He waved toward the ruffians who were about to disappear beyond a bend in the road. "I'm still a bit agitated."

Victor nodded with indifference, then smiled. "Of course you are. Something like that'll get you going." He paused, and there was a moment of awkward silence. "Where are you two headed?"

Louis shrugged off the awkwardness and placed an arm around Victor's shoulders. "We're wandering," he said. "Nowhere in particular. Just wandering, talking, admiring the day." He hesitated, and gave Colette a questioning look. He didn't want to be rude, but he didn't want to make Colette uncomfortable, either. Finally, he said, "Would you care to join us?"

"Me?" Victor said, brightening. He held his palms to his chest. "Me, walk with you? Why, I'd be honored." Louis knew then that he had hoped to be invited.

Louis maneuvered Victor so that he was on the opposite side of him from Colette, and he turned to walk south, the way from which they'd come.

"Where do you live, Victor," Louis asked. Colette leaned forward to look past Louis at their new friend.

"Not very far from you," Victor said with a wry smirk.

"No?" Louis said. "How close?"

"We're tenants of your father," Victor said. "We tend your fields."

"Ah," Louis said. "I thought so. I didn't recognize you at first, but now I remember seeing you around…in the fields, mostly. Your family is comfortable?"

"We get by," Victor said. "We're fortunate. Your father's a good man. Our work is steady. We're content."

"I suppose I should have recognized you sooner," Louis said. "I'm sure you work very hard for us. It wouldn't be too much for you to expect me to know who you are."

"Yes, it would," Victor said. "I've no place expecting anything of you. Besides, I know it must be hard to notice little things when you're caught up in the heat of battle," he added, stifling a laugh.

"In the heat of…" Louis's voice trailed off as he realized what Victor meant by that. Victor was the tenant moving through the brush that day in the field by the stream years earlier. Maximilian had noticed him, and brought him to Louis's attention. "In the heat of battle," Louis said. He nodded his head, feeling sheepish.

Victor beamed.

"You watched me," Louis said.

Victor nodded.

"How long?"

"Years."

"Years! You watched from the woods all that time, and you never thought to say hello? That's a bit disturbing."

"You were…engrossed. I was passing through, coming from the fields. I didn't think you'd appreciate having your private conquests acknowledged. I left you to it. I'd have wanted you to do the same had I been the dreamer and you the witness."

"I suppose I *was* engrossed," Louis admitted. Colette looked from one to the other, perplexed. Louis caught her questioning look. "Never mind," he whispered to her.

"Anyway, I saw you all the time," Victor said. "I watched you riding with your uncle, the Templar, and I wished I could have been you. Not to be with the Templar, of course," he said, giving the word *Templar* a peculiar inflection, "but to ride that fine horse of yours."

"You like horses," Louis said.

"I love horses. I hung around the stables all the time, and more than once I felt the back of my mother's hand for it. I've always longed to work in the stables instead of the fields."

"Why didn't you?" Louis said.

Victor gave him an incredulous look. "Are you serious?" he said. "Do you really think that would be wise, to complain about my work, or to ask for special treatment? My father would have whipped me for that. 'You take the work you get,' he'd say to me. A laborer with special requests is usually taken for a trouble maker. There are too many others ready to accept what little comes their way." He peered at Louis. "Do you truly not know these things?"

Louis did not answer. He had never thought of such things. It seemed a shame to him that a lad could not do a job he enjoyed rather than one he loathed. He tried to remember seeing Victor in the fields or around the stables, and something that would have indicated that the boy was miserable in his work, but he just could not.

"You're a shepherd now?" Louis asked. Victor nodded, shrugging as if it should be obvious. "How do you feel about that?"

"I'm glad for the food on my family's table," Victor said. He smiled broadly.

"Do you still want to work in the stables?"

Colette gave Louis an admiring look. She obviously liked that he was thinking of a laborer's welfare.

Victor nodded thoughtfully. "I want to work," he said. He let that statement stand on its own for a long moment before he added, "But if you're asking me where my working days would fly by on a happy breeze of joy and satisfaction, I'd have to admit that it would be in the stables, working with the horses."

Louis smiled to himself. There might be a way to reward his new friend after all.

Chapter 7

"Tell me more!" Louis insisted. He leaned forward, his elbows propped on the heavy oak table in the center of the vaulted stone hall. He had been listening wide–eyed as the Templar wove his heroic tales of adventure.

Louis's father, Raimon, held up a hand to silence him. "Patience, son," he said.

The handsome, battle–hardened Templar, Louis's Uncle Willem, smiled kindly at Louis's eagerness. He disregarded Raimon's admonishment and continued with unflagging enthusiasm.

"We won that battle, of course," he said, "though, once again, we were badly outnumbered. Sir Bertrand was the champion of that battle." Sir Willem turned and indicated a slender knight with intense blue eyes seated at the end of the table. "He fought like he was God's own First Knight."

Sir Bertrand de Rennes nodded in humble acknowledgement. The other knights nodded with him.

Louis held deep admiration for his Uncle Willem. Willem's rare visits from Outremer, the Christian kingdoms across the sea, were among the highlights of Louis's life. He anticipated them with eagerness as they approached, and he tingled with excitement long after they had passed.

"We were fifty knights," Willem said, "seventy sergeants, and three hundred soldiers. Scouts had spotted Mamluks the previous night, in the south of Tripoli. They were forward detachments, pressing closer, and we were out to meet them. What we didn't know was that their main force had been close behind, and had arrived in the night. We expected an easy victory that would send a swift and stern message to the main Mamluk force to fall back."

"There were Mamluks behind every dune," Bertrand said. "We were unprepared for that."

"Quite," Willem agreed. "As we made our way between two large dunes, pressing south, a lone Mamluk stood tall at the top of one of them, waving to us as if he were lost and in need of our assistance. We stopped in our tracks and stared. A moment later, a dozen more stood with him. We believed we'd come across Mamluk scouts, but in another moment hundreds stood at the top of each dune. We realized then that we'd stumbled into an ambush."

"Little did we know," Bertrand added, "there were more than a thousand Saracen devils on the far sides of the dunes. We were, as your uncle said, surrounded and outnumbered."

"We formed a tight circle, facing all directions, and we waited for the charge," Willem said, "but it didn't come." He shrugged. "They stood looking at us, doing nothing."

"It was unnerving," a tall, gangly, dark-skinned knight said in a thickly accented voice. Antonio Bollani was Venetian. Willem had joked that he was darker than the Saracens, and that if it weren't for the crimson cross emblazoned on his pure white mantle, he'd be taken for one and swiftly cut down. Antonio's smile had implied his doubt about that. "The sun beat down on us," Bollani said, "and the silence was deafening."

"Two horses broke from the Mamluk formation on the eastern-most dune," Willem continued. "They approached, while the rest stood ready. Their leader, a magnificent general, of no less than kingly countenance, came face to face with our commander and his aide. The Saracen general – Kala'un himself – gave our company a choice."

"Kala'un!" Louis gasped. He had heard much about the enigmatic Mamluk leader. Willem nodded solemnly.

"We would all go free," Willem said, "if only we would deny Christ, and convert to Islam."

"But that was not an option!" Louis exclaimed.

"Kala'un knew that before he offered the terms," Willem said, "but he was bound by honor to propose them…in the event that even one of us were disposed toward the faith of Muhammad."

"The faith of dogs," Louis said, his lips curled in contempt. He expected his comment to be met with hearty approval, but instead there was a brief silence. Willem looked hard at him for a moment, his eyes narrowed. Louis sensed, with puzzlement, reproof lingering on Willem's lips, barely restrained. Willem blinked once, tightly, as if to suppress a response.

"Kala'un advised us that the alternative to conversion was death," Willem said. "Beheading, to a man."

"Our commander corrected him," Bollani said, "and reminded him of a third and more likely option: that the Templars would defeat and destroy the Mamluks, to the last man."

"Did he tremble?" Louis asked, thinking that any living man would tremble in the face of a fierce Templar force.

"Kala'un is not given to trembling," Bertrand said. "I'm not sure he has ever known fear."

Louis was intrigued by that. Courage was not an attribute he had ever ascribed to Saracens. It must have been foolishness, rather than courage. "What did he do, then?" he asked.

"He looked long and hard into the commander's eyes," Willem said, "and he asked him if he was certain of his reply. The commander nodded, and Kala'un turned his steed without a word and returned to his troops."

"We braced for the onslaught," Bertrand said.

"But they waited, still," Bollani added, "as if to make us ponder our impending doom." The Venetian's gloomy voice conveyed a hint of that doom.

"Or as if he were paying homage to the force that was about to defeat him," Willem said. Louis nodded. That was more likely… or at least he would like to think so.

Louis considered what it must be like, waiting wordlessly in the midst of distant desert dunes, baking in the sun, surrounded by fierce Saracen warriors bent on massacre. He tried to imagine the courage that could stay a man's fear in such a moment. He was certain he possessed such courage, and that it would rise up and fortify him when the time came for him to face such peril.

"And finally…, " Bertrand said, "*finally*, they charged."

"We held formation," Willem said. "The knights encircled the soldiers to fend off the cavalry charge. They came upon us, wave after wave, breaking as the sea upon a rocky coast. They lost a tenth at every thrust. Then, as they retreated to regroup for the fifth or sixth time, we, seeing that the tide had begun to turn, broke and charged at their rear. They fell into disarray.

"Their infantry fell upon us, then, and our soldiers joined the fray. Bertrand fought like a madman, as I've never seen him fight before. He was unstoppable – until a Mamluk killed his horse, and he was thrown into the midst of a raging melee. He was back on his feet in a flash, slashing left and right, sending heads and limbs flying like weeds in a whirlwind. The infantry parted quickly, giving his lightning blade a wide berth. Those closest to him stared in astonishment; some lowered their swords and fell to their knees in surrender."

"It did them no good," Bollani said solemnly.

Raimon turned to look at Bertrand with heightened respect. Bertrand flushed, embarrassed by the attention and the accolades.

"Suddenly, the Saracens broke into retreat," Willem said. "We gave chase with a fierce roar." He raised a cautionary finger. "But Saracen cavalry is generally quicker and more nimble than ours. Their horses are lighter, and better suited for galloping across sand. They slipped away into the distance."

"Sir Bertrand," Louis said, "how did it feel to kill so many Mamluks?"

"Louis—," Willem said, raising his hand to stop him. Raimon gave a slight shake of his head.

"It's all right," Bertrand said. He smiled, but there was vague melancholy in his eyes. He nodded slowly. "It's all right," he repeated.

"One should not ask a warrior such questions," Willem said, giving Louis a stern look.

"He has so many questions," Bertrand said. His voice was kind and patient. "Is he always so inquisitive?"

"Relentlessly," Raimon said. "I apologize—"

"It's all right," Bertrand repeated. Louis shrugged off Raimon's comment and looked expectantly to Bertrand for an answer. Bertrand smiled and said, "I suffered a slight wound, so it didn't feel very good."

"But...what's that like, to kill so many men?" Louis asked.

Bertrand blinked, as if he was unsure how to answer.

"Louis!" Willem snapped. "Enough!" He stared hard at Louis and mouthed the word, "*stop*."

"I...could not describe to you how it feels to take another man's life," Bertrand said, "nor the weight of having taken so many. Your uncle is correct in this. One must avoid turning a Christian warrior's attention to such things. Regarding such things, we pray for forgiveness and a peaceful heart."

Louis was puzzled. He'd imagined feeling powerful and victorious in the glory of defeating heathens on the battlefield. He had long imagined the pride he would carry after his own battlefield triumphs.

"You're disappointed," Willem said.

"No," Louis said. "I'm confused. That's not how I've always imagined it. One feels wounded after killing heathen devils?"

"It does not matter what our enemies believe, or the cause for which they die," Bertrand said, "or what God they beseech in their final moment. When one takes a life, it's a human life endowed with an immortal soul. By separating another man's body from his soul, one has sent that soul to its eternity, with no further chance for redemption. It's a weighty thing to send a soul to its eternity, whatever that may be. One cannot take that lightly and still love Christ."

Louis had not thought of death in battle from the enemy's perspective. He'd considered his own death, of course, and his assurance of eternity with God when that day came; he regarded death as an inevitable transition into the presence of God. He pondered that for the heathen, death was the irreversible beginning of eternity in the torments of hell.

"I fear I've done you a disservice, Louis," Willem said.

"How so?" Louis asked. He was ashamed of a momentary quiver in his voice.

"I've long filled your head with only the notions of glory. I've made crusading sound wondrous and alluring. In many ways, it is just that. There's great satisfaction in winning battles for God and His kingdom. I have not told you, though, of the side of battle that stays with us in the days between battles, and in the nights when all is silent but the voice of our conscience."

Louis felt profound disappointment. This was not what he wanted to hear.

"It's not all glory," Willem continued. "We celebrate our victories, yes...but we respect the lives and mourn the deaths of good warriors, of worthy men."

"And it gets harder when one begins to wonder why they die," a third knight said. Everyone turned to look at Richard Osbourne, an English knight, thickly bearded and badly scarred.

Louis was incredulous. "Why would anyone wonder why an infidel died?" he asked.

"It's a complicated matter, Louis," Willem said. His tone had turned solemn, and his eyes were dark. "Sometimes the lines between darkness and light begin to blur, and it gets harder to maintain one's original convictions. The distinctions are easier the more distant one remains from the tempest."

"I don't understand."

"I know. You may not, until you've experienced it for yourself."

"Kala'un respected us for our victory in that battle," Bertrand said. "He saw honor in our commitment to our faith, and in the way we fought that day. We show him and his men the same regard. His respect for us led to his bid for peace, and to a treaty that has since held fast. That has bought us time. It has allowed Kala'un to focus his efforts on the Mongols, who press him from the east, and it has allowed us to focus on managing unceasing conflict among the Christians."

"I've heard that the Christians bicker like children," Raimon said.

"They do," Osbourne said. "The Genoese and the Venetians are impossible...no offense, Antonio, but it's true. They fight one another more vehemently than they have ever fought the Mamluks. They wage war on one another while the Muslims grow stronger. Without fail, and with infuriating frequency, we are pulled into that conflict."

"Pulled into it?" Bertrand said. "Sometimes I think we fly to it like moths to a flame, for the influence it affords us."

Willem shook his head sadly.

"That's precisely what drives the bickering," Raimon said, "the struggle among the European nobility for power and influence in Jerusalem."

Louis felt bitterness rising within him. He could not believe his ears. He could not restrain himself. "Peace with Saracens," he said, "and war between Christians." He shook his head in consternation and mounting disappointment. He felt he was about to throw up.

"Yes," Willem said, "affairs in the Holy Land have become very complicated. At times it seems that we languish there, caught in a web of irony and intrigue. We're here now precisely because of that – to petition Europe's nobility to put an end to the political infighting, and for the pope to pressure them into compliance. We need a recommitment of the money, men, leadership, and diplomacy that it will take to reunite and rebuild our forces. Conflict with the Mamluks will resume, unless we are willing to settle for what's left of our kingdom and accept its ultimate demise."

"We can't accept that," Louis said. He felt dizzy.

"We've already lost most of it," Osbourne said. "We've gained nothing in decades, but rather lost more ground as time has passed. One of two things is inevitable: we will rally and regain our kingdom, or we will leave the Holy Land forever. We have a respite in which to rally, thanks to the Mongols. If we do not take advantage of it, all will be lost when it ends. We're here now to see to it that we rally. If we rally, we won't stop until we've retaken all of Jerusalem."

"We should be joining forces with the Mongols, truth be told," Bertrand said. "For the life of me, I don't know why we haven't done that."

Louis wondered how Willem's wondrous tales of adventures in Jerusalem had spiraled into this unexpected, unbelievable nightmare of doom and despair. He knew that these Templars were speaking the truth; they would surely not conjure such gloom. But his uncle had never spoken of it, and he had not prepared him for the revelation. He suddenly resented Willem for that.

Since his earliest days, Louis had carried the images of glorious victory, of shining knights and cowering Mamluks, the glory of God and His host of angels accompanying the charge with trumpets and fanfare and the certainty of triumph in His name. He had imagined Christians unified in a consecrated company of indomitable strength, parting the seas of their enemies and laying them low, for now and forever. Willem had handed him the brushes with which he had painted his images. But the picture that Willem and these knights were painting for him now was hell to the heaven of his dreams.

Louis had also believed that faith was the core of a Templar, yet these Templars seemed driven by inconceivable doubt.

"How can you talk of these things as if they are simply tidings of the day?" Louis asked.

"Because they *are* tidings of the day," Willem said. He tilted his head and gave Louis a look of concern. "This is truly the current situation in Jerusalem today."

"You never told me."

"It wasn't time."

"But it's time now?"

"Yes, it's time. Your dreams got you this far, Louis. You're a squire now, and soon to be a knight. But you've reached the place where dreams can get you killed, if they're all you can see. You must add to them now the sober knowledge of the realities you will face, and the wit and the insight that will guide you through them. Yes, Louis…it's time."

"If the Christians in Jerusalem care more for petty squabbling than they do for the good of the kingdom, what is there for me to do? What reason do I have to fight?"

"To make it right," Bollani said.

Louis's anger peaked. "How could Christians act in such a way at the expense of the Crusade?" he said. "How could they so dishonor the cause of Christ? I would go there myself right now, if I could, and give my life, if necessary, for something they scorn!"

"We're counting on that!" Bollani said, gesturing excitedly. "That's the kind of enthusiasm we need! But we need it in the thousands. This is the kind of passion for which we search. You will join the Order one day soon, will you not?"

"I had planned on it," Louis said. "But should I? Is there anything left for which to fight?"

The room fell silent. Louis knew that nothing they could say would make him feel better about it anyway. He wanted them, though, to come up with something. He wanted optimism, and resolve, and strength, and not the tired, powerless dejection that seemed to have consumed his exalted heroes. He wanted someone to burst into laughter and applaud them all for the prank they had played on him, and drink to the impending success of a new and glorious crusade, which would begin at any moment, just as soon as the kings and the pope finished assembling the necessary resources.

"Yes," Willem said simply. "There *is* a reason to fight." He stood and paced the length of the table as he spoke. "I have always told you that we Templars do not surrender. We fight until the last man draws his last breath, or until the beauseant is lowered on the field to signal retreat. We were born to be soldiers of Christ, Louis, and we will fight for Christ until we go, against our will, to rest at the foot of His heavenly throne. But we are still alive, and the beauseant still flies high. Retreat has not been called, at least not among the Templars. Do not mistake our grim demeanor for craven defeat, Louis. I should think you would know better than that."

"But why have you never told me these disheartening things? Why do you tell me them now?"

"There's a time for encouragement, and I gave you that. You've dreamed of this day because of the stories I told. There's also a time to face stark realities, and for you that time is now. You're closer now to facing an enemy that, until now, you have only ever fantasized. To defeat your enemy, Louis, you must first know him. We're telling you now that, at the moment, Christianity is its own worst enemy. *We* are the enemy we must overcome, if we are to recapture the vision of God's Kingdom in Jerusalem. And you will be part of that vision soon...as you have always longed to be. You must perceive that vision clearly if you wish to be of use."

Perhaps there was something someone could say, after all, to make it better, Louis thought. Willem had found the words.

"Then I will join you," he said.

"When it is time," Willem replied.

"I want to go now."

Willem glanced nervously toward the stairs that led to the private quarters where his sister, Louis's mother, no doubt strained to hear the muffled sound of their voices. Louis and Willem both knew that she dreaded that day more as it approached.

"If there *is* time," Louis said. "I'm starting to get the impression that I may not have the opportunity, for it will be too late."

"We need knights like you," Bollani said. "It would be good to have you with us, and an honor." His voice was always gruff, it seemed, even when his words were buoyant. Louis got the impression that some ancient slight had permanently annoyed the imposing Venetian. The incongruity of his words and his tone was peculiar.

Louis smiled sardonically. "You don't think it will be too late?"

"Our presence in the Holy Land has indeed grown tenuous," Bollani said. "City after city has fallen – Jerusalem, Nazareth, Cæsarea and Jaffa all in one year, and then Antioch." He counted each loss on a finger of his left hand.

"But all is not lost," Willem quickly added. "Stalled, yes, but not lost. Not yet."

The other Templars nodded in agreement.

"It just seems as though everything I've held dear was an illusion," Louis said.

"Louis," Willem said firmly, "our mission in Europe is to revive the crusade. We're here to fight for your dream, which each of us has always shared. I'll meet with bishops and nobles across Occitania. De Beaujeu is meeting with the pope. Gaudin and de Molay are in Paris and London. I believe this effort will bear fruit."

Raimon raised his eyebrows. "The highest ranks of the Templar Order, all here in Europe," he said. "That *is* significant."

"Quite," said Antonio Bollani. He nearly spat the word.

"The Grand Master is with the pope…" Raimon said. He seemed to be mulling the implications. "The pope is driven to distraction by his pursuit of heretics. Do you think de Beaujeu will be convincing enough to overcome that distraction?"

Willem had spoken highly of the Templar Grand Master, William de Beaujeu, and through Willem's stories, Louis had come to idolize him. He knew that de Beaujeu would prevail.

Thibaud Gaudin and Jacques de Molay were de Beaujeu's closest advisors. For those three men to have left the holy land simultaneously was indeed a portentous sign, and Louis was glad to hear of the endeavor. It gave him reason to hope.

"I think he will," Willem said. "He can be persuasive in his passions, and he is passionate about revitalizing the crusade."

"Europeans have turned their attention away from the crusades," Raimon said, "and toward more pressing concerns. There is danger here, close to home, and more turmoil with each passing year. The holy land is still important to people here, but less so than in the past."

"I'm not so sure of that," Bollani said. "I'm not sure it's important to them at all."

"There is deep and growing distrust," Raimon said. "Inquisitors have cast wide nets in their hunt for heretics, and they snare more of the innocent than the guilty. Fear has cooled the ardor of religious passion and nurtured wary, self–protective pretense in its place."

Louis grew perturbed by his father's words. Raimon never spoke of such things. He customarily sat and listened quietly while Willem and his Templars spoke, occasionally nodding, or laughing, or perhaps adding a vague or innocuous observation.

Uncle Willem gazed tentatively at Raimon, with concern, while Raimon looked from knight to knight, searching their faces as if weighing the wisdom of speaking further. Bollani leaned into the table toward Raimon and gazed intently into his eyes.

"It's all right," Bollani said. "Speak freely. None of us will take issue with your words, or repeat them, ever." The gangly knight seemed to soften a bit. Raimon nodded. *If the knight said it, it is so,* Louis thought.

"Many have grown deeply concerned," Raimon continued, "with the...conduct and integrity of the clergy. Many still sting from the persecutions in this land. It comes in waves, unpredictable, and often, some think, misguided." The Templars nodded in understanding. The enthusiasm of their response surprised Louis.

"The Templars were called into the Cathar crusade," Willem said. "Not many supported it, and many refused to take part."

"Most of those who did participate," Bollani said, "did so with little zeal or effect."

The crusade against the Cathars was the Church's first organized persecution of professing Christians. It had outraged many in the Languedoc and in Venice, where the Cathars were widely regarded as pious Christians.

The monks had taught Louis the truth about the Cathars, though, and he knew that they worshipped Lucifer as the god of light, the god of heaven. They believed he created heaven and dwelt there, along with everything holy. They called the God of the Old Testament evil, and they said that He created only the earth, and all that was sinful. It was a twisted theology, and Louis understood clearly why they were persecuted.

The Templars – and Raimon – sounded sympathetic toward them. "Why," Louis asked?

"Why what?" Bollani said.

"Why did the Templars refuse to take part?"

"Our mission is to fight Saracens," Bollani said, "and not Christians – particularly pious Christians who have done no harm."

"But they're not Christians," Louis protested. "They're heretics."

Bollani looked thoughtfully at Louis. Despite its gruffness, his voice was kind. "They profess Christ," he said. "I don't presume to judge the professions of others. To claim Christ is enough for me." He continued quickly to belay Louis's protest. "Yes, I understand the accusations against the Cathars. But I've rarely encountered people more pious, more gentle, or more forgiving. More importantly, I've never seen anyone but a Cathar face death with perfect serenity. Only the faith of saints could inspire such peace with eternity."

Louis resolved to contemplate that point further.

Bertrand said, "We understand that the matter of the Cathars has sullied popular regard for the Church in some places. Truth be told, it has driven a wedge between the Brethren and the pope." He leaned forward and moved his hand in a slashing motion for emphasis. "But that's a separate issue, distinct from Christian support for God's Kingdom in Jerusalem. It should not interfere with support for the Crusade."

Willem motioned for Bertrand to allow Raimon to continue.

"I'm not suggesting what should or should not be," Raimon replied. "I'm simply saying what *is*."

Louis noted rising tension.

"It's difficult," Raimon continued, "to hold enthusiasm for a far off crusade for Christ when Christians feel threatened at the hands of their own clergy."

"Suspicions run deep," Willem added quietly, nodding. "Trust has been weakened, if not broken. Good people have grown wary of those they should trust the most. We have been hindered by our ignorance of that fact. We," he said to his brethren, "are as separated from the troubles of this land as its people are from the reality of Jerusalem. We would do well to reacquaint ourselves with such things."

"Meanwhile," Raimon continued, "we hear tales of Templars embroiled in conflict between the Genoese and the Venetians, and not in the crusade, and Mongols fighting Mamluks while Christians fight among themselves. Such things make it difficult to maintain moral support, let alone financial support."

The words stung Louis. His mother and father had nurtured his love for the Church. They had encouraged him to worship God and to serve the Church, much as the Templars did. The words he was hearing now stood in opposition to their guidance, and to his firm convictions about the Church's infallibility.

Willem suddenly waved the discussion aside. "In any event," he said loudly, clearing his throat, "we are glad to be back in the company of my beloved sister and her family!"

Louis turned to see that his mother had appeared at the foot of the stairs to the upper chamber. Willem bowed in Marie's direction and smiled warmly.

Louis's mother held both fierce pride and frustrated anxiety for her valiant younger brother. Louis could see that even when his mother disapproved of Willem's stories and talk of war, she reserved those emotions in favor of her tenderness toward him. Louis could not imagine anything moving his mother to anger, save the vaguest threat to her brother or her son.

Now, though, her lips were tightly pursed. Louis guessed that she considered the Templar lifestyle to be just such a threat.

He was nearly overcome by the emotional undercurrent of the room. He longed for the resumption of more pleasant discourse. "Tell me more about your travels, Uncle Willem," he said. He added in a whisper, "And perhaps a bit more about the battles."

A look from Marie made it clear that there would be no more

tales, and no more talk of politics, or of battles with Mamluks.

"Tell us of the Saracen food, perhaps," she said with a dry smile, "or of their markets, or the latest fashions of their women's clothes. How do they entertain their guests?" She flashed a triumphant smile.

Louis sighed and resigned himself to the end of relevant conversation.

Chapter 8

The Martis arrived toward evening. In the dining hall, Uncle Willem introduced Jacques Marti to each of the visiting Templars. Jacques eagerly shook each of their hands, and wasted no time engaging them in conversation. He expressed grave concerns about the state of the Kingdom of Jerusalem, and keen interest in anything to do with the Templars and the Church.

Colette stood beside Louis. She placed her hand on his elbow and kissed him softly on the cheek. "It's good to see you, Louis," she said quietly. She glanced at the visiting Templars and leaned closer to him. "You must be thrilled to see Uncle Willem."

Louis nodded slightly, with uncharacteristic stoicism. He was consumed by other thoughts.

"Have they been telling you stories?" Colette asked.

Louis sniffed contemptuously, but he didn't answer. Colette stared at him with startled concern.

"Louis?"

"Of course they've been telling me stories," he said.

"And...that upset you?" she asked.

Louis shook his head curtly. “That’s all they have done, is tell me stories…tall tales, all my life.”

Marie beckoned to them to join the guests at the crowded table.

“Louis, Colette,” she said softly, “come…sit.”

“I don’t feel much like visiting,” Louis said. Willem glanced sharply at him, but Louis ignored the look. “I’d rather go for a walk. I’d like some fresh air.” He turned to Colette with a questioning look, and she nodded, looking uncertain. Louis turned his attention to Jacques Marti.

“Monsieur Marti,” Louis said respectfully, as he bowed slightly, “may we?” He indicated Colette, and then the door, with a nod.

Jacques Marti seemed disconcerted by Louis’s abruptness. He regarded his daughter with a mixture of affection and concern. She smiled shyly back at him, and he deftly returned Louis’s bow. It was a gracious bow, as exaggerated as those he and Louis had always exchanged at this point in their visits, which usually came much later after a bit of conversation and refreshment.

Marie frowned at her son’s indelicacy in taking leave without engaging in the customary pleasantries.

“You may, young man,” Jacques said graciously. He, too, noted the irregularity with slightly narrowed eyes. “Look after her well,” he added with mock sternness.

“I shall, Monsieur,” Louis vowed.

Colette nodded curtly to her father and followed Louis to the door, her brow furrowed with apprehension. Louis held the door for her as she walked past him, her head bowed, into the afternoon sun.

As Louis shut the door behind him, she turned abruptly to face him.

“What is it, Louis?” she said.

He shook his head and brushed past her, breaking into a rapid stride across the field. She rushed to catch up. They headed toward Louis’s refuge by the stream, Louis quietly grim, and Colette casting glances of growing concern.

"Louis...," she said.

"It's nothing," he snapped. "I don't want to talk about it."

"You're not yourself. I'd think you'd be excited that Uncle Willem is here. How could that not be so? What could be amiss?"

Louis groaned with frustration. Colette took the cue and let a long moment pass in silence, marked only by her breath as she hurried to match his pace. Finally, he had gathered the words to vent his aggravation, and he halted mid–stride.

"The Templars say the Crusade is a disaster," he said, throwing up his hands. "It sounds hopeless. It sounds as though the Christian presence in the Holy Land is doomed. I didn't expect such news from Uncle Willem. I expected the usual stories of bravery and triumph. I expected heroic optimism. Instead, I heard of nothing but turmoil among the Christians, and the Saracens gaining strength." He spun and resumed his drive toward the stream.

They soon arrived there without further conversation. Louis stood glaring at the water that gurgled past them in pleasant disregard for his mood. He cursed the peacefulness of the place, which suddenly seemed a mockery of his turmoil. Colette sat quietly on their favorite rock and waited.

Finally, wordlessly, Louis sat beside her. He huffed to himself several times and angrily threw a rock into the water, wishing it would cause more turbulence than it did.

"Louis," Colette finally ventured once more, "talk to me. Please."

"The abbot was right about one thing," he said. "Even those whose faith seems strongest are given to doubt, and to lapses of devotion."

Colette looked puzzled, but she waited for him to continue.

"I've believed as I've been taught to believe," he fumed. "I've believed that Uncle Willem and my father shared those beliefs. I've listened to what I've been told, and I've built my future on that foundation."

"Yes, you have," Colette said softly.

"And now I'm suddenly faced with doubts and pessimism,"

he said. "It makes me angry."

"What do you doubt?"

He looked at her in dismay.

"Me?" he said. "It's not my doubt, Colette. I don't doubt anything, except for the courage and the spiritual integrity of those who've taught me my faith."

"Oh?" She furrowed her brow. She was clearly taken aback by his words. He huffed again, incredulous at the realizations he was trying to absorb.

"My father—" he began; he was about to repeat some of the things his father had said earlier in the day, but it occurred to him that his father had probably said those things in confidence, not expecting them to be repeated. *My words are for you, and for no other, ever,* he had cautioned Louis more than once. Louis had never forgotten it. Indignant as he might feel now, he would not betray his father's confidence, even with Colette.

"Your father?"

"Never mind. It's just that I was taught to believe so many things, and to be loyal to those beliefs, to hold fast to them. I've learned to hate whatever opposed those beliefs, and to fight against the things I hate. Now, I hear Templars speaking of the Crusade with loathing in their voices, and deriding the Christians for whom it was undertaken in the first place. They speak of infidels with reverence, and of Christians with repugnance."

"I don't understand," Colette said.

He nearly lost his line of thought when he turned and saw her face, her eyes bewildered, her brow furrowed, and her nose wrinkled as if she smelled something dreadful. Her expression was almost comical in the intensity of its perplexity. He nearly laughed, but he caught himself.

"The Muslim sultan," he said. "Kala'un. They spoke of him as if he is one of the greatest warriors. They spoke of his fearlessness, his dignity. They are at peace with him. Yet they see the Christians in Jerusalem as bickering children, defeated already by their own foolish in–fighting."

"Yes," Colette said, nodding. "I can see how that would disturb you."

"Disturb me? It enrages me."

"Yes, I see." She smiled dimly, and then looked thoughtful for a moment. "So," she said, "you believe that only Christians are fearless and dignified?"

"I can't imagine the leader of the infidels as noble. I never thought I'd hear Christians – Templars, no less – describe an infidel in such lofty terms."

"And you also have difficulty imagining Christians as backbiting and foolish?"

"The Crusaders, yes."

"But they're human, Louis. It's not so hard to understand, if you really think about it." After a long silence, she spoke more lightly. "Perhaps we should talk about more pleasant things." She turned and smiled widely at him.

"You never like to talk about these things anymore," he observed. "Mother is the same. She reacts much as you do at the mere mention of Crusades. She always discourages Uncle Willem from telling his tales of battle."

"Perhaps—"

"She interrupts often," he continued. "I don't know why she hates his stories so."

"You don't?" Colette said it in a way that made clear that she understood completely.

"No," he said, peering at her. "I don't. He speaks only of faith, and loyalty, and courage, and victory in God's name. These are the highest ideals, and she knows I am anxious to hear about them."

"Too anxious, perhaps...for her liking."

"It's long been my dream to follow him," he reminded her. "It's the purpose of my life. Why would she have misgivings about such a noble ambition?"

"Well, for one thing, Louis, while you have made Templars and crusading your life's ambition, others may see those things as threats to your life, or at least to your welfare. Perhaps some cherish your life more than you do. That shouldn't be difficult for you to see."

"It honors God to commit one's life to such things. There are eternal rewards."

"Yes...as long as you understand that by living for eternal rewards, one may overlook earthly gifts, and perhaps miss out on daily blessings."

"The things of this world pass away," he said flatly.

"Or so we are taught," she said slowly. She gazed at their reflection in the rippling stream, and in the pause that followed, he wondered at her strange remark. "Anyway," she said, "I understand why it makes you so angry. I don't blame you, but I wish it wouldn't consume you so. Can you let it go enough to enjoy the rest of the day?" She leaned toward him and gazed into his eyes, beaming a cheery, affectionate smile.

Louis felt his anxiety begin to wane as he contemplated the question. "You're right, of course," he said grudgingly. "It *is* good to see Uncle Willem again. I've waited a long time for this visit. It's also very good to see *you* again." He winked at her and forced a smile.

"That's more like it," she said.

A disturbance in the gently swaying field grass drew their attention, and they laughed when Maximilian emerged, his ears flapping wildly as he bounded toward them.

"Max!" Colette called. She opened her arms to receive him. Max snorted and trembled as she embraced him. Louis admired the two of them, and the simplicity of their affection. His anxiety diminished as he allowed the company of his closest boyhood conspirators to dominate his attention.

Colette picked up a stick and threw it for Max to retrieve. As Max ran after it, she turned back to Louis.

"Can we let all of this go for now?" she asked. "I'd just like to enjoy being here with you, talking of lighter things and enjoying this glorious day." She turned in a slow circle, her arms outstretched, turning her face to the warming sun. "Isn't it just perfect?" she said.

His gaze was drawn to the young woman. "It is," he readily agreed.

"He didn't take that very well," Raimon observed.

"No, he didn't," Willem said. "But it's time he balanced his dreams and ideals with a healthy appreciation for political realities."

"I worry about his idealism," Raimon said. "He's almost fanatical in his commitment to the Church. We've encouraged his faith and piety, and loyalty to the Church, of course. But our lessons in religious observance took root more deeply than we intended."

Willem nodded and said, "He'll face the truth of it soon enough. I think it's important to start preparing him now."

"Perhaps it's time," Marie said quietly, "to offer Louis not only a more balanced perspective, but also the opportunity to reconsider his future, based on truth."

Raimon raised an eyebrow in consideration.

Willem answered quickly. "I'd prefer that he not reconsider," he said. "If good men give up their dreams in the face of discouragement, there shall be no hope. We need men like Louis to bring their ideals into the Order, to counter the cynicism and despair that are growing more prevalent throughout the Holy Land. I'd rather see him hold fast to his commitment, and to his dreams, despite the sobering truth."

"And I'd like to know my son will be safe," Marie said, "or at the very least, that if he does find danger, he will face it prepared, and not mired in disillusion. Do not lead him into hopelessness, Willem."

"Marie," Willem said, "when I look at Louis I see myself. I was at least as idealistic at his age." He thought back to his early Templar days. "I imagined myself riding into battle every day, triumphant and proud, cutting down the heathen horde to the sound of angelic hymns. But when I got to Outremer I learned the reality of it: crippling sickness and unbearable heat throughout the land, and boredom and backstabbing among the Crusaders. It was a hard lesson, to be sure. For many months I was plagued by disillusion and regret. But my dreams are what led me to the cause, and the cause is greater than the disillusion."

"His disillusion will be immense," Marie warned.

"It is true," Willem conceded, "that the trauma of disillusion is proportionate to the degree of idealism. I shall never forget my own introduction to reality "

"I want my son safe, and whole in every way," she insisted.

"I will watch over him," Willem said. He had promised this to Marie long ago, when Louis first expressed his Templar dreams. He'd never doubted his ability to keep that vow. "I've already promised you—"

"Yes, I know you have," she interrupted. "But I see now that you are pressed from both sides – on the one side by your promise to me, and on the other by your promises to him. I wonder if you will be able to honor one promise without breaking the other."

Willem swallowed hard. She had identified his greatest fear. No matter how hard he tried, he had never succeeded in concealing anything from his sister. Her perceptiveness both amazed and annoyed him.

"I will do everything in my power to honor both your wishes and his," he said. He paused, considering his capacity to deliver on a further commitment to Marie.

"And if they conflict?" she said.

"I swear that if my support for Louis's ambitions should clash with my promise to you, I shall honor your wishes above all, dear sister."

Marie peered intently at her brother for a moment. She weighed his words, and then she smiled, her eyes sparkling with appreciative affection. "You shouldn't swear," she whispered. "Your word is good enough."

Willem smiled at his sister's gentle, familiar scolding.

"Where do the Templars stand with young Philip the Fair?" Jacques Marti suddenly asked, drawing attention from Willem and Marie. He continued, addressing Antonio Bollani. "Philip appears intent on amassing more territory and power, and eager to recover the influence his father squandered. Some say he will intensify French aggression against Aragon."

Bollani shrugged. "It's difficult to predict what this king will do," he said. "He's intelligent, but he lacks his father's passion. Dispassion can lead to thoughtful, reasoned rule, but also to calculated cruelty. He is hungry for power, so I believe continued hostility with Aragon is assured."

"Our Grand Master, de Beaujeu, will try to persuade him to turn his attention to the Crusade," Willem said.

"I doubt he'll succeed entirely," Bollani said. "The support we'll receive from Philip will most likely be nominal, and it will come at a high price. More likely, he'll expect financing for the expansion of his domain."

"Will the Templars support his military ventures?" Raimon asked.

"The Grand Master will loan him money," Willem said, "but he won't offer troops. De Beaujeu is intent on recovering Jerusalem. I don't see him sacrificing that vision for any cause. He would sacrifice the king's good graces before he'd jeopardize his sacred mission. Besides, de Beaujeu's loyalty to Aragon is strong."

"As is that of de Garonne," Raimon said with a nod to Willem.

"Oh?" Bollani said. "Why is that?"

"Aragon strongly supported the Languedoc nobles against the Albigensian Crusade," Willem said. "Raimon's ancestors formed firm alliances among the Aragon nobility. Those loyalties have always run deep. They were strengthened by France's forays into the Languedoc, and the Church's expansion of power here. Alliances with Aragon, though unspoken, remain strong."

Raimon said, "My ancestry extends far into the misty past, to a time when the Languedoc was left defenseless by the disintegration of the Roman Empire and its protection. The Languedoc nobility banded together to protect itself then, and they formed lasting fraternal bonds."

Bollani nodded understanding.

"Those bonds were tested," Willem said, "but ultimately strengthened by decades of the Church's crusading against the Cathars. The Albigensian Crusade destroyed nearly half a million souls, most of them friends and relations of the nobles."

"France's aggression against Aragon led ultimately to the theft of our land," Raimon said with an edge of rising passion. "That aggression destroyed the peace we had managed to attain. We have had no peace in the decades since our annexation to France. Inquisition and abuse are a constant fear. Only independence from France and renewed ties with Aragon could renew our peace."

Bollani nodded again. "Perhaps, then," he observed, "it is better for young Louis to pursue the more noble conflict in Outremer than to be caught up in conflict among Christians in his homeland. Such conflict, should it escalate, could be a far greater blow to his youthful idealism."

Willem nodded appreciatively at Bollani's reasoning. Marie appeared only to grow more deeply alarmed.

Chapter 9

A BITTER WIND HOWLED across the frozen fields of Lord Bertrand Jacquette's estate, blowing tattered leaves and broken branches through the open stable doors. Louis dropped the stallion's hoof and moved to pull the heavy doors closed.

It was nearing dawn, and a feeble glow crept into an overcast sky. He had woken early, as usual, to the sound of the red deer's antlers tangling branches in the tree line at the edges of the fields. He had come to wake easily every morning, and always with the urgency for another chance to demonstrate his fitness for knighthood.

He had excelled in most aspects of his squiring in the six months he'd been at it. Jacquette was not given to praising his squires, but he made no secret of the frustration and disappointment they generally caused him. Jacquette criticized Louis rarely of late, and that was a sure sign that Louis's performance had improved. Louis sensed, though, that there was something about him that Jacquette did not like. He forced himself not to let that distract him.

He wondered now what it was. He was obedient. He studied hard and practiced ceaselessly, mastering both his horsemanship and his sword. And he was as pious as any man could be.

He was worrying that point when a tumult broke the silence of the cold, gray morning. Someone or something crashed recklessly through the trees, moving toward the house with an urgency that could only mean danger. As the sound grew louder, Louis recognized the panicked panting of a man who had run farther than he was conditioned to run, but who was too afraid to stop. The dogs outside the kitchen lunged to the ends of their leashes and raised a howl that would surely wake the entire estate.

Louis seized his sword belt and rushed from the barn to investigate. As he emerged from the barn, the door of the estate house flew open and men–at–arms hurried toward the disturbance.

A gaunt, gray–haired man ran wildly from the tree line toward the house, his black cloak tattered and flapping behind him as he ran. The men–at–arms formed a line between him and the house, their hands upon the pommels of their swords. As the man approached, he slid to his knees and skidded to a halt before them, bowing his head in submission.

Bertrand Jacquette emerged from the house. The men–at–arms made way for him as he approached. The man looked up at Jacquette with pleading eyes, his hands clasped in frantic supplication. Jacquette waited expectantly for the man to speak.

"Lord Jacquette," the man began, gasping for breath. "We need your help…"

"Explain," Jacquette said, holding up his hand.

The man took several breaths and composed himself. The men–at–arms relaxed their stance.

The man said, "They've come for us. I need you to shelter my wife."

"What makes you think I would do that, Cathar?" Jacquette said sternly.

Louis looked at the ragged man in surprise. So this was a Cathar! He had never seen one, and his interest was suddenly piqued. He had an image in his head of what a Cathar must look like, given all that he had been told of their evil, and their despicable rituals and beliefs. This man did not fit his preconceptions of the bloodthirsty demons.

The Cathar said, "I am Eustache, of Pieusse. I know who you are, Lord Jacquette. I know you will help me. That is why I'm here." Eustache of Pieusse clasped his hands at his chest as if he were praying for deliverance.

"How do you know of me?" Jacquette asked, his eyes narrowed with suspicion.

"Christophe, in Toulouse," Eustache said.

Jacquette's eyes flashed recognition. He glanced at the men–at–arms. "Take him to the hall," he said with a sharp gesture. His nervous gaze scanned the tree line, then the horizon beyond the fields. The men–at–arms lifted Eustache gently to his feet and hurried him toward the house. Jacquette followed them, glancing back toward the fields as he went.

Louis's heart pounded. He'd come face to face with a Cathar, the scourge of the Holy Church. And his mentor, among the most respected of the Languedoc nobility, was sheltering the heretic from authorities of the Church, who must surely be following in close pursuit.

He turned back to his task and resolved to remain mindful of his place. It would not do to question authority, but as Louis was learning, restraint in that regard was one thing he had yet to master.

"Prepare to ride," a voice said gruffly, startling him yet once again. He turned toward the knight who had appeared at the stable doors. Gervais was stern after the fashion of their master, but Louis respected both his intellect and his authority. Gervais had provided Louis with most of his training, and he seemed to approve of his performance. "We'll need six horses," he said.

"Yes, sir," Louis answered. He turned to the task.

"We'll ride to retrieve the woman," Gervais said. "One should be a palfrey."

Louis nodded his understanding. "She's alone?" he asked.

"With an escort," Gervais said. Louis nodded again. "You'll

come with us." Louis looked up in surprise. He was pleased that someone thought he should go, and he welcomed the break from routine now that his blood had been quickened by the excitement.

"I need but a few minutes," he said. Gervais nodded and hurried back to the house to assemble the rest of the party.

Louis, Gervais, and two men–at–arms rode quickly into the woods. Louis led the palfrey, and one of the men led a courser. None spoke. Gervais seemed exceptionally alert; he was clearly anticipating trouble. They rode in the direction the Cathar had indicated, toward the stream that ran south toward Saint-Polycarpe. The woman was about a mile to the south.

Louis searched Gervais' eyes for signs of distaste with their task. While the Cathars had once enjoyed the warmth and admiration of the people of the Languedoc, the Church's protracted inquisition against them had almost thoroughly alienated them from the rest of their neighbors. One risked all to be seen, or whispered to have been seen, in the company of Cathars. Gervais betrayed no such aversion. His blue-gray eyes were sharp, but expressionless as he scanned the trail and the leafless woods ahead of them.

Presently they arrived at the crook in the stream where Eustache had said they would find his wife and her escort. The woman stood gazing into the stream. Her movement was ethereal as she turned to face their approach. She wore black robes like her husband's, and she was equally gaunt. Her skin was nearly translucent, but the evidence of remarkable beauty lingered upon her face.

At the sound of the hooves, the escort sprang to stand between the lady and the approaching horses. He wore no arms. He, too, was a Cathar, Louis thought. Cathars abhorred violence, and never took weapons in hand. While they would often rely on secular knights to defend them, they would not defend themselves.

"We are Lord Jacquette's men," Gervais called out as they approached. The man bowed deeply, his hands clasped in the same supplicating gesture Eustache had displayed. The woman stood calmly, her shoulders held high in stately resolve.

Louis studied the woman as he dismounted and led the palfrey to her. She was neither haughty nor proud; she radiated strength and self–assurance. Her eyes betrayed no fear, though she faced considerable danger.

"I am Mathilde of Benoit," she said. "My companion is my brother, Pierre." Pierre nodded to Jacquette's men.

"Madame," Louis said, gesturing toward the palfrey's sidesaddle. The woman smiled kindly at Louis and allowed him to help her up. Once everyone had mounted, they reined toward the manor house without delay.

The Cathars fascinated Louis. He studied Pierre, and noted differences between him and his sister, and Eustache. While Eustache and Mathilde were very thin, and apparently undernourished, Pierre seemed adequately fed. His robes and cloak were gray. He was less self–assured than Mathilde, and he lacked the burning passion Louis had seen in Eustache's eyes. Louis assumed that Pierre was a *credente*, a believer, and had not yet been elevated to the station of Perfect.

The group rode in silence, though Louis felt compelled to question Mathilde, to learn more about her and her ways. He reproved himself silently; he had learned all he needed to know about the Cathars at the abbey, and from the priests in the village. A crusade would not have been launched against these people had they not demonstrated diabolical heresy.

Finally, he could not help himself. "You're a Cathar," he said with a hint of wonder.

Mathilde turned to him in surprise. "Yes," she said. "have you never met a Cathar?"

"I haven't," Louis said. He hated that it felt like a confession of ignorance.

"They say that I eat my babies," she said, "and drink their blood." Louis cringed at her bluntness; she smiled as if she was genuinely amused by the charge that would justify her execution. Almost as if she knew his thoughts, she added, "Death is but a form of birth, a passing from one place of growing to the next. I do not fear it." She paused, and then grew solemn. "I assure you that I am not a monster."

Louis said nothing. He doubted that the monks would lie about such things, or be so badly mistaken. And yet this woman could have been his mother. She had the same saintly bearing, the same kindly eyes, and the same gentle demeanor. Purity emanated from her like warmth from a winter hearth. He did not see how she could be what he believed her to be.

Wolves in sheep's clothing, he remembered the monks saying. It was Satan's trickery to appear as a shining, beautiful thing, they said. Men are repulsed by the ugliness of evil, and tempted by the beauty of Godliness. It was the way of the Evil One to take the forms of pious, saintly people.

"Yes," Louis said. "I've heard the accusations. I've heard of contemptible rites, abominations. I thought you'd look like the demons I've envisioned." He paused, regarding the stately woman. "You don't seem like the sort that burns babies and eats their remains."

Gervais shot Louis a look of disapproval and shook his head to silence him.

"The irony of that accusation," she said, "is that Cathars avoid both procreation and the consumption of flesh. We encourage chasteness, even among the married. We do not consume anything that is related to procreation – no meat, milk, eggs, or cheese. The very thought of consuming flesh is abhorrent to us, yet that is precisely the nature of the despicable charges of our persecutors. But surely you already know these things." She glanced at Gervais, who shrugged and looked straight ahead.

Strange customs, Louis thought, *but hardly evil.* He considered the woman's words, wary of being tricked into sympathizing with her.

"That's the way they work," said Nicolas, a man–at–arms. Nicolas, about twenty–two and from the foothills of the Pyrenees, never said much. Louis looked at him quizzically, surprised by his interjection. "They attack your greatest strengths, the things they fear the most," Nicolas continued. Gervais nodded in agreement.

"Who?" Louis said.

"The Inquisitors," Nicolas said, shrugging. "They know they cannot diminish your strength, so they attack it instead, saying it is the mask that hides – and therefore exposes – your true evil." He paused and looked up through the trees in thought. "It's like this," he said. "An order of monks fulfills its vows of poverty so perfectly that it shames the rest of the clergy; one day those monks are accused of being puffed up with pride, and perhaps of stealing the Church's money and hiding it away for their own surreptitious use. Or a group of Gnostics demonstrates greater chasteness than the Church's clergy; they are accused of conducting perverse orgies with their own daughters and mothers."

Louis was outraged. Nicolas spoke as if the Church's accusations were lies. He was about to protest when Gervais spoke, nodding again in agreement.

"The Cathars," he explained, nodding toward Mathilde, "believe that procreation is Satan's tool for enslaving Godly souls, binding them to this God-forsaken world, which is Satan's creation, and his domain. To a Cathar, procreation is fundamentally evil, as it serves only the purposes of the Evil One. And yet, the chief charge against them is the usual one: that they engage in wild orgies with their own sons and daughters."

"Do you not know these things, Louis?" Nicolas asked. "Surely you've heard all of this before."

Louis realized that in this group he was probably alone in his beliefs about the Cathars and heresy. He decided in favor of discretion. "I only know what I've been told," he said. "I've never met a Cathar until today."

"Ah! Then I'm honored to be your first," Mathilde said with a smile. "I pray that I may be a worthy exemplar of the Good People."

"You remind me of my mother," Louis said. Mathilde was clearly pleased. Louis did not want to discuss Cathars anymore. He turned his face toward the woods and set his jaw.

The group dismounted outside the front door of the manor house. Jacquette emerged with several of his knights, followed by Eustache. Mathilde straightened her robes and her cloak and turned to face them.

"You're safe," Eustache said when he saw her.

"Yes," she answered. To Jacquette, she said, "I thank you for the kindness of your escort."

"I understand you intend to return to your congregation," Jacquette said. "That is not advisable."

"I must," Mathilde said. "I'm responsible for them. I must make provisions for their survival, if at all possible."

Jacquette shook his head and said, "That may not be possible. Their survival is unlikely. If, as Eustache says, an agent of the Church has infiltrated, the Church knows everything now, and everyone. It's only a matter of time."

"I must try," Mathilde insisted. "You will do your best to delay them, then?"

"We'll say we are waiting on you, and that we expect you presently," Jacquette said. He was nonchalant. "We'll present Eustache as our prisoner, and explain that we await your arrival, upon which we will arrest you, too. They'll no doubt wait with us."

Mathilde nodded appreciatively. "Very well," she said.

"We'll hold them as long as we can, but at some point they'll tire of waiting and go for you."

"I'll hurry," Mathilde said.

"My men will take you wherever you need to go."

Jacquette sent a knight and two men–at–arms to escort Mathilde and Pierre to their congregation.

Louis approached Gervais, perplexed.

"Why are we helping them?" he said. "Doesn't protecting them put us all at risk?"

"They've done nothing wrong," Gervais said. "They're innocent."

"But they're heretics."

Gervais nodded. "That's always been a convenient and malleable term. It could be applied to anyone, given the right set of circumstances."

"How so?"

"We all know who leads the Inquisition," Gervais said, shrugging.

"The Dominicans, yes."

Gervais nodded again. "And yet, in his day, Dominic himself urged the Church to embrace humility and austerity. He recognized the piety of the Cathars, and its stark contrast with the excesses of the Church. He preached what the Cathars exemplify. Why he sided with the Church against them is a mystery to me."

"They believe in two gods," Louis said flatly.

"They make a good argument," Gervais countered. "With a cursory look, one might reasonably wonder if they're right: that the god of this world is not God, but the Devil."

"They also say the Old Testament is the Devil's book."

"The God of the Old Testament ordered the slaughter of innocents," Gervais said. "The Midianites, the Canaanites, and so many others were utterly destroyed, to the last woman and child. Virgins were taken as slaves, and to be the unwilling wives of the Israelite army. The God of the New Testament, Our Holy Savior, could not have condoned such brutality. It is reasonable to wonder at that disparity."

"The Israelites slaughtered unbelievers who did not love God," Louis said. "The unbelievers deserved to die for their rebellion against God."

Gervais looked intently at Louis. He seemed to be formulating an argument, but then he seemed to think better of it. Finally, he gave a slight nod.

"Your faith is strong," he said simply. He stood deep in thought for a moment more. "Stable the horses now," he said, "and meet me at the training field. We'll review your lance work, and then sharpen your swordsmanship."

"Yes, sir," Louis said. He was glad to end the conversation. He had sensed an emotional reaction in Gervais, and it was something he was not yet fully prepared to confront.

✠ ✠ ✠

The Inquisition arrived the next day. A friar in black, a Dominican, with a clerical entourage and a detachment of soldiers, rode hard into the compound and clattered to a halt on the frozen ground outside the manor house. Jacquette's men emerged from the house, and Jacquette followed.

It was Friar Diego de Mondragón, the Dominican who had visited the de Garonne estate almost five years earlier. He was heavier, and his face bore deeper lines. He wore the same heavy black cloak over pure white robes. His thick, black hair was unkempt. His dark eyes glowered beneath ample brows, and they looked weary, as though he had not slept. Louis got the impression that things had not gone entirely well for Fra Mondragón.

"Friar," Lord Jacquette said, "we've been expecting you."

Mondragón seemed surprised, as if he had expected resistance. "You have?" he said doubtfully. "Then you know why I'm here."

"Yes. I have something for you." Jacquette motioned to a man–at–arms, who moved toward the rear of the house, toward the cell that held the prisoner. "He arrived yesterday, desperate for shelter. He said that the rest of his party would follow, by a week at the most. He said they were hunted by outlaws, but I know a Cathar when I see one." The contempt in his voice sounded real. "I held him so that his party would assume that he was, in fact, sheltered, rather than turn him in and risk spreading word of his arrest."

Mondragón's piercing gaze lingered on Jacquette. "That was good thinking," he said. "What did you plan to do next?"

"Wait a week, or until his party arrived. Then bring him, and if possible his accomplices, to you."

"We'll wait here as well," Mondragón said. "When his wife arrives, we'll take them both into custody. It'll save you the travel to Carcassonne."

Jacquette nodded. "Very well," he said.

The Dominican sent his troops to make camp a short distance away while he and his clergymen made themselves comfortable in the Jacquette residence. Jacquette assured the troops that he would send for them the moment the Cathar Perfect Mathilde arrived.

It took but a few days for Mondragón's patience to wear thin, though, and finally they seized Eustache and left to hunt the countryside for Mathilde.

Louis struggled for those few days with his impulse to divulge the Cathars' deception to the Inquisitor. The loyalty of his heart was to the Church. But he understood that his duty as a squire, and the duty of all knights, was firm and unceasing loyalty to his liege. Treason against his lord would be a felony, punishable by dispossession, disenfranchisement, and death by hanging, or worse.

His loyalty to the Church was a powerful force. Yet, something in Mondragón's countenance restrained it. Louis sensed malevolence in the man. Worse, the contrast between the friar and the Cathars was stark. It made the Cathars appear saintly, and the friar corrupt.

Louis held his tongue.

In time, he pushed his troubled thoughts and the incident of the Cathars from his mind. He resolved to focus on his training, to be made knight as soon as possible and be finished with the rigors of his training.

The friar left with his entourage dragging the unfortunate Eustache behind them, tattered, weary, and somehow imbued with a profound, inexplicable peace.

Chapter 10

Guis, a fellow squire in training, tightened his grip on the throat of a hissing, flailing cat that he had captured behind the barn. He carried it to a stake in the clearing behind the main house, struggling to restrain the frantic clawing that shredded the skin of his forearms. He cursed at the animal as it fought to escape his grasp.

Louis and the other squires watched in silence. Simos, a rebellious lad from a village at the foot of the Pyrenees, laughed and shifted his weight from foot to foot in nervous anticipation.

Bouchard, an oafish commoner who was raised a ward of the Church, approached the stake with a leather cord. He tightened a noose around the cat's neck, and tied the other end fast to the foot of the stake.

The cat hissed and spat and hopped madly at the end of the cord. The boys laughed at the grotesquely comical sight, and Louis wished that it would stop at that.

"Now," Guis said grimly, facing the boys, "we're going to teach that little bastard a lesson." He bent to pick up a handful of stones. Blood dripped from deep scratches on his arms, but he pretended not to notice them.

The other boys also collected rocks. Louis selected stones that were shaped for a comfortable throw, and heavy enough to put a quick end to the game.

The first to kill the cat would win the prize: honorary knighthood for the day. For him, there would be no chores: no cleaning the stables, nor polishing swords, nor carrying wood for the fires. Instead, the 'knight' would spend the day in weapons training with the knights, and riding and sparring, and eventually even dining with the men-at-arms.

Simos threw the first stone. He hit the cat squarely in the ribs with a sickening thud. The cat screeched and leapt several feet into the air.

Guis followed, catching the cat on the rump, and Bouchard missed because the cat had been driven into frenzy. Guis shoved Bouchard, sending him sprawling in the gravelly dirt.

Aimes glanced shyly at Louis, yielding him the next turn, while Piere hung back with an air of bored detachment.

Aimes de Lomnha did not want to be a knight. He had never said as much, but to Louis it was painfully clear. He would never have a choice in the matter, or the apparent will to make one if he could. He did what he was told to do, without fail, but only because he was told to do it. He seemed disinclined to think for himself, or to challenge the mildest opposition. Louis imagined that he would die in his first battle, and that today he would rather be chasing butterflies than throwing rocks at a feral cat.

Piere wanted to throw rocks, probably more than any of them did. His ambivalence was a practiced shield. He wanted them to believe that he could do without any of it, and that he was humoring them, and nothing more.

Louis took careful aim. He didn't want to hurt the cat, but he wanted to end its misery. It would die today; that much was certain. The more they played these games, the less he cared about that. They were part of his training. But he saw no point in prolonging the process. It was better to die from one quick blow than from a dozen ineptly placed wounds.

A knight must kill without qualms, he reasoned, for that was their primary station. But a knight must also show mercy, for that was their highest calling. He aimed to kill with mercy.

He cursed himself for misplacing his first throw, and hitting the cat solidly on the shoulder. Bones broke, and the cat fell twitching to the ground with an eerie, pain-wracked cry.

Piere peered curiously now, as if concerned he might not get his turn. Since Louis's throw felled the cat, he got another chance to finish it.

Louis aimed the second stone carefully. He controlled his breathing despite his eagerness, and concentrated on his target. Finally, he threw a perfect stone and cracked the animal's skull. He breathed a sigh of relief when it stopped twitching and lay lifeless in the dirt.

Piere nodded his approval and sniffed, obviously feeling cheated, and Aimes gazed appreciatively at Louis. Guis threw his hands into the air in a celebratory gesture and approached Louis to congratulate him. He began to speak, but was interrupted by the hurried approach of cavalry from the road.

Men-at-arms rushed from all corners of the estate at the cavalry's approach. Nearly a hundred knights in azure and gold, the colors of King Philip IV, arrived in a turbulent cloud of dust.

Lord Jacquette emerged from the house flanked by his highest commanders. The French captain dismounted and approached Jacquette, his dark, close-set eyes squinting in the sunlight and the settling dust.

"We're riding to Navarre," he said abruptly, without introduction.

Jacquette nodded acknowledgement, his hands clasped behind his back.

"I expect you'll send men along with me," the captain added.

Jacquette surveyed the large host of horsemen with puzzlement. "For what purpose?" he asked.

"We've heard of Cathar enclaves protected by renegade nobles there," the captain snapped. "To whom do I explain myself?"

Jacquette smiled dryly. "To someone of whom you have come to beg support," he said, "and whose name you should already know."

"Am I wrong to expect you to serve your king?" the captain asked in an ominous drawl.

"Is the king conscripting nobles?" Jacquette countered. "You must have his order, then." He held out his hand for the document.

"There's no conscription," the captain said. "I'm asking you to support your king."

Jacquette shook his head. "I haven't the resources," he said. He turned and raised his palms to indicate his land. "I have farmland. Tenants and shepherds. A few knights and men-at-arms, and a handful of squires in training."

"What better training than a real campaign?" the captain said.

"They're not ready," Jacquette said forcefully. He glared at the captain and added, "I don't have what you need."

The captain took a long look around at the gathered men and the squires. He seemed to make a mental note.

"What did you say is your name?" he asked.

Jacquette laughed. "I am Bertrand Jacquette," he said. "Give my regards to our young king when you see him next. He's sure to welcome it."

The captain blanched slightly at that, and then nodded and quickly remounted.

"We would welcome any support you care to send, should you reconsider," he said. He ordered the cavalry to move on.

The men and the squires watched until the French soldiers disappeared into a distant dust cloud, and then they returned to their business.

Jacquette turned to the squires. He raised an appraising eyebrow. "Who is 'knight' for the day?" he asked.

"Louis," Simos said proudly, pointing.

Jacquette seemed pleased. "Ah," he said. "Very well." To Louis, he said, "Ride with Gervais and Nicolas," he said. "Enjoy the honor while it lasts." He turned to go.

"My lord," Louis called after him, and Jacquette turned back.

"May I ask you something?" Jacquette nodded. Louis hesitated, doubting he should ask the question. But his curiosity prodded him. "Why did we not send men with them?"

Jacquette walked to Louis and stood before him. His powerful build made Louis feel slight, even though he was nearly as tall, and quite strong for his size.

"I was put on this earth to do God's work," Jacquette said, "just as were the rest of you. That work does not include helping Christians who are convinced they are right destroy Christians they believe to be wrong. I possess neither the divine wisdom nor the personal inclination to cast such judgment, and I'll be damned if I'll allow anyone in my charge to do so."

Louis nodded. He admired the clarity of Jacquette's reasoning, though he found the truth of it jarring.

"Have you any other questions?" Jacquette asked.

"No, my lord," he replied.

"Then go and be a knight for the day." He turned and strode toward the house.

Gervais stood holding the reins of his solidly muscled warhorse, regarding Louis with a strangely appreciative grin.

Chapter 11

AUTUMN APPROACHED on a brisk north wind that blew leaves and ominous clouds ahead of its chill. Louis was home for a few days on a break from his training with Lord Jacquette. It had been a good visit; he missed his mother badly, and they spent much of the time catching up on the past months.

For the first time in his life, he noticed the subtle signs of age in the lines of his mother's face. He realized that he would see far less of her over the coming years, and the thought brought sadness to his heart.

He rose early because he wanted to spend an hour riding with Victor before he returned to Jacquette's estate. He pulled his wool cloak tight against the cold as he headed toward the stables. He was due to return to Jacquette's before noon, so he'd have to be on the road shortly after sunrise.

Victor had been working in the stables since the day after the confrontation on the road to Carcassonne. He was appreciative; he demonstrated it by tending more meticulously to Louis's horse than to the others, and by gracing Louis with a wide smile whenever he saw him.

Louis sensed restraint, though, in Victor's gratitude. He suspected that Victor resented the inequity of their status. He understood that, of course, but there wasn't anything he could do about it. It was the way of things. It pleased him, though, to think that Victor aspired to higher standing

They had become fast friends after that eventful summer day. They were an unusual pair, the peasant boy and the noble's son, the serf and the squire, who hunted and rode horses together as if they were fellow knights. Louis had grown to cherish their friendship.

He blew on his hands and rubbed them briskly as his feet crunched the grass grown stiff by the deepening chill. As he neared the stable he called out to Victor, who appeared in the doorway with his customary toothy grin.

Victor had both horses saddled and ready to go. Even at the earliest hours, he was always energetic and alert. Louis marveled at that as he stifled a yawn. Victor held the reins of both horses, one in each hand, and he spoke to them in a low, soothing voice.

Louis's new courser was of average size, but exceptionally strong and agile. It's chestnut coat was smooth, and it carried itself with majestic bearing. Raimon had surprised him with it, as it had been given to him in payment for an outstanding debt, and all of his men–at–arms were already amply equipped. None had need of another courser, so this one went to Louis. He called his new courser Invictus.

It was unusual for a squire to ride a horse of such caliber, and Louis appreciated the richness of the blessing. He did not take such fortune for granted. In turn, he gave his older, less agile rouncey, Soranus, to Victor – not to own, but to ride whenever he wished. The gesture was unconventional, and his father protested vigorously until Louis told him of the care with which Victor had tended the horses, and the skill with which he trained and exercised them.

Soranus was Louis's first horse, a well–trained warhorse that once belonged to one of the men–at–arms. Raimon had given

Soranus to him when the man acquired a younger, more valuable mount. Louis rode Soranus for years, and he had developed a bond with the faithful steed.

Victor was ecstatic the day Louis handed him Soranus's reins. He thanked Louis profusely; he'd never really expected to have a horse that he could ride as if it were his own. Louis knew that even nominal possession of a horse like Soranus was, for Victor, an unlikely dream come true.

Victor smiled cheerfully as he handed over Invictus's reins. Invictus stomped, and his breath steamed in the chilly air.

"He's anxious to ride," Victor said. Louis smiled. Victor always knew, or at least believed he knew, what the horses were thinking or feeling. He liked to speak for them. "How'd you sleep?" he said.

"I slept well," Louis said.

"You're lying," Victor said. Louis looked at him with a start. Victor grinned widely at him, with a hint of his characteristic mischievousness.

Louis *was* lying. In fact, he hadn't slept well at all. He'd woken in the middle of the night from a terrible dream that had shaken him to the depths of his soul. After it woke him, he'd been haunted by shame through long, harrowing hours that dragged toward dawn. Even now, the memory of it disturbed him. He wished he could turn to Victor for reassurance that the dream wasn't horrid, or at least that it wasn't nearly as dreadful as it felt. He couldn't do that, though, for he knew that Victor would only confirm what he already knew: that the dream was twisted and bizarre, an abomination born in the depths of hell, sent by Satan to shame him.

Louis had dreamed of Colette.

He'd dreamed about her before, of course, but never like this. She'd been his closest friend. She'd filled his childhood with companionship and joy. Her thoughts and observations had helped him to reason through problems, to see things more clearly, and to form more sensible opinions. His cousin had always been a source of wisdom and support. He'd never permitted his sentiments to wander toward romance or sex, even as a passing fancy, even in those brief and fleeting moments when the disturbing prospect had beckoned to him. But in this dream, he had done so much worse. He had seized her, covered her, and consumed her with passion he never knew existed. His desire for her had possessed him, and they'd made frenzied love amid the gently swaying barley in the field beside the stream. He awoke in the grip of his torrid desire.

The dream had drawn from him passions he had refused to acknowledge. He couldn't deny them now, and he knew that the devil had seized him. He resolved to find the priest as soon as he arrived at the Jacquette estate, to confess and do his penance before the Good Lord got around to leveling His judgment. He shuddered at the thought of God's retribution, but more at the images of his vile dream, and he did his best to push it from his mind.

"Lost in your dream?" Victor said, with a nearly imperceptible touch of scorn.

Louis froze, dumbfounded, his throat constricted by fear. *How could he know?* he wondered frantically. It truly was Satan's work if Victor knew of the dream without having been told. What would he say? How could he explain? He flushed with embarrassment and trembled in fear. His voice cracked when he finally spoke.

"What do you mean?" he said.

"What do I mean? You know what I mean." Victor shook his head as if it were obvious. "There's only one thing I know that can take you so far from here, even when you're standing right next to me." Louis stared blankly. Victor leaned into him, as if he were coaxing an elusive memory. "Fighting another Templar battle in your head?" he said. "Chasing that God-forsaken dream, even at this early hour?"

It took a moment before relief swept over Louis. His mouth dropped open and his knees grew weak so that he feared he might collapse. "No," he said, but only a squeaky croak escaped his mouth. Victor gave him a curious look.

"No? Something else has you so lost in thought? Do tell!"

Louis shrugged it off and shook his head briskly.

"It's nothing," he said. "A nightmare. It was really vivid."

"Well, it must have been, to have you shaken up so. Are you all right? You'll tell me about it, of course."

"No," Louis said, with a little too much emphasis. "It was evil. I can't speak it." He exaggerated a shudder to make his point, and he crossed himself.

Victor laughed softly. He wasn't superstitious, and he thought of religion as mostly superstition. He was unusual in both of those things. But he was smart enough not to express his disbelief openly. He had confided in Louis, and because of that trust, Louis ignored his religious ambivalence. He wondered to himself, though, how trust and disbelief could coexist. How was it possible for a person to trust another human, yet not trust in God?

They mounted up and headed across a field that ran a furlong to the edge of the woods. The field had gone fallow this year, and the ground was firm beneath them.

"So it was pure evil," Victor prodded with a mischievous grin. "You won't tell it to me, then?"

"No," Louis said firmly. He fixed his eyes on the line of oaks and ash at the far edge of the field.

"Okay, then," Victor said. "Keep it to yourself. If it was that bad, I don't want to hear it anyway." Now he was the one telling the untruth. He was intrigued, and it would be hard for him not to hear the details. That was unusual, too, Louis thought. In a subtle way, Victor seemed all too eager for the intimate details of Louis's thoughts, while feigning casual indifference. At times it was unsettling, and Louis found himself reacting with instinctive evasiveness. They had grown close, but some things were just too intimate to share, even with the closest of friends.

Well, nearly so, anyway. His mind drifted again toward the dream, but he resisted.

"You're good with horses," Louis observed, changing the subject.

Victor smiled and nodded.

"They respond to you, and you to them. It's almost as if you feel a kinship to them."

"I do."

"Why?"

"Why not? They're strong and uncomplicated, they work hard for little thanks, and despite an independent spirit, they accept bondage gracefully, without complaint. They labor," he said with a meaningful look, "because it's their lot in life."

"Ah," Louis said. He looked straight ahead and thought for a moment. He had turned to idle conversation, but it seemed to have led precisely to the matter he wanted to discuss with Victor. "How do you see your lot in life," he asked. "What future do you see for yourself?"

Victor looked blankly at him. "What do I see for myself? You mean for my future?"

"Yes."

"What else would I see for myself?" Victor replied with a shrug. "This is my life. Tending horses, thanks to you, at least until you leave. Working the fields, otherwise. Or shepherding. I like that fine. It gives me time to think—"

"You'll stay here, then?"

"Where else would I go?" Victor was obviously puzzled by the question. "Unless your father threw me off the land, why would I leave?"

"Don't you want to travel, to see faraway places and incredible things?" Louis asked.

Victor seemed annoyed. "What if I did?" he said. "What does it matter what I want? You forget who I am sometimes, don't you?"

"You could come with me."

"And how could I do that?" Victor exclaimed. "Will we be minstrels? I'm for God's sake sure not going to be a knight, even if you are. How do you suppose I could I tag along with you?"

Louis could see that he had angered Victor, but he didn't understand how. He was about to propose the opportunity of Victor's lifetime, and he'd thought that it might go more smoothly. He hesitated as Victor urged Soranus into a trot. They were nearing the wood, and Victor reined toward one of the numerous deer trails that dotted the tree line. Louis squeezed into Invictus's solid ribcage and urged him to keep up with Soranus. Invictus needed little urging; he'd already quickened his pace.

They rode in silence for a while after they entered the woods, minding tree branches and fallen limbs, and watching the roe and red deer as they sprang from the brush at their approach. A huge stag bounded away to the north. They watched in awe as the stag, with a massive frame and heavy rack, sprang noiselessly through the wood, with only the faintest swishing of leaves to betray its flight. It carried the weight of the burliest of men with the grace of the noblest of queens.

When the stag disappeared into the distant foliage, Louis took advantage of a widening in the trail to draw closer to Victor. He cleared his throat softly. Victor glanced at him with eyes still awed by the stag.

"Victor," he said. "I have something to ask you."

"Anything," Victor said, but Louis wasn't sure he meant it.

"I'll be squire to Lord Jacquette for two more years, maybe three." Victor nodded. "If all goes well, and I don't see why it shouldn't, I'll be knighted then – probably before my eighteenth birthday."

Victor nodded again. "I suspect that's a given," he said. "You were born a knight; it's just a matter of time and formalities."

"Well, it's more than that," Louis said. "It's hard work. Squiring involves rigorous training and discipline, learning combat skills, and carrying armor, and otherwise laboring in service to one's knight."

"I know. I just meant that you'll do all that well enough. I didn't mean you wouldn't have to work for it."

Louis reproved himself silently for his touchy response. Of course that was what Victor had meant. He couldn't help feeling guilty sometimes about the privileges of his life compared to Victor's. He nodded ruefully.

"I know. I'm sorry. Anyway, when that day comes, I'll also petition for acceptance to the Templars."

"I know that too."

"I'd like you to come with me."

Victor reined in and turned to look at Louis in disbelief. "How?"

"Be my squire."

A long moment passed as Victor stared hard at Louis, in silence. Louis tried to read his expression, but failed. It was not what he had expected, and it made no sense to him. He sensed that Victor was pained, but once again he found himself oblivious to the cause and the composition of Victor's reaction.

"Your squire…," Victor said.

"Yes." Louis beamed. "Why not?"

"You're serious? Have you forgotten who I am?" Victor was clearly restraining anger. "Look at me, Louis. Do you see the son of a noble sitting here? I'm a damned peasant, acting like the son of a noble, and God knows why. You know I'll never be a knight, much less a Templar Knight."

Louis was taken aback. "And whom did you think I would choose, of all the people in this world, to be my squire?"

Victor sniffed in contempt. "You want me to be your squire," he repeated slowly, reflectively. Then he laughed. "Surely you could find a better squire."

Louis tutted. "You're a good man, Victor. I wouldn't have anyone else as my squire."

"Your father will see that you do."

"My father likes you," Louis protested.

"Your father never forgets that I'm merely one of his laborers."

"That doesn't matter—"

"You can find a better squire."

Louis shook his head. "No, I couldn't. You always underestimate yourself."

"What I mean when I say a better squire is one who actually wants to be one," Victor said sharply.

"Oh…," Louis said. He looked at Victor skeptically. "You wouldn't want to be a squire?" Louis furrowed his brow in thought. "Do you know what squires do?"

"Of course," Victor said. "You just told me what they do, even though I already knew it. Rigorous training, discipline, honing combat skills, carrying armor, cleaning stalls, dressing knights, and fetching water. Laboring in service to one's knight from dawn to dusk." He especially emphasized the last sentence.

"And you don't want that."

"No."

"What then?"

"To labor – here, close to home. What does it matter if I labor here for my food, or in some godforsaken land I never wanted to see, fighting against people I've never known, over something I'll probably never believe?"

Louis was astonished. He had never suspected Victor's contempt for his dream. He had always assumed that Victor understood, and even shared it. He didn't know what to say.

"You want to remain a laborer," Louis said, trying to fathom the idea.

"I want to be a *knight*," Victor said. He said it with passion, and it was clear that he meant it. "But that won't happen, will it? A squire is the most I'd ever be, and that's nothing more than a laborer going into battle too lightly armed. No...I'll remain a laborer, and I'll remain here."

"With the horses."

Victor nodded. "If your father will have it."

"The horses will come with me." Louis half-smiled, mischievously. "They'll miss you. You'll miss them."

Victor looked incensed. He opened his mouth to argue, then closed it. He thought for a moment, then said, "There are other horses. Your father and his men-at-arms have plenty of horses."

"You want to be a knight."

"Is that so hard to imagine?"

"Squires become knights."

"*Noble* squires become knights."

"Squires become nobles, if they prove themselves."

"And if they can afford horses, and armor, and squires, and men-at-arms, and an occasional meal and lodging. I don't have a father to help me with all of that. I'll be happy for the occasional meal. How do you suppose I'd finance my knighthood?"

"I imagine you never will," Louis said in resignation, "as you've already decided not to try."

"It would be pointless," Victor said.

"Maybe. It's rare that a peasant is ever made a knight." He hated the words as they left his mouth, but they were true.

"Yes," Victor said. "It is."

"One thing's certain, though," Louis continued. "While you might never be knighted if you come along as my squire, you will *never* be knighted working here in the stables and plowing the fields. It you wish to seal your fate, I'll argue no further. It's sad, but it's your life." Louis paused for emphasis. "But if you wish for the slightest chance at knighthood, you'll come with me, and put aside your grudge, and strive for something few peasants ever realize."

An uneasy silence lingered between them. Finally, Louis broke it.

"Do you really aspire to knighthood?" he asked.

"I'd be as good a knight as any," Victor said. "Perhaps without the horses, the money, and the farms and villages. But it's not the money or the land that swing the sword and take the field. It's this..." He raised his right fist and placed his left hand on his biceps. Then he placed his palm against his chest, over his heart. "And this," he said.

"Yes," Louis said. "Sometimes that's more than enough. It helps to have a sponsor. It helps more to have courage and honor. Accomplishments in battle have transformed lives and built fortunes. The plow would never offer you such things.

It was unusual, Louis thought, for a peasant to so openly despise his lot in life, especially in front of the nobility for which he toiled. It was even more strange for one who despised it so to hesitate at the only opportunity he would probably ever have to rise above it. He was an uncommon lad. *An uncommon commoner,* Louis thought to himself.

"Your squire," Victor finally said. He said it with resignation, as if he had resolved a fierce internal struggle. "It would be almost like losing a friend," he said, "the only true friend I've got, and gaining in return yet another superior."

Victor's words stabbed Louis. He hadn't seen it that way.

"It wouldn't be like that at all," Louis insisted. "We'd still be friends. Nothing could change that."

"You just can't see things from my perspective," Victor said. Louis didn't reply. Victor shook his head and said, "You're the only *chevalier* I have ever known who would treat one of his father's serfs as a friend." He laughed. "It's really quite noble." He seemed amused by the irony of his own words. "But you have to see that one day you'll inherit these lands, and everything on them – including me. You could order me off to war any time you choose, and I'd have no choice but to go. So when you ask me now, it rings hollow, because I wonder if I were to refuse, if you would honor that."

"I would honor it," Louis said fervently. "I haven't forgotten the road to Carcassonne." He was pained by Victor's words, but he couldn't deny their truth. "I swear to you now, before God's eyes, that if it's not what you want, I will leave you here. You'll continue as a groom, and one day, no doubt, be made head hostler. You'll live your life in peace, and I'll see you from time to time when I return home." Louis's eyes blazed with sincerity. "I don't think of you as a serf," he said.

"No. But as a squire, ever in your service." The contempt was back in his voice, despite Louis's vow.

Louis shook his head. "No…as a future knight!" he said, growing frustrated. "Why do you distrust me so?"

Victor held up a hand and shook his head. "It's fine," he said. "It's no matter. I don't hold you responsible for my station in life. It's just that if I go with you, I won't be content to be your squire." He nodded ruefully. "I don't know, Louis. It's a generous offer…I'm aware of that much. You have to let me think it over."

"I'd help you to succeed," Louis said.

Victor wore a complicated expression, a strange mix of grudging appreciation, simmering resentment, and sincere fondness. Louis wanted desperately to fathom its depths, but he knew he hadn't the time.

"I'll think about it," Victor repeated. "I owe you that much. But I ask you for just one thing in return, in place of every other thing you might ever be moved to give me. I swear I'll never ask you for anything else."

"What thing?" Louis asked.

"Let me make this decision on my own, without pressure or penalty," Victor said. "Give me this one freedom, to give you the answer I choose, even if you don't like it. Promise me you won't make me pay for it if I say no."

Louis nodded firmly. "Done," he said. He leaned far out of his saddle and extended a hand to Victor. Victor reached also, and they clasped hands to wrists in a solemn, silent oath.

"Till the death!" Louis exclaimed, repeating the oath they had shared from the beginning, since the summer they met on the road to Carcassonne. He attempted to dispel his own anxiety with a wild, toothy grin.

"Till the death," Victor said.

Louis hoped that Victor's misgivings would fade as he considered the prospect of an adventure they would share as compatriots, as warriors, as brothers, and as friends.

They spurred their horses and rode at a gallop toward home.

Chapter 12

A YEAR HAD PASSED, and Louis was glad to be with his family for an extended summer break from his training. It had been a year and a half since he began his training with Jacquette. He had immersed himself in the rigors of his training, and spent little time away from his liege's estate. He avoided visiting the Marti's despite his close proximity to their home.

He couldn't avoid them now.

The Martis had arrived to accompany him and his parents on a trip into Carcassonne for market day. The journey, the warming breeze, and the approaching culmination of Louis's training lifted his spirits to new heights. He even allowed himself the inevitable euphoria of riding at a leisurely pace beside the person whose company he enjoyed most: his cousin Colette.

Shame flushed his cheeks, though, when his thoughts returned to his dream of her. He shrugged them away, willing them not to return. But they did, maddeningly often. He resented their interference with the joyous beauty of the day.

They approached Carcassonne from the south on the dusty

road from Limoux, which paralleled the meandering path of the Aude River as it flowed north and east toward the Mediterranean coast. The imposing walls of the fortified city, which had often withstood the most formidable armies of Europe, loomed ahead of them as they approached. The walls had served their purpose often enough, but they had failed to stop the invasion of the Inquisitors nearly eighty years earlier. Carcassonne had since grown to be, in addition to the cultural center of the region, the headquarters of the Dominican Inquisition in the Languedoc region.

It was a minor market day, but the throngs that clamored at the city gates were larger and more boisterous than the usual market crowd. It was clear that something extraordinary was planned for the day. Louis wondered what it might be. The excitement that permeated the air was characteristic of an execution day; the Cathar Perfects, Eustache and Mathilde, whom Louis had met at the Jacquette estate, came to mind.

Even though the pedestrian crowd made way for the nobles' horses and carriages, Louis and his family were delayed in their entry to the city. Louis nodded to a sentry and gave him a quizzical look. The sentry drew his hand slowly across his throat to indicate that there was indeed to be an execution, and he traced the shape of a cross on his chest, mimicking the cross of yellow cloth that convicted heretics were required to sew into their clothing, to confirm that the condemned were heretics. Louis nodded his acknowledgement.

A glance at Colette told Louis that she had caught the gestures, too. Her jaw tensed, and her eyes flashed indignation. She caught herself quickly, though, and her expression softened abruptly.

While the peasants closest to them did their best to make way for them, Louis's party was jostled and blocked by the teeming crowd. It was several minutes before they got through the gates, but when they did, the street beyond seemed calm in comparison to the mob at the gate.

They made their way toward the market. Businessmen anxiously supervised the movement of their wares – bales of wool, saddles and boots, tools and foodstuff and ale – toward the market square outside the western entrance to the cathedral. Peasants from the countryside marveled as they always did at the breathtaking architecture, the crowded quarters, and the frenetic commotion of the city.

Louis and Colette exchanged nervous glances. They had vowed to make this day as glorious as it could be, to take full advantage of the time they had together, and with their families. Louis knew the pall that an execution would cast over their leisure. He felt growing resentment toward the frequency with which such things had come to dominate market days. He wanted to turn back and leave Carcassonne, and plan instead to return on a day that would see no suffering or death.

He thought again about Eustache and Mathilde. It had been a year since they passed through Jacquette's land and into the hands of the Inquisition. They could certainly be among today's condemned. His gut tightened at the prospect, and he hoped it would not be so. Despite their crimes, and in spite of himself, he felt empathy for their plight. They were gentle and kind; they would have caused no harm to anyone, save for the deception of weaker, impressionable souls. He wondered against his will if such a crime was just cause for execution. He crossed himself and mumbled a quick prayer of repentance.

The market stalls were doing sparse business in spite of the unusually heavy attendance. Most of the visitors walked or rode past them on their way to the cathedral. An excited buzz filled the air in the manner of a wedding or a feast day, but more fevered. As was characteristic, the impending execution infused the multitude with a palpable giddiness. Louis felt his stomach start to churn.

He looked to his father, hoping he would remain a comfortable distance from the front of the crowd. He wondered at his aversion to the impending spectacle.

Raimon's watchful eyes scanned the crowd. As a noble, he would be expected to show proper enthusiasm for a public display of justice by taking a prominent position close to the platform. To do otherwise could be seen as evidence of sympathy for the condemned.

They made their way toward the front of the crowd, where an execution platform stood with four wooden stakes on raised pedestals, each surrounded by stacks of bundled kindling.

A commotion arose at the far side of the square as a wagon made its way from the inquisitors' jail to the market square, drawn by ancient nags with grayish coats, and driven by an official of the court, a slight and crooked man of about forty.

At the head of the procession, Louis spied the Dominican friar, the Inquisitor Diego Mondragón, accompanied by the Bishop of Carcassonne, the sheriff and his bailiff, three Dominican monks, and six heavily armored men–at–arms.

The guards seemed an excessive measure to secure the weary, tattered prisoners who stood unsteadily, chained together in the bed of the lurching cart. In light of incidents past, however, where Inquisitors and their underlings had been beaten or even killed in the countryside surrounding Toulouse and Carcassonne, Louis understood the precautions.

As the wagon drew nearer, Louis realized with a start that two of the four prisoners were, in fact, Eustache and Mathilde. He was shaken by the realization, and by the horror of their countenance.

Eustache's face was a ghastly, misshapen mask, bruised and broken by the rigors of his interrogation. His limbs hung limp, one arm ending in a blackened stump just below the elbow, and the other arm twisted and badly swollen.

Mathilde leaned heavily against the constraints of her bonds, too weak to hold herself upright against the wagon's erratic motion. Her face was a hollow mask of clouded pain and confusion. Louis could not fathom the torment that had reduced the stately woman to such devastation.

The wagon ground to a halt yards from the wooden platform. The crowd taunted the condemned heretics, shouting and pelting them with vegetables and stones.

Fra Diego Mondragón stood from his seat on the platform reserved for officials, both of the town and of the Inquisition. He walked to the edge of the platform and read from a scroll.

"These prisoners stand before you accused of heresy," he shouted, to a chorus of boos and cheers. "May God show them His mercy." He folded the scroll and abruptly returned to his seat.

The executioner and his apprentices led the heretics from the wagon to the platform. They climbed the wooden steps to the stage, where they draped the prisoners in water-soaked cloaks. The cloaks would slow their burning, and prolong their suffering in the hope of eliciting repentance before they died, so that they might be returned finally to God's grace.

The executioners bound the prisoners to the stakes with ropes around their ankles, thighs, abdomens, and chests, and with chains about their necks. They piled yet more twigs and straw as kindling at their feet, and then placed sticks and logs atop the kindling. The Dominican friars stood close to the condemned, whispering into their ears, exhorting them to confess and abjure so that they might gain entrance into Heaven upon their deaths.

Mondragón rose again and read the rest of the condemnation from the scroll.

"Those we bring before you today," he said, "stand convicted and condemned for the crime of heresy." He recited the words with impassive, practiced precision. He was clearly familiar with such pronouncements. He continued: "Despite relentless efforts to turn them from the path to eternal damnation, they have remained unrepentant and refused to abjure their heresy. As the Holy Mother Church has exhausted its recourse in securing their liberation from evil, there is no alternative but to separate them from the Church that has sought their salvation, and to abandon them into the hands of their secular authorities. By the authority of the Holy Mother Church, and in the name of the Father, and the Son, and the Holy Ghost, I so remand these heretics. We pray for them even now, that their eternal souls may yet find release, that they may find mercy, and that their lives may yet be spared."

Louis knew that the prayer was in vain, and that it was meant only to relieve the Church of responsibility for the deaths of the heretics. He also knew that the Church would promptly accuse the secular authorities of fautorship, the crime of supporting or abetting heresy, should those authorities fail to carry out the expected executions.

The monks attending the heretics stepped away as a hooded executioner brandished his torch and approached. They scurried down the steps and took their places on the dais that was set for the official observers. The executioner touched his torch to the kindling at Mathilde's feet. He stood back and regarded Eustache, appearing to appreciate his expression as the flames caught and flourished at Mathilde's feet. He snickered scornfully and touched the flame to Eustache's kindling.

A gentle breeze fanned the flames higher. The executioner put the torch to the two remaining stakes, and then he turned to savor the expressions on the faces of the condemned. He tilted his head and gazed curiously at Mathilde, who had somehow summoned the strength to stand tall, and who stared calmly into his eyes as though nothing were amiss. Her eyes remained serene and forgiving as the flames blackened her bruised and swollen legs.

Eustache turned his face to the sky and prayed. "*Pater Noster,*" he intoned, "*qui es in caelis…*" Pain wracked his voice to the point of breaking, but he completed the Lord's Prayer in Latin, barely faltering. The monks who had sought the heretics' last-minute repentance looked on in pained silence.

One of the heretics screamed as his clothing burst into flames. The fourth lost consciousness almost instantly, more likely because of the rigors of his interrogation rather than the intensity of his immediate pain. Eustache and Mathilde prayed solemnly, stoic against the flames that consumed them.

Mondragón peered keenly into the crowd, searching for signs of revulsion or opposition to the dramatic display of justice. Louis glanced nervously at his mother's face and found reassurance in her placid expression. His father, too, had succeeded in affecting a mask with which Mondragón could not find fault.

Colette had not been as successful; her eyes were wide with

shock that would betray her compassion. Mondragón's eyes lingered on Colette for a moment, but an anguished wail from the crowd offered a timely distraction.

Mondragón's eyes snapped to the source of the commotion, and soldiers moved to investigate. A moment later, they dragged a woman out of the crowd, wracked by torment and howling curses in the direction of the pyres. Tears formed in Colette's eyes, and Louis moved to shield her from the inquisitors' view.

"Don't," Louis whispered. Colette looked into his eyes and shook her head gently. He placed his arm around her and held her tightly. "Be strong," he said.

"Why?" she whispered. "Why does this have to happen?"

"Hush," he said more firmly. "Not here. Not now." Colette set her jaw firmly. Her eyes hardened and her shoulders drooped as helpless acceptance swept over her. A murmur of excited appreciation went up from the crowd as the flames at Mathilde's feet, which had built slowly until now, shot high into the air with a frightful sound, in a fierce blaze that engulfed her. Mathilde let out an involuntary moan that sounded more of surprise than of agony. Louis felt the heat on his cheeks, and he tried to hold his breath against the smell of burning flesh.

Three more whooshing sounds followed as flames consumed the rest of the heretics. Eustache closed his eyes as fluid escaped to trickle down swollen, distorted cheeks. The man next to him howled as his hair and beard, already singed from previous torture sessions, burst into flames that ringed his contorted face.

Louis stood transfixed by the sight of human bodies so utterly and violently destroyed, and by the fact that he was neither expected nor permitted to rescue them. His inherent drive to save the afflicted heaved in rebellion against his inaction.

Within minutes, each of the figures was reduced to charred, melted likenesses of the humans they had been. Another cheer went up from the crowd. The spectators spoke excitedly, demonstrating animated approval of the justice that had been done, while the more pious among them knelt and prayed in thanks.

Louis sensed that much of the reaction was staged for the

benefit of the inquisitorial officials, who now stood alert to the reactions among the crowd as it dispersed.

The Bishop of Carcassonne moved to the front of the officials' platform. He cast a somber gaze over the crowd, and then solemnly crossed himself. A hush fell over the spectators.

"Our Father in Heaven," the bishop intoned, "we ask for your blessing as we effect justice in your name, and in the defense of your Holy Word. In your name, we absolve any sin that may lay upon the souls of those who have borne the terrible task of dispensing Your justice today." The executioner and his assistants crossed themselves. "We pray that all who have witnessed these proceedings will take heed, and take care to choose the side of righteousness; to aid and not impede the Holy Inquisition; to abandon and not assist the heretical enemies of the Faith; to aid and not hinder the apprehension of those enemies wherever they may flee or seek solace; to offer themselves today and every day as good soldiers, and as a source of strength and encouragement for your servants in this holy war on heresy."

The crowd murmured its assent. People crossed themselves repeatedly to demonstrate the sincerity of their faith. Louis prayed silently for the strength to hold fast to his own faith despite his involuntary empathy for the condemned.

The bishop spoke at length about the glory that is given to God in the war against heresy, and the extent to which the Church would go to win that war. He justified whatever measures had been taken, or might be taken in the future, to keep the faith safe from the pernicious wiles of Satan's heretics. Nothing less than the destruction of the faith, he said with certainty, was the goal of these filthy fiends. He warned any among the crowd who might entertain such evil that they would do well to mind themselves, their actions, and their speech.

"Mind your words," he said, "and how you speak them."

During the sermon the fire cooled. When it had cooled sufficiently, the executioner and his assistants poked and prodded the charred corpses to break them apart and reduce the remains to piles of ash and bone. They swept the remains into a pit beside the platform to be burned again to further reduce them to ash. The ash would then be brought to the city's edge and dumped into the garbage pit.

As the secondary fire built, the Bishop of Carcassonne blessed the crowd, and it dispersed toward the well–stocked market stalls. The Martis and the de Garonnes moved away in silence. Despite their practiced indifference, Louis felt the anguish that had possessed them. He hoped he was the only one who could sense it.

Chapter 13

A WEEK HAD PASSED since the market day *auto de fé*, the burning of the heretics in the market square. No one had spoken of it, though it hung heavy over every meal, and lurked beneath every conversation. Louis hoped for the lifting of the gloom, so he restrained his desire to discuss it. Now that he was alone with Colette, he resisted it still, and chose a more innocuous topic to avoid its draw.

They meandered along the path from the de Garonne house to their favorite clearing by the stream.

"I've almost completed my training," he said proudly. "Lord Jacquette appears to be pleased with my performance these last few months. I'm sure I'll be knighted soon."

Colette smiled with exaggerated approval. "I'm proud of you!" she exclaimed. A light glinted in her eyes, but Louis suspected it was more the mist of sadness than admiration of his success.

"You're not happy," he said with narrowed eyes.

"I *am* happy, for you, yes," she said, nodding. "I truly am."

"But...?"

"Well, it's just that I know what it means. And that doesn't terribly please me. I haven't longed for your leaving."

He gazed at her, and after a moment, he nodded. "I understand," he said. "I'm going to miss you, too."

"I know how much you've looked forward to this, though, and how hard you've worked for it. I want you to be happy."

"I'll be happy in Jerusalem," he said, "Everything still makes sense there. There, one can be certain of who is the enemy, and who is not. Things will be simpler there."

"And yet more dangerous," she said grimly.

"This past year has been complicated, and confusing," he said. "That has caused me more apprehension than the threat of a thousand Saracens. I welcome the simplicity of clearly defined danger; such things, I know how to confront."

"What has troubled you most in your time with Lord Jacquette?" Colette asked.

Louis considered the question at length.

"The degree to which I hold for him both admiration and contempt," he finally said.

"Contempt?" she said with a gasp. "What could possibly cause you contempt toward Lord Jacquette?

"I understand his political loyalties well enough," he said. "Those, I can reconcile. But I'm dismayed by his support for the Cathars. He risked all of our lives to help them. I've tried, but failed to understand that."

"Why?"

"They were heretics," he said with conviction. "Filthy heretics."

"Filthy," she repeated. The word clearly displeased her. Her jaw tensed, and she glared into the distance. "They were people," she said simply. "Humans. People who thought differently from you, who had different ideas about God and salvation. Do not all people deserve our compassion, if not the mercy of the Church?"

"Is it not more compassionate to lead them from their error into the light of truth than to fautor their heresy?" he asked.

She turned to him in horror. "Is that how you see it?" she asked. "I mean, I understand that that's how the Church sees it...but you? Do you truly believe that the Inquisition is simply leading lost sheep to the Good Lord's bosom?"

He hesitated. He wanted to say *no*, that whatever Colette believed was good enough for him. But he could not lie. With an apprehensive look, he nodded. "Yes," he said. "I do."

She shook her head furiously.

"I've respected your opinions on this subject all along," she said. "I've avoided having this discussion with you. But *how*? How can you still believe such things, even after what we witnessed at Carcassonne? Those were good people who were burned alive, Louis! They hurt no one!" She paused, fuming. "The charge of heresy is nothing more than a ready sword, wielded at will by the powerful against those they despise...or fear."

"Heretics lead people away from the truth," Louis said, growing defensive.

"Truth!" she scoffed. "What truth? For what truth do angry men burn pious and peaceable men, and women, and children? Those Cathars preach nothing but love and forgiveness. They demonstrate those very things even as the inquisitors' flames consume them! The people we watched burn did not curse their persecutors. They demonstrated love and forgiveness as evil men destroyed them. And simply for speaking these words, I could be next. I could be burned. You would see truth in that?"

"No! I could never let that happen!"

"Then you're as guilty as I," she said, "and we are as guilty as the people they burned at Carcassonne: I for speaking, and you for fautoring my heresy. *This* is your truth."

"No..."

"No?" She huffed and crossed her arms. Her anger surprised him. He had never witnessed it before, and he would not have believed it possible. He wanted to do or say anything to make it go away.

"Why does this affect you so deeply," he asked. He spoke softly, tenderly. He wanted to understand, but at the same time he feared what she might say.

She turned to face him with a fierce and unfamiliar intensity. "You really don't think about it, do you?" she said. "You've never considered...never wondered?"

"About what?"

She bit her lip for a moment. "Louis, what if those Cathars at Carcassonne had been your parents?" she said. "How would you feel about their murder then?"

"But they weren't. My parents are not heretics."

"What if they were?"

"I don't know. You're right. I've never considered that. There was never a reason to consider that."

"I'm asking you to consider it now."

Louis saw no point in wondering about something that could never be, but he was anxious to accommodate Colette. He tried to conjure the feeling. It was true that Mathilde reminded him of his mother, but even the slightest effort to visualize his parents as heretics provoked shame and disgust. He shuddered and shook it away.

"You love your parents," Colette said. "You've said often that you would die for them without hesitation. But I want you to tell me now what you would do if you learned that they, too, were deemed worthy of those flames – that they, too, questioned the dogma of your precious Church."

"*My* Church?" he said, shrugging quizzically. "Not *our* Church...?"

She shook her head with exasperation. "Please!" she said.

"I suppose I should feel obligated to..." He faltered. He couldn't say the words. "I don't know," he said.

She waited expectantly, then said, "Your hesitation has condemned you." She said it with the same dispassionate finality with which Mondragón had delivered his pronouncement. She allowed her words to sink in. "Now, do you see?" she said. "That's all it takes. In one brief moment, you would be judged worthy of death."

He felt shaken. He had never seen this side of Colette. He didn't know what to make of it.

"I don't understand," he said. "Why? Why do you feel so

strongly about this?"

She looked at him as if he should see it clearly. "Because I feel so strongly about you," she said, "and about your heart and what moves you. Because I know your heart is pure, even when it is misguided. Because I know that when you realize you've been misled, you won't forgive yourself for not seeing clearly from the start. And most of all, because I love your family and mine, and I don't want to see happen to us what has already happened to so many because of this bloody Inquisition."

"It couldn't."

"You don't know that."

He realized that she was right. While the Inquisition targeted the evil conspiracies that led Christians from the path of righteousness, he knew that innocents had suffered. He'd taken comfort, however small, in the monks' assurances that suspicion would not exist in the absence of cause, and that whatever the cause, it was enough to justify the most strenuous effort of the Church to return the lost to their faith. If, on occasion, a random innocent suffered in the process, well, it was all for a good cause. Better that, they said, than for so many others to be lost. And yet...what if the random innocent *were* his mother?

What if it were *Colette*?

He shuddered as the thought struck deeply, in a place he had not anticipated. The image of Colette under torture, or taken from him and killed, horrified him. His soul was shaken by the thought of it. With a start, he realized that he did not want to be apart from her, ever.

"Louis," she said. Her voice sounded far away as his mind swirled with the gravity of a dawning realization. "Are you all right? I'm sorry..."

He loved her.

"I shouldn't have...," she said.

In a way that he should not.

"I got carried away," she said.

In a way that was worse than heresy. He felt he might faint.

"Louis?" she said softly as she reached for him.

"My God," he finally whispered.

"Louis…?"

"I'm sorry," he said. The earth slowly steadied beneath him, and his focus returned. Conflicting emotions roiled in his core. "I…don't feel well."

"I've upset you. I'm so sorry. I shouldn't have said those things."

"It's all right," he said. "You're right. I have to think about what you've said."

"Louis," she said softly, "I love you."

His hand went to his mouth to stop the words he wanted to say. There were too many, and they conflicted too much to make sense. He stared at her, wide–eyed.

"I love you, too," he finally said. He nodded at nothing in particular and stepped away.

Apprehension still filled her gaze. "I didn't mean to upset you so," she said gently.

He shook his head. "It's all right," he said. He was anxious for distance from the feelings that had overtaken him.

"You're sad now," she said.

He wanted to change the subject. They had reached their clearing by the stream, and he held her hand as she sat on the wide, flat rock that jutted over the gurgling water. He sat beside her and turned the conversation back toward the topic that troubled him only slightly less.

"It was hard to watch them burn," he said.

She nodded sadly.

He grew more somber as he recalled the scene. Until that day, the burning of heretics had been, for him, an academic and impersonal reality. Years of training at the monastery had led him to equate heresy with filth, and heretics with the diabolical influences of Satan in his protracted conspiracy against God's Church. Meeting Mathilde had put a human face on heresy. In her spirit, Louis detected none of the devil's influence, but rather much that was exemplary of Christian character. The strength with which she had met her end moved him; surely such strength could only have come from God.

"It's a tragic waste of human life, this Inquisition," Colette said. "Such things debase us, and do nothing to edify our spirit or magnify God. It's…unchristian."

"How can the will of God's Church be unchristian?" he said. "Does not the fact that it is done by the Church make it Christian? Is it not done in the defense of Christianity?"

"Louis, can you imagine Our Lord Jesus Christ subjecting anyone to torture, or condemning any human to be burned at the stake?"

"In the Gospel of John, he did say that branches that turn from him should be gathered up and thrown into the fire. God also commanded us to fight his enemies, to defend his kingdom."

She sighed. "He was talking about burning in hell, and not in the market square at Carcassonne, at the hands of politicians and priests. How could God, on the one hand, command us to murder his supposed enemies, and on the other hand, exhort us to love our own enemies even as we love ourselves? How does one reconcile 'Thou shalt not kill' with 'Burn whoever you suspect of heresy?'"

"God is at war with Satan," he replied. "This is what I have been taught. Heretics follow Satan. They are a danger to God's Church. Should the Church not protect itself from its enemies, the soldiers of Satan?"

"Did Christ protect himself from his enemies?" she asked. "Or did he say that we should turn the other cheek? Did he not offer the greatest example of this for us? And do you really think that poor woman was a soldier of Satan?"

"I don't know, Colette," he said. "I thought I knew how I feel about these things, but now I'm confused. It was easy to defend the persecution of heretics when I saw them as less than human. But I came to regard two of them as human, and I watched them die as humans."

"They're all as human as you and I," she said, "no more and no less."

"You seem to like them," he mused.

"I don't hate them," she said. "I find some of their beliefs intriguing."

"Which ones?"

"Reincarnation," she said. "I wonder about that."

"It's a crazy belief," he said. "I don't know how anyone could believe such fantastic lies."

"Do you not ever wonder about it?"

"Why would I?" he asked. "What would be the point of such a thing?"

"Spiritual growth," she offered, "beyond what we've already attained. The chance to do more good, to live better lives. Perhaps our souls would be strengthened and made more perfect by the effort."

He looked hard at her. Such ideas were fundamentally opposed to Church doctrine, and many had been burned for entertaining them.

"The Bible is clear on that," he said.

"Is it?" she replied. "Some even think that Jesus taught such things."

"What could make anyone think that?"

"Are you sure you want to discuss this?" she asked. He nodded reluctantly. "Some believe that's what Jesus meant when he told the Pharisee Nicodemus that a man must be reborn in order to see the kingdom of God."

"He meant 'baptized.'"

She shook her head. "Nicodemus heard 'reborn,' as in physical birth. He spoke the same language as Jesus. He understood the words. He understood Jesus to be speaking about physical birth, and not spiritual. How could he have misunderstood such a thing?"

"But being reborn into this world would not allow a person to see God's kingdom…unless he were reborn in Jerusalem." He smiled wryly at his own wit.

"Right," she said with a smirk. "Anyway, the Cathars believe that we're born into this life as often as it takes for us to transcend the evil nature of our flesh. They believe it takes extraordinary faith to do that while we're still in the flesh. If we fail, we're condemned to another life, and another opportunity to succeed. If we succeed, we are allowed into God's true kingdom, in heaven."

"I suppose I can see that," he said, "but I don't think that's what Jesus meant."

"Jesus asked his apostles once who people thought he was," she said. "One of them said that some people believed he was Elijah the prophet, and others believed he was one of the other prophets from the Old Testament."

"Yes."

"Why would people think Jesus was a prophet who was long dead, if they didn't believe in reincarnation, at least for the prophets?"

"But Jesus didn't say that he was reincarnated."

"He didn't correct them," she said. "He didn't ask why people would believe such a thing. He didn't rebuke the belief. Instead, he asked the apostles who *they* thought he was." Louis nodded. "Why would he ask them that? They *knew* who he was. He was asking them who they thought he was in a previous life."

"You believe that?" Louis said.

"What else could it be?"

Heresy, Louis thought. That's what it was: heresy. He said nothing.

"What would be the point," she said, "if this life is nothing more than one chance to get it right or suffer for all eternity? Why would life not serve some greater purpose for the soul?"

He shook his head, at a loss for words.

"How can anyone say these ideas are wrong," she continued, "without ever giving them a moment of honest consideration?"

He wasn't sure what to say.

"Do you ever wonder about our friendship?" she asked.

"Our friendship?"

"Yes," she said, peering into his eyes. "I felt I'd already known you forever that day when we first met."

He was uncomfortable with the shift of topic. He furrowed his brow.

"Did you feel that way?" she prodded.

"I'm not sure what you mean," he said. She waited expectantly for his answer. "I mean, yes, in a way, I felt familiar with you. But it was nothing, really. We'd never met."

He thought back to that time. He was captivated from the start by the gentle, refined beauty of her face, and by the pleasantness of her voice, which was subtly accented by the combination of Scottish and Occitan influence. He was unsure of her, though. She was probing and direct, friendly and warm, and in his shyness he shrank from her outgoing demeanor. He warmed to her quickly, though, and his shyness passed. He had wished that she weren't his cousin, and then he had thrashed himself without mercy for the thought.

As he considered her question, he realized that he had, in fact, felt a deep familiarity from the start, as if they had known one another forever.

"But you felt it…" she said, pressing him. "The same way I did." Her eyes grew more animated. "I've thought about that a lot. I felt comfortable with you from the start, as though we were old friends. You seemed so…*important* to me, though we were strangers. It feels odd even saying that we were strangers."

He agreed. "I've never experienced that, before or since, now that I think about it."

"The moment we met," she said, "you felt closer to me than a brother. I felt safe with you. Protected. And that was before we even spoke."

"I felt like I wanted to protect you," he admitted, "even though you didn't need my protection."

"You've experienced the opposite, too," she said. "Do you remember a time when you felt animosity toward someone you didn't even know, the first time you saw them, for no good reason?"

"Yes," he said. "I've never understood that, but then, I never really gave it much thought."

"Gilles, on the road to Carcassonne," she said.

"That's who came to mind."

They sat in silence then, thinking and dangling their feet

into the cool water.

Finally, she gazed sideways at him, and said, "These are the things that make me wonder if there might be some truth to reincarnation."

"That belief is heresy," he repeated flatly.

"There are no inquisitors here," she said, looking around as if to confirm it.

"The lies of heresy are designed to make sense, to trick us into thinking the Church is wrong, and that it doesn't matter how we live our present lives. God said there's the Judgment at the end of this life, and that's what I believe."

She sighed and shook her head. "And then the eternal consequences of our failure or success," she said. "That makes less sense to me than the Cathar beliefs. I should think a merciful God would want us to learn, to grow, and to succeed, even if it takes a hundred tries to get it right."

"I suppose one day we'll both know the answers to these questions," he said. "Until then, there's not much sense discussing them. I think I'd rather just enjoy your company while I still can."

She smiled at him, then gazed thoughtfully at their reflection in the rippling stream.

Chapter 14

An autumn wind, hot and humid, blew across the rolling Languedoc hills. The Jacquette estate was a flurry of activity as servants prepared for impending festivities.

Louis turned to Roland, a squire nearly three years his junior. "We're nearly finished; gather and straighten the tack while I finish spreading the fresh hay." Tending to the stables was their last task of the day.

Roland nodded with a smile. At fifteen, he was among the youngest of Lord Jacquette's squires, and he was, by far, the most agreeable. He admired Louis almost to the point of worship, which sometimes embarrassed Louis. It humbled him to be seen as a role model by other squires, even one so young.

He liked Roland. He was pleased whenever they were assigned as work mates. Roland worked hard, and with a cooperative spirit. His slight build, his narrow, hooked nose, and his dark and close set eyes made him look more like a young monk bound for the scriptorium than a budding future knight. But his fighting skills had proven remarkable: his swordsmanship rivaled that of the older squires. He had earned Louis's respect quickly after his arrival.

They finished their task and left the stable.

"Tomorrow's your big day," Roland said with an admiring grin. "It must be wonderful. How does it feel?"

"I often thought it might never come," Louis said. "It seems that I've trained for ages. But then, sometimes it seems like yesterday that I was a fledgling colt like you." He slapped Roland playfully on the back of the head, and Roland recoiled in mock outrage. "But yes, it's almost overwhelming. I can't believe the day has finally come."

"Well, I'm proud of you," Roland said. "I can't wait to witness your adoubement." They were walking toward the squires' hall, where supper was ready to be served. "Well, I'm off to supper," Roland said with a wave. He turned toward the hall. "Blessings to you, my brother!"

"And to you," Louis called after him.

Louis walked on past the hall. He retired instead to the bathhouse for a warm, cleansing bath. Afterward, he dressed in fresh, white linen reserved for this day, and he proceeded directly to chapel, skipping the supper in the hall.

Tomorrow would see the culmination of his training, and the realization of his lifelong dreams in a ceremony that would elevate him to knighthood. In a ritual prescribed by centuries of tradition, he would purify his body through fasting, his mind through contemplation, and his soul through confession, penance, and prayer.

He approached the chapel slowly, deep in thought. He savored the feeling of these final steps toward his destiny. His heart swelled with pride and boundless satisfaction.

He entered the chapel and paused for a moment as his eyes adjusted to the darkness. Candles glowed warmly on the altar and in the corners of the room. Father Esteban, Lord Jacquette's Castilian priest, sat in the front pew waiting to hear his confession.

The priest rose to his feet as Louis entered. He bowed curtly and indicated the small confessional in the corner to the left of the altar. Louis took his place in the penitent's box, and Father Esteban took his in the confessor's.

"Bless me, Father," Louis began. "I have sinned…" He related to the priest his venial sins, exaggerating a few to compensate for the absence of real ones. His venial sins were not his greatest concern. He wrestled with the proper delivery of the most egregious, the mortal sin that had lately plagued his conscience. As he finished with his minor litany of petty offenses, he faltered and fell into silence.

"There is more yet to tell, my son?" the priest prompted. Louis's throat went dry. "There is something troubling you, yes?"

"I hold inappropriate affections," Louis finally said.

"Inappropriate, how?" The priest said, leaning closer to the screen that separated them. "It is a girl, yes?"

"Yes." *Of course it's a girl,* he thought. *What else?*

"Then that would seem appropriate enough."

"But she's my..." He couldn't form the words. "Uh, it's just not appropriate."

"She is your…what?" Esteban's voice had taken on a conspiratorial quality. Louis sensed that his interest was inordinately keen, and he decided that it would be too dangerous to divulge everything at this moment.

Instead, he lied. "She's…betrothed," he said. "To another man…a knight."

Esteban's form withdrew from sight as he sat back, sighing in apparent disappointment. "This is hardly a sin unless you acted upon your affections," he intoned. "Did you act upon your affections in any way?" He almost sounded hopeful.

"No," Louis said.

"Well, my son, for this trivial infraction, there is only a minor penance." His voice turned perfunctory. "You are to pray to Our Holy Mother Mary for renewed purity of heart. When she grants you this, you will find your affections dispersed and gone far from you."

Louis berated himself. He had failed to confess his most grievous sin. How could he proceed with his knighting with that stain yet upon his soul? He bit his lip hard in self–rebuke. There was nothing he could do. He could not confess this sin, and he could not forestall his ceremony. He decided to spend the entire night begging directly for God's forgiveness.

Louis said his prayer of contrition with as much sincerity as he could muster. Esteban instructed him to devote the hours until morning to prayer and self–examination, in accordance with knightly tradition, and he offered Louis's absolution:

"God, the Father of mercies, through the death and resurrection of His Son, has reconciled the world to Himself and sent the Holy Spirit among us for the forgiveness of sins; through the ministry of the Church may God give you pardon and peace. I absolve you from your sins in the name of the Father, and of the Son, and of the Holy Spirit. Amen."

Esteban exited the confessor's stall and was nearly out of the church by the time Louis emerged from the confessional. Louis took his place at the foot of the altar. As he knelt, his eyes fell upon the prize that was to him most glorious, placed with care upon the altar where he would pray. A magnificent sword, new and brightly polished, gleamed beside a finely crafted shield, it's tough leather painted crimson and embellished with the de Garonne coat of arms. He savored the sight for a moment, and then he crossed himself and commenced a long night of earnest, fervent prayer.

✠ ✠ ✠

The black sky beyond the church windows took on a dreary gray glow, which lightened gradually as Louis rubbed his bleary eyes. In a sudden burst, sunlight pierced the gloom and streamed boldly into the choir, illuminating the chapel and filling Louis with reviving, reassuring warmth.

The hours of reverent supplication, reasoned consideration, and solemn self–assessment had done little to diminish his persistent shame. He took a deep breath and prayed a final, ardent prayer, bringing all of his renewed vigor to bear. Yet, he knew his prayers were in vain. He could not curb the passions that had taken root so insidiously, and as he realized, so very long ago. He believed that he was irretrievably damned.

Father Esteban returned to the church shortly after daybreak. He was garbed for mass, in a white cassock and a purple alb with gold piping. He was followed by two dutiful altar boys in black cassocks who carried the incense and the thurible for Louis's mass.

Louis heard the murmuring of a crowd that was growing outside the church. All of Lord Jacquette's household – family, knights, squires, servants, and men–at–arms – would attend. None would enter the church until the organist signaled the start of the service, which Louis hoped would be soon.

He watched as the altar boys set the altar, and then disappeared into a room behind it, to which Esteban had already retreated. He pretended to be immersed in prayer, but he could think of nothing more for which to pray. The thought crossed his mind that if God had not heard him yet, he would probably not, but the thought seemed to him impertinent, and he dismissed it. He asked for God's forgiveness.

The organ sounded and the church quickly filled. As the last of the attendees took their seats, Lord Jacquette entered with a flourish and took his place in the front pew, which had been left empty for him.

The organ hymn ended, and a new one began to herald the reentrance of Father Esteban and his assistants, one carrying the processional cross, and the other the smoldering thurible. The incense reached Louis's nose as he knelt in contrition before the altar, and it filled him, as it always did, with the comfort and the power of God's glory.

Father Esteban bid him stand, and he did. His knees ached, and his legs felt cramped.

A solemn mass sanctified Louis's knighthood. Esteban spoke at length about the duty of every knight to dedicate his life and his heart to God, and to forever follow the time-honored code of chivalry. He admonished Louis, and all the knights who were present, to walk in purity. At the end of his homily, Esteban came around the altar and stood facing Louis, gazing solemnly into his face.

"Humble servant of God," the priest said, "do you stand before me wholly purified in body, mind and soul, acceptable for service to our Lord Jesus Christ?"

"I do," Louis said.

"Are you prepared to take your most solemn oath?"

"I am."

"Do you promise to God your unfailing devotion to the Church?"

"I do."

"To speak only the truth?"

"I do."

"To be ever loyal to your lord?"

"I do."

"To be prompt and faithful in all things, and in all ways?"

"I do."

"To be ever brave, and to avoid no danger out of fear?"

"I do."

"To always defend the lady, and the poor, and the weak, and the helpless?"

"I will always, without fail."

"To be charitable?"

"I do."

"To fight with fairness and honor, above contempt or reproach?"

"In all things and in all ways," Louis said, "I promise."

"On pain of death," Esteban said with a grim look.

"On pain of death," Louis replied, firmly.

Father Esteban nodded toward Lord Jacquette, who rose from his seat to stand beside the priest.

"I find the squire worthy of the honor of knighthood," Esteban said.

Jacquette nodded. He took Louis's sword from the altar and held it aloft, regarding it with admiration. He turned and addressed the congregation in a booming voice that made the chapel feel suddenly smaller.

"I have been honored yet again," he said, "to witness a wondrous transformation. I have watched a child of God grow to become a man of God. I have watched as youthful ideals blossomed into formidable conviction, as untrained desire gave way to forcible strength and indomitable power. The imagination and impatience of youth have coalesced into the sturdy foundation for a lifetime of knightly service.

"Having trained and nurtured the talents and convictions of this brave squire over the years, I enjoy the privilege of performing his noble adoubement. It is a privilege I prize." He turned to look toward Raimon with a stately smile and extended a magnanimous hand. "But today, I prefer to offer the honor to a more deserving man than I, and it would please me well if he were to accept it."

Louis followed Jacquette's gaze to see his father standing astonished, his eyes brimming with inestimable pride. Raimon moved to stand beside Jacquette, who offered him the gleaming sword. Raimon took it and turned to face Louis, who marveled at his father's unprecedented emotion.

"I have been blessed by God with the honor," Raimon said, "of conferring upon you the accolade of knighthood." He extended the sword and tapped Louis lightly upon his left shoulder. "In the name of the Father, and of the Son, and of the Holy Ghost," he said, passing the blade over Louis's head to tap his right shoulder, "I dub thee Sir Knight, Louis de Garonne."

Louis crossed himself and murmured thanks to God.

"Arise, Sir Knight, and take up your sword and shield," Raimon said.

Louis rose, took the sword from Raimon, and gently kissed its hilt. He took his new shield from Lord Jacquette's outstretched hands. A roar of approval went up from the congregation, and the service was ended. The ceremony of Louis's new knighthood had just begun.

He turned from the altar to face the congregation. He looked toward the future of which he had always dreamed, but with lingering shame in his heart, and the hint of tears in his eyes.

✠ ✠ ✠

"It doesn't require a mother's instincts to see that you are troubled, my son. On this day, of all days, what could anguish you so?" Louis turned to face his mother.

Music played, and maidens sang. Squires danced, and nobles schemed. Celebration filled the air, and gaiety filled the faces of all but one. Marie maneuvered Louis toward the privacy of the servant's dining hall. She bid the servants to leave them their privacy, and in a moment they were alone.

"I'm troubled in ways I'd never thought possible," Louis said. He wondered if he could speak the words, especially to his mother. He couldn't even tell the priest. But he respected her unequivocally, and he had to trust her not to condemn him, and to help him to find freedom from his troubles. He had to confess to someone, if only to ease his conscience to some degree.

"Speak freely, Louis," she urged him. "You are my son. Nothing you say or feel will ever change that. Nothing you could do would cause me to turn from you."

He still struggled with the enormity of the truth. Finally, he drew a deep breath and began.

"I have realized that I hold affections that I cannot check, no matter how hard I try. They're despicable, and intolerable. I believe that if I cannot purge them from my heart, I'll be damned. It is hypocritical to accept the mantle of knighthood, even after spending a night in prayer. If I cannot confess and receive absolution, I fear I'm in danger of living a lie."

Marie gasped. "Oh, my," she said. "What affections could possibly afflict you so? Surely you have overestimated their significance." Louis shook his head sadly. "In any event," she continued, "it's nothing I'll condemn."

He was thankful for his mother's unconditional love for him. He prayed that his revelation would not diminish it.

"I'm afraid I'm in love," he said weakly.

Marie brightened at that, but apprehension curbed her enthusiasm. "But that's wonderful!" she exclaimed. "Or it should be so. I realize that it might complicate your ambitions, but it can't possibly be cause for sorrow."

Louis held his breath and nodded to indicate that it could, in fact, be that bad.

"Who is she?" Marie asked tentatively.

He held a long pause. Finally, he sighed and looked directly into his mother's eyes. His voice was barely audible.

"We've always been close," he said. "She has been my best friend. We've shared our deepest secrets, our darkest fears, and our brightest hopes and dreams. I've felt happiest in her company, and until now I thought that was normal affection."

"Colette?" Marie's eyes grew wide, and her hand flew to her mouth.

"My cousin," Louis said firmly, as if he needed to clarify the problem.

In the long silence that followed, a series of expressions washed over Marie's face. Dismay, realization, recollection, misgiving, and finally, apparent acceptance.

"I should have known," she said. "At some level, I suppose it's possible that I actually did know. I've watched the two of you together. It pleased me to see your closeness. I suppose I ignored the more weighty potential of your affection. My God...my dear son. You must be tortured by this."

"I don't know what to do," he said.

"This is a complication. I should have anticipated it," she said.

"How could you have anticipated it?" he said. "It's unnatural. It should never have happened."

She wrung her hands and paced the room. She looked at Louis several times as if to speak, but seemed to think better of it. He could see that she was deeply troubled, and he began to regret his revelation.

"I'm sorry, mother," he offered.

Marie shook her head quickly. "No, Louis," she said. "Don't." She walked to him and placed her hands firmly upon his shoulders. "The fault is mine. It's my doing. There are things I should have told you long ago. It's time for you to understand some things I've never wanted to tell you."

Now he was perplexed. "What things? How could this be your doing? This is not your fault."

Marie turned toward the dining table. "It is," she said. "Please, Louis. Sit with me. I'll explain." She had become visibly distraught, and Louis grew alarmed. He sat.

"What is it, mother?" he said. "What could you tell me that could be worse than what I've told you?"

Her expression turned resolute. "The things I will tell you now may change your regard for me forever. I don't know what will be their full effect, but I have no right to continue to keep them from you. You have a right to know the entire truth."

"Tell me, mother," he said tenderly. "Whatever it is, I promise you that I will always love you, and I will never turn from you, either, just as you would not turn from me."

She sighed heavily and stared away to a distant place that only she could see.

"It was so long ago," she said, "nearly four decades, but it seems an eternity. I was a small child. So much had happened – some that I could comprehend, and some that I never would. It was as if the world had come apart before my eyes, and fallen into darkness and ruin."

Tears welled in her eyes as she drifted back to a dark and terrible day.

Chapter 15

THE FORTRESS AT MONTSÉGUR stood stern and majestic, in defiance of the turbulent drama that surged around it. The fortress peered stolidly upon the breathtaking scenery that surrounded it, from the peaks of the magnificent Pyrenees to the south, to the exquisite vista of the walled city of Carcassonne away to the northeast.

In the winter of 1244, a bitter wind blew relentlessly from the north, and with its deathly chill, it carried across the land a strange and ominous threat of impending doom. The inhabitants of Montségur had grown all too familiar with suffering and tragedy in recent times. Further anguish loomed for the remote and cloistered community of pious souls.

Marie was unusually aware for a child of so few years. At six, she was accustomed to austerity and hardship. In the absence of distractions or diversions, she'd spent a lot of time alone with her deepest thoughts.

She felt the menace that filled the air, and the anxiety that shook her small community to its core. She saw the strain of struggle and starvation in the lines of her neighbors' faces, and she sensed the despair that simmered beneath the calm of their virtuous veneer.

She bore the intensity of the foreboding with strength and calm, and little fear, but its effect on her parents and the community saddened her deeply. She worried too for her younger brother, Willem, a beautiful boy barely four years old.

Marie's family lived in a tiny community of Cathars, the devout adherents of a simple, humble faith. They were the tattered remnants of a sect that had once numbered half a million souls, and that had exerted a profound influence on the culture and the convictions of the people of the Languedoc. But now fewer than five hundred Cathars survived in the region, and two hundred twenty-four of them were here, huddled together in the tenuous security of an imposing fortress perched at the peak of Montségur.

At twelve hundred meters above the rolling green Languedoc hills, the peak of Montségur was the closest the Cathars could get to their heavenly God.

It had been almost ten months since French soldiers had begun to mass at the foot of Montségur. The Catholic pope had sent them to destroy these last of the Languedoc Cathars. The French King Louis IX had sent his soldiers, too. While the pope wanted the Cathars dead, the king wanted control of the Languedoc region.

Cathar contempt for the excesses of political and religious leaders complemented and encouraged the independent spirit of the local nobility, most of whom had stubbornly resisted the domination of both popes and kings.

The sincerity of the Cathars' faith had irrevocably sealed their fate.

Since the beginning of last summer the soldiers had come. Their trebuchet launched a steady volley of huge rocks at the fortress walls and into the village that nestled just below it on the northeastern face. Most of the time the missiles fell short of their targets, but the constant pounding of rock on rock unnerved

Marie. It made the ground shudder beneath her feet, and it made her think of what would happen if one were to fall on her or upon their little house. She wished that it would go away, but instead it grew closer as the summer passed into autumn, and the autumn to winter.

Two months earlier the soldiers had scaled the northeast tip of Montségur and taken the outer defenses. The Cathars' defenders ceded their strategic position at Roc de la Tour, the fortified tower at the tip of the lower plateau, and they had retreated upward behind the fortress walls.

The pope's French army moved its trebuchet closer, to a glen at the foot of the steep green hill just below the east wall of the fortress. The army and its trebuchet stood where the slope leveled into the plateau that stretched away toward the majestic Roc de la Tour. The trebuchet was now well within range of the fortress and the tiny village just below it, to the north.

Prior to the army's arrival, Marie would take Willem for walks in the glen, among the grass, and they would play in the woods beyond the glen for hours. She remembered those idyllic days, and it was hard for her to comprehend that the glen was now filled with angry men of death, intent on destroying her community.

The boulders were bigger now, since they didn't have so far to fly, and they were crashing directly into the fortress walls. The stone missiles were also demolishing the tiny houses of the village, so the refugee Cathars had moved their families inside the fortress walls.

The siege had cut off the main supply lines to the mountain top. Supplies still got through sporadically by way of a grueling and tortuous climb up the southwestern face of the mountain. The nature of the climb limited what supplies could be brought, and the brave souls who risked the endeavor faced death upon capture. Marie didn't know who brought the supplies from time to time, but she was happy when they did. The siege was taking its toll on everyone inside the fortress.

Marie was hungry. She was cold and tired and drawn, and

if it were not for her family she would care little how their predicament ended, as long as it came to an end.

At night she could hear the soldiers below singing songs – songs of love, songs of war and death, songs of victory, and hymns to the glory of God. Marie wondered how those songs could all be sung by men who were hungry for the blood of innocents.

The crashing of rock on rock continued as the trebuchet pounded the fortress with brutal, merciless accuracy. In places, the walls appeared ready to crumble. It was clear that their collapse was imminent. The Cathars knew that the siege of Montségur was nearing its dreadful end.

On the morning of March the thirteenth, Jean de LaGarde, a member of the *Perfecti*, the leaders of the faith, called the community to prayer. It was time, he said, for all to prepare for the inevitable. Those who had not yet received *consolamentum* should wait no longer. The *consolamentum* elevated a believer, or credente to the station of Perfect, one of the elect of the Cathar faith. It should be taken before the passage from life to death, and this was no doubt their last opportunity.

"The beginning," de LaGarde said firmly, "not the end. We go soon to be with our God in heaven. Let us make ourselves ready."

The credente gathered close in the chapel. They nodded at de LaGarde's solemn words. Some murmured that they were prepared, and even joyful at the prospect of departing this evil world for the presence of their Almighty God. They were going home, and there was nothing tragic in that.

Marie wondered if they all truly felt that way. If so, then their faith was incredibly strong.

The most solemn consolamentum that Marie had ever witnessed took the better part of the afternoon and the evening. Twenty-one of the credente, including Marie's parents, affirmed their faith and prepared for the laying on of hands that would confer upon them the presence of the Holy Spirit of God, and that would condemn them to death at the hands of their impatient Inquisitors. While the credente might be spared by the Inquisitors upon the renunciation of their heresy, there was no such forgiveness for the Perfecti.

The congregation knelt and prayed for spiritual deliverance, and then de LaGarde took his place at the head of the gathering. One by one the credente took their place at the Perfect's feet to receive the consolamentum.

Marie watched as each of her parents took their place before the Perfect. Her father, Peires, knelt first. De LaGarde held his well-worn Gospel aloft, over Peires's lowered head, and recited the Lord's Prayer. He then explained the significance of the consolamentum, and that the indwelling of God's Holy Spirit would elevate the recipient to the station of Perfect, and a new Son of God.

"Repeat now the Lord's Prayer," de LaGarde said.

"Our Father," Peires began, "who art in Heaven, hallowed be thy name—"

De LaGarde interrupted now, repeating the line of prayer and saying a few words to elucidate its significance. He did the same with each new line as Peires intoned the prayer. It was important that the postulant understand each subtle inflection and connotation of the prayer that was given by the Savior Himself, to be recited by the believer to mark every significant moment, so that the glory of each would be properly given to God.

The Renunciation followed.

"Do you renounce the Church of Satan?" de LaGarde asked.

Peires's voice was strong and steady.

"I renounce the Church of Satan," he said, "its pagan rituals, its hunger for filthy lucre, and its celebration of the despicable cross, the instrument of the agony of my Savior."

De LaGarde placed his hands upon Peires's head, and several other Perfects approached and joined him, placing their hands also upon Peires's head.

"The Perfect carries the obligation to honor Christ, and to live each day in the path He set for us. The Perfect must love his enemy, and forgive all trespasses against him and against others. The Perfect must not carry arms, neither sword nor shield, and must turn to one who smites him the other cheek also. The

Perfect must offer his mantle to one who seizes his tunic. The Perfect must neither judge nor condemn, for that is not our place. The Perfect must neither swear, nor take oaths, but rather let his actions speak alone."

Peires bowed in humble affirmation of each instruction.

"The Perfect must hate this world and all its works, and abjure all things of this world, for if any man loves the world, the love of the Father is not in him. The world and its lust will surely pass away, but he that does the will of God will have eternal life."

De LaGarde paused to ensure that Peires appreciated the gravity of his affirmations, and then he continued.

"Will you, Peires Domergue, fulfill each of the obligations of the Perfecti of the faith?"

"It is my will to do so," Peires said. "Pray God for me that He gives me His strength." He prayed for forgiveness for his sins.

De LaGarde placed the Gospel against the top of Peires's head. Several of the other Perfecti placed their hands upon his head as well.

"Adoramus, Patrem, et Filium, et Spiritum Sanctum," de LaGarde said. Peires and de LaGarde repeated the words three times in turn.

Raymond de Belvis, one of the credente and Peires's closest friend, spoke the necessary plea.

"Good Christians, we pray that you, by the love of God, grant this blessing that God has given you, to our friend here and in our presence."

"For all the sins," Peires said, "that I have ever done, in thought, in word, or in deed, I ask pardon of God, of the congregation, and of you."

The congregation responded in unison: "By God, and by us, and by God's Church, may your sins be forgiven. We pray God to forgive you them."

De LaGarde led the congregation in the Adoration.

"Adoramus, Patrem, et Filium, et Spiritum Sanctum." The congregation repeated the Adoration three times, and Peires's consolamentum was complete. Peires stood and took his place among

the new Perfecti, and Marie's mother took her place before de LaGarde for her own consolamentum rite.

The rites continued throughout the afternoon and into the night as boulders crashed relentlessly into the crumbling fortress walls, and the defending archers tried desperately to quell their attack. Twenty credente were raised that day to the station of Perfect in preparation for their passing into the presence of God.

✠ ✠ ✠

Two days later the elders of the community convened with their loyal defenders, knights and soldiers who had dedicated themselves to protecting the Cathars. Many of the defenders had been excommunicated and become fugitives as a result. Pierre-Roger de Mirepoix was a fierce defender of the Cathars, and had led the knights who massacred a band of Inquisitors at Avignonet two summers earlier.

"We will not hold out for much longer," Pierre-Roger said. "The trebuchet is too effective. It's a matter of days, at the most."

The collapse of the fortress walls was imminent. The French soldiers would massacre the inhabitants when the walls were breached.

"Yes," de LaGarde agreed. "It is time. You may request our terms. You and your knights have been valiant in our defense, but it is time for all of us to move on to our next station, whatever for each of us that may be. You will be forever blessed for your faithful service to God."

De Mirepoix bowed to the Perfect in thanks.

While the Perfecti were doomed, the credente would have the choice of martyrdom for their faith or leniency upon repentance. The Perfecti firmly believed that each of the credente should have this choice, and they made that choice the chief of the terms of surrender. They also demanded that their defenders be unconditionally spared.

De Mirepoix chose a detachment of knights to ride out from the fortress to the soldiers below to formally present the terms of surrender. They returned to announce that the terms had been accepted by the captain of the papal troops.

The next morning the inhabitants of Montségur gathered in the courtyard of the fortress. De LaGarde prayed for the deliverance of the knights and the believers, and for the sanctity of those who would face their martyrdom. He prayed for the forgiveness of their persecutors, and for God's mercy upon all who worked in the service of the pope's Church of Satan.

Finally, when the prayers were complete, de LaGarde turned to address the believers one last time.

"The time has come," he said, with finality. "This day we commit ourselves into the hands of our persecutors, and so into the hands of our merciful God. There will be the great reward of heaven for all who stand fast and proclaim their faith in the living God. There will be no shame for those who choose leniency. The choice is yours alone. Your God will abide with you no matter how you choose. You have fought the good fight, each of you. Whatever shall come this day will be a testament to the strength of your will and the purity of your spirit. May God's blessings be upon each of you as we leave this sanctuary."

The believers gathered their meager belongings and formed the line that would proceed from the fortress gate and down the slope to the plateau, where they would meet their conquerors. De LaGarde and de Mirepoix retired to the chapel for last-minute arrangements, and de Mirepoix called for four of the defending knights to join them. The knights soon emerged from the chapel carrying overstuffed packs upon their backs. They hurried to a hidden portal on the southwestern wall of the fortress, and they disappeared through it without delay.

Marie knew that the secret portal led to a treacherous climb down the steep, craggy southeast face of the mountain. Whatever the knights were spiriting out of the fortress must have been precious, and she hoped that they would succeed in their mission.

Peires Domergue placed a steady hand on his daughter's

shoulder.

"Marie," he said quietly, "it is time."

Marie moved to join her parents and her brother, glancing briefly at the point in the brush where the knights had disappeared. Bruna, Marie's mother, took Marie by the hand and held Willem close to her side.

✠ ✠ ✠

On the lower plateau, the pope's French soldiers waited impatiently. They had besieged this fortress for ten long months. Now that they had taken the plateau, they were close enough to storm the fortress and finally end it, and most of them failed to see the point of further delay.

Among them, a rugged, battle-hardened Templar watched with steely eyes and a rigid jaw as the climax of the siege unfolded. He grimaced in contempt. In all of his days, Arnaud had not seen a moment as shameful as this. He and his Templar contingent had been sent by the pope to participate in this unholy crusade, to root out the last of the Cathars, but it was a mission that most of them loathed. Many of his men had long-standing Cathar ties, and none bore the Cathars ill will. An army of ten thousand Crusaders against a rabble of pacifistic refugees was a shameful farce.

Arnaud's left fist clenched the reins to steady his muscular steed as it bucked and snorted at the acrid smoke that seared its flaring nostrils. Arnaud's own body was taut with anxious tension, and his gut churned as tragedy unfolded in the morning light.

The Templar detachment stood in tight formation, a slight but notable distance from the French soldiers who had moved to the higher plateau, nearer to the summit of the mount and far above the massive army gathered below. The soldiers on the plateau shivered in the cold, crisp dawn as the sun rose higher over Montségur. The rising sun cast brilliant rays across the rooftops in the expanse of the valley below, and warmed the faces of those waiting to carry out the Lord's sacred work.

The fortress gates cranked open at the touch of the sun's soft glow, slowly and with a muted, reluctant groan. A solemn procession of exhausted, failed defenders emerged from the darkness within, from the spare sanctuary of the fortress's battered but unyielding walls. Two hundred twenty-four unarmed Cathar men, women, and children, and another two hundred lightly armed knights and soldiers moved slowly down the slope to meet the first of the massive army that had finally overwhelmed them.

The Cathars blinked in the sunlight and shivered in the cold as they surveyed the sight of ten thousand soldiers spread out across the valley, standing in silent witness to their final defeat.

Arnaud watched, his chiseled face stoic. His expression did not betray the wrenching nausea and contempt that churned inside him. Having vanquished countless enemies in a lifetime of fierce battle, he was not inclined to pity those defeated in an honorable fight; the scene unfolding before him was the result of no such thing.

It was not the skills of the army they faced that had finally defeated the Cathars, but rather the distress of persistent starvation and mounting sickness that finally compelled them to surrender.

According to the terms of surrender, the confessed would go free on their assurance of repentance. Those who refused to abjure would be burned in the flames of the inquisitors' execution pyre. The defending knights, as agreed, would go free.

The chill of the early spring breeze carried the quiet murmur of solemn prayer down the slope from the shuffling column, through gaps in the fagots of kindling that stood beneath the execution platform to the ears of the waiting soldiers. Even the soldiers who tended the roaring fire of the torch pit shivered at the sound.

Arnaud searched the faces of the tattered Cathars as they reached the small plateau. Except for a few, he detected no sign of fear or sorrow among them. He was struck by the prevalence of peaceful resolution and acceptance on the faces of the condemned.

A contingent of French soldiers met the Cathar column, and one by one they heard each of their personal decisions on the surrender terms. The Cathars were separated into two groups based on their decisions: those who chose to live were herded to the Inquisitors who would receive their depositions and abjurations, while the others would climb seven rickety steps to the funeral pyre, built to accommodate at least two hundred heretics.

The knights who defended the Cathars were promptly arrested, against the terms of surrender, to be led to Paris dungeons in shackles and chains.

There was no wailing of grief from the defeated Cathars. They walked steadily, calmly, and fully composed with a peace that defied the understanding of those who were preparing to destroy them.

Arnaud turned casually to meet the eyes of his brethren knights. He could see that they, as he, felt compassion for these brave souls. He spurred his horse forward, moving closer to the approaching procession, and his brethren followed him closely.

He studied the peaceful faces of the doomed. He tried to fathom the conviction of faith that allowed them victory over their fear, but he could not. He was no stranger to courage in the midst of battle, or a warrior's valor in the face of a death that fulfilled a sacred duty. But the courage to walk calmly as sheep to slaughter, to face death without the aid of a warrior's rage, was for Arnaud an unimaginable thing. He was awed by their strength, their composure and resolve, and he longed to save these fearless, helpless people from their fate.

His gaze was drawn to the sight of a man and a woman, who walked huddled with two children pressed between them. They were dirty and tattered and deeply fatigued, but stately in the strength of their bearing. They walked purposefully, unflinchingly toward the men who would be their judges.

The children, a girl and a boy, clung tightly to their parents' coarse woolen cloaks, staring wide-eyed as they approached the inquisitors.

The husband, strong and wiry and calmly subdued, declared

his decision firmly and clearly when they reached the captain of the soldiers, who wordlessly and abruptly pushed him into the line for the pyre. Arnaud shook his head at the heartrending sight.

The wife then delivered her own declaration to the captain, who gazed briefly at the children by her side. The soldiers looked at the woman with incredulous dismay. One soldier shook his head with consternation and spread his hands wide to indicate the children.

The woman glanced wordlessly at her dirty, swollen feet. The captain shook his head impatiently, and several of the soldiers pushed the woman with her children toward her husband, who stood waiting. The family proceeded with grim determination toward the waiting pyre, the children's eyes wide with apprehension.

The fire-tenders stood ready with the torches that would ignite the kindling stacked beneath the platform.

Arnaud was astonished and deeply moved by this family's final, wrenching drama. He ached to take some action to prevent their execution, but he knew that there was nothing he could do. Then, his eyes met those of the father.

The man looked into Arnaud's eyes with a sad smile of compassion and forgiveness. Arnaud was stricken by the realization that the man counted him among the executioners. While Arnaud had secretly forbidden his Templar contingent from active participation in the capture of Montségur, or in the ensuing massacre, he knew that the man who silently forgave him now couldn't possibly know that. And yet the man's forgiveness was clear and unmistakable. Arnaud's inaction filled him with unbearable guilt.

Arnaud nodded almost imperceptibly to the condemned man, and then toward the children who stood shivering by his side. The man grasped Arnaud's meaning, and he looked thoughtfully at the children. When he returned his gaze to Arnaud, he nodded slowly and purposefully, and then closed his eyes tightly in profound thanks.

The man whispered into his wife's ear. She turned in dismay toward the bearded, scarred, and grim-faced Templar, and shook her head. *No*, she mouthed. Arnaud gave the woman a slight but meaningful signal with his mail-gloved hand, a signal that he knew only a Cathar would understand. The fear and doubt faded from the woman's face, and in seconds she realized the significance of this fleeting opportunity.

The woman leaned close to her children. She gathered them to her bosom. She spoke urgently to them, and then she turned them around to face the waiting knight. The children pushed back into their mother's arms, but their father stilled them with a sharp rebuke. He softened a bit, but repeated his firm instruction to the children.

The man and the woman pushed the eldest of the children toward Arnaud. The young girl hesitated still, leaning back into her mother's arms. Tears filled her eyes as her mother whispered passionately into her ear, and she struggled against the words. As the mother pleaded, the girl relaxed, accepting the terrible reality. She gazed numbly at the waiting Templar.

Finally she stood straight. She threw back her shoulders and wiped the tears from her eyes. She turned to her father and looked into his solemn face, and she threw her arms around him and held him tight. After a moment she turned and embraced her mother, burying her face in her bosom before pushing away and grasping her brother by the hand. She pulled the boy hastily away from the procession and toward the waiting Templar.

One of Arnaud's men, witnessing the exchange, instinctively sprang into action. He spurred his horse and shouted a command to his brethren. The Templars fell into chaotic disarray, riding wildly toward the French captain, yelling that some of the defending knights had escaped. All eyes turned to the disruption, and away from Arnaud and the children.

Arnaud nodded to his close friend Guillaume and spurred his own horse in a dash toward the children. He leaned far to grasp the small girl's arm, and he pulled her onto the horse. She threw her arms tightly about his waist and watched as Guillaume snatched her brother amidst the clamoring chaos.

The French soldiers gawked as the raucous Templars rode in

wild circles, shouting nonsensical orders to no one in particular. In a flash Arnaud, Guillaume, and the children disappeared from view.

The Templar band settled and grew quiet only when they were certain they'd covered their commander's escape. With a rambling, apologetic explanation to the irritated French captain, they turned back toward the pyre. The French captain glared ill-concealed annoyance at the Templars.

The tattered Cathar couple stared calmly through the dust cloud to the brush at the edge of the plateau, into which their children had disappeared. They turned with a whisper to the heavens and stepped with resolution onto the steps to the execution platform. They climbed the steps slowly, holding hands and nodding their thanks to the Templars.

Arnaud and Guillaume rode hard along the tortuous trail that led down the steep slope from the plateau to the valley below. They rode until they were satisfied that they had not been followed. They finally reined their steeds to a skittering halt below a rocky outcropping on the mountain's northeastern face.

They dismounted and extended their hands to help the children to the ground.

"Your name?" Arnaud asked the girl as he placed her gently to the ground. She was perhaps five years old, maybe six. She looked up at the towering knight with a convincing show of defiance that was betrayed only by the slight trembling of her chin. The boy, about two years younger, pulled himself roughly from the grasp of his rescuer. Neither child spoke.

Arnaud lowered himself to one knee. He held an open palm toward the resolute girl.

"Do not fear me," he gently assured her. "You're safe now."

The boy pushed his way to stand defiantly between his sister and the knight. Arnaud drew back a bit and cocked his head, half-smiling in surprised appreciation.

"You're protective," Arnaud said. "That's good. But don't you worry, lad. I mean no harm to either you or your sister."

"You're a soldier," the boy said with contempt. "We don't

like soldiers."

The girl grasped her brother's slender shoulders and pulled him close to her. She wrapped her arms around him protectively.

"Shhh," she whispered to him. "Say nothing."

Suddenly a loud crack, followed by a slithering sound, rang out from above their heads. Arnaud and Guillaume spun in alarm, each drawing his sword with blinding speed. They moved to stand on either side of the children, extending their swords in anticipation of conflict.

A small rock landed with a solid thud on the ground a few feet from Arnaud. It had been jarred loose by someone who was descending the rocky slope above them. He held a forefinger to his lips to caution the children. Guillaume motioned for the children to move closer to the rocks for cover, and they quickly complied.

The knights moved to the place where a water-worn gully emerged from the brush that covered the steep, rocky cliff. A moment passed, and then a sudden crash and the sound of tumbling was punctuated by barely muffled curses of surprise and frustration.

Arnaud relaxed slightly. The curses were not uttered in French, but in Occitan; the clumsy climbers were the knights who had escaped the fallen fortress, and not French reconnaissance soldiers. Arnaud and Guillaume waited at the gully to intercept the frustrated knights.

The clamor moved closer, growing louder, and suddenly a filthy, tattered, and badly scraped man slid face first into the bottom of the gravelly gully. He sat up with a grunt and stared in horror at the sword-wielding Templars.

The man scrambled to his feet, and he half turned as if to shout a frantic warning up the slope. Guillaume silenced the man with a sword point to the base of his throat. The sound of more scrambling came from some distance above them.

"Quiet," Arnaud warned. The man looked warily at the Templar.

Within minutes, three more men slid to the bottom of the gully, and they stood to face their unexpected reception. The four knights trembled in panic. The packs they carried prevented them from drawing their weapons.

Arnaud noted the protectiveness with which they clutched the packs, which were filled to capacity. He eyed the packs with interest. The children watched intently, their mouths slack with rapt fascination.

For a long moment all stood silent, absorbing the implications of the unexpected meeting. Finally, Arnaud pointed meaningfully toward one of the men, and to the bundle he clutched tightly to his chest.

"The relics," Arnaud said simply and directly. It was not a question, but rather a stern observation.

The man nodded slightly, warily.

"Then pass," Arnaud commanded, "and pass quickly. And do so with far more caution than you've just demonstrated. It is only by God's good grace that we, and not the king's soldiers, caught you here."

The man nodded nervously. *"Òc,"* he said in acknowledgement. He nodded curtly to his companions, and they started off to the winding path that led farther down the slope to the southwest.

"There will be a small Templar garrison farther on," Arnaud called quietly after the men. "Give them the word, and they will keep you safe."

The clumsiest of the men turned to nod his acknowledgement, and his thanks. In a moment the men had disappeared into the thick, concealing brush.

"And now," Arnaud continued, turning again to face the young girl. "What, pray tell, is your name?

"Marie," she answered quietly. "Marie Doumergue. My parents are Peires and Bruna Doumergue."

Arnaud nodded. "Marie," he repeated. "It's a beautiful name." He turned to the boy. "And you, Master Doumergue? What shall I call you?"

"I am Willem," the boy said proudly. "Willem Doumergue."

"Wil—"

"You let them go…," Marie interrupted, speaking quietly,

and with wonder, nodding in the direction of the fleeing knights. "And you saved us. Why? You are a soldier."

"I am no mere soldier," Arnaud replied, his voice even and intense. "I am a Templar Knight. My name is Arnaud Marti. I did not come here to participate in the destruction of your people. The truth is too complex to explain to you here and now. You will have to trust me until I can help you to understand. You have no other choice."

"Our parents…," Marie said quietly, "they are dead."

Young Willem looked plaintively into his sister's solemn eyes as dreadful realization dawned in his own.

Arnaud did not immediately answer. His throat choked with emotion. He took a moment to compose himself, and to think of a gentle reply. He failed. He closed his eyes for a moment, and then looked directly into Marie's eyes.

"Yes," he said. "But you are safe with me. You will be safe from this day on. You have my word. I swear it on my life."

"You should not swear," Marie scolded him. "Never swear. Your word is enough."

Arnaud raised his eyebrows in surprise. The girl had insight beyond her years, and he knew that she had probably seen more in her short life than most others could imagine.

"We must go," he said brusquely. He mounted his horse in one smooth movement, and he held out his hand for Marie. She took it eagerly, and he hoisted her up to sit snugly behind him. She turned to ensure that Willem was seated safely behind Guillaume, who had remained strangely silent, and whose name she still did not know.

"Who is he?" Marie asked, tugging at Arnaud's shoulder and pointing toward Guillaume.

"A good man," Arnaud said simply. "You can trust him, too. Your brother is in good hands."

Arnaud spurred his horse, jolting Marie into silence as she grasped at his waist to hang on. Guillaume and Willem followed, and they rode in silence until Montségur was far, far behind them.

Chapter 16

"So a Templar saved your life!" Louis gasped.

Marie nodded, still gazing into the distance of her memories. Finally, she shifted her attention to her son and watched him as he struggled with the truth.

Louis was stunned by the magnitude of his mother's revelation. He stared at her in silence, nodding occasionally as the implications of her story occurred to him.

"Who was this Templar? What happened next?"

Marie gazed out the window and across the fields. She took a deep breath before she spoke.

"He was Arnaud..." She paused again, and then said softly, "He was Arnaud Marti. He took us to live with his brother's family. His brother was François."

"François Marti...," Louis whispered in disbelief. "Your father. And your Uncle Arnaud was the Templar who saved you." Louis pieced it all together with wonder. "Then François was not your real father. And...he was a Cathar."

"Yes," Marie said.

Louis sucked in his breath. “And your real parents,” he said, “they were also Cathars.” He narrowed his eyes. “And Arnaud was there at Montségur to arrest the Cathars, but he saved you and Uncle Willem instead.”

“He was there against his will, by the order of the pope,” Marie said. “He resolved to do what he could to ease the suffering of the Good People. His own parents and his grandparents had been Cathar. His brother and his brother’s wife were Cathar. He shared their beliefs, but privately. Those were days when Cathars were not yet considered to be heretics, except by the Church and precious few others.”

“Why did he not refuse the task?” Louis asked.

“Refuse the pope? Refuse the French king? No man is invincible, Louis. All must choose their battles wisely. It would have helped no one, had he chosen that battle. It would have meant his own death, ultimately. He was doing much to help, wherever he could, under circumstances he did not choose. His death would have gained nothing.”

Louis sat silent for a long moment, staring at his mother.

“So why, then,” he asked, “do you hate the Templars so?”

Marie stood and paced for a moment, her hands clasped in front of her.

“I don’t hate them, Louis,” she finally said. She stopped pacing and sighed again, deeply. “I despise what they represent. I despise what they have defended, and all for which they have died. I despise war and murder and the evil of powerful men. The Templars themselves are not evil, but they do serve evil men and an evil cause.”

The shock of the heresy of his mother’s words shook him. Once again he struggled with discoveries that exceeded his capacity to understand or accept.

“François Marti adopted you and Uncle Willem, then,” he said. “He was not your real father.” Marie nodded with a look of remorse as he still struggled to grasp that truth. “And Uncle Jacques, then…” His face clouded over as his words trailed off. The magnitude of this new perspective overwhelmed him.

She looked at him expectantly.

"Uncle Jacques..." he continued, "is not your brother."

"No, he is not. Not of blood."

"And so, Colette..."

"...is not your cousin. Not of blood."

His eyes grew wide, and his mouth fell open. The weight of his guilt lifted, but it was quickly replaced by budding resentment. His feelings for Colette were *not* obscene. They were *not* an evil perversion. They were natural, and pure before God. They were...acceptable.

But not to the Church, he thought. Nor to anyone who did not know the truth. As far as anyone knew, Colette was his cousin, and it was obvious that no one could ever know the truth. Anyone suspected of even tenuous ties to Cathars was hunted, tortured when found, and often burned. None betrayed them unless tortured beyond bearing, but the inquisitors were ever vigilant and madly aggressive in their search for signs of their presence. The inquisitors did not hesitate to act upon the flimsiest shred of evidence in their pursuit.

"It may be just as well," Louis mused aloud.

Marie looked at him questioningly.

"What may be just as well?" she asked.

Louis shook his head. He stood from his stool and paced the room.

It's impossible, he thought. *It's just as well.*

"Louis...?" Marie said.

"A Templar cannot marry," he said with finality. "A Templar cannot fall in love, or even be close with a woman. It's just as well. It's God's will. All is as it should be." He nodded firmly and set his jaw. He was succeeding at convincing himself, for now.

Pain filled Marie's eyes. She tried to speak, but the words caught in her throat.

"I'll go to my calling," he continued. "I'm not to marry anyway. I'm to be a Templar and to fight God's fight. It's my calling, and my destiny."

"No...," Marie said. "That's not your destiny. It's your choice, and you're free to reconsider it."

"It's clear," Louis insisted. He turned to face her, his eyes hard with forced determination. "If this were not my destiny, then all other things would not be as they are...as they have been. If anything other than this were meant to be, then it would be."

"We've tried to protect you from the truth, Louis," Marie said.

"Protect me?"

"We kept you safe from the Church by placing you in its arms, by nurturing your devotion to the Church and to God."

"The same Church that burned your parents at Montségur," Louis said. His voice was suddenly calm and even.

"We spared you that knowledge, and the rage that would have consumed you because of it. You could not have hidden that, and it would have destroyed you."

"You did not think I could bear it."

"There was no reason to burden you with it. What end would that have served?"

"The truth," Louis said, raising his palms. "I would have known the truth."

"And what would you have done with it?" She looked sorrowfully at him. "The truth of this would be our condemnation. It would destroy us if it came to light. It would have been stupid to have burdened you with such a thing." Louis stood in silence. "The Martis have suffered much for this truth," she continued. "They were watched constantly. Arnaud Marti's sympathies were not entirely secret. His truth was only thinly veiled. No matter how hard he tried to hide it, discovery was always a whisper away. It was so dangerous that the Martis eventually had to leave. They had no choice."

"Colette has known this all along?"

"Yes," Marie said.

She kept it from me, too, he realized. He felt foolish.

"For how long?"

"Her awareness is what forced them to leave for Scotland," she said. "She was barely four years old when she began to show contempt for the parish priests." She laughed wistfully. "It was as though she knew instinctively what she had never been told. She compared the faith of her parents to that of the churchmen, and she knew the difference, even at that young age. She seemed to sense the enmity of the churchmen toward people like her parents. Her intuition was unusual, almost supernatural...and exceedingly dangerous."

Louis imagined Colette as an innocent, precocious child.

"There were incidents that sparked the suspicions of the local Inquisitors," Marie continued. "It was prudent for the Martis to leave, and to stay away until Colette learned to mask her feelings."

"She learned that well, it seems" Louis said wryly.

"Yes."

"And I've lived a lie."

"As this world often forces us to do," Marie said, frowning. She rarely frowned. "We would not have chosen that for you, but we did what we felt was necessary."

Louis labored with the thought that his lifelong loyalties and affections were contrived. He had been taught to love the Church that had murdered his true grandparents, that would have murdered his mother and Uncle Willem when they were children. He lived to serve that Church. He was loyal to men for whom his mother had long held profound, if well-concealed contempt. He'd suppressed his natural love for Colette when he should have been free to revel in it.

He'd idolized the Templars. That sentiment, at least, was well–founded. If all else was a lie, that was not. He briefly reconsidered even that before he pushed the thought from his mind.

"And what am I to do with this, mother?" he asked. "How do I reconcile this truth?"

Marie lowered her eyes. "You needed to know," she said. "I see you torturing yourself. I've wanted for so long to tell you the truth, and to get you to change your mind about crusading. But even now I don't know if it was best to tell you at all, or if it would have been any better to have told you long ago."

Louis shook his head. He pulled at his sleeve to even the hem, and he straightened his shirt beneath his coat. "It doesn't matter," he said. "What's done is done. It is as it is. And what will be, will be. I shall be a Crusader and a Templar Knight."

Marie watched in silence as Louis made his way to the door. As he reached it, she called softly to him. He turned and nodded curtly.

"I love you, my son," she said in a faltering voice.

He nodded again, then pushed through the door and headed for the beckoning solitude of the fields.

His thoughts careened out of control as he struggled to assimilate new realities. He struggled to pull them back into a semblance of order. His mother's tale of Arnaud Marti's heroism at Montségur only spurred his Templar ambitions. His crusading desire intensified, and his resolve to sate it strengthened. His love for the Church remained undiminished, though he could not help questioning its wisdom, and its motivations.

He walked aimlessly, lost in those thoughts, until he arrived at his favorite place at the creek that ran to the Aude.

He was pleased to find his good friend Victor lazing at the water's edge, a fishing pole clutched loosely in his hand. Louis knew that Victor would help him to reason through this madness.

Victor appeared perplexed when Louis finished recounting all that had transpired.

"So, allow me to sum up your problems," Victor said. Louis thought he sounded oddly disingenuous. "You were taught to love the Church in order to protect you from a deadly truth, from which you still have to hide; you're free to marry your cousin, who you mistakenly thought you shouldn't love in the first place, and who you can't love now because then everyone would know about the first problem; but your Templars are still the heroes you've always thought they were, and you're still going to run off and join them, sacrificing everything else that you care about anyway."

Louis scowled at Victor.

"That sums it up, doesn't it?" Victor said.

"You make it sound ridiculous," Louis replied.

Victor shrugged. "I should have your problems," he said. He tossed a pebble into the water with his free hand.

"I shouldn't have told you," Louis said. "Especially the part about Colette."

Victor chuckled. "You're right. The part about the heresy isn't so bad. It's the thing about being in love with a beautiful girl who's no longer your cousin that you should have kept to yourself."

"I thought you'd help," Louis said with exasperation. "I thought I could confide in you."

"And you did," Victor said. He paused, eyeing Louis with what appeared to be disdain. "Relax, Louis," he said. "I'm teasing you. And you deserve it." Louis shook his head, incredulous. "Come on," Victor said. "It's just that some people face problems every day, and most are a lot more tragic than yours. Yes, there's a danger that someone might one day accuse your family of heresy. But everyone faces that danger; I'd be accused sooner than you. Some people have no food to eat, and they struggle to make it through every new day. They can only wish they had your problems. And yet, you're overwrought by yours."

Louis considered Victor's point. He decided that Victor simply did not appreciate the gravity of his troubles, and that he was probably wrong to expect that of him.

"It's easy to minimize it when it's not your problem," Louis said.

Victor shook his head. "I'm not minimizing it. You're leaving, aren't you? What will any of this matter then? It'll be forgotten. You'll never speak of it again. Your future is secure. Not everyone is so lucky."

Louis thought of Victor left alone to his labors, and largely friendless when he left. Raimon was not particularly fond of Victor, and there was no guarantee that Victor would remain in the stables after he left. In fact, Louis thought, there was a good chance that Victor would be shipped off to war with one of Raimon's noble friends, if the occasion presented itself. Louis would not learn of such a thing until he eventually returned from Jerusalem. He wondered if Victor was still considering his request to join him.

"Victor, this is a weighty thing for me. I understand you just can't see it, but that's all right. I shouldn't have burdened you with it anyway. It's my decision to make, and not your problem."

"What decision?"

Louis was curious at his own choice of words. He was suddenly aware that at some level he had begun to question his own plans.

"I suppose...whether I really want to leave now," he said. "I wonder if I should just stay, or at least delay my leaving and see what happens."

"Damn," Victor muttered. "I was hoping you'd go quickly and leave Colette to me."

Louis wheeled and slapped Victor hard across the top of his head. He hated when Victor talked like that. It had always been clear to him that Victor wanted Colette for himself. He had never pursued her, probably knowing that she would have no interest in a common laborer. But he had not concealed his desire for her, and Louis was suddenly aware of how deeply that had annoyed him over the years.

"Hey!" Victor yelled. "Don't do that! You'll be sorry."

"You deserved it," Louis said. "Stop talking like that. I don't want to hear it anymore."

"I was kidding. Why would you act like that?" Louis shrugged as if it were obvious. "You know," Victor said, "for a noble and a would-be knight, you're pretty damned thin-skinned. You know Colette would never have me, and you know I'd never betray you."

Louis nodded doubtfully. "I know you wouldn't," he said. He knew he sounded unconvincing. He offered Victor a conciliatory hand, which Victor clasped. "I'm struggling with this. It helps to talk to you about it. You're straightforward, and I was counting on that."

"Louis, you've had your mind made up for years. You've talked about going off with the Templars since you were a child. What is there to decide?"

"I didn't know what I know now," Louis said. "Colette was my cousin, and we would never be more than close friends. But that's changed. Everything has changed."

"I'm sorry I've taunted you," Victor said. "I do understand, and I sympathize."

"I can see it now, me walking arm in arm with Colette for everyone to see. I can hear them whispering behind us."

"You've walked arm in arm with her since she returned from Scotland."

"As cousins," Louis said. "But I'd know better now, and the truth would almost certainly come to light. The truth can never come to light. It's no use. I have no choice."

Victor nodded slowly. "I can see that," he said.

Louis grinned dejectedly. "Alas, the Crusades have always been my fate. It couldn't be otherwise. My dream and my fate." He paused for a moment, then sighed. "God surely works in mysterious ways."

Victor looked off into the distance. "Yes," he said with a faint smirk. "He certainly does."

Louis got the distinct impression that Victor's thoughts in that moment were far different from his own. It occurred to him that he had *two* reasons to convince Victor to join him.

"I don't want you to stay behind," he said.

Victor blinked in mock confusion, as if he didn't understand the statement.

"Come with me," Louis said.

"As your squire," Victor said dryly. "You're still going to try to talk me into that? I still can't think of a good reason to do that."

"Just come with me, Victor," Louis said. "Come with me to the Templars. To Jerusalem."

"We've talked about all of this before. Again, I have to ask you: why would I do that?"

Louis felt that Victor was trying to goad him into ordering him to go, in violation of the promise he had made to Victor.

"I need a squire," Louis said. "I would have you over anyone else. I'd like to have you with me. You're my closest friend."

"Your squire," Victor snapped. He paused, then said, "I can't imagine how that would be better than this. Why do you think I'd want to be your squire? What makes you think that would be good for either one of us?"

Louis could not speak the truth. Now that he'd considered it, more than ever he did not want Victor to stay behind with Colette. His misgivings were illogical – Colette would never fancy Victor romantically – but they were visceral, and he couldn't shake them. He had to talk Victor into going with him.

"You'll have a horse," Louis said.

"Soranus?"

Louis smiled. *It couldn't be that easy,* he thought. "Soranus," he said. "And you'd have clothing, and weapons. Good food, excellent training, and of course, the very best of company."

Victor nodded, his face twisted with grim doubt.

"Most of all," Louis continued, "you could very well one day be made a knight, if you were to prove your valor in battle."

"You're going then," Victor said. "It's decided? There's no talking you out of it?"

Louis looked away into the forest at the edge of the field. As if startled by his gaze, a flock of starlings flittered into the air and wheeled away to the south. He did not want to reaffirm his commitment without Victor's firm reply.

Victor out-waited him.

He sighed. "Of course I'm going," he said with finality. He looked questioningly at Victor, who shook his head briskly.

"I just don't know," Victor said. After a long pause, he added, "I'll think about it some more and let you know." He pulled the fishing line from the stream to check his bait. He peered dubiously at Louis. "I can think of better fates," he said with a grin.

Part II

Chapter 17

"You're certain about this decision, then," Sir Willem Marti said. He peered into Louis's face for signs of doubt. They walked along a path that led through the woods that lined the meandering creek.

Louis nodded. "I'm certain," he said.

"Your mother told me that you know about Montségur," Willem said. He placed a hand on Louis's shoulder. "Now you understand the truth about our past." Louis nodded. "The knowledge must change things for you, at least somewhat." A long silence passed. Louis felt pensive, but he remained resolved. "I'd understand if that were the case," Willem added.

Finally, Louis shook his head. "It does change things," he said. "Everything has changed. Almost everything I ever thought I knew is different now. The one thing that hasn't changed is my determination to join the Templars and go to Jerusalem. That will not change."

"You're angry," Willem said. "I understand that, too."

"Since I didn't know the truth, I never really had a choice.

What if I had wanted things to be different? What if I was meant to be with Colette from the start? I never considered that, because it wasn't in the realm of possibility."

"Would fate not have allowed it, if it were meant to be?" Willem asked. "Would God not have seen to it?"

"I don't know," Louis said, shaking his head.

"Let me pose it to you thus: for things to be different, several things would have to have happened. My parents would have to have lived. Your mother and I would not have ended up with François Marti. Cathars would have to be tolerated by the Church, and we would not have had to hide from it. Even if all those circumstances had been different, you would still have to have met Colette and developed a relationship with her that was close enough to inspire the feelings you have for her today. If God had intended for you to be with her, would He not have allowed for the proper circumstances to occur?"

Louis nodded hesitantly.

"And yet, He did not," Willem continued. "We must ask ourselves why."

"Yes," Louis said. "We must." He shook his head sadly. "And we must accept the only possible answer to that question, and follow the path to which it leads us."

If Louis had no future with Colette, then she would surely, inevitably marry someone else. He could not imagine living day to day with that truth, now that he had realized the depth and the nature of his affection for her. If she was going to marry someone else, he wanted to be as far from that as he could be. Jerusalem might just be far enough.

"You may need some time to think," Willem said.

Louis shook his head again. "No," he said. "I won't. I know what I'm going to do, and I'm not going to delay it for even one day. Take me to the Templars, Uncle. Take me to Jerusalem."

Willem nodded. "I will. But I must be satisfied for myself that it is still your heart's desire. I will not be party to a life altering decision made in the heat of emotional turmoil. I will give you the time I think you need, even if you deny it."

"How long?"

"As long as it takes."

"You're not in league with my father now, are you," Louis said, "in attempting to dissuade me for the sake of my mother?"

"I would not do that," Willem said. "You should know that by now. It's your resolve that I must trust completely; if I am to look into your mother's eyes from this day to my last, I must know without doubt that I have done right, that I was no party to foolishness that led to her grief, and that I have no cause for shame. I will go to the ends of the earth, and toil until the coming of the Lord to make sure I am secure in that knowledge."

Louis nodded. He admired Willem's indomitable, unwavering devotion to his sister, Louis's mother.

✠ ✠ ✠

"I'll have a word with your father," Willem said to Louis as they approached the main Garonne house. He nodded toward the entrance to the hall. "In private." A hint of trepidation flashed across Louis's face.

"All right," Louis said, and he turned to walk away.

"Louis," Willem called. Louis turned back to him. "It will be all right." Louis nodded and went on his way. Willem empathized with his nephew. The simultaneous passage from youth to man, from squire to knight, and from lay person to ordained warrior monk was wrought with profound and contradictory emotions. Louis's were further complicated by a deeper and more poignant emotional drama that he was forced to keep to himself. Willem would do what little he could to ease Louis's pain.

The Templars rose from the table as Willem entered the hall. Willem nodded toward the door to indicate his desire for privacy with Raimon. He turned to Raimon and waited for them to leave.

"I will speak to you plainly of things that are only whispered within the order," Willem said, once they were alone. He took a seat across from Raimon, his face dark and grave. "Then you and I will forever deny that these words have passed my lips."

Raimon nodded, his interest piqued.

After a long silence, Willem continued, quietly, looking suddenly weary and forlorn. "Jerusalem is all but lost," he said. He shrugged and raised his hands in resignation. "It is only a matter of time."

Raimon's eyes grew wide. "So definite," he said, the shock evident in his voice.

They had discussed the Crusade frankly on many occasions, including the apparent inevitability of its demise. But their dire speculations had been distant and theoretical probabilities. Willem knew that as they became more of a reality, the impact of that reality across Europe would be profound. He saw a vague shadow of that impact forming in his brother–in–law's expression.

Raimon worked to maintain his composure. "Interest in the Holy Land has faded," he said, nodding in agreement. "Crusades have failed. Kings have been captured and ransomed for the wealth of their kingdoms."

"It's clear," Willem said, "that Europe has turned its attention inward. Kings are more concerned with building their own kingdoms rather than God's, and popes have turned their inquisitorial crusading against dissent in their own flock. They care less and less about infidels a world away, and sacred sites that cost both men and money to retain."

Still, no one had ever admitted publicly that the end of the Crusade was imminent.

"The Crusade has inspired us for nearly two centuries," Raimon said. "It's hard to imagine a Europe without a Crusade off in the distance, beckoning and rousing us to action. It's hard to imagine Jerusalem without Christians there to safeguard our sacred birthright." He paused to reflect. "Can nothing be done?" He looked to Willem for reassurance.

"The Mongols have emissaries in Europe," Willem said, "searching in vain for support for their own efforts to subdue the Mamluks. They have offered total and permanent Christian control of Jerusalem once the Mamluks are defeated, in return for our support. The pope rejected their plea, and no king will respond to it without the pope's support."

"The Mongols," Raimon said. "They would eventually become our enemies, though, would they not?"

"The Mongols realize they will have to draw their border somewhere. They're not interested in Europe. They want Asia to the Mediterranean, and they're willing to give us the sliver that we treasure in return for our support."

"They would maintain peace with Christians at their borders?"

"They are at peace with Christians in their own lands. Kublai Khan's closest advisors are of many and various faiths, including Christian – the Venetian merchant Marco Polo is among them. The Mongols tolerate all religions, and fear none. The Muslims despise that tolerance as godless disbelief, and that aggravates Muslim hostility toward them. And the Muslims occupy land the Mongols want. The Mongols' interests are purely political; they are equally tolerant of Islam, but they will not let Islam stand in the way of their empire."

"I've heard of Arghun Khan's emissaries," Raimon said, nodding. "They've been greeted warmly by Nicholas and the kings, and assured of Christian support."

"In word alone," Willem said. "Their letters to the Khan were vague and noncommittal. To the Khan, they were nothing more than ornately veiled rejection."

"What would Christian support do for the Mongols, truly?" Raimon asked. "Would it assure their success, or would Christians end up stranded in the midst of victorious and vengeful Mamluks, while the Mongols flee back to Asia?"

"The Mongols and the Mamluks are evenly matched," Willem said. Our support would tip the scales. We would be guaranteed control of lands that we have steadily lost to the Mamluks ever since we first won them. And yet, Europe isn't interested in the proposal."

Raimon was appalled. He understood that zeal for the Crusades had faded, but the idea that there was virtually no support for regaining Christian control of the Holy Land staggered him. After all the blood and money that had been expended in winning that presence, he considered its abandonment despicable.

"And you intend to take my son there?" Raimon said. "Why would you do that? How could I allow that, knowing what you've just told me? I have no other heir."

"I doubt that either of us could stop him.," Willem said. "He's going, with or without me, I fear. It's best that he go with me."

Raimon shook his head. "Don't tell his mother," he warned.

"It would not be for long, Raimon. When the moment is right, I assure you, the Templars will withdraw most of our forces and consolidate on Cyprus, and back here in the Languedoc."

"Don't patronize me, Willem," Raimon snapped. "Templars don't retreat. I'm not an idiot."

"I'm sorry, Raimon," Willem said. He had not told Raimon everything, so Raimon's reaction was understandable. "There's more. What I am about to tell you is of the utmost secrecy, and must not be breathed to another soul. I tell you now only to give you hope for your son's future, and for that of your estate. My punishment would be severe should anyone learn that I've told you."

"I'm listening," Raimon said with a nod.

"The Grand Master has hinted at a petition for a Templar state...here, in the Languedoc." Raimon's jaw dropped in disbelief. "Louis could be home before you know it. We believe that the pope will support our petition, and if he does, the French king would have to honor it."

"This king exerts influence over the pope, and not vice versa."

"At times," Willem agreed. "But with the support of Europe's other monarchs and nobles on our side, perhaps he won't this time."

Raimon considered Willem's startling disclosure.

"If this comes to pass," Willem said, "the Languedoc would be safe once again for the Cathars. Many Templars supported them, albeit in secret, and most of them abhorred the Albigensian Crusade." He looked meaningfully at Raimon and added, "Our family would be safe."

A long pause ensued as both men contemplated that future, and the implications of its realization.

"And while Louis is in Jerusalem?" Raimon said.

"I'll watch over him," Willem reassured. "I'll be assigned to Sidon, away from the turmoil of Tripoli, and close to the safety of Acre. Louis will be with me always. I will see that he is reasonably safe from harm, and I'll personally see him onto the first ships that withdraw to Cyprus."

Raimon nodded his approval.

"You know that he'll be anxious for battle," Willem said. "He's an assertive lad."

"That he is."

"I will keep him close, to the extent of my ability."

"On pain of death," Raimon said with half a smile and smoldering eyes.

"On pain of death," Willem agreed. He didn't smile. He meant it. He would rather die than bring tragic news home to his sister.

Willem and Raimon rose and went outside to join the others. The Templars had gathered around the well. Louis had joined them, and they were in the midst of regaling him with the usual tales of heroic battles, honorable deaths, and massacred Mamluks left to the vultures and the carrion crows. Willem placed his hands on Louis's shoulders, which had grown noticeably more broad, and he jostled him playfully.

"You must have your father's blessing," Willem said. "You are his son, and he will always be your father. You must respect that, or you will never truly respect anything else. You must request his blessing, and it must be given freely."

Louis nodded and turned to Raimon. He placed a steady hand on his father's shoulder.

"Father," he said, "I would be honored to have your blessing. This is what I want, and what I have always wanted, for all of my life. But your blessing is yet more precious to me, and I pray for it."

Raimon placed his hand over Louis's and he shook his head in sadness.

"I can give my blessing only with the deepest reservations, my son," he said. "You must know how it pains me, and it pains your mother more. Please do not make me regret this any more than I already do. You must see yourself safely through. Do nothing foolish or rash. You *must* return to us safely."

Raimon turned to Willem. "I place him in your charge," he said. "It would be most unpleasant for both of us should you return to me without him, or with sorrowful news."

Willem nodded solemnly and extended his hand to Raimon.

"On my honor," he swore.

✠ ✠ ✠

Willem stood at the head of the table in the dining hall. Louis sat to his right, feeling solemn and determined. Raimon sat next to Louis, expressionless. Antonio Bollani, Bertrand de Rennes, and Richard Osbourne occupied the other chairs, waiting for Willem to speak. Lord Jacquette sat deferentially at the far end of the table.

For the first time in his life, Louis sat among them as equals, as a knight in his own right, recognized but as yet untried. The mood was cheerful and congratulatory.

"My brothers," Willem began, "I stand before you to offer my heartfelt sanction of a young knight's fervent request for the honor of joining our order. I will pledge my name to vouch for his moral strength and character. I have examined him at length and found him worthy, and I offer him now for your consideration."

The Templars nodded, and Willem took his seat.

"How does it feel, Sir Louis, to have received your accolade?" Antonio Bollani asked, smiling. The gruffness of his voice contrasted the enthusiasm that glowed in his eyes.

Louis beamed. "Like I have awoken from a dream to find it real," he said.

"Well said," Richard Osbourne said. "It was the same for me.

I still fancy I'm dreaming from time to time." The other Templars laughed and nodded.

"Nightmares, often enough," Bollani quipped.

"The honor of knighthood carries with it many burdens," said Bertrand de Rennes. "Are you ready for those?"

Louis nodded.

"He is," Jacquette assured the powerfully built knight. "We have discussed the challenges and the responsibilities endlessly, so that I thought he might reconsider. But he never has. He is ready."

"Are you ready, young Louis?" Bollani asked.

"Ye—"

"This is not a glamorous path," Osbourne said, interrupting. "It will be grueling and treacherous, dangerous at every turn, and unforgiving, should you slip or fall."

"You will be tested beyond your wildest imagination," Bertrand said. "You will often wish that you had not taken your oath; you will wish that you could come back to this day and retract it."

"I'll not," Louis said quickly, before anyone could interrupt him again. "Nothing could make that so."

"How do you know this?" Bollani asked.

"I have lived for this," Louis said with passion. "And I would die for this."

A faint smile played at Willem's lips.

"But you have never seen death," Bertrand said. "How could you possibly know how you will face death?"

The image of the burning at Carcassonne filled Louis's mind: Eustache and Mathilde burning at the stake, the skin of their faces melting into grotesque masks as fluid spilled from their eyes and sputtered in the flames. It sickened him even now. He grimaced as his stomach churned.

"I've seen death," he replied. "It sickened me. I would not welcome it, but for the assurance of my heavenly reward should I die in service to my Savior. I realize that the reward is eternal, while the passage into it but momentary, if painful."

In response to the knights' inquisitive expressions, Louis related the story of the Cathars' burning. They listened with rapt attention, and they appeared to evaluate his perspective on the event.

"I know, then," he concluded, "that death is a dreadful thing, to be avoided if at all possible." The Templars laughed and nodded. "But I also understand that death is inevitable, and that it is best embraced in the name of something precious. What could be more precious than one's faith?"

"Indeed," Bollani said, as if he were pondering the idea.

"Well said, Sir Louis," Osbourne said. "Well said, indeed. You felt compassion, then, for the Cathars?" A sudden nervous charge filled the air as the others reacted to Osbourne's question with bewildered looks and silencing gestures.

"His feelings about the heretics are irrelevant," Willem interjected. Raimon fixed a mildly menacing glare upon Osbourne, who held up a hand to retract his words. "I thought it safe for him to answer in this company."

"They were human," Louis said firmly, with clear eyes and no apology. "I should feel compassion for all humans. Does not the Church even feel compassion toward the victims of the Devil's wiles?" He grinned slightly, pleased with his ability to deliver the appropriate words while only barely masking the sentiments that the burning had inspired.

Bollani cleared his throat. "I fear that one auto de fé does not compare with the suffering and carnage you will witness in the battles you will face."

Louis noted that Bollani spoke in the definitive; there was no question about the outcome of this vetting. "I will face them," he said, "as each of you have faced them, when you were young and newly dubbed initiates."

"We were also challenged by our mentors," Bertrand said, "the same as we now challenge you to determine your awareness of what you face, and your resolve to face it well."

"I know," Louis said. He stood, and said, "I will die before surrendering, converting, or allowing others to be captured or killed. This is my firm resolve."

"In many battles," Bollani said, "that is precisely the choice that is offered. The Battle of the Horns of Hattin is but one of the worst examples. I can tell you of similar tragedies, from my earliest days in Jerusalem." Bollani appeared to grow morose at the memories he had conjured. The other Templars sat back, prepared to yield to his reminiscence, and he continued. "As a young Templar, I was assigned to a new outpost, a small castle on the coast of Tripoli. It was my good fortune that our contingent had been delayed in its departure, for the scene upon which we arrived was terrible to behold. There was but one surviving Templar, hobbled and blinded, left alive to tell the awful tale to any who came upon him before he died." Bollani clenched his jaw and looked away. He seemed momentarily lost in the memory.

"It's all right," Louis said. "I have an idea what you are about to tell. I know of these things."

"No," Bollani snapped, turning to glare at Louis. "You don't. You will hear it now. I insist."

Louis was taken aback. He nodded. "All right," he said.

"We rode up to the castle. Its walls were blackened, and collapsed in places. The battle had been fierce, and only recently ended. More than a thousand Templars, and nearly three thousand others had defended that castle. All but the Templars were taken into slavery." He paused, and then said purposefully, "Templars are never taken into slavery."

"I should think that worse than death," Louis said. All the Templars nodded their agreement.

"The blinded knight was the seneschal of the company commander," Bollani continued. "He was forced to witness the choice that each of his brethren would make, starting with the commander: either to deny Christ and convert to Islam, or to die. The commander refused, of course. He was told that if he refused again, two of his men would be flayed alive, and then thrown down the side of a dune. He refused again, and the Saracens did what they had promised, to the horror of every last knight."

"They flayed them both?" Louis was horrified. "Alive?" He had not heard of such cruelty at the hands of the Muslims.

"That was only the start of it," Bollani said. "The seneschal said that the sight of it was nearly enough to make every Templar convert on the spot. But they remained stoic, betraying no horror. The commander refused again, and then stood silent as they did the same to him." Bollani paused, and silence hung in the air. "They gave the choice to each knight in his turn," he continued quietly, "offering his life in exchange for his conversion. Each knight refused, and each knight was promptly beheaded. The last of them stood silent and resolute as the first, having witnessed the systematic slaughter of a thousand of his brethren. He, too, fell without a word. They tore out the seneschal's eyes so that the carnage was the last thing he would ever see."

Louis was astonished by the brutality the Templars had suffered at the hands of the Saracens. He tried to imagine facing such a fate, and the courage it must take to do so with unyielding faith and unwavering loyalty to the cause.

"One cannot know," Osbourne said, "when one might face just such a scene. One must understand that the reality that such things are possible at any given time."

"Such sacrifices are made in the defense of Jerusalem," Louis said. "And yet, the Christians there continue to bicker over money and power. Good men go to their death in their defense, and still they bicker." He stuck his jaw out in defiance. "Well, I will do what I must to make a difference. I will go to fight beside the warriors of God, and do my part to see that as few of them as possible face such a fate. It will make a difference when good men join them, and fight beside them to the end."

"And you will be one of those good men?" Willem asked.

"You know that I will," Louis replied. "Are there not still good and strong men fighting for Jerusalem?"

"There are," Willem said.

"Then I'll join them, if they will have me," Louis said, looking at Raimon. "Even if it means my death. If enough like me join the cause, the tide will turn and the Kingdom of God will prevail. But I won't wait for others to join before I meet my own obligation."

Raimon shook his head sadly as Willem gave Louis a long,

appraising look. Louis's face beamed with conviction.

"Spoken like a seasoned Templar," Willem finally said. The other Templars nodded in agreement.

"His fervor burns brightly," Antonio Bollani said. He turned to Louis. "So, you are ready to take upon yourself the mantle of a Knight of the Temple, though it means the end of all you have known, and the path to an end unknown."

Louis looked around the table at the knights, each in turn, until his eyes rested upon his uncle. He nodded, and then he turned to Raimon. He looked directly into his father's eyes and spoke in a firm voice.

"I am ready, father. I have never wanted any other thing. I will never want any other thing. This is my destiny and my dream, and I am ready for it, more now than ever."

Raimon gave a restrained nod, though his eyes registered poorly veiled resignation. He extended his hand, which Louis grasped. "I give you my blessing," he said. "Go with courage. Go with strength. Go with God, my son."

Bollani clapped his hands and sat forward. "That's good enough for me!" he exclaimed.

"And for me," Willem said. The other knights nodded in unison, and they smiled approvingly at Louis.

"I propose acceptance of the candidate," said Antonio Bollani. "I've long known him to be pious and sincere in his desires, and worthy of the honor. I have no cause to doubt him."

"I, too, accept this candidate," said Osbourne. Bertrand also voiced his approval, and Louis was passed into candidacy for acceptance into the Order of Poor Knights of Christ and of the Temple of Solomon.

They made plans for the journey to the commandery at Avignon, where Louis would be initiated into the Templar order. Before they could leave, however, Louis had one more challenge to overcome.

He found Victor at his labor in the stables, working industriously, brushing Soranus with an almost angry fervor.

"So you'll be leaving soon," Victor said without looking up

from his work.

"Soon enough," Louis said. "I have a few things to accomplish before I do. One of them is uncertain, but I have to give it one last try. I think you know what it is." Victor nodded absently. "I've thought of putting it off, but there is precious little time left now."

"You promised no pressure," Victor said sharply.

"I'm not trying to pressure you," Louis said. "I want you to know how important it is to me."

"I know how important it is to you," Victor replied. He threw the grooming brush to the ground and bent to inspect a hoof.

"Fair enough," Louis said. "But I'd really like to have you with me. I know you've given it a lot of thought, but you've never actually answered the question since we last spoke of it. I can't leave without asking you one more time." Victor glanced up in annoyance. "Will you go with me?"

Victor releases Soranus's hoof and turned to Louis.

"I'm not a noble," Victor said. "I'll never be a noble. To tell you the truth, despite whatever I've said, I'm not sure I'd even *want* to be a noble. In any event, I just don't crave crusading the way you do...certainly not enough to change everything I know on the slim chance that my dreams might be fulfilled."

"So, you do have dreams!" Louis said triumphantly.

"Dreams of nobility," Victor said, "are foolish for someone like me."

"Quite the contrary," Louis said. "You just don't see it."

"See what?"

"The nobility."

"What nobility?" Victor asked with exasperation.

"Yours," Louis replied. Victor shook his head. "Real nobility, I mean, and not some inherited status."

"What do you mean?"

"Nobility is, on the one hand, a title that one inherits with fortunate birth," Louis said. He leaned toward Victor and peered into his eyes. "Real nobility, though, is something different, something that one cannot inherit or buy. It's the power to exert one's will, tempered by the strength to do so sparingly, and only when necessary to the pursuit of good. It's the determination to triumph over fear, and do what's right. It's a sense of justice and the will to see it done, and indignation at the sight of innocent blood. Few men have that, Victor, and you're one of them. You know that. I knew it long ago, on the road to Carcassonne. And I've never forgotten it."

Victor looked up then, with an expression that surprised Louis. He started to speak, but said nothing.

"I knew then that I would always want you by my side," Louis said.

"I don't know what to say," Victor said. "I just don't know."

They spoke into the wee hours of the night, until Victor finally relented and agreed to join Louis in his crusading adventure. As dawn broke gray and gloomy in the eastern sky, they sealed their commitment with a solemn oath.

The week flew by, with too little time for too many sad farewells. Louis's most painful parting was with Colette. Louis suspected that she knew full well his feelings for her. He also grew convinced that it was mutual, and that she was grieving their parting as much as he.

He wondered if their parting would be as profound a loss for her as it was for him.

Chapter 18

THE FIVE-DAY JOURNEY to Avignon took them through the market towns of Beziers, Montpellier, and Nimes. They lodged at Templar houses and commanderies along the way, and on the fourth night they stayed at a small Templar estate just outside of Nimes. They began the final day of the shortest leg of their journey well–rested and amply fed.

A more leisurely pace and the anticipation of reaching their destination imbued the party with light–hearted good humor. The knights joked and chattered in a manner uncharacteristic of Templars, and Louis counted it a pleasant change from the quiet intensity that had dominated the journey to this point.

Avignon came into view, its clay tile rooftops glowing brilliantly in the light of the afternoon sun. A massive cathedral dominated the town; it was the first thing they saw as they approached from the west. Louis thrilled at the sight of it.

Victor did not appear to share his delight. His glum mood contrasted that of the rest of the party. Noting it, Louis recalled his father's misgivings about Victor, which he had voiced yet again the evening before their departure. He resolved to discuss with Victor his sour disposition at the earliest opportunity. For now, though, he focused on his memories of Avignon as they drew closer.

He had been here twice before with his father, and both times he had wanted to stay and explore it longer. It was an ancient town with a past as turbulent as the river that rushed past its walls.

Avignon's political evolution had helped to shape the character of most of the surrounding area. When he had come here as a boy, several old men who loitered at the market told Louis stories of how, just sixty years earlier, Avignon had been a major Cathar stronghold. But the French King Louis VIII ravaged, and then annexed the city after it closed its gates to his crusade against the Avignon Cathars. Since then, life in the town had gradually resumed its quiet repose, but it never regained the air of gentle tolerance that had been the distinctive mark of the Cathars.

In Roman times, Avignon was an important way station on the salt road from Arles to Lyon, the main passage from northern to southern Europe. The strategically located and heavily fortified town, with a conveniently positioned island river crossing, drew conquerors from the farthest reaches of the continent. Frankish barbarians devastated the town in their conquest of its Roman inhabitants. The Vandals came, and then the Goths, and eventually even the Saracen Moors, from whom the Franks eventually succeeded in taking it back.

Avignon flourished as the most important city on the pilgrim and trade route between Italy and Spain. Over centuries, it amassed great wealth, most of which during Frankish rule was shared and controlled by an independent mercantile commune. Louis VIII's conquest brought that golden age to an end, but even after centuries of devastating conquest, scattered remnants remained in silent testimony to Avignon's former glory.

Louis loved Avignon. It pleased him that he would take his initiation into the Templar Order in one of the most charming cities in Europe.

They came to the foot of the storied Saint Benezet Bridge,

built a hundred years earlier to connect the west bank of the Rhône to the Avignon gate on the east. The bridge originally consisted of twenty-two stone arches that spanned the breadth of the raging river. Torrential currents had since washed fourteen of those arches away. The frustrated bridge builders replaced them with wooden arches that, while flimsier than stone, could be repaired more quickly and with less hindrance to the commerce that depended on the bridge. Any impediment to travel or trade was costly not only to the merchants, but to the city as a whole, so timber was the more expedient choice.

It was a narrow bridge, allowing only one or two men or horses to travel comfortably side-by-side in each direction. Willem and Antonio Bollani moved onto the bridge first, proceeding gingerly onto the first wooden section, which creaked and swayed slightly with the weight of their fully laden palfreys.

The horses whinnied nervously at the swaying at first, but they settled quickly as they made their way along the planks. Louis glanced nervously at the water rushing below them, and he was glad when they reached the more stable stone sections a little more than halfway across. Two by two the knights crossed the bridge to the chapel at the eastern end, where a monk collected tolls from all who crossed.

The monk was a slight, stooped old man with snowy hair and watery gray eyes. He looked up into the faces of each of the travelers as if they had disturbed him unannounced.

"Three deniers per mount," the old monk croaked. He extended a bony hand as Willem withdrew a purse from beneath his white linen surcoat.

"Three!" Willem said in exaggerated surprise. "A month ago it was two." The monk looked up at Willem accusingly as he counted thirty coins into the leathery palm.

"It's costly to maintain," the monk barked, nodding toward the bridge. "And times have been hard."

"I'd rather pay than swim," Willem said good-naturedly. He glanced at the ghastly sight of two battered heads mounted on pikes, prominently displayed for visitors to the city to see.

"Thieves," the monk said in a seething voice. He spat in the direction of the heads, but most of his spittle dribbled harmlessly down his chin. He wiped it with his sleeve. Willem nodded his acknowledgement.

Victor glanced uncomfortably at the thieves' heads as the party continued on past the chapel to an open wooden gate that led to the ramparts of the city walls. They crossed the rampart to a ramp that descended into the city proper. The cathedral loomed in front of them as they descended the ramp.

Louis was awed by the cathedral. He gaped at it as they turned south and weaved their way through rows of shops and temporary stands where merchants sold wool, Egyptian cotton, and a dizzying variety of clothing, crafts, ales, and food. The aroma of the market was an odd mixture of deliciously spiced foods, sweaty merchants, and smelly livestock. They turned to the left at the end of the row of shops, and the Templar commandery loomed among a group of smaller buildings a short distance ahead.

Maison du Temple d'Avignon was a squat stone building, built of the same ashlar block of which the cathedral was built, but in the Templar fashion, simpler and less ornate. It was a magnificent structure, Louis thought. His eyes grew wide at the sight of it, and his escorts grinned at his boyish wonder.

"Is it as I have described it?" Willem asked.

"Better," Louis whispered. "It's hard to believe I'm finally here."

The party dismounted, and a group of novice monks rushed forward to take charge of their horses. As the novices led the horses to the stables, Willem knocked loudly on the heavy oak door. A steel hatch mounted at eye level slid open, and a muffled voice demanded the visitor's identity. Willem mumbled an unintelligible phrase that sounded oddly foreign, and the door swung open, its hinges groaning under the weight of the heavy oak. A Templar guard appeared, holding a ready sword. The guard recognized Willem, and the two men embraced. Louis, Victor, and the rest of the Templars followed them inside.

"I've been expecting you," the guard said as he closed and

bolted the door behind them. "You bring aspirants to the Order, I'm told."

"You know my companions," Willem said, indicating his Templar brethren. The guard nodded and shook their hands. "And you know all that I have told you of my nephew, Louis de Garonne...now *Sir* Louis de Garonne." The guard raised his chin and nodded in approval. Willem turned to Louis. "Louis, meet my old friend and Brother, Sir Hugh Bardsley." Louis nodded.

Bardsley was a stout man, more stout around the middle than in the shoulders, with wispy blond hair and pale blue eyes. He squinted when he looked at Louis, more out of habit, Louis thought, than difficulty seeing. Bardsley did not look hard enough to be a battle–tested knight.

"I have indeed heard tales of you, lad," Bardsley said. He grasped Louis's hand. "I've looked forward to meeting you. And this is your squire?" he asked, turning toward Victor.

Louis caught Victor's ill–concealed wince at the word, and he momentarily reconsidered the wisdom of having convinced him to come along.

"Yes," Louis said flatly. "This is Victor Guyot." Victor bowed respectfully and extended his hand.

"Guyot," Bardsley repeated as he studied Victor's face. Louis wondered if Bardsley had detected Victor's fleeting grimace. "Welcome to you," Bardsley said. "Welcome, one and all!" Bardsley turned and led them from the vestibule into the adjacent hall with an oddly loping gait, his Templar surcoat with its crimson cross flapping behind him.

The traveling party settled into their dormitory cells, two to a room, and they met for a refreshing meal of fresh vegetables, spiced mutton, and mugs of watered ale. They took the meal in silence in accordance with the Templar Rule. It occurred to Louis that the rule of mealtime silence would be among those he would like the least. Meal time for him was the time for tall tales and jovial camaraderie. It was an adjustment he would have to manage.

Vespers followed supper, and afterwards Louis's party joined the commander and his senior knights for wine and talk. The commander, Henri de Villeroi, was a wiry, powerful man with closely cropped hair and an energetic manner. Unlike Bardsley, he had clearly seen more than his share of battle. His silvery hair was peppered with the remnants of what had once been dark black, but his face bore the youthfulness of someone half his age.

De Villeroi addressed Uncle Willem with an aristocratic air.

"How familiar is your nephew with the initiation rite?" he asked.

"I've explained it to him in general," Willem said. "I have not divulged the symbolism of its parts, or the significance of its form." De Villeroi nodded. Louis understood that it was forbidden for anyone outside the Order to know the symbolism of Templar rites and rituals. Strict secrecy served both to bind the brethren knights and to provide the means for discerning between true brethren and spies and imposters. A simple quiz could easily reveal the authenticity of a stranger's claim to brotherhood.

De Villeroi turned to indicate a tall, gaunt Templar with a hawkish face and piercing, blue-gray eyes.

"Pierre Rosencroix," the commander said, looking at Louis. "He will train you."

Louis and Pierre Rosencroix exchanged bows. Rosencroix listed to one side, the apparent effect of an injury to one of his legs. He held his hands folded in front of him, giving the impression that he was more monk than warrior, but the hardness of his features offered balance.

"You will be trained vigorously," de Villeroi said, "and examined relentlessly. You will learn all the Templar customs and rituals, and the meaning and purpose of each. There is no way you can imagine the intensity of what you are about to endure, but this I can tell you: only the best knights are accepted, and almost to a man, they succeed. But for a weakness or a flaw that has escaped detection until now, you will come through it, and it will change your life. You will never be the same."

Louis nodded respectfully.

"Now tell me why," de Villeroi continued, "knowing all of this, you would subject yourself to this ordeal, and to the life of hardship and sacrifice that will follow for the rest of your days."

Louis spoke at length of the things that had led him here, from his battles among the meadow grass, to his fascination with the tales that followed his uncle from the battlefields of Outremer, and finally to his passion for the final and long overdue building of the Kingdom of Jerusalem on the ashes of infidel rule.

When he finally finished, all sat quietly. De Villeroi gazed at Louis as if he were lost in distant thoughts. Suddenly he turned and fixed his eyes on Willem's. He stared intently for a moment, and then he nodded slowly.

"A truer knight I have not seen in a very long time," de Villeroi said. "This one seems from a different time, as if he had stepped into this day from the golden days of Montsigard, from Baldwin's victorious arms into our own."

Louis detected sadness in de Villeroi's laudatory words. He was mildly annoyed by his thinly veiled melancholy over long gone glory days, and the implication that they might not be resurrected. He had encountered this attitude all too often in recent years, and it disheartened him. He could not understand passive acquiesce to the fading of Christian glory in Outremer.

"Am I truly so unusual?" he asked. "Does passion for the battle not rage among all true warriors of the Cross?"

De Villeroi stared stolidly at Louis for a long, silent moment. "Our hopes and dreams," he finally said, "are often at odds with the realities we face."

"But that can change," Louis insisted.

De Villeroi nodded slightly and said, "Yes, it can. That is a possibility. I suppose one must always hope."

"And fight," Louis said.

"And fight," de Villeroi agreed. His jaw tensed as he spoke.

Louis sensed that the commander might regard his enthusiasm as impertinence, and he softened his manner. "I will contribute all that I can toward revival of the cause," he said. "I will do my part."

"I know you will," the commander said. "and tomorrow you will begin to do just that. Preparation for your initiation will begin promptly after Prime. You will not yet be a Templar, but in that moment you will become subject to the Templar Rule. Do you understand the Templar Rule?"

"I do," Louis said.

"Good. Then you understand that from this point forward, you will not question the valor or the enthusiasm of this Order, or of any of its brethren. You will keep your considerations of such things to yourself, unless and until you are placed into a position where your considerations count for something. Do not forget your place, young knight." De Villeroi was not angry; his words carried a greater force than anger. His voice was low and even, with an intensity that did not entertain a response. "If I order you to march into an inferno for nothing but the greater glory of God, you will do so without question or delay. You will trust my judgment, defer to my authority, and know in your heart that I do nothing unless it is for the good of all that is holy."

Louis's heart skipped a beat. It had begun. With a sense of wonder he realized that he had passed through the door to his dreams, and that on the morrow there would be no turning back. In the same moment, he knew that there was no force on earth that could induce him to consider turning back. His dream was real.

"I understand," Louis said. "I give you my word."

✠ ✠ ✠

Each morning for the next twelve days Louis arose well before Prime. He barely slept through each night, though the pallet of straw in his cell was comfortable enough, and his excitement woke him long before dawn. He arrived first for Prime, and his mentors duly noted his daily promptness. He was content to let them regard his enthusiasm as piety.

The Psalms of Prime were sung, and prayers were said for the customary causes of each day. The final prayer of the early morning hour was for the diligence and the strength of the initiates as they prepared for their acceptance into the Order. Louis focused especially on those prayers.

The intensity of his examination exceeded his expectations. At times, he imagined that an inquisitorial trial might have been similar, and at times he feared that he might actually fail the ordeal. He saw nothing of Victor, who was lodging with a group of squires at a monastery a half day's journey from the commandery.

After Prime on the seventh day, Louis went quickly to the room in which most of his training and all of his examinations were held. Pierre Rosencroix waited for him there, as he did each morning.

Rosencroix was a stern tutor. Louis did not know each day if he would walk into a lengthy training session, where he would study Templar history, customs, battle strategy, or the Rule and its application, or into a terse and grueling examination, which would grow harsh and quite loud if he should stumble.

"You're early," Rosencroix said flatly as Louis entered the room. "That is what I expect: punctuality and enthusiasm, and nothing less. A Templar will be where he is supposed to be, precisely when he is supposed to be there. Tardiness foils plans and imperils our brethren."

Louis nodded. "Yes, master," he said.

"What is the significance of the color of our cross?" Rosencroix snapped.

"The blood of our passion for Christ," Louis snapped back without hesitation.

"And the beauséant?"

"The darkness of the world into God's purity and light."

"What attribute is most dear to our Christ?"

"Obedience," Louis said, again without the slightest hesitation. Rosencroix's face relaxed as he smiled. Louis was surprised, but happy that his tutor appeared to be in a good mood. This day would see more instruction than examination, and perhaps even a casual conversation or two.

"Today we will discuss your initiation," Rosencroix said. "You will need to understand every move and gesture, every command and question, and the exact form and meaning of the answers you will offer when you are addressed. There is no room for error in this rite; it *must* be completed perfectly. I cannot stress this nearly enough."

They went over the ritual in tedious detail, time and again, Rosencroix explaining patiently the significance of each, and Louis committing every word to memory. Nothing was written. Nothing ever would be written. The Rule prohibited recording one word of the ritual to vellum and ink.

By the end of the seventh day, Louis believed he had everything memorized, but the true test would be the next morning, when he was certain Rosencroix would grill him mercilessly until he had it right from start to finish.

He absorbed his lessons as if his life depended on it, as indeed he knew it would. Rosencroix grew increasingly pleased, and less stern with every passing day. On the twelfth day, the two of them spent more time talking, and Louis learned a great deal about Rosencroix – about his life as a child in Lorraine, his days as a young Templar knight, and the battle in which a Mamluk blade crippled his leg and relegated him to a life of teaching aspirants to the Order. Louis learned that he liked Rosencroix a great deal, not least of all because, if not for his leg, he would be on the first ship to Jerusalem to wield his sword once again for the glory of the Kingdom of God.

On the evening of the thirteenth day, just after Compline, the knights gathered in the upper chamber of an octagonal tower that stood off the inner courtyard. A small altar dominated the eastern side of the great room, and the seating was arranged in an open–ended square with the open end facing the altar.

Rosencroix gave his testimony of Louis's performance, and his fitness for initiation. When Rosencroix finished, de Villeroi called for Louis to come forth and stand before the altar. Louis approached and stood facing the commander and two knights who stood on either side of him.

Rosencroix rose and took a wooden box of painted balls, half black and half white, and began to distribute one of each color to each of the seated knights. The knight to the commander's left approached and blindfolded Louis. The blindfold smelled as if it had been perfumed with incense. De Villeroi told Louis to kneel, and the knight helped to guide Louis to his knees. De Villeroi called for the vote.

The vote was held in the customary fashion: a plain black box with a small hole in its lid was passed from knight to knight, into which each knight would place either a black or a white ball, depending on his vote. When the vote box returned to the commander, he would count the votes and announced the result. One black ball would disqualify Louis, and he would be sent back home in the morning.

Louis bit his lip and toyed with the edge of his heavy brown mantle. The future that he had envisioned his entire life was in the hands of these warrior monks, who had thoroughly discussed and carefully considered his progress of the past two weeks. Whichever way the vote went, it marked the culmination of his stay with the Avignon knights: he would leave either an initiated knight, or a crestfallen aspirant with shattered dreams. He could not envision the latter possibility.

Through what seemed a considerable length of time, Louis followed the sound of the wooden balls as they dropped into the box, as the box moved around the room. At first the sound was sharp and distinct, as the balls hit the bottom of the empty box, but it grew more muffled as the box filled with the harbingers of his destiny. Finally the box reached the seat closest to him on his right. He prayed and envisioned the inside of the box as white as freshly fallen snow.

He imagined that it was Rosencroix who moved across the room to retrieve the wooden box and carry it to de Villeroi. He tried in vain to see through the heavy cloth of his blindfold. Someone fumbled with it, and it was lifted from his eyes. De Villeroi poured the balls into one of two large bowls on the altar and proceeded to count them as he moved them into the other.

"Twenty–eight brethren have cast their votes," the commander said, "and I have counted twenty–eight votes of affirmation." Louis caught his breath and fought the feeling that he might faint. He realized that his heart was pounding like a war drum, and he steadied himself with great resolve, hoping that his face had remained impassive. "The candidate is approved. Initiation will commence after Matins."

Louis nodded respectfully to de Villeroi and then bowed his head in prayer. The hall remained silent as he prayed, and when he rose they began to file out. Rosencroix motioned for Louis to follow him through a door set into the shadows behind the altar, into the room where his final preparations would be made. He studied with Rosencroix, going over the ritual one more time in detail to make sure he had it right. They took full advantage of the hours between Compline and Matins.

Louis could hardly sit still through Matins. The hymns seemed interminable, and the Psalms muffled, as if they were spoken from afar. He prayed fervently for strength and guidance to carry him through his initiation, and for the courage to serve God with honor. Finally, Matins was over, and the knights filed silently from the chapel and back to the hall in the octagonal tower. His initiation had begun.

He knelt on the cold stone floor in front of the altar, as he had been instructed to do in his training. The knights resumed their places in the wooden chairs. De Villeroi's voice rang out clearly and echoed from the far walls as he addressed the knights from behind the altar.

"Is there an objection among the brethren to the initiation of this novice into the Order?" he asked. Silence answered his call. The question was purely ceremonial, as the vote had already confirmed Louis's candidacy. Twice more, the commander repeated the question; twice more it was met with silence.

"Your candidacy has raised no objections," de Villeroi said to Louis. "And so the following questions are for you. As you know, the Rule forbids brethren to marry, or to carry debt. Are you married or betrothed?"

Louis shuddered. His mind went immediately to Colette. He

missed her so, and more than anything he would have liked to answer loudly for all to hear that, yes, he was indeed betrothed, and to the love of his life. He pushed the thought from his mind and answered, "I am not."

"Are you indebted to any man for any sum of money, or for any other value or consideration?"

"I am not."

"And to whom do you owe your allegiance?"

"To the Lord my God, and no other."

"Do you submit yourself to be made servant and slave to the Order of the Poor Fellow–Soldiers of Christ and the Temple of Solomon, bound to obedience by an oath before God and the Blessed Mother?"

"I do, with all my heart!" Louis said.

The commander reminded Louis that the penalty for discussing his initiation with anyone outside of the Order was death, and that anyone worthy of the knowledge had it already, while those who didn't had no right to it.

Louis understood that the commander was not exaggerating the penalty for indiscretion; Templars took seriously the pain of death as punishment for violating the most serious Rules of the Order.

"Raise your right hand," de Villeroi said. Louis complied, and he placed his left hand on a book he had never seen, which lay open on the altar in front of him. "Do you swear that you believe in the Immortal God, Who has never died, and will never die?"

"I do," Louis said. He wondered at the words, as he had through the duration of his studies, and how they conflicted with the crucifixion of Christ, but he let it pass as he had before and focused only on what followed.

"Do you swear to commit your life to the Order, and to the building of the Kingdom of Jerusalem, even to the sacrifice of your own life?"

"I do."

The examination began in earnest, as Louis learned in his training that it would.

"Do you believe in Our Lord Jesus Christ, and in the Holy Catholic Church and all of its teachings, and are you willing to fight to the death in the defense of them?"

"I do, and I am."

"Are you an excommunicate of the Church for any reason of your own failing, or that of another?"

"I am not."

"Are you free-born, the son of a noble, and in wedlock?"

"I am."

"Are you petitioning for acceptance to the Order of your own free will, and free of any devious design to undermine or otherwise harm the Order?"

"I am."

"Are you in good health, ready and able to wield the weapons of war?"

"I am."

"Are you now, or have you ever been, a member of any other monastic or military order?"

"I am not, and have never been."

"Once again, are you willing to die for your Christ, for your Church, for your pope, for your Master, and for your brother knights?"

"I am."

De Villeroi told Louis to stand and walk to a crucifix that stood behind and to the right of the altar.

"Do you, thou son of man," he said, "deny this crucifix, and that you have ever known the man who was crucified upon it?"

Louis hesitated for the briefest moment. "I do," he said with a quiver in his voice. "I know him not."

The commander repeated the question two more times, and twice more Louis repeated the answer.

"Then you are already dead," the commander said. He grasped Louis roughly by the collar and dragged him to the ground, forcing him into a prone position on the stone floor in front of the altar. The commander motioned to the knights, and six of them surrounded Louis.

"Strip the corpse of its garments," de Villeroi commanded. The six knights roughly tore away Louis's coarse, brown mantle and tunic, and he lay naked and prone on the floor. The commander allowed Louis to lay there for a long moment. The cold floor drained the heat from his body, and he began to shiver uncontrollably.

Then, de Villeroi said, "Do you yearn for rebirth?"

"I do," Louis said through clenched teeth.

"Then rise, Judas, and kiss your Savior in atonement for your betrayal. Repent the evil you have wrought." The knights lifted Louis to his feet and placed him naked and shivering before the commander. Louis moved forward, timidly, and stretched his neck to kiss the commander once on each cheek.

"What is it that you seek as a new man of God?" de Villeroi boomed.

"The wisdom of the Christ," Louis answered, as he had been taught.

"Then behold the only true Wisdom: the holy countenance of your Savior!"

The commander stood aside and turned to a small table behind him, upon which an object was covered with black cloth. De Villeroi pulled the cloth away, revealing the sculpted likeness of a severed head, its flowing hair strewn around its neck, and its long beard spread before it on the table. Deep lacerations marked the stony forehead. Rivulets of blood were frozen in their tracks upon a tortured face.

Louis knelt, as he was ordered to do, and he prayed to the likeness of the Christ for strength, for wisdom, and for salvation from his human depravity. After his prayer, he arose and turned to face de Villeroi, who continued his questioning.

"Do you, new son of God, accept the cross of the Holy Lamb of God?"

"I do," Louis answered, without hesitation, grateful to have arrived at this point in the ritual. He looked upon the crucifix with passionate pride. He genuflected to his right knee before it and made the sign of the cross with his right hand, reciting, *"In nomine Patris et Filii et Spiritus Sancti."* He remained kneeling.

"Do you, new son of God, swear your life in service to this cross, upon which was crucified the Holy Lamb of God?"

"I do."

"And do you, new son of God, swear to give your life in battle, if so directed or required, to defend the Holy Church of the One True God, this Holy Order, its masters, and its brethren?"

"I do."

"Then rise, Sir Brother Knight, and join your brethren, who have also sworn the same. You are, this day and forevermore, a Knight of the Order of the Poor Fellow–Soldiers of Christ and the Temple of Solomon. Take up your Cross and wear it with piety, with honor, and with courage."

One of the six knights stepped forward with a fresh white linen mantle emblazoned with the bold red Templar cross, and he placed it around Louis's shoulders, covering his naked body. Louis's heart filled with the pride and elation of having finally, after what had seemed endless anticipation, attained that goal for which he had longed since he could remember.

He was finally, at long last, a Templar Knight.

Chapter 19

Louis rode high in the saddle, his shoulders straight and proud. The detachment of thirty Templars and their sergeants forged steadily toward Marseilles, where they would board a Templar ship for passage to Cyprus. At Cyprus, they would join a larger force and sail to Sidon, on the Mediterranean coast of Jerusalem.

Victor rode beside him, looking not as straight and proud. He shot a furtive look of annoyance at the friend he'd sworn to serve. While for Louis the Templar life was an idealistic boyhood dream, it was far from that for Victor. Victor was anxious to fight no one, and there was no cause for which he cared to risk his life. His demeanor since their departure from Verzeille had made that much clear to Louis. He seemed to have regretted following Louis into the Order almost from the start.

Louis had meant to discuss Victor's discontent with him, but the initiation process took priority, and he never got the chance. Now was as good a time as any.

"You're unhappy," Louis said casually, glancing past Victor

at the horizon.

"You don't miss a thing," Victor said dryly.

His tone annoyed Louis. "Why did you go through with this?" he asked.

"I almost didn't," Victor replied. "I almost changed my mind at the monastery. It was a horrid place. I was ready to head back home when a fat jackass of a monk said I wouldn't last a week with the Templars anyway. There was no way I was going to prove him right."

"That made you stay?" Louis was incredulous. "Wanting to prove an old monk wrong?"

Victor shrugged. "I can't think of a better reason," he said.

"What about your future?" Louis said. "I thought that was the reason you came in the first place: to build a better life for yourself." Victor sniffed. "Was that not what we agreed?" Louis pressed. "That the Templar life would offer you a chance to earn a better life. That maybe you'd be asked into the Order, too, and perhaps by then you'd see some benefit in that. That was what we discussed." Victor remained dour. "Look, Victor, if I knew you would dislike it so, I would not have tried so hard to talk you into this. I thought this would be good for you."

"I know you did," Victor said, turning abruptly to glare at Louis. "But that's just it…it was always what you thought. I'd argue, and you'd only try harder to convince me. It has always been futile trying to explain anything to you that you didn't want to hear. All your life, you've had this ideal, and as far as you were concerned, anyone who didn't see things as you did just needed a little more convincing. I know you thought this best for both of us, and now look at us: you, riding off to war like you're the Lionheart himself, and me following after you, the hapless squire, the would–be knight, unlikely to survive your grand adventure."

"I don't know what to say," Louis said. He was genuinely perplexed. "This has got to be better than cleaning stables." Victor seemed to consider that for a moment, but he only shook his head and said nothing. Silence reigned for a long moment, then Louis said, "Was the training at the monastery not interesting?"

"It was a pompous, ridiculous charade," Victor said.

Louis blinked in disbelief. They rode on in silence for several miles. He noted that the other Templars, especially Uncle Willem, were watching them and straining to hear their conversation. For the first time Louis began to consider the validity of Willem's and his father's misgivings. He wondered again if he had made a terrible mistake bringing Victor with him.

"My initiation was very impressive," he said. He knew at once that the statement was absurdly irrelevant, and he resolved to say no more.

A long silence passed before Victor suddenly said, "I'm sorry." Louis turned to face him. "It's a hard change for me," he continued. "In the stables, I had solitude. I was safe from scrutiny. I didn't have to worry about making a mistake and paying the price for it. I knew the job well, and I liked doing it. But here," he said, nodding toward the other Templars, "everybody has expectations, and I'm not sure I can meet them. I don't know what will happen if I fail."

"You're not going to fail," Louis said.

"I was certain of that as a stable boy. I knew my lot in life. I knew it would probably never change. Now..." He looked off into the distance. "Now I don't know if I'll be alive a month from now."

"Victor," Louis said, "this will be a fantastic adventure. It will be glorious. We will prove ourselves among the most capable, the most noble. We'll be respected and rewarded for our strength and our valor. This is going to be the best thing you've ever done, better than you ever could have dreamed. You will see. We will live, and the lives we live will be rich and rewarding. And more importantly than anything, we will be guaranteed our place in heaven when it's all over. Where else could you get such a guarantee?"

Victor nodded grudgingly. "Yes," he said. "I suppose you're right."

"I am," Louis said. "And Victor..."

"Yes?"

"I'm glad you're here. I'm glad you decided to come with me."

Victor stared at the horizon as the port of Marseilles came into view. Louis rose up in his stirrups at the sight. As they drew closer, the sails of three Templar ships, their crimson crosses standing in bold contrast to the brilliant white of the sails, came into view.

"La Templere," Uncle Willem said, pointing toward the ships. "And to the right of her, *Le Faucon* and *La Buzzard*. Those are three of our finest ships."

"How many ships do the Templars have, Uncle?" Louis asked.

"At least sixty," Willem replied.

Louis had always thought of Templars as mounted knights in desert battles; he had rarely considered the Templar fleet that ferried pilgrims and armies to Outremer, and commercial goods to ports throughout Europe. He realized that the Templar fleet must be as proficient as it was large to carry out the logistics of supporting the Order from England to Acre.

When they reached the docks at Marseilles, they loaded their equipment and provisions onto *Le Faucon*. It was a heavy cog that accommodated a considerable cargo of horses, men, and provisions. After they had stowed their cargo, they walked the short distance to the Marseille commandery for a hot, refreshing supper, and then prayers and the mass in the chapel. They retired early in preparation for the fifteen–day journey to Cyprus, which would begin an hour before dawn.

The next morning, as the ships sailed smoothly out of the Port of Marseille, Louis found Victor working on the deck, helping several of the deckhands with the rigging. Louis noted that the only times he had seen Victor truly happy was when he was performing some physical labor, exerting himself in ways that most men tried to avoid. He marveled at the exhilaration that shone on Victor's face. It faded as Louis approached.

"Victor," he said quietly as Victor left his work and approached him, "I want to finish the discussion we started yesterday."

"I'm working," Victor said.

"Yes, I see that. But talk with me now. For weeks now, despite my best efforts, you are clearly, deeply unhappy. It's troubling me, and I want to understand. I'd hoped you would find your way to happiness."

"I'm reasonably happy."

"But you're much happier working with the deckhands," Louis replied. "You know you don't have to do this work."

Victor shrugged and said, "Why wouldn't I? What else would I do?"

"Come walk with me," Louis said. They turned and walked along the deck until they came to the stern, and they leaned on the railing to gaze at the receding shoreline of Marseille. "What is it that displeases you most?"

"I don't know," Victor said.

"You must."

"No. That's just it: I don't know. I don't know anything. I don't know what we're doing, where we're going, or why. I know all about your dreams, but as far as I can see, that's not where we're going. We're going to some place that is real, that you've never seen, that you can't possibly know. We're not going to the place that's in your head. And it bothers me that you don't know that yet." Louis didn't know what to say. He opened his mouth to speak, but Victor continued, waving toward the shoreline. "Everything I do know is back there, beyond Marseille, in your father's fields and stables, and in the streets of Carcassonne." He turned toward the front of the ship. "But over there, across this sea? I don't know anything. I'm lost."

"But that's just it," Louis said. "You're not lost! We're the opposite of lost. Don't you see that all we will do in our service to the Templars, in service to God, will gain us our place in heaven? It's a guarantee."

Victor shrugged, looking uncertain. "I suppose," he said.

"Our futures are certain, Victor! Our futures are secure."

"Our futures are certain to be brief," Victor retorted.

It occurred to Louis that Victor was afraid. It was reasonable to be afraid, he thought. Victor had never been fired by the passions Louis held. Louis suddenly felt sorry for Victor. He wished Victor could share his passion.

"The things we do from here on out will make the world a better place," he said. "Less evil."

"The world will always be evil," Victor said. "As long as there are men in it, it will be evil."

"When the Kingdom of Jerusalem is built," Louis said, "there will be less room in the world for evil."

"If God wants Jerusalem to be built," Victor said, "why has He not yet blessed the Crusades with lasting victory, or better yet, just built it Himself?"

Louis blinked in dismay. He didn't expect the question.

"The sins of men," he finally said, "have thwarted victory in the past. God cannot be present where there is sin. Sinfulness has surely stood in the way of lasting success. And God wants man to turn from his sin and build His kingdom of his own free will, as a manifestation of faith."

"Why can't you just accept that the world and most of the men in it are evil?" Victor asked.

"Because I believe that surrendering to the depravity of the world is no better than dying, and I am not ready to die. I would rather die believing in something better, and doing something to build it. If I die in that effort, my life will not have been wasted."

"You're more idealistic even than I thought you were," Victor said, almost laughing.

"Answer me this," Louis said, pausing for a moment to frame his words. "If we're destined to fail in the pursuit of my idealistic dreams anyway, what have we lost in the effort that we ever really had in the first place?"

Victor didn't answer immediately. When he did, his tone had changed. "I suppose you have a point," he said, "and for once I cannot think of a meaningful argument. It's not just that I won't say it to you. I really can't argue."

"Fight by my side, Victor," Louis said. "Try to believe in this. Try to believe that in return for the things we will do for God's earthly kingdom, we will be rewarded in God's great heaven. I promise you, you will not regret it."

Louis extended his hand, but Victor shook his head.

"Maybe I'll get used to the idea," Victor said. "But regardless, I'm here now, and I can't change that. I'm not going to abandon you, and I'm not going to shrink from my duties. Of course I'll fight by your side; I said I would. Perhaps I'll even grow to understand why I agreed to it, and maybe I'll even be glad I'm here with you." He took Louis's hand and gripped it firmly.

"I won't let you down," Louis said.

"Nor I you," Victor replied.

They leaned on the railing in silence for a long, quiet moment watching the coast disappear into the morning sun's reflection on the widening sea.

"Thank you," Louis said, almost in a whisper.

"I have to get back to work," Victor said.

Chapter 20

"Over the years, Cyprus has grown crucial to our operations in Jerusalem," Willem said to Louis as the first leg of their voyage drew to an end. "Its ports and our bases here are convenient to the Levantine coast. We can reach any point in less than twenty-four hours, and most of our ports in half a day."

The island measured one hundred fifty miles from west to east, and sixty miles at its widest point, from the modest mountain range on its northern coast to the imposing Mount Olympus to the south. As they approached, it rose majestically, an emerald oasis in the vast emptiness of the Mediterranean sea.

The ships rounded the coast and landed at the port at Limassol, in the Akrotiri Bay on the island's southern coast. Victor joined the deckhands as they guided *Le Faucon* into port.

They had enjoyed good weather over the past two weeks and made good time, but Louis was ready for a stroll on solid land. They would not stay long. They would consolidate their force with another that had waited for them, and then sail for Sidon on the Jerusalem coast.

The Templars owned Cyprus briefly a hundred years ago, having purchased it from Richard the Lionheart when he lacked the resources to maintain it. But they divested themselves of it in short order after an insurrection among its Greek inhabitants nearly wiped out the garrison that guarded it. Since then, the island was under the control of the King of Jerusalem. The Templars maintained houses in two of its towns, and castles in three others. They used Cyprus now only to gather and plan, and to launch invasions, supplies, and reinforcements to Jerusalem.

A group of knight–Brothers and sergeants approached as the ships docked. They were led by their commander, an intense man with overly animated features.

"Brother Willem Marti!" he called as the group approached. "Welcome to Cyprus, once again!" The commander embraced Willem as he disembarked, and then each of the others in Willem's party, speaking their names as he embraced them. When he came to Louis, he gazed at him appraisingly. "Who have we here?" he asked.

"It's good to see you, Brother Barthélemy," Willem said. "This is my nephew, Sir Louis de Garonne. He is a new knight, and our newest Brother." Louis was aware of Victor hurrying down the gangplank from the galley. "Louis," Willem continued, "this is Sir Barthélemy de Quincy, Marshal of the Cyprus commandery. He is responsible for the organization of all expeditions that launch from Cyprus to Outremer."

"I am honored," Louis said, bowing slightly. Victor came up beside Louis, straightening his tunic and out of breath from his labors and his haste. "I have heard a great deal about you," Louis continued. He turned toward Victor. "This is my squire, Victor Guyot. He has proven his valor and his loyalty many times over. He, too, is a new Brother."

Barthélemy looked appraisingly at Victor. "It's a pleasure," he said.

Louis realized that for reasons he did not fully understand, Victor had inspired cool receptions from nearly everyone they had met since they left Verzeille. He wondered if he was the only one who recognized his inherent strengths and potential nobility. Victor would have to prove himself, he thought.

Barthélemy's eyes blazed with intensity. He spoke quickly, seeming impatient to discuss something of importance.

"Follow me," he said. He waved at a group of Templar sergeants at the dock. "Get their things," he called. The sergeants rushed to comply. "Only the essentials!" he yelled after them. "They'll be embarking again soon enough." He turned back to Willem. "Much has happened. The news is bad. We have little time to waste."

"What news?" Antonio Bollani asked.

"From Tripoli," Barthélemy said. "Disaster!" His excitement and his haste left him gasping for breath as they hurried toward Kolossi Castle, the Templar headquarters that stood guard over the port from a short distance away.

"Tripoli!" Willem exclaimed. "An attack?"

"A massacre! The Mamluks have taken the city. Few survived."

Louis's gut froze as the words hit him with tremendous force.

"My God," Willem said. He shook his head, speechless.

"The Grand Master sent Geoffrey de Vendac with reinforcements, but de Vendac returned without his troops, accompanied only by Lucia of Tripoli, Prince Amalric, and the Hospitaller Matthew de Clermont.

"The marshals left their troops?" Bollani exclaimed in disbelief.

"They chose to escort Lucia to safety."

"A small detachment could have done that," Bollani retorted, incensed. Louis shared his outrage, but he said nothing. De Villeroi's admonition still rang in his ears, and he was careful to keep his silence, as the Rule commanded. Barthélemy shook his head, but said nothing.

"And the population?" Willem asked.

"Massacred. None survived. Every Templar killed. Every Hospitaller, every Crusader, every soldier, every merchant – every man older than twelve years of age – all dead. Even those who escaped to Saint-Thomas were hunted down and butchered within days. The women and children are gone into slavery. So many have been enslaved, we have heard that the price of slaves in the Levant has dropped to a pittance."

They had arrived at the castle drawbridge, and they all stopped to absorb the horrible news, as well as its grave implications for the future of the Christian Crusade.

"Then...Peter de Moncada is dead," Willem said. He sounded vaguely uncertain, but Louis knew that it was a mournful statement, and not a question.

"He fought to the death," Barthélemy replied.

"Of course." Willem's face hardened. He nodded tersely and turned toward the castle. "Let's get started."

We're going to war, Louis thought. "So soon...," he whispered. No one responded. He glanced up at the machicolated battlements and the marble scorcher balcony from which defenders had often poured boiling oil or molten lead onto attackers at the door. The knights crossed the drawbridge and entered the castle, while the sergeants remained outside.

The heavy oak door opened into an immense marble hall. To the left of the door, a fireplace lay dormant in the early summer heat. To the right, on the western wall, a large window at floor level looked out on the expanse of sea beyond the port of Limassol. A smaller window near the peak of the ceiling allowed additional sunlight into the room. The largest windows, one on the southern wall directly opposite the entrance, and another on the eastern wall beyond the head of a massive oak table illuminated the white stone walls that stretched upward and curved inward to a high arched ceiling. The room glowed brilliantly in the morning sun. Even at the peak of the ceiling there were no shadows.

The hall had been converted into a war room. It was crowded and thick with tension, teeming with the urgent voices of dozens of outraged Templars. The highest ranking Brethren of the Order were here, including the Grand Master, William de Beaujeu, who sat at the head of the table. Several knights paced aimlessly, deep in thought or quiet conversation, but most sat around the busy table arguing the proper reaction to the loss of Tripoli.

De Beaujeu sat quietly, slumped in his chair and cradling his head in his hand.

When Willem's band arrived, de Beaujeu stood and called the meeting to order. Silence settled instantly. Willem and the Grand Master greeted one another with the Templar salute and silent bows.

De Beaujeu was of medium height, with a powerful build, a straight nose, and clear blue eyes that shone brilliant against his deeply tanned face. His eyes seemed to absorb everything that was happening around him. He exuded a sense of calm despite the chaotic emotion that surrounded him. He stood quietly for a moment and waited for his brethren to settle.

"Kala'un has broken the truce," he finally said, simply, and quietly. Most of the brethren nodded, and some gritted their teeth in anger. "And so, we must decide on our next course of action." Louis sensed that many in the room wanted to shout out their suggestions, and perhaps adjourn the meeting and load the ships for battle. Everyone waited for de Beaujeu to continue. "But first," he said, "we must understand what happened in Tripoli. What happened to the truce?" De Beaujeu directed his gaze toward Geoffrey de Vendac. "Brother Geoffrey?"

Several of the knights dropped their gaze at the mention of de Vendac's name. Antonio Bollani glared at him openly, while Willem attempted to distract Bollani from his hostility. De Vendac's round, boyish face radiated pride, and a smugness that made Louis share Bollani's sentiments in spite of himself.

"The Venetians ended the truce," de Vendac said with disdain. Bollani's jaw tensed, and he appeared ready to lunge across the table at the marshal. "They invited Kala'un to take their side against Lucia. Simply to cut the Genoese out, to tip the balance of trade in favor of Venice, they asked the infidel to intervene on their behalf."

"That can't be true," Bollani snapped.

"I assure you," de Vendac said, "it is quite true." Louis was appalled. "I know they're your countrymen, Brother Bollani, but *you* know the merchants have been bickering for years. It's impossible to please them, or assuage their hostilities. They have all come to value profit more highly than peace, or unity, or even their Christian faith. They have found agreement only in their relentless, reciprocal hatred."

The authority in de Beaujeu's voice contained the hostility. "Kala'un fought for the Venetians against the Genoese?" he asked.

De Vendac shook his head. "No. He took advantage of the merchants' disunity, and the Venetians' invitation. He brought ten thousand men and laid siege to the city. The walls crumbled under their catapults. They massacred the Venetians as well as the Genoese, at least those who had not taken flight with their treasure and left the Templars and the peasants to face the fury they had unleashed. The Saracens massacred everything that moved within what was left of the city walls."

Bollani glared hotly at the marshal, but he softened under the Grand Master's gaze.

De Beaujeu said, "For one hundred eighty years the County of Tripoli has been under Christian control. Now it is lost, not to the enemies of God, but to an enemy far more insidious: ourselves." He gazed into the distance, deep in thought. "And what do we do now? I'm thinking that we should go to Sidon. Kala'un will surely go there next. We must meet him there. Brother Geoffrey, what do you say?"

"I believe we should return to Tripoli," de Vendac said. He seemed to concentrate his attention on the tip of his narrow nose as he spoke, and it made him look mildly cross–eyed. "If Kala'un is moving against Sidon, our arrival at Tripoli will draw him back. We will protect Sidon and regain Tripoli at once."

Bollani leaned forward, barely concealing his anger. "That's an ambitious plan for one who abandoned Tripoli to the Saracens in the first place," he said. His seething words drew a cacophony of protest and agreement.

"Enough!" de Beaujeu shouted, raising his hands. The room fell silent. "This is not the time for yet more bickering."

Barthélemy de Quincy, the Marshal of Cyprus, said, "Kala'un is demolishing Tripoli brick by brick." He spoke quietly, but emphatically. "Stone by stone. There's nothing to recapture."

"We'll rebuild," de Vendac said.

"There's no one left to live there," Barthélemy retorted. "There's nothing there for us now. There's nothing left."

"May I speak?" an English knight said.

"Brother Andreu," de Beaujeu acknowledged.

"Andreu de Renham," Willem whispered into Louis's ear. Willem never failed to assign the names to the faces of the people Louis met along the way.

"It's clear that Brother Barthélemy is correct," Andreu said. He looked sharply at Geoffrey de Vendac. "To rush to Tripoli would be pointless, as much as many of us would like to reclaim what we have lost." De Vendac looked at the floor. "Kala'un will not double back to confront a force much smaller than the one he has just destroyed. We should not spread our forces thin. In this case, I believe that unity is our strength. We must join forces at Sidon and thwart Kala'un's advance. Time, and not haste, will rebuild our strength."

Louis was impressed with Andreu's demeanor. He was at once kind and firm, his voice gentle, but clear and unwavering. His hair was longer than the Rule proscribed, and curled under in the style of secular nobility, but his beard was long and well-groomed in the Templar manner.

De Beaujeu was apparently equally impressed with Andreu de Renham; he nodded energetically in agreement.

"There is little more to discuss, I think," de Beaujeu said. "We'll have a show of hands, of course, but of the two choices, only one makes sense. We will reinforce Sidon, and I will take a contingent to Acre and remain there indefinitely. We must stem the losses and redeem this Crusade before we are pushed entirely into the sea. Show your hands, and then make ready to sail before dawn. I will meet with the marshals now."

All but three of the knights raised their hands in concurrence. De Vendac pursed his lips and shifted his weight from side to side.

As the knights left the hall, de Beaujeu said, "Sir Willem Marti, please stay."

Geoffrey de Vendac and Barthélemy de Quincy remained behind, along with Willem and several of the higher ranking knights, the Grand Master's most trusted advisors. Louis and the rest of the knights left the hall to rejoin the sergeants and prepare for the voyage to Sidon.

"What's happening?" Victor asked Louis. He was sweating in the simmering heat, and Louis imagined that he would have rather stripped off his mantle and tunic and gone bare–chested.

"We leave for Sidon," Louis said. "There's no time to lose. We'll remain garrisoned there while the Grand Master continues to Acre with a smaller contingent."

"So, we'll be seeing battle before too long."

Louis nodded. "So it appears." He felt an unfamiliar gloom rising within him as he contemplated the certainty of real battle. It disturbed him, and he shook it off and forced a smile. "Finally," he said.

Victor shook his head and walked away.

Chapter 21

SIDON FROM THE SEA was majestic in the golden morning sun. The silhouette of a great castle dominated the dun–colored shoreline, its massive towers standing resolute between the twin basins of the busy port. The Crusaders built the castle sixty years earlier on a small island that lay two ships' lengths from the shore, connected to the shore by a narrow, fortified causeway. The castle appeared impregnable, and it ensured safe landing for merchants and armies alike.

Victor and the deckhands guided *Le Faucon* smoothly into the dock and tied her in. Most of the Templars would stay at Sidon, so the bulk of the provisions were to be unloaded and carted to the castle.

The Grand Master William de Beaujeu hurried to the great hall with the marshal, Geoffrey de Vendac, and Thibaud Gaudin, the Grand Commander of the Templars in Jerusalem. De Beaujeu motioned for his advisors to accompany him, and he beckoned to Willem Marti as well. Willem hurried to follow the leadership of the Order into the castle.

Louis was proud of his uncle's good standing among the Templar high command. He turned to Victor with an air of satisfaction.

"My uncle has done well for himself," he said. Victor nodded, looking after the group of men as they disappeared through the castle gate. "I imagine there are great things in store for him," Louis added.

Victor nodded again in agreement. "No doubt," he said as he turned toward the ships. "We should help with the unloading." Louis followed him down to the docks, and they pitched in with the deckhands.

"You enjoy labor," Louis observed.

Victor nodded. "I'm accustomed to it. It feels good to do honest work, and it helps me to think."

"Something troubles you?" Louis said. Victor ignored the comment, but Louis persisted. "You can talk to me," he said.

Victor heaved a heavy sack in Louis's direction, and Louis lunged to catch it and throw it onto a waiting cart. Victor did not respond, and they worked in silence for nearly an hour. Finally, they broke for a drink of water and a short rest. Louis decided to give it another try as they leaned back against the cart and drank.

"Victor," he said, "it disturbs me that you're so unhappy. I didn't expect you to be as cheerful as I about this adventure, but I didn't think it would make you this miserable, either." He looked quizzically into his friend's face. "Will you talk to me?"

Victor shrugged and looked out to sea. He shook his head dolefully. "It's just hard not knowing from day to day where we're headed, or where we'll end up," he said.

"What do you mean?" Louis said. "We both knew we were headed to Jerusalem."

"We knew we were headed to Outremer," Victor said. "We still don't know which town, or which camp we'll sleep in tonight, or whether we'll rush to Tripoli to fight the Saracens or stay here and wait for them to come to us. It's the not knowing that makes me uneasy. I'd like to know where I'll be tonight, and whether I'll be fighting or resting easy."

It occurred to Louis that Victor's life had always been certain: he had always been told where to go, and what work he would do, and what would happen to him if he wasn't where he was expected to be. Louis realized that the uncertainty of their journey was foreign to Victor, and that it must be disconcerting.

"I'm sorry," Louis said. He felt rising resentment. "I suppose I assumed that things would be the same for you as they are for me, but I can see now that they are not. There's not a lot I can do about that now. You followed me here, Victor. You have a job to do. Wherever you go, you'll have a job to do, and while you're here with me your job is to be my squire. I can see now how much you hate that. If you hate it so, I can surely make arrangements for you to return home, where you will work for my father, and eventually for me, as a stable hand. I'll make the arrangements now, if you wish. But if you don't go now, you must accept your choice and be the kind of squire I need: one who will follow me, trust me, and above all, be at my side whenever your duty requires it, even in the worst of the heat of battle. I will not trust my life to someone whose heart isn't in that pursuit."

"That's what I needed to see," Victor said with a look of resignation.

"What?" Louis asked.

"The truth."

"What truth?"

"That you are my lord," Victor replied. "You are the knight, and I am your squire. You can stop trying to act like you're still my friend now, because you're not my friend...not any more. You are my master, no more and no less."

A long silence passed between them. Louis stared hard at Victor, who gazed sullenly across the sea to its distant horizon. Louis started to speak, but thought better of it. What would he say? Victor was right; there was no denying it.

Finally, Victor abruptly stood and threw back his shoulders. "It's no matter," he said. He shrugged again. "I go where you go. That's the way things are." He tossed his leather tankard at the barrel of drinking water that stood a few feet from them and returned to work.

The deckhands raised a teasing fuss about the length of their break. Louis would normally have joined in the good-natured teasing, but he waved them off with a scowl and hoisted a sack of flour.

One of the deckhands called out and nodded toward the castle. Louis turned to see the Grand Master returning with his entourage.

"I'll be back," Louis said, and he joined the rest of the knights as they dropped their tasks and converged upon their leaders.

"The Marshal will remain at Sidon with most of our force," de Beaujeu said, nodding at Geoffrey de Vendac. De Vendac nodded in unnecessary acknowledgement. "I'll proceed to Acre and take command there, along with the Grand Commander. The Venetians have sent reinforcements to Acre; Brother Gaudin will welcome the assistance of Brothers de Molay and de Sevrey, and our newest commanders, in training them properly for battle." The Grand Master paused and gazed at the senior knights who had accompanied him to the castle. "Brothers Bollani and Marti will take command of their own troops upon arrival at Acre."

Murmurs and nods of approval ensued. Louis beamed at his Uncle Willem, his heart bursting with pride. He remembered the Rule's caution against pride, and he dismissed it out of hand. He wondered if he would be assigned to Willem's command, and Willem nodded as if in answer to the unspoken thought.

I'm going along, Louis thought. He could not have received better news.

Chapter 22

Le Faucon and two Venetian cogs left Sidon at noon to carry the Grand Master de Beaujeu, Thibaud Gaudin, Jacques de Molay, and thirty of the Cyprus knights with their sergeants and squires south along the coast to Acre. It was late afternoon when they arrived at the stronghold to find dark, ominous clouds rolling in from the sea.

"Does it rain often?" Louis asked Willem, eyeing the storm clouds with concern. Lightning flashed eerily deep within them, and deep, rumbling thunder shook the deck of the ship.

Willem shook his head. "It rains occasionally in winter, but *that's* unusual," he said, pointing at the darkening sea. "I hope it's not portentous." Louis nodded in agreement. "Sandstorms are much more common," Willem continued, "but mostly in spring and summer. We'll have to disembark quickly; it looks like it's going to hit hard."

Louis looked to the imposing profile of the largest structure at Acre, a thick-walled fortress at the city's southwestern tip, which jutted into the sea like a protective arm cradling a busy harbor. The massive walls rose from the sea, presenting a seemingly insurmountable defense. Doves cooed peacefully atop them, their presence contrasting the purpose of the battlements.

Louis nodded toward the fortress. "Templar?" he asked.

"The Templar fortress, surrounded by the Templar Quarter of the city," Willem said. "It's the grandest fortification in the region, a hundred years old, and never taken."

"That will be home for us," Louis mused. He was pleased.

"For a long while, God willing," Willem said.

As *Le Faucon* rounded the point and turned eastward into the harbor, a mountain range loomed in the distance, across the harbor to the southeast. Louis gazed at its impressive profile against a darkening sky.

"Mount Carmel," Willem said. "Elijah's home for many years. His grotto would have been near the top." Willem pointed toward Mount Carmel's peak, which rose to nearly eighteen hundred feet above the sea just beyond the southern shore of the harbor.

The ships turned in through the sea gate, into the military port. A bridge stretched from the walkway at the edge of the harbor to a tower built away from the shore, from which the port captain would lower a heavy iron chain each night to protect the port from marauders.

Sailors and dockworkers scurried quickly, anxious to avoid the approaching storm. The port captain waved impatiently, as if he could will *Le Faucon* to dock more quickly.

Willem laughed softly. "Gaston," he murmured to himself, shaking his head.

As the ship drew nearer to the dock, Louis made out Gaston's rugged features. He was a stout, powerful man with a face that had seen its share of hardship. A bulbous nose dominated a deeply lined face with deep set eyes that seemed fixed in a permanent squint, and with several scars in the places that weren't wrinkled by perpetual ill–temper. Gaston barked orders and arbitrary abuse at the dockworkers who hurried to comply. Suddenly, Gaston spied Willem on deck.

"You're back," he said, the gruffness of his voice lending an air of contempt to the greeting.

"Happily," Willem called out.

"Well, get a move on, before this storm blows the lot of us out to sea!"

Willem laughed. "You'll be at your supper soon enough, you miserable dog. Stop your complaining and bring us in."

Louis smiled and relaxed. They disembarked as soon as the ship was safely docked.

The rain did hit hard. It drove into them with gusty winds and the biggest raindrops Louis had ever seen. The drops stung and made slapping sounds as they pounded into him from above and from behind. He was drenched before he could even comment.

"I've never seen rain like this," he yelled above the sudden squall.

Willem glanced back to the sea and anxiously shook his head. "Nor have I," he said. His face was grim.

"Go on," Gaston called out to Willem, nodding toward the fortress. "I'll be along soon enough. We'll unload later, after this passes."

De Beaujeu and his advisors were already well ahead. Willem nodded and motioned for Louis and Victor to follow him. They moved with haste toward the gate in the city wall, longing for the shelter of the fortress. Their haste was futile; they were already thoroughly drenched.

They slogged into the fortress's great hall to the greetings of more than a dozen knights, who offered to relieve them of their burdens, the personal effects they carried with them from the ship. They exchanged their wet garments for dry ones from the draper's stores and gathered around a roaring fire at the hearth.

"I am Renier de Vichiers," said a sandy–haired knight of about forty. "I'm the Seneschal of the Acre command. Welcome to Acre. We're glad for the reinforcements." De Vichiers was a thin man, with a puffiness to his face that gave the false impression of excess weight. His eyes squinted as if they were swollen, and Louis wondered if he did not drink a bit too much ale. "We're particularly honored," he continued, "to have the company of our esteemed Grand Master, and our most exalted commanders."

William de Beaujeu nodded his appreciation. De Vichiers introduced the rest of the Acre Templars who were present, and de Beaujeu responded by introducing the knights who accompanied him.

"We'll meet after supper," de Beaujeu said, "when everyone is rested and fed." De Vichiers nodded. "You, Brother de Vichiers, will attend, along with Marshal de Sevrey, myself, and Brothers de Molay, Gaudin, and Marti. There's much to discuss. We'll prepare for a meeting with King Henry."

Louis sensed grave concern in the Grand Master's voice, but no one in the room acknowledged it. Louis had heard that Henry was a reckless king, and not given to the counsel of the military Orders, the experts at preserving his domain. He suspected that the meeting with Henry would be less than genial.

"Marshal de Sevrey will be along shortly," de Vichiers said. "He is with de Villiers at the Hospitaller fortress."

De Beaujeu nodded, apparently pleased with the information. "Very well," he said. "How are relations between the Orders of late?"

"Minor strains," de Vichiers said. "But for the most part, cooperative...positive. The Hospitallers are deeply committed. They'll fight to the last, if necessary."

"And among the factions?" de Beaujeu said.

"Tense. Verging on open hostility." This clearly did not please de Beaujeu. The rift between the Venetians and the Genoese was a constant and growing concern. "We work to keep the peace among the Italians, but we find that task more difficult than open warfare with the Saracens. The Venetians are intractable, and the Genoese impetuous. Their profits mean more to them than the welfare of this populace...even more, it seems, than their own lives. They diminish rather than reinforce our unity, and should we face a Saracen attack, they can be trusted more to abandon than to defend our position. The consensus among the Crusaders is that they will flee with their gold rather than stand against an attack, which they themselves, undoubtedly, will invite."

De Beaujeu's face hardened into a quiet sternness. He thought for a moment, then said, "In that case, it would be prudent to reevaluate the priority of defending their assets in the event of attack," he said. "The safety of the citizens and supporters of the Crusading Orders is paramount." Many of the knights nodded in agreement. "It would be foolish to defend those who do more to harm than to help even themselves."

"So be it," de Vichiers said. He seemed gratified by the Grand Master's conclusion.

Chapter 23

THE GRAND MASTER William de Beaujeu and the senior Templars filed into the great hall of the king's Grand Maneir. King Henry sat stolidly at the head of a long oak table with his advisors sitting on either side of him.

Amalric, Henry's brother, sat to Henry's right. He was the Constable of Jerusalem since he fled the final fall of Tripoli. He had initially defended Tripoli in the final siege, but he fled to Acre when the inevitability of Tripoli's collapse became clear. Amalric, a tall and powerful warrior, was respected among the Templars, but he had garnered grumbling ill will with his decision to abandon Tripoli.

Philip, the king's bailiff, was a mouse of a man with wavy black hair and nervous, almost fanatical black eyes that shifted tensely, as if he were anxious to absorb every detail of the activity around him.

He's a fearful man, Willem thought to himself. He shrugged off the thought and nodded agreeably as platitudes were exchanged.

“Welcome, Grand Master,” King Henry said, nodding to de Beaujeu.

“Thank you, my king,” de Beaujeu replied.

Henry turned to Willem. “You’ve returned safely from Europe, Sir Willem,” he said. “It’s good to have you back. Your nephew, was it?”

Willem bowed and smiled at the king. “Louis de Garonne, Your Highness,” Willem said. “A new knight, and a newer Templar Brother.”

“Ah,” Henry said with disinterest.

“You’re a commander now,” Philip observed with a twitch of his nose. Willem nodded deferentially. “Congratulations. The losses at Tripoli have made room at the top.” Willem froze in dismay at the remark, and de Beaujeu glared hotly, first at Philip, and then at Amalric, who averted his gaze. Henry groaned at his advisor’s ineptitude.

“It is my poor fortune to have lost beloved brethren at Tripoli,” Willem said icily. “But they died for their God, and so shall reap their reward. For that, I praise God.”

“Well spoken,” Henry said. “A true knight you are, and a man of God.”

Willem retreated from the attention of the king and his aides feeling sick to his stomach. He fought the feeling and adopted an impassive demeanor.

“We’re here to discuss the future of Acre,” de Beaujeu said quickly. “We are at a crossroads, I think.”

“That we are,” Henry agreed. “How do you propose to guide us safely past it?”

“We all know the Venetians and the Genoese are the greatest threat to our strength and unity.” Henry nodded in bland acknowledgement. “Kala'un is acutely aware of the weakness their division causes. He has demonstrated that he will exploit that weakness and division if he is incited and finds just cause. At the same time, discipline is nearly nonexistent among the newest recruits from Europe, and we cannot expect that condition to improve with subsequent reinforcements.”

"What's wrong with our recruits?" the king demanded.

"They only want to kill," de Beaujeu said. "And after a night of ale, they are ready to do so indiscriminately."

"They are soldiers," Henry cried. "They *came* here to kill. It's not their fault that the Templar Order has crafted peace with the enemy they came to kill. What else are they to do?"

"You know as well as I," de Beaujeu argued, "that we are in no position to wage war against Kala'un. You know as well as I that the war between the Italians cost twenty thousand lives that we could ill afford to lose, and we have not recovered from that loss."

"It sounds as though you are afraid to face Kala'un," the king said. Once again, de Beaujeu glared at Amalric, who again averted his gaze.

"I see no profit in suicide," de Beaujeu said.

"And you, Sir Willem," the king said, turning to Willem. "What is your assessment? How do you view the Grand Master's trepidation?"

"I am in firm agreement," Willem said, failing to disguise his dismay at the question.

The king looked appraisingly at Willem for a moment, then turned abruptly back to de Beaujeu. "What do you propose?" he asked.

"For two years now," the Grand Master said, "the knightly Orders have been patrolling the streets of Acre to keep the peace. Until recently that has been no great task. However, with the arrival of a somewhat less law–abiding element, the task appears to have grown daunting. I'd ask that you make it abundantly clear that the Templar patrols have your full authority to dispense justice and arrest violators whenever and wherever they deem it necessary."

"You want full authority," the king said.

"You've tasked us with peace," de Beaujeu said. "We need the tools to effect it."

"It's the king's jurisdiction," Philip interjected sharply.

"Which makes it the king's responsibility," de Beaujeu said, no less sharply. "If the Templars are to carry out the king's responsibilities, they are entitled to the king's authority to do so."

Willem cringed at the boldness of the Grand Master's challenge. Philip opened his mouth to speak, but the king waved him to silence.

"Very well," Henry said. "It's not unreasonable. You have whatever authority you need to keep the peace."

"Among the Christians," de Beaujeu said, "*and* between them and the Muslims."

Henry peered keenly at de Beaujeu as if he suspected a trick that he could not spot. He looked troubled as he waved with abandon.

"So be it," he said.

"But you will report to us," Amalric said quickly, "every action, every suspicion, and every arrest. Each is subject to the king's summary annulment."

"Of course," de Beaujeu said.

"What is your assessment, Grand Master, of the Mamluk situation?" Amalric asked.

De Beaujeu thought for a moment, then said, "Kala'un would have been content with our peace. When the Venetians summoned him to Tripoli to support them against the Genoese, they obviously aroused his ambitions. Now that he has Tripoli, he must taste ultimate victory and our expulsion from this land. Most often, the sultan would choose peace for his people over a costly war. But the improved prospect of a Muslim Jerusalem may have whet his appetite to the point where war may be inevitable."

"How will we fare?" Henry asked.

Willem thought to himself that Henry must not have been listening at all, or that some sort of dementia had set in, preventing him from grasping de Beaujeu's dire assessment of only a moment ago.

"My king," the Grand Master said patiently, "we will lose. Without reinforcements of solid fighting men, without substantial commitment on the part of Europe's pope and kings, we do not stand a chance. We must prevail upon Europe, in due haste, for reinforcements and a revival of sincere commitment."

"There's little chance of that," Henry said. "Europe is weary of the Outremer question. We have become, for most, a distant and foreign land, autonomous and self-sustaining. Many believe that with the Orders here, there is little need for material support from outside." He looked meaningfully at de Beaujeu. "To most Europeans, the myth of Templar invincibility exceeds the reality of Templar strength. It is an irony that with you here, there is little perceived need for anything else."

Willem detected the flash of anger that the Grand Master deftly concealed.

King Henry continued. "It appears that as far as Europe is concerned, this is no longer the Crusade," he said, waving his hand to indicate all of Jerusalem. "The Crusade is there now, back in Europe...against the heretics who are the more immediate enemies of God's Church. No one cares about this Crusade anymore. In the eyes of Europe, it is over. It is done."

"We've got to make them care again," de Beaujeu said. "We've got to make them understand the reality that two thousand Templars, almost as many Hospitallers, and an army of mercenaries and militias face nearly two hundred thousand Mamluks from here to Cairo. We must make them see the impossibility of those odds, and the certainty of a Muslim Jerusalem if they are not improved."

Henry sat quietly and absorbed the Grand Master's argument. "I'll send messengers," he finally said. He turned to Philip and said, "Make it so."

"And we need to keep the peace," de Beaujeu added.

"Yes, you've already said that." The king sounded exasperated. Willem believed that if anyone had a right to be exasperated, it was the Grand Master for whom his esteem had only grown in the recent weeks he had spent with him.

Chapter 24

WILLEM AND LOUIS WALKED the cobbled streets of Acre, stopping to talk with merchants and shake hands with townsfolk with whom Willem had been acquainted for years. An unusually cool breeze blew in from the Mediterranean, and a cloudless sky allowed the sun to warm the air to the perfect temperature. While Louis missed the green fields of his home, he loved the temperate climate and the rich beauty of the Jerusalem coast.

"It doesn't feel much like we're building God's kingdom, Uncle," he said. "What do we accomplish by maintaining peace with the Muslims? Why are we here, if not to work to defeat them and rebuild the Kingdom once and for all?"

"The Kingdom of God is not made up of only Christians," Willem said. "It cannot be. To make it so, we would have to kill every Muslim and Jew who refused to convert: the men, the women, the elderly, and the children. Many among us are not Christian, but may yet turn to Christ. Annihilating them would please God far less than persuading them to His Word." Willem smiled sardonically as he waved to a Venetian merchant hawking hand tools from an open stall. "Our Savior taught us to love our neighbors, not to destroy them in His name. If we are able to restore the Kingdom through peace and prosperity, as opposed to violent conflict, thereby adding to it the seasoning of contrasting cultures, should we not do so?"

"I suppose so," Louis said. "But the Mamluks gain strength in peacetime just as we do, and it appears that this peace is better for them than it is for us." He indicated an Arab merchant selling fruit from a stand in front of a small shop several yards away. The man was talking amiably with several Christians as he pocketed their money. "This man does not fear the coming of God's Kingdom. What motive does he have to convert, or even to consider Christianity over his infidel faith?"

"How do you know he's an infidel?" Willem asked.

"Isn't he?"

"If he is today, he may not be tomorrow. It is not for me to judge. If he is an infidel, what is more likely to convince him to turn to our faith: our kindness and tolerance when that is possible, or the threat that he will die at our hands?"

Louis considered Willem's words as they approached the fruit vendor. They did not sound like the words of a Crusader.

"Ahlan wa sahlan, ya akhi!" the merchant called to them. He was a handsome man with clear black eyes and a close–shaven beard. His robes were clean and brilliant white, and his genial smile revealed straight teeth that gleamed in contrast to the dark skin of his face.

"Marhaban, ya Ahmad," Willem said. *"Kaifa halluk?"*

Louis looked at his uncle in surprise. He had never heard him speak any foreign tongue but Latin, and he wondered how – and *why* – he had learned the language of the Saracens.

"I'm well," the Arab said. *"Alhamdulillah."*

Willem introduced Louis to Ahmad Abd al-Karim, whose ancestors had lived in the vicinity of Acre for untold centuries.

"There is no news today," Ahmad said, "and that is good."

"How is business?" Willem asked.

"Steady and unremarkable. It feeds my family."

"I would like to introduce you to my nephew, Louis. He returned with me from our home in Europe." Willem placed a hand on Louis's shoulder.

"Louis...like the Christian king," Ahmad said, tilting his head in studied interest.

"Exactly like the king," Willem said with pride. "As noble a knight as ever there could be."

Ahmad shook Louis's hand. "Welcome to Jerusalem," he said.

"Thank you," Louis replied.

"Shukran," Ahmad said. Louis looked quizzically at him. *"Shukran* is the Arabic word for thank you," Ahmad explained with a smile.

"Ah," Louis said. *"Shukran."*

"Afwan." Ahmad nodded enthusiastically. "I like this man, your nephew," he said to Willem.

Willem and Ahmad exchanged a few more pleasantries before taking their leave. Louis repeated to himself the Arabic words he had learned as he and his uncle continued down the street.

"Ahmad is a good man," Willem said. "He has done much to promote peace and strengthen the fabric of the Acre community. He demonstrates equal respect for Christian, Jew, and Muslim. He promotes understanding in place of ignorance."

Louis nodded. "I get a good feeling from him," he said. An odd thought troubled Louis. "Tell me though, Uncle," he continued, "how does one wage war against a people, having developed fondness for them? Does it not become difficult to face them across the battlements if necessary, and wish them dead?"

Willem looked thoughtful. "That's an excellent question, Louis," he said. He thought for another moment as they strolled city streets chaotic with the din of merchants and shoppers haggling, children chasing wildly through the crowd squealing and raising both smiles and irritated scowls, and dogs barking for scraps from the street side butchers who irritably shooed them away.

Finally, Willem stopped and turned to Louis. "It raises an important point," he said, "which is that a true Christian never wishes the Saracens dead, but would rather see them alive in the Holy Spirit and the grace of God. To get to the point where one wishes another dead, one must first demonize the other to the point where they appear no longer human. The Church has done this in its crusade against the Cathars. This crusade, though, is different. Here, honorable warriors fight in the name of their deity, against a worthy adversary who is similarly compelled. Both sides believe their mission is sacred, and that their God would have them honor even their enemy. In a holy war, both sides seek their heavenly reward, and many on both sides find it. There is no sorrow in that. Therefore, it is no crime of conscience to send a worthy adversary to his heavenly reward in the presence of his Almighty God."

"So, you would face Ahmad on the battlefield if he were a soldier, and kill him without remorse?"

"Not without remorse. But without hesitation, yes…as he would me."

Louis nodded slowly. The easy familiarity he had witnessed between his Templar brethren and the Muslims had disturbed him because it seemed contrary to the Crusaders' obligation to fight against Muslims for the glory of God. He was learning that familiarity was expedient, even necessary to the functioning of social structure in time of peace, and not an impediment to the military mission when circumstances brought it to bear. It felt complicated compared to his boyhood conceptions of hollow, nameless Saracens whose single earthly purpose was to stand between him and the realization of the Kingdom of God.

Ahmad would die, Louis realized, unless he turned from his flawed faith and embraced the God of Christianity. It was only a matter of time.

"Why is it so hard for them to see the superiority of our faith?" he asked.

Willem flinched. His face grew grave.

"They believe that Jesus was a prophet of God, a perfect soul sent to lead men to God." Louis was surprised. He had always believed that Muslims rejected or denied Christ.

"Then why are they not Christian?"

"They don't believe that Jesus *was* God," Willem said.

"Just a man...," Louis mused.

"A prophet, like Muhammad. And that he was murdered like a dog on a cross of shame by his own people because they rejected his holy message."

"That explains why they reject Judaism. But what do they have against Christians?"

"That we're worse: that we celebrate the instrument of Jesus' murder, the cross, rather than his life and his message. They believe that we worship the execution of God's prophet, that we elevate his agony over his teaching. They despise our faith because they believe we fail to honor God's prophet."

"You make them sound more pious than we are," Louis said.

Willem shrugged and looked away, as if to say, "so be it." Louis wondered if Willem agreed with the Muslims. He wanted to ask the question, but he thought better of it.

"So, they don't believe the Savior is God," he said instead.

"They don't believe in the Trinity of God. That is why they say, '*la ilaha illa Allah,*'—'there is no god but Allah.' The notion of Trinity is, to the Muslim, sacrilege. There is only one true God, and not three. When Constantine's Council at Nicea ruled that Jesus is God, the Muslims believe that Christianity stood in violation of God's first commandment. When we pray at the foot of the Cross, they believe we violate the second. From the Muslim perspective, Christianity glorifies the contravention of God's own foundational commandments. We have boldly claimed heresy in God's name."

Louis struggled with his curiosity, and ultimately he lost.

"What do you believe, Uncle?"

Willem looked around them, and up and down the street to ensure that no one had shown undue interest in their conversation. He fixed a hard look upon Louis's inquiring eyes and pursed his lips. He spoke in a lowered voice.

"It doesn't matter what I believe," he said. Each of us must find our own peace with the thoughts and ideas God gives us.

We must pray that our ideas are in fact from God, and not borne of evil. I could be as wrong as any other man, and so I conceal my deepest thoughts within the depths of my own heart, where they can harm no one but me."

"I do not ask in order to trap you, Uncle, but out of respect for your opinion and admiration of your spirit. It matters to me what you believe, as I suspect that I may one day reexamine what I myself believe. I would value your thoughts, should that day come."

"To believe anything other than Church doctrine is heresy," Willem said flatly.

Louis accepted the conclusion of the course of their discussion and returned to his original question.

"How does this peace work?" he asked. "How is it maintained, and when and how is it broken?"

"The population of Acre is diverse," Willem said. "There is an underlying tension to every interaction, whether it is between Christian and Muslim, Crusader and merchant, or most notably, Venetian and Genoese nobles. The hostility among the Italians is unrestrained and unrelenting. It exceeds the hostility between Christian and Muslim. Our primary function in Jerusalem of late has been to keep the peace – especially among the Italians – and to enforce the civil laws. Occasionally, we fail."

"That's not quite what I had imagined I would do here," Louis said.

"There is much you could not have imagined," Willem said. "War is sporadic in nature, Louis. Battles brew, but they don't always come to pass. Most often they're avoided through skillful diplomacy or by the need for both sides to rebuild. Also, in peacetime, commerce thrives, and commerce pays for armies. War drains resources and weakens the fabric of the communities we're trying to build."

"But we compromise with the infidel to that end."

"Only as a means to an end," Willem said. "Ultimately, we want to fight, and to win, and to push the Muslims from the Holy Land. One day we will do that; it is our grand vision. But that day is far off, and we must survive until it comes. And that means peace with the Muslims…for now."

"That distant day is why I'm here," Louis said. "I'll do all I can to expedite its arrival."

"Then, for now, we will protect the peace," Willem said.

They resumed their stroll and turned their discussion toward lighter matters.

Chapter 25

On a cool April evening, Louis and Victor walked along the Mediterranean shore, talking and watching the sun sink toward the sea. They had been in Acre for nearly six months, and their duties had so far been routine and uneventful.

"So," Victor said, "this is why you brought me here, then, to help you police the locals?" He laughed. The Templars were functioning primarily as the administrators of the secular government of Jerusalem. There were no glorious battles, and the only Muslims they saw were happily trading their wares alongside Christians in the town markets, and paying taxes to their Christian rulers.

"It's our presence here that holds these lands for the Church," Louis reminded him. "Besides, from the looks of things, we'll get to see battle soon enough. The Mamluks broke the treaty at Tripoli, so we're actually no longer at peace. Tripoli whetted Kala'un's appetite for conquest, too, and the Arabs' desire to be rid of the Christians. They'll probably look to Acre next, and then to all of Jerusalem. Sidon is the only thing that stands between Tripoli and Acre. If Sidon falls, it's only a matter of time and we'll be lost."

"Well, I appreciate that cheery thought, Louis," Victor said sarcastically. "It's hardly encouraging. Somehow, though, I don't get the feeling that all will be lost."

Victor seemed to have finally accepted his role in the Templar Order, and the opportunity it afforded him. Had he not joined, he'd said, he would have led a Languedoc peasant's life, with no hope of fulfilling even the most modest of ambitions. He had finally realized that he did, in fact, want more than the peasant's life into which he had been born. He also knew that Louis had offered him the only possible way to achieve more. But he still did not share Louis's unrestrained zeal for the arrangement. For Victor, it was a necessary evil.

"We could yet play a critical role in winning the Holy Land back for the Church, and for Europe," Louis said.

"They shouldn't be losing it again," Victor retorted.

"Agreed. But they are, and it falls to us to prevent it."

"While I hate these patrols," Victor said, "they're better than dying in the desert. I'll be content if we don't fight for a while. We'll do no good for Jerusalem if we're dead."

"We will if we each take ten Saracens with us."

"Your logic reassures me," Victor said dryly. "I'll do my best to take ten with me when my time comes."

"That should be our agreement: neither of us goes unless we take ten of them with us."

Victor laughed. "Agreed," he said. "So I shall kill nine in every battle. That will ensure me of a long life."

"These castles and fortifications," Louis said, waving toward the coastline, "guard the shores of Christian Palestine from north to south. They are the achievements of the Holy Crusades, and the Templars who gave their blood for them. We owe it to those souls to continue the fight, and to keep what they have won. It's our obligation."

"You make it sound so nice, and so noble," Victor said. "You're always the romantic."

"As they were, too," Louis countered. "Romantics are driven to great accomplishments. I'm proud to count myself one."

"You realize you already have everything, don't you?" Victor said abruptly.

"What do you mean?" Louis asked.

"I'm not sure why you would welcome battle, and a chance to die. You've realized your goal: you're a Templar. You have a beautiful girl at home who would give anything to be your wife, even if she will never have that. You have land and wealth just waiting for you to return home and claim it, but you won't. Instead, you're here, keeping peace, but discontent with it. You crave battle and glory, even when it's clear that everyone else around you has grown tired of it and considers it pointless. Sometimes, Louis, you astonish me, and I can't help thinking you a fool."

"You're quite comfortable being direct with me."

"I've always given you the truth."

"Do you have any other truths for me today?"

"Questions," Victor said.

"What questions?"

"Well, for instance...do you really think God wants all the blood, and the constant suffering and death of these Crusades? Do you ever think that maybe if God really wanted a kingdom here, He would have it, and it would be a place of peace and safety that did not require Templar enforcement?"

"It's not my place to question God, or to doubt the Church when it calls us to Crusade."

"And when it calls your mother a heretic?"

Louis stopped in his tracks, stunned. "What are you talking about?" he demanded.

"You didn't think I knew that," Victor said, "but I do. It doesn't matter to me, though, and I don't know why it matters to you. Except that it's hard for me to understand why you'd still serve the church that accused your mother and killed her family."

"How do you know this?" Louis asked.

"I've always known it," Victor said.

"How?"

"I don't remember where I first heard it. Probably from my mother. I only heard her whisper it once, but I knew it already, so she must have told me before that."

"If you know this, then others do, too," Louis mused with growing alarm. Victor nodded once. "Why did you never mention it?"

"It was none of my business," Victor said. "It's a private matter, and unfounded, in any event. I never saw a point in discussing it, but as I said, it does make me wonder why you remain so committed to your ideals."

Louis blinked in amazement. "How could you not see that they're all I have?" he said. "They're the only thing of which I can be sure anymore."

He stared blankly at the disappearing sun. His heart sank with it as jumbled thoughts flooded his mind, from the unthinkable notion of his mother as a heretic, to concern for her safety, and to the lies that had been woven so neatly through his life, and so subtly that he had failed to discern them. He leaned against the wall of a shuttered shop as the weight of all that had been troubling him, all that he had pushed into the shadows, came to bear.

"Well, I suppose that's reason enough," Victor said, "except that you're badly mistaken."

"What do you mean?"

"Do you really believe this is all you have?" Victor said. He shook his head. "Then you're blind. I've already told you: you have so much more than this. But you have always refused to let anything else be more important."

Louis was about to argue, but he knew that Victor was right, and he said nothing. He also knew that no good could come of discussing Colette on this balmy, golden evening as the sun set on this beautiful and distant Outremer town.

✠ ✠ ✠

The hulking soldier sauntered toward the merchant while his seven ragged companions hung back to observe. The merchant glanced nervously up and down the street. Other merchants avoided his gaze and sent their children scurrying to the safety of their shops.

"How much for one of your fine linen shirts?" the soldier asked. His tone was belligerent, and as he spoke, he leered lasciviously at the merchant's young daughter, who sat quietly in the shadows inside the shop.

"Seven dinars," the Muslim said. He was visibly frightened.

"Seven! So much?" The soldier leaned close to the merchant. "That's robbery," he said. The merchant choked against the heavy stench of stale ale on the soldier's breath.

"For you, my lord, it is but five."

"One," the soldier growled. The merchant stepped backwards, away from him.

"It cost me five, my lord."

"One," the soldier repeated, advancing menacingly. The merchant backed into his shop and motioned for his daughter to retreat. She moved quickly to the rear of the shop. The soldier grasped the merchant's cloak and pulled him close. The merchant's daughter yelped involuntarily as she hurried away.

"I'll just take that linen shirt as a gratuity," the soldier bellowed. "Why should an infidel dog profit from an exchange with a Christian? You're lucky to be allowed to live among us, much less reap profit from us!" The soldier twisted the merchant's collar and shoved him hard against the shop's weather-beaten wooden doorframe.

The man cried out in anguish as blood gushed from a gash in the back of his head. He pressed a palm against the wound and moaned. The soldier drew a fist to punch him.

"Stop!" a voice bellowed from the intersection at the end of the street. A Templar patrol, two knights and two sergeants, had come around the corner in time to witness the soldier's first blow. They ran to the scene. "What's the meaning of this," Louis yelled.

The soldier turned slowly toward the source of the interruption. He drew himself to full height and squared off before his challengers. He blanched almost imperceptibly at the sight of the crimson crosses on the Templars' surcoats, but he quickly masked his anxiety.

"Who wants to know?" the soldier demanded. His accent was of the Languedoc.

Louis peered intently into the man's face. He seemed familiar, though he could not imagine where he would have made the acquaintance of such an oafish man. Since he was clearly from the Languedoc, though, it was possible. The soldier was a mercenary, hired by the Italians, no doubt, and sent to fight for them in Outremer. He wore bits and pieces of armor, none of which matched the others, and most of which fit him badly. He wore a dirty dagger on his belt, and a rusty sword slung over his shoulder. Louis guessed that he had not come upon his weaponry entirely honestly.

"Who are you?" Louis demanded. "What is your name?" The mercenary ignored him. A crowd had gathered a safe distance from the commotion, and a group of Muslims stood fearfully in a close group on the edge of the crowd. The tallest among them, an Arab with a warrior's build, had fixed his solemn, dark eyes upon Louis. Louis met his gaze for a moment, and then turned back to the mercenary. "I asked you a question," he said firmly.

"Louis," Victor said urgently. "Wait." He beckoned to Louis.

"What is it," Louis said, leaning into Victor.

Victor cupped his mouth at Louis's ear. "The road to Carcassonne," he whispered. "The outlaws." He nodded toward the mercenary, and Louis's eyes snapped back in his direction, widening with recognition.

My God, Louis thought. It was Gilles, the thug who had accosted him on the road to Carcassonne so many years earlier, when Victor came so gallantly to his defense.

"It's *you,*" Louis said, moving ominously toward the oaf. "You are Gilles." The mercenary peered at Louis in dismay, trying to determine where they had met. "Gilles *le Dadais Grand!*"

Gilles' mouth twisted into a ugly, seething grimace. He balled his fists and leaned toward Louis.

Victor moved to intervene. "You still haven't learned your lesson, have you?" he taunted.

Recognition dawned in Gilles' eyes as he turned his gaze to Victor. "You!" he said, seething.

Victor grinned acerbically at Gilles, his eyes flashing contempt.

"Back away from that man," Louis said, pointing at the merchant.

"He tried to rob me," Gilles protested.

"Did he?" Louis said in mock dismay. He walked to the man and inspected him carefully. The man stood shaking, clutching the back of his bleeding head. "With what weapon did he threaten you?"

"Do you defend an infidel against a Christian?" Gilles demanded with righteous indignation.

Louis glared at Gilles. He recalled his Uncle Willem's words. "I know not whether this man is an infidel," Louis said. "For all I know, he may be a good Christian. But you...I'm certain that you are no Christian. Christians do not go heavily armed against defenseless merchants."

"Don't they, now?" Gilles said.

Louis ignored the irony in Gilles' voice. "On my watch, they don't," he said. "I told you to move away from that man. Now, step back." Louis advanced toward Gilles with his hand on his sword. Victor and the other two Templars placed their hands on their own swords, as well. Gilles assessed the odds and backed away. "That's better," Louis said.

The merchant looked at Louis with uncertain gratitude. His daughter ran from the rear of the shop with a cotton scarf to clean the blood from her father's face.

"Disperse," Louis said to the crowd. The onlookers complied with varying degrees of haste. Several of the Arabs, including the tall one, lingered a brief moment longer than the rest. The tall one never took his eyes off Louis. Louis nodded his reassurance to the man, who turned and disappeared into the shadows. Louis was intrigued by the man, and he made a mental note to discover his identity.

Gilles stood glowering at Louis from the end of the street. Louis nodded curtly for him to disappear. Gilles slowly drew an index finger across his throat, and then quickly covered the threat by jerking his thumb to the rear and barking at his men to retreat.

Louis gazed after them until they disappeared into the darkness at the far end of the street. He felt a sickness rising within him at the promise of escalating conflict.

Chapter 26

Louis and Victor returned from their street patrols well after midnight. Tension was mounting in all quarters of the city. Disturbances were erupting more frequently, and among larger mobs. Quelling the quarrels and carousing of restless soldiers had sapped Louis both physically and emotionally. He took his leave of Victor, who went to his squire's quarters near the stables, and headed toward the knights' cells in the Templar castle. He was weary and numb, and reluctant to face the stone stairways that would take him to his cell.

He went instead to the kitchen in search of scraps to tide him over until morning. He felt his way in the darkness, remembering the layout of the stair and the hallway that led past the kitchener's quarters to the larder. The soft glow of moonlight filtered into the hall from the larder; the oak door stood slightly ajar. As he approached the door, a shadow moved across the patch of moonlight on the floor. He pushed carefully on the door, to open it as quietly as he could. A soft moan emanated from the pantry on the other side of the kitchen. The sound stopped him in his tracks.

He imagined what could have made such a sound, and a chill went up his spine. When he heard heavy breathing, he realized he'd come upon a man, possibly another knight who was also rooting around in search of food. He moved into the kitchen and peered into the pantry, where he made out the indistinct form of a stoutly built man kneeling on the floor and moving in an oddly rhythmic manner.

"Hello?" Louis called. The figure jumped, startled by Louis's voice. He fell backwards into the shelving and moved quickly to conceal himself in the shadows. Louis realized that there was someone else on the other side of the wall and out of sight, who was working hard to restrain their own frightened panting. "Who's there?" Louis repeated, more sternly.

"Sir Louis?" a weak voice whispered, almost fearfully. He recognized the voice, but he could not place it.

"Who's there?"

"It is I," the voice said. "Richard Osbourne."

"And who else is there?" No one answered. Louis grew bewildered. "Who is with you?"

A form moved out of the shadows of the pantry and into the moonlight that streamed through the kitchen window. Louis gasped. It was the Venetian, Antonio Bollani, his face a mask of breathless panic and frustration, and his garments disheveled.

"This is none of your concern," Bollani snapped. He brushed past Louis, followed quickly by the shadowy form of Richard Osbourne. Osbourne glanced fearfully at Louis as he passed. The men disappeared into the hall, and their padding footsteps faded into the distance. Louis stood silent, paralyzed by his incomprehension of what he had discovered. He leaned against a wall and sank to the floor, and he sat there staring into the darkness into which the men, his heroes and friends, had melted. Numbness overtook him. He gladly allowed his thoughts to succumb to it, and his mind went blank.

He sat in the darkness for more than an hour, taking in the smells of the kitchen and the whispery, scurrying sounds of the night, trying to isolate and identify each. He allowed his mind to find occupation with arbitrary, irrelevant things, anything to ward off the reality of what he had discovered.

Eventually, the reality crept in. It started with memories of Bollani and Osbourne and the other Templars with whom Uncle Willem traveled back to Verzeille, and the marvelous stories of bravery, brotherhood, and undying devotion to all for which they stood together. Then, the images of both men, quiet and self–possessed, at once humble and exceedingly strong, who had always been the most avid advocates of his quest for a Templar future, took sharp focus.

He wondered how such men could carry such strength, exude such piety, pray so devoutly, and fight so fiercely for God when they bore upon their souls the most despicable of all iniquities.

They couldn't, he thought. This was impulsive, unplanned… the product of momentary blindness or a dastardly trick of the Devil in the shadows of a cursed night. Something had overtaken them, but it was momentary, and it was to their shame. An hour with their confessor would put it right, clean the stains of their sin, and restore them to God's good graces. It had to be so. It could be no other way.

He recovered his wits and left the kitchen without the scraps he had sought, and he hurried to his cell. He tried to sleep, but found it impossible. He went over the scene in the pantry a dozen times, trying to convince himself it was different from what he thought he saw, and searching for all the possible explanations that would eliminate the one that seemed most obvious. Finally, with no hope of finding sleep, he got up and went to find Willem.

The light of the full moon reflected brightly off the surface of the shimmering sea, silhouetting the ships in the harbor and illuminating the castle rampart, almost as if it were day. Willem stood in silence, his hands clasped behind him as he gazed out over the tranquil seascape.

"Uncle," Louis called softly. His throat was dry, and his voice cracked as he called out. Willem turned toward him.

"Louis," he said. "What is it? Can you not sleep?"

"I'm troubled," Louis said. "I can't find sleep."

"What troubles you?"

"Several things. Many things. I need to talk with you."

"Of course."

"I came upon Brothers Bollani and Osbourne unexpectedly..."

Willem's eyes narrowed. He waited expectantly. "Yes?" he finally said.

"They were..." Louis paused. He conjured the courage to speak the words. "I found them in a compromising position."

Willem groaned almost imperceptibly. He looked off to the sea for a moment, and then turned to Louis. "What do you mean?" he asked. Louis had the impression that his uncle knew full well what he meant. "Explain."

"They...embraced."

"Men often embrace."

"Not like this."

Willem drew a deep breath and sighed. "Like what, exactly?"

"Like...lovers."

"Ah," Willem said, almost in a gasp. He turned back toward the sea. "It was nothing, I'm sure."

Louis stood beside his uncle and matched his posture, clasping his hands behind him and gazing at the sea. He stood quietly for a long time, allowing Willem the chance to speak. Willem remained mute.

"I'm sure you're right," Louis finally said. "I'm sure it was nothing. Perhaps it was only the shadows playing tricks on me." Willem nodded, and Louis continued. "I know such things would not be tolerated. It was foolish of me to jump to conclusions." Willem nodded again.

They stood in silence watching wispy clouds glide across the moon and listening to the lapping of the waves against the shore and the hulls of the ships in the harbor. Louis could keep the silence no longer.

"It's just that there have been rumors, and I've refuted them vehemently whenever they arose, and now it seems to me that there might be something to them."

Willem turned to face Louis.

"What if you did see what you think you saw?" he said. "What difference would that mean to you?"

"It's the sin of the Sodomites," Louis said. "It would be an abomination."

"To you?"

"To God."

"But what is it to *you?*"

"An abomination."

"Why? How does an act between two other people affect you? Is it not between them and their God alone?"

Louis thought for a moment. He understood that if he had not stumbled upon the men amidst their embrace, his regard for them would not have changed; they were still the same men they had been before the embrace.

But only because he had not known of their sin. His thoughts went to his own sin: his courtly love for his own cousin, Colette – before he knew she was not his cousin by blood. He wondered what that sin made him, despite his highest aspirations.

"Their sin is not my concern," Louis conceded. "But has God not commanded that such men should be put to death?"

"God has commanded that a great many men ought to be put to death. *All* men, as a matter of fact."

"*All* men?"

"Without exception," Willem said. "You've studied the scripture, Louis. Levitical law condemns us all to death by stoning for one infraction or another."

"Which part of Leviticus condemns me?" Louis asked.

"Several, actually," Willem replied. He pointed at Louis's chest and said, "Your surcoat – the cross of silk sewn into a linen cloak. Leviticus, in verse nineteen of the nineteenth chapter, condemns you for that." Louis looked down at the mantle of which he was so proud. He found it hard to believe that God would condemn its construction. "Your hair," Willem continued, "the same chapter, verse twenty–seven. It's good that we do not shave, but our custom of cropping our hair condemns us. Those verses are written in the same chapter, with the same sternness, and in the same spirit as the verse that condemns Antonio and Richard for what you think you saw. In the darkness of the night, on rare occasions, having suffered pain or loss or watched a brother die, I have cursed my God. For that, I am more condemned than any. Must not each of us be stoned, then, in the manner the Bible prescribes?"

"Then what is the point?"

"Just that: that none of us is perfect, that we are all worthy of death in God's eyes...but that our Savior died to free us from that penalty."

"So, are you saying that the Church should now accept the behaviors for which God has said we should die?"

"I'm saying that it is no man's business what another man does in the darkness of his cell. I'm saying that none of us is any better than the next man, and to judge anyone when we ourselves are unclean is the worst of all our offenses."

"But the Church condemns such things, and it requires us to do the same."

"The wages of sin, Louis, are a weapon in the hands of the clergy," Willem said. "The Church wields the weapons of condemnation and absolution with precision in its battle to control all men. The clergy's worthiness of its own condemnation is not enough to induce it to lay down those arms. The Church will never discard the means to punish any who dare stand against it."

"The Savior would forgive these men," Louis said with sudden insight. "He would tell them to stop, but he would forgive them."

"Of course," Willem said.

"And so, should they not repent, and put away their sin?"

"That is for God to say," Willem said. "I have no authority to judge, and my efforts are better spent on my own sins."

Again, the two men stood in silence. Louis contemplated the vastness of the sea, and the wisdom of Willem's words. He likened the sea to all there was to know, far more than he could ever comprehend. Willem's words were like a feeble beacon, casting a yellow glow upon the promise of better understanding. He recalled the time when everything seemed so simple, and so definite. He found himself longing for those days.

He peered at his uncle in the pale moonlight and marveled at how little he really knew of him. He wondered how much more he had yet to learn.

Chapter 27

Ahmad Abd al-Karim, the generous and affable fruit merchant who had been blessed with a richly melodic voice, greeted Louis with the flowery prose of the fabled Arab balladeers, from whom he boasted descent.

"Sabah al-khair, ya sadiqi!" Ahmad sang out as Louis approached with Victor and two companions, a Venetian Templar named Marcello Venier and his squire. *"Assalamu alaikum, wa rahmatullahi, wa barakatuhu!"*

"Good morning to you, Ahmad," Louis replied with a smile. "God's blessings to you, as well, my friend." In the months since his arrival, Louis had learned the most common Arabic phrases, and what he did not understand, he knew to be kind and complementary coming from Ahmad.

"Thank you, good knight," Ahmad said. "Is everything, *insha'allah,* peaceful and calmness today?"

Victor glowered at the Arab as Louis nodded for Marcello to proceed with the street patrol.

Louis nodded and said, "Yes, thank God."

Ahmad smiled broadly. "*Alhamdulillah*," he said, reminding Louis of the Arabic phrase he had previously taught him.

"Yes, *alhamdulillah*. Of course."

"I've heard stories about you, Ahmad Abd al-Karim," Victor said. His tone was abrupt and accusing.

For a brief moment, Ahmad's eyes flitted from side to side, as if to ensure that no one had heard. Louis scowled reproachfully at Victor.

"Stories?" Ahmad repeated nervously. He clearly did not want the stories aired publicly, whatever they were.

"Yes, stories," Victor said. He paused to gauge Ahmad's reaction. "About a Christian woman," he prodded. Ahmad shrank away from Victor as if he were a leper. "A *married* Christian woman," Victor pressed.

"I don't know what you mean." Ahmad appeared on the verge of panic.

"Victor," Louis said quietly. "Stop."

Victor did not relent. "You don't know anything of Marguerite d'Auberive?"

Ahmad trembled visibly, his face filled with fear.

Victor laughed aloud. "You're a sly one," he said, jabbing a finger toward Ahmad. "Don't worry, infidel. I don't care to tell your secret to anyone...just yet."

"Victor!" Louis grew angry. "What are you doing? You can't throw an accusation like that around in public. What proof do you have? More importantly, what are you trying to gain here?"

"I want to see him squirm," Victor said.

"For God's sake, why?"

Victor shook his head with contempt. "Why not? He's dallying with the wife of a Christian. He's lucky I don't haul him in, or better yet, beat him to a pulp for that. It's only a matter of time before someone else does it, and he should be smart enough to know that." He turned to Ahmad. "But you don't fear us, do you, infidel? You think we're too weak or stupid to do anything about it."

"Victor!" Louis shouted. "Enough! Ahmad, is any of this

true?"

Ahmad hung his head. "It is an accusation," he said quietly, "and nothing more."

Louis studied Ahmad's face. "Well, if it is more," he said, "you'd best put an end to it before it can be proven. You know the penalty for such things."

Ahmad looked up sadly, his eyes pleading with Louis to believe him. "I have done nothing wrong," he said.

"I'm sorry, Ahmad." Louis said. "I'm sorry for my squire." He emphasized the word *squire*. It was the first time Louis had ever used it to disparage Victor. He realized that for the first time he actually wanted to see Victor wince at the word, for the way he had treated Ahmad. Victor glared bitterly at the cobbled street.

Louis took Victor by the elbow and led him away. They hurried to the end of the street and turned the corner, out of sight of the fruit merchant.

"What is wrong with you," Louis demanded.

"Everyone's talking about it," Victor protested. "It's going to cause a problem. I was trying to avoid that."

Louis knew better. "Do you think you accomplished that?"

"There's going to be trouble," Victor said. "Word has gotten out that Ahmad has been romancing the wife of a Hospitaller commander. When word reaches the commander, there will be trouble that our patrols will not be able to quell. I don't want to get caught up in that, especially on account of a Muslim dog who can't confine his manhood to his own Muslim bitches."

Louis's intended rebuke was cut short by a ferocious yell that echoed from Ahmad's direction. Chaotic shouts and the clanging of weaponry reverberated from the rows of houses and shops that lined the street. They raced back to the corner in time to see a mob descending upon Ahmad, who screamed in helpless terror. Louis called out to Marcello and his squire to rejoin them as they ran to the scene.

"Stop!" Louis yelled. No one paid him any mind. The mob was a conglomeration of Hospitallers, mercenaries, and Frankish soldiers of several of the various Crusader armies. A Hospitaller knight marched grimly beside his commander, dragging Ahmad by a rope around his neck. Louis was horrified to see that another knight also dragged a prisoner, a petite woman with golden hair and petrified azure eyes. They were headed for the city square.

Louis chased after the mob, trying futilely to pull men away and get to the commander to stop the rampage. To his chagrin, he spied Gilles among the rabble, cheering it on. He stopped in his tracks at the sight of a priest standing beside the public stocks in the square, accompanied by a soldier with a bucket of pitch in one hand and a horsehair brush in the other. A group of Hospitallers stood behind the priest waiting for the mob.

"Commander!" Louis yelled. The commander turned in Louis's direction, but he only looked past him with glazed and bleary eyes. His face was ashen, and his hands shook with rage. "Stop this," Louis pleaded.

The commander ignored Louis and turned back to the priest, who beckoned the knights to bring the prisoners to him. Muslim townsfolk gathered at the edge of the square, murmuring excitedly among themselves.

Ahmad and the woman were thrust in front of the priest, where they stood petrified by fear.

"Madame d'Auberive," the priest intoned, "you stand accused of adultery, and of consorting with the heathen. The penalty for your sin is death. How do you plead?"

Marguerite d'Auberive gaped helplessly, her trembling lips silently mouthing the word *no*, over and over.

"Very well," the priest said. "Has anyone witnessed the sin of the accused?"

Several hands and a chorus of affirmation were raised among the crowd. Ahmad gasped and swallowed in terror.

"No—," he cried before one of the knights struck him hard in the mouth.

"Quiet, dog," the knight said.

"I have seen them," a Frankish merchant called out.

"And I," said another.

"It is done," the priest declared, and he motioned to the

soldier, who painted Ahmad from shoulders to feet with pitch.

The soldier turned to the panic-stricken woman and painted her as well. He tossed the empty bucket to the side and accepted the torch another soldier offered him.

With a horrible shriek, Ahmad burst into flames at the touch of the torch. Marguerite d'Auberive also cried out, and tears streamed down her cheeks as the torch was put to her.

Louis's stomach wrenched violently at the grisly scene and the anguished howls of the condemned. He remembered Eustache and Mathilde, and the horror of their market day execution at Carcassonne. Now even more than then, he failed to see justice in the barbarity of these hasty executions.

His attention was seized by a sudden roar from the edge of the square. The gathering of Muslims had grown to a teeming crowd, and that crowd surged menacingly toward the much smaller group of Christians.

The fascination with which the Christians had witnessed the execution turned to alarm at the Muslims' approach. Louis realized that he and his three companions were caught between the forces of an impending clash. He hesitated to draw his sword, but he knew he would have no choice.

A Muslim picked up a weighty stone and threw it into the pack of Christians. Someone bellowed as the rock found its mark.

"Kill them!" a voice rang out from among the Christians. Most of them moved toward the advancing Muslims, leaving only a few to stand vigil as the conflagration consumed its victims. The Christians were outnumbered, but undaunted. Louis drew his sword.

"Stop!" he yelled to no one in particular.

"Out of the way," a gruff voice commanded him. Someone pushed him from behind, and a moment later he realized it was Gilles, who now led the advance toward the Muslims.

Louis thought briefly that he would witness the end of Gilles, but a chorus of shouts from the headquarters of the Hospitaller Order gave the Arabs pause. A detachment of twenty knights and more than a hundred soldiers attacked the Muslims from behind as the execution mob reached them with their weapons drawn. Louis hung back, his mouth agape.

"We have to help," Victor urged.

Brother Marcello held up a restraining hand and shook his head. Victor gave him a bewildered look.

"We'll do no such thing," Louis said. He felt shaken as he turned to Marcello. "I'm not sure on whose side we would fight," he said. Marcello shrugged and continued to shake his head, spellbound by the spontaneous violence.

Shouts and screams filled the air as swords and maces flailed, and unarmed Muslims fought with rocks and fists and walking sticks in a desperate attempt at self-defense.

Gilles wore a fiendish grin as he lashed out with brutal force. One of the Muslims, a merchant with a reputation for being peaceable and honest, shook a fist at Gilles in defiance of his upraised sword. Gilles brought the sword down hard upon the Arab's head, splitting it in two before the blade lodged itself near the man's heart. Gilles tilted his head backwards and let out a deep–throated, maniacal laugh.

He's possessed, Louis thought. He wondered for a moment if Gilles was even human. Gilles withdrew his blade as the Arab fell and swung wildly toward another, a teenage boy who tripped frantically over fallen bodies in his efforts to escape the carnage. He too fell, his back laid open like an overripe pomegranate.

Finally, Louis moved. He headed for Gilles. Victor hurried to stay with him. Louis glanced over his shoulder at the Hospitaller Commander d'Auberive, who stood stoically over the smoldering bodies of his wife and her accused lover, before he refocused his attention on the ruffian Gilles.

"What will you do?" Victor yelled. Louis ignored him.

The last of the defiant Arabs were falling quickly, dead or dying, into the pooling blood. Louis reached Gilles as his last victim fell. He seized Gilles by the shoulder and spun him around. Gilles reared to strike, but Victor stopped him with a sword point to the throat.

"Don't move," Victor commanded.

"What are you doing?" Gilles sputtered. "Get away from me!" He slapped at Victor's blade.

"You will hang," Louis said.

"For what?" Gilles cried. He looked about as if he had been accosted by a madman. "You saw it yourself! We defended ourselves against rabid dogs."

"This did not have to happen," Louis said. "You incited a riot." He glared at Gilles with contempt. "What are you doing here, anyway?" he asked. "I should think you'd be spending your life in a dungeon in Toulouse. How is it that you've found your way here, in the guise of a Crusader of the cross?"

"It's my penance," Gilles said, sneering and wiping blood from his cheek with a ragged sleeve. He added in sing–song sarcasm, "I'm forgiven. My soul is white as snow. The pope himself has guaranteed it."

"You were released from prison to do your penance?" Louis said, incredulous.

Gilles laughed. "It was this or the gallows," he said. "Here, I have a fighting chance."

"Here, you'll see the gallows just as well," Louis said. A crowd had gathered around them.

"What has this man done?" asked a knight of the Genoese army.

"He has incited riot," Louis said.

"What, this?" the knight said, surveying the square with a wave of his hand. "We all saw what happened here. This man protected you." He leered at Louis. "You'd be laying among the fallen if not for him."

Marcello placed a hand on Louis's shoulder and gently pulled him away. "Come," he said. "Leave this."

"Mark my words, Gilles of Roullens," Louis seethed, "you will hang, and you will burn in hell."

Gilles blanched visibly, but he caught himself and bared his teeth.

"It won't be in your lifetime, Templar," he said. "*You* can mark *my* words on *that*."

"We need reinforcements," Louis sputtered as he turned from the mob and walked hurriedly away. "This is getting out of control. We can't contain this."

Victor pursed his lips. He, Marcello, and Marcello's squire hurried after Louis as he stormed toward the Templar fortress.

Chapter 28

The clinking and clanging of trinkets and tools followed a dozen Muslim traders as they made their way past the sheriff's station and toward the inner gate of the city. Louis squinted at them briefly in the morning sun, and then did a double take as he realized that their carts and pack horses were loaded with more than trading goods. He saw, too, that not all the Arabs were traders. It was a family group, and they were leaving town with all the household goods they could carry.

Only recently had it become common, Uncle Willem had said, for local Muslim families to uproot after countless generations and move far from their ancestral town.

Louis sighed with frustration. More Muslims left Acre with every passing day since the arrival of the peasant crusaders. Templar patrols had increased, and the Italian mercenaries did not hide their resentment of them. By night, the city teemed with an unruly carnival spirit. Mornings were solemn as the townsfolk awoke to the aftermath of drunken mischief. Hapless Muslims fell victim to the harassments and assault with increasing frequency.

"The more that leave here, the better," Victor said. "There will be less tension with them gone."

"Yes," Louis said, nodding. "But where are they going? And what tales are they carrying with them?"

"What does that matter?" Victor asked.

"How do you think the Saracen leaders will react to a steady stream of refugees from abuses and suffering?" Louis said. "I think we're inviting vengeance."

"Kala'un would attack us over poor treatment of a few merchants and craftsmen?"

"I believe he might," Louis said. In fact, Louis was sure of it. He believed it was only a matter of time before Kala'un brought his entire army to the gates of Acre to atone for unfortunates like Ahmad, and countless others who had done little to invite poor treatment by the mercenary rabble.

"I doubt he would," Victor said.

"I hope you're right."

"I thought you wanted to fight," Victor said incredulously. "You complained because we were at peace and all we had to do was patrol the streets to keep that peace. Now that trouble is brewing, you're suddenly afraid we might actually have to fight the Mamluks." Victor shook his head in exasperation.

Louis stared straight ahead as they made their way toward the market square. It was rare that they had free time away from their duties, their training drills, and a heavy schedule of prayer and tutoring in the business matters of the Order. They had found themselves with an hour to spare, and they intended to make the best of it.

"Do you have nothing to say?" Victor persisted.

"It's just that since we've been here, I've seen for myself that we may not be very well matched against the Mamluks," Louis said. He didn't want to say too much about his concerns. It occurred to him that a degree of distrust had grown between them, and that for him that distrust was mounting. He resolved to meditate on that troubling realization later, alone, at the prayer hour.

"Really," Victor scoffed. "You came here certain that we had them all but beaten, and now you tell me we may not be evenly matched? It's just now occurring to you that if we stood a chance of defeating them, we wouldn't be at peace?"

"I knew we'd receive reinforcements; I didn't know they would be sixteen hundred murderers, rapists, and thieves, spared the gallows or life in prison and absolved in exchange for going to a faraway place from which they'll never return. We asked for support; Europe took that as an opportunity to empty their dungeons and rid themselves of lawless barbarians."

"I see your point," Victor said.

"I also did not believe until I saw it for myself that the Venetians and the Genoese truly are more interested in their petty quarrels than in the unity it would take to stand firm against the Mamluks. We lost Sidon to their foolishness. If not for that, I think we would stand a chance."

"I see that, too." Victor nodded in understanding. "Things are not as you thought they would be."

"No, they're not. Not in the least."

"What do we do?"

"The best we can," Louis said. "We keep the peace. And if we fail, we fight. I just wish the fight would be purposeful and planned, and not the result of bickering and backbiting among ourselves."

"What do you make of Gilles?" Victor asked. "He's the last person I'd expect to see in Outremer pretending to be a Crusader."

"He's just another one of the barbarians," Louis said, "absolved of his sins and freed to sin with reckless abandon. I can't imagine a pope, priest, or bishop that would allow such a travesty."

"And yet, here he is," Victor said. He cast his eyes down the street as Gilles sauntered toward them, not yet aware of their presence.

Gilles glared sullenly at the people he passed on the street. Louis felt a fleeting compulsion to slip down a side alley and avoid a confrontation, but the feeling turned instantly to anger for having felt it. He squared his shoulders and readied himself.

Merchants averted their eyes as Gilles swaggered past. Louis watched them and wondered what they would give for the chance to cut him down.

Gilles stopped abruptly as one merchant boldly met his gaze. It was the tall man who had watched stoically when Gilles beat the innocent merchant, and again at the burning of Ahmad. Gilles took the man's eye contact as impudence, and he moved to confront him.

"Gilles!" Louis called.

Gilles flinched warily and cast an angry gaze in Louis's direction. His eyes flashed as he recognized Louis and Victor.

"You again," he growled. "You don't learn."

"Keep moving," Louis ordered. "Move along and keep the peace."

"You're the one disturbing the peace, Templar," Gilles said. "*My* peace."

"You know no peace," Louis said. "You know only hatred and violence. Well, not today, my felonious friend. Not today. Move along…*now*."

Gilles noted Victor's hand on the pommel of his dagger, and he reconsidered the odds. He glared at the tall Arab and stormed past Louis and on his way. The Arab nodded his thanks.

Louis was intrigued by the man. He projected a peculiar presence, a reserve and an awareness that Louis had only seen in the best of warriors. Louis was certain that he must be a warrior.

He approached the Arab. "Who are you?" he asked.

"I am a humble merchant," the man said.

"A merchant," Louis repeated doubtfully.

The man nodded and said nothing. Louis gazed steadily into his dark, unblinking eyes. He wanted to know more about him.

"What is your name?" he asked.

The man squinted and tilted his head, gazing sideways at Louis as if he should already know the answer to that question.

"You've recently arrived at Acre," the man observed. "From Europe?"

"Yes," Louis answered. He realized the man had not answered him, and he was about to challenge his refusal. Instead, he nodded sharply. "I'm sorry for the disturbance," he said. "Good day."

The man nodded slightly, with a vague twinkle in his eyes. Louis turned on his heels, and the man watched as he and Victor continued on their way.

"He's no merchant," Victor muttered.

"I know," Louis said. The vague apprehension he had been feeling of late felt suddenly more pronounced.

✠ ✠ ✠

Evening fell, and the sounds of commerce gave way to the nascent din of carousing. As the sun sank lower, the din grew louder. When darkness reigned, the transformation was complete, and the streets of Acre had become a different world from the one that had melted away. Sullen mercenaries, tipsy sailors, and gaudy, painted prostitutes appeared on the street as Louis and Victor walked past.

"And so it begins," Victor said.

"We'll find another patrol," Louis said. "Double our forces."

"Good idea."

They passed shuttered shops as they approached an intersection where the lights were coming up in the corner pubs. Louis spied a pair of Templars just past the intersection, headed their way. He was relieved to recognize Hugues de Canteleu, a knight who had been in Acre for nearly twelve years, and his sergeant, an Englishman named Gregory Longford. He hailed them.

They seemed as relieved as Louis felt at their meeting.

"How goes it?" de Canteleu said.

"Nothing strange," Louis said. "Yet," he added.

De Canteleu nodded. "Soon enough," he said. "We've heard grumblings. We'll need to be on our guard, especially here in the Venetian Quarter. There are rumors of a concerted attack on the Muslims."

"It's inevitable," Victor said.

"These latest arrivals with the Venetian fleet are particularly unruly," de Canteleu continued. "They're frustrated that they didn't disembark from their ships swinging their swords and lopping off Saracen heads from the gangplank before they even set foot on the docks. Now that they've found nothing but troubled peace, and restraint at the hands of the Orders, who knows what will happen? God knows half of them wouldn't know what to do with a proper sword, but that doesn't curb their enthusiasm for blood. It's a perilous situation."

Louis nodded grimly in acknowledgement. "We'll step lively," he said. "We should patrol in fours."

"Agreed," de Canteleu said.

They walked for several blocks, chatting lightly as they went, but focusing tightly on the ragged gangs and loitering thugs who seemed unified only in their longing for strife.

A dull roar rose upon the wind from the direction of the main city gate. It sounded like an approaching sandstorm. Louis considered seeking shelter, but as the sound grew louder and more distinct, he realized that it was not a storm. It was the sound of voices raised in a cacophony of fury and fear. It came from a mob that must surely dwarf any they had suppressed until now. With an exchange of alarmed glances, they raced toward the sound.

As they got closer, the sound grew deafening. A yellow-orange glow danced gaily above the rooftops ahead, and acrid smoke burned their eyes and throats. Whatever was burning was more than a bonfire. Louis did not smell burning flesh, and for that he was, for the moment at least, grateful. He cringed, nevertheless, at what they might find at the scene.

They came upon a drunken, malevolent mob that filled the street near the sheriff's station and stretched the distance to the bolted main city gate. There appeared to be no violence yet, except for the torching of several prominent Muslim shops. There were no Muslims in view. Louis spied a small group of men making their way up a set of stone steps that led to the parapet atop the city wall.

A booming voice rose above the din, and many stopped their

carousing to hear its message. Louis shushed Victor mid–sentence so they could better hear.

"How long?" the voice roared. "How long do we languish here without a purpose, without pay, and without the fight we came here to fight?" Louis strained to identify the speaker, a Corsican with the look and dress of an itinerate tradesman, who had climbed atop a wagon in the square outside the sheriff's station.

The sheriff, a skinny knight named Gervais who came from Troyes, stood powerless to quell the commotion that raged around him. He spied the Templars and raised his hands in a desperate plea for help. Louis, Victor, Hugues, and Gregory made their way toward him through the crowd.

"I've had enough!" the Corsican yelled. "I didn't come here for peace, or to trade with the paynims, or to be bullied by Templars and Italians!"

The crowd cheered wildly and pounded on walls and doors up and down the street.

"To hell with the cowards!" someone yelled from the crowd, to another round of raucous cheers. Louis glanced at Hugues with concern. Some in the crowd closest to them turned to stare as if gauging their reaction. All of them had obviously taken more than their share of ale or wine. All were in a surly mood.

"The paynims rob us!" the Corsican yelled. "Every day in these filthy streets! They call it commerce, but it's naught but robbery in the name of Allah! They leer at our women, they drool over our children. They're rats and dogs, scavengers for their false god!"

"Allah be damned!" someone screamed in a drunken rage.

"And we'll do the damning," the Corsican replied.

"Victor," Louis said quietly, "go to the castle. Quickly. Call out the Templars." One man obviously heard him, as he grasped another man's elbow and motioned for them both to depart. Victor nodded to Louis and left quickly. Louis watched warily after the two demonstrators as they disappeared into the crowd.

He turned in time to see a mercenary strike the sheriff in the face with a leathered fist. The sheriff reeled backwards and caught himself before he fell. Ruffians surrounded the sheriff, bent on venting their rage upon him. Louis and Hugues pushed toward them.

"Stop!" Hugues yelled. He positioned himself between the sheriff and the attackers while Louis restrained the man who seemed most likely to strike. Gregory Longford made a conspicuous move toward his sword, inducing the crowd to back down. "What in God's name do you think you're doing?" Hugues demanded. "This is the sheriff! You don't raise a hand to the sheriff."

"We're not going to live like this," said the man Louis had restrained. His accent was English. His face was dirty, and his clothing tattered. It was clear he had been deprived of both sleep and good food, but not of ale. He swayed unsteadily on his feet.

"Like this?" Louis said, nodding toward the commotion that filled the square. "You're right. You're not. It ends now, and you go home."

"No!" the man screamed. "Like this!" He clutched at the rags he was wearing and stuck a defiant jaw toward Louis.

"Are those the clothes you wore in prison?" Louis asked.

"Yes—" The man stopped abruptly.

"I thought so," Louis said. "You're here straight from the dungeon…in Lombardy?" The man nodded with a shamed look. "And this is worse than that?" Louis asked.

The man glared, recovering from his shame. "It's not what I was told it would be," he said. His indignation revived. "I was absolved! I was promised the chance to turn my life around, to find heaven in fighting for the pope. I did not come here to continue to starve or to return to a life of thievery to survive. What am I supposed to do?"

Louis did not have an answer. He shook his head. "You can't do this," he said, motioning toward the sheriff and the mayhem around them.

A small crowd had gathered around them, and the newcomers were prodding and whispering to the man, inciting him to further defiance. The Englishman drew himself to his full height, still wavering on his feet.

"Look!" a voice cried from the parapet. "Outside the gate!"

The crowd hushed and turned in unison toward the voice.

"What do you see?" someone shouted.

"It's an army!" The crowd gasped and moaned. The man continued: "It's an army of Mamluks come to kill us all! To arms! *To arms!*"

Louis knew there could not be an army outside the city walls about which the Templars had not been forewarned. There was no glow from torches or the flames of houses burning outside the gate. Surely, an invading army would have torched the outer city. He was shaken, just the same.

"How many?" Louis yelled.

"Thousands!" came the reply. "Mamluks!"

A new disturbance arose behind them, in the direction of the Templar castle. Louis turned to see the first of the knights responding to Victor's summons. A louder commotion resumed among the riotous mob.

"Kill them!" people screamed.

"Open the gate!" others screamed, and, "Kill them all!"

"Oh, my good Lord," the sheriff moaned, clasping his hands to his head.

Bolts and chains creaked as the townsfolk opened the city gate.

"My God," Louis said with a gasp.

The crowd poured out of the gate as it opened, brandishing swords and daggers and anything else that could serve as a crude weapon. The knights pushed through the mob and toward the gate, but their progress was slow against the crush.

Before they could reach the gate the air was filled with screams and chaos from the neighborhood just outside the gate. Now the glow appeared, and Louis knew the mob was setting fire to houses. When they finally got through the gate, he was appalled by the scene that greeted him.

The mercenaries and recruits had lost control. They rampaged through streets and alleys kicking through doors and dragging screaming residents from their homes. Some lobbed torches into houses or onto their roofs while others savagely beat their terrified victims.

The brutality immobilized Louis until he saw a filthy vagrant dragging a young girl by her hair from her home into the alley behind it. He bound toward the alley.

He entered the alley as the man slammed the girl, who was perhaps twelve years old, against the wall. He punched her in the mouth and pressed himself into her as she fell limp.

Louis felt a rage that he had never felt before. It took him by surprise, but he did not ponder it. His body moved before his mind could grasp it, and he brought his mailed fist down upon the base of the attacker's neck. The man crumpled to the ground, clutching at the girl's nightclothes as he fell. The linen gown was torn from her slender, olive–skinned body. She slid slowly down the wall until she was sitting naked at her attacker's feet, her onyx eyes filled with a dull, disoriented fear.

Louis found himself straddling the man's chest, hammering at his face in mindless rage. The girl yelped in dismay at the violence of Louis's reprisal, and the sound made him pause and turn to her. Seeing her nakedness, he forgot his rage and rushed to offer her his cloak.

"Louis!" someone yelled. It was Hugues, at the end of the alley. He and Gregory were struggling to subdue the beating of a sleepy Muslim man who had been torn from his bed.

Louis helped the girl back to the door of her home, where her mother waited in terror. The woman pulled the girl into the house, and she threw Louis's cloak, smeared with the girl's blood, out the door and into the dusty street. Louis retrieved it and joined Hugues and Gregory in subduing rioters.

Louis and Gregory seized a man who swung a rusty, pitted sword in a drunken, wavering arc with no particular aim. He nearly connected with Gregory's helmet, but Gregory deflected the blow with a crack of his heavy oak club on the man's elbow. Louis drew his own club from his belt and brought it down upon the back of the man's head. The man crumpled to the ground.

The streets were teeming with chaos. Moans and yells and

blood–curdling screams cut through the heavy night air. It was clear that countless people were dying or in terrible pain.

A crowd of twelve or fifteen rioters surrounded a pair of Muslim men who had been caught in the melee and were trying to make it to their homes with their lives. Shouts of rage went up from the crowd as it fell upon them, and the pair disappeared into its midst, shrieking in terror.

The three Templars exchanged glances as they calculated the odds.

"Swords," Hugues said.

"Yes," Louis agreed. He turned and saw to his relief that the Templars had finally made it through the gate. He drew his sword and lunged at the marauders. Hugues and Gregory were already upon them, and several had already fallen. He picked a target and swung mightily.

The man's back split open with a grisly sound. Louis cringed, aghast. He was seized by the realization that the first man he had ever killed in battle was Christian. He couldn't help feeling as though his world had turned upside down, and that he would never again understand it. He had killed a Christian in defense of the infidels.

A hideous scream rang out from the center of the throng, and it ended abruptly in a gurgling, choking sound. One of the men in the center stood up straight and triumphantly lifted the head of one of the Muslims, horribly severed and still feebly mouthing a futile plea for mercy.

Another man beheaded the second Muslim and held his head aloft.

Louis recoiled in horror. Everything had turned surreal. He felt as though he were suddenly under water, disembodied from what was happening around him, the deafening cacophony of sound moving far into the distance so that he could barely discern it.

He noted that Hugues had gone into a blind, frenzied rage. He was slashing and hacking at the crowd that beheaded the Muslims, and Gregory had followed suit. Louis worked to shrug off his shock and rejoin the fight.

The rioters turned to confront Hugues and the Templars, but the sight of crimson crosses on white dispersed them, and they melted into the chaos. Four of them lay dead at the Templars' feet.

The Templar army waded into the melee, some mounted but most on foot, and wherever possible they rescued unfortunate villagers from their attackers.

When the rampage finally subsided, the streets were littered with Muslim bodies, some raped, many killed, and the survivors wailing in pain and despair. Templars rounded up all the lawless they could capture and led them to the dungeons at the points of their swords. Swaggering, staggering, or trudging along, the rioters submitted to the force of arms.

Louis spied Gilles among them. Almost proudly, only barely unsteady on his feet, he marched in front of a pair of Templars. His eyes settled momentarily on Louis, blazing in anger at the sight of him. His lips curled in contempt, and he spat in Louis's direction. One of his captors shoved him violently so that he fell hard, landing on his face. The other dragged him blinking to his feet. Gilles apparently forgot about Louis as the knights propelled him toward the dungeon.

Louis surveyed the carnage. There were too many casualties to count, but he estimated that there were close to a hundred. Most were stabbed through with swords, or had their throats cut or their heads crushed. They were murdered with a brutality that Louis could not grasp, and what was left of them lay scattered in the streets.

Fires blazed as houses burned, and acrid smoke choked Louis and stung his eyes. The crackling of the fires grew evident as a somber silence settled over the scene.

Angry and fearful Muslims peered from doorways and windows. They avoided eye contact with the few Christians who remained in the streets, including the Templars and the Hospitallers who had fought to quell the crowd.

One Muslim, however, did not avert his eyes. A tall, powerfully built figure stood boldly in the doorway of a house, arms crossed and feet spread wide in confident defiance. Louis recognized the man from the scene of Gilles' attack on the merchant in the marketplace. The man met Louis's eyes with a steady gaze of his own, tinged with a mixture of sadness and resolve, and something else that Louis perceived as pity. He was disconcerted by the look.

Louis shook his head in helpless dismay at the carnage. The man turned slowly, his gaze lingering on Louis as he disappeared into the darkness of his house.

"Salim Abd al-Majid," Hugues said, nodding toward the empty doorway.

Louis looked at Hugues, then followed his gaze. "Who is he?" he asked.

"He's an important man," Hugues replied. "An informal liaison between the Grand Master and the Sultan...a secret ambassador. That man has been instrumental in the crafting of treaties and accord whenever such things proved necessary. Under normal circumstances, he is one of the most valued Muslims in Acre, if not in all of Jerusalem." Hugues shook his head. "Tonight, however, I suspect that he is simply the attentive eyes and ears of the Sultan Kala'un."

Louis nodded solemnly, surveying the death and devastation the rioters had wrought. "Then God help us all," he whispered softly.

Chapter 29

DAWN BROKE ON A SOMBER TOWN. Smoke rose from various locations outside the city walls. Christians and Arabs alike watched in silence as Templars stood guard and Arabs collected their dead. Anguished wails occasionally pierced the silence, echoing through the cobbled streets and alleys.

After decades of peaceful coexistence in Christian Acre, encouraged by the practical tolerance of the Templar Order, the unspoken truce was broken. Almost overnight, the city teemed with thousands of seething Arabs.

As the details of the massacre spread through the city, Arabs gathered in restless, murmuring groups. Venetians and Genoese merchants distanced themselves from the mercenaries, as well as from one another. The Arabs were encouraged by the appearance of growing division among the Christians, and the Templars prepared to counter violent reprisals. Civility deteriorated quickly.

Salim Abd al–Majid prepared for his journey to Cairo. Twelve would travel with him, close friends and relatives of the riot's casualties. They had collected blood–soaked remnants of the victims' clothing that they would use to strengthen their plea for the sultan's vengeance.

Salim had tried to discourage their thirst for revenge. He had pointed out differences between their long–time Christian neighbors and the latest arrivals from Lombardy. He suggested appealing first to the Templars for justice, noting the equanimity with which they generally managed conflict among the citizenry. His suggestions were met with outrage, and he realized the futility of his efforts.

They are right, after all, he thought. Who was he to dissuade them? They had the right to seek their own justice, and he had an obligation to champion their pursuit.

They left quietly long before dawn, as embers still burned and wives and mothers wailed. The streets were nearly empty but for wary Templars with ready swords, grieving survivors collecting their dead, and a handful of the most curious citizens. The rioters had all gone, either to jail or to their homes, to lay in sleepless anticipation of the consequences of their lawlessness.

Salim and the survivors set off for the court of the sultan Kala'un.

On their arrival in Cairo, Kala'un seemed hesitant to receive them. Salim pleaded with him, reasoning that if innocent Muslim merchants feared for their lives in Acre, then no Muslim in the Levant would travel there to trade, and the impact on commerce would be considerable. The sultan appeared to reconsider, but then shook his head and dismissed Salim with a wave.

Before Salim could respond, a guard appeared at the entrance to Kala'un's council hall.

"My lord," the guard said, "they insist." He shrugged and nodded toward a small, clamoring throng behind him.

Kala'un grew cross and snapped, "They'll wait until I call them."

The guard bowed deeply. "A thousand pardons, my lord," he said. "They insist that it has bearing on the matter at hand." Again, he shrugged, as if he could do little to dissuade them.

Kala'un huffed, then said, "Very well. Admit them. But not

all of them." The guard looked puzzled. "Three," the sultan clarified, raising three fingers.

The twelve briefly bickered before three were chosen to approach the sultan. The three entered the hall, an elderly merchant, a brawny sailor, and a young, grief-stricken mother. They approached the sultan respectfully, and placed their bloody bundles on the floor before him.

Kala'un eyed the clothing, then peered at the three with narrowed eyes. "What is this?" he asked.

"It's all we have left," the old man said. His raspy voice was feeble with grief, and his ancient eyes swollen and damp. "They attacked us in the middle of the night and killed our families like dogs in the streets."

"My wife and my daughter," the sailor said, stepping forward and pointing to their blood-stained clothing, "were raped and butchered before my very eyes, while the bastards pinned me to the ground and forced me to watch." His body shook with rage, and he shook his head. "I demand vengeance," he said.

The young mother knelt and clasped her hands. "I beseech you, lord Sultan: hear us, and seek justice for our beloved. They murdered my husband as he tried to stop them from dragging us into the street. And then, in the street, they murdered my children. They were so young, and so beautiful. To see them would melt your heart and convince you to spare nothing to keep them from harm. I beg you to fight for them now."

"You were not killed," Kala'un said. "Why not?"

"The man who killed my husband pressed a knife into my throat," she said. "Before he could kill me, a soldier stopped him."

"How?" the sultan asked.

"He killed him," she said.

"What kind of soldier was he?"

"A Templar knight," she said.

"The Templars intervened, then?"

"They stopped the rampage," the old man answered. "If not for them, we'd all be dead." The sailor nodded in agreement.

"Very well," Kala'un said. "I am sorry for your grief, and for your loss. You are all welcome to remain here in safety for as long as you like. I will see to it that you receive proper care, and comfortable homes."

"What will you do?" the sailor asked.

"If you choose to return to Acre," the sultan said to Salim, "I will see you before you leave." Salim nodded. "That will be all."

The guard escorted the grieving delegation to the door. Salim nodded his thanks to the sultan and followed them out.

The sailor turned to Salim. "What now?" he asked.

"We wait," Salim said with a curt nod.

✠ ✠ ✠

Kala'un summoned Salim to his council hall toward evening.

"You'll return to Acre?" the sultan said. Salim understood that it was less a question then a statement. He nodded. "I want you to deliver something for me."

He handed Salim two letters that bore his personal seal. One was addressed to King Henry of Jerusalem, and the other to the Templar Grand Master, William de Beaujeu.

"Give them both to de Beaujeu," Kala'un said. "He is to personally deliver Henry's letter, and keep his own private until it no longer matters. He will understand what I mean by that."

"Yes, lord," Salim said.

"I expect de Beaujeu to guarantee your safety until you return to me with his reply. I'll await your return before I take further action, but if you don't return in ten weeks' time, I will wait no longer, and I will proceed as if you had been executed."

Salim nodded his understanding. "Thank you, my lord Sultan," he said. "Will that be all?"

"One more thing," the sultan said. "Tell the Grand Master that I expect him to prevent a recurrence of this outrage. Tell him my patience is worn."

Salim nodded and left to prepare for his return journey.

When the council was seated in King Henry's hall, de Beaujeu handed Henry the letter from Kala'un. The king gazed at the letter in silence, and then he ordered de Beaujeu to read it aloud.

The letter was clear and direct. The sultan demanded immediate custody of the ruffians who had perpetrated the violence against the Muslims at Acre, all of whom were henceforth under the sultan's protection. The attackers were to be transported to the sultan's camp at Cairo immediately, under Templar guard. Immediate compliance carried the promise of peace. Failure to comply would be tragic.

King Henry sat stolidly, looking around the room for advice.

"It would be the prudent thing to do," offered de Beaujeu.

"Preposterous!" shouted one of the king's advisors.

"Under Templar guard!" another shouted derisively.

A furor broke out in the hall. Someone shouted, "*Traitor,*" and several others shouted their agreement. The king stared at de Beaujeu in astonishment.

"These are ruffians," the Grand Master said above the din. "They came here in disarray, untrained and unkempt, and they have brought with them nothing but trouble. Now, through their capricious stupidity they have broken the truce and inspired war."

"The Mamluks broke the truce at Tripoli," the king interjected.

"The Mamluks were called to Tripoli by Christians," de Beaujeu retorted, "to assist in a fight between Christians. We defeated ourselves at Tripoli, and then we abandoned it. The sultan took only what we lost to our own disunity."

"You are a traitor!" shouted another of the king's advisors. "You care only for Templar interests in these matters. You care nothing for the Christians that you would happily betray to Kala'un! How do you call yourself a Christian?"

"The *pope* calls me a Christian," de Beaujeu seethed, "and you would do well to mind your tongue. I am the kind of Christian that believes in honoring agreements, and would prefer to retain the Kingdom of God for at least a while longer." His nostrils flared in anger. He took a moment to compose himself. "The sultan only wants justice," he said, more calmly. "Those mercenaries should not have engaged in riot. They should not have attacked those Arabs. Some of you saw the victims yourselves. Many of them were children. Would you not seek the same justice, were they Christian children?" He turned to face King Henry. "We are honor bound to seek justice, and to maintain order in this city. We must do so if we are to retain control of this, our last real foothold in Jerusalem. We will be outnumbered nearly ten to one in war with the Mamluks, and you, my lord, may lose your kingdom to them...irrevocably." His words hung in the air. "I must insist…this is the only prudent thing to do."

"What you *will* do," thundered Philip, the king's bailiff, "is sit down, and cease your treason!" Philip stood and turned to the king, pleading. "My lord, do not give thought to the words of a self-interested man. He and his Templars stand to lose much if peace ends with the Saracens. They do business with those demons of the desert, and this man would forsake his own church and king to prolong his own profit."

De Beaujeu stood glowering at Philip. "Mind yourself, bailiff," he warned. "I'm a self-interested man? We'll leave well enough alone rather than follow that road to your own profiteering, both here and elsewhere." The Grand Master paused. "You'll not want to make an enemy of me, Philip." He glanced at the king and continued. "Unless, of course, you think yourself capable of protecting your king without me…"

Henry's face paled. Everyone well knew that the Templars owed fealty to none but the pope. Henry well knew that the Grand Master had no compelling reason to protect him, even while defending Acre. The realization held the room in silence for a long moment.

"We'll keep to the business at hand," de Beaujeu finally said. "Had these men killed Christians, they'd be at trial now, and hanged in the morning. Because they killed Muslims, we do nothing. Lest we be hypocrites, we are obligated to satisfy the sultan's reasonable request for justice. If we refuse, it will be to our great loss, in many ways."

He turned to the king. "My lord, my brothers and I are sworn to fight to the death in defense of God's Kingdom. Forgive my interest in preventing needless deaths, and the loss of precious resources. I have spoken wisdom here today. You must do with it what you will, and I will do as you command...to the extent of my conscience and my vows." He bowed slightly and returned to his seat.

The hall fell silent again as the king considered de Beaujeu's words. Finally, he made his decision.

"We will give no Christian over to the infidel for punishment," he said. "We will deal with the matter ourselves. It was an infraction against my subjects, within the walls of my city, and there is the lingering question of whether the Muslims instigated the affair in the first place. I will see that justice is done. I will not answer to a Saracen general, now or ever."

All but one in the hall agreed heartily with the king's decision. The advisors sneered at de Beaujeu as they prepared to leave the hall. The king gestured for de Beaujeu to remain. When the advisors had left, he spoke evenly and directly.

"Were you not a Templar, your words would be deemed treasonous. You implied that you would withhold your protection from my kingdom, my crown, and my person. You must know that your impudence is wearing thin. And your suggestion that we hand Christians over to the Muslim idea of justice is contemptible.

"Now, Sir William, I appreciate all that you have done until now, and all that the Templar Order has sacrificed in defense of my realm. I realize that many here owe you much for your loyalty and your efforts. But this is still a secular realm, and not a vassal of Rome. Do not forget that, and do not presume to dictate to me the manner in which I rule." He paused for a moment, then said, "The ruffians will be fined for their infraction against the peace. My answer to the sultan is 'no.' I will not convey the offenders, nor any other Christian, ever, as prisoners to him."

De Beaujeu shook his head. "Then you must know this, my lord," he said, producing his own letter from the sultan, which he had held beneath his tunic. "I am to go personally to Kala'un with your answer. He will offer to me his terms for your surrender. When I return to you with his terms, he will not be far behind me. You must prepare for war... and more wisely, for evacuation."

The king peered at de Beaujeu, as if he were lying. "You would do his bidding," he said with contempt. "You give in too easily. Have you no more courage than that? Can you see so clearly the outcome of a battle not yet begun?"

"I can see one hundred sixty thousand Mamluks waiting anxiously to spill our blood, and two hundred thousand more behind them, not far off in Egypt. They are all prepared to descend upon fifteen thousand of the finest Christian warriors in the world, who have defied their lawful request. And I can also see beyond the Mamluks, away to the east, where there are more than six hundred thousand Mongols whose requests for an alliance with us have been snubbed. I see a pope and kings who have ignored your own requests for reinforcements and support, and I see a ragged crew of misfits sent from Venice who are doing far more harm than good, setting torches to the kindling of a conflagration that will turn our dreams to ash."

The king glared quietly at de Beaujeu for a long time before he spoke. "Be that as it may," he said icily, "God will protect us against the heathens. And so will the Templars, to the death." He smiled sardonically as de Beaujeu dropped his eyes in disgust. "The answer is still no," he said with a dismissive wave.

Chapter 30

WILLEM'S FOOTSTEPS ECHOED in the darkness of the empty cobbled streets as he hurried toward the Templar commandery. The Grand Master had summoned him on some urgent matter, and his mind raced to imagine what it might be.

Grand Master William De Beaujeu was an introspective man who spoke only when it was necessary, and who divulged nothing more than what he absolutely must. To gain his personal confidence was a rare honor. Willem hurried out of respect, but also out of burning curiosity.

At the commandery, the lights were dim. De Beaujeu stood alone in the council chamber gazing through a window to the silent city below. The soothing sound of the Mediterranean waves washed over the room. The Grand Master did not turn to face Willem when he entered.

"Master, it is I, Willem Marti."

"Sir Willem," de Beaujeu said, "I appreciate your promptness. I have an urgent matter to discuss with you, in confidence." Willem caught his breath. He had never served as the Grand Master's confidant. He waited for de Beaujeu to continue. Finally, de Beaujeu turned to him with the exasperated look of a defeated man.

"Things are grim," de Beaujeu finally said. He related to Willem all that had happened in the king's council, and the contents of the letters from Kala'un.

"I depart in the morning for Kala'un's court, to bring him this unfortunate news."

"You won't return alive," Willem protested.

"I'll return alive," de Beaujeu assured him. "The Sultan and I have an understanding. He respects me more, it would seem, than does our own king. But I will return from Kala'un with an army at my heels." He paused and sighed. "Perhaps then I shall die."

Willem shook his head, speechless.

"Kala'un is a clever man," de Beaujeu continued. "He does nothing frivolous, or in vain. He sent me with letters offering peace, while I know he was preparing for war. He requested that I return personally with the king's answer, and I am wondering what he has planned for Acre in my absence. Surely, he too has anticipated Henry's reply."

"We'll stand ready," Willem declared. "You need not worry about Acre in your absence."

"Of course," de Beaujeu said. "But I didn't call you here to discuss the defense of Acre. I want to speak with you of a more personal concern." The Grand Master gestured toward the council table.

Willem was perplexed.

"Personal concern?"

De Beaujeu looked intently at Willem. "Louis," he said.

Willem raised his eyebrows, surprised.

"My nephew?"

"Of course, your nephew. He is in your charge, is he not?"

"In a sense, yes."

"Not in a sense. He is your greatest personal concern."

"Yes, he is. I'm sorry, Grand Master…of what interest could he be to you?"

De Beaujeu was silent for a long time. He paced the room

as if he were searching for words. Finally, he too sat in a chair and faced Willem.

"I know of your family, and its history."

Willem paled. De Beaujeu dismissed Willem's alarm with a wave of his hand and continued.

"It's something we have in common," he said. He grew contemplative, and sat quietly for a long moment, until he said, "One of your earliest memories must be that fateful day on the mountain top – the day of the burning at Montségur – and a battle-weary Templar astride a great warhorse..."

Willem's eyes grew wide. "Arnaud..."

"Yes, Arnaud. He was a close friend of my father, almost a brother to him. My father was there with Arnaud at Montségur. He covered Arnaud's escape with you and your sister. My family revered Arnaud, almost as a saint. For obvious reasons, I have never spoken to you of this. But the fact is that I have always been charged with your welfare, to the degree that I could influence it. By extension, I am naturally charged, just as you are, with your nephew's welfare."

Willem was dumbfounded by the Grand Master's revelation. De Beaujeu paused for a moment to allow it to sink in, and then he spoke with intensity. "There may be great things in Louis's future, Willem, should we get out of this God-forsaken place alive. I am beginning to fear, though, that we may not."

Willem nodded his acknowledgement. "What great things?" he asked.

"A future in the Languedoc," de Beaujeu said. "Our New Jerusalem. The Order has known for years that it is only a matter of time before the Mamluks push us into the sea. Since the beginning, and for almost two hundred years, this kingdom has been the sole reason for the Order's existence. But it has grown clear that no one cares about this kingdom any more. It has become a millstone around Europe's neck, and little more than an irritation to the papal throne. The Mamluks know this, too; they have offered us refuge with them, and a kingdom of our own, autonomous and secure in their land. We could coexist with them, if we chose to do so. We would trade with the Arabs and the peoples beyond their lands, and not rely upon Europe for our sustenance and support. But that arrangement would carry one intolerable condition: our conversion to Islam. While many of us have learned to respect the Mamluks, and to regard Islam as a legitimate faith, to claim that faith under those circumstances would be hypocrisy, and nothing more. Our oath is to Jesus Christ, and we will embrace that oath unto death. The riches of the world are not worth the defilement of hypocrisy or apostasy."

The magnitude of the Grand Master's revelations numbed Willem. He shook his head in awe. "The condition of the Crusade and the future of Jerusalem are self-evident," he said. "But offers of Muslim sanctuary, and discussions of conversion...these things I have not imagined."

"Not a word of it has ever been whispered outside the leadership of the Order," de Beaujeu said, "for obvious reasons."

"What future do you foresee for us?" Willem asked.

"The one we began to tell you after we spoke with Emir Salih," de Beaujeu said. "The Languedoc faces French domination. King Philip is even more ambitious than his father. He will employ any means to appropriate more territory. The so-called crusade against believers in the Languedoc, and the extermination of both the Good People and their culture were nothing more than tools of that domination. The king and his minions accused the population of heresy to gain the pope's blessing upon its subjugation. It is nothing more than theft by deceit; it will inevitably be reversed. As I say, if we leave this place alive, we will hasten that reversal."

Willem marveled at the magnitude of the treason in de Beaujeu's words. But he also understood their truth. Finally, he spoke, his voice cracking.

"What does this mean for us, here and now?"

"You and Louis will accompany me to Cairo," the Grand Master said. "The Sultan guarantees safe passage, and our visit has been arranged. Upon our return, we will defend Acre against Kala'un, but we will do so with prudence, and ultimately we will make our way back to the Languedoc."

Willem listened solemnly and nodded his understanding as the Grand Master laid out his plan. But as he left the Grand Master's company, he remained shaken. He realized that he had been mistaken in thinking his Cathar roots were long buried. He saw now that those roots had probably bolstered rather than threatened his standing in the Order. He wondered about the extent of Cathar sympathies in the Order, and he suddenly saw the history of the Languedoc in a new light.

The thought of the Templar Order without a Crusading mission troubled Willem. Whatever support the Order still enjoyed came from local Christians who counted upon the Templars to retain control and protect their business interests in Outremer. If Jerusalem were lost, that support would give way to bitter resentment. Templars would become but one more group of displaced warriors in search of a sovereign domain, should Jerusalem fall.

Willem contemplated that as he made his way back through the gloomy streets to advise Louis of their impending journey.

✠ ✠ ✠

The knock came soft but urgent. Louis rose as the door opened and Willem stood squinting in the light of the lantern that hung by the door.

"What is it, uncle?" Louis asked.

"We need to speak," Willem said.

Louis motioned for Willem to enter.

"It's late," Louis observed.

"Later than you know, Louis," Willem replied. He entered quickly, then turned and closed the door. Louis looked at Willem expectantly.

"You and I will rise early," Willem said. "You must have your squire and your equipment ready at dawn. We're going with the Grand Master to Cairo."

"Cairo!" Louis exclaimed. "To the Mamluks? Why?"

"Yes. To Kala'un, with the king's reply to Kala'un's demand for custody of the rioters." Louis noted the foreboding in Willem's voice.

"It's not good, then?" Louis asked, knowing the answer.

Willem shook his head in annoyance. "Kala'un will not be pleased," he said.

"We'll be in danger…" Louis said.

Willem shook his head again. "Kala'un respects de Beaujeu. He will not harm the messenger. We won't have to worry until we return to Acre with Kala'un's army on our heels."

"You're right. It's not good."

"Not good at all," Willem agreed. "On the way to Cairo, we'll discuss with the Grand Master many sensitive matters. You must be mindful to listen carefully, question sparingly, and maintain strict secrecy." Louis nodded. "Winds of change are blowing, Louis. You must prepare yourself for unexpected turns, and commit your support to all that is expected of you. Now, though, you must sleep well and rise early. Be ready with Victor at dawn." Louis nodded again. "And tell Victor nothing for now," Willem added.

Willem disappeared into the night, and Louis sat on the edge of his pallet, wondering what new adventures awaited him.

Chapter 31

A FAINT ORANGE GLOW teased at the eastern horizon, and the clinking of gear echoed in the empty courtyard below the solid fortress walls of the Templar quarter.

"Do you think Acre could fall?" Louis asked Willem.

He looked anxiously to his uncle as he checked the tack of his palfrey and Victor packed the equipment and supplies for the journey.

"It appears inevitable," Willem said. "The Venetians and the Genoese will not look past their differences. As they did at Tripoli, they will allow those differences to undermine our unity, and our ability to defend against attack."

"Why would we defend them, then?" Victor asked.

Willem looked patiently at Victor, whose doleful eyes betrayed smoldering anger.

"It's not the Italians we're defending," Willem said. "We're defending two hundred years of blood and sacrifice for the Kingdom of Jerusalem. If Acre falls, Jerusalem falls with it, and it will never be recovered. We will prevent that at any cost, and to the last. We will not abandon the Kingdom of God."

"Templars do not retreat," Louis reminded Victor.

"Yes, I know...even when it's hopeless," Victor said.

"Nothing's hopeless," Willem stated flatly, with a stern look. "We've sworn to fight to the death, if necessary. Remember that you made that oath as well, and pray to God for the strength to fulfill it, should it become necessary."

Victor glared briefly before he dropped his gaze. Willem's face betrayed growing misgivings about Victor.

The Grand Master de Beaujeu appeared from the shadows of the commandery doorway. His own squires had finished preparing his horses and equipment, and he seemed anxious to begin the journey. He motioned for Willem to walk with him a short distance from the others. They spoke in hushed tones, but in the early air their voices carried, and Louis overheard some of their discussion.

"How goes it with our young charge?" de Beaujeu asked.

"He's well," Willem replied. "His devotion is absolute. He'll give his life to support whatever serves the Order, and the Church."

"He's an impressive young knight," de Beaujeu said. "Men like him are reason to hope for the future."

"He struggles—" Louis strained to hear, but Willem's words grew muffled with distance. He thought he heard the name Montségur, and something about the Church, and then the Grand Master nodded in Victor's direction, and they appeared to be discussing him. Willem shrugged and shook his head as if resigned to something.

"What do you think will happen at Cairo?" Victor asked. His sudden question startled Louis, and his voice was edged with barely perceptible fear. Victor had grown increasingly uneasy over the past few months, and Louis had tried, in vain, to reassure him.

"De Beaujeu will deliver the king's answer to the Sultan, and the Sultan will be displeased," Louis said. "De Beaujeu will offer an alternative solution. We'll return to Acre with Kala'un's reply."

"Do you think they'll take hostages?"

"Not likely," Louis said. "There's no value in a Templar hostage, as everyone knows that the Rule forbids ransom for captured brethren. They'd sooner kill us, but that's not likely either. Kala'un would not harm a Templar diplomatic mission, even if he were inclined to do so. As deeply as some Muslims hate us, they wouldn't incur Templar wrath for no good reason. I believe we're safe." He placed a reassuring hand on Victor's shoulder.

"They wouldn't kill us," Victor said hopefully.

"They wouldn't kill us," Louis said. "De Beaujeu is friendly with the Sultan. While they are foes, they share a deep mutual respect. And this Sultan has never violated an agreement with the Order."

"He did at Tripoli."

"Had the rulers of Tripoli listened to de Beaujeu, that attack might never have happened. They were obstinate. They mocked de Beaujeu when he tried to broker peace among the Italians. The Italians called upon Kala'un, instead, to intercede in their bickering. He obliged them in his own fashion, and Tripoli fell."

"I'll have to take your word for that," Victor said. "But I don't like this. I don't trust the paynims."

"From what I've learned of them, their honor is legendary, and their treatment of enemies fair and civilized," Louis said.

"I'll take your word on that, too."

Willem and the Grand Master returned to them, and the party mounted and set out on their journey to Cairo.

✠ ✠ ✠

The knights marveled at the shimmering outline of Cairo as they approached, rising from the desert floor in the autumn heat, like a mirage nestled snug against the Mediterranean shore. An Arab shepherd stared in surprise as the Templar troop marched steadily toward the city, apparently free of earthly cares. De Beaujeu waved curtly at the shepherd, who raised a nervous hand in reply.

Victor glared as Louis nodded genially toward the Bedouin, who returned a narrow stare.

As the delegation approached the city, a Mamluk contingent rode out in battle dress to meet them. De Beaujeu and the knights did not break stride at their approach. Victor's right hand moved toward his sword, and Louis stopped him with a glare.

As the Mamluks surrounded them, they halted, and de Beaujeu held up his hand in greeting.

"*Marhaban*," de Beaujeu said in Arabic. "*Assalamu alaikum*."

"*Wa alaikum assalam*," the Mamluk commander replied. "Follow me. The sultan awaits."

The Mamluk commander took his position beside de Beaujeu, and the rest of the Mamluks surrounded the knights to escort them into town.

"Marwan," the commander said in introduction. He extended his hand to de Beaujeu.

"William de Beaujeu," the Grand Master replied.

Marwan laughed. "I know. I have heard much about you." Marwan turned to assess de Beaujeu's companions. "Kala'un will be pleased to have your company. He speaks highly of you."

"The Sultan is an honorable man," de Beaujeu replied.

"He is, indeed, praise be to Allah."

As the procession entered the city, people stopped and stared. Louis marveled at the industriousness of the place. The market was noisy and crowded as merchants hawked and buyers haggled. To Louis's surprise, some of the younger children waved to the Templars, smiling. Older warriors looked on with a mix of enmity and admiration.

Louis and the other knights noted, with knowing glances, that the Mamluk army appeared to be in a high state of readiness. Large units marched and drilled, lending a martial air to the demeanor of the population.

Marwan signaled them to halt when they arrived at the sultan's great hall. As they dismounted, he gestured to de Beaujeu to follow him. De Beaujeu signaled for Willem and Louis to accompany him as well. Marwan looked questioningly at de

Beaujeu, but then nodded his assent. The four men entered the hall under guard of eight Mamluk warriors.

As Marwan approached to announce de Beaujeu, the sultan uncharacteristically rose and approached them with his hands outstretched. Kala'un and de Beaujeu locked hands and kissed one another on each cheek.

"*Assalamu alaikum, ya sadiqi!*" exclaimed Kala'un.

"*Wa alaikum assalam. Allah ma'ak,*" de Beaujeu replied.

"And God be with you, my friend."

Louis was amazed by the display. He was beginning to see the Muslims as something more than the one-dimensional infidels of fable and myth, and the mindless oafs he battled beneath the oaks of his Languedoc home. There was warmth here that Louis found oddly comforting.

Willem leaned toward Louis and whispered.

"Don't be misled, Louis. They would take our heads in an instant, if it pleased them to do so." Louis was startled. "It's a warrior-friendship, Louis. In battle, Kala'un and de Beaujeu would not hesitate to kill one another. They would do so with respect, of course. Their friendship is based solely upon the mutual respect of noble warriors. Noble warriors respect the truce."

Louis nodded in understanding.

De Beaujeu and Kala'un spoke quietly for a moment, and then they turned to Willem and Louis. De Beaujeu placed his hand on Willem's shoulder and led him forward.

"My deputy, Sir Willem Marti, of the Languedoc," de Beaujeu announced. Willem was visibly surprised by his impromptu promotion to deputy to the Grand Master. "And his honorable nephew, Sir Louis de Garonne." De Beaujeu gestured widely toward Louis. "These are some of my most trusted men," he added.

"I am honored to make your acquaintance," Kala'un said in perfect French.

"As are we to make yours," Willem replied.

While refreshments were served, De Beaujeu and Kala'un exchanged more pleasantries before maneuvering deftly toward the business at hand.

"You've brought King Henry's response," Kala'un finally said.

De Beaujeu's face clouded over for a brief moment, and then he spoke with firmness and sincerity.

"The king would like to thank you in advance for your confidence in both his ability and his commitment to see that proper justice is done in the matter of the unfortunate clash." Kala'un's face grew dark as the king's rejection of his demand registered. "The perpetrators are in custody," de Beaujeu continued. "The king intends to try them in accordance with Christian law."

Kala'un was silent for a long while before he responded.

"There is no Christian law against killing Muslims," he said. "What penalty is there for an act that violates no law?"

De Beaujeu remained silent. The answer, which both men knew, would lead inevitably to war.

"My friend," Kala'un continued, "please do not patronize me. Let us speak plainly, so that we may both retain our honor. You have spoken well for your king, in his words. Now use your own, that we may find a solution to an impasse."

"These murderers are not Crusaders, as you well know," de Beaujeu said. "They're not even knights. They are peasants, mercenaries, and outlaws, and they are the best that Europe could offer in response to Henry's request for reinforcements. They came here looking for a fight, and instead they found us living in peace, side by side with Muslims. They've languished in the taverns with no income and no prospects for enrichment.

"On the other hand, these men are Christians. To turn them over to you would be to submit Christianity to Mamluk rule. Henry might just as well hand you the keys to Acre and sail home. No one would have such a thing; Henry might not survive the wrath of his subjects, should he acquiesce to your demand."

"He may not survive my wrath, should he not," the sultan said. "He will fight us, then?"

De Beaujeu nodded. "We will all fight you."

Kala'un appeared genuinely sad. He gazed at Louis, who admired the thoughtfulness that shone in his eyes.

"*All* of you?" Kala'un's question seemed directed at Louis.

De Beaujeu looked at Louis for a moment, and then he nodded, permitting Louis to answer.

"All of us," Louis said. "Each of us must do what our honor demands, and nothing less."

Kala'un nodded in agreement, pleased with Louis's forthright, measured words.

"Not only is he fearless," Kala'un said, tilting his head toward de Beaujeu and gazing appraisingly at Louis, "but he is a true chevalier as well."

"I regret the intractability of my king," de Beaujeu offered. "I had hoped he would be more conciliatory, and that he would take a more reasonable position despite criticism."

Kala'un shook his head curtly. "How could he? You spoke well. He has no choice, and I knew that all along. Of course, I am also left with no choice. Your king should have maintained better control of his men, and for that he is at fault. The question that remains is what will be the next move toward the inevitable." The sultan sat quiet then, in contemplation.

"I would seek with you an acceptable solution to this unfortunate situation," de Beaujeu said, "and some way of restoring the truce that has been broken. These seven years of peace have been fortuitous for all. The peace should not be ended over the actions of a handful of undisciplined mercenaries."

"The peace has ended," Kala'un said, "because of Henry's refusal to offer justice. Innocent, unarmed Muslims have died at the hands of criminals, my friend." He fought for a moment to suppress his anger, and then he offered a possible solution. "I have no compelling desire to kill more Christians," he said. "It is not the people of Acre that I want, but the city itself. I would be pleased to take possession of Acre peacefully, and I am sure it would please you to see no more Christians killed." De Beaujeu nodded. "I have a proposal for your king, though I suspect I already know his response. I will hold you to the task of making him see the obvious. You must make him see the light."

De Beaujeu nodded solemnly.

"Your time here is finished," Kala'un said flatly. "You know this as well as I. The only question is when you will all leave, and under what circumstances. Even if you were to defeat us at Acre in defiance of the terrible odds against you, and even if you were to go on and recapture all of Jerusalem, you would then face the Mongols, who are even greater in number than we. Your Kingdom of God is gasping for life, and it shall soon expire. I offer the opportunity for it to expire with grace, and with your lives and your possessions intact."

De Beaujeu nodded for Kala'un to continue.

"Your king will direct the Christians of Acre to remit to me one gold ducat for every soul. For each gold ducat paid to me, one Christian may leave in peace, together with all of his possessions. In any event, no Christian will remain in Acre. All will leave, either in peace, or in slavery, or in death. The Muslims of Acre will abide the Christian presence no more.

"As you have surely seen, I am prepared for war. I have pressing matters in Africa, and I shall go to deal with them within the month. It will not take long to regain the submission of the Sudanese. I will expect to have your king's answer before my return, and I will expect to find the gates of Acre open to me upon my arrival there. If I should find it otherwise, my disappointment shall be great, for in that event every Christian at Acre will surely die."

De Beaujeu considered the sultan's words at length. He knew full well that the sultan's army was preparing for Acre, and not for Africa. He did not believe for a minute that the sultan expected King Henry to consider his terms.

Kala'un's price for forty thousand Christian lives was a pittance. The amount made it clear that the principle was more important than the price, and that negotiation was irrelevant. To counter with a lesser amount would have been absurd.

"There are many Christians at Acre who would live in peace with the Muslims," de Beaujeu said. "Having been born there, some would prefer to remain among your people, even under your beneficent rule."

"None will remain," the sultan said. "At least, not as Christians."

De Beaujeu nodded his understanding. He did not see a viable alternative to the sultan's demand. He could conjure no respectable compromise. He would return to Acre with Kala'un's ultimatum.

"Understood," de Beaujeu said. "I'll depart at dawn to present your terms to Henry."

Chapter 32

THE COMMANDERS AND THE LEADERS of the Templar Order at Acre sat in conference with their Grand Master in the great hall. The night air was damp and musty, and uncommonly cool. It chilled Willem Marti to the bone.

The journey from Cairo seemed interminable. They stopped only when necessary, and slept very little. When they reached Acre, they left their mounts with the stable boys and went directly from the stables to the hall. Willem felt as though he could fall asleep walking, and he longed for the respite of his straw pallet. Now he sat wearily at the table in the hall, struggling to hold his bleary eyes open in the flickering, pale yellow candlelight.

De Beaujeu briefed the Seneschal, Jacques de Molay, and the Marshal, Peter de Sevrey, on his visit to Kala'un. De Molay recounted the mood and the events of the weeks since the party had departed. Things were quieter, the Seneschal said, but not better. Hostility still simmered.

A knock came at the door, and the Tyler entered to advise de Beaujeu of a visitor.

"An Arab," he said simply. "With news."

"Bring him," de Beaujeu said.

A very old Muslim, whose flowing robes of gold–trimmed scarlet attested to noble rank, entered and stood just inside the doorway. Without a word, he scanned the room, identifying each of the commanders. His eyes rested briefly upon Willem, and he turned with a questioning look to de Beaujeu.

"Sir Willem Marti," de Beaujeu said, "a new and trusted commander."

The man cocked his head momentarily, and then accepted the introduction. He walked to Willem and leaned into him, extending his hand.

"I am Emir Salih," he said graciously. "I am pleased to make your acquaintance."

"*Allah ma'ak,*" Willem said.

"May God be with you also," Salih responded with a smile before turning back to de Beaujeu. His ornate robes shimmered in the candlelight, and the skin glowed golden-brown. He clasped his hands against his chest, interlacing his long, bony fingers, and bowed slightly. "I bring news," he said.

"Sit, please," de Beaujeu said, indicating a chair at the table.

The emir sat gracefully. "*Shukran,*" he said. "The news is not good, my friend. You must prepare immediately to defend yourselves."

De Beaujeu shook his head with a troubled look and said, "Kala'un told me himself...he's off to the Sudan to quell rebellion. It was clear that he hadn't time for Acre, and that he would prefer to resolve this issue diplomatically."

The emir narrowed his eyes. "Yes," he said, "he told you that. But that was a ruse. At this very moment his agents are at Château Pèlerin, cutting wood for the siege. There is nothing more important to Kala'un, I assure you, than avenging the Muslim blood that was spilled in Acre."

"Why would he not tell me that?" De Beaujeu mused. He strummed his fingers anxiously on the oak table, pondering the news.

"He feels that you've broken the truce," Salih said.

"That *I've* broken the truce?" de Beaujeu said. He was about to say more, but instead he frowned and gazed through the window to the moonlit sea.

"Of course not you," Salih said. "But the Crusaders have broken the truce. He's heard enough tales of abuses, and that they grow more frequent and vicious with each passing week." He leaned toward the Grand Master. "You know of these things, no?"

De Beaujeu was hesitant, but he nodded his acknowledgement.

Salih said, "The sultan believes that an attack on a single Muslim is an attack on all of Islam."

"We've tried to keep them under control," de Beaujeu said.

Salih nodded.

"They're not Crusaders," said Jacques de Molay. Salih raised his eyebrows, and de Molay said, "They're mercenaries and murderers from the dungeons and gallows of Lombardy. They were absolved of their sins and sent here to do penance."

Willem Marti was shocked by de Molay's candor in the presence of the Saracen, but Salih appeared to empathize, and he smiled sadly.

"'*Go and sin some more,*'" the emir mused, distorting the Christian phrase of absolution with a wry smile. He nodded and said, "It was a weak show of support for your cause."

"Yes," de Beaujeu said. "More trouble than it was worth."

Salih sighed and sat back, folding his hands over his abdomen and staring pensively at de Beaujeu. The Grand Master waited patiently until the emir finally shook his head and spoke.

"They have lost Jerusalem for you," the emir said with finality.

De Beaujeu rose and walked to the window. He crossed his arms and shook his head wistfully. For a long time no one spoke, until finally the emir spoke again.

"What will you do?" he asked.

De Beaujeu turned from the window with a determined look.

"We will fight," he said.

The emir sighed in obvious disappointment.

"What would you have us do?" said Thibaud Gaudin with exasperation. "Surrender?"

"Depart," Salih said. "The sultan would much prefer that you leave peacefully. Go back to Europe."

"We haven't the ships to evacuate the city," de Beaujeu said.

"No one suggested evacuation," Salih said with a shrug. "Take your Templars and go in peace."

"And what of these people?" de Beaujeu asked. "They are our responsibility. They cannot protect themselves. We will not abandon them."

"It will be suicide if you stay," Salih said.

"The Christians of Jerusalem are our reason for existing," de Molay said, waving toward the city center. "If we abandon them, we abandon our very purpose. Without that purpose, our Order would cease to exist."

"It may cease to exist if you stay," Salih countered.

The Grand Master moved to stand beside the emir's chair. "Tell the sultan," he said firmly, "that I appreciate his concern for our welfare. I'm sure he understands what I must do, as surely as I myself understand it." The emir rose and nodded his understanding. "Go with God, my friend," de Beaujeu said.

"I will not see you again, *sadiqi*," Salih said. He grasped the Grand Master's shoulders and kissed him once on each cheek. "It has been good to know you."

"And you, Salih," de Beaujeu said.

"Fi aman Allah," Salih said.

"*Wa anta aidhan*," de Beaujeu responded.

Emir Salih left the hall, and the Grand Master took his seat. His shoulders sagged, and he sighed deeply. Willem had never see him quite so fatigued.

Willem leaned toward Jacques de Molay. "Why does that Saracen come to us?" he asked in a whisper, nodding toward the door that had closed behind the emir.

"He's a good man with a crucial purpose," de Molay answered. "He's part of the informal communication between the Grand Master and the sultan. If not for men like him, slights and misunderstandings would have unleashed bloodbaths over the last decade."

"There are others?" Willem asked.

"Several," de Molay said.

Willem shared the Grand Master's despair. There were eight hundred Templars at Acre. Reinforcements from Cyprus and Sidon could increase the number to two thousand. In addition to the Templars, there were another eighteen thousand fighting men at Acre, and that included the latest arrivals, whose fighting skills had yet to be tested against real opponents.

The fighting force of twenty thousand was half the population of Acre, and about a tenth the size of the army Kala'un could launch against it. Willem agreed with the emir: departure was the more appealing option. But as Jacques de Molay had said, it was not one they would consider.

"We'll send for reinforcements," Thibaud Gaudin said in a perfunctory tone.

De Beaujeu turned to face him with grave intensity. He shook his head. "No," he said.

Willem's mouth dropped open. He wondered if he'd heard the Grand Master correctly. Of the knights present, only Gaudin and de Molay displayed no surprise. Instead, they nodded in somber acknowledgement.

"Why not?" Antonio Bollani asked in disbelief.

De Beaujeu turned to his most senior knights, eyebrows raised. Gaudin shrugged in apparent ambivalence. De Molay nodded sadly. De Beaujeu turned to Bollani.

"We have long understood the inevitability of this day," he said. "What we are about to discuss here tonight remains secret until I say otherwise. You are not to repeat a word of it on pain of perpetual imprisonment. Do you understand?"

Bollani was taken aback. "Of course," he said. Willem nodded solemnly.

"Jerusalem will fall," the Grand Master said flatly. "Nothing will prevent that now. No European king cares enough to prevent it anymore, and the pope stands impotent before them.

The Italians would raise money and arms if they saw profit in it, but they prefer to expend their resources diminishing the profits of their rivals. Twenty thousand fighting men were lost to their bickering warfare, and in twenty years we have not recovered from that loss. King Henry wonders why we go to such great lengths to maintain peace with the Saracens; what else is there to do when we can't even raise an army strong enough to keep peace among ourselves?"

The Grand Master stopped abruptly, staunched his anger, and took a moment to compose himself.

"We have discussed the future of the Order," de Molay said to Willem, Bollani, and de Sevrey.

Willem raised an eyebrow, intrigued.

"Twenty years ago," de Beaujeu said, "after the War of Saint Sabas, Grand Master Bérard lost hope for the future of Jerusalem." Willem and Bollani exchanged puzzled looks. "He beseeched the pope and the kings of Europe to influence the Venetians and the Genoese, to convince them to forsake their rivalry and work instead to help revive the flagging Crusade. His pleas were ignored."

"I never heard a word about Bérard's disillusionment," Willem said, almost beneath his breath.

"Of course you didn't," said Thibaud Gaudin. "Until this moment, only three living men knew anything of it."

"And this would change the future of the Templar Order?" Peter de Sevrey asked. De Molay nodded. "In what way?"

De Beaujeu, Gaudin, and de Molay exchanged looks before the Grand Master answered.

"Without the Kingdom of God in Jerusalem," de Beaujeu said, "the Templar Order has no further purpose. With no purpose, we will lose whatever support for us remains. We are forced to establish a new purpose." He paused and fixed the newest commanders with a meaningful look. "We have done so," he said.

"May we know it?" Willem asked.

"You *must* know it now," the Grand Master said. "But first, you must swear to secrecy on the matter."

Willem sat back in his chair, astonished by the Grand Master's gravity.

"Of course," he said. "I swear it."

"As do I," said Peter de Sevrey.

"And I," Bollani said.

"Very well, then," said de Beaujeu. He rose and walked to a heavy, locked cabinet. He withdrew a key that hung from a chain in the folds of his tunic. He unlocked the massive cabinet and withdrew a sheaf of vellum, tightly bound. He undid the binding as he returned to his place at the table.

"It's time," the Grand Master said, "for us to look toward an alternative future." He nodded slowly, sadly. "It's time to shift our focus to a New Jerusalem."

Chapter 33

Grand Master William de Beaujeu entered the council hall at the Grand Maneir with the king's advisors, and they took their seats to await the king's arrival. The advisors nodded curtly toward de Beaujeu.

"How went the trip?" asked the constable, Amalric.

"Uneventful," de Beaujeu answered. He smiled weakly. "I'm alive." Amalric returned the weak smile.

"We are all anxious for the news," Philip, the bailiff, said. "We'll await the king, of course."

"Of course," de Beaujeu said in a caustic tone.

Several awkward moments passed as the king's advisors fussed with their sleeves or drummed their fingers on the heavy oak table. Amalric's chair scraped the floor suddenly as he pushed it back and stood for the king's arrival. The rest of those present in the room followed suit. The king quickly waved them back to their seats.

"Welcome back, Sir William," Henry said. "What news have you from Cairo? Are we at war?"

"Not at this moment, my lord, but war is not far off. I bring another proposal for peace from the sultan, and failing that, the certainty of war."

The king's advisors nodded solemnly. They did not appear to be surprised by de Beaujeu's words.

"And what is his latest proposal?" the king asked. "Does he now wish for me to hand him the crown of the Kingdom of Jerusalem?"

"Not exactly, my lord. He would, however, prefer a peaceful resolution."

"Excellent," the king said. "At what price comes the sultan's peace?"

"Forty thousand ducats, my lord."

The king sputtered in indignation.

"That much!" he roared. "And you're serious! You are? You're serious?" The king shook his head in fierce consternation. He struggled to resume a calmer demeanor. "Very well," he said through clenched teeth. "Go on. Tell me more of this so–called 'peace' proposal…"

De Beaujeu pursed his lips for a moment, and then continued.

"The sultan demands one gold ducat for the safe departure of every Christian in Acre." Everyone sat in stunned silence. "Respectfully, my lord," the Grand Master continued, "I urge you to consider the offer."

Amalric stood glaring at de Beaujeu. "You the king to consider this outrageous demand?" he said. "You suggest that we should just leave…without a fight?"

"I suggest that Henry should consider the proposal," de Beaujeu said. He failed to mask the weariness in his voice. "Or perhaps the more assertive alternative."

"What alternative?" Philip said with contempt.

"To stand firm and utterly defeat the Mamluks when they come," de Beaujeu said. He stood and paced around the table. "I would prefer, however," he continued, "that we not wait for them…that we take our army south immediately, and pitch it into the face of the craven infidel before he even departs from his camp." De Beaujeu glared at Philip as he continued to pace the room. "Our fifteen thousand warriors and two thousand murderous mercenaries will overwhelm Kala'un, though outnumbered ten to one!" The Grand Master's voice had risen in incredulous scorn. "We will crush them there, and then we will return to Acre victorious. Then we'll march north and retake Byblos and Tyre. "We'll recapture the True Cross," he said, seething, "and then when we return, we will rebuild Haifa, at long last. It will be the jewel of the newly revived Kingdom of Jerusalem."

The room fell silent as de Beaujeu's outburst echoed away down the empty halls. The king gaped at him in dismay.

Amalric nervously cleared his throat and extended a hand as though to calm de Beaujeu. "It's clear," he ventured, "that the Grand Master is already convinced that we should accept Kala'un's proposal."

De Beaujeu slumped into his chair, irritated and drained.

"Are you?" Philip demanded, leaning toward the Grand Master.

De Beaujeu heaved a weary sigh. "We have fifteen thousand seasoned troops," he said. "And of course, the additional two thousand mercenary 'Crusaders'. There will be no further assistance from anywhere, unless someone here is privy to something to which I am not." He glanced around the room as if expecting a response, and then continued. "Kala'un has more than a hundred thousand infantry and sixty thousand cavalry, all well-trained and primed for battle. His siege units alone outnumber us." The Grand Master shook his head in frustration. "And if, in spite of all that," he added, "we prevailed against impossible odds...what then? We'll be left to our peace in Outremer?"

A stony silence filled the room in response. De Beaujeu rose and paced the room again, with less fury.

"There are half a million Mongols to the east," he continued, his voice rising in genuine dismay. "They've cast their eyes on the Mamluk empire. They begged us for an alliance that would have tipped the balance in their favor and guaranteed our kingdom, in peace and in perpetuity. The pope and the Christian princes flatly refused. What do you suppose will become of us once we've miraculously vanquished the Mamluks, only to face the Mongols we rebuffed?"

Again, a sullen silence reigned. The king and his advisors stared stolidly at the Grand Master, who resumed his seat.

"I do not see that we have any choice," he said with finality. "We must accept Kala'un's proposal."

"Then you carry your treason too far," Philip charged.

De Beaujeu stood once more and placed a purposeful hand on the pommel of his sword.

"Take one step toward me and you will be hanged for treason," Philip warned.

De Beaujeu noted the fear in his eyes, and he advanced a step.

"I'm warning you," Philip continued. "Your cowardice and treason will not be tolerated here."

King Henry stood suddenly, blocking de Beaujeu. He turned to face Philip.

"There will be no violence here," he said firmly, "and no one hanged." To de Beaujeu he said, "And there will be no agreement. We will defend Acre to the last, and we will prevail. I will not abandon the Kingdom of God. You will prepare immediately to defend my realm." The king turned his back on de Beaujeu, ignoring his bow. He cast a regal gaze around the room, and then he spun on his heel and disappeared.

"You will carry out the king's orders," Amalric said quietly. It was more of a question than a command.

"Of course," de Beaujeu said. His jaw tensed as he regarded the king's fools. He bowed slightly and turned to leave the room. Philip opened his mouth to call after de Beaujeu, but he was stopped cold by Amalric's piercing glare.

Chapter 34

THE KNIGHTS HAD DOUBLED their patrols, and Louis now led a unit of four armed Templars on local rounds. He tried to maintain his affable relations with the local merchants, but most were unreceptive. His greetings drew awkward stares or averted eyes. Resentment rang in the voices of those who did bother to respond to his efforts.

"Why do you bother?" Victor asked after Louis suffered yet another icy reaction. "Why does it matter so much to you?"

Louis realized that he was not entirely sure why it mattered to him. He considered that he had come here to kill Mamluks, or drive them from Jerusalem forever. He had not given much thought to his desire to maintain friendly relations with the locals. He imagined that it must have been Uncle Willem's example that set the tone.

"I don't know," Louis said.

A foot soldier named Simon Cripplegate, who had entered the Order first as a serving brother before rising to the rank of sergeant, snorted.

"You're not afraid of them, are you?" he said. His expression indicated that he was jesting, but Louis felt he had meant it. "You can't possibly like them," he added.

"Why not?" asked Laurence de Eure, an older knight who had seen his share of battle in the thirty years he had spent in Outremer.

Simon turned to Laurence with an inquisitive look. "Why not?" he echoed. "They're paynims...infidels...pagans."

"They're people," Laurence said quietly, "worthy of our respect, at least, if not our Christian compassion."

"How many have you killed?" Victor asked brusquely.

Laurence stopped and looked blankly at Victor. "I—"

"These merchants," Louis said quickly, "have done nothing to harm us. They are not the enemy."

"If they're not, then who is?" Victor asked.

Louis looked past Victor to a group of Arabs who had entered through the Tower Gate at the eastern end of the city. He spied among them the tall, watchful man named Salim Abd al-Majid. Louis waved Victor to silence and led the troop toward the Arabs.

"Salim Abd al-Majid," Louis called out as they approached.

Salim turned in surprise. He nodded a subdued greeting. "*Assalamu alaikum,*" he said.

"*Wa alaikum assalam,*" Louis responded. "You've returned."

"Obviously," Salim said.

"Welcome," Louis said. He wanted to ask Salim for news, but he had abruptly recalled that Salim's association with the Grand Master was secret, and he stood awkwardly for a moment, saying nothing.

Salim sensed Louis's misstep. "Thank you," he said quickly. "*Ma'a salaam.*" He turned to walk toward the marketplace. Louis caught up with him, motioning to his companions not to follow.

"Salim," Louis called. Salim turned to face him. "Will you accompany me, please?"

Salim peered keenly at Louis. "If you wish," he said.

Louis turned and nodded toward the Templar castle. He would find Willem and turn Salim over to him; surely Salim carried a message from Sultan Kala'un. Laurence de Eure watched their departure with narrowed eyes.

Louis found Willem in the courtyard working with Antonio Bollani on battle training for a company of knights and foot soldiers. Willem withdrew from the training immediately upon seeing Salim, and the two men exchanged customary greetings.

Willem escorted Louis and Salim on a circuitous route between outlying buildings and to a rear entrance to the castle, concealed from public view. He brought them to a private chamber and went to find the Grand Master.

Salim studied Louis. Louis nodded at him, but held his tongue rather than appear to pry into matters that did not concern him.

"I've watched you," Salim finally said.

"I know," Louis responded.

"You are unlike the others." Louis raised his eyebrows inquisitively. "You demonstrate no hostility toward my people."

"I came here to kill them," Louis confessed.

"No, you didn't," Salim said. "You came here to fight for your Christ. That's different. Since the Muslims here have shown no hostility toward your Christ, you have found no cause to kill them."

Louis smiled at Salim's assessment, a conclusion that had evaded him until now. "I suppose you're right," he said.

"Yes," Salim agreed.

Willem reentered the room and beckoned Salim to follow him. He paused to consider Louis, then gestured for him to follow, too. They walked wordlessly down a long hall to a room in a distant corner of the castle, remote from the common areas.

In the Grand Master's private quarters, de Beaujeu stood and greeted Salim with a kiss on both cheeks. He noted Louis's presence and glanced at Willem briefly before nodding his approval. They sat at a small oak table with a single candle at its center.

"It's good to see you again, my friend," de Beaujeu said. "What news have you brought?"

"The sultan has died," Salim said.

De Beaujeu stiffened, his eyes wide with surprise. "How?" he asked.

Salim shrugged and raised his eyebrows. "It was sudden," he said, "and unexplained. Some suspect poison, and some suspect his emir Turuntay."

"Has Turuntay succeeded Kala'un?" the Grand Master asked.

"No," Salim said with pursed lips. "The son, al-Ashraf Khalil, has been confirmed as Kala'un's successor, and Khalil had Turuntay executed."

De Beaujeu sat back in astonishment. "The sultan worried over Khalil's competence, did he not?"

"He did," Salim said, nodding. "It is said that he privately lamented that he could not allow Khalil to succeed him. Most believe that Turuntay was the rightful successor."

De Beaujeu nodded, looking troubled. "What does this mean for us?"

"That is why I'm here," Salim said. His tone was grave. "Kala'un implored Khalil to proceed with his plans to attack Acre in retaliation for the massacre. Khalil intends to go farther than that; he intends to take all of Outremer and expel Christianity from the land." Salim paused to allow de Beaujeu to absorb his words. "And then," he added, "he intends to follow you to Cyprus."

"To Cyprus!" de Beaujeu exclaimed.

"He is more eager than ever to prove himself," Salim said.

The Grand Master absorbed the news in silence for a long moment. Finally he said, "I must meet with Khalil."

"No," Salim quickly replied. "You must understand that Khalil will receive neither gifts nor delegations; gifts will be burned, and delegations executed. Nothing will turn him back; do not waste your time. I tell you truly that if you do not have the good sense to abandon this land forever, then you must prepare for war."

De Beaujeu nodded in solemn silence.

Louis's heart pounded. Suddenly, he thought, the Crusade of his childhood dreams had become real, and the anxious peace that had disappointed those dreams was gone. The peace he had been tasked to protect since his arrival was turning out to have been an illusion. He began to realize that the world may yet turn out to be exactly what he had always thought it to be.

Salim departed, and the grand master went immediately to alert the King of Jerusalem.

✠ ✠ ✠

Henry and his advisors met grudgingly with de Beaujeu to hear the news he had received from his Saracen messenger. The Grand Master feared that his meeting with Henry would follow suit with his previous warnings, most recently to Henry, and a few years earlier, to Lucia, the Countess of Tripoli. He entered the room quietly and did not take a seat.

Henry received the Grand Master coldly.

"What is it now?" he demanded.

"News from Cairo," de Beaujeu said.

"And what are the infidel Kala'un's latest demands?"

"I would imagine," de Beaujeu mused, his hands clasped in front of him, "Allah's mercy and prompt admittance into paradise."

Henry narrowed his eyes as if he were being mocked. "What do you mean?" he asked.

"Kala'un is dead," de Beaujeu said flatly. "Khalil is sultan now."

"Wonderful!" Henry exclaimed. He stood, his arms extended to welcome the news, and his eyes animated with glee. "That's excellent news! The Saracens will be in disarray, and we have nothing to fear." The king paced excitedly. "Perhaps," he said, "we should send an army against him after all, as you suggested, while he is weak and in chaos."

De Beaujeu shook his head in exasperation. He was about to respond when Henry continued.

"But tell me," Henry said, his head cocked in puzzlement, "what of Turuntay? Did you not tell me he was to succeed Kala'un? How could you have gotten that wrong?"

"Turuntay is dead, too," de Beaujeu said, a bit too sharply.

"He is…?" The king seemed truly perplexed by that.

"Khalil had him executed."

Henry nodded. "That was a bold move," he said.

"Yes," de Beaujeu said. "Quite."

"What do you make of it?"

De Beaujeu finally sat and folded his hands on the table in front of him. "I make of it only what I have been told," he said, "by a trusted source from the sultan's court."

"By a spy," the king said.

"By a liaison."

"You have liaisons with Khalil, too?" Henry cast a deprecatory look around the room.

"This man was a trusted liaison between Kala'un and myself." De Beaujeu's voice was acid. "His future with Khalil is uncertain."

"And what has your 'liaison' told you?"

"To prepare for attack."

"Oh?" the king said doubtfully.

"He said that Khalil means to finish what his father had started," the Grand Master said. "He's certain that Khalil will send the bulk of his force against us, and that nothing will sway his resolve. He advised us to abandon Acre, and the rest of Jerusalem, or risk annihilation. He said that if we stay, Khalil intends to pursue us all the way to Cyprus, and relieve you of your kingdom in its entirety."

Henry smirked, and then chuckled. "And you believe him," he said.

"Yes," de Beaujeu said. "I do."

The king's advisors also laughed, and the king turned to them. "What do my advisors think?" he asked.

Amalric seemed uncertain. "Perhaps we should question the messenger ourselves," he suggested.

"Absolutely not—" de Beaujeu began.

"No," said Philip. "We would be fools to believe anything he says. Instead, we should send a delegation to Kha—"

"No," de Beaujeu snapped. "Khalil specifically demanded that we *not* send gifts or emissaries. He will burn our gifts and execute our messengers."

"Then we will send a Templar," Henry said with an imperious air.

"To his death?" de Beaujeu shouted.

"A sultan would not kill a Templar messenger," Philip said dryly. "The Templars are his friends."

De Beaujeu stared at him in disbelief. "No Templars will go," he said.

"They will if I say they will!" the king bellowed.

"I command them," de Beaujeu said.

"And I command you," Henry said. "Do you defy your king?"

"I won't send my men to certain death for no good reason," de Beaujeu said.

"You would defy the King of Jerusalem?" the king asked. "You're willing to explain your defiance to Pope Nicholas?"

"Your delegation will accomplish nothing," the Grand Master said. "The sultan himself has made that clear. Sending good men to certain death is folly. I will not support it."

"Your support is irrelevant," Henry said. "You answer to the pope, but you serve your king, and I am your king. Your cowardice is bordering on treason; your defiance exceeds all bounds."

The king's advisors leaned forward in anticipation of the Grand Master's response.

De Beaujeu glared at each of them and shook his head in contempt. "You have no idea what you're doing," he said. "You have no one to blame but yourselves." He huffed and pointed at the king, saying, "It will be you, my lord, who will one day explain to the pope the consequences of this decision."

The Grand Master bowed curtly, then turned and stormed from the room.

✠ ✠ ✠

"Find Salim," de Beaujeu snapped.

Louis looked up in surprise. He had not heard the Grand Master return from the king's Grand Maneir.

"Yes, Grand Mas—," Willem began.

"Not you," de Beaujeu said. He pointed at Louis. "You!"

"Yes, lord," Louis said. "Right away."

"Tell him," de Beaujeu said, "that I beg of him…hurry to the sultan, and plead with him for the safety of my men. Khalil must know that Henry sent them against their will and mine."

"Yes, my lord," Louis answered. He ran into the darkness to find Salim. He had an idea where to find him.

He ran to the entryway beside the bolted city gate and pushed it open. He hurried through the streets until he turned a corner onto an alleyway that was forever burned into his memory. He slowed and approached the merchant's house with reverence.

The merchant's young daughter had died a few days after the rampage from the injuries she had suffered at the hands of her rapist. He had subconsciously avoided the house out of shame for the actions of the marauders. He approached it now because he had no choice.

He knocked softly, dreading the response.

The door opened a crack, and then slammed shut. Louis waited a moment and knocked again.

"I'm sorry," he called, as gently as he could. "I must speak with Salim." He thought with a start that Salim might very well not be inside, in which case he would have to search the town for him, and in which case the occupants must be terrified by his late intrusion. He was about to turn from the door when it reopened.

Salim's figure filled the doorway. He exited the house quickly and pulled the door shut behind him, fixing a piercing gaze upon Louis.

"What do you want?" Salim asked in a hushed voice.

"I'm sorry," Louis said. "I've a message from the Grand Master." Salim nodded for him to continue. "The king is sending messengers—"

Salim gasped and shook his head.

Louis continued, "—with gifts. He is acting against the Grand Master's counsel. He's sending Templars among them, out of contempt for the Grand Master. My lord begs that you will plead for the lives of these men, and try to prevent their execution."

Salim glared at the stars, curling his lips in anger. "There is no end to the arrogance," he lamented. Louis was inclined to agree. "Tell Sir William," Salim finally said, "that I will do what I can, but I make no promise."

Louis nodded. "Thank you," he said. He bowed to Salim and turned to go.

He had taken a few steps when he suddenly turned back.

"Salim," he called. Salim stopped halfway through the door and turned back to Louis. "Why?" Louis asked. Salim furrowed a questioning brow. "Why do you do this?"

Salim stepped back into the alley and closed the door behind him.

"For Allah," the tall Saracen said with tranquil, thoughtful eyes. "So that you may see how my God teaches me to live."

The two of them locked eyes for a long moment, until Salim smiled warmly at Louis. "God be with you," he said. "I will do my best."

Louis turned and walked through the darkness to report that the message had been delivered.

Chapter 35

The Grand Master, William de Beaujeu, gritted his teeth and glared over the rampart into the desert plains that lay between the sea coast to the north and the mountains to the east, beyond which lay Lake Huleh and the Sea of Galilee.

Louis marveled at the composure with which the Grand Master had shrugged off the ridicule and abuse he had suffered at the council of Acre, at the hands of the various factional leaders and the King of Jerusalem's advisors. They had gone so far as to call for his hanging for treason, but it was an empty cry, as none but the pope had the authority to judge, let alone to punish a Templar knight.

De Beaujeu declared that his persistent appeals to King Henry's common sense had failed, and that the partisan divisions among the leaders of the town were crippling. He had no choice but to muster the most effective defense of Acre that was possible, in spite of them. The stubborn dismissal of his advice was a maddening repetition of that of Tripoli's leaders just two years earlier, and the Grand Master was certain that the outcome at Acre would also be the same.

It was April 4th, and the king's delegation had not yet returned from as–Salahiyah. There was no official word of their fate, but merchants and seamen were whispering down the alleys and along the wharves ghastly tales of the envoys' demise. They had been skinned alive, some said, and roasted on spits. Others had heard that their limbs were removed, one joint at a time, until the sultan himself, driven by their screams, beheaded them with his own scimitar. They'd been fed to dogs; of that, all were certain.

The Grand Master's stoicism in the face of such tales made Louis wonder if he had received more credible news. If he had, he was keeping it to himself.

King Henry, on the other hand, was frantic. Before he departed for Cyprus, he had sputtered furiously about godless infidels and wrathful revenge, and he ordered the Templar Grand Master to prepare for war.

Louis had smiled inwardly then, as Henry, at once regal and disarrayed in his fluttering robes, descended the steps to the dockside; the Grand Master had started preparing weeks ago, the morning after the king sent his men to the sultan. The armies at Acre were as ready as they would ever be for the Saracens' attack.

De Beaujeu went off to inspect troops and weapons. Louis accompanied his uncle as he made his rounds among his troops, and the evening sun set upon eighteen thousand anxious and eager Crusaders. They were knights and squires, sergeants and sailors, merchants and mendicants, Templars and thieves – a motley assortment that was the last great hope for the Kingdom of God in Jerusalem. Louis shook his head as the evening darkness fell.

Dawn came early, and the chapel bells chimed the call to Prime. Louis was thankful, for his fitful efforts to sleep had grown frustratingly futile. He roused Victor, who did not share his disquiet, from a sound slumber.

They made their way to the chapel. The stone hallway echoed with muffled murmurs and yawns that were silenced by the sudden shrill of the call to arms.

The attack had begun.

Louis and his brethren raced to the armory to supplement their standard weaponry with lances, bows, arrows, and maces. From there they streamed to the ramparts through city streets that were lit by the ghostly glow of the pre–dawn moon.

At the rampart, Louis was stunned by the magnitude of the horde that stretched like an ink–black stain that filled the space between the edges of the city and the reaches of the dissipating darkness.

As dawn broke, Louis stared in silent awe. A vast sea of Saracen tents filled the Phoenician plain as far as the eye could see, from the sea coast toward Tyre in the north, to the foothills of the Naftali mountains to the east, and extending south to the foothills of Mount Carmel and back into the plain of Megiddo. Louis had never seen so many people, let alone heavily armed warriors, gathered together in one place. He was staggered by the thought that every last one of them would kill him where he stood.

Clamoring throngs from the village outside the city wall were straining at the gates, their panic pushing them to the brink of deadly stampede. Hospitaller knights barked urgent orders in an attempt to forge the mob into an orderly procession. Louis looked beyond the chaos once more to the Saracen tents.

The sultan's tent, the largest of all, stood atop a small hill by the seacoast to the north, just beyond the reach of Acre's most effective trebuchets. It was pitched with its entrance facing Acre. Its crimson fabric, hemmed in gold and festooned with the sultan's intricate rosette, undulated softly in a gentle breeze. It stood in stark contrast against the white and tan tents of the Saracen army.

"The sultan's tent," Willem said, "is pitched in the direction of the sultan's objective. It's symbolic." He pointed toward the crimson tent. "He intends to overrun Acre. If his *dehliz* were facing to the north, it would indicate Sidon as his ultimate intention, and Acre as a distraction along the way."

"*Dehliz?*" Louis said.

"It means 'vestibule,'" Willem replied. "It's the sultan's command tent, where he meets with his emirs, or discusses terms with his enemies." He nodded grimly toward the tent. "That," he said, "is the head of the demon."

Throughout the day and most of the night, the Mamluk army occupied the plains in quiet repose. Before dawn on the second day, a lone drum sounded a plaintive beat from the far eastern edge of the plain. For almost an hour, it pounded a slow, solemn rhythm that eventually started to grate on Louis's nerves. It finally faded, but before Louis could thank God for that, another drum took up the beat far away to the north. When that drum ceased, another sounded from the south, somewhere on the plain of Megiddo. Louis was curious at the random progression of the drumming until he realized their insidious purpose: they were illustrating for the Christians the vast breadth of the enemy arrayed against them.

The drums continued, slow and doleful, day after day, without a break. Occasional forays outside the walls inspired clashes that brought no great losses to either side. The Crusaders probed and the Mamluks parried until finally, on a cool and sunny morning, the Grand Master assembled a troop to launch a frontal assault against the Mamluk force.

He rode with Jean de Villiers, the Hospitaller Grand Master, leading a hundred Templar knights and three hundred foot soldiers against the front line that opposed the Lazarus Gate, on the sea coast at the north of the city.

The gate opened briefly, and the knights charged hard in the standard Templar V–formation. They charged directly into the front lines, their swords and maces wreaking devastation. As they pushed into the Muslim ranks, they swung hard to the right, driving a wedge between a segment of the front line force and the rest of their army. The foot soldiers rushed to the destruction of the isolated forward line.

The expedition took a turn for the worse as the Mamluks recovered from their surprise and rallied against the Templars. De Beaujeu shouted the command to retreat as more than a thousand Mamluk horses rode hard against them. The Templars made it safely to the Lazarus gate as the Mamluks closed in, having lost eight knights and more than two dozen foot soldiers, but having taken more than three hundred of the enemy's front line infantry.

The Mamluks retreated to their line and did not retaliate. The drumming continued as if nothing had happened, and night fell on the first brief day of fighting.

Similar clashes punctuated the next four days, but the Mamluks still did not attack the wall. After each clash, they retired to their line and waited – for what, Louis could not imagine.

On Friday, April 13th, dawn broke to the louder sound of many drums, pounding a new rhythm in unison. The Crusaders rushed to their positions at the walls and the gates.

Louis found his uncle on the ramparts near the Lazarus Gate with the Grand Master William de Beaujeu and the Templar command. They were shouting orders as their contingents formed and took their prearranged positions along the wall. Dozens of siege engines lumbered slowly across the hilly plain toward the garrisoned walls, urged along by the teeming Mamluk horde. One of the engines took a position north of the city, opposite the Templar defenders. Others moved to similarly strategic points along the walls, facing the Hospitallers, the Pisans, and King Henry's forces.

"This does not look good," Victor muttered in Louis's ear.

Louis nodded grimly, gazing out from the wall as the first feeble rays of sunlight illuminated the army arrayed against them. It seemed to have grown larger with each passing day.

"There must be a hundred thousand," Louis said in muted awe. "Or more," he added.

Victor crossed himself in silence. He pointed to the massive trebuchet that had approached their position, and the single Arabic word painted across its front. "What does that say?" he asked Willem.

"*Ghadhban,*" Willem said. "It means 'furious.' I'd say it reflects Khalil's disposition just now."

A horn sounded from the sultan's tent. At the sound of the horn, the vast horde moved as one.

In the silence on the parapet, a choked gasp came from among the defenders. Louis turned to see the king's brother,

Amalric, the constable of Jerusalem, standing wide-eyed, his mouth agape at the sight of the Mamluk force. His hand moved absently to his mouth. The Grand Master, a few yards away, had also heard Amalric's involuntary gasp. He turned at the sound, and he failed for a fleeting moment to conceal his contempt for the king's brother.

Another horn sounded from across the plain, and the trebuchets and a dozen mangonels launched the first of their projectiles. Boulders crashed against the city walls and into the houses that clustered around them. The shuddering impacts roused the Crusaders from their astonishment, and Amalric turned and fled down the steps from the rampart.

"Launch!" the Grand Master screamed to the trebuchets on the ground. Boulders the size of ale barrels sailed overhead, arcing toward the Mamluk horde. It seemed to Louis that the teeming mass simply absorbed the massive projectiles. The trebuchets had no apparent effect.

"Again!" de Beaujeu shouted. In moments, the air was filled with the wail of sailing projectiles, and the stone beneath Louis's feet shuddered and swayed under crushing blows. The defenders steeled themselves for the inevitable approach of the siege towers.

Hours passed as the two sides traded boulders. Louis stood in anxious silence on the ramparts with Willem and Victor.

"What will happen?" he asked.

Willem sighed heavily and pursed his lips. "Just this, for a couple of days," he replied. "Maybe longer. Then they'll send a messenger to offer terms."

The hours dragged, and Louis was left with little to occupy his mind. A feeling of futility and despair gnawed at him, and he found himself increasingly troubled by a sense of incalculable loss.

Nothing had turned out the way he had imagined it would.

He contemplated his childhood fantasies, which seemed to him more absurd with the passage of time.

He had imagined the Crusade as a relentless, heroic conquest of the Saracen infidels by faithful and cohesive Christian legions, the signature wedge-shaped charges of the Templar vanguard splitting enemy armies asunder so that other Crusaders could crush them into the ground. Yet, here they languished day after day, lining the crumbling ramparts of the last Crusader stronghold waiting for a Saracen messenger to offer the terms for their surrender.

He had fancied himself Colette's champion, her pride and her protector. He would probably never realize that childhood role, and he felt foolish at the memory of it.

The pounding continued day and night for nearly a week, and still there was no sign of messengers, or terms. The defenders slept fitfully, when they slept at all, in their places atop the ramparts.

"They're not going to offer terms," Victor said on the fourth evening of the steady trebuchet siege. The trebuchets had taken a toll. The Christians of Acre had fallen into a woeful pall.

Louis suspected that Victor was right. "We can't just sit here and wait to be slaughtered," he said.

"What else is there for us to do?" Victor replied.

At that moment, Willem left the commanders who stood huddled around the Grand Master and approached them. Louis sensed that a decision had been made, although he couldn't imagine what it might be. Willem nodded curtly to Victor, and then spoke to Louis.

"We'll send out an attack," he said. "A third of our horsemen, when night falls."

Louis was surprised. "Two hundred knights?" he said. "Against two hundred thousand?"

"Three hundred," Willem said, as if it made a difference. "It's better than waiting."

Victor nodded reluctant agreement.

"One thing is certain," Willem continued, nodding toward the Saracen horde, "it's the last thing they'll expect."

Louis agreed. He shook off his torpor and rallied his fervor. "Who will go?" he asked.

"They're deciding that now," Willem said. "Brother Bollani wants to lead." He paused, then said, "I'll go, too."

Louis looked past Willem to the commanders. Antonio

Bollani stood tall and resolute, his feet firmly planted and his shoulders thrown back, and his face set in an expression of firm defiance. Of all the commanders, he cut the most imposing figure. Louis had never quite reconciled the curious disparity between Bollani's fierce warrior's demeanor and the shadowy image in the softly moonlit corner of the kitchen pantry.

"What will we do?" Victor asked.

"They're discussing the details," Willem said. "We'll slip through the Lazarus Gate under cover of darkness. We'll attack in silence and kill as many as we can before the Mamluks can mount a resistance, and we'll return, God willing, before we take losses."

"I hope the good Lord is smiling upon us," Louis said. He was torn between his desire for battle and his reluctance to die. He was about to speak when Willem held up a hand.

"You'll stay with me," he said. "*Close* to me." He turned to walk toward the commanders, and Louis followed. Willem said over his shoulder, "I'll take our men and a Venetian company. Bollani will take his own men, and Osbourne's. De Grailly's regiment will go, too."

Louis nodded as they approached the commanders and caught the tail end of the Grand Master's plan.

"—with Grandison and the Pisans," de Beaujeu was saying. Willem gave him an inquiring look. "We've decided," de Beaujeu said, "to send Grandison and the Pisans through Saint Anthony's gate to provide a distraction in the event we raise an alarm or face opposition too early." He nodded to Louis. "You'll fight with us this time," he said. "I pray we will do well tonight. It's a good plan."

Louis nodded enthusiastically.

✠ ✠ ✠

The full moon rose high. A sentry quietly opened the Lazarus Gate long enough for the Templars to slip out onto the moonlit plain. The knights moved cautiously so as not to raise an alarm.

De Beaujeu assigned a knight named Percival to the task of carrying a cloth–bound bundle of Greek fire, and a glowing ember with which he would ignite the bundle before he threw it directly onto the great trebuchet called 'Furious'. Percival betrayed only a momentary hint of reluctance at the task before he grasped the bundle and the ember with a flourish and tied it to the neck of his mount.

Louis reined Invictus back to steady his anxious gait, and he steeled his own tingling nerves. He had trained for this, of course, but for the first time in his life he would engage armed Saracens in battle. Until now, the only Muslims he had known he had met in Acre, and many of those he had befriended. He mentally separated those he had befriended from those he intended to kill.

The moon shone brightly, which increased the risk of getting close enough to the Furious to destroy it.

They roused no response from the Saracens as they approached the Furious. Percival lit the missile and drew his arm back to launch it toward the trebuchet. He glanced around nervously for a moment, as if he had heard some noise. He shrugged it off and launched. A split second before he released the missile, it flared prematurely with a deafening *whoosh*. He panicked and released the Greek fire a moment too soon; it flew in too low an arc, landing harmlessly on the ground a full twenty feet from its target.

The flames flared high, sputtering and illuminating the field around it. The sound and the light alerted the Saracens in the vicinity, and they sprang to their feet and to their weapons.

The knights rallied and rode hard into the mustering Mamluks, swinging their swords and maces for all they were worth. Louis bore down on a sergeant who had barely gotten his sword from its scabbard, and he swung hard to sever the arm that held it. He flinched in spite of himself and withdrew his sword at the last moment, riding harmlessly past the bewildered sergeant. He cursed himself and spun around for another pass.

Enraged by his reluctance, he spurred Invictus and drove hard toward the Mamluk sergeant. This time he swung his sword without hesitation and took off the sergeant's head. His sword passed through the man's neck like steel scraping on stones. The sound of it turned his stomach.

He turned and watched as the body sank to the ground beside its gruesome, lifeless head. He imagined that the sergeant still saw him, for he couldn't imagine that death could be so sudden. A surprising amount of blood pooled on the ground.

"*Louis!*" Willem cried.

The sound jarred Louis, and he realized that his uncle had been frantically calling his name. He turned toward Willem.

"*Fight!*" Willem screamed.

Louis nodded and turned as several mounted Mamluks headed toward him. He raised his sword in his right hand and his mace in his left and set his mind to battle. He drew a deep breath and charged at the approaching Mamluks.

Templars appeared from all sides as if they'd been conjured by magic, and they closed in on the group of charging Mamluks. Louis swung hard and blocked the carnage from his mind. His training took hold and his movements became automatic. Before the reality of it registered, he had felled three more Saracen knights.

De Beaujeu signaled retreat. The Templars had moved farther into the Mamluk encampment than they had planned. Most of the Mamluks closest to them scurried for safety, but others were taking up arms to counter the Templar attack.

The knights turned hard to retreat, as the foot soldiers had already done. Louis wheeled Invictus around and leapt over fallen Mamluks and their weapons that were scattered on the ground. Invictus ran up against the ropes of a Mamluk tent, throwing him momentarily off balance. Louis cursed and held tight as Invictus reared to avoid the ropes.

A loud crash sounded from among the tents, followed by several more and an anguished scream. Louis realized that other knights were also getting caught up in the ropes of the tightly grouped tents, and some were being thrown from their mounts. More screams followed as Mamluks slaughtered the ill-fated knights.

He looked frantically for a clear path to the perimeter of the encampment, and when he saw one he spurred Invictus to a gallop. He broke the perimeter and raced a dozen yards toward the wall. He turned to assess the status of the retreat, and to locate Willem and the Grand Master. The Templars were in chaos as they tried to escape the close quarters, but most were breaking free.

Willem emerged from the fray with two Saracen knights close behind him. Louis spurred Invictus again and raced to head them off. Willem saw him coming and turned to join his assault. The Saracens veered in a wide arc to avoid them, returning to their camp.

De Beaujeu repeated his call to retreat. His voice rang out from a short distance away, just inside the perimeter of the camp; he would be the last to retreat, and he would go to the aid of any of the fallen who had not been killed. Finally, as the screaming had ceased, he too emerged from the camp and raced toward the wall. The knights dashed toward the Lazarus Gate, slowing as they caught up to the retreating foot soldiers.

Once inside the gate, the Grand Master and the commanders assessed their losses. Eighteen knights and two dozen soldiers had fallen. Grandison and the Pisans had barely gotten out of Saint Anthony's Gate when Mamluk sentries spotted them and beat them back to the gate.

Louis tasted blood in his mouth and a rawness in the back of his throat. He put his hand to his lips to see if he was bleeding, and he felt no wound. His skin was slippery, though, with the blood of the men he had killed. The nausea had faded, though he couldn't remember when it had. It its place he felt the euphoria of having survived his first real battle, and the pride of having overcome his momentary squeamishness and performing well enough.

Willem approached Louis in the darkness between the double walls that defended Montmusard. He, too, was covered in blood, as was his mahogany warhorse. He wore a strangely distant expression as he approached, but it turned to grim approval as he focused on his nephew. He nodded solemnly.

"You've reassured me," he said, "and made me proud. You fought like a true Templar."

"For a moment—," Louis began, but Willem stopped him with an abrupt wave of his hand and nodded again, solemn and resolute.

"You fought well, nephew. I thank God for the strength and the skill with which he has blessed you." He reached to place a blood–stained, mail–clad hand on Louis's shoulder. "Arnaud would have been proud, too."

I'm glad, Louis said with a satisfied smile.

Willem brightened. "I've no more reason to worry!" he said. He turned to those who had gathered around them. "My nephew is a true knight, now tried in battle. The whole of the Mamluk army had best take heed. As long as this knight treads on the ground of Jerusalem, their days are numbered!"

The other knights laughed heartily, but their laughter was tinged with subtle melancholy.

Chapter 36

King Henry returned from Cyprus with forty ships, three thousand soldiers, and a smug, imperious air. When he got to the ramparts and took in the sight of the vast Mamluk encampment. His face froze in dismay at the magnitude of the army that stood against his troubled city.

He ordered Amalric to muster his army and inspire his men to mount a valiant defense.

The Mamluks clearly knew of Henry's arrival. They launched the most aggressive assault of the siege, moving a dozen more trebuchets to the front and preparing the siege towers for an inevitable attack on the parapet itself.

By the afternoon of Friday, the fourth of May, ominous cracks had formed along the King's Wall and in the parapet atop the walls by Saint Anthony's Gate. Rubble fell from the inside surface of the wall, and softening of the structure had rendered the sound of the boulders' blows less pronounced. The king raged at his brother to do something to counter the bombardment, to push the trebuchets back, but Amalric answered his rage with a dull, indolent stare.

Henry stormed from the wall. The spectacle of a powerless king overcome by his own vulnerability astonished Louis. He wondered why Henry would not at least attempt to appear noble, resilient, and strong, if only to motivate his men. He noted that it took more than a crown and royal attire to conjure regal majesty.

The following dawn, the Muslim call to *Fitr*, the sunrise prayer, echoed its song across the plain. The Crusaders arose to face another day of brutal, disheartening assault.

King Henry, accompanied by Amalric and the rest of his advisors, rode into the Templar camp as it mustered by the Lazarus Gate. Henry appeared disheveled and in a state of mild shock. De Beaujeu sighed with exasperation as he turned to face him.

"We need more troops at Saint Anthony's Gate!" the king fumed. As if to punctuate his plea, a boulder crashed into the wall quite close to him. Henry jumped in alarm, and his horse whinnied and reared at the impact. The king regained control of his mount and turned to the Grand Master with a wild look in his eyes. He opened his mouth to speak, but the Grand Master spoke first.

"We need more troops everywhere," de Beaujeu said wryly, nodding toward the point of the impact.

"The King's Tower is about to fall," Henry said, only slightly more composed.

"We'll do what we can," de Beaujeu said. "But I think it's time we discussed a truce, and terms."

It was clear that the king wanted to rage at the Grand Master, to hold him responsible for their dire situation, but he held his peace.

"What terms?" he demanded.

"We'll discuss that," de Beaujeu said.

"What do you recommend?" the king asked more insistently, sneering.

Another boulder crashed into the same section of the wall. It seemed as though the Saracens knew where Henry stood. Before the Grand Master could speak, a flaming ball of Greek fire crashed into the top of the wall, and several Templars fell screaming and in flames to their deaths, not fifty feet away.

De Beaujeu's faced tensed as he glared in the direction of the casualties. "Peaceful withdrawal," he said through clenched teeth. He shifted his glare toward Henry as if to dare him to challenge the suggestion.

Henry faltered for a moment before answering. "We'll call the council together," he finally said. He shook his head and turned to go.

"Henry," de Beaujeu called after him.

The king froze, as did his advisors, at the Grand Master's impetuous use of his given name. He turned slowly.

"I'll expect your support in council," de Beaujeu said, and then he turned his back on the king. The king glared at his back for a moment before he spun and galloped away.

✠ ✠ ✠

The council convened a few hours later, just before noon.

Willem and Antonio Bollani walked into the council hall behind the Grand Master. Willem observed that de Beaujeu's typically composed demeanor had been ruffled, and reasonably so. It was not enough that two hundred thousand Saracens threatened the city from outside its walls; the Italians' squabbling, the king's obstinacy, and the pope's failure to raise effective reinforcements doomed it from within. De Beaujeu walked with uncharacteristic stiffness, his shoulders rigid and his jaw tight.

Henry's bailiff, Philip, called the council to order. He sat to Henry's left, and Amalric, the Lord of Tyre, to his right. The commanders of the English, the French, and the Venetians lined one side of the table, and the Genoese, the Pisans, and the Germans the other. The Hospitaller Grand Master, Jean de Villiers, sat at the far end of the table next to an empty chair that was reserved for de Beaujeu. Willem and Bollani took seats on a bench against the wall.

"I sense disunity," the king thundered, staring at de Beaujeu as he moved to his seat. The Grand Master glowered. "Are you unable to remedy this?" the king demanded.

"The factions have pulled together," de Beaujeu said, "as well as they are able." He was being tactful, Willem thought, and generous. "Every point of the defense is sorely tested. None is in any position to assist any other for very long."

The Pisan commander smirked while the Genoese smoothed the wrinkles of his tunic.

"The King's Tower is about to fall," Henry repeated, "as is Saint Anthony's Gate. Why are we not moving troops to those points?"

"From where would you have them moved?" de Beaujeu asked. He looked to the Hospitaller de Villiers for support. De Villiers shrugged quietly. "Your Highness," de Beaujeu continued, "we are stretched thin at the walls. With all due respect to all the commanders in attendance, it appears that forces have been withheld from some quarters."

The king glanced at each of the Italians. "Is this true?" he asked.

They hesitated for a moment before the Venetian responded.

"I have withheld a modest contingent," he admitted. "It is prudent to do so in view of the large Pisan and Genoese forces that have remained in their quarters protecting their own assets."

The king rolled his eyes in exasperation.

"My reserves are nothing compared to yours!" the Genoese commander protested.

"Nor are mine," the Pisan added.

"There are no reserves!" de Villiers snapped. "We do not have that luxury."

"And you," the king said, turning to de Beaujeu, "have been unable to contain this pettiness and rally the troops?"

De Beaujeu smiled and turned to the Pisan commander. "Are you saying that you have failed to comply with my command?"

The Pisan looked indignant.

"And you?" the Grand Master said to the Genoese. "You have also disregarded my authority?"

De Villiers barely concealed a sardonic grin.

"My lord," de Beaujeu said to the king, "do you truly hold me accountable for the intractability of the merchants? If you will put them under my command, I will get them to the wall. Perhaps you could coax them there yourself." He rose and walked to the Patriarch of Jerusalem, Nicholas of Hanapes, who sat behind the king. "Or better still," he said, "perhaps we should appeal to the pope, and *he* can inspire the Italians to put aside their differences long enough to defend this city with zeal."

Nicholas looked at de Beaujeu with shamed thoughtfulness, as if he were realizing it was something to which he should already have attended. Henry turned to Nicholas, who nodded his assent.

"Still," de Beaujeu said as he returned to his seat, "it's only a matter of time. The fall of Acre appears inevitable. These merchants will not unite, and our pope will not send reinforcements. Even if he would, there is no more time for that."

"You are prepared to give up?" the king said.

"The sultan has offered no terms," de Beaujeu said sharply. "Our envoys have yet to return from as-Salahiyah. It appears unlikely that Khalil is interested in anything less than our annihilation. It's more unlikely that seventeen thousand Christians will overcome two hundred thousand Mamluks. I will fight to the death, of course. To that, I am sworn. But I will do so with something less than my customary optimism. If you call grasping the obvious giving up, then yes, I suppose I'm prepared for that, too. I've never been given to fancy, and I am not at the moment so inclined."

Philip scoffed. "So we simply throw open the gates?" he asked. "Lay down our arms?"

"I suggest we call a truce and request terms," the Grand Master said.

"What terms?" the king asked.

"The terms his father first offered."

"Khalil won't agree to them now," Amalric said. "I'd think

it's too late for that, too."

"It's a starting point," de Beaujeu said.

Philip peered at de Beaujeu with narrowed eyes. "You'll offer up the rioters?"

De Beaujeu shrugged. "Or convicts who are already sentenced to die for their crimes."

"You're a coward!" the Pisan commander snapped as he sprang to his feet. Many among the condemned were his men.

De Beaujeu turned and gazed coolly at the Pisan. "I've heard that before," he said slowly, "from the lips of men who share your tenuous understanding of courage. Forgive me if I miss the offense in hearing it from your own."

"Your treasure is locked away in your fortress," the Pisan shouted, pointing toward the Templar quarter. "Sure you don't care! Ours is out here, vulnerable to pillage. It'll be the first to be taken by the infidels!"

"And you believe they will settle for your pittance and leave my Order's property untouched?" de Beaujeu said.

"You'll bargain that, sure!" the Pisan replied.

"I will not," the Grand Master said. "I will bargain for our lives. If I win that, I'll push for our treasures as well." De Beaujeu shook his head. "Is your gold more precious than your lives? We squabble here while both our treasures and our lives hang by a thread. What good is your gold after the walls come down? We have no other option."

"You can't bargain with them," the Pisan protested. "We can only fight or flee. I'm inclined toward the latter, truth be told."

"We'll let the Grand Master bargain," Henry said. "We can lose nothing, but we may gain time."

"It will show them we're weak," the Venetian commander protested.

"They already know we're weak," Amalric growled. Henry turned to him with a scolding look. Amalric slouched in his seat with an air of resignation that Willem had never seen in him. "Otherwise," he said, pouting, "they wouldn't be here."

"We'll convene after the parley," the king said. To de Beaujeu, he turned with contempt and said, "Go and do your bargaining."

✠ ✠ ✠

Under a flag of truce, Willem and Antonio Bollani rode through the gate and toward the sultan's *dehliz*. Their mounts picked their way through the rubble of the siege and the tents of the besiegers. Boulders lay in the fosse outside Saint Anthony's Gate and littered the perimeter of the wall.

Willem surveyed the condition of the walls with alarm. Gaping cracks had formed around the King's Tower, snaking their way ominously toward the ramparts and to the ground. The King's Wall was riddled with fractures, and portions had caved inward. Collapse was clearly imminent.

The Mamluks watched their advance in silence, some glaring and others nodding politely. Willem made eye contact with a soldier he thought he recognized, but from where he did not know. The soldier seemed also to recognize Willem; he placed his clenched fist to his heart in a solemn salute. Willem nodded in response.

At the *dehliz*, the knights dismounted and handed the reins to an attendant, a boy about twelve years old dressed in the garb of the sultan's servants. They entered the *dehliz*, where Willem noted a dozen of the sultan's emirs, and several servants and courtiers, among them his good friend, the messenger Salim Abd al-Majid. Willem nodded briefly at Salim, who smiled.

Willem and Bollani stood before the sultan for a moment before they knelt and bowed their heads. They rose and knelt twice more before Willem stood and addressed Khalil in Arabic.

"*Assalamu alaikum, ya Saidi*," he said. "*Jazzahallahu khairan.*" The sultan seemed pleased with his greeting.

"And the peace of God be upon you, too," Khalil said. "Have you brought me the keys to the city?"

Willem shook his head. "No, I have not. I have come rather

to discuss terms for peace."

"The treaty is ended," Khalil said.

"We should like to resurrect it," Willem replied.

"Of that, I'm sure," Khalil said. He shook his head. "We have tolerated your presence here in the name of peace and commerce. My father trusted your Grand Master. But when you murdered unarmed merchants and raped their daughters in our streets you demonstrated clearly that peace and commerce are no longer possible. Your presence is intolerable, and will no longer be suffered."

"It was not the Christians of Acre who murdered those merchants," Willem replied. "It was the work of foreigners, vagabonds and criminals who acted of their own volition."

"And you have protected those criminals from the justice of Allah," Khalil said, his eyes blazing indignation. "There is nothing more to say about that."

Willem understood the futility of his approach. He said, "Your father, the great Kala'un, proposed that we pay a ransom for our lives. The Grand Master asks that you extend that same graciousness to us now."

"Your king rejected my father's generosity," Khalil snapped, "and he blamed the victims themselves for the atrocities they suffered. Henry's petulance drove my father to vengeance. I am here to claim that vengeance. Your money means nothing to me."

"Then I beg your mercy on the inhabitants of the city," Willem said. He gazed earnestly into the sultan's eyes. "Let them leave in peace before we finish this fight."

Khalil peered back at Willem with narrowed eyes. "You're an honorable man," he observed. He turned and took a few steps away from the two Templars, contemplating Willem's request. Finally, he turned back to them. "Your people will live if you surrender the city peacefully and leave in orderly haste."

"I will—"

A gasp went up from the Mamluk host, followed by a crashing thud a dozen yards from the sultan's *dehliz*, behind Willem. Willem spun to see a massive boulder embedded in a crater barely a yard away from a group of ashen-faced Mamluk guards.

The sultan bellowed as Willem turned back to him in horror. Khalil had drawn his sword halfway from its scabbard. "You filthy swine!" he screamed. "For that, you will die!"

"My lord," said Salim Abd al–Majid softly, moving toward the sultan, "do not foul your sword with the blood of pigs." He placed a calm hand upon the sultan's sword hand and eased the sword back into its scabbard. "They didn't launch the stone, for they are here with you." He nodded solemnly, and the sultan appeared to heed his council. Willem sighed in relief.

"Lord sultan," Willem said carefully, "I know how this looks. But that missile was not intended for you."

"What do you mean?" the sultan demanded.

Willem turned to glance at the boulder. "It's a Pisan stone, and it was intended for me."

"For you...," the sultan said dubiously.

Willem nodded. "To drive a message home."

"What message?"

"That I'm a coward, on a cowardly mission."

The sultan was incredulous. He paced quickly for a moment. "I will never understand your kind," he said. "It amazes me that you have survived in this land for so long." He stopped and faced Willem. "If I were a patient man, I'd withdraw and simply wait for you to exterminate yourselves. It would only be a matter of time. However, you have utterly exhausted my patience." He shook his head. "I don't know what to do with you."

Salim leaned toward the sultan and whispered into his ear. The sultan nodded and turned to Willem with an air of finality.

"I will have every last one of you dead or gone forever before the month is out," he said. "It does not matter to me which fate you choose. Go back now and tell your master that all is lost, and there is nothing more to say."

Willem and Bollani bowed to the sultan and turned to go.

"Templar," Khalil called after them, and they turned. "Tell your Grand Master to send no more delegates to my *dehliz*. If he does, I will execute them myself."

Willem and Bollani remounted and rode back to the city.

Mamluk knights and soldiers stood and watched them go, and more than Willem could count placed their clenched fists over their hearts in a silent salute. Willem understood that they were bidding reverent farewell to worthy opponents for whom they held high regard. Willem threw back his shoulders and met their farewell with the composure for which his Order was known.

Chapter 37

Willem and Bollani no sooner entered the gate when the bombardment resumed. Khalil concentrated his attention on the King's Tower and the King's Wall, the most exposed and vulnerable section of the city's fortification.

Willem summoned Louis, and together they accompanied the Grand Master de Beaujeu to the council to deliver the sultan's response, which was already clear from the shuddering impact of the boulders.

The Pisan commander barely acknowledged the Templars as they entered, and Louis wondered what retribution he faced at the Grand Master's hand over the trebuchet attack upon the parley. De Beaujeu had said nothing of the incident as yet.

The king glowered as de Beaujeu relayed Sultan Khalil's message. His council reacted with shouts of rage and fear, and the Italians stormed out of the hall, presumably to protect their own factions and interests.

Henry swore to battle the Mamluks to the end, but Louis suspected that the king's bravado would fade in the face of the threat to his Cypriot kingdom and the futility of defending Acre.

Louis ached at the realization that this battle, his first true conflict of the Holy Crusade, presaged the collapse of his lifelong dreams. He tried to maintain his zeal for the fight, but the pounding of the trebuchets mocked his resolve, and the squabbling of the factions shattered his hopes. The division, the animosity, and the incivility that plagued the Christians clawed at his gut. He could conjure no hope that Jerusalem might yet be won.

"Nicholas," de Beaujeu said to the Patriarch of Jerusalem, ignoring the frantic debate of the commanders who remained in the hall, "you must do something. Someone must induce the Italians to unite and to join the fight. I believe you're the only one who might influence them."

Nicholas was a dispassionate man. He shrugged defensively and turned up his palms. "What can I do?" he asked. "What am I supposed to say to them?"

"Think of something," de Beaujeu snapped. "They see you as a man of God. As such, they fear you. Say anything. Just get them to the wall. Our lives depend on it."

Nicholas thought deeply for a long moment before he rose and left the hall to do the Grand Master's bidding. Louis had difficulty imagining the patriarch inspiring the merchants to selfless cooperation.

"Do you think the Italians will make a difference?" asked Otto de Grandison, the commander of the English forces at Acre. "Is this not futile, even with them in the fight?"

"Yes," de Beaujeu said. "It's futile. The best we can hope for is Khalil's impatience, and the improbability that he will tire of the siege and withdraw until his anger cools. There's no hope of that with half our forces barely defending the wall, and the other half sticking daggers into each other in the streets and alleys." De Beaujeu paused, shaking his head with frustration. "I'd rather we all die fighting than bickering like children while the Mamluks cut us down. In any event, with or without the Italians, I'm going to the wall. My men have been patient long enough, and now there's only one thing left to do. The sultan rejected our overture; now we fight, to the death if necessary."

He turned and motioned for his knights to follow.

They crossed through the square on their way to Montmusard, and to the wall by the Lazarus Gate. The Patriarch of Jerusalem had ascended to a landing on the stone stairway of a palace on the square and was calling out exhortations to the citizens who had begun to gather in curiosity.

"It is your Godly duty to defend this holy city," the patriarch shouted, "this, the capital of the Kingdom of God in Jerusalem! We have built it, tended it, and protected it for two hundred years..."

De Beaujeu shook his head as they passed the throng and the patriarch's voice faded into the noise of the crowd. They cut through an alley and moved toward the north to join the Templar army at Montmusard.

As they approached the northern wall near the Lazarus Gate, Louis noted that the store of boulders for the trebuchets had dwindled, as had the oil and the water for the ramparts. The armory had been emptied of arrows for the archers' bows, and craftsmen were working non–stop to replenish the supply. Missiles from the Mamluk trebuchets continued to rain down, crashing with dull thuds against the walls and smashing against the ramparts, sending defenders dead and dying to the ground below.

Louis mounted the steps to the rampart to take his position among the archers. The siege towers were drawing closer, and it would not be long before they succeeded in latching onto the ramparts, allowing the Mamluks to breach them.

The walls were buckling, and the defenders' nerves were worn to the breaking point. The incessant pounding on the walls irritated Louis, and it filled the pit of his stomach with hollow fear. From the roadway between the inner and outer walls, they could hear the Mamluk miners weakening the foundations, while the arrows, rocks, oil, and torches that the Crusaders rained upon them from the ramparts had little effect.

Amazingly, the patriarch appeared to have found the right words to inspire the Italians to fight. They trickled in sporadic throngs to their appointed stations at the city's perimeter. It took several hours, but their arrival nearly doubled the defenses at the wall. But just as they took their positions, the king's forces abandoned the barbican at the King's Tower. The tower swayed ominously before its front wall finally collapsed, taking part of the outer wall with it.

The English and the French rushed to the ramparts to try to defend the breach. They were able to prevent the Mamluks from occupying the King's Tower, but they could do little to stave off the relentless trebuchet and mangonel offensive.

✠ ✠ ✠

The rubble of the front half of the King's Tower had collapsed into the fosse, leaving the inner wall of the tower exposed to the Mamluk trebuchets.

At the sight of the tower's collapse, some of the Italians reconsidered their newfound commitment and withdrew from the wall as quickly as they had arrived. Louis shook his head and moved to chastise them.

"The king!" someone cried from the rampart to the east.

Louis turned to see Henry approaching the Templar camp on horseback with Amalric, Philip, and his entourage. Louis had grown to share the Grand Master's visceral contempt for the king's presence. He resented Henry's willingness to depart in the midst of turmoil, and to reappear on a whim with instructions and demands for those who had not left the fight. He curled his lip at the king's overstated royalty.

The Grand Master turned from his commanders to face the king.

"The Italians have withdrawn," the king said. He seemed weary, and resigned to the fact.

The Grand Master nodded curtly and shrugged. "Yes," he said. "Of course they have."

"We need them back," Henry said. De Beaujeu closed his eyes and sighed heavily. "I need you to get them back," the king said.

"With what authority shall I accomplish that?" de Beaujeu said. He pointed to the ramparts. "The fight is here. I haven't the time to nurse cowards into a fight in which they will be little more than a liability."

Henry frowned and pursed his lips.

"You have allowed your advisors to undermine my position," de Beaujeu continued. "How do you expect me to sway the merchants?"

The king stared blankly at the Grand Master. It was clear that he could not argue the point, but he was verging on panic and desperate for help.

Henry said, "I will send my men to spread the word that the city is at your command, in my name. Send your men to round them up. Get them to the walls and lead them."

Henry whirled his steed and galloped back toward the city. Amalric hesitated for a moment, then gave de Beaujeu an apologetic shrug. "I'll send out the word," he said in an unconvincing tone before he turned, too, and followed the king.

De Beaujeu beckoned to Willem. Louis bounded down the steps from the rampart to join his uncle.

"Have a few of your men try to get the Italians back," de Beaujeu said. "Tell them to do the best they can, and to bring them here, if they will come. If they refuse, leave them where they are. They'll all be dead soon enough."

Willem nodded. "Yes, Master," he said. He turned to Louis. "You go. Take de Valery, du Perche, and Cripplegate with you." Louis nodded his acknowledgement. "You heard what he said," Willem added. "Don't waste time. Try to convince them, but hurry. Leave them if they argue."

Louis and the other knights ran through the city to the Venetian Quarter, where they fanned out to confront and cajole every able-bodied man they could find to go to Montmusard and man the walls. Many complied, but far more argued or outright refused. Every refusal stoked Louis's anger higher still.

"These are Christians," he fumed as Victor hurried to keep step with him. "Their behavior is despicable." Victor nodded and grunted in agreement. "By God's eyes, I'll kill the next bastard who argues with me!" Louis glanced at Victor, who gaped at him in surprise. He was about to question the look, but he reconsidered. He understood it well enough. Victor was taken aback by the rage he had never seen in Louis. *Well, so am I,* he thought to himself.

Fortunately for the next Venetians he approached, they readily agreed and said they would head to the wall as soon as they could collect their equipment.

"No," Louis snapped. "Go now, directly. You'll find weapons there. Don't let me discover that you've dallied!" The Venetians hurried toward Montmusard without delay.

They turned a corner and moved westward into the Pisan Quarter. A group of five soldiers stood idly outside a small, fortified church that stood in the shadow of the massive walls of the Templar fortress to its west. Louis and Victor approached the soldiers in haste.

"What are you doing?" Louis demanded. "You are to join the defenses immediately, in the name of King Henry. Why are you not there already?"

The soldiers turned and looked curiously at Louis. The ranking soldier descended the church steps toward him. He stopped a few feet from him and said, "We are protecting our church, and the nunnery." He pointed in the direction of a small nunnery built against the Templar wall. It appeared to be deserted, but Louis knew that the nuns were locked inside, praying for the salvation of the city and deliverance from their inevitable fate. Louis turned back to the Pisan.

"If you want to protect them, get to the wall," he said.

The Pisan shook his head. "If we leave, the Venetians will sack our church."

"If you don't leave," he said, placing a his hand to his sword, "I will kill all of you where you stand, and *I* will sack your church."

The Pisan stiffened and glared angrily at Louis. Victor gripped his own sword and moved to stand with Louis. The soldiers exchanged glances, and one of them disappeared into the church.

Louis advanced and drew his sword. "Stop!" he shouted.

The Pisan captain held up a hand. "Please," he said soothingly. "He is only seeing to our treasure. It must be secured if we are to leave it unattended."

Louis spied the Templar, Simon Cripplegate, half a block away and called to him. Cripplegate turned and hurried toward them.

"We're not going to fight you," the captain said. "I swear it." The man who had entered the church emerged and nodded to the others. The captain smiled wryly. "To the gate," he said, and the Pisans headed toward Montmusard.

Just then, the door to the nunnery opened, and a group of nuns emerged, beckoning to Louis.

"What is it?" Louis asked.

"We paid them," a young nun said. "To protect us."

Louis had seen the nun before, but only from afar. His heart skipped a beat at the sight of her face. She was a pretty girl of no more than twenty, but that was not what captivated him. Wisps of chestnut hair poked out from beneath her coif, and her green eyes shone with devout purity. Though her face was thinner and her lips less full, her resemblance to Colette was remarkable.

He knew from her accent that she was Irish.

He caught his breath and blinked, confused. "You paid them?" he asked. "You have the protection of the Templars."

"There are no Templars here," she said.

"They are at the wall," he replied, "keeping the Saracens out of the city. As long as that is so, from whom do you need protection?"

"From them," she said, pointing at the departing Pisans.

Louis turned to look after the Pisans, and then he turned back to the nun, his eyes wide. He wondered why the nuns feared the Pisans, but he marveled more at the ingenuity in how they had managed their predicament. They knew that Pisans would do anything to avoid the dishonor of harm coming to someone who had paid for their protection.

"Perhaps you should take up residence inside the Templar castle," Louis said. "You'd be safe there." He noted the strength of the nun's bearing, and a frank fearlessness in her expression. He wondered whether it was true fearlessness or simple naïveté.

"We must minister to the people out here among the chaos," she said. "What would it say to them about our commitment to God, and our faith in Him, if we were to abandon them for our own safety?"

Louis shook his head. "I don't know what more to suggest, Sister…"

"Mairead," she said. "Sister Miriam Mairead."

"Sister Miriam," Louis said. "I can't protect you here. We must round up soldiers and return to the fight."

Mairead smiled kindly. "Thank you, knight, for thinking of us. God will protect us. He sent you, after all, to send those soldiers away. We will stay here and do what we can to minister to those in need. We'll ask the Good Lord to keep us safe, and you."

Louis nodded. "As you wish," he said. He knew she was being foolish. He turned to go.

"Knight…," Mairead called.

He turned back to her. "Louis," he said. "Louis de Garonne."

"Louis," she repeated. "I'll pray for you, Louis."

Louis nodded. "Thank you," he said. There was a time when Sister Miriam's prayers would have reassured him. Now the promise struck him as futile and irrelevant. He appreciated her sentiment, nonetheless. It occurred to him, too, that he had been captivated by the grace and her resolve, as well as by her plain but stunning beauty. He felt himself flushing, and he quickened his steps.

"I'll check on you from time to time," he called over his shoulder as he hurried away.

"She's pretty," Victor said.

"She's a nun," Louis retorted.

"A *pretty* nun." Victor craned his neck for another look.

"You'll go to hell," Louis said flatly.

"We may already be there," Victor said. He slowed suddenly, and his mouth dropped open.

Ahead of them, a melee had broken out and spilled from an alley behind a church in the Genoese Quarter. At least thirty men flailed and kicked wildly, screaming and pushing at one another in blind fury.

Louis and Victor, four other knights, and a dozen sergeants and squires converged on the scene. More than a dozen Genoese mercenaries and as many Pisans were fighting as if to the death. A back door of the Genoese church had been kicked in, and that was no doubt the cause of the fray.

The Templars drew their swords, and Louis yelled for order.

"What's the meaning of this?" he demanded. The men stopped thrashing and fell into a sullen silence at the sight of the Templars.

"They broke into our church," a Genoese sailor said with a snarl, pointing at the Pisans.

"They have our treasure in there," a Pisan yelled, "stolen from *our* church."

"Do you mean the church that was under heavy guard until just now?" Louis asked.

The Pisan glared at Louis. "That's why we're guarding it," he said, fuming. "Because they pillaged it!"

Victor walked close to the Pisan and gazed deeply into his eyes. He turned to Louis with a grave look.

"I think he's lying," Victor said. The Pisan struggled to swing at Victor as one of the sergeants quickly restrained him. Louis frowned at Victor's theatrics.

"What does it matter?" Louis yelled in frustration. "Why do you people continue to bicker?" He wanted to thrash them all for their stupidity. "What do you hope to gain? We will all lose our lives to your quibbling!" He paced, enraged and fingering the pommel of his sword. "There are Saracens at the gates!" he yelled. "They're days away from breaking through. And when they do, they will kill *you,* and *you.*" He pointed at the Pisans and the Genoese in turn. "They will kill your families! Your priests! Your nuns! And then they will take your precious treasures to their sultan, and all of this will have come to nothing!" He raised his arms in futility.

The fight seemed to drain from some of the Italians, giving way to awkward embarrassment, but a few of them seemed intent on continuing their quarrel.

"If you want to fight," Victor said, "you can go and fight. There." He pointed north toward Montmusard. Louis glanced at Victor in surprise.

"We're going to leave this place," the Pisan said. "There's no fight for us here. If there's no more trade with the paynims, there's no more reason to stay."

"You're cowards, then," Louis said. "And your man called *us* the cowards."

The Pisan shook his head.

"I'll scuttle your ship myself before you get out of the harbor," Victor said. Again, Louis looked at him in surprise. Victor pointed his sword at the Pisan. "Get to the fight," he growled.

The Pisan took a step back and hesitated for a moment, and then he turned to his men. "Let's go," he said. They sheathed their weapons and straightened their clothing and hurried up the street toward Montmusard.

"You, too," Louis said to the Genoese soldiers. "All of you."

Wordlessly, they complied.

Louis turned and looked in the direction of the Templar castle, and the small nunnery that nestled in its shadow. He wondered briefly how long the pretty nun would be safe outside the castle. He suddenly longed to return to her, to urge her into the castle, and to stay with her to ensure that she was safe. He subdued the longing and returned to his task.

Once they had rounded up all the able-bodied men they could find, they returned to the Templar command tent by the Lazarus Gate to find the commanders in excited discussion.

"The Mamluks have filled up the fosse with bags of sand," Osbourne reported, "on top of the rubble of the King's Tower. They're moving their siege towers to the walls."

"We've got to defend it," Willem said.

De Beaujeu nodded.

Antonio Bollani shook his head. "The other towers are falling, too," he said. "And the walls by Saint Anthony's Gate. If they come down, the Mamluks will follow the road to the Lazarus Gate. We must stay here to meet them."

"We must do both," the Grand Master said solemnly. The commanders looked at him in silence. "Richard, Willem…take your men to the King's Wall. Defend against the siege towers. When the Mamluks can no longer be contained at the breach, hurry back here to join us in defending the northern gates."

Willem and Osbourne nodded. A glance passed between Bollani and Osbourne. Louis understood instinctively that it was a brief and heartfelt farewell. He was surprised that his heart broke for them, and the emotion felt surreal.

Willem and Osbourne mustered their troops and departed for the King's Wall. A runner passed them at a gallop coming from the east.

"Anthony's Gate is breached!" he yelled.

"Halt!" Willem cried to his troops, and they stopped to wait for the news.

"We're holding them back," the courier said, "but I can't say for how long!"

De Beaujeu approached Willem and Osbourne. "Proceed to the King's Wall as ordered," he said. He glanced at Louis. "But send Louis with some men back to the city. We must evacuate now."

Louis's heart sank. *So this is the end,* he thought.

The evacuation plan had been laid at the beginning of the siege. The Grand Master sent word along the ramparts that the ships' captains should ready their crews for departure. Louis and his men would supervise the orderly boarding of the women, the children, the old, and the infirm. They would also discourage the mischief and bribery that would push the evacuees aside and buy passage for the wealthy and unscrupulous instead. Louis hoped that he would be able to fulfill his duties without murdering unruly scoundrels.

Chapter 38

LOUIS TOOK VICTOR AND a company of knights back into the city for the evacuation. They fanned out through the markets, neighborhoods, and quarters spreading the word for the women, the children, and the feeble to flee to the docks.

They encountered little resistance; most seemed long ready to go. Only the priests and nuns insisted on staying until the end, against the knights' strenuous urging.

Malingering able–bodied men had emerged from their homes and churches after the knights had returned to the wall. Louis enlisted them to assist in the evacuation, despite his desire to pummel them. He kept a wary eye for opportunists who would try to buy passage ahead of the evacuees. He found a darker part of himself almost wishing he would encounter such cowardice.

They made their way south through the city again, through the Genoese Quarter, and then the Pisan, until they came once again to the square between the Pisan church and the little convent of the Nuns of Saint Mary Magdalene, huddled in the shadow of the Templar castle.

"Into the church, Gaston," Louis said to one of his knights. "There are bound to be spineless cowards in there, along with the priests. Bring them all out. Get as many of the priests to the ships as will go." Gaston nodded and dashed toward the church. "You, Frederick," he said to another, "clear out these shops. Hurry." Louis nodded to Victor to come with him.

They walked to the convent, where Louis rapped on the heavy oak door. An old nun with wispy gray hair slid the peephole open and peered out at him.

"Who knocks?" she said in a tremulous voice.

"Louis de Garonne, a Templar knight," he said. The nun unbolted the door.

"What is it?" she asked through the cracked door.

"Evacuation," Louis replied. "It's time to board the ships for Cyprus."

"Just a moment," the old nun said. She shut the door and disappeared from the peephole.

Minutes passed. Louis grew impatient and knocked again. This time, Mairead opened the door. He caught his breath at the sight of her.

"Just a moment," she said.

"We haven't much time," Louis said.

"Perhaps you can evacuate others and come back for us," Mairead said.

"Why?" he asked.

"We're still in prayer and discussion," she said.

"Discussion about what?" Louis asked. "There's no time for discussion."

"Come back," Mairead said as she shut the door.

Louis banged impatiently on the door until Mairead returned. She had retrieved a cloak and was pulling it on as she exited the convent.

"You're impatient," she observed.

"How could I be patient?" he asked incredulously. "You may not realize it, sister, but the Saracens are at the gates, and the gates are about to fall."

"I know that," she said. "Let's go."

"Where are you going?" he asked.

"With you," she said. "As you said, there's not much time. We'd best get moving."

"You can't come with me," Louis said.

"I'll help you get people to the boats." She moved down a street toward the center of the city with the quick, graceful steps of a resolute woman.

"You need to get yourselves to the ships!" Louis snapped.

Mairead glanced back at the nunnery with a quick shake of her head. "They're not leaving," she said curtly. "They're praying."

"It'll take more than praying to save them," Victor said.

"They need to go," Louis insisted. "*You* need to go."

She turned and smiled sweetly at him, and then hurried on. "Where have you yet to move people out?" she called over her shoulder.

Louis looked at Victor with exasperation. Victor shrugged and shook his head. They hurried after the nun.

"We don't need help," Louis said.

"And yet, I'll help you anyway," Mairead said, still smiling. She knocked hard on the door of a house and yelled out to the occupants to evacuate.

"We have a plan," Louis protested.

"I'm sure of it," she said. "You've gone through the Italian quarters to rally the crews to the ships, and now you'll be heading to the hospital to get the sick and infirm to the docks." She paused to look at Louis for confirmation. "You'll need help with that."

Louis shook his head. This was not part of the plan. He raced to keep up with her.

At the end of the street they turned a corner toward the west. They had barely turned the corner when an angry chorus of shouts arose from a crowd at the sea wall. A group of dirty men in tattered clothing broke away from the gathering, and the rest pursued brandishing knives, clubs, and iron chains.

Templar and Hospitaller knights in the area reacted with alarm and moved to converge on the clash. The mob was headed in Louis's direction, and he worried for Mairead's safety. He pulled her from the path of the mob as Victor joined the rest of the Templars.

Louis pulled Mairead down an alley and stopped in the shadows, holding a finger to his lips. Footsteps rang against the cobbled stones of the alley. He peered around the corner to investigate. The armed vagrants shouted when they saw him, and they dashed toward him.

Louis grabbed Mairead's hand and pulled her farther down the alley. There were nearly twenty of them, too many to fight off and still protect the nun. He longed to whirl on his pursuers and lay into them with his sword, but he feared for Mairead's safety.

"Hurry!" he said, urging her on. They ran down the alley as fast as Mairead's habit would allow.

"You should have gone to the ships," Louis scolded. He saw the door of an abandoned shop standing ajar, and he pulled her inside and slammed it. He dropped the latch to lock them in.

The angry voices grew louder as they drew nearer. The pursuers swore angrily as they searched for signs of their prey.

Louis cupped his hand gently over Mairead's mouth as the men grunted and swore just outside the door.

"Find them," a gruff voice commanded. "The bastard saw us. We'll be hunted if we don't put him down." Footsteps retreated in several directions while two or three of the men remained outside, panting and grumbling.

"Damn Venetians," one said in a thick Pisan accent.

"Bastard Templars," another one spat. His voice was familiar, but Louis couldn't place it.

"They're all the same," the first one said, fuming. "They drag us here to fight their battles, and then push us around and lock us away for killing the infidels we came here to kill."

"Well, it got us freed from prison, anyway."

"Yes, and right back into prison the minute we're here," the Pisan said.

"We're out now," the second man said. As he spoke, Louis placed the voice, more hoarse and strained than he remembered it.

"*Gilles,*" he whispered to himself, grimacing.

"*What?*" Mairead whispered back through Louis's cupped fingers. Louis held a finger to his lips again and gently squeezed her mouth. He wondered how Gilles had gotten out of the prison. Obviously, the chaos of the siege had played in his favor, and he was using the opportunity to stir up more of his own.

One of the men hushed the others and said, "Did you hear that?" They stood very still for a long moment, listening. Louis and Mairead barely breathed. "Ah, I'm hearing things," the man finally said with a hint of relief, and their footsteps moved away from the shop.

Louis exhaled and leaned against the wall as Mairead relaxed in his arms. He recoiled instinctively at the feel of her body against his, but he was pinned between her and the wall, and he could not pull away. He caught and held his breath, hoping she would mind herself and spring away. She did not.

Instead, she leaned comfortably against him. He felt her heart pounding against his chest, and her breathing returning to normal. He fought the heat that rose inside him, but in vain. His head spun and his mouth went dry, and though he willed himself to loosen his arms from around her, he could not. Instead, he pulled her closer, and she did not protest.

They stood in their awkward embrace as the world around them went silent and still. Mairead moved her hand to Louis's forearm and gently squeezed. His breath came heavy, and he flushed with desire. Her breath soon matched his, and she pressed harder against him. Louis no longer wanted to move; he was content to remain frozen in their unexpected embrace.

Suddenly, she turned to face him. She gazed at him with hooded eyes and trembling lips.

"Louis," she whispered.

He tried to speak, but he only managed a gasp. He was lost for words.

Her eyes were moist, and fixed on his.

"We're going to die here, Louis," she said.

Louis shook his head and mouthed, "No."

"Yes," she insisted. She glanced about the shop fearfully. "I don't want to die." Suddenly, the nun whose commanding will had eclipsed her delicate stature seemed a frightened girl.

He held her close. "We're not going to die," he said. "We've got to get to the ships. We have to go."

She placed a finger to his lips and gripped his arm. "No," she said, shaking her head. "Not yet." She loosened her grip and laid her head on his chest.

He felt panicked. *The devil has breached the walls,* he thought. It was not the Mamluks, for they were still outside the city, but a far more terrifying demon that had entered and conquered his soul. He suddenly cared for nothing but this woman's touch while the city was falling around him. He tried to pray for strength, but the words evaded him, and he needed no further proof. He was damned.

He pulled her close and kissed her. Part of him hoped that she would resist. Another part of him didn't much care anymore. She kissed him back.

Louis recoiled. He pushed Mairead away and held her at arm's length. "We can't do this."

Breathlessly, she said, "I don't want to die without this."

He realized that he felt the same, but he had not yet resigned himself to it. He suspected that he would live with this moment longer than he would like. Nonetheless, his sudden lust for her consumed him. He craved her body, her velvet skin, and the radiant warmth of her spirit.

A roar arose from the east, near Saint Anthony's Gate. Louis knew it could mean but one thing: that the gate had fallen and all was lost. His momentary reason dissipated, and he gave in to the flesh's temptation.

He pulled Mairead to him and kissed her again, pressing his lips to hers as if it would save their lives. The demon took over completely, and his body moved of its own volition, automatically, surrendered to his hunger.

Louis's hands moved to release his belt with practiced precision.

Her coif and veil slid from her head as she raised her face toward his, and her thick, chestnut hair fell about her shoulders. She gazed into his eyes.

He pulled her close and turned so that her back was against the wall, and he pressed into her. He inhaled deeply, intoxicated by her scent, and buried his face in her hair. He closed his eyes and imagined that this was the only chance he would ever have to be with the woman he loved, the only woman he would ever love, before they were lost to one another forever.

"*Colette...*," he whispered softly.

He was astonished by the intensity of the pleasure that flushed over him at the thought of her. This would be the real heaven, he thought, just the two of them together and all the world to themselves, with all of its beauty and none of its cares. His longing raged and drove him into her with a passion he had never imagined, much less felt. It built to a crescendo and exploded in a release of temptation, fear, and need.

Mairead let out a soft, muffled cry, her face buried in his chest.

They clung tightly to one another as if they were afraid to move. Slowly, the stillness returned. The sounds of battle grew louder, and they reluctantly released their grip on one another. Collapsing against the wall, they lay against each other, their hearts pounding.

Louis's senses slowly returned, and with them arose the dark realization of what he had done. He drew back and looked into the face of the nun with whom he had committed the ultimate sin. She looked back at him with despair. He knew that they would both burn for this, both in this life and in the next.

But he was perplexed. How could something so evil feel so perfectly glorious? How could such wickedness mimic divine ecstasy? Evil, he knew, is ugly, but this was no such thing.

"I'm sorry," he murmured.

"No," she said firmly, shaking her head. "Don't ever be sorry." She straightened her clothing, smoothed her disheveled hair, and carefully replaced her coif and veil. Louis pulled himself together, straightening his tunic and fastening his belt. "It may be the last thing we will know," she said. "If I'm wrong, and we survive, I shall cherish this for the rest of my life."

"We are damned," Louis said.

Mairead shook her head and looked toward the approaching sound of battle. She nodded toward it.

"If there's absolution for an evil such as that," she said somberly, "how could a just God rightly condemn us for this?"

Louis nodded absently. He swore to confess, and to beg absolution at the first opportunity. He agreed with her, though. Their intimacy came as close to his notion of heavenly as almost any other thing he could imagine. If only it had been Colette, he thought...that would be heaven. But alas, he was unlikely to ever see that heaven. The mere vision of it would have to suffice.

The sounds of battle beckoned him, and he pulled himself from the torpor that had enveloped him, and forced himself to duty. He turned hesitantly toward the door, then turned back to Mairead. He felt there was something he should say, but words failed him.

"What is it?" she asked softly.

"Do you...do you feel shame?" he asked.

She looked thoughtful for a moment.

"I've seen a lot of things in my time here," she said, "that have given me cause to re-examine what brought me here in the first place." She paused for a moment, reflecting. "I've seen atrocities absolved, and venial sins condemned...innocents destroyed for their faith, and scoundrels blessed for destroying them. Perhaps I've lost my sense of right and wrong, but I simply wanted just one more taste of the love I forsook to be here." She hesitated for a moment, then said, "I'm sorry, Louis, for bringing you into my sin."

He touched her face gently. "No," he said. "It is my sin, and no fault of yours." He kissed her on the forehead. "Let's go," he said.

They hurried through the alleyways and back to the main streets to resume their efforts to shepherd evacuees to the ships. Louis tried once more, in vain, to convince the nuns to embark. They resolved to stay to minister to the city's defenders. Louis escorted them to the convent and posted a Templar guard outside their door.

The ships put out to sea, and Louis returned to the ramparts at Saint Anthony's Gate.

✠ ✠ ✠

At Saint Anthony's Gate, Louis found Victor among the defenders. Mamluk siege towers had approached the wall, and the miners were digging at the foundations beneath them. Victor clapped Louis on the back.

"Welcome back!" Victor shouted above the din. "I'm sure you haven't missed the best part." He flashed a toothy grin that Louis thought jarringly incongruous. "You look a little flushed. Are you all right?"

"I'm fine," Louis said. "The non-combatants are safely to sea."

"And the nuns?" Victor prodded.

"Man the oil pots," Louis said. He pointed to the siege engineers at the base of the wall. "We've got to stop the miners."

Victor nodded and complied while Louis turned to face the approaching towers. As they lumbered closer, he could see the faces of the Mamluks crowded onto the elevated platforms waiting to drop their drawbridges and stream onto the ramparts. He seized a longbow and took aim at the wheelmen who pushed the towers along the uneven terrain.

The archers rained arrows down on the wheelmen, but as quickly as the wheelmen fell, reserves rushed in from behind, pushing the fallen out of the way and pressing on. There were just too many, Louis thought. He worried that they would run out of arrows and spears long before the Mamluks ran out of men.

"Take your time," he yelled out to the archers. "Make every shot count!" He held his breath and took steady aim, and sent an arrow into a wheelman's jugular. The man was quickly replaced, and Louis strung another arrow for his replacement.

Victor heaved an oil pot with the aid of another man, pouring boiling oil onto the miners at the foot of the wall. Screams reverberated from below as they set the empty pot down. Victor set an arrow to flame and loosed it into the pooled oil. The oil erupted into an inferno, incinerating the miners. Just as quickly, another siege team rushed forward to smother the flames and continue the mining.

The siege tower continued its lumbering approach. There were not enough archers to hold it back. Louis threw off his longbow, retrieved his shield, and drew his gleaming sword.

The tower slammed into the wall with a thud. The Mamluks on the platform unlatched the draw bridge and pushed it onto the rampart. The first Mamluks to emerge met a barrage of arrows that cut them down like grass.

The second row of attackers pushed through their fallen comrades. Some of the fallen fell screaming to their death among the miners at the foot of the wall. Another volley of arrows cut the second row down, too, but most of the archers abandoned their bows for swords as the third wave flooded onto the rampart.

The wooden steps that led up to the platform were crowded with screaming Mamluks anxious to get to the rampart and engage the defenders.

Louis swung fiercely. Mamluks streamed across the drawbridge as if a dam had broken and unleashed a torrent of death. His sword glanced off shields and rang out against Mamluk blades, but contact with flesh was difficult in the rush of bodies. Mamluks pressed him back into the Crusaders that pushed forward from behind.

For a moment, the crush pinned Louis's arms against his chest, preventing him from maneuvering. He spun and ducked and twisted free, nearly pitching headlong off the rampart. He regained his footing and turned back to face the drawbridge.

Victor had taken up a longbow and was firing arrows into the Mamluks as fast as he could. Louis shoved an attacker who had focused on Victor, and the dark, wiry man turned to face him.

The Mamluk threw up his sword and lunged, growling. Louis

parried and blocked the Mamluk's blade with his shield. They fought furiously for several minutes, neither besting the other, until finally the Mamluk struck a blow with the flat of his sword, knocking Louis off balance and to his knees. The Mamluk raised his sword to deliver a fatal blow.

Louis's timing was true. He sunk his blade deep into the Mamluk's underarm, nearly severing the arm at the shoulder. Blood gushed freely, and the man collapsed at the edge of the rampart. Victor rushed forward and kicked the man hard beneath the chin, sending him flailing off the rampart and into the void.

Attackers and defenders fell under a rain of arrows, maces, and swords. Several knights used long pikes to rock the tower, trying to achieve the momentum that would topple it away from the wall.

Louis leapt to his feet and chose another foe from the gangplank. He engaged the Saracen, an oddly shaped Syrian with a roundish, scowling face, whose eyes flashed enthusiasm for battle.

He was slower than Louis, but more powerful. Louis grimaced at the blows against his sword, which sent shuddering shocks through his forearms. He allowed the Saracen to continue to strike at him, while he moved deftly, avoiding more blows than he took.

The Saracen began to tire, apparently more quickly than he had expected, judging from his troubled expression. He backed away slightly to allow himself more room. As he did so, an errant Saracen mace swung around from behind him and caved in the right side of his head. The blow sent him headlong off the parapet to the forty foot drop to the rocks.

The Saracen who had swung the mace watched in dismay as his own man sailed through the void. He turned, snarling, and swung the mace at Louis.

Louis dodged the mace and spun to the right, completing his turn to bring his sword across the man's back, laying him open and nearly severing his mace arm. The man screamed in agony and twisted his head to glare defiantly back at Louis. Louis swung again against the back of the Mamluk's neck, nearly decapitating him. The dead man sank to the ground.

The pike men finally gained the momentum to throw the tower off balance. It hung in an uncertain balance, at an impossible angle for a moment. The Mamluks who were crowded on the stairs looked out from its framework in alarm. Angry exclamations erupted as the siege tower crashed to the ground on top of a mining team.

The siege towers began to pull back.

The battle had raged into evening, but in the fading light the sounds of it receded. Louis could not believe the day had already passed.

Both sides had taken nearly equivalent casualties, but as the Mamluks withdrew, their teeming mass still stretched far away into the falling darkness. Unlike the Crusaders, their numbers appeared undiminished by a brutal day of conflict.

"*To Montmusard!*" a voice yelled from the distance. A Templar sergeant ran along the parapet calling his brethren to their home camp. "*To Montmusard!*" he repeated.

Louis glanced at Victor to be sure he had heard the call. Victor nodded. They retreated from the battle and descended the steps to the ground. They leapt to their horses and joined their brethren in a gallop toward Montmusard.

Chapter 39

THE FOLLOWING DAY PASSED quietly without a Mamluk attack. Toward evening, just before Vespers, the calm was broken as the Mamluks clamored once more at the foot of the crumbling King's Wall.

The defenders rushed to their posts and resumed casting heavy rocks, boiling oil, and Greek fire onto the attackers, and the archers decimated their ranks. But the siege towers drew nearer again, intent on breaching the walls.

The trebuchets fired relentlessly. Rocks crashed into the walls in a deafening crescendo. For nearly an hour they pounded what remained of the King's Tower and the walls on either side of it. Finally, with a shrieking groan, the rest of the tower collapsed. A roar arose from the multitude on the plain. It was clear to Louis that the end had finally begun.

After the collapse of the King's Tower, other towers fell in quick succession. The Countess's Tower fell, then the English Tower. Walls buckled, and at Saint Anthony's Gate and the Saint Nicholas Tower, they fell.

The corner of the city that jutted northeastward into the plain became the focus of the Mamluk attack. They turned trebuchets to the Accursed Tower on the eastern wall, where a breach would open directly into the heart of the city, abandoning for the moment the walls that protected the Templar camp at Montmusard.

Before night fell, the northeast walls were in rubble, and the attack inexplicably ceased. An eerie silence fell over the city. The Mamluks withdrew a hundred feet from the walls, and the Christians reinforced positions from which they had withdrawn. It was going to be a long, sleepless night.

✠ ✠ ✠

Dawn broke to the sound of thousands of Mamluk drums pounding the thunderous beat of Acre's impending destruction. For Louis, the sound was as a terrible awakening from a short, troubled slumber to a dreadful, wrenching nightmare.

The trebuchets were silent. In forty–two days they had accomplished their task, reducing defenses that had never been breached to pervious ruin and rubble.

The enemy's drums called the Christians to arms, and the battle for the breaches began. Both sides converged at the remnants of the Accursed Tower. It did not take long for the Christian defense to disintegrate before the surging Mamluk force.

King Henry's forces, and then the English and the French, retreated in disarray from the crumbling wall. Each army fled to its own quarter of the city to attempt to protect its own interests. As soldiers and horsemen turned to flee, the Mamluks cut them down from behind.

Henry's retreat ceded the eastern half of the city to the victorious Mamluks.

A sudden violent storm blew up along the coast as if it had been conjured by the Mamluk triumph. The sea grew ugly and gray. Waves crashed against the bows of the evacuation ships and sent them reeling against rocks and shoals. The ships limped back to the harbor to avoid being dashed to pieces. Frantic and desperate refugees disembarked to escape the sea's wrath and made their way back into the city, to the flimsy sanctuary of their churches and homes.

Streets on the east side erupted into chaos. The main Mamluk force drove through the King's Wall and into the city proper. The Hospitaller knights mounted a hopeless defense, outnumbered nearly five to one. A massive secondary enemy force rushed north along the road between the inner and outer walls toward the Lazarus Gate at Montmusard, burning merchants' shops and rich men's palaces as they surged past them. The arrows and missile from the ramparts were impotent to stop the advance, and the Mamluks pressed on toward the Templar stronghold at Montmusard.

At Montmusard, the Templars fought savagely to repel the onslaught. Archers rained arrows upon the Mamluks from the ramparts, and soldiers dropped rocks and hot sand as the attackers threw ladders against the walls and ascended to engage them.

Siege towers lumbered toward Montmusard from the north. They slammed into the outer wall, where nearly a thousand Templars were cut off from the main force by the Mamluks that filled the roadway between them and the inner wall.

Louis fired flaming arrows from the inner wall into the siege towers. Victor stood by him with his sword drawn as the Mamluks ascended ladders to their position. Pike men pushed the ladders away, but for every one that fell, two more appeared. each that fell was quickly replaced by two more. It was not long before the wave of Mamluks overpowered the defenders and scrambled onto the ramparts.

Louis cast his bow aside and drew his sword.

A Mamluk roared victoriously as he scrambled from his ladder and rushed Louis with a heavy spiked mace. Louis whirled toward him, his sword whistling through the dusty air and slicing deeply into the Mamluk's right shoulder. The Mamluk lurched and fell screaming from the parapet to the ground below.

A knight next to Louis took an arrow to the throat and staggered backward, clutching at his gurgling wound. Louis turned, thinking that Victor had been hit, as the knight tumbled over the edge of the wall. Victor traded blows with a swordsman, oblivious to Louis's concern.

Knights were falling quickly. It was clear that those on the outer wall were doomed. Louis searched for Willem, and caught sight of him farther down the wall, fighting by the grand master's side. They too were locked in fierce hand-to-hand combat.

Louis caught Willem's eye, and Willem nodded toward the rear. Willem called to the Grand Master, and de Beaujeu shouted the order to fall back.

"To the ground!" the Grand Master bellowed. The knights began an arduous retreat down the steps to the open ground of Montmusard.

By noon the Mamluks had taken both walls and were streaming over them unimpeded. The Templars retreated deeper into the town. The crashing din of swords on shields and the screams of mortal battle rang through the streets and alleys.

William de Beaujeu called for the Templars to mount a charge against the Mamluks in the field just inside the wall at Montmusard. Louis raced to join them, and a line of Templars charged the Mamluk foot soldiers. The Templar charge devastated the Mamluk infantry. Bodies piled high at the breaches in the wall, and archers fought furiously to stem the tide from the ramparts. The Templars regained the ground inside the wall.

As the knights dismounted, Mamluk trebuchets resumed their attack, lobbing boulders into the battling throngs and laying into the weakening Lazarus Gate. Within an hour the gate and the surrounding walls collapsed, and with the fall of the gate, the Mamluks streamed freely into Montmusard.

The Templars sent their horses to the rear as squires carried javelins to the front line. The knights launched their javelins, and the Mamluks responded with a torrent of arrows and spears. The sky grew thick with deadly darts, and the Templars retreated toward the city center.

Louis turned as the Grand Master bellowed a rallying cry. De Beaujeu prepared to release a javelin, raising his left arm high for aim and balance. An enemy spear sailed in a long, low arc and found its target just below the Grand Master's armpit. Louis watched in horror as de Beaujeu reeled under the impact, and his javelin slipped clumsily from his grip to the dusty ground.

De Beaujeu stood unsteadily for a moment, and then turned and staggered away from the raging battle.

"Master!" Antonio Bollani cried out. "Where are you going? We can't retreat! We've got to hold them here!"

Louis wanted to cry out that de Beaujeu had been horribly wounded.

"Sir William!" Willem called. "What are you—"

De Beaujeu turned toward his knights, his face dazed and drained of blood. Crimson stained his tunic at the chest.

Louis turned and launched his javelin, and before it found its mark in the hollow of an advancing Mamluk's throat, he turned and raced toward the Grand Master.

De Beaujeu gazed blankly around the battlefield as his commanders turned their attention to him.

"I can fight no more," he said plaintively. Flecks of blood spit from his mouth as he spoke. He raised his left arm for all to see. "I have been killed," he said with astonishment. A light Mamluk spear had pierced his armpit and sunk deep into his chest. The bleeding was severe, and Louis didn't understand how de Beaujeu was still standing.

De Beaujeu stumbled, then caught himself. His commanders rushed to catch him. They hurried to fashion a litter from pikes and tunics, and they placed him on it to carry him to the Templar castle. A company of knights surrounded the litter to protect it as they withdrew from the field.

"All is lost," Bollani muttered.

At the sight of de Beaujeu's mortal wound, the Crusader defense faltered, and their forces withdrew toward the old city proper.

Louis did not want to retreat. He wanted to beat the Mamluks back to the wall and chase them back out to the plain. He was newly enraged and more determined than ever to avenge his Grand Master and revive his fading dreams. He wheeled and lunged toward the battle as the Mamluk line advanced. He swung his sword viciously into the face of the nearest Mamluk, killing him instantly. He yanked his blade from the corpse and swung again. He screamed with an animal rage as the lust for blood overtook him.

Mamluk cavalry emerged from the breach in the wall and scanned the battlefield for targets. One of the horsemen spotted the Grand Master's litter a few yards from the cherished Templar beauseant. He shouted excitedly and pointed, and six mounted Mamluks spurred to a gallop. Louis sprang into action as they bore down on the wounded Grand Master.

The Mamluk horses, Arabians, were fast and agile. There was no way that Louis could get to the Grand Master's litter before they did, though he ran as fast as he could.

The knights who guarded the Grand Master lay down the litter and turned to face the charging cavalry. Horror registered on their faces as they realized the futility of their position. Bollani and Osbourne exchanged glances, and Osbourne nodded toward the litter. Bollani motioned for two of the knights to join Osbourne, and for the rest to take up the litter and resume their retreat.

Osbourne and the two knights turned to face the charge. Osbourne drew his sword and lifted a spear from the ground, brandishing it in his left arm like a lance.

The cavalry charge flew past Louis, nearly close enough for him to swipe at them with his sword, the thunder of the horses' hooves nearly drowning out the clanking of his armor as he ran.

The three knights formed a line between the Mamluks and the Grand Master. Osbourne raised the spear and crouched in anticipation.

The leader of the charge reached Osbourne first. The tip of the spear glanced off the Mamluk's shield and drove upward, catching beneath his chin. The impact drove him from his horse and tore the spear from Osbourne's grip. The Mamluk landed with a thud as Osbourne quickly regained his balance and turned to face another horseman.

As the second horse bore down on him, Osbourne stepped aside and swung his sword low, catching the rider mid-calf and severing his right foot. The man screamed and lurched from the saddle. Osbourne pounced and drove his sword through his chest.

A third horse followed close behind the others, too close to allow Osbourne time to recover. Louis screamed a warning, but it was too late. The third horseman rode hard into Osbourne, and as the horse's muscled chest slammed into him, the Mamluk swung his gleaming crescent sword in a wide, powerful arc that cleanly severed Osbourne's head.

Louis cried out in anguish as Osbourne fell beneath the horse's hooves. He ran after the Mamluk in futile rage, driven to avenge his fallen brother.

Mounted Templars appeared from beyond the Grand Master's protectors and swept past them into the remaining Mamluk cavalry. They cut them down in short order and moved on toward the wall.

Louis stared for a moment at Osbourne's broken body, numb with shock and fury. He glanced up at the retreating party to see that they were safely away, and then he turned to follow after the mounted Templars.

He drove into a group of advancing foot soldiers and swung his sword with a vengeance. He no longer felt the rending of flesh, or the gravity of extinguished life. He felt only the torrent of blind, brutal rage, and the drive of bitter vengeance.

"Retreat!" he heard someone yell from behind him. The call sounded distant, and disconnected from the battle he waged. He thought he heard it again, plaintive and small amidst the fierce din. He shrugged it off and dismembered another attacker, grinning at the carnage he wrought.

"Louis!" a louder voice cried. He turned impatiently toward it. Antonio Bollani loomed before him, his eyes blazing, and his

face twisted and covered with blood. "Retreat! Now!"

Louis glared at Bollani and nearly swung his sword, unable to check his rage.

"Now!" Bollani shouted. He grabbed Louis's collar and pulled him off balance as he dragged him toward the rear.

Louis recovered and hurried to keep up with Bollani as the Mamluks clamored madly behind them.

Willem caught sight of Louis. "Hurry!" he screamed.

"We must evacuate," Bollani called out as he turned to engage an advancing attacker.

Willem nodded his agreement as he parried against two others, who were trying to drive him into an alley. He struck a fatal blow to one and spun out of the path of the other's brutal mace.

"Louis!" Willem shouted, nodding toward the south of the city. "Go! Evacuate!"

With one last look at the carnage of the losing battle, Louis joined the Templars in a general retreat to the south, toward the castle, the port, and the waiting ships.

✠ ✠ ✠

There were almost as many Mamluks in the streets of old city Acre as there were in the suburb of Montmusard. Chaos reigned to a chorus of screams. Christian merchants stood defiantly outside their homes in a vain attempt to protect what was left of their families, while Arab merchants watched impassively from their own windows. The invaders cut the Christians down where they stood.

Louis faltered at the sight of two hulking Mamluks restraining a man in front of his house, forcing him to watch as half a dozen others raped his wife and daughters in the street. Louis's hand went to his sword, but Willem grabbed his wrist and dragged him along.

Louis resisted, transfixed by the scene. One of the Mamluks

drew his *khanjar* and raised it to put out the man's eyes. Louis wrenched free from Willem's grasp and drew his sword. In one swift movement, he leapt onto the steps and his blade passed through the Mamluk's muscled neck. The other Mamluk barely registered surprise before Louis dispatched him, too.

Willem sprang into action the moment Louis's sword left its scabbard. "There are too many," he yelled as he drove his sword into one of the rapists. "We can't fight them all!"

They turned and ran through the city to the docks. As they made their way through the chaos, Louis gaped in disbelief. Mamluks were pressing in from all sides, destroying every Christian in their path, while Christian merchants argued with one another, pushing and shoving, still bickering away the final, gasping breath of their crumbling Kingdom of God.

✠ ✠ ✠

Flames licked the skies in every corner of the city. The garitas at the corners of the ramparts spewed smoke and flames, and bodies lay broken and burning on the ground beneath the walls. Acrid smoke filled the air so thickly that it seemed like dusk.

The Templars reached the Templar castle, and Louis broke away from them and ran to the little convent by the Pisan church. He banged hard on the convent door.

"Louis!" Willem called.

Louis shook his head. "Go on," he shouted. "I'll follow. The nuns must move into the castle."

Victor arrived at his side, and Louis turned to him.

"They won't answer," Louis said.

The door creaked open, and the blood drained from Victor's face. Louis follow his gaze to the convent doorway.

The nun who stood there was drenched in blood. Her face was a mass of deep gashes and tattered flesh. Her habit was shredded, and blood flowed freely from deep lacerations across her breasts.

"Good God," Louis whispered. "What..." His voice trailed off as another nun appeared from the darkness beyond the door. She was also badly disfigured and covered with blood.

"Sister!" Willem yelled. "What has happened?"

Victor stared in astonishment.

Nuns began to stagger from the convent, dropping to their knees as they emerged. Louis searched for Mairead, although he was unlikely to recognize her if she were as mutilated as these. He looked from one nun to the other.

Then he saw her hair, strands of chestnut flax, poking from the sides of that familiar coif and veil. There, kneeling in a pool of blood, her hands clasped in silent, solemn prayer, was Mairead – the beautiful, vibrant nun whom he had wrongfully loved, torn and disfigured by her own hand to deny the invaders her beauty.

Every Christian knew the fate of virgin nuns in the hands of Muslim captors. They were raped, of course, until their captors had their fill. Then they were sold as virgins, nonetheless, to the slave traders who supplied the harems of the wealthy emirs. European nuns brought the highest prices for virgin slaves.

Not these nuns, Louis thought to himself. Not now.

He knelt before Mairead in horror. She turned her face from his.

"Mairead," he said softly. She looked up at him slowly through blood–drenched eyes. His throat closed and the blood drained from his face. He felt dizzy. Her nose was gone. Her cheek bones gleamed through deep lacerations, and her lips were cut to shreds.

She murmured incoherently. He leaned closer to her.

"Why didn't you just go?" he asked, aware that it no longer mattered. She shook her head sadly.

In the distance, the streets were filling with combatants, Christians retreating grudgingly before the inexorable push of the Mamluks. The sound of it grew louder with each passing moment. Fleeing civilians clamored in a crush at the Templar fortress gate, a massive, reinforced structure of thick oak and iron set into an impregnable wall, twenty–eight feet thick, and nearly twice as high. Knights and sergeants toiled to manage an orderly flow of refugees into the safety of those walls.

Louis looked up at the magnificent tower that rose high above the gate. The corners of the tower were crowned by turrets, each mounted with a gilded *passant*, nearly life–sized likenesses of lions with outstretched paws, and brilliant silk *beauséants*, flapping in a gentle breeze.

The incongruity of serene beauty, impervious to the horror that surrounded it, infuriated him. He turned back to Mairead.

She gazed sorrowfully at him through the blood that covered her butchered face. Hot tears welled in his eyes, and he wiped them angrily away.

The roar grew louder as the light in Mairead's eyes grew dim. She had lost more blood than Louis thought possible, and he wondered how she was still alive. He cursed silently and pulled her to him, cradling her in his arms.

"Louis...," Willem called softly.

Louis rocked Mairead gently. "It's all right," he whispered to her. "It will be all right."

"Louis...," Willem called again.

"I'll stay with you," Louis said.

"Louis," Willem repeated, placing a hand on his shoulder. Louis turned his eyes to Willem, who shook his head and said, "She's gone."

Willem was right. Mairead had gone lifeless in Louis's arms. He held her tightly as tears streamed freely down his cheeks.

The battle sounds grew deafening, and they were coming from barely half a block away. Louis saw that all the nuns were dead or dying, and that nothing more could be done to help them now. He lowered Mairead's body gently to the ground.

Her passing drew his mind into sharp focus. This street, the little convent, the gilded Pisan church, and the imposing Templar castle – all of this was the final refuge on the farthest promontory of the last Christian stronghold in the promised Holy Land, and it was crumbling. Louis stood and turned toward the raging battle. He resolved courage in the face of the calamitous fall of his cherished, magnificent Jerusalem.

Chapter 40

Ten thousand refugees fled to the Templar fortress ahead of the Mamluk tide. They crowded the castle's courts and alleys, streets and shops, and any space that could hold just one more body. Blind confusion and palpable fear drove many past the point of hysteria. Templar priests circulated among them offering absolution and futile comfort.

The Templars could attempt another evacuation, but their access to the docks was limited to the narrow exits and pathways from the Templar castle, and it would be impossible to move so many people through them. Besides that, the ships in the harbor were now vulnerable to the Mamluk trebuchets, which had moved inside the city.

Enemy siege engineers were mining beneath the walls of the castle, a magnificent fortress that had stood impregnable, until now. Templars on the walls and in the towers continued to repel their attack.

In the Grand Master's palace, William de Beaujeu lay on the table in the great hall. The mood in the room was grim, the silence charged with despair. Louis would never have believed he would end up standing in the company of these men, the most prestigious of all the Templars, in agony, despair, and defeat.

They stood in a semi–circle a short distance from their fading master. Thibaud Gaudin, Jacques de Molay, Peter de Sevrey, and the surviving Templar commanders spoke softly among themselves.

Louis looked to Bollani, who stood rigid, stone–faced and fierce. His dark eyes smoldered, fixed upon something unseen. Louis shifted his gaze to Willem, who nodded almost imperceptibly before dropping his gaze to the floor.

He still could not believe that Osbourne was dead. His heart ached at the loss, and at what it must mean to Bollani, whom he had grown to admire deeply, if not to completely understand.

The Grand Master gasped in pain. He coughed, spraying blood into the air. He raised his hand and gestured for someone to come close. Gaudin and de Molay approached him.

De Beaujeu grasped the collar of Gaudin's tunic and pulled him closer. De Molay leaned in toward him, too. The Grand Master's voice was too raspy and weak for Louis to comprehend what he said, but he understood that the Grand Master was issuing final directives to his potential successors.

De Beaujeu turned his head to the right as if he were straining to see out of the high window on the far wall of the room, to the east. He scowled as the sounds of battle grew louder.

"They're outside the walls," de Molay said quietly.

"Of the castle?" de Beaujeu asked with a pained groan.

"Yes," de Molay said.

The Grand Master closed his eyes and exhaled. "Leave me," he said with a wave of his hand. "See to it. You're wasting your time here."

The seneschals nodded. Gaudin bent and kissed the Grand Master first on his right cheek, then on his left, and de Molay did the same. They backed away and nodded to the servants to tend to him.

With a grim look, Gaudin nodded for the knights to follow

him, and they left the hall to lead the castle's defense.

Louis and Victor went to the docks to oversee the frenzied evacuation. King Henry, along with the Hospitaller Grand Master and the armies of the European kings, had already embarked and set sail for Cyprus, resigned to the loss of Acre and all of its citizens.

The Italians were following suit. As Louis supervised the boarding of the Templar ship *Le Faucon*, a skiff carrying three Venetian sailors pulled in to the dock. They eyed four large chests that were stacked on the dock waiting for transport to a ship. The chests belonged to a church dignitary who stood next to them with his back toward Louis.

Louis approached the dignitary, noting his familiar build. "Those chests will take the space of four people," he said. The man tensed, but did not turn to him. "Better to sacrifice things to save living souls, wouldn't you say?"

Nicholas, the pope's Patriarch of Jerusalem, turned to face him with a haughty look.

"I'm sorry, Your Eminence," Louis said, bowing slightly. Victor turned and looked out to sea, shaking his head.

Nicholas waved a hand and said, "That might be the case if those trunks carried anything less than the relics of Saints Cyprian, Omechios, Leontius, and John Chrysostom."

Louis stared in awe at the chests for a moment, but then he grew doubtful. He glanced at the patriarch sideways as Victor chuckled quietly.

"Relics?" Louis said. "Four chests of relics?" The relics of saints were typically bone fragments, some teeth, or an internal organ, ideally the heart. In rare cases the hands, the feet, or even the skull of a martyred saint were the most highly prized relics. Louis had never heard of venerated relics that consisted of much more than that. "The four saints, you say?"

Nicholas grew indignant. "Is that not what I just said, my son?"

"Eminence," a Venetian sailor shouted from the skiff, "we're ready for your treasure." The patriarch blanched, and Louis scowled at him.

"They *are* in there," the patriarch protested. Louis glared at him. "The relics of all four saints...they're in there."

"With your treasure," Louis said dryly.

"With the *Church's* treasure," the patriarch said. "You don't think I'd leave it for the Saracens."

Louis shook his head. "No, of course not," he said. Four chests of treasure would cost the lives of as many women or children. *One should think the Church would choose children over gold,* he thought. He had come to know better.

"You will not question the pope's patriarch," Nicholas scolded.

Louis shook his head, then turned and walked away. The sailors started loading the chests onto the skiff.

"Do you suppose it even occurs to him?" Louis asked.

"What?" Victor said.

"The choice he's making."

They stopped and turned to watch the loading of the chests.

One of the sailors turned from securing the chests and reached out to help the patriarch onto the skiff. The other two sailors prepared to pull away from the dock.

"How many men do you think would choose differently?" Victor asked.

Louis gave him a look of reproof and said, "Many, especially if they were men of God!"

"Ah," Victor said with a nod.

A startled, high pitched scream came from the skiff, followed by a thunderous splash. The patriarch had slipped from the sailor's grasp and fallen from the dock into the water. The sailor stood with his hands on his hips watching with insipid pity as the patriarch struggled to stay afloat. The other two continued to row the skiff away from the dock.

"You!" Louis shouted, hurrying back to the scene.

The sailor wheeled, surprised that Louis was still watching them. He raised his hands in helplessness and shook his head. "He slipped!" the sailor yelled. "He has the grip of a woman!"

"Save him!" Louis bellowed.

The sailor shrugged helplessly as the skiff pulled away with the chests.

"Stop!" Louis called.

The patriarch's robes were heavy in the water, and they quickly pulled him under. He flailed frantically as his muffled cries bubbled to the surface. Louis and Victor watched helplessly, powerless to do anything to save him. In their armor, they would drown faster than he was if they dove in after him. The patriarch's flailing slowed, and then finally ceased. His vacant eyes froze in an expression of unspeakable betrayal.

Louis glared furiously at the receding skiff. "Burn in hell!" he screamed. He paced the deck, fuming. He wanted to fly to the skiff and cut the sailors to shreds.

"Louis," Victor said, "there's too much more to do."

Louis clenched his fists. "What in God's hell is wrong with people?" he cried. He turned and stormed back toward the ships. "One day I'll find those pigs and gut them," he fumed.

"You'll never see them again," Victor said as he hurried to keep up with Louis.

All along the docks, ships jostled for berth and struggled to take on refugees in as orderly a fashion as possible. In the harbor, a Venetian galley listed badly to its port side not a hundred yards from the dock it had just left. It was clearly overloaded, and badly manned. Louis watched in horror as the ship rolled over on its side and began to sink.

"Too heavy," a dock hand said needlessly, nodding at the ship. Louis stared blankly at him. The dock hand shrugged. "Too much gold," he added.

"What do you mean?" Louis asked.

"A hundred florins a head for passage," the laborer said. "That's a lot of gold...from a lot of people." He looked casually out at the wreckage. "One too many, I'd say," he muttered.

"They're charging for passage," Louis said to Victor. Victor shook his head.

They approached a Genoese captain who was loading evacuees onto his gang plank. A young woman wearing fine silk and a velvet cloak pleaded with the captain, proffering a bejeweled locket from around her neck. A wealthy merchant pushed in front of her, shoving a bag of coins into the captain's face. The captain eyed both treasures with studied indecision.

"Women and children first!" Louis bellowed. He shoved the merchant to the side and confronted the captain. The captain motioned impatiently for the woman to pass. Another woman, perhaps thirty, rushed to embrace Louis, sinking to her knees.

"I'll give you whatever you want!" she pleaded. "Anything. Just get me onto that ship!"

Louis grasped her arm and pulled her to her feet. "There's no charge for passage," he said. He turned to the captain. "Isn't that right, captain?" The man nodded. "Just wait your turn, mademoiselle, like everyone else." The woman nodded and moved to the back of the line for the gangplank.

Up and down the dock, women offered favors and men offered indentured servitude in exchange for passage on evacuation ships. Captains exploited the panic-stricken fray by accepting desperate bribes.

The merchant Louis had pushed out of the line returned to plead with him, his sack of coins cupped in his hands as if he were praying for entry to heaven. Several other merchants accompanied him, each with his own sack of gold.

Louis shook the man by his collar.

"Go find a sword," he roared, "and fight! You'll fight until the last Mamluk is dead, or I'll kill you all myself."

The merchants backed away from Louis in dismay.

"Don't come back," Victor warned.

"I don't want to see any of you," Louis added, "until the Mamluks are gone or the city has fallen, and the women and children are on Cyprus. Then your passage will be free of charge."

The men shuffled away toward the city, grumbling as they went.

The last ships sailed for Cyprus as the first to have left reappeared on the horizon, returning to continue the evacuation. Louis and Victor trudged toward the castle to continue the evacuation. Thousands still waited, and the task promised to be long and arduous.

Excited voices drew Louis's attention as two Templars, Eudes de Valery and Simon Cripplegate, hurried breathlessly from the sea gate toward the docks.

"Louis!" Simon called. "He's dead. De Beaujeu is dead."

Louis stopped in his tracks and bowed for a respectful moment. He said a quick prayer and crossed himself, and then nodded.

"The sultan has heard," Eudes said. "He's asked for our surrender."

Louis was startled. "On what terms?" he asked.

"Safe conduct if we lay down our arms," Eudes replied. "Everybody leaves."

"Are we surrendering?"

"The marshal advises it," Simon said. "They'll stop the siege engines and allow us to board the ships in peace."

They hurried into the fortress and found the commanders discussing the surrender with the marshal, Peter de Sevrey.

"They'll send men in," the marshal was saying, "to assist in the evacuation."

"Why should they do that?" Bollani asked angrily. "They can enter when the last of us is gone."

"Those are their terms," de Sevrey said. "We haven't much choice. Fighting might buy us time, but that is all. Survival is out of the question, especially if the trebuchets keep us from loading the ships."

"How many men?" Willem asked.

"Three hundred," the marshal said.

"Fair enough," Willem answered. "There are at least three hundred of us remaining. They'll do no harm."

The knights agreed, and the marshal ordered the gate guards to admit the Mamluk contingent. An emir entered through the gate followed by three hundred horsemen. When the last of them entered, the guards closed and barred the gate.

De Sevrey stood to meet the emir, who dismounted and

bowed lightly to him.

"Assalamu alai—," the emir began to say when a disturbance arose at the rear of the Mamluk guard. The emir turned toward the commotion.

Dozens of the Mamluks had dismounted and stood gaping at the trembling refugees. They appeared to be taken with the number of young women among them. They began to touch and fondle the women, as well as, to Louis's horror, some of the young boys.

Templars and other knights shouted their protest, but still more Mamluks dismounted and joined in the mischief. Within seconds, the square erupted with shouts, cries, and bedlam.

Around the square, Mamluk soldiers accosted women and boys, tearing their clothing and forcing themselves upon them. Innocents were dragged screaming into alleys and shops, and some were raped on the spot, in full view.

A Mamluk soldier close to Louis seized a woman and forced her to her knees in front of him. She cried out in protest, and the soldier clenched her hair in his hand and twisted, forcing her head to an impossible angle and choking her. He thrust her head into his groin.

Louis flew into a rage. He drew his sword and rushed the Mamluk as a cry went up among the Templars. He buried his sword between the man's shoulder blades. He withdrew his blade and threw the Mamluk to the ground, turning to prepare for a counter-attack.

A thick–built Mamluk dragged a frantic young boy by his wrists into a darkened shop, and bellowed for the refugees to move out and make way for him. Louis followed him into the shop.

Those who could not escape watched in horror with their backs pressed hard against the wall, as if to gain greater distance from the scene.

"Let him go!" Louis yelled, preparing to strike with his sword.

The Mamluk held a *khanjar* to the boy's throat and sneered.

"Let him go, or you die," Louis said, seething.

In one swift movement, the Mamluk drew his *khanjar* across

the boy's throat, threw the blade to the ground, and drew his sword. Anguished screams filled the room as the boy fell lifeless to the floor, nearly beheaded. The Mamluk parried.

Louis maneuvered to allow the others to leave the room while he kept his eyes on his foe. The man jabbed at him angrily, craning his neck to see through the open door what was happening in the square. Louis guessed by his expression that the rising pandemonium wasn't going well for the Mamluks.

The Mamluk laughed.

Something about that laugh, and the slimy, sickening stench it carried forth from the man's foul belly, sent Louis into a rage. Images flashed in his mind, each stoking his rage higher still: the helpless look on the doomed boy's face; the sad defeat in the butchered nuns' eyes; and the dastardly drowning of the wretched, wealthy prelate. The world had gone mad, Louis thought, and he along with it.

Even the way the Mamluk danced before him, thrusting, parrying, working his feet to gain the position of advantage, infuriated Louis. *As if he deserves to win this,* he screamed to himself. With that thought, Louis's world went red.

He sensed violent movement. He heard growling voices, and he felt the snapping and twisting of sinewy flesh. He held no thoughts, but rather the vague awareness that he had thrown himself into a fight to the death – his own, his enemy's, or both. He exploded into a blind, animal fury.

After a moment he grew aware that he was hacking at a lifeless corpse. What was left of the Mamluk was unrecognizable. Four refugees who had not escaped the shop stood in a corner, stunned and speechless, staring at the carnage.

Louis turned to them. He felt blood dripping from his face. He knew he was covered in it, and that he must be a frightful sight. The old man, two women, and a very young girl, also splattered with the Mamluk's blood, looked at him for a moment before they lowered their gaze to the floor. Louis turned and went into the square.

Nearly all the Mamluks were dead or dying. De Sevrey held

the emir at the tip of his sword as both men watched the slaughter in silence.

When the last Mamluk soldier died, de Sevrey shook his head at the emir. "It will be a fight to the death, then," he said. He swung his sword in a wide arc and struck off the emir's head.

De Molay approached from the center of the square. His tunic and sword were covered in blood. He moved with urgency, gathering commanders as he went.

"It's time," he said as he led the commanders to the Templar chapter house. Willem signaled for Louis to wait for him.

A half hour passed before the commanders emerged from the chapter house. Each sought out his own men, and Louis hurried to join Willem.

"We'll be sailing to Sidon," Willem said to Louis.

"What?" Victor said.

"We can't leave," Louis said.

"We must," Willem said. "It was the Grand Master's final order. We're to sail with Gaudin and de Molay to Sidon, and then to Cyprus, to save what is left of the Order."

"Everyone else here will die," Louis said.

"Yes, they will," Willem said, "with us or without us. We'll take as many with us as we can, but all is lost here. We must look to the future."

"We can't abandon them," Louis insisted. Victor glared at him, as if willing him to shut up.

"Louis," Willem said patiently, "they are already dead. And so are we, in a matter of time. The Grand Master's instructions are clear. The remaining assets of the Order are here and at Sidon. They must be taken to Cyprus, where we will regroup and, in time, return. We can only do that if we get our assets, our plans, and our leaders to Cyprus. This is our mission now."

Three Templar ships were loaded for the journey. The ranking Templars gathered on the edge of the square by the sea gate as smoke and flames billowed over the castle from the town outside its walls. The stench of death and destruction stung Louis's eyes.

"Godspeed," Antonio Bollani said. He extended his right

hand, placed it on the pommel of his sword, and bowed slightly in the Templar salute. The others who would remain behind followed suit.

"God be with you," Gaudin said solemnly. "We will return with reinforcements as soon as possible."

The look on Bollani's face made it clear that he believed they would arrive too late. But the look was serene, and his demeanor resolute. He betrayed no trepidation at the battle he was about to face, or its outcome. Louis sensed that he welcomed the fight to the end.

"God save the Poor Fellow-Soldiers of Christ and of the Temple of Solomon," Bollani said.

"We will return," Gaudin promised.

Chapter 41

Louis boarded Le Faucon once again, his disposition profoundly changed from the one with which he first arrived on the sleek, agile ship. He barely remembered that voyage, or the energy and optimism that filled him then. Now he felt oppressed by gloom. It was wrong, he thought, to sail away while others still fought. He understood the reasoning well enough, but it still offended his honor.

The sail caught wind and *Le Faucon* pulled strongly to starboard as she nosed toward the west, where the setting sun edged closer to the dark blue horizon. Louis stood on deck leaning heavily on the railing and staring back at the smoldering city. Smoke billowed from each of the quarters, and flames leapt eagerly into the sky above Montmusard.

As Louis watched, a huge section of the Templar fortress collapsed into the chasms the miners had dug beneath its walls, and a panicked roar arose from the Christians within. Thick smoke billowed from the heart of Acre. Louis knew that there would be no survivors.

He thought of those who lay outside the Templar fortress, in the streets of the walled city, dead or dying the most horrible of deaths. Some would be spared for the slave market; theirs was the worst fate of all.

"So many," he said, shaking his head. Victor stood silently beside him.

Those inside the fortress would die, too, in a matter of time. It might be days, or even weeks, but even with Gaudin's reinforcements, the towers would fall, as surely as the evening sun would set.

Louis leaned against a crate and folded his arms, propping a foot against the rail for balance. He thought about the last few days and the passions to which he had so easily surrendered. Rage, hatred, and the lust for flesh and blood had consumed him.

"I came here to secure my place in heaven," he mused.

Victor shifted his weight and cleared his throat. "Do you feel that you've done that?" he asked.

Louis sniffed. "No," he said. "To the contrary. I feel damned."

"For what?" Victor asked. "You've done what you were supposed to do. You fought well. That's what you came here to do, and that's what you did." He raised his palms, perplexed.

"And now all I can do is wonder why," Louis said. "For what, exactly, did I fight so well? The Kingdom of God?" He pointed at the smoldering city receding into the darkening distance. "For that?"

Victor raised his eyebrows, but said nothing.

"It wasn't what I thought it would be," Louis continued. "I came here bold and certain. I'm anything but that now."

Victor gave Louis's shoulder a sympathetic squeeze. He turned and walked away without a word.

"I *am* damned," Louis muttered to himself. He shook his head as anger grew within him, and the heat of it flushed his cheeks. He wasn't sure what angered him the most. Was it the failure of the Crusade, or that of his own imagined honor? The treachery of the Italians, or his own veiled perfidy? He decided that he was most infuriated by the death of his dreams, but just as quickly he realized that it was the naïveté of his belief in them that enraged him more.

The naïveté was gone. He had learned hatred in Jerusalem, unlike any he had ever felt. He had come here to earn his place in heaven, but instead he had assured himself of hell. He'd learned sympathy for the Saracens and loathing for the Christians. He'd violated his vow of celibacy, and with a nun! The guilt of that alone was weighty, but it was nothing compared with his remorse for having violated it with someone other than Colette. He could find absolution for his sin, and do penance, but he would never find release from his remorse.

Louis felt lost in a life built on little but lies.

Le Faucon sailed silently into Sidon four hours later. The light of the crescent moon was a diffuse glow behind heavy, billowing storm clouds. The wind whipped angrily up the coast, as if to admonish the fleeing ships to never return to the place from which they had been driven.

Soldiers and dock hands waited at the docks to tie them in and escort them to the Templar compound.

In the hall, Gaudin recounted the tale of Acre to the commander and his knights.

"The Grand Master fought valiantly," Thibaud Gaudin said. "He was a champion to the very end. He was struck by a javelin as he raised his arm to lead another charge, despite the losses, and against the odds."

The commander of Sidon, Nicholas de Brienne, nodded solemnly. "As was his way," he said. "He would not have left alive." The commander peered at Gaudin with dark, contemplative eyes.

"He instructed us to depart," Gaudin said defensively.

"Oh, I know that," de Brienne said quickly. "I implied nothing. I knew when you arrived that de Beaujeu was dead, and that Acre was lost. He had sent word to us: should he arrive, then Acre is safe, and peace restored; but should you arrive without him, then Jerusalem itself is lost, and our future forever altered. We are to choose a new master immediately, as was his wish."

Gaudin nodded and glanced nervously at Jacques de Molay,

who sat silent, as if deep in thought.

Serving brothers brought a meal of meat and bread, but Louis had no appetite. He took a few mouthfuls only because he knew he would need his strength, but the food sat heavy in his stomach, and he could eat no more. He felt compelled to find a priest and make his confession, but he knew he could not confess the worst of his sins to just any priest. He wasn't sure he could bring himself to confess it at all.

The future was in fact forever altered, as de Beaujeu had said. Those words were, for Louis, particularly apt. The future is not only altered, he thought, but utterly and terribly unknown. It occurred to him that at no point in his life had he ever, even briefly, lacked certainty about his future.

"We'll hold chapter tomorrow," Gaudin said. " We'll hold the election then." De Molay and de Brienne nodded their agreement.

The Templars elected Thibaud Gaudin to be the twenty–second Grand Master of their Order. In chapter, the Sidon Templars agreed to vacate Sidon and move to the Sea Castle, two ships' lengths from shore.

At the Sea Castle, Gaudin called a chapter to debate the future of the Order in view of Jerusalem's fall, and the merits of further crusading.

"Of course we will continue the Crusade," said Jacques de Molay, the new Templar Commander of Jerusalem. "As we promised, we will bring reinforcements to de Sevrey and recover Acre. But we must move carefully, calculating every step, and every commitment."

Gaudin nodded and said, "We'll retake Sidon, too. The sultan will not hold his armies here for long; he has Cairo to defend, and Mongols to his east. He has taken his revenge. He will go away sated and care little about Acre in three months' time."

Louis saw doubt in De Molay's glance at the new Grand Master, but de Molay pursed his lips and said nothing.

"It will be no easy task to retake Acre," Willem said. Gaudin glared at him, but he continued. "We lost most of our finest, most powerful and seasoned men at Acre. With what will we take her back?"

"You're suggesting that the loss of Acre ruined the entire Templar Order?" Gaudin snapped.

"I'm suggesting that it weakened us," Willem said, "enough that it will take considerable time and effort to win it back."

"I did not—"

"He's right," de Molay interrupted, to Gaudin's indignation. De Molay smiled blandly. "And we will take whatever time is necessary to make it so. But in the meantime, we must think shorter term. How do we get our men from Acre to safety, and what must we do to rebuild strength, and more importantly, the necessary resources and support for our return?"

A tense silence ensued. At long last, de Molay cleared his throat.

"Perhaps," he said, "it is also time for us to entertain our contingencies."

"It's too soon for that." Gaudin said quickly.

"Perhaps not," de Molay replied. "The other Orders have taken steps of their own toward sovereignty. The German Order has established their influence in Prussia, and their Grand Master is headed there now to assert Teutonic authority."

"You're proposing that we abandon Outremer altogether," Gaudin said.

"I'm proposing that we face realities that we have refused to believe, and that we begin to reconsider our destiny," de Molay said. "The Grand Master...Brother de Beaujeu suspected that the time was near. I believe he was correct."

"The time for what?" Louis whispered to Willem.

"Not now," Willem said with a terse wave of his hand.

"I tend to agree with Brother Jacques," said Andreu de Renham. Andreu was a quiet, unassuming man who rarely spoke out in chapter. He had been close to de Beaujeu, almost a confidant, and when he did speak, his thoughts commanded considerable credence.

"Explain," Gaudin said.

"As much as we might desire to continue the Crusade, and

to one day recapture the Holy Land," Andreu said, "we cannot do it alone. Even if we were to return to Acre restored to our full might, and with the vigorous support of the Church, we would fail without the material support of secular Europe. I'd further say that even if we had that, we would still fail without the support of the Mongols."

"You believe Europe will not support further crusade?" Gaudin said.

"How could I believe otherwise?" Andreu said. "The answer to our last request was shiploads of vagrants and felons, an army of murderers and thieves. That so–called support only hastened our fall. That was the clearest sign of what we can expect from Europe in the future."

"Even if we did recapture the coast," Willem said, "I agree with Brother Andreu's assertion that we would not hold it without a Mongol alliance, which we will never have since the pope and our kings spurned their overtures. The Templar Order, though unmatched in might and nobility, would stand alone as a feeble voice in the wilderness, surrounded by hordes of Mamluks and Mongols, and clinging to the memory of a dream long forsaken by the rest of Christendom."

Louis turned to Willem in astonishment. He wondered at what point Willem's assessment of the Holy Land Crusade had turned so starkly negative. He wanted to scream at Willem and demand to know why he had led him on this preposterous quest only to assess it so scathingly now.

Gaudin sat back and placed his fingertips together in front of his face, and the room fell into a troubled silence.

Jacques de Molay cleared his throat. The others in the room turned to him expectantly.

"I don't believe it's too soon," he said. His words were patient and carefully measured. "I believe it's exactly the time to pursue our alternate destiny."

Gaudin peered at him dubiously.

"What destiny?" Louis asked aloud in spite of himself. The question drew stares, but no response.

De Molay continued. "Without firm assurances from the kings of Europe, I believe it's prudent to proceed as if they will not be offered. We can return at a moment's notice to that which we do best, should things turn out otherwise."

"What destiny," Louis whispered to Willem. Again, Willem waved him off.

"A sovereign Templar state, fashioned with a new – and revolutionary – social order," Gaudin announced dramatically, standing as if he were about to deliver a monologue. "You're suggesting that we turn our attention now to the establishment of that fairy-tale sovereignty, before we are certain the Crusades are lost?"

"Fairy tale?" de Molay said. "We have discussed this at length. You have never questioned it as such. Whence comes your change of heart?"

"It will fail," Gaudin said flatly. "It would not last a decade."

"Why not?" de Molay said. "The Hospitallers have their eye on Rhodes. The Germans have their Prussian plan. It would be foolish to proceed as though the Crusade will continue undiminished, as it has for two hundred years, as if nothing has changed. All but the Templars seem to have more promising interests. England, France, Aragon, the Byzantines, the other military orders, and inevitably, even the Italians will all have their sovereign nation states. We will truly be utterly alone in the wilderness of Jerusalem until the Mamluks and the Mongols push us finally and irretrievably into the sea." He paused for emphasis. "The time is *now*. There will be no better time."

Louis finally grasped the nature of the plan to which de Molay referred, a plan that the Templar leadership had held in reserve, apparently for some time, and in absolute secrecy.

He turned to look at his uncle. This was one more secret Willem had kept from him without ever betraying the slightest clue to its existence.

"It's a matter for a vote," Gaudin said. "We'll not decide today. We'll discuss it among ourselves and reconvene tomorrow. We'll vote, and then we'll sail to Cyprus before dawn on Monday. At Cyprus we'll confirm our vote, and then we can look to the future upon which we all decide in the customary fashion."

Murmurs of assent filled the room, and the chapter was brought to a close.

Louis and Willem walked quickly from the hall, Willem leading at a hurried clip.

"Can you tell me what that was about?" Louis asked. He was thoroughly vexed. His greatest aspirations had dissipated. Doubt had engulfed a future he once thought certain. Now, as if that were not enough, there existed a secret plan for his future of which he had not the vaguest clue. "*What* alternate destiny?" he asked.

"Not now," Willem snapped. His eyes flitted warily about the courtyard as they hurried through it. "Not here."

They strode through the Sea Castle gate and onto the dock, and then turned toward the beach on the northern end of the tiny island. Finally, when they were alone at the edge of the sea, with gentle waves and sea foam lapping at their boots, Willem spoke.

"We've known for some time that it would come to this," he said.

"To what?"

"To hard decisions about the future of the Templar Order, in the event the Kingdom of Jerusalem fell and our mission in Outremer was lost."

"And there's a plan..."

Willem nodded.

"Why did you never tell me?" Louis asked.

"I was not at liberty," Willem said. "You should already know that. This is not a matter of my loyalty to you. Our oath to the Order is inviolable. You know I had no right to divulge to you a secret I was sworn to protect."

"Why was it secret?" Louis asked.

"For obvious reasons, I would think," Willem said. "It's a last resort, and nothing more, in the event of the collapse of the Crusade. We hoped against hope, but in vain." He paused, scowling at a seashell that rocked idly in the frothy water. "We expected the Italians to bring seasoned armies. We expected sixty thousand seasoned troops from England, France, and Spain. We didn't count on the rabble they released from the dungeons." He sighed. "I might not have brought you here if I had known how things would turn out. But I must ask you, Louis, in all sincerity." He peered intently into Louis's eyes. "Would you have allowed me to prevent you?"

Louis had to admit that Willem was right. He couldn't imagine what his uncle could have said that would have dissuaded him from joining the Templars and the Crusade. Had Willem painted a bleaker picture, he would only have hardened Louis's resolve.

"No," Louis finally said. "You couldn't have stopped me. You did tell me in the end, before we left Verzeille, that things were going badly. It angered me, but it could not have stopped me." He nodded sadly. "The hounds of hell could not have kept me from my dreams." He looked out to the sea for a moment. "I've been unfair to you," he said. "I've blamed you for my own choices."

"I know," Willem said.

"Things have not been what I expected them to be."

"I know that, too."

"I'm not—," Louis began, but his voice cracked, and he choked on the words. After a pause, he said, "I'm not what I thought myself to be."

"Of course you're not," Willem said. "None of us are. Our ideals are founded in fantasy from the start. We build them when we're young and hopeful, and we pursue them for all we are worth. We fancy ourselves heroes before we've ever had to fight. Our ideals are what drive us to conquer, but we expend them in the process. They end up ravaged by reality." He nodded slowly and said, "That happened to you too quickly."

"Your stories were so wonderful," Louis said.

"I began telling them when I was young...your age, in fact. Unlike you, I started out with good stories to tell."

"So tell me the one about this new order of things, Uncle," Louis said. "Tell me this new story."

Willem cocked his head and furrowed his brow. "That's a complicated tale," he said. "It has its roots at Montségur."

"Montségur!" Louis exclaimed. "The Cathars?"

Willem nodded. "And the French," he said, "and the pope. And the Templars who witnessed the evil of that day."

"I know the story of my grandparents," Louis said. "Mother told me about your escape with the Templar."

"Then you know that Arnaud and the Templars were appalled by the Church's ruthless eradication of harmless, if errant believers."

Louis shrugged and said, "Not entirely. But what has that to do with the Order's destiny, or a new social order?"

"Eighty years ago," Willem said, "for the first time, the Church turned its crusading zeal against Christians. The Cathars held strange and ancient beliefs, which were to the Church something of an inconvenience."

"Yes," Louis said. "I know their criticism angered the clergy."

"More importantly," Willem said, "it was their ideas about the God of the Old Testament as opposed to the God of the New. The idea that the Old Testament God, the God of Creation, was actually the Devil, and that the earth and everything physical is the Devil's creation, is blasphemy in the eyes of the Church."

"I can see that," Louis said.

"But it takes more than a profane inconvenience to move a pope to exterminate an entire sect, particularly one known for its strict adherence to the teachings of Christ."

"What drove Pope Innocent to destroy them?" Louis asked.

"It was not so much Pope Innocent," Willem said, "as it was Louis IX."

"My namesake..."

"Yes. 'The Saint.'"

"Louis must have hated their heresy," Louis said.

Willem shook his head. "Not as much as he hated their influence on the nobles of the Languedoc," he said.

"Their influence?" Louis said, frowning quizzically.

"Many saw logic in their beliefs," Willem said. "If Christians were to reject the Old Testament, they would likewise reject Levitical law. Levitical law is the foundation of the Church's control over its flock. Without Leviticus, there is no fear of God, and without that fear, there is no control. Take away the Old Testament, and you're left with forgiveness and love, God's love, which we are to extend to our enemies as to our friends. While fear brings control, love brings freedom, and freedom is not the pope's desire for his flock."

"The Cathars were too free," Louis observed with a nod.

"They were spiritually free," Willem said. "They exalted neither king nor clergy over any other man. To the Cathars, all men – and all women – were equal: each spirit equally sacred, and each body equally wicked. The material world is evil, and the spiritual divine. The Cathars considered the Church's affluence, its materialism, and the men who pursued it sinful, and not of God."

"I can see why that would offend the pope," Louis said. "That explains why the Church hated them. But what did King Louis have against them? I thought they were loved by the nobility."

"They were," Willem said enthusiastically, "by the *Languedoc* nobility. The Cathars' independence appealed to them. It inspired them. The people of the Languedoc have always harbored a desire for autonomy, and the Cathar spirit complemented and intensified that. But such independence threatens tyrants. It threatened Louis's designs on the Languedoc, which he wanted badly to annex to his empire."

"And the nobles resisted," Louis mused.

"Vigorously," Willem said, "and Louis blamed the Cathars. He instigated the popes to action against the Cathars, and he provided the troops. There were ten thousand French soldiers at Montségur, but only a handful of Inquisitors and their attendant clergy. Montségur was more a French military campaign than the workings of the Church."

"Yes," Louis said, "I can see that, too." He paused, troubled. "How does that lead to the Templar plan?"

"Louis," Willem said, "our world has long been ordered under the dominion of popes and kings. Kings rule in temporal matters, and priests in the spiritual. The delicate balance of power between them, as long as it is maintained, affords the rest of us a measure of protection from each against the other. But when those forces combine in common pursuits, such as the extermination of the Cathars and the annexation of the lands they influenced, that power is formidable. And there is little that stands in the way of that collaboration but their mutual distrust."

"What would be the alternative?" Louis asked. "How could men be governed in the absence of such power?"

"As I said, things have been that way for centuries, but it has not always been so. The Greeks established government by the people to end the dictatorship of petty kings and cruel aristocrats. The incomparable magnificence of Rome was built on a government in which the power of its kings was checked by a self-governing citizenry. Only when the emperors seized absolute power did Rome's glory fade."

"Are you saying that kings should not have the power to govern?" Louis asked.

"The power to govern," Willem said, "is destructive in the hands of too few men. History has shown that despotism cannot survive the insanity it breeds. Until the power of tyrants is balanced by the will of the governed, kingdoms will rise and fall, and peace will never reign. God's kingdom would be one of peace. It cannot be built on the foundation of the current social order."

To speak heresy would get his uncle arrested, Louis thought. But this was treasonous speech, and it would get him executed without a trial.

Willem continued: "A lot of consideration has been given to the idea of a new kind of order, a social structure the likes of which has not existed for nearly a thousand years."

"A social structure that failed nearly a thousand years ago?" Louis asked pointedly.

"A social structure that faded in the face of the despotic greed that rules us to this day."

Louis gasped and said, "You shouldn't speak that way, Uncle, not even to me. It's suicide to speak such things."

"Louis, there are men among us who dream of such a society, and who are willing to die trying to build it." Willem pointed to the shores of Sidon. "There are men who *have* died to build such a kingdom here." He drew a deep breath and turned toward the sea. "Imagine," he said softly, "a social order ruled not by priests and kings, but rather by nobles and free men, by parliaments and judiciaries that govern through a system of elections, debates, and ballot boxes...a system in which every free man has an equal voice. Imagine a society governed only by a common rule of law."

"No king would allow such a thing," Louis said.

"Perhaps not readily," Willem said. "But ultimately, one may. That may lead others to do the same, because greatness will come of it. Seventy–five years ago, the English Magna Carta was a small step toward just such a thing. Simon de Montfort made great strides in creating a parliament in England. He was one of those of whom I spoke, who are willing to give their lives to create a new order."

"He was killed," Louis said. "As I said, no king would allow it."

"De Montfort set a spark to the kindling," Willem said. "The English nobility have had a taste of self–governance. They will not forget the taste of it, and they will inevitably resume their quest for it. I believe King Edward is aware of that."

Louis nodded slowly, then said, "And what of the Templars? What has this to do with us?"

A commotion in Sidon drew their attention. Saracen soldiers were gathering along the shore, clearly in preparation for attack. Willem sighed again.

"This is not our destiny," he said. He shook his head and turned to Louis. "We answer to no king. We will build that sovereign Templar state in the Languedoc, from the Pyrenees to Auvergne, and from Toulouse to Avignon."

Louis was stunned. "Philip would surely never allow that!" he exclaimed.

Willem shrugged. "It may not be a matter of him allowing it," he said. "He's deeply in debt to the Order. It's not likely he'll acquire the financial means to satisfy that debt. It may turn out to be in his financial interest to support the plan."

As the concept of a Templar state grew clearer in his mind,

Louis felt excitement rising within him. A Templar state in the Languedoc would bring him home. His ambitions for Outremer would be over, but he would still be a Templar, and he would be home. His mind raced to Colette.

At the thought of Colette, he understood the conflict he would face. How could he be near her and not be with her? How would he observe his Templar vows?

"Uncle Willem," he said, "the Order is to be based in the Languedoc, then?"

"Eventually," Willem replied. "I imagine it would take some time to effect the plan...a decade or so. But then, of course, it would make sense. Until then, Cyprus will remain our base."

Willem raised his eyebrows. "The Languedoc would be difficult for you," he ventured.

Louis nodded uncomfortably.

"That has occurred to me," Willem said.

"It has?"

"Of course it has."

"Why?" Louis asked.

After a long silence, Willem spoke softly. "I've thought that perhaps you may want to consider an alternative destiny of your own," he said. "Perhaps one where you might find true happiness instead of the endless pursuit of elusive dreams."

"That's not possible," Louis said. "I made a vow."

Willem looked thoughtful. Finally, he said, "Vows have been broken. Vows have been retracted and dissolved." He folded his arms and walked slowly along the waterline. "Especially in the last decade," he continued, "as things have grown less certain. You're not the only one who has discovered that the things that drew you here are past and gone. Many before you have reassessed their vows in the harsh light of reality. A few rejected them so completely that the only honest thing to do was to renounce them, and to be on their way."

"It's a shameful thing," Louis said.

"Less shameful than the pretense of vows no longer cherished," Willem replied. "Far less shameful than vows inevitably broken."

Louis winced. "I don't want to renounce my vows," he said.

"I know you don't," Willem said. "And I don't want that for you. But you must know that it is an option."

Louis said nothing. He could not imagine publicly renouncing his vows. He had set the course for his life, and it could not be changed.

Willem said, "Just know this, Louis, that a formal request from you and a supportive word from me would likely gain release from your vows and allow you to pursue a life for which you may have greater longing. There would be no shame in the forthright declaration of what is in your heart, or in having enough respect for the Order, and for yourself, to renounce vows you can no longer honor. It would be far better than to fail those vows in an inevitable moment of spontaneous passion."

Louis hung his head. *It's too late for that,* he thought. Nevertheless, he knew Willem was right. He had already begun to feel the longing that would draw him back to Colette. He knew that once they arrived at Cyprus, he had a lot to consider. He had much for which to pray. He had much to confess. There was a good deal for which he owed God penance.

Chapter 42

EUROPE REELED FROM THE LOSS of the last Christian stronghold of the Kingdom of God, and Europeans began to question the need for the military Orders whose purpose it was to defend it.

Templars from all corners of the Levant gathered at Cyprus to recover from their loss of the Holy Land. Casualties had crippled the Order, and rebuilding would take many years.

The new Grand Master Thibaud Gaudin focused his efforts on reviving the Crusade. He sent knights throughout Europe to recruit and to campaign for a new Holy Land Crusade.

But after two hundred years of vacillation between triumph and collapse, the likelihood of such a revival was remote. The occasions when Europe committed its full passion, power, and wealth to the Crusade had produced only fleeting success; each subjugation of Jerusalem inspired a more crushing retaliation than the last. Few thought such enthusiasm for Crusade would ever rise again.

Therefore, Gaudin introduced to the commanders of the Order a closely guarded contingency. He formed a council to work out the planning for a new, sovereign Templar state.

Louis spent a year on Cyprus studying the administrative duties he would assume upon the formation of the new Templar state. He understood that he was about to begin forging the foundations for a new world order. It was not the foundation of an invincible, enduring kingdom of God, but rather precisely the opposite: a society of free men governed by the common good rather than by tyrants or popes.

He longed to return to his home, to put his experiences in Acre behind him, and to set about building the foundations of that state. He also found himself thinking more about Colette with each passing week, and before long he could not get her out of his mind. He had accepted that he loved her deeply, and her letters to him made it clear that she was heartsick for him. He pursued his work with deep and growing uncertainty. He puzzled over the outcome of their inevitable reunion.

✠ ✠ ✠

Late one evening, Louis sat with Willem in the courtyard of the commandery at Douzens making small talk and musing about the future. Louis also mulled questions that still nagged him about his past.

"Uncle," he said tentatively, "could you tell me more about my grandparents and our connection to the Cathars?

Willem did not answer for a moment. Finally, he sighed and said, "My parents were good people. In fact, they were two of the finest people to have walked this earth. I do not say that only because they were my parents. All who ever knew them said that. The example of their lives inspired many others to seek greater closeness to God, and greater goodness in their own hearts."

"Are you talking about François and Marguerite Marti," Louis asked, "or about the parents you lost at Montségur?"

"I'm talking about Peires and Bruna Domergue. They were

my mother and father."

Louis nodded. "The Cathars," he said.

"Yes," Willem said, "the Cathars. The pope's Albigensian Crusade drove them to Montségur. They survived the ten-month siege of Montségur, but in the end they were marched down the mountainside and into a waiting bonfire, along with more than two hundred others."

"Mother told me the story," Louis said quietly.

"They were godly people," Willem said, "and they were burned alive by so-called 'people of God.'" Sadness overtook him. He paused for a moment, then said, "The Templar who rescued us—"

"Arnaud."

"Yes, Arnaud. He took us to the great castle at Quéribus, to which most of Europe's Cathars had fled from the terrible crusade."

Louis nodded.

"I was three years old, and your mother five when we were taken to Quéribus."

"To the home of François Marti," Louis said.

"Yes," Willem replied. "François and his wife Marguerite were Cathars, too. Publicly, they had been good Catholics, but they fled to Quéribus to protect us. They told their neighbors they were off to their Scottish estate."

"How long did you stay at Quéribus?"

"Eleven years," Willem said. "I was fourteen, and your mother sixteen, when we fled Quéribus ahead of the French army. Most went to Aragon, and some to Piedmont, but the Martis, along with four other families, chose to return to Languedoc." He paused, reflecting and shaking his head. "It was a terrible mistake."

"Why?" Louis asked.

"The Inquisitors caught up with several of the other families. Suspicions about the Martis were vague and unsubstantiated, but the other families were not so fortunate."

"They were arrested...," Louis mused.

"And tortured," Willem added. "And imprisoned for life."

"Not burned?"

"They had confessed under torture and begged forgiveness," Willem said. "Life imprisonment was their reward. It was not a long sentence, though. Two years later, they made the mistake of defending their faith in a debate with another prisoner. They were burned as relapsed heretics. All but one."

"Why not that one?"

"One son reaffirmed his repentance," Willem said. He looked thoughtfully at Louis. "He rejected the Cathars. He denied their beliefs. They allowed him to live. The Inquisitors released him as a demonstration of the good will they offered to repentant heretics."

"Why did he repent?" Louis asked.

"Because he was furious with God," Willem replied, "for allowing such horrors to destroy his family, and to ravage so many innocent Christians. He rejected God altogether, and he said what he needed to say to gain his release. He retained one Cathar belief: that God cares nothing for the fate of a soul born into this life, and that if He cares for anything at all, it is only for the spirit that eventually escapes it."

"I can see why he would feel that way," Louis said.

"Yes," Willem agreed. "His anger with God eventually waned, but his hatred for the Church did not."

"That alone will get him killed, eventually," Louis observed.

"Louis," Willem said pointedly, "that son is your father."

Louis's jaw dropped. "My father!" His mind reeled. "But, he's a good Christian..."

"Yes," Willem agreed. "He is...as good a Christian as any. And his devout Catholicism assures his survival, as it did your own."

Louis shook his head. He was losing patience with seemingly endless discoveries that upset his cherished images of his family as simple and devout, and of his life as valiant and noble. "My life is a lie," he muttered.

"No more so than anyone else's, Louis," Willem said with a shrug.

"How much more is there that I don't know?" Louis asked, still shaking his head.

"Louis, whether we like it or not, this world forces us to hide who we are, and for the most part, the things we feel or believe most deeply. Honesty is rarely a rewarding attribute."

"The Martis?" Louis asked. "Are they what I believe them to be?"

"They're saints," Willem answered. "Jacques Marti's parents took your mother and me into their home as orphans of the Inquisition. They raised us as Catholics, teaching us how to navigate a complicated gauntlet of scrutiny and judgment. Jacques' parents were highly regarded members of their local parish. They were also among the most devoted Cathars I have ever known.

"And Colette," Louis said. It was an acknowledgement rather than a question.

"A wonderful, beautiful, and brilliant little Cathar, she is," Willem said with a smile. He paused for a moment, mulling a question he finally voiced. "You want to marry her," he said.

Louis jumped and nearly lost his balance.

"I'm a Templar!" he protested. He felt his face flush hotly.

"Yes," Willem said, nodding.

"I took a vow," Louis said solemnly.

"You did," Willem agreed.

"It's not relevant what I want."

"But it *is* what you want..."

"I took a vow," Louis repeated.

"You could trade it for another."

"I don't take my vows so lightly," Louis said. "It doesn't matter whether or not I would like to marry Colette. It's not possible."

"It is, actually," Willem said

Louis wanted to ask him what he meant, but he refrained from pursuing the idea.

"My vows are everything to me," he said.

"I know," Willem said. "It's an admirable trait. But the truth is that no one would blame you. She's a fine girl. She'd make a finer wife. The Grand Master would understand, and agree to it."

"Things make ever less sense to me," Louis said. "To whom, then, did I make my vow? To the Order, certainly...yet the Grand

Master would agree with my breaking them. To the Church, also. I doubt the Church would agree, but then I have come to suspect that the Church possesses more the evil of men than the glory of God, and perhaps the pope's blessing is of little meaning anyway. So what, or whom, do my vows serve?"

Willem thought for a very long time, until Louis began to think that he would not answer.

"Your vow," he finally said, "was to those things for which the Poor Fellow-Soldiers of Christ and of the Temple of Solomon stand. You may perceive as time goes by that the things for which the Order stands often have little to do with the Church and its inquisitions. There is much I can tell you, and much I should not say, but of this you may be sure: the Templar Order has stood and fought for virtuous ideals. Of that, you can be both certain and proud."

"And yet you think I should renounce my vows."

"I think you should be true to yourself," Willem said. "By being true to yourself, you are being true to the Order. You should not be here if it is not in your heart."

"It *is* in my heart," Louis said. "It has always been in my heart." He looked off into the distance and felt his shoulders sag. "But I suppose there are a lot of other things in there with it."

"Yes," Willem said. "That's plain for all to see." He placed a reassuring hand on Louis's shoulder. "All who care for you want only for you to find happiness, and your true destiny."

"Would it not be failure to forsake this destiny for another?"

"This destiny has failed all of us," Willem said sadly. "It would be failure to cling to it when another, truer destiny beckons."

"When the time is right, we will bring this to Gaudin and de Molay," Willem said. "When we settle at Cyprus and our future grows more clear, we can request a release from your vows, and we'll discuss your future in the new Templar state. I believe you could still play an instrumental role in that endeavor."

"I'll give it prayerful consideration," Louis said.

Lightning streaked across the sky as Louis's ship put in to port near Perpignan. Most of the knights who accompanied him had been reassigned to the Perpignan commandery. Willem, Victor, and Louis would continue on to the commandery at Douzens, just east of Carcassonne.

The night at Perpignan was restless for Louis. His heart pounded with the excitement of going home. The four long years since he had left home seemed like a lifetime.

Thibaud Gaudin had died before they broached the subject of Louis's release. Jacques de Molay was promptly elected Grand Master, and the concerns of an Order in turmoil left him no time to entertain the private matters of individual knights.

De Molay moved quickly to effect the sovereignty plan. In less than a week, the knights were bound for new assignments throughout Europe, and Louis was on the ship toward Perpignan, his ultimate fate yet unclear.

"Was it this way for you?" Louis asked Willem. "A lifetime between your visits home?" He tightened the straps on his saddle as they prepared for the journey from Perpignan to Douzens.

Willem smiled and nodded. "Sometimes," he said.

"And the uncertainty?"

"That's new," Willem said. "I suppose we'll get used to it, at least for a while."

Rain fell hard on their early morning departure from Perpignan. The squires grumbled and the horses whinnied in the weather to which they had grown unaccustomed. The road was thick mud, and the going was slow. The tediousness of their progress frustrated Louis, but he maintained an impassive demeanor, resolved to repress his eagerness. He reminded himself that the journey would take two long days or two short days, but two days nonetheless.

They arrived at the Douzens commandery, along with their squires, in the afternoon of the second day. Three days later Willem, Louis, and Victor set out on the five hour journey to Verzeille. They passed Carcassonne at noon. The sight of it set Louis's heart aflutter; they were barely two hours from home.

Just after noon they passed the village of Leuc on the road to Saint-Hilaire, not far from where Louis and Colette first met Victor. Verzeille was less than an hour to the south, and Louis could barely contain himself. His home was a half mile beyond Verzeille.

"They may not recognize you," Willem said, giving Louis an appraising look.

"I've not changed that much," Louis replied.

"You have," Victor said.

"Not so much that Col…that my family wouldn't recognize me," Louis said. "Surely not that much." Victor shrugged and Willem grinned.

"We'll see," Willem said.

Louis wondered about Maximilian. Surely he would know Louis, if he was still alive.

They crossed a small brook that flowed into the stream that ran along the right side of the road. The road and the stream curved slightly to the right, and beyond that curve was the sight Louis longed to see. He felt as though he were approaching heaven. He wondered if it had been like that for Willem all those times he had approached this curve on his return from his Outremer adventures. He was too excited to ask.

They rounded the curve and caught sight of a man bent over to some task in front of the house. At the sound of the hooves, the man straightened and peered at them across the fields. It was Hervé, the steward.

Hervé threw his shoulders back and hurried excitedly into the house. As the troop approached the dusty drive that led from the road to the house, Hervé reappeared, followed by a jubilant throng.

Louis's heart pounded. First came his mother, waving excitedly. Then his father, calm and composed, yet clearly buoyant at their return. Louis looked past them to the open door. His heart leapt and his throat went dry as Colette emerged, radiant and graceful as ever.

The sight of her captivated him. He dismounted and embraced

his mother as she wept with joy. He turned to his father and embraced him firmly for a moment. Jacques Marti rushed to embrace him next, and as he did Louis fixed his gaze on Colette and her mother, Isabelle, who stood patiently behind Jacques.

"God's eyes, son, how you've grown!" Jacques exclaimed. "What a fine, strong lad you are! Welcome home."

Finally, Jacques released Louis, and Louis stood facing Colette and Isabelle. He bowed toward Isabelle.

"Madame Marti," he said graciously. He took Colette's hand in his and tenderly kissed it. "Dearest Colette," he said.

She drew her hand from his and touched her lips. Tears filled her eyes, and the sight of it broke Louis's heart. Her shoulders shook with a silent sob. She threw her arms around him and held him for a long moment. "Louis," she finally said, "I've missed you so. I'm so glad you're back!"

"So am I," he whispered.

Colette looked past Louis and smiled at Victor. "It's good to see you, too, Victor," she said.

"Mademoiselle," Victor said, rather too stiffly. He nodded curtly at Louis and said, "I don't mean to be rude, but I'd like to—"

"By all means," Louis said. "Go, my friend. Visit with your family. Give them my regards."

Victor nodded and remounted Soranus.

"Is he all right?" Colette asked as he rode at a quick canter down the drive.

"I'm sure he is," Louis said with a shrug.

Hervé disappeared toward the kitchen, and Louis thought with delight of the dinner he would surely prepare. He was famished.

"Into the hall," Marie said in a playfully commanding tone. She shooed them all toward the house.

"Come, sit," Isabelle said when they entered the hall. She motioned Louis to a chair at the table. "Tell me how you have been."

"Quite well, Madame," Louis said as he sat. "Although I must say, I have longed to be home with my family and friends." He smiled at Colette. *She's so much more beautiful than I remembered*, he thought to himself, although he hardly thought that possible.

Colette blushed as though she knew his thoughts.

"We've missed your company as well, Louis," Jacques said. "Will you be home long?"

Louis looked to Willem.

"We'll be garrisoned here," Willem said. "At Douzens."

"Douzens!" Jacques exclaimed. "That's wonderful! Then we shall see you all the time."

Colette beamed.

Louis was struck by the joy that shone in Colette's eyes. He was also haunted by an anxiety that had lurked beneath his excitement for most of the last few hours. It grew as they neared Verzeille, and now it was palpable. He could not banish the image of Mairead that appeared when he looked at Colette. He cursed himself and his sin.

"What will you be doing there?" Jacques asked. "Oh, I'm sorry," he quickly added, catching himself. "Never mind that. It's Templar business, of course."

"Yes," Louis said, forcing a smiling. "Templar business."

"With the fall of Acre," Willem said, "we're faced with rebuilding the Order's strength and its finances. We hope to resume the Crusade eventually, but the possibility and the timing of that are uncertain. Our duties here are primarily administrative. I'll work to bolster support for the Order. Louis will train for administration and finance."

"At least you will not be fighting," Marie said, squeezing Louis's shoulders and kissing the top of his head.

Louis grimaced. "I had always imagined a life of adventure and heroism," he said, "and not one of administrative drudgery."

"Well, I prefer the latter," Marie said.

Louis was surprised to see his father nod in agreement.

Raimon grinned and said, "You may find navigating local politics somewhat more brutal than combat with the Saracens."

Louis nodded. "It's not my preference," he said.

In fact, it occurred to him that some degree of his anxiety

was at the prospect of life as a cleric rather than a warrior of God.

"Eat," Marie said, gently scolding, "and drink. Talk, but of simpler, more peaceful things."

Louis sat for hours talking with his family, and along with Willem, answering a steady flow of questions about their Outremer experience, and in particular the details of the fall of Acre. As they told the tales of all that had happened over the last few years, Louis marveled at all that had happened in such a short time. He could hardly believe that in a mere four years he had experienced the exhilaration of joining a glorious cause, and the anguish of its thunderous collapse.

He could not resist his desire to walk with Colette, and to talk with her alone. That much, at least, had not changed. He caught her attention, and she nodded her acknowledgement. At long last, he chose an appropriate lull in conversation, and he quietly stood from his chair.

"Monsieur Marti," Louis said respectfully, bowing in his customary fashion, "may we?" He indicated Colette with a weak grin and a nod of his head.

Jacques glanced at Colette with a smile, and then returned Louis's bow. "You may, young man," he said. "Look after her well, Sir Knight."

"I shall, Monsieur," Louis vowed. He took Colette's hand and led her to the door. Outside, they walked slowly, side by side, gazing warmly at one another, until they arrived at their favorite spot by the stream.

Chapter 43

THEY SAT FOR A VERY LONG TIME, watching the water swirl in the stream and the clouds drift across the azure sky. They were content to savor one another's company in silence.

Finally, she turned to him and said, "Tell me about Jerusalem. Was it anything like what you expected it to be?"

Louis watched a hawk circle high above a field in the distance as he contemplated the question.

"No," he finally said. "It wasn't what I expected."

"In what ways?"

Again, he struggled with his reply. He bit his lip and forced his most shameful memory aside.

"There were no glorious battles," he said.

Colette suppressed a smile. "I'm not sure I ever believed such a thing exists," she said.

"What I mean," Louis explained, "is that we didn't sweep across the deserts subduing Saracens and reclaiming vast swaths of Outremer for the Holy Church and the Kingdom of God."

Colette nodded.

"Instead," he continued, "we patrolled the streets of Christian cities in an effort to prevent Christian merchants from causing the collapse of the meager scraps of the Kingdom we still controlled."

"But you're alive," Colette said, placing a gentle hand on his arm. "That's all that really matters to me."

He smiled weakly and said, "But you know it's not all that matters to me."

"I know it's not," she said. "I'm sorry. I'm just so glad you're home. Tell me about what you've done."

He was haunted once more by the image of his desperate tryst with the alluring nun amid the dust and din of the collapsing Crusade.

"What I've done?" he said. He felt his face flush. He shook off the image. "There's not much to tell, really."

"I don't believe that," she said. "You're being modest."

"No." He shook his head. "I'm really not. Not at all." He paused while she waited patiently. "Until the end," he continued, "it was mostly just patrols – not against the Mamluks, but to control the Christians in the city."

Colette furrowed her brow. "Why?" she asked.

"They bickered, mostly," he said. "The Italians' hatred for one another exceeds their desire to live. They cheat one another at every opportunity, and they betray one another to the enemy if they think it's in their interest to do so."

She nodded in understanding. "They're merchants," she said.

"They stop at nothing to gain the upper hand against their competitors," Louis continued. "They found unity only in their abuse of the local Arabs. I spent more time protecting Muslims from Christians – and *Christians* from Christians – than I ever did protecting Christians from Muslims. Only in the end did I find myself fighting Muslims for the Kingdom of God, and that was for its very survival."

"You seem disillusioned," Colette said softly.

"I imagined a Jerusalem filled with ardent Crusaders," Louis said. "I thought I'd fight alongside others who thought as I did, who dreamed the same dreams." He tore a pinch of grass from the earth and flicked it into the swirling water. He sighed heavily and said, "I was wrong."

She stroked his forearm and gazed into his eyes. He marveled at the warmth of her expression.

"I'd heard the stories," he said, "but I was not prepared to see with my own eyes Christians tearing at each other's throats. I did not expect cruelty among Christians and kindness from Muslims. It was unsettling."

She cocked her head and peered at him. "It seems to have changed you in some way," she said. "Has it?"

He sensed that she wanted badly to hear that it had not. He shrugged. "It was discouraging," he said.

"I'm sure it was," Colette said. "It goes against everything you believe in. But you can't let it make you angry, Louis."

He gave her a reproachful look. She couldn't possibly understand. "I can't?" he asked. "Why not?"

"Because it won't make any difference to them," she replied, "and it will only make you very unhappy...as it seems to be doing now."

"People should be loyal," he said, but even as he said the words they cut like a dagger to his heart, and he faltered.

"Perhaps you should be more forgiving," she said in a softly reassuring voice.

He gritted his teeth, more angry with himself than anything. "Yes, I know you're right," he said. "It will take time. It's like I lost everything – my dream, my future, even my own sense of myself." He gazed into her eyes and said, "I've missed you terribly."

"Oh, Louis," she said, "I've missed you, too. It was as though I'd lost my lifelong friend. I've wandered these fields without you, and they seemed to have all gone fallow. I've gazed into the stream for images of you, but the currents were empty and dark. This place is lifeless without you, Louis."

A painful lump formed in his throat. "Colette," he whispered, "you know that I love you."

"I do," she whispered.

"You love me, too..."

"Yes."

"I've wished that things were different."

"As I have, also."

"I made my choice," he said. "I took my vow."

"Yes, you did."

"There are times—"

She pressed a finger to his lips to stop the words. She leaned into him and pressed her cheek to his, and slid her arms around him. He felt a fluttering in his chest, and his mouth went dry. He closed his eyes and saw the desperate nun.

"What's wrong?" Colette asked. She must have felt him shudder.

He pushed the image from his mind.

"Nothing," he said. "It's all right." He embraced her, and rising passion overcame his nagging regret.

"I've dreamed of holding you like this," she said. Her voice grew husky in a way he had never heard, and her breaths grew deep and heavy. His heart pounded as she pressed into him.

He leaned to kiss her brow. She turned her eyes toward his, and he felt her breath on his lips. He stopped, transfixed by the feel of it.

Finally, his hunger overwhelmed him, and his lips found hers. They kissed long and deep, and the passion that had tugged at the fringes of his heart rose in thunderous waves, as if driven by an ocean storm. Her body responded to his, and she pressed into him with surprising strength.

"I've craved you," he said, surprised by his own words.

"And I you," she said in a husky, breathy voice.

Louis's breath caught in his chest as Colette's hand moved from his back to his thigh, pulling him tighter against her.

The touch of her hand on his thigh caused a stirring in his groin and enflamed his desire for her. He longed for her to consume him, to smother him in the magnificent beauty of her soul, and to banish forever the memories of all the blood, the pain, and the war of deceit from his mind. He wanted to bury himself inside of her, as close to the warmth of her heart as he could be.

As the world faded around them, he surrendered to his desire and pressed his mouth harder against hers. He wrapped his arms around her body and hoisted her to his chest. A hungry gasp escaped her lips, and their tongues found one another.

The pleasure of her mouth on his dispelled his discipline. He felt a fervor that was new to him, that had nothing to do with conviction, loyalty, or belief. It was a visceral hunger that only her body could feed.

"Colette," he said in a low, husky voice, "I have dreamed of nothing but you. Your love is my breath." He pulled back and gazed into her eyes, driven to finally, fully, and freely communicate to her what he felt in his heart for her. "Your love has been my strength through all these years."

Unable to respond, she nodded and held his gaze. She pulled him back to her as she closed her eyes and opened her mouth to his.

Tears welled in the eyes of a warrior who had wept for no other thing: not the carnage of war, nor the ache of betrayal, nor the burning of innocents, and not even the utter devastation of his dreams. Nothing had touched him so deeply as his desire for her, which had grown into a burning need.

He felt the softness of the worn white fabric on her back, and he turned and laid her down in the green meadow grass. His hand explored her warm, soft flesh.

"Yes, Louis…yes," she said. "Make me yours."

He was not sure if she actually said those words, or if he had imagined them. He gazed at her. Her chest heaved, and her eyes clouded with emotion. His hunger for her intensified. He wanted to take her quickly, as he had the battlefields of his life, but at the same time, he wanted to savor her, to memorize the softness, the scent, the contours, and the warmth of her body. He contained his urgency. He had time to make love to her. He looked into her eyes.

He felt the heat of her gaze. His mouth found the curve of her neck, and his lips caressed her skin. The musky scent of her hair mingled with the fresh smell of clover.

She ran her fingers through his hair and gently pushed his head toward her breasts. She loosened the ties of her blouse. He pulled them free, and his calloused hands explored flesh he had never seen with his eyes. Her body moved rhythmically beneath his touch, and her breath came heavy and deep. She pressed her fingers into the muscles of his back.

"Take me," she whispered.

He fumbled with the hem of her dress and slid his hand up her thigh. She moaned softly as he caressed her in a way she had never been touched. He lingered there, allowing her to savor his attention. Her hips rose to meet his touch, and she placed her hand on his and pressed him into her.

He raised the folds of her dress over her hips. She pulled him toward her and reached to unfasten his buckle. He pressed his body against hers and kissed the hollow of her throat. She tensed and gasped as he entered her, and their bodies came together.

They moved in a slow, intoxicating rhythm and the feel of her filled him with ecstasy. He felt as though their spirits had become as one, and that his would never again be complete apart from hers. Their movement built to a pulsing crescendo of pleasure, passion, and love.

In an explosion of intensity, he lost all awareness of anything outside of their union. His body trembled, and he felt as though his heart might burst. Rapturous waves washed over him, consuming him, and uniting his essence with hers. He collapsed into a sea of euphoria.

"I love you, Colette," he finally said as his heart slowed and he caught his breath. "I want to live my life inside of you."

She moaned softly. "That's all I've ever wanted," she said. "This…is all I've ever wanted."

They lay on the soft, green grass, the sunlight warming their faces and their passion subsiding into gentle, enveloping warmth. Neither of them noticed the furtive movements of a figure in the darkness of the tree line.

"What will I do?" he mused as he nuzzled her neck.

"About what?" she asked.

He turned his head toward her, pressing his cheek to the ground.

"About my vows," he said. "They're firmly broken."

"Are you sorry?" she asked.

"No," he said. "That's why I believe they're truly broken."

They gazed at one another in silence.

"What do you want, Louis," she finally asked.

He struggled for a long moment with his powerful and mutually exclusive desires. "I want to marry you," he finally replied. "I want to spend every day of my life with you." He reached for the cloak he had cast aside in the heat of their passion and clutched at the silk crimson cross stitched to its breast. "But how can I turn from one solemn vow and presume to make yet another?"

"Do you truly want to marry me?" she asked, her brow furrowed in doubtful surprise.

"More than anything," he said. "If only I could."

Colette sat up and pulled her clothing close. "I would never ask you to leave the Order," she said. "I wouldn't expect that."

"I know you wouldn't," he said. His lips twisted into a sad smile. "That's all the more reason to consider it."

"It's very sweet of you to say that," she replied. "It's a fantasy I'd like very much to see come true. But you don't have to do anything yet. There's no hurry, especially for a decision of such gravity. I'd really prefer right now to enjoy this moment. We can worry about the rest as we go along." She rolled over and rested against his chest and kissed him softly on the lips. "I love you, Louis," she said. "I would die for you. I can certainly wait for you, and I'll take what I can get in the meantime."

"You're the only thing that's true," he said. "I went to Outremer to fight for God, but in Outremer I found no sign of God. I found that my dreams were empty, and that I love you in way I'd never imagined. I'm confused, and more than a little angry, and right now I want only to sweep all of that away and be back here with you forever, and never leave again. I don't know what I will do, Colette, but I can tell you what I want to do, most desperately, and that is to be with you."

She looked away with darkened eyes.

"What's wrong?" he asked. "Have I angered you?"

"No," she said. "It just saddens me."

"It saddens you?" he said.

"You were so in love with your dreams," she said. "It breaks my heart to think they've been shattered." She turned to him. "Are you certain they have been? Perhaps you are only discouraged, and it will pass."

"Perhaps," he said. "But I don't think so. I thought about you every day I was gone. I couldn't wait to get back to you. Now that I'm here, I don't want to leave." He paused, and then he said as if he had only now discovered it, "I never felt that way about Jerusalem."

"Louis," she said, pressing a finger to his lips, "I don't want promises you cannot keep. Should I ever have you, I want you fully, and with no regrets." She gazed into his eyes. "Think hard on this. I will always be here. You will not lose me to passing time."

But Louis had already made up his mind. Nothing meant more to him than this magnificent woman, and there would be no more passing time.

Part III

Chapter 44

After the fall of Acre, the framework for the new Templar state, the New Jerusalem, was nearly complete. Willem and Louis had toiled, both at Cyprus and at the Templar commanderie at Douzens, to build it. Douzens had become their home, and Louis preferred it over Cyprus.

Victor worked quietly alongside Louis, accompanying him wherever his duties took him and taking fastidious care of their equipment and their mounts. As time passed, he grew more reticent, and obviously discontented. Louis grew less concerned about Victor's disposition, and a chasm formed between them.

The Grand Master Thibaud Gaudin died within a year of Jerusalem's fall, and Jacques de Molay succeeded him as the Templar Grand Master. De Molay was driven by his fervor for New Jerusalem, but he also developed an inexplicable enthusiasm for recapturing the old Jerusalem, despite his initial rejection of a renewed Crusade. For nearly a decade he launched failed attempts to revive the Crusade, which periodically interrupted Louis's work. On those occasions, with grave resolve and inspiring speeches, the Grand Master drove the expanding Templar force to the brink of battle on the shores of Outremer, only to reconsider at the sight of Saracen might and withdraw to Cyprus, where Louis and Willem resumed their painstaking labors.

Except among themselves, Louis, Willem, and a handful of others never discussed their work on the new state, even with the most trusted of their brethren. King Philip of France coveted the Languedoc, and he would react harshly to the slightest challenge to his claim on it.

Louis visited with Colette whenever he could. He spent more time with her with each passing year. Each visit strengthened his growing awareness that she, and not the Templar Order, was his purpose.

Willem noted that many of the knights had quietly returned home to resume their former lives, with no intention of returning to active roles in the Order. Their superiors had done little to dissuade them, and had, in fact, turned an increasingly blind eye to even more blatant infractions of the Rule. He speculated that the Order's laxity could portend some imminent, profound change to which he was not privy, and he encouraged Louis to at least consider his own options.

They sat at a table in an alehouse a short distance from the commanderie. Louis sipped his ale and tore a mouthful of bread from the loaf on the table. A pretty serving girl, Madeleine, brought bowls of stew while the innkeeper tended the dying fire.

Willem leaned forward to speak when Madeleine had moved out of earshot.

"We have finished the race at long last," he said with a heavy sigh. "God knows it has taken long enough."

"It's a staggering plan," Louis said in a low tone. "I never would have imagined a nation without a king, or a people free to choose their church and faith."

Willem nodded. "It's still hard to imagine kings and popes tolerating the very idea, much less the plan. The greatest challenge has yet to be confronted: the current order of things."

"I wonder if it's even possible," Louis said. "We've proceeded as if it is, but do you believe in your heart that it is?"

"We shall see," Willem said. "The Grand Master makes a good case, at least in council, that with the freedom to choose, most men would willingly choose much of what they already know, though more fervently for having been given the choice. It's not the religion or the governance they despise as much as the manner in which they are imposed." He took a sip of his ale. "We can only hope he makes the case convincingly."

"And if he doesn't?"

Willem smiled sardonically. "The Order has significant leverage against King Philip. His debts are not modest."

Louis laughed. "He has borrowed heavily from the Order."

"I also suspect that Clement will go along with whatever Philip does," Willem continued. "The papacy is in disarray, and mostly subject to Philip's whims. Some in the Church, though, might actually like to see his hold on the Languedoc loosened, if only to dilute his growing power, particularly if the new state declares sole fealty to the Church."

"What happens now?" Louis asked. "When will the Grand Master move to establish New Jerusalem?"

"That's hard to say," Willem replied. "When the moment is right, I imagine he will broach the subject with King Philip." Willem swallowed a mouthful of ale. "God only knows how that will go."

"I'm anxious for that to move forward," Louis said.

"It'll happen in its time," Willem said. "Philip must see a compelling advantage in a neutral buffer between France and Aragon. Perhaps conditions will arise that will make a buffer more ideal than a shared border."

Louis nodded. An escalation in tensions between Philip and King James of Aragon would do just that. He imagined such an escalation might be instigated.

"I suspect the reason for your eagerness," Willem said. Louis looked questioningly at him. "You envision a secular role for yourself in New Jerusalem?"

Louis considered his answer carefully. "I've wondered about

the possibility," he said. "If it were possible, I could have the two things I most cherish."

"You see yourself married to Colette, then," Willem said.

Louis nodded solemnly. "God willing."

"Perhaps—"

There was a commotion as the door to the alehouse swung open and Victor swaggered in, accompanied by three other squires, all very drunk. Louis frowned, and Willem sat back and pursed his lips.

"Victor," Louis said with an icy stare.

"Ah!" Victor exclaimed. He flashed a sneering smile at the other squires. "My brother! Uh, I'm sorry…correction! My master!" He bowed deeply toward Louis.

Louis and Willem exchanged glances.

"You've been drinking," Louis said.

"We've all been drinking," Victor replied, waving his hand toward the mugs in front of Louis and Willem. "And so?"

"But you're drunk," Louis retorted.

Victor stared unsteadily at Louis. "What do you care?" he finally said.

"Come sit down," Louis replied.

Victor waved his companions toward another table, and he took a seat with Louis.

"What's wrong with you, Victor?"

"What's wrong with me?" Victor replied with a sniff. "I don't know what you mean by that. Nothing's wrong. I'm enjoying a little time away from working, and drilling, and services, and cleaning, and being your squire. Is there something wrong with me that I don't know?"

"You're not acting yourself," Louis said. Willem sat back gazing at Victor in silence. "You're discontented. What's bothering you?"

Victor shook his head. "What is there to be happy about? I do my job from day to day. That's all well and good. But I train for battles I'll likely never see, and I languish in an existence I never really wanted, but cannot escape without shame. Your life may be what you wanted it to be – if indeed it is – but mine is nothing that I wanted. So I'll live it the way I damn well please. Perhaps you should worry less about that."

"It's my responsibility to worry about it."

"Don't you have bigger worries without concerning yourself with me?" Victor asked.

"It's not right for a Templar to go about drunk," Louis said.

"Is it not?" Victor replied. "Perhaps you should worry about your own conduct, and not mine."

"What do you mean by that?" Louis snapped.

Victor bit his lip and leaned back with an appraising look. "We do not consort with women, either, my lord," he said, "be they married, or single, or...consecrated."

Willem's face clouded with anger, and Louis gasped in horror.

Victor continued with a sneer, "There are far worse things than drinking a bit of ale."

Louis held his breath.

Victor squinted at him through watery eyes for a long, uncomfortable moment, then blurted, "Does Colette know about the nun?"

Willem's gaze shifted to Louis, whose face froze in a horrified mask. Louis rose slowly, his hand moving to the pommel of his sword. Victor leered at him with his own hand on his dagger.

Victor continued: "I think she has a right to know about that. Perhaps she could choose a better man."

Willem glared hard at Victor.

"Don't speak her name," Louis said, seething.

"Whose," Victor said, tilting his head with a questioning look, "Colette's, or the nun's?"

Louis lunged at Victor, who pulled his dagger from its sheath. Willem moved quickly to pin Victor's arm and wrench the dagger from his hand.

The other squires rose to their feet, uncertain about coming to Victor's defense. Willem turned on them with an upraised finger, and they fled the inn. Louis grasped Victor by the collar and nearly lifted him off his feet.

Willem leaned close to Victor. "You forget yourself, boy," he growled. "You'd better learn to mind yourself, ale or no ale."

"I don't think you want to do this," Victor said to Louis. They glared at one another for a moment before Louis released Victor.

Victor straightened his cloak and backed away from Louis. "You question my conduct?" he said. "Perhaps you should worry more about your own."

Louis nodded. "Perhaps you're right. But you need to leave now, before you regret your words."

Victor nodded threateningly, but he backed toward the door.

"Don't speak to me of Colette again," Louis said. "That's the last I'll hear of it from you."

Victor turned and left the tavern. Louis gave Willem a worried look as they both sat down.

"I don't think I want to know," Willem said before Louis could speak.

They sat in silence for a long moment. Finally, Willem took a draft of his ale and said, "I'll say two things before we drop the matter." He paused, and Louis waited expectantly. "First, you're not the only one with something to hide. You should know that. You've shielded others from scrutiny. Allow yourself the same consideration."

Louis nodded.

"Second…and more important: you should petition for release from your vows." Louis began to protest, but Willem held up a hand. "You have other, more pressing concerns," he said. "You have a woman who loves you, and a friend who hates you." He pointed toward the door through which Victor had disappeared. "That one is consumed by his jealousy. Nothing good can come of that. Things as they are could destroy you."

"Would you not be disappointed in me?" Louis asked. "Would you not think I had failed?"

"No, Louis," Willem said. "I think you should do the right thing, so you can't disappoint me by doing it. I believe you owe it to yourself, and to the Order, to do what is in your heart. And this is no longer in your heart."

"I wouldn't be the only one," Louis pointed out.

"No, you wouldn't," Willem agreed. "Many have realized that things are not what they were. Many have gone home to their old lives, either openly or in secret. I think your decision should be open and clear, and that you should be who you are. But tell me this...what is the greatest source of your disillusion?"

"There is no Kingdom of God," Louis answered flatly. "There never was a Kingdom of God. I fought for a kingdom of men, of merchants and mercenaries, and nothing more."

"And now we are building something more," Willem said.

"But I don't have to be a Templar to build that," Louis countered. "I can do that as a secular knight."

"You can," Willem agreed. "And you should."

"You would approve of my marriage to Colette?" Louis asked.

Willem considered the question for a moment before answering.

"She's not your cousin," he said. "You were the only one in our family who thought she was, and there was a reason for that. That reason no longer exists. You can protect the sensitivity of our past much better now that you understand it, and if you were to marry Colette, it would only support that secrecy."

"In what way?"

"If you were to marry her," Willem said, "that would further conceal the fact that she is a Cathar."

"How?"

"Cathars don't marry," Willem said.

"I know that," Louis replied. "You said that Colette is a Cathar. I understood that some of her family were Cathars, and that she sympathized with them, but I did not know that she is one."

"You never discussed that?"

"Often," Louis said. "She discussed the faith, but she never professed it."

"I've overstepped," Willem said.

Louis shook his head. "No, Uncle. As a Cathar, she wouldn't marry me, then."

"Don't be ridiculous," Willem said. "Of course she would. Cathars *choose* not to marry. It's a choice that only the most devout among them make, and there are very few of those still living."

"And you think she would choose me."

"I think she chose you long ago," Willem said.

Louis smiled weakly. "I suppose you're right," he said. "But I almost dare not hope for it."

"Well," Willem said slowly, "you've always been one to pursue your dreams with all your God–given strength. I've no doubt that's exactly what you'll do...and exactly what you *should* do."

They rose to leave, and Willem tossed a few coins onto the table beside their empty mugs. As they turned to go, he placed a hand on Louis's shoulder.

"Louis," he said with a purposeful gaze, "forget about the nun."

Louis winced, but he nodded his appreciation.

✠ ✠ ✠

"I've decided to leave the Order," Louis said. His voice was somber, but resolute.

Colette gazed back at him in silence. They walked slowly along the Carcassonne road, unhurried and deeply engrossed in one another's company.

"I've discussed it with Willem, and with the commander," he continued. "They have agreed to it. They say there's no harm."

"I had all but given up on that possibility," she said.

"I never did," he replied.

"But are you certain?" she asked. "Louis, I don't want you to do something you will regret. I don't want to become the reason you gave up your dreams."

"The dreams I pursued," he said, "are long dead. Jerusalem fell long ago, and it will not likely rise again in my lifetime. My old dreams gave way to new ones. I was given the honor of helping to build a new and different Jerusalem, one that I believe will soon be established."

"You seem happy with what you are doing."

"I am," he replied. "I'm pleased with what the future holds."

"Then why leave it?" she asked.

"That's the beauty of it, Colette," he replied. "I don't have to leave it. I could serve New Jerusalem as a secular knight. There's no requirement that I retain my monastic vows. Uncle Willem believes that it may actually be better to be free of the constraints of my vows."

"Why would that be so?" she said.

"It will be a secular nation," he said. Colette raised her eyebrows in dismay. He continued: "New Jerusalem will be a nation of citizens, free men, loyal to the Church, but not ruled by it; friendly to the kingdoms, but not subject to them."

"How is that possible?" she asked.

Louis smiled. He had never discussed with her the things over which he had labored for so long. It felt good to divulge them to someone he knew he could trust with his life, even though he knew he shouldn't. He was surprised by how good it felt to break the secret.

"It will be a nation of bankers," he said with a satisfied air.

Colette frowned in puzzlement. "Bankers?" she said.

"The Templars have long filled the role of bankers across Europe and the Levant. The integrity with which they've guarded the wealth of nobles, kings, and nations, and the efficiency with which they have managed the currency of a vast and burgeoning commerce have put the Order in a unique position. The world has come to trust the Order in that role. Their ability to persist in that role demands autonomy from both popes and kings."

"And the popes and kings would allow this?" she said. "Why?"

"They're all indebted to the Order," he said with a grin. "And to one another through the Order. Their financial strength will depend upon it."

Colette seemed doubtful.

"Why would it be better for you to renounce your vows?"

she asked.

"Uncle Willem says – and I agree – that free men should not be led by priests or soldiers."

"And you intend to lead?" she asked.

"I do," he said.

Colette stopped walking and cocked her head in a long, appraising look.

"Yes," she finally said. "I can see that." She nodded, then repeated, "Yes." She smiled with what appeared to be profound satisfaction, and continued walking.

"This is an unusual plan," she said.

Louis nodded in agreement. They walked on discussing the plan, and the ideas that formed its foundation. The more they talked, the more Louis grew convinced that their framework was the basis for a stronger, more equal society where every man could have some say in his fortune and his destiny. Sharing his thoughts with Colette infused them with a brilliance they had not acquired in the years he had labored over them. He wondered at the ability of her mere presence to do that.

They neared the entrance to the estate. Louis slowed, mulling his words and mustering the courage to say them. Colette slowed with him, and turned to him expectantly.

"Colette," he finally said in nearly a whisper.

"Yes?" she whispered back.

"I love you," he said. "I have always loved you. I want to marry you. I want you to be my wife. There is nothing I have wanted more."

Her eyes grew wide at the magnitude of his words. "Nothing?" she whispered.

"Nothing," he replied.

"There are things you have wanted so badly that it seemed you would have died without them," she said.

He nodded. "I want you more," he said. He paused, then breathed deeply. "Will you marry me?" he said.

"Of course," she said. "As badly as you say you want me to be your wife, I have wanted it more. And while I know I wouldn't die without you, I know that I would never really live, either."

Hot tears filled Louis's eyes, and his throat choked with the intensity of his love for her. He felt his lip trembling despite his effort to control it.

"Yes, Louis," she said with a nod. "I will be your wife."

"We should not tell anyone yet," he said. "We must wait until I conclude my withdrawal from the Order."

"Agreed," she said. "Although it will be hard to keep this to myself."

They continued to the house, resolved to act as if nothing remarkable was afoot.

Chapter 45

Louis petitioned for release from his vows within the month. He went with Willem to speak with Nicholas de Brienne, the former Commander of Sidon, who now held the office of Commander of the Languedoc Templars.

They met at a chateau a few miles outside Douzens, where Brienne had taken up residence. Serving brothers tended sheep and split wood in the bitter cold as Louis and Willem made their way up the drive to the door of the chateau.

Brienne appeared uncharacteristically tense. He seemed preoccupied with something more important than Louis's petition. His greeting was cordial, but distant.

"You seem troubled," Willem said.

Brienne stared out the window across the frozen, barren fields to where the woodcutters worked the edge of the distant tree line.

"Trouble is brewing," he said absently.

"Trouble?" Louis said.

"What sort of trouble?" Willem asked.

"There's been disturbing talk about the Crusading orders,"

Brienne said, "mostly out of Paris, and mostly unfavorable for us."

"In what way?" Willem asked.

"There's talk of merging the orders," Brienne said, "or at least of merging the Templars with the Hospitallers. Or worse."

"What could be worse?" Willem said.

Brienne gave him an ominous look. "Dissolving the Templar Order," he said.

Willem sniffed in disbelief. "That's only talk, of course," he said. "Surely, only a fool would consider such nonsense!"

"Surely," Brienne said. "You've said it yourself: only the most dangerous fool that sits at the French king's court."

Louis guessed that Willem knew well to whom Brienne referred, but Willem did not speak a name.

Brienne smiled craftily. "You're a prudent man, Brother Willem. Graceful and wise. But of course you know that I refer to William of Nogaret, the king's most unduly trusted advisor."

Willem pursed his lips.

"That treacherous business at Anagni," Brienne continued, "was just the start. Nogaret is on a mission. I believe he will stop at nothing to end the pope's authority, and to supplant it with Philip's power. I believe he wishes to install Philip as the head of the Church." He shook his head in disgust at the thought, and said, "Clearly, the Templars are an obstacle to that aim."

"But what could he do, really?" Willem said. "Nogaret doesn't wield that kind of power. Anagni demonstrated that."

"For a moment, yes," Brienne said. "But that only strengthened his resolve." Brienne toyed with the long whiskers of his beard and stared at the wall. "'What could he do?' you ask. I'll tell you what he could do, and what I believe he has long plotted to do. He'll manipulate the merger of the orders, to which the Hospitallers would not object, and the confiscation of all Templar properties and wealth. That would serve the dual purpose of eliminating his only real obstacle and replenishing the king's empty coffers. That's not only what he *can* do, Willem, but what I believe he damn well intends to do."

"Philip would support this," Willem mused.

"Why wouldn't he?" Brienne said. "De Molay rejected his bid for acceptance into the Order. Surely, such rejection would justify an assault on the Order."

Louis was taken by surprise. He could see by Willem's expression that he was not alone. The implications of de Molay's rejection were portentous. Willem stood and paced the room before stopping by a window to gaze out at the fields.

"Si non amplectar te, vos interficite," he murmured.

"I'm sorry?" Brienne said.

Willem turned from the window and sighed. "It's something my uncle told me long ago," he said. "He heard it said at Montségur." Willem stroked his beard thoughtfully for a moment, and then continued. "He said the Inquisitor used the wrong words when he gave the order for dealing with the captured Cathars. Those words swayed my uncle, and saved my life."

Both Louis and Brienne looked expectantly at Willem.

Willem continued: "The Inquisitor said, 'If they don't embrace you, kill them.' He should have said, 'If they don't embrace *the truth*,' but the words he used were revealing. Arnaud said that if the Cathars were to die, it should have been for the truth, and not to gratify an Inquisitor's lust for power."

"I see," Brienne said.

Willem smiled sadly. "It would seem that the Inquisitor's words apply to Philip's intentions toward the Order."

"De Molay will not present your plan," Brienne said. "It would be the worst thing he could do at this moment."

Willem nodded. "Perhaps, then, the timing of our petition is fortunate," he said.

Brienne raised his eyebrows and waved to a chair. Willem returned to his seat.

"What can I do for you?" Brienne asked.

Willem folded his hands and looked at Louis. Nodding in his direction, he said, "Louis has put a lot of effort into the new state," he said. "He has sacrificed much for the Order, and served faithfully."

"Yes," Brienne said. "He has. He was courageous at Acre."

"The time he has spent serving the Order has been..."

"Discouraging?" Brienne said.

Willem paused to consider the interruption. "No," he said. "I was going to say that his service has been richly rewarding, but I suppose that now that you've said it, perhaps it has been—"

"Disappointing, to be sure," Louis said. Willem and Brienne turned to him in surprise. "But I have never regretted one day of my service. I would be pleased to remain a Templar to my last days."

"But?" Brienne said.

"But it has not been what I had imagined it would be," Louis said. "I can accept that. However, I hold less enthusiasm for administration than I did for soldiering. I'm happy to serve in an administrative capacity, of course, but I fail to see the importance of my vows to the administrative function."

"You want to leave the Order," Brienne said.

"Not as much as one might think," Louis said. "But there is something for which I long even more than I longed to be a Templar."

"A woman?" Brienne guessed.

"Not just any woman," Willem said with a meaningful look. Brienne nodded. "A girl he has loved since his boyhood days."

Brienne raised his eyebrows. "How is it," he asked, "that you chose the Order over her in the first place?"

Louis grew flustered. "I didn't...," he began, but he faltered at the odd truth. "I thought—"

"He thought she would never have him," Willem said quickly. He smiled knowingly at Brienne. "He had far greater confidence in his military skills than his romantic prowess."

Brienne smiled and nodded. "And now that has changed?" he said.

Louis blushed. "It has," he said quietly, nodding appreciatively at Willem.

Brienne sighed deeply, drumming his fingertips on the table. "I am inclined to refuse your petition," he said. "I don't approve of men who abandon their vows. When one makes a vow, one is bound by that vow, and the Templar vow is a vow unto death." He paused for a moment that was, for Louis, lengthy and uncomfortable. He took a sip of his wine and gave Louis a look of sad resignation. "Alas, in better times," he said, "I would have dismissed you out of hand. However, these are not better times. Some would argue that the Templar vow itself has perished, along with our purpose. I do not agree, but the argument has been made. I must give it its due."

Louis brightened.

"Our mission has changed," Brienne continued. "There is yet much to do. But I grant you the point that your place in it does not of a necessity require a vow of monastic chastity. While the nature of battle demands a devotion undivided by the temptations of home and family, the leadership of free men might benefit from the embrace of such things. In any event, there is no defensible reason to deny your request, save my objection to broken oaths."

"That is our line of reasoning, as well," Willem said.

"I suspected it might be," Brienne said. With a wave of his hand, he said, "Your petition is granted, Brother Louis. I'm confident of the Grand Master's approval, under the circumstances."

"Thank you," Louis said.

"When the reasons for my approval grow more clear to you, my friend," Brienne replied, "you may not be so thankful."

"What do you mean?" Willem asked.

"You have done much to effect the creation of our Templar state," Brienne said.

"We have."

"Your work may have placed you especially in harm's way."

"How so?" Willem asked.

"It's hard to say, exactly," Brienne said. "An ill wind is blowing. While it's hard to say exactly what form it will take, I believe trouble is coming. We must be watchful. And you, Brother Louis... put your Templar past behind you. Marry your young woman and start your new life. Remember your strict vow of secrecy; of that, you will never be free. In any event, it shall serve you as well as it does the Order."

"I believe he is overly cautious," Willem said to Louis as they left through the chateau's main gate. "It's hard to imagine a cause for such trepidation."

"Yes," Louis said, nodding. "But I'm pleased with the commander's approval."

"I am, as well," Willem replied. "I suspect that neither of us is nearly as happy as Colette is bound to be, when you tell her the news."

Louis smiled broadly at the prospect of that.

✠ ✠ ✠

An October chill settled over the fields of the Garonne estate. Louis and Colette had married in the spring, and Louis turned to tending the estate as his father battled failing health. Domestic tranquility had grown on him, and his life with Colette made him happier than he had ever imagined possible.

He gazed into the fire contemplating that happiness, and the sobering thought that he had nearly forsaken it.

Near midnight, an insistent knocking startled Louis and brought him to the front door. The man who stood before him wore the simple garb of a shopkeeper from the city, but the solid build of a soldier was obvious beneath it.

"Marhaban, ya akhi," the man said. The Arabic greeting could only mean that the man was a Templar messenger who had spent time in the Levant, and who bore grave news.

"Salaam," Louis replied. It had been years since he had spoken the word.

"Ominous tidings, my lord," the messenger said.

"Come in," Louis said. He stood back from the door and waved the man inside.

Louis led the messenger to the oak dining table and offered him a glass of wine, which he politely refused.

"Water, if you please," the man said.

Louis brought the water, and wine for himself. He took a seat across from the man.

"Marchand," the man said, introducing himself. He offered the gesture that confirmed his status as a Templar, and Louis returned the sign.

"Welcome to my home," Louis said.

"Thank you, Brother Garonne. I must tell you that a terrible thing has happened." Marchand was solemn, but his words were practiced. He had already repeated his news countless times.

"Is it what we feared?" Louis asked.

"Yes, and worse."

"Tell me." Louis couldn't imagine it any worse than what they had feared.

"King Philip issued orders for the arrest of all French Templars within the week."

"All of them?" Louis said with a gasp.

"To the last man," Marchand replied.

The blood drained from Louis's face. He stared at his guest, speechless. "Good God," he finally said.

The messenger nodded. "He won't succeed," he said. "He'll target the knights first, but he'll not take them all. As many as we can warn, and who are able to do so, will have escaped before the order is executed."

"How can Philip do this?" Louis said. "He can't possibly have the pope's permission. Who would support him in this?"

"Only his men," Marchand said. "But that's enough for Philip. I understand that the pope has not so much as acknowledged the information we've received."

"What information, exactly?"

"One of the king's men in Richerenches opened his orders early, in defiance of the king. They were to remain sealed until the twelfth, and executed at dawn on the thirteenth. This man suspected the nature of the orders. We are fortunate for his loyalty."

Louis nodded in agreement. Should that man be exposed, his execution would be swift.

"The orders are for the arrest of every knight in France at

dawn on the thirteenth. Should any slip away, they will be hunted. Their property will be confiscated, and their families watched or arrested, until they are caught."

"I've heard that de Molay is in Paris," Louis said.

"Yes."

"He knows."

"Yes, of course."

"What will he do?"

"He is under the king's nose. He'll do nothing to tip him off to the escape of his men."

Louis shook his head. This was terrible news indeed, worse than any he could have imagined.

"What shall *we* do?" Louis asked.

"All who escape will meet at Mas Deu," Marchand said. "You are, of course, to tell no one. If you tell anyone of your plans, you will have placed them, as well as all of us, in grave danger. You must disappear without a trace."

"And then?"

"Mas Deu is all I know. You will learn more when you arrive there. I suspect that once everyone who has escaped has met there, the Order will sail from Perpignan to Cyprus. Beyond that is anyone's guess."

Marchand gave Louis the passwords and signs that would gain him access to safe houses and the ultimate meeting place of the fugitives.

"And now, I must go," Marchand said. He pushed back from the table and stood, straightening his cloak. "I've tarried. I have much yet to do before dawn."

Louis stood, too. "Thank you," he said. "Be safe. Go with God." Marchand smiled wryly. "I am grateful for your service," Louis added.

"My duty," the messenger replied with a bow. "Thank you for the water, Brother Garonne. Be safe as well, and may God be with you."

Louis embraced Marchand and saw him to the door.

As he turned, the flickering firelight caught a movement at

the top of the stairway to the bedchambers. Colette hesitated before she padded down the stair, and she stopped at the bottom, waiting expectantly.

"Louis?" his mother called softly from the top of the stair. "Is everything all right?"

"I have to go," Louis said. His voice was grim, and his eyes dark.

"Why?" Colette asked. "You're no longer with them. What have you to fear?"

"I am no longer a Templar only as far as you and I are concerned," he replied. "But my vow was for life, and to many I am still – and will always be – a Templar. More importantly, I'm privy to sensitive matters. That alone places me in jeopardy."

Colette nodded. She bit her lip and clasped her hands so tightly that her knuckles went white. She paced the room for a minute, and then took a seat by the fire.

Marie had descended half the stair, her eyes wide with worry.

"It's all right, mother," Louis said. "Go to bed now, and look after father."

Marie peered suspiciously at him before she turned and went back upstairs.

"I've been thinking," Colette said. "It's been a very long time since I visited with my cousins at Arbroath."

"I had thought that, too," he said. "It will be winter soon, and not ideal for Scotland, but perhaps it would be best."

Colette nodded. "It will be best," she said.

Louis stood behind her and caressed her shoulders.

"Men–at–arms will escort you and my parents to your father," he said, "and then to Arbroath. I won't be far behind."

Colette turned to look at him with alarm. "Why?" she asked. "Why won't you come with me?"

"There are things to which I must tend," he replied. "I cannot abandon my work, or the men with whom I have labored for so long. There is too much to lose, and I have an obligation to defend it."

"How long will you be?" she said. "I'll be worried to death.

It will be unbearable."

"I don't know," he replied. "I'll follow you as soon as I can. I swear it. I'll come to you."

She reached to place a hand on his

"I love you, Colette," he whispered. "I long to be by your side. But you must go quickly. I will not rest until I'm with you again."

She sighed heavily as he gently squeezed her shoulders. She rested her head on his hands and wept.

Chapter 46

The king's captain knocked heavily upon the door of the Garonne house. He peered warily toward the stables as if to detect an attempted escape. A dozen powerful horses carrying heavily armed soldiers shifted anxiously, as if they sensed the tension of an impending encounter. The soldiers were flushed with excitement.

Willem hunched painfully against the bars of a caged cart that was tethered to a team of drays. He and four other Templars had been dragged from their homes before dawn and thrown, bound and disheveled, into the cart that would carry them to prison.

Willem glared at the captain and prayed that the door would not open. He hoped that Louis had fled, and that he was a safe distance from the evil of King Philip that was spreading like the morning sunlight across the land.

The captain motioned for soldiers to encircle the house, and for two to fetch the ram to smash in the door. Hatred burned in Willem's eyes, but his lips curled with satisfaction at the thought of Louis's escape.

The door gave way with a splintering crash on the third blow.

Willem had waited a moment too long for word that the warnings had been delivered. The last of the messengers returned with the king's men close on his heels. But Willem's mission had succeeded; most of his men would escape. He was not so fortunate.

Willem pondered King Philip's motives for his attack on the Templar Order. He was dismayed by its audacity, and by the pope's failure to prevent it. The Grand Master, Jacques de Molay, had spoken of Philip's growing resentment toward the Order, but with no suspicion that it could lead to this ruthless assault.

Frustrated shouts from the house confirmed Louis's escape. The king's men rushed to the stables to find them empty, and they shouted orders for any armed men to show themselves and surrender. Servants, cooks, and farmhands emerged from their hovels in silence.

The captain cursed and kicked at the dusty ground. He motioned for the soldiers to interrogate the peasants, and he stormed back to the front of the house.

He glared at Willem and spat.

After questioning the peasants, the soldiers returned empty-handed. The captain cursed again as Willem nodded his grim satisfaction. The detachment remounted, and the cart lurched violently as they wheeled toward the road to Carcassonne.

✠ ✠ ✠

Willem sat on a rickety wooden stool at the center of the interrogation room, his hands bound behind his back. He was naked, bruised, and bloody, and his eyes were nearly swollen shut. His back and shoulders bore the deep lacerations of barbed whips.

The Inquisitor, a bishop, glared contemptuously at him from a high-backed chair across the room. His silk robes glistened in the shimmering torchlight. Two large-limbed brutes stood behind Willem with folded arms and vacant stares. The instruments of their profession lay on a table behind them, along with a length of sturdy rope.

Willem struggled to hold his head upright. He squinted through his swollen eyes at the bishop, who repeated his relentless, ridiculous accusation.

"Did you not worship a devilish cat, and kiss its anus during midnight rituals?" the bishop asked, his voice rising to an exaggerated pitch.

It was clear to Willem that there would be no reprieve from this ghastly charade, and that he would not awake to find that it had been but a terrible dream.

Why? he wondered in a silent, plaintive scream. His thoughts reeled in a cloud of confused indignation. *What have I done to deserve this?*

"It would be much easier for you if you would just tell me the truth," the bishop said. "Get it out and be done with it. You have had enough, have you not?"

"I have told you the truth," Willem croaked. His throat was swollen and parched, and it screamed with pain when he spoke. "I can't say what you want to hear. Why would you want me to speak such a lie?"

"You say, then, that I lie?" the bishop said.

Willem repeated his answer for what seemed like the hundredth time. "I say that someone has told you a lie," he said. "I say that I love Christ, and that I have served Him all of my life."

The bishop shook his head sadly.

"You will die a horrible death if you do not repent," he said. Willem's head dropped to his chest. "Again, confess, and you will know God's mercy. Tell me how, during your initiation into that unholy order, you spat upon the holy cross of Jesus, and you denied that He is God."

Willem sat silent. He felt faint.

"Tell me of the abominations in which your Order engaged," the bishop droned in a perfunctory, singsong voice, as if he were saying the Mass. "Tell me of your heresy. Tell me something truthful so that your pain may end, and God's mercy may be offered to you. Confess to the charges against you, I beg of you, so that I may help you to find release."

Willem raised his tortured eyes to the bishop.

"I don't know the charges against me," he said. "You have not stated them. You've only asked me strange questions that I do not understand."

"Of course you know the charges," the bishop snapped. "It won't do to toy with me. You know what you have done. You know of the abominations in which you participated, either willingly or not. You know all, and you must confess all, or you may not survive the hour."

Willem's head dropped once more. He shook his head slowly, hopelessly.

The bishop gestured to the men behind Willem. One grabbed Willem from behind and forced him to his feet. The other threw the long rope over one of the ceiling rafters and bound one end to the bindings on Willem's wrists.

When they finished, they stood waiting for the bishop's order. The bishop turned to Willem one last time.

"Confess," he said.

"I've done nothing wrong," Willem replied.

The bishop shook his head curtly and turned away. He raised a hand, and the men drew the rope, wrenching Willem's arms upward behind him, and raising him nearly to the rafter. The weight of his body tore at the tendons in his shoulders and elbows.

He hung there for what seemed eternity as pain wracked his body and the voice in his head screamed for a reason for his torture. At long last, he began to grow numb.

The men released the rope a bit, just enough for Willem to drop several feet to a jarring halt. Pain seared anew through his body, worse than he could have imagined it. His involuntary scream seemed alien to him, as if it had come from someone else. It echoed in the chamber and rang in his ears.

"Confess!" the bishop bellowed.

Willem drew his head back and looked to the heavens without responding.

They released the rope again, and he dropped another foot. He felt the sinew snap in his shoulders, and again the room reverberated with an eerie, echoing scream.

"Confess," the bishop whispered, his voice intense, and almost pleading.

Willem hung silent. His weight stretched his arms nearly vertical behind him, his hands pointed toward the ceiling. His shoulders were torn and burning with excruciating pain.

He collapsed to the floor when they lowered him. They lifted him to the rickety stool. He listed, as though he would fall to the floor.

The bishop took his seat. "There is one question," he said, "to which you surely do know the answer."

One of the men grasped Willem's hair and raised his head so that he faced the bishop, who peered intently into his pain-wracked eyes.

"Where," he said, "will we find Louis De Garonne?" Willem moaned involuntarily. "You're his uncle...his mentor. You sponsored his acceptance into your damnable brotherhood. You know where he is. Tell me where to find him, and you will suffer no more."

Willem stared stolidly into the Inquisitor's eyes. His lips tightened in defiance.

Why, the voice repeated more feebly. What terrible wrong could he and his brethren have done to deserve this torture? What false accusations had the king of France concocted to justify it, and more importantly, *why?* Was it his fear of a Templar sovereignty in the Languedoc he so coveted? The vast sum he owed to the Templar treasury? Was it Jacques de Molay's refusal to admit him into the Order? He realized that it could be any of these things, or all of them.

But why had the pope failed to intervene?

One of the guards came around to face Willem. He held a battered, bloody club.

The pope condones this, Willem thought. He retched at the notion, and tried to reject it. He could not. *He is complicit, or he is a dupe.*

"You refuse to answer even this?" the bishop demanded. "Your silence confirms your nephew's guilt, and it seals your fate."

Willem averted his eyes as the guard raised the bloodied club high. In a blur of movement and a blinding crash, it shattered his jaw and cast him into a pitch-black void.

✠ ✠ ✠

Colette and Louis's parents fled south to Limoux with a company of knights and men–at–arms. Louis departed with six of his knights to the Templar commanderie of Mas Deu, at Trouillas.

Bérenger Guifre was among them. Bérenger had once been squire to Willem Marti, and over the years had grown to be one of his closest friends. He was a pleasant man of humble means and a generous spirit. He was born a peasant and raised to nobility along with his father at a very young age; he bore innate compassion and profound respect for his station. Louis admired Bérenger's loyalty to his uncle, and he had also grown to like him a great deal.

They arrived at Trouillas late the following evening. When they got to the commanderie, they found it a flurry of anxious activity. The air in the meeting hall was charged with a mixture of urgency, anger, and fear. The commander stood grim–faced as a young, sandy–haired squire named Alain led Louis and his knights into the hall.

"Have you traveled far?" the commander asked gruffly.

"Two days," Louis replied. "From Verzeille."

The commander nodded in recognition. "Louis de Garonne," he said. "Willem Marti's nephew."

"Yes," Louis said.

The commander looked past Louis and the knights to the empty vestibule. "Is your uncle not with you?" he asked.

Louis shook his head, and the commander gave an angry huff.

"We fear—"

"—he's arrested," the commander snapped, shaking his head with contempt.

"I'm hoping not," Louis said.

The commander looked at him as if he were naïve. "I'm Peter of Castellón," he said. "Commander of Mas Deu."

Louis shook the commander's hand and turned to introduce his knights. Castellón waved his hand to clear the room and gestured for Louis and his knights to sit at the table.

"Everyone got the same word?" Louis asked as they sat. "To meet at Mas Deu?"

"Yes," Castellón said. "Mas Deu has always been a secret rallying point in the event of sudden mobilization…primarily for returning to Outremer. Every high ranking Brother knew of it. I never imagined we would meet here under these circumstances."

"Who could have foreseen this?" Bérenger Guifre said.

"Some began to suspect the possibility in recent months," the commander replied. "Not many, but a few." Bérenger raised his eyebrows. "De Molay," Castellón said. "And a handful of others." To Louis, he said, "Your uncle was among them. I'm surprised you didn't know. In fact, he feared this possibility most – he and de Molay. Most others thought them overly suspicious." The commander looked quizzically at Louis. "I'm surprised he never mentioned his fears to you," he said.

"Yes," Louis said, nodding. "So am I."

"Your uncle devised the contingency that we will put into motion," the commander said.

"The move to Cyprus," Louis said.

"No," Castellón replied. "Not Cyprus."

"No?" Louis said. "I don't understand."

"That's what every soul in Europe will be expecting us to do," Castellón said. "No, there's a plan of which only a few were aware, and those few will take it to the grave, if necessary."

"What is the plan?" Louis asked.

Castellón peered around the table at Louis's men. He appeared to be appraising them.

"My men are trustworthy," Louis said

"It's not a matter of trust," the commander said. "It's a matter of prudence. Choose one to stay; the others must leave."

Louis nodded to Bérenger, and the rest of the knights stood and left the hall.

"We'll scatter from here," Castellón said, "in groups of two or three. We'll cut our beards and dress as peasants and merchants, and head northwest on a hundred different routes."

"Northwest!" Louis gasped. "Away from our ships?"

"To La Rochelle," Castellón said. "Toward our ships."

Louis was stunned. "Our ships are at La Rochelle?" he asked.

"We'll sail from there," Castellón replied.

"To where?"

"For now," Castellón said, "let us focus on getting the troops to La Rochelle. That will be enough of a challenge without worrying about what happens afterward."

Louis nodded. He wondered where they might go from La Rochelle. They could get to Aragon by road, so it must be England, or Ireland...perhaps even Scotland. His heart leapt as he imagined Colette standing on the shore to welcome him.

"Many of the Brethren will not know we are headed to La Rochelle," Castellón was saying. Louis nodded quickly. "It's important that it stays that way. There's no need for them to know. It will make no difference to their fate." Again, Louis nodded his understanding. The commander eyed him for a moment, and then leaned toward him. "Your uncle spoke highly of you," he said.

"He's my uncle," Louis said modestly.

The commander shook his head. "Everyone spoke highly of you," he said. "You may be called upon to stand in for your uncle."

Louis shuddered at the weight of Castellón's words. He had tried not to think of Willem's fate, but he was all too aware of it. Willem would be one of those tortured for information on the fugitive Templars.

"Are you up to it?" the commander asked.

Louis shook off his anxiety. "Yes," he said. "Of course."

"Do you have any questions?"

Louis shook his head.

"Get some rest, then," Castellón said. "There is much to do, and no time to lose."

Louis and Bérenger rose to leave.

"Brother Louis," the commander called just as Louis reached the door. Louis paused and turned back. "I'm sorry about your uncle," he said. "I'll be praying for him."

"As will I," Louis said. He nodded and left the hall.

He walked into the cool autumn darkness torn between his trepidation over Willem's fate, and the thrill of the possibility that he might see Colette far sooner than he had expected.

✠ ✠ ✠

Willem sat in the interrogation chair once again. This chair sat high, leaving his feet dangling several feet above the floor. His shoulders throbbed where the ligaments had been wrenched and torn. He struggled to see through swollen eyes, and he could feel with his tongue the gaps left by teeth he had lost.

The guards were doing something to his legs. It took him a moment to realize that his torturers were strapping his feet into heavy iron boots. He knew their purpose, and he closed his eyes in dreadful anticipation.

The guards filled the boots with oil, and they set a torch to a pan of embers on the floor. The Inquisitor stood in front of him, watching him with exaggerated pity.

"Willem Marti, I only require your confession and your repentance. Repentance will bring you freedom, and a light penance. You were led to your transgression by evil men, but I know that your intentions were honorable. You need only to confess, and to repent, and all will be well once again."

Willem imagined that dozens of knights must have already died under this torture since the first arrests. He was certain they had remained steadfast in defense of Templar honor. They had surely chosen death over betrayal and dishonor. He resolved to honor their sacrifice by refusing to trade his freedom for the lies the Inquisitor demanded.

"Let's start again from the beginning," the bishop droned. "Tell me of your initiation rite..." The words lost their meaning for Willem. His mind reduced them to toneless noise. He knew that engaging with the noise would do nothing to alter his fate.

The interrogation continued relentlessly. The guards pushed the pan of coals directly beneath the boots to heat the oil. For a brief moment the warming oil soothed Willem's aching calves, but the moment passed, and the heat intensified.

He braced himself, restraining the scream that begged for release. He prayed for strength and a quick death. He turned his thoughts to the Cathar belief that transcendence of earthly pain brought spiritual release from the bondage of an evil world. He embraced that notion.

He thought of the two hundred Cathar souls that marched solemnly from the heights of Montségur, singing resolute hymns, transcending their fear of the bonfires that waited below. He thought of his parents, pious and stoic in the face of their own cruel deaths. He prayed for a measure of their spirit, and for swift release from the agony he faced.

✠ ✠ ✠

Peter de Castellón, commander of the Templars at Mas Deu, spoke urgently to eighteen of the most senior knights. The hall was dark, lit only by low candlelight.

"We'll make our way to camps in the countryside a day's distance from La Rochelle," he said. "Each group will be led by a captain. Captains will make contact with one another and coordinate the exodus from that point forth."

Castellón's seneschal, Dagobert, circulated among the knights handing out small wax-sealed vellum envelopes.

"It's of paramount importance," Castellón said, "that none of the lesser brethren know the details of our escape. If any should be captured, the rest would be placed at great risk." The knights nodded solemnly. "You each have brethren you trust," he continued, "but that trust is irrelevant. Confide in no one. The success of our flight depends upon it. It's not a matter of trust, but of prudence."

"How will we reassemble once we get to La Rochelle?" Louis asked, fingering the vellum envelope.

"We'll set up camp in the countryside between Surgères and La Rochelle," Castellón said. "Each group will pose as travelling merchants or artisans, and avoid contact with other travelers or villagers. By the time anyone reacts to the influx of strangers, we'll be on our way. Each captain will travel from camp to an inn at Surgères. The name of the inn will be revealed to you by that time. The innkeeper will tally our names until all have arrived. From there we will depart from La Rochelle."

Louis held up his envelope with a questioning look.

"The envelopes remain sealed, Castellón said, "until after we've made camp at Surgères. And if you face capture, if it's the last thing you do, destroy them." He returned to his seat and continued. "They contain the final arrangements and the specific timing for our gathering at La Rochelle, and our departure from there. These steps may appear to be unnecessarily complex, but it's of necessity."

"How many do we expect will gather at Surgères?" Bérenger Guifre asked.

"It's hard to say," Castellón said. "We'll know better over the next few days, as more fugitives arrive. We already know of dozens who have been captured. If I had to guess, I would say perhaps a hundred fifty, possibly two hundred." He shrugged his shoulders and added, "Some say I'm optimistic."

"Let's hope not," said Ramiro de Vria, in a thick Castilian accent. "I should hope there would be more. Although I haven't seen my squire for quite some time."

Louis thought of Victor. He tried to remember when he'd last seen him. It had been at least six months, and that was unusual. Victor had grown more distant over the years, especially since Louis left the Order and married Colette. He couldn't blame Victor for resenting him for coaxing him into the Order, and then leaving it when it no longer suited him.

But he'd left the Order for Colette. Surely Victor understood that.

"In any event," Castellón said, "we've planned to transport two or three hundred Brothers. We should have enough ships available to accommodate that number."

Dagobert, the commander's seneschal, added, "That will be an unusual influx of wanderers into the forests around Surgères. It will draw notice. Fortunately, there's a market at Surgères, and we'll arrive in the vicinity near the time of the autumn market fair. Traders travel to and from the area routinely, especially for the market fair. Travel as traders; that will be your most effective cover."

"The market draws artisans," Castellón said, "and merchants, and farmers. Some of you may pose as pilgrims passing through. Each of you must ensure that you blend into the populace if we are to succeed."

"Stay into the woods as much as possible," Dagobert said, "to minimize the attention to our arrival."

Louis wondered if the other knights felt as demoralized as he did by the prospect of hiding from view, and sneaking around like wary animals. From their general demeanor, he suspected that they did.

The plan was laid in detail. Groups were chosen, and leaders commissioned and briefed with passwords, contacts, and secret signs and symbols. As dawn broke and the assembly dispersed, Louis knew that their chance of success was good.

He slept for an hour and a half before the bells rang the call to Terce. He rose and rubbed the grittiness from his eyes. He made his way down the convent stairs and into the morning light. He was hungry, but he didn't want to eat. He felt as though food would lay heavy in his stomach.

On the way to the chapel, he stopped short at the sight of a familiar figure by the stables. A man with his back to Louis handed the reins of a warhorse to the stable boy. His heart leapt.

"Victor!" he called, changing course to hurry toward the stable.

Victor turned and stared for a moment as if he failed to recognize Louis. Finally, he opened his arms to receive him.

"Where have you been?" Louis asked. He hugged Victor warmly, and then held him by the shoulders at arm's length, waiting for an answer.

"In Bruges," Victor said, almost self-consciously.

"What were you doing there?" Louis asked.

Victor shrugged. "Living," he said. "Helping to tend the commanderie." He paused, as if trying to remember. "Tending horses…livestock."

Louis nodded. "It's good to see you!" he exclaimed. He glanced at the chapel, and then nodded in its direction. "To prayers?" he asked.

A look of distaste crossed Victor's face, but he dropped his gaze and nodded, and they made their way.

"Are you all right?" Louis asked. Something was clearly wrong with Victor.

Victor nodded and shrugged again. "As well as can be expected," he replied.

"You've escaped," Louis said. "That's well enough, I suppose. How did you avoid capture?"

"I was lucky," Victor said with a troubled look. "You've heard, I suppose, about Willem?"

"I know he's captured," Louis said sadly.

"And that's all?" Victor said. "You've heard nothing more?"

A chill cut through Louis. He stared anxiously at Victor. "What else?" he asked.

Victor turned and continued toward the chapel, shaking his head.

"What else?" Louis repeated more firmly.

Victor stopped and faced him. "He's dead," he said flatly.

"They burned him with fifty others just outside Paris."

Louis caught his breath. His heart froze in his chest, and his throat choked with anguish. His mind spun suddenly out of control, and he felt faint.

"My God...," he whispered. He stumbled backward a few feet to lean against the side of a storage hut. He looked up at Victor. "How did you hear?" he asked.

Victor hesitated for a moment. "One of the Brothers who was imprisoned with him," he finally said. "I don't remember his name, but he had confessed and received absolution. He said that...Willem refused to confess despite the torture. He died proclaiming his innocence."

Louis nodded absently. "Yes," he said. "Of course he did." He furrowed his brow and said, "Confess to what?"

"The charges," Victor replied with a shrug. "The ritual. The blasphemy. Spitting on the cross." He gazed down the street for a moment as if he were tired of telling it, and then said, "The demon worship. That's the worst of it, I suppose...worshipping demons and kissing their assholes."

"What?" Louis gasped. Again, Victor shrugged. "Those are the charges?" Victor nodded. "That's preposterous."

Victor nodded again, but something in his manner disturbed Louis. Something about his sudden appearance nagged at Louis, too. Louis narrowed his eyes and said, "You were not arrested?"

An uncomfortable expression crossed Victor's face. "You've already asked me that," he said quickly. Louis held his gaze, and Victor added, "No! I wasn't arrested."

"You didn't *see* Willem?"

"No!"

"I was hoping," Louis said with a sigh.

"I'm sorry," Victor said. "I don't know what to say."

Louis felt something inside him grow hard and cold. He tried to imagine the Inquisitor, that man of the Church, questioning his uncle, accusing him, torturing him, tearing at him, and bringing upon him the terrible might of the Holy Catholic Church. Louis loved the Church...but he loved his uncle more.

And the Church murdered his uncle. It had sent his wife into hiding, and him into flight like a frightened hare.

"I'm sorry too," Louis said icily. Victor glanced at him, surprised by his tone. Louis stood and set his jaw and continued toward the chapel. Victor hurried to keep pace.

"Are you all right?" Victor asked.

Louis continued in silence for a moment. Finally, he stopped and wheeled toward Victor.

"We have a mission to execute," he said through clenched teeth. "That's all I care about now." He turned on his heels and entered the chapel.

After Terce, Louis and Victor went about the task of preparing for the journey to La Rochelle. They cleaned and packed their weapons, and bundled provisions.

"So, the plan is to camp outside of Surgères?" Victor said. He seemed perplexed by the destination.

"Yes," Louis said. "To rally and take roll before we head to the port at La Rochelle."

"I thought we would go to Cyprus, or Ruad," Victor said.

"If the plan were for another Crusade," Louis said dryly, "I suppose we would. But it's clear that's not to be. Under the circumstances, I doubt we'd be welcome at Cyprus. At Ruad, we'd be trapped, surrounded by Mamluks and pursued by the French. Either way would be suicide."

Victor looked troubled.

"Where then, from La Rochelle?" he asked.

Louis hesitated. He still did not know of their ultimate destination. He considered pondering the possibilities with Victor, but he thought better of it.

"We'll find out when we get to the ships," he said flatly.

Victor studied him. "You know, though," he said. He waved a finger. "You do know, don't you? If you do, you should tell me. I've followed you everywhere. It's the least you could do now."

Louis peered at Victor through narrowed eyes. Victor's eagerness was uncharacteristic. Though he was tempted to discuss the plan with him, a vague suspicion nagged at him.

"We'll find out soon enough," he said curtly, turning to his task as if to end the conversation.

Victor said no more, but Louis's refusal to confide in him clearly irked him.

The next morning, Louis noted that Victor did not attend Prime. He was still reeling from the news of Willem's fate, so he gave it little thought. When Victor also failed to show for breakfast, Louis realized that he had left the commanderie. He checked the stables for Victor's horse and tack, and they were gone.

Puzzled over Victor's brief appearance at Mas Deu, and his sudden departure, he worried for Victor and wondered where he would go. Victor had seemed evasive, though, as if he were hiding something. It was strange that he had chosen not to accompany the Templars on their flight to La Rochelle. Louis suspected that something was amiss with his old friend.

Alain, the sandy–haired squire, approached from the direction of the refectory.

"We're to depart in the darkness," Alain said. "I'll do a final check of the equipment. The commander would like to see you right away."

"You're my new squire," Louis observed.

"Yes," Alain said.

Louis nodded curtly and strode toward the hall.

Chapter 47

A BITTER WIND DROVE icy darts of lashing winter rain across the skin of Louis's face. He pulled the hood of his ragged mantle close and huddled at the foot of the lighthouse at La Rochelle, on the west side of the heavily trafficked port.

He glared at the surly, steel gray sky. It reflected the somber coldness that lay heavy in his heart. He growled with contempt at the numbing chill.

"This is it," Louis snapped. "Be alert."

Alain nodded and blew into his cupped hands. His breath steamed through his fingers. His blue-gray eyes darted to the shadows, and to the faces that passed them by. He shifted an appraising gaze toward Louis.

Louis had grown irritable, and he knew that his disposition unsettled his new charge. He was not inclined to explain himself, despite the squire's discomfort. In fact, he had found himself increasingly less disposed to any conversation at all.

They were there to make silent contact with other fugitive Templars as they arrived at La Rochelle. Word had been passed of further arrests by King Philip's men and of an exodus to safety for any who could find their way to this dreary place.

The message had been placed inside the bundles that Castellón distributed in the hall at Mas Deu. It was neatly printed in the secret Templar cipher, and crafted in cryptic English verse that would mystify any but a Templar. But to any Templar, the meaning of the cryptic code would ring clear. Louis pulled the parchment from the folds of his cloak and opened it carefully once more, reading to himself:

Pass by the light at the rock of the knights,
'neath the glow of the last bright orb
Then three nights on, at three before dawn,
join the troop by the belt of pearls.
There shall be cast the lines for the pass
to the white mists of Albion,
The departure unseen, concealed by the screen
of the mists of the new orb's dawn.

Louis had received his own verbal instructions in addition to the cryptic verse. He and Alain would tally their fellow fugitives as they passed by the lighthouse, to determine whether any more were captured, and to note any who had since escaped. Louis, Alain, and the Templars passing by looked nothing like Templars in their ragged peasants' garb. Only their subtle, secret hand signals identified them as brethren.

"Two hundred years…," Louis murmured. He shook his head almost imperceptibly.

"I'm sorry?" Alain said.

"Two hundred years," Louis repeated with disgust. "For two hundred years this town has been a Templar stronghold. Now we hide in the shadows as if we should not be here."

Alain stared silently. Louis had said little since they left Mas Deu. His mood had been as dreary as the weather, and Alain's attempts at conversation had failed. His station barred him from probing, but he was obviously anxious for answers. He would have them in due time.

"The *rock of the knights*," Louis continued, as if to himself. "This place, La Rochelle. *The little rock* of the Templars." He looked thoughtfully at Alain and then nodded into the distance. "Seven roads stretch away from here," he said softly, waving his hand toward the west, "to the farthest reaches of Europe. All built by Templars."

"I've never been here before," Alain said absently. After a pause, he continued. "The cryptic is in English," he said.

Louis nodded. He turned and stared at the threatening sea.

The lighthouse had long stood at the mouth of the port, guiding ships safely through darkness or fog. The fugitives were to pass by the lighthouse throughout this night, so that he could identify them in the light of the last full moon of the year. They were to make visual, but not physical contact as they passed. Louis cursed the misty rain and the clouds that obscured the moon's glow. He would have to be very alert to his brethren's subtle signals.

"The light at the rock of knights," Alain said, nodding, repeating the verse from the cryptic.

"You read it!" Louis exclaimed. "Over my shoulder! How dare you?"

"I'm sorry," Alain said. "I didn't mean to. I glanced at the parchment. That's all it takes sometimes, to glance at a verse, and somehow it's in my head. I can't help it." He shrugged helplessly. "Maybe because I read too much as a boy. My eyes just capture the words."

Louis shook his head, more with wonder than disapproval. "No amount of reading is too much," he said. "Unless, of course, you're reading something you have no business reading."

Alain dropped his gaze to the cobblestones.

"The lighthouse at La Rochelle, yes," Louis said, more gently. Alain nodded grudgingly. Louis pointing across the harbor to the east. "Over there," he said, "builders set markers into the paving long ago. The markers, along with the lighthouse, mark the positions of the Orion Belt."

"The belt of pearls...," Alain said cautiously.

"Alnilam," Louis said, "the middle star. *Alnilam* is the Arab name of the middle Orion star. Its marker is on the other side of the port, next to a Templar storehouse." The storehouse was where the fugitives were to meet three nights hence.

"Pardon the question, sir," Alain ventured. He waited for Louis's acknowledgement. Louis gazed at him through lowered brows. "How long do you think we will be gone?"

Louis sighed deeply. The squire was ignorant of the extent of their plight, and of their destination. He would surely miss his family and his home. Louis thought it might be best to prepare him.

"Philip le Bel is working up another arrest," Louis said. He snarled at the name he had grown to despise. He resented the title of king attached to Philip's name, and he chose instead the popular misnomer that he loathed slightly less. "It'll come at any moment. There's little to stop it, or to contain its fervor. The pope remains silent...impotent...a coward." It was hard for Louis to mouth those words, but his anger had trumped his piety.

Alain's eyes grew wide. He touched his hand to his throat as if he were about to be hanged.

"Without the pope's justice," Louis said, "there is no safe place in France, nor in most of Europe."

Alain appeared pale and shaken.

"Where will we go, then?" he asked. "To sea?" Alain pointed anxiously at the roiling waves.

Night was falling. Louis shivered in the drenching rain that fell unabated from the slate gray clouds. A group of three passers-by peered at the figures huddled by the lighthouse. Louis made eye contact, and one of the men nodded slightly. His right hand emerged from his cloak, fingers extended to form an inverted "V," with the split spreading the middle and ring fingers. Louis nodded and returned the sign. He tallied the Templars he'd seen so far.

Forty-three. Surely there would be more. Each acknowledgement lifted his spirits a little more – yet one more brother had escaped, and would live.

"There's one safe place," Louis said, "where one brave man has stood up to popes and kings, without fear. There's one place where Templars might retain their honor, and perhaps find a new purpose."

Alain quietly anticipated the revelation.

Louis indicated the parchment in his hand. *"Albion,"* he said.

"Scotland," Alain said after a moment's thought. He did not appear pleased by the prospect.

"Three days from now," Louis said, "Thursday evening. We'll meet the others at *Alnilam*." He pointed again across the harbor toward the storehouse. "We'll tally the troops and plan the passage."

"How many do you suppose will arrive?"

"It's hard to say," Louis said. He wondered what his new squire thought of his short experience as a Templar. He felt for the youth, wondering if he was feeling the disillusionment Louis had come to know too well, the sharp sting of staunch loyalty betrayed.

Alain had been initiated into the order on a muggy summer day little more than three months ago. He had mostly stared wide-eyed since then as an inexplicable drama played out around him, and as his sponsor, an uncle, was arrested and not seen again. Alain escaped arrest simply by keeping his mouth shut through the confusion, and escaping the notice of Philip's men, who did not yet have him on their list. He was left hanging, helpless in the vacuum that followed Philip's first lethal blow.

"Do you regret it?" Louis asked.

Alain blinked and said nothing. Louis allowed the question to hang between them.

"I don't know," Alain finally said, slowly. "I don't know what to feel. I've wanted this for as long as I can remember. But I wanted something different, and not this." He shrugged and nodded at the dreariness that surrounded them. "I wanted to fight for my Church, not against it. I wanted to be a soldier of the pope, and not a fugitive of his inquisition." Alain's jaw tightened as he looked off into the darkened streets. "How can he be of

God?" he finally said, whipping around to face Louis with sudden, dark anger. "How can this be of God? We swore our lives to God. How can this be our reward?"

Louis was taken with compassion for the young man, and sorrow for the wreckage of his ideals. He too doubted all he had ever held dear, and all he had ever thought true. He too had come to curse God, in spite of himself, with nearly the same fervor with which he had once praised Him. He wanted to comfort the squire, but he couldn't summon the words. He could not bring himself to utter a blatant untruth.

"There's little profit in such words, Brother," Louis said, placing a hand on the squire's shoulder. "They'll reach the ears of no one, god or man, who would see fit to change what has been done."

"I've believed," Alain said, nodding angrily. "I have lived my belief. I need to understand. I need to know how I could have been so wrong."

"The wrong is not in you, my friend," Louis said, "but in our persecution. You have not been wrong; you have been wronged."

"I feel foolish," Alain said. "I worked so hard, for so long to be a Templar. I sacrificed everything for this."

Louis shook his head and sighed deeply.

"We're all foolish," he said. "Men are fools, from their first day to their last. We pay a price for that, but if we have the heart, we still do right. We'll go on from here to try again, to find purpose elsewhere and do some good."

"Do good for whom?" Alain asked. "If not God, whom will I serve?"

"I've come to believe, Brother, that perhaps our God was never in the men our Order served," Louis said. "That was our error: thinking Him there. I've seen no evidence of Him there."

Louis did not say that he had come to believe that God was but a hope upon which evil men preyed, a creation they employed to harness and exploit idealistic men. He kept that thought to himself. *There's little profit in such words,* he repeated to himself yet one more time.

"And you think we will find Him in Scotland?" Alain asked.

He seemed incredulous.

"We're not going to Scotland to find or to serve God," Louis said, "but rather for sanctuary from so–called men of God, in the only place that might still offer it. We go there to remain free."

Alain's face tightened again at the prospect of exile to Scotland. He'd known one climate in his short life: the temperate Mediterranean coast.

"You'll adjust," Louis assured him. "It's a small price to pay for your life, and for refuge from the inquisitors. It's really not a terrible turn of events." Louis forced a small smile and forgave himself the lie.

They passed the remaining hours in silence, shivering in the dampness and struggling to keep their spirits. A faint glow arose in the east, and their task was coming to a close. Louis was encouraged to have tallied ninety-seven knights and their attendants, or more than two hundred souls, throughout the night. There would be a sizable gathering at the storehouse.

The darkness was turning to murky gray when Louis laid his head upon his pillow at last. The innkeeper's wife was already hard at work in the kitchen when they'd come in, and she gave them a wary look as they climbed the creaky steps to their room. The thin straw pallet upon which Louis lay felt luxurious to his weary, aching bones. He slept without uttering a prayer.

Chapter 48

THREE NIGHTS LATER, three hours before dawn, a vagrant stood stoic in the shadows of the Templar storehouse. Shadowy figures in peasant's cloaks approached and offered the proper obscure greeting. Louis followed suit. The vagrant directed the knights to an entrance in the rear of the storehouse, down an alley barely wide enough for a broad-shouldered man to navigate.

Louis offered the sign to yet another sentry who stood by the nondescript entrance.

"Welcome, Brothers," the sentry said. He fished a key from his shirt and turned it in the lock.

There was no light in the storehouse. It took some time for Louis's eyes to adjust to the heavy blackness. He felt the musty dampness on his skin, and the smell of dust and mold filled his nostrils. As his eyes adjusted, the figures of men became apparent, and he recognized faces he had seen passing by the lighthouse in the rain.

Most of those present were dirty, weary, and worn. They looked around the room with cautious wonder, their wary eyes drawn anxiously toward the door. No one spoke aloud as an hour slowly passed, and the last few arrivals trickled into the crowded room.

An older knight, perhaps sixty years old, sat on a chair in the far corner of the room gazing intently at each newcomer. He seemed to be lost in thought, as though he were calculating yet one more time a great and complicated plan. Louis had seen the man before, but he could not place him. He reckoned him to be of lofty rank, though it was a guess without his Templar garb.

Finally, a few minutes after the last attendee entered, an armed guard drew the bolt on the door and latched it fast. Three more knights moved toward the door and took their places by his side, swords drawn.

The tylers at the door brought an odd sense of safety to the gathering. A tyler's duty was to watch over meetings and rites, to prevent unauthorized intrusions; here they stood guard against the unfathomable hostility that all knew lay beyond the bolted door, from which they were in dire need of respite.

The older knight rose and walked stiffly to the side of the room opposite the entrance. Louis nearly gasped as he suddenly recognized the man. He was stunned by how much François Andelieu had aged since he'd last seen him.

Alain looked quizzically at Louis, who pointed toward the aging knight.

"François Andelieu," Louis whispered. "He was a Provincial Master on Cyprus. I met him there after the fall of Acre." Alain nodded. "He was a key figure in the Templar administration. He taught me intricacies of financial management of the Order. He's well known throughout France. I'm surprised he's yet free."

Louis remembered Andelieu as powerful and energetic. He was thoughtful and introspective, and a brilliant strategist. Louis had been struck by the depth of his patience. But now he appeared weak and broken. Louis saw upon closer inspection that his leg had been fractured, and badly healed. His limp was almost imperceptible, but Andelieu's face betrayed intense pain.

"He has suffered a great deal since I last saw him," Louis

whispered.

Andelieu stood quietly before the gathered knights, awaiting their full attention. Under his gaze, the barely audible murmur in the room faded to silence. Specks of dust floated in the dim shafts of light that filtered through gaps in the burlap that covered the windows.

Andelieu's eyes scanned the room. He searched the faces of those he could see. His gaze found Louis and paused. A small, sad smile flitted across his face.

Andelieu finally spoke in a hoarse voice, barely above a whisper. The knights leaned forward, straining to hear.

"I am thankful," he said, "that each of you has made it to this place, and survived unto this day. I grieve with you for our Brothers who have not. We are fortunate to have survived this tragedy thus far. To my last breath, I will ensure our continued survival."

Knights nodded and murmured. Their tangled emotions were palpable: forlorn sadness, grinding grief, bitter anger, and tentative fear. Such things were not typical in a gathering of Templars. Louis sensed in all of them the same profound weariness that had consumed him.

"We must avoid recapture," Andelieu continued. "Many are going to England, since Edward II has challenged Philip's actions. They believe they'll be safe there, at least for now."

"'*Recapture,*' he said," Louis murmured. "So he *was* captured."

"Is that where we'll go?" asked one of the knights.

Andelieu shook his head. "No," he said. "Our final destination will be divulged once we've set sail. We're here to discuss the next few days, to ensure that we all get safely to the ships."

A murmur arose among the knights. It was all so very alien to them, Louis thought, to be fugitives on the run from authorities that had once paid them deference, facing an unknown future which they would not be trusted to protect.

"We'll form groups of five," Andelieu said. "There will be one captain for each group. The captains will maintain communications. The others will hunt and keep camp, well away from towns. If you must go to town for provisions, two, and *only* two will go, making as little contact as possible with the townsfolk." He paused and gazed around the room, as if waiting for questions. "Form your groups now."

The knights moved quickly, with an efficiency born of years of training and practice. Each knight gravitated toward the brethren closest to them, or sought friends with whom they were familiar. There was a momentary rustling of cloaks, and the scraping of chairs against the stone floor, but it quickly subsided. The knights had organized as quickly as if they faced impending battle.

Andelieu smiled weakly at their efficiency. "The discipline remains," he said quietly, with appreciation. Then more loudly, "Captains, step forward."

With brief, wordless glances, each group acknowledged a captain. The men in Louis's group looked to him expectantly, and he moved toward the old Master in unison with the other captains.

Nineteen knights stood in silence before the Master's gaze.

"Commanders?" Andelieu said.

The captains separated into four groups, and in the same silent manner selected their commanders. All but one from each group of captains stepped respectfully back from his commander. Louis stepped forward with the other three commanders.

Andelieu nodded appreciatively. The knights had chosen well, as was their practice. Each commander was an accomplished, battle-hardened Crusader. Andelieu greeted each of them with a firm grip and an embrace, and then he stepped back to look upon them in appraisal. He turned to address the assembly.

"Commanders will meet here tomorrow night," he said. "They will communicate my instructions to you through the captains. From this moment on, your captains will be your only communication, your only guidance. Their words shall be the same as my own." The knights murmured their acknowledgement.

Andelieu stood with his hands behind his back peering into the assembly with reassuring certainty.

He took a deep breath, and said, "Keep this thought close, my Brothers: before a month has passed, we will be beyond the reach of our new enemies."

Andelieu's seneschal stood and faced the gathering. He raised his hands, indicating that all should stand. He turned and motioned to the Chaplain, who stood to lead the brethren in prayer.

"My brothers, let us bow in prayer."

Many of the brethren exchanged glances that betrayed uncertainty about to whom they would pray.

"We pray to a God forsaken by the men of this world," the Chaplain said, "but not by His true believers. We stand before You this day, Our Holy Father, hunted by unbelievers who would persecute us in Your Holy Name. We pray now for Your mercy, for Your deliverance from this evil. We pray that You will see us to safety."

While many bowed in reverence, Louis stood erect facing the Chaplain and the Master. Andelieu, too, held his head high. Their eyes met, and Andelieu held his gaze for a moment. Louis sensed that they shared a cataclysm of faith at the rending of all they had known.

Louis broke their gaze to look around at the gathered knights, with their heads bowed solemnly in the darkened, musty room. It occurred to him that these fierce, fearless warriors of the Holy Crusade, these men of unshakable faith and indomitable spirit, were suddenly much like sheep driven into the wilderness, by a shepherd that had gone deranged.

"Lord God," the Chaplain intoned, "our Father in heaven, hear our prayer. We stand before you in humbleness and sorrow, our faith in You unshaken by this villainy perpetrated in your Holy Name. We ask that You deliver us from the grip of the Great Satan, who has revealed unto us his true nature."

The mournful murmur of the ever-faithful, woefully betrayed knights filled the musty storehouse with the essence of their agony. A sense of loss was palpable. The Chaplain blessed the knights with a solemn sign of the cross and whispered to them Godspeed on their impending voyage.

Louis turned to the knights in his charge.

"Brother de Bouverie," he said to the most senior knight, "take the troop to an encampment – Alain knows the place – and set up camp. I'll be along shortly, after I've met with the captains and commanders."

Erard de Bouverie began to protest, but Louis raised his hand.

"Alain knows the place," Louis repeated. "I'll meet you there."

"Humbly, I must protest," de Bouverie said. "I've sworn my life to the safety of each of my Brethren. You are my Brother. I should stay with you."

"You're released now from that vow where it concerns me," Louis replied, almost impatiently. He waved the knights away.

"Brother," de Bouverie insisted, his voice rising, "I have kept that vow through the Inquisitor's flames. I must keep it now." He raised the sleeve of his tunic to reveal ghastly burns.

Louis gazed at the wounds and considered de Bouverie's plea. After a moment he nodded his assent. He did not want his troop divided, but he also knew that de Bouverie was right: he should not travel alone. Templars had been declared outlaw, and so they were in the eyes of kings and the pope. Fugitive Templars enjoyed no protection of law. Any ruffian, robber, or murderer could do as they pleased against them with impunity. None would dare to attack a Templar troop, but a lone knight could find himself cornered by villains filled with contempt for the virtuous, fallen knights.

"Wait with the tylers," Louis said quietly. He glanced at the tylers and saw that de Bouverie would not be alone. Escorts had gathered to wait for each of the captains.

Fourteen captains and five commanders gathered around the Master and his seneschal, in a semi-circle of worn oak chairs.

The seneschal, Berenguer de Coll, leaned forward and spoke.

"James of Aragon has helped us in preparing our flight. Our ships from Cyprus are docked at Barcelona under his flag, with our assets in their bellies, under guard. Those ships will meet us under the new moon at La Rochelle."

The knights nodded their understanding and exchanged brief glances.

"And what of Cyprus?" asked one.

"A nominal detachment will go there, but little else," de Coll said. "They will attempt to maintain our properties for as long as they can."

Many of the Templars had assumed that Cyprus would be their asylum. It stood to reason that if they were to be driven from Europe, they should resume their Holy Land Crusade, even if the rest of Europe had abandoned it, and seek to regain their home there.

"What I am about to say will not be repeated until we are under way," de Coll said. He took a deep breath and paused, looking around at the knights. "Our ships will carry us to Scotland," he continued. "King Robert has refused to arrest Templars. In fact, he has offered asylum...in exchange for our services."

"Our services?" one of the commanders asked. Louis did not know the man who spoke. He was younger than Louis, and Spanish. He'd no doubt spent most of his Crusading service fighting for Aragon against the Moors.

"In his war for independence from the English," de Coll said. "He has the will, and his soldiers have the spirit, but they lack military training and expertise. The war has taken its toll. We have much to offer. We've agreed to help."

"Fighting against Christians," the commander said. His jaw tensed. "Fighting against English Christians."

"Edward II is nothing like his father," de Coll said of the English king. "He is weak. It's a matter of time until he gives in to Philip's pressure and starts arresting Templars. He'll no doubt realize the property he can seize, and that will sway him."

"He's Christian," the commander insisted. "Our oath is to defend Christians, and not to fight them. I cannot kill a Christian."

"Our oath to whom?" Louis quietly interjected.

"Our world has changed," de Coll said evenly, patiently.

The Spanish commander turned and glared at Louis. Louis looked at the Spaniard with compassion. He understood all too well the bonds of their oaths. But the world had indeed changed, profoundly.

"To whom?" the Spaniard repeated.

"Yes," Louis said. "Our oath to whom? To the pope? To the Church?"

"To God," the Spaniard said.

Louis moved toward the man and extended his hand.

"I am Louis de Garonne," he said. "I am your Brother. I share your oaths."

Andelieu looked at Louis in surprise.

"Garvisso de la Fuente," the Spaniard said, hesitantly taking Louis's hand.

"But I'm no longer sure to whom those oaths were made," Louis said, "or for whom I am to risk my life in keeping those oaths. Perhaps you have retained your sense of such things, but for many of us, that certainty is gone."

"An oath to God is an oath to God," Garvisso said. "It is eternal."

"This Church," Louis said calmly, "has allowed a king to take our very lives – our Rule, our name, our mission, our Brethren… my uncle." Louis choked back an involuntary sob. "Some have died horrible deaths…crushed, burned, torn to shreds. All in the name of God." His eyes narrowed with purpose. "By *Christians*," he added.

Andelieu placed a hand on Garvisso's shoulder. "Things are not as we would have them," he said softly. "But things are as they are, in spite of what we would like them to be. The days are gone when the Knights Templar exemplified nobility and righteousness. This is our world no more. Our oaths were made to a Kingdom of God that does not exist in this world."

"It feels like blasphemy," Garvisso muttered.

"It is reality," Andelieu said.

"A shift has taken place," the Chaplain said. "Bishop Wishart of Glasgow has expressed the sentiment that it is as noble to defend Scottish Christians against the English as it is to fight the Saracens in the Holy Land."

While Garvisso considered the point, Andelieu drove it home.

"Christian oppression of European Christians seems to me

more heinous," he said, "than the enmity of the Saracens, who are, after all, our natural enemies."

"Robert the Bruce is a good man," de Coll said of the Scottish king. "A good king. He shares our ideals. Those ideals lend foundation to the social order we seek to create, where tyranny is replaced with equity, and where kings and popes serve the common good, if they serve at all."

Garvisso gasped. "What ideals support such sedition?" he asked.

"The ideals that all men are equal in the sight of God," the Chaplain said, "and that all men deserve the benevolent affection of their rulers. These are Templar ideals. It appears that they are no longer compatible with the current order of things."

"We've sought a nation of our own," Andelieu said, "to be founded upon the ideals of freedom and equality, respect and human dignity. While it appears that our Templar nation is not meant to be, Scotland is a nation ready to embrace such things. And Scotland is oppressed by a tyrant king."

Garvisso nodded slowly, weighing the words. He was clearly grieving the Templars' predicament.

"We will do what we must," Andelieu said with finality, "to survive, if not to flourish, and to continue to defend the things we most cherish." He turned to the captains. "Go to your troops," he ordered. "We'll meet twice, commanders and captains, before we sail. I'll see you at the inn at Saint-Xandre, at the twentieth hour of Monday the fourteenth. Keep your troops hidden and well–disciplined. Draw no attention. The commanders will contact you when necessary. Until then, Godspeed."

Most of the knights left, and a few lingered by the door with Erard de Bouverie while Louis remained behind to speak with François Andelieu.

Their eyes met, and Andelieu nodded to Louis in recognition.

"It soothes my heart to see you here, my son," Andelieu said. "I've prayed for you and your uncle."

Louis nodded in appreciation. "Thank you," he said. "I'm glad you're well."

Andelieu smiled sadly. "Not extremely well," he said. "A bit the worse for wear. And you…" Andelieu peered closely at Louis's face. "…you are worn, as well."

"We've all suffered," Louis said. He thought of Willem, then shook his head tersely against the pain. "But here we are… brethren till the end. In that, at least, we may retain our trust."

"Each of you has led your brethren well," Andelieu said. "You have fought bravely in battles past. Ahead of you may lay the greatest challenges of all. Our own home, our own Church has become our gravest danger."

"Are we certain of sanctuary in Scotland?" Louis asked. "Has Robert the Bruce committed to that?"

"He has," Andelieu said.

"And we trust him? We trust the Scots?"

"We do," Andelieu said with certainty.

Louis thought for a moment, then said, "Scotland, then… will it be our New Jerusalem?"

Andelieu gave Louis a long, appraising look. He nodded and said, "In a sense."

"The Bruce would allow that?" Louis pressed.

Andelieu smiled. "Scotland will be King Robert's 'New Jerusalem,'" he said. "The Bruce wants for the Scots precisely what we intended for our Templar nation. Fortune frowned upon us, but all is not lost. A new world will arise, and we will champion its rise. But in Scotland, for now, and not in the Languedoc. It will yet be, but it will not be as we had planned."

"We've been driven underground," Berenguer de Coll said. "But that doesn't change our future. We must simply function behind a veil, as if we no longer exist."

"In many ways," Andelieu added, "that may be to our advantage."

"If they don't see us, they can't fight us," Louis said.

"Exactly." Andelieu nodded approvingly. "Philip cannot harm what he believes he has already crushed."

"Stay in contact with your captains," de Coll said. "Maintain discipline and morale. At the inn, on the fourteenth, we'll share news of the fleet and discuss our preparations. Secrecy is paramount. We intend to vanish in the night, without a trace, leaving no rumblings or rumors behind us. See to it."

Louis nodded.

"Blessings upon all of us," the chaplain said.

Louis started to cross himself in response, but he could not bring himself to complete the gesture.

✠ ✠ ✠

The fourteenth came quickly. Incessant rains cast dreariness over the troops as they went about the business of survival in what had become a hostile land. Hunting, meals, and the maintenance of horses and arms filled the gaps between regularly scheduled prayers and training. The Templar lifestyle was rigorous and demanding, and it left little idle time. If not for that, the grayness would have seemed interminable.

Louis saddled his horse and tightened the bridle and buckles. He mounted briskly and turned to ensure that Alain was ready, too. He turned back toward Berenguer de Bouverie, who stood to see them off. With a nod, Louis clicked his tongue and reined toward the road to Saint-Xandre.

"Safe return," de Bouverie called. Louis's cloak billowed as he nudged the steed to a trot.

"We go for news of the fleet," Alain said, not as much questioning as making idle conversation.

Louis nodded, his eyes intent on the road and the brush that lined it. He was alert to the presence of robbers, who might have gotten wind of fugitive Templars around Surgères. He knew, too, that Templar gold was not the only prize an outlaw or a peasant might covet. Many commoners had come to equate the Templars' vast power and esteem with undue arrogance and wealth. Even for little or no profit, some would welcome the opportunity to vent hostility upon an isolated Templar, particularly in the absence of legal consequence.

"You're nervous," Alain said. "Should I be, also?"

"There would be no penalty for our murder," Louis said.

Alain seemed shaken by that. "You're right," he said. "I hadn't thought of that."

"Be vigilant."

"Yes, lord," Alain replied.

"Our own countrymen have become our enemy," Louis fumed. "I'd feel more at home in a Muslim camp than I do here in my own land."

"You've been to a Muslim camp, then?" Alain said.

"Often," Louis said. He looked off into the damp trees as he remembered the visit with Kala'un.

"Yet, you're alive," Alain mused.

Louis turned to Alain with a reproving look, and said, "The Muslims are as honorable hosts as they are fierce warriors. Their ways are noble as any I have seen." He paused as they rode on. "More noble than most," he added. "I feared for nothing as a guest in their camps."

Alain seemed surprised. "I thought they were demons," he said.

"In battle, they are," Louis said with a smile. "We all were. But few more fearsome than a Muslim fighting to regain his land."

"They let you leave their camp in peace?" Alain said with wonder.

"We came in peace," Louis said. "They honor that peace, and would not defile it. They fight with purpose, and their purpose is peace...*their* peace, of course...the peace of undisputed Muslim rule."

"Why would they not coexist with us in our Kingdom of God?" Alain asked.

Louis smiled wryly, remembering Kala'un's answer to a similar question.

"Why would we not coexist with them in their Kingdom of Islam?" he replied.

Alain blinked at the question, but then he understood.

"They call our Christ a prophet of God," Louis said. "We call their Muhammad a demon from Hell. Which view is hostile, and which is more tolerant?"

"You seem to like them," Alain said after a moment. "And yet you fought them."

"Fiercely," Louis said, "and with deep respect. They were the most worthy of enemies, and the most loyal of friends. There are madmen among them, of course. Can we not say the same of ourselves? But in general, the Muslims are humble, God-fearing men who hold genuine respect for all of God's creation...including Christians. They think we are lost, but aside from that, they respect us." He let his words hang in the heavy air for a moment, and then he turned to Alain and spread his arms wide. "Tell me, Alain," he said, "in all honesty...are we not lost? Even in our own country, we are lost. Perhaps we are more lost than any pagan."

Alain narrowed his eyes and furrowed his brow, and he did not answer.

"I think that now I would sooner fight the English in defense of the Scots," Louis said vehemently, "than the Muslims in the name of religion."

Alain made no more idle conversation. They rode rest of the way to Saint-Xandre in stony silence.

At Saint-Xandre, they approached the inn door just as it was pulled open from the inside. A drunken peasant lurched into the drizzle and nearly sent Alain sprawling. Alain deftly sidestepped the collision, and the man careened into the descending darkness.

Louis laughed. "Our plight is more dangerous than I'd imagined," he joked.

Alain stepped into the doorway and held the door for Louis. Murmuring voices and comforting warmth filled the musty inn. Chairs scraped the floor as patrons shifted for a better view of the newcomers.

Close to the door, a ragged farmer sat at a table facing them with a mug of ale in his fist. Louis recognized him from the storehouse. The Templar nodded toward the stair that led to an upper hall, and Louis and Alain ascended the stair without acknowledgement.

At the top of the stair, Andelieu and the commanders sat around the table. Louis took a seat, and Alain moved to a bench by the fire. Straw littered the floor, and a serving girl moved around the table filling mugs with ale.

Andelieu nodded and began.

"We'll gather outside La Rochelle after midnight on the second day of Christmas. Scouts will make sure all is clear, and we'll go to the docks in pairs, in stealthy haste, until the last of us has boarded. It should take two or three hours at the most."

"Those ships are provisioned?" Louis asked. He had thought that no one would have ventured near the sixteen Templar ships that had sat idle at La Rochelle in the months since the initial arrests. Surely they were under surveillance by the local authorities.

Andelieu smiled. "They're more than provisioned," he said. "They're loaded with some of our most treasured assets."

Louis thought he knew what that meant: artifacts and scrolls from deep within the Temple Mount, charters and contracts with popes and princes, some of which the signatories might prefer did not exist, and a vast accumulation of business and banking wealth from two centuries of prudent financial management. The combination of treasure, legalities, and knowledge was possibly the greatest accumulation of wealth in the world. Louis doubted that either the pope or Europe's kings would spare any effort to acquire it.

Andelieu continued. "Philip's spies have been watching the ships since the arrests," he said. "They send dispatches to the king every Friday, reassuring him that they remain secure."

"They'll surely alert him the day we depart," said one of the commanders, a Venetian named Ponç de Veneto.

"Normally, they would," Andelieu agreed. "But these aren't just any spies." He raised his hands in mock helplessness. "They're our spies, more than they are his."

Louis laughed and shook his head. Of course the king's spies owed loyalty to the Order, or at least held sympathy for it. If they were well–placed nobles, they had friends or relations among its ranks.

"The king will get his report," Andelieu said with a smile, "just as soon as his men are able to get it to him." He turned and nodded to a knight Louis didn't recognize.

The knight said, "We'll sail under the flag of Aragon. No one will attack sixteen ships under the flag of King James, even if they suspect we're aboard...perhaps *because* we're aboard." The knights in the room laughed, and their momentary levity pleased Louis. "We'll cast off before dawn," the knight said.

Andelieu nodded to the knight and said, "Remember, we will not discuss our destination until we are safely at sea. The fewer who know of it, the less likely it is to be exposed. Be sure that your men are well–fed and rested for the journey, and above all, that they get to the ships timely."

Chapter 49

THE SHIPS PUT IN AT ARDROSSAN in the darkness of the Twelfth Night of Christmas. The moon was nearly full again, and its light danced on the waves like brilliant jewels. The air was crisp and cold. The imposing hostility of the rugged landscape that stretched from the sea into the midnight sky felt welcoming to the fugitives.

It was the perfect haven, Louis thought.

Bitter wind whipped the sails as they were furled. Knights sat huddled in groups, shivering and praying for warmth. Many appeared to Louis lost and wretched, seasick, and worn. The ten day journey felt like a month, and Louis was glad it was over. He had never longed so deeply for dry land.

Louis watched in anticipation as the Scottish coast came into focus. He was barely conscious of the chilling mist that sprayed over him from the bow as he gazed at the welcoming sight. He felt sudden, inexplicable pride at the sight of the dramatic emerald coast and the bluish highlands that rose into the clouds just beyond it. He felt a mysterious familiarity, as if he were arriving home after a long and arduous absence. He felt a sense of belonging, as if it had always been his fate to arrive at this magnificent place.

A delegation of Robert the Bruce waited for them at the docks. The Scots were hearty, and apparently unaffected by the cold. They wore heavy shirts and woolen kilts with the ends draped over one shoulder. Laced leather sandals more suited for warmer climates protected their feet.

One of the Scots, a bulky man with a flowing red beard, surged to the foot of the gangplank to welcome Andelieu, who moved slowly, with the assistance of the chaplain.

"Welcome!" the Scotsman bellowed. He grasped Andelieu's hand and roughly embraced him. "Andrew," he said proudly, "of Clan Douglas! You are François Andelieu?"

Andelieu nodded and smiled faintly as he and the chaplain walked off to speak with Andrew privately. Dozens of Scots scrambled up gangplanks to assist with the unloading of the ships. At the gangway to the trading ship *Le Pèlerin*, Templar guards firmly blocked their way. The Scots backed off with puzzled shrugs. Louis guessed that *Le Pèlerin* held the most precious cargo.

"What can I do to help?" a young man of about twenty said as he approached Louis. The young man surveyed the disembarking Templars with curiosity.

Louis thought for a moment. He still had his sea legs, and the ground swayed beneath him. He longed only for sound sleep.

"Lodging," he said. "Most of us will be needing a bed, more than anything else."

"I'm James," the young man said. "James of Douglas." He was slim, almost dainty, with dark hair and deep blue eyes. Something in those eyes reminded Louis of Colette, as did the young man's elegant demeanor. James Douglas spoke quietly, and with a faint lisp.

Louis took James's hand and said, "I'm Louis de Garonne."

"Ah!" James exclaimed. "So you are!" He nodded excitedly. "My darling Colette will be glad to hear it. She's been anxious for you."

"Your darling?" Louis said with a frown.

"My cousin," James said, grinning. "Don't worry, Louis. You've nothing to fear on that count. You're dearer than breath to that lass. She'd die to see you smile."

Louis relaxed, relieved. He could hardly believe he would soon be in her arms.

"She's all right, then?" he asked.

"Aside from the longing, yes," James replied. "She's fine. She's down in Ayr, barely a day's journey. She's working hard there, ministering to the wounded and orphans of war."

Louis smiled. He could have guessed. "How goes the war?" he asked.

"Fits and starts," James replied. "Victories, mostly, but small ones with heavy casualties. Most of Edward's men are lackluster; they fight with fear. They don't want to be here, and they're not comfortable with the way we fight."

"The way you fight?"

"Raids and ambushes, sudden strikes from the shadows and bushes...not their conventional battle on the open field."

"This is effective?" Louis asked.

"More than one might expect," James replied. "It demoralizes the bastards." James turned to watch his countrymen helping the Templars unload their provisions. "But it's not enough," he added.

Louis nodded as he, too, observed the bustling activity on the dock. "Perhaps your fortunes have changed for the better," he said.

"My friend, that's what we're hoping," James said. "No offense to you and your brethren, but it appears that your misfortune is our gain. The Bruce has few friends in Europe; we're grateful for any that come our way."

"That's a practical assessment," Louis said dryly.

"Pardon my frankness...," James said.

"No," Louis said, shrugging, "I appreciate it. Honesty is no fault."

"That depends to whom one is speaking," James said with a laugh. "Come now, though...and meet my compatriots."

Louis walked up a small but steep hill dotted with thistles and ferns, and strange pink flowers that he had never seen, with two blossoms at the top of every stem, hanging in what seemed like modest deference to the world. He stopped to inspect the flowers.

"Twinflowers," James Douglas said. "Have you never seen them?"

Louis grinned. He had thought that Colette made up the word she used so long ago to describe them together. It never occurred to him that there might actually be such a thing. Now the word drew him back to those sunny fields. "I've heard of them," he said with a smile. "But no, I've never seen them." He turned and continued on with James Douglas toward a group of Scottish captains.

"Sir Robert!" James called out as they approached the group. Louis gave a start at the name and peered keenly at the man who turned toward them.

"That's the Bruce?" he asked in a low voice.

James turned to him in amusement. "No," he said, laughing. "The Bruce is far off from here, but on his way." He nodded at the tall, powerful man with long, reddish hair and a wind burned face, and introduced him to Louis.

"This," he said with a flourish, "is Sir Robert Keith, Justiciar of Scotland, and hero of our fight for independence."

Robert Keith waved the introduction off and extended his hand to Louis.

"This is Louis de Garonne," James continued, "a knight among knights, as I've been told, and a nephew of Sir Jacques Marti."

Robert nodded approvingly.

"Not a nephew, exactly," Louis began, but he faltered. "Well...I—"

The Scots looked perplexed, but they seemed to work out the complexity for themselves, and James nodded hesitantly.

"My mother was his adopted sister," Louis said quickly, feeling awkward.

"Well, that's the same damn thing!" Robert exclaimed.

"I supp—"

"No matter," James said. He turned to the other men and introduced them in turn.

Thomas Randolph, the Earl of Moray, seemed exceptionally wary. He shook Louis's hand without a word.

Sir James Stewart, a lanky man near fifty, with long, graying hair, carried himself with a royal air; he was, after all, the High Steward of Scotland...among the closest advisors to the king.

When all the introductions were made, Louis sent for the Templar commanders to join their Scottish hosts for a welcome meal of fresh meat, warm bread, and strong ale. The Scots dove into the meal, but stopped and shifted uncomfortably as the Templars bowed their heads for solemn prayers. Finally the knights crossed themselves and attacked their own plates.

"We're glad to have you here," Robert Keith said with weary gruffness.

The swarthy Venetian knight, Ponç de Veneto, said, "Do you think we'll make that much of a difference?"

James Douglas nodded, chewing furiously in an effort to answer. "Oh, yes," he said as he swallowed. "In many ways. First, many of our soldiers are ragtag, and untrained. They could use a bit of training in the arts of war. You'll help with that, of course."

"Of course," Veneto said.

"Your mere presence will embolden them," Thomas Randolph added. "Already their spirits are lifted to know you're coming."

Louis doubted that two hundred knights could make such a difference, even if they were Templars. "There must be at least twenty thousand English against you," he said.

"More," Robert Keith said. "And none of them have faced a Templar in battle."

"There may be Templars among them," said Bérenger Guifre, Louis's close friend. "Surely the English Templars have not been arrested...and they may never be. We'll face them." He looked uncertainly at Louis.

Louis nodded and said, "Things have changed dramatically. It's a new world, and we'll face profound adjustments...especially in our notions of who are our enemies, and who are our friends."

The Scots exchanged nervous glances, and an awkward silence ensued.

Louis continued: "I never imagined myself, for instance, fighting the English, though they have always been mortal enemies of France. The bond of the Templar Order made English knights my brethren. Now, I'll have to think of them simply as Englishmen." The other Templars nodded in agreement. "I would not have chosen for it to be so. It has been made so against my will. That doesn't change that it is so."

Again, the other Templars nodded, with lingering uncertainty.

"So, we don't have a problem, then," Robert Keith said in a booming voice. "Is that what I'm hearing?"

"That's what you're hearing," Louis said.

James Douglas raised his tankard high. "To our new guests, then," he said. The Scots joined the toast, and the Templars followed.

"To Scotland," Louis said. A raucous chorus of shouts startled him for a moment. When it subsided, he turned to James Douglas.

"So, tell me news of Colette," he said. James smiled broadly at the shift to a more pleasant topic.

They talked late into the night, drinking ale and singing songs that grew more silly by the hour. Louis's longing for Colette swelled until it nearly consumed him. It was not long before seeing her became the solitary purpose of his life.

✠ ✠ ✠

"It's an odd twist of fate," Louis said to James Douglas, "that would bring the pope's most loyal army to the aid of the pope's most defiant foe."

They sat around a heavy oak table in the upper hall of a tavern on the quay at Saltcoats, a small fishing village a short walk east of Ardrossan.

"To say the least," James Douglas replied, wiping a droplet of ale from the corner of his mouth. "But then, we Scots are well accustomed to odd twists of fate. Who would have thought before Stirling Bridge that one minor, obscure noble from the western Lowlands could rally a ragtag Scottish army to defeat an English force more than five times its size?"

Louis nodded. "That was quite a feat," he agreed. "I have to say, though, that this is the last place I thought I'd end up... fighting for an excommunicate king."

"In an excommunicate country," Douglas said with a shrug. "The pope hates all of us, not just the Bruce."

"I suppose we have that in common, then," Louis said. "What set King Robert at odds with the Church?"

"Ach," Douglas said, "it was a number of things...not least of all the murder of Comyn at Greyfriars."

"That was bold," Louis said with a nod.

"Aye, and quite unpopular with the papacy," Douglas said. "Mostly, it was the blood all over the greyfriars' altar. You know how the Franciscans hate blood." He winked and smiled sardonically. "But aside from that, the Bruce is disinclined to allow anyone outside of Scotland to control Scotland. It's hard enough to keep Scotland in control of Scotland."

"I can see the pope taking opposition to that," Louis said. Douglas nodded.

Louis imagined the pope's reaction to King Robert's stubbornness. No other European king had demonstrated such disregard for the papacy. Even Philip of France made a show of diplomatic convention as he ruthlessly manipulated Clement V.

"I want to meet him," Louis said.

"Oh, that you will, lad," said Robert Keith, who had sat quietly, lost in thought. "You'll meet him soon enough. He'll be joining us shortly."

"Ah!" Louis said. "Excellent."

Robert Keith laughed heartily, and the rest of the Scots joined him. "And he'll be pleased to meet you, as well," he said, "and to hear of how you'll be helping him with his Balliol problem."

"His Balliol problem?" Louis said. Of course, by killing John Comyn, of the House of Balliol, the Bruce had made sworn enemies on that side of the dispute for the Scottish crown. Of course it was a problem for the Bruce, but Louis could not imagine how it could involve him.

James Douglas said, "We're worried that the sodomite king of England will bring his army north in a few months, and we can't be distracted by Balliol rebellion when that happens. We must defeat the Balliols and gain their homage, and we have little time to do that."

Louis flinched at Douglas's epithet for Edward II; its use against the Templars was a raw wound. It gave him cause to question the veracity of any such charge.

"Have you the troops?" he asked.

"Three thousand," Douglas replied.

"That's all?"

"For the time being. We expect twice as many to gather from across the country."

"And Balliol's numbers?" Louis asked.

"About the same," Douglas said. "You seem troubled."

Louis nodded. "Yes," he said. "I knew before we came here that the Scots were fighting the English. I reconciled myself to involvement in that. But I didn't realize that the Scots were still fighting among themselves, and that we'd be drawn into a civil war."

"It's housekeeping," an authoritative voice boomed from halfway up the stairwell to the hall. Heavy footsteps trudged up the wooden stair, each step a solid, determined blow. The Scots sprang to their feet at the voice, and the Templars quickly followed. They bowed as the king arrived at the top of the stair.

The Bruce was tall and broad-shouldered, with a modest waist. His ample red hair and thick beard framed an uncommonly attractive face that bore the effects of recent illness. His fair skin was pale and moist, and his piercing blue eyes rimmed with fatigue.

The Bruce scanned the room with the intensity of a man on

guard. His gaze settled on the Templars.

"I am consolidating my forces," he continued in that booming voice. "This is not a civil war. It's the effort to which one must go when one's kingdom has been torn by decades of domination and betrayal."

"Welcome back, my lord," said James Douglas. He drew the head chair, newly vacant, away from the table for the king. Servants rushed into the room with hot food and fresh tankards of ale.

The Bruce took his seat, and his men followed while James Douglas introduced each of the Templars.

"We were telling our new friends of our current challenge," James said.

"So I gathered," the king said. "And it troubles them."

James turned to Louis, gesturing for him to explain.

"Not troubled, my lord," Louis said. "Surprised. I had wrongly assumed that the Scots were united in their opposition to the English."

"Oh, the Scots are united in their opposition," the king said firmly. He turned to Douglas and said with a hearty laugh, "What's never entirely certain is behind whom they are united."

The rest of the Scots laughed loudly at that, and nodded genial agreement.

"But you're their king," Louis said, smiling weakly.

Again, Robert laughed. "You're French," he said.

"Occitan," Louis replied.

The king acknowledged the distinction. "But not Scottish, so you may not understand that a Scot lays down for no one, particularly one who presumes to be his king...and most assuredly, not one who kills the man he thought should be his king. I knew when I killed Comyn that I'd be fighting to get his men onto my side. I'd have it no other way. I have no use for a soldier who is easily turned."

Louis nodded. He admired the philosophy, despite its obvious difficulties.

"Will we be going up to Argyll?" asked Thomas Randolph. Randolph was the king's nephew, and the Earl of Moray. A solid man of average height, he had the fair hair and pale skin of a Norseman. "It's high time we did so," he said. "MacDougall will be thinking we've gone soft."

"We're going," the king said. "Without delay. Young John Bacach will be leading the MacDougall army, and he'll be anxious to prove himself to his father. We must teach him the wisdom of a united Scotland, once and for all."

"Where will we meet them?" Randolph asked.

"They know we'll be heading to Lochaber, to attack them there," the king said. "Our scouts have told us that John has his men in the hills above the Pass of Brander waiting for us to pass." He paused for a moment, grinning. "It's a crafty trap. It would be difficult, if not impossible to face them in that narrow pass. We'll have to come up with something more ingenious."

"It's good that they're at the pass," said James Douglas.

The Bruce looked thoughtfully at James and said, "What do you have in mind?"

"It *would* be treacherous fighting in that narrow pass," James said, nodding, "with the mountain on one side, and the lake on the other. No room to maneuver, or to turn and retreat. It would be treacherous indeed...for us, and for Argyll."

"Yes," Randolph said, "but we would be the ones marching into their trap. We know they're there, but we would still be at the disadvantage. They're uphill; we're in the open, below their archers."

"Yes," James said. "Some of us would be. But then, some of us could be up above them, on the ridge. Our archers could take them by surprise, raining arrows from above while the rest of you charge from below."

The king raised an eyebrow. "It's a good plan," he said. "You're certain you'll get behind them unnoticed?"

"I'll see that we do," James said.

It was a brilliant plan, Louis thought, and the lanky, boyish knight James Douglas saw it as clearly as if he were there. Louis nodded appreciatively.

"We'll leave in the morning," the king said. "James and Walter Stewart, and Andrew Douglas will meet us at Paisley, and my brother Edward will be at Dumbarton waiting for us. By the time we get to Stronmilchan, we'll have fifteen thousand men to their ten. Stronmilchan is where you'll take your army into the mountain, James?"

James nodded. Stronmilchan lay at the north end of Loch Awe, just before the road turned southwest into the narrow pass, with the lake on the left hand and the mountains towering straight into the clouds on the right.

"I'll need a head start," James said. "About a day, to be certain. We'll engage Argyll the following morning."

The king nodded and said, "That's good. Argyll is the last of the holdouts. A victory here will seal our unity once and for all." He peered curiously at Louis and the Templars. "Now, though," he said, "let's hear from our guests."

"Well, as for me," Louis said, "I'm still a bit disoriented." He glanced at the other Templars, who murmured their agreement. "The entire world has changed for us. It may take some time before we regain our footing on solid ground."

"You had no warning?" the Bruce asked. "It seems to me there would have been some sign or signal to tip you off."

"No," said Bérenger Guifre. "Well, perhaps in retrospect. But who would have believed that Philip would attack a crusading order in such a manner?"

"Even Jacques de Molay was in the jaws of the devil the night before the arrests," said Ponç de Veneto. "He was by Philip's side, as a brother-in-arms."

"That doesn't mean he didn't know," Louis said.

"Why would he have borne Princess Catherine's coffin," Ponç replied, "if he'd known that Philip was about to have his entire Order arrested?"

"If he'd refused the honor," Louis said, "Philip might have realized that he had been warned. Perhaps Nogaret would have moved sooner, and fewer would have been warned."

"Philip is crafty," the king said. "You may be correct."

A French knight, Rogier Garic, said, "So, you think he

feigned ignorance and allowed himself to be arrested just to give us the chance to escape?"

Louis nodded. "I suspect that he sacrificed himself. Perhaps he believed Philip would deal kindly with him."

"If so, from what I have heard, he was wrong," Ponç said.

Again, Louis nodded. In fact, they had heard that Philip's Inquisitors subjected their Grand Master to grievous torture, to no avail. Louis wondered if de Molay could not have concocted a more effective plan. But on such short notice, perhaps not.

"He had to have known," said Bérenger Guifre. "*We* were warned. Surely he knew long before we did. I'm awed by the courage it took for him to feign ignorance to protect our escape."

"Philip has made some dreadful accusations," James Douglas said.

"I'm not sure I even know what they are," Louis said dolefully. James and the king exchanged glances. Obviously, the Bruce had received communication from King Philip. "What have you heard?" Louis asked.

"Some of the standard accusations," the king said. "Heresy, of course. Idol worship. Sodomy." He appeared pensive for a moment, and then said, "The more disturbing charges have to do with the initiation rites, and the nature of the most secret rituals of worship. Those are troublesome, and of course, easy targets. Their strict secrecy invites speculation."

"I don't understand," Louis said. "The pope blessed our Rule. Nothing has ever been hidden from the popes. There are no secrets from him. He has but to ask, and all would be answered him."

"And you think he wants the truth...," King Robert said. "You think this is about truth?"

"Obviously not," Louis replied. "But I don't know why."

"Domination," the king said. "Nothing more or less. It is always about domination, Sir Louis. I am excommunicate, not because of John Comyn, but because I have refused to allow my nation and my church to be dominated by foreign kings and foreign churches."

"We were loyal to all of Christendom," Louis said. "That

included Philip's throne."

"You threatened Philip's throne…or at least the expansion of its power," the king replied.

"How?" Louis said.

"You had designs on the Languedoc, did you not?"

Louis was astonished. No one had known about that. He had worked with Willem and the others in the strictest secrecy. How could either Philip or Robert the Bruce know anything of those plans? He sat speechless, his mouth agape.

"You thought no one knew?" Robert asked, incredulously.

"How could anyone know that?" Louis said.

"How could anyone not?" the king countered. "It made perfect sense. The Hospitallers have Rhodes. The German knights have Prussia. The Templars no longer have the Levant, while the Languedoc welcomes them with open arms…in the hope, one might guess, of resisting Philip's total domination."

Louis saw now the futility of concealing the obvious.

"I'd have been surprised to learn that you did *not* have designs on the Languedoc," the king added.

Louis suddenly felt foolish.

"So, this is why Philip has attacked your Order," James Douglas said with certainty.

"Well, yes, certainly," Louis said, "if in fact he knew."

"It was a fine plan," the king said.

"We appreciate your willingness to welcome us here," Louis said, shifting the topic.

"Of course you do," the king replied. "But of course you know that it's self–serving, as well, and not simple charity."

Louis nodded.

"Scotland *will* be free," James Douglas said. "That is more certain now than ever, particularly with your assistance. With Argyll and the rest of the clans in line, and the presence of seasoned Templars, England's domination will be too costly for Edward to maintain. Tomorrow we go to Brander to make that so."

"Perhaps then," King Robert said with a grim smile, "we can all go together to resume the Holy Crusade against God's pagan foes."

Douglas furrowed his brow in surprise.

"I'll have to earn my absolution eventually," the king said with a shrug. "What better way than that?"

The Templars exchanged uncertain looks while the Scots nodded casual acquiescence.

"Well, for now," Louis said with a nod, "It's to Brander. Let's see to our victory there."

"To Brander," James Douglas said with a toast.

"To victory," the king replied.

Chapter 50

Every mile of the march from Ardrossan to Glasgow intensified the ache in Louis's heart as it took him farther from Colette, who waited for him in Ayr, a mere day's ride in the opposite direction.

At Glasgow, they crossed the River Clyde. As they turned to the northwest and followed the Clyde, he resigned himself to his task. Another month would pass, at least, before he would see her.

They camped the second night on the west bank of a vast and magnificent lake dotted with dozens of islands and surrounded by Highland peaks. They drew an ample variety of trout, pike, and perch from the misty, brooding lake, and picked bowls of wild blaeberries from the leafy shrubs that grew thick along the shore. It was the best meal Louis had ever eaten on a march into battle.

Despite the vague chill that almost always hung in the air, he found an odd comfort in the rugged richness of this magical land. The warmth of the fire and the camaraderie of his new Scottish friends made him feel strangely at home.

After two more days and a wide-ranging arc around the

northeast side of a harsh and craggy mountain, they camped on a riverbed plain at the edge of Loch Awe. In the morning, James Douglas and nearly a thousand archers scaled the rocky face of Ben Cruachan, an immense emerald mountain riddled with towering ridges and spectacular, treacherous cliffs.

The Bruce's main force broke camp before dawn the next morning and proceeded along the road to the Pass of Brander.

The road was narrow, allowing a column of no more than three horses abreast. To the right, the mountain ascended sharply into the mist. To the left, the bank of Loch Awe lapped at the hooves of the outermost mounts. In places, the road narrowed, thinning the column further and slowing progress still more.

The king was in no hurry; it was better to allow the archers ample time to settle into position on the ridge.

Louis noted the scouts of Argyll concealed within the deep brush, and he caught their movements as they rushed to alert the MacDougall army. He knew that the Bruce's men detected them too, but they masked their awareness.

As they rounded the southern edge of Ben Cruachan and turned west, Louis spied a long, slender, clinker-built galley about a mile up the Awe, hanging on the edge of the misty river. Its single sail was tightly furled, but its oars were manned and ready. As the galley came into view, a horn blared from its deck and a tumult arose in the hills above the king's army. Argyll's attack had begun.

Thousands of warriors rose from the brush with a shout and descended upon Bruce's men. The king's men braced themselves for the onslaught. Louis briefly wondered whether James Douglas had secured his archers' position in time. His thought was answered by an ominous hum from the ridges and peaks above, as thousands of arrows arced through the air toward the Argyll attackers.

Argyll's men fell into disarray. The Bruce gave the word, and his men charged up the hill. A chorus of shouts rang out from above – of confusion from the Argyll army, and of triumph from James Douglas's men.

The Argyll men broke and ran to the west, descending the hill on a diagonal toward the River Awe. The archers pursued them, firing into their ranks, and the men in the pass rushed to block their escape. A frenzied chase ensued, and it grew clear that the enemy would be routed.

As the Argyll men reached the river and proceeded to cross, the Bruce held up a hand and reined his horse to a slower pace. Louis turned to the king with a questioning look.

The king nodded toward the retreating army. "They'll be my men soon," he shouted with a grin. "I'll be needing as many of them as I can spare."

John Bacach sailed away to the south on his galley as the Bruce pursued his Argyll army at a leisurely pace to Dunstaffnage Castle, where Alexander MacDougall promptly swore allegiance to King Robert the Bruce.

✠ ✠ ✠

Over the course of several weeks, King Robert and his commanders established control over the fierce Argyll warriors who had, until their defeat at Brander Pass, staunchly opposed his kingship.

Alexander MacDougall, the Lord of Argyll, was aged and ill, and too weak to resist the conquest of his castle. His son fled and his men were defeated; he had no choice but to embrace the king. The Bruce warmly accepted the old man's allegiance.

Finally, Louis was free to ride to Colette on the fastest palfrey he could acquire. Five of his closest brethren went with him, along with their squires. None shared Louis's enthusiasm for squeezing the four–day journey into three, but they understood his motivation well enough. None complained, even late into the third night when Louis refused to make camp with two more hours of travel yet ahead of them.

They rode into Ayr under a high, yellow three–quarter moon and dark, wispy clouds that slid furtively across its face. Louis ached to find Colette in that moment, but they found an inn and settled in for the night.

The innkeeper unbolted the door with a string of ornery expletives. At the sight of a dozen Templars in battle dress, he fell silent, and his eyes narrowed in suspicious curiosity. He pursed his lips and stood staring at them, unsteady on his feet.

"Rooms for the night," Louis said simply. "Stables for our mounts."

The innkeeper waved with annoyance toward the rear of the inn, and the squires led the horses in that direction. Louis and the knights entered the hall.

"There's porridge in the pot," the innkeeper said, waving toward the hearth with a scowl. The embers were cold, and so, Louis guessed, was the porridge.

The thought of cold porridge turned his stomach. It was just as well. He wasn't hungry anyway. Despite his impending reunion with Colette, he longed for a thick straw pallet. He refused the porridge with a shake of his head, and the innkeeper shrugged.

"I could have my lady warm it up," he said in a noncommittal tone. He continued before Louis could refuse. "I've two rooms open, so you'll have to snug in." He pointed toward the door, and said, "Your squires can sleep in the stable. Best I can offer." He turned and shuffled painfully off to his chamber. The knights exchanged glances and laughed softly.

"I'm glad I'm not hungry," said Ponç de Veneto. Bérenger Guifre nodded his agreement and Louis grimaced.

"I only want bed," Louis said. He peered after the innkeeper and said, "I suppose he'll take his pay in the morning. He'd best rise early, then."

Louis slept fitfully despite his fatigue. As he relaxed into the straw, his mind raced with images and thoughts of Colette. He tried to imagine their meeting. His heart pounded with excitement the way it always had so long ago. He imagined what they would say, her first words, and his. He would kiss her first, of course – and the thought of that caught his breath. He struggled to banish the thoughts in the hope of getting some sleep, but they were beyond his command. It was long toward dawn before his weariness won out, and but a brief moment more before the clamor of the roosters roused him.

Ponç and Bérenger accompanied him, along with three of the squires. They followed a narrow road south across the lazy River Ayr. A cool breeze blew in from the Firth, and it chilled them despite the rising of the summer sun into a cloudless sky.

They arrived at the village of Alloway, and the small church that James Douglas had said they would find just before they reached the Marti estate. It was a small, rectangular stone church with a modest bell tower at the peak of the roof above the front door.

Louis's heart pounded with excitement. He stopped reluctantly at the church and dismounted. His companions watched with puzzled expressions as he went into the church.

Bérenger dismounted and followed Louis. They walked into the church, and Louis genuflected at the rear of the main aisle. Bérenger stood by the doors as Louis walked to the front of the church and knelt at the altar.

Louis blessed himself and pressed his forehead into his folded hands. His thoughts went back to the fierce and terrible last days of Acre, where events and emotions laid waste to much of his faith, and to most of his dreams. He thought of all that had ensued, leading him to this place of renewed hope and promise. He prayed that he would find the strength to finally put away the guilt that had followed him since that time.

He thought of Mairead and prayed one last time for forgiveness for his sins. He prayed that she had been welcomed into the arms of God despite that sin, and he prayed that she would one day cease to haunt his troubled conscience. He prayed that he could one day soon know peace.

He blessed himself again and hurried back to his horse. He mounted and spurred it to a gallop.

They rode up the drive that led to a modest stone castle. Servants tended to a meticulously manicured landscape. A small chapel stood to the left of the castle, and stables off to the right.

A servant boy drawing water from the well beside the house let the bucket slip as he stood erect, gaping at the sight of the band of Templars. A woman by the door hesitated, then ran inside.

Several men–at–arms came from the direction of the stables, their hands on their swords. As the knights drew closer, one of them recognized Louis and let out a cry. He broke in to a run to meet them.

"Lord Louis!" he exclaimed.

"Mathieu!" Louis called out.

Louis dismounted, and Mathieu threw his arms around him. "I didn't expect to see you again so soon." He turned toward the stone castle. "We…thought it would be many months, or even years. Madame Colette will be ecstatic, once she recovers from the shock."

Mathieu waved frantically for one of the men–at–arms to fetch Colette, but as he did so the front door opened, and Louis caught his breath at the sight of her in the doorway.

She stepped outside and gazed across the short distance between them. She shielded her eyes from the sun and stared.

Louis approached Colette slowly, savoring her beauty. He intended to kneel and kiss her hand, but his desire overwhelmed him. He rushed to her arms, and they embraced.

He felt her shudder against him, and she drew a deep breath.

"I didn't expect you so soon," she said in a trembling voice.

"I didn't expect to be here so soon," he replied. "The Lord has smiled upon us."

Colette tensed for a moment, and then she leaned away from Louis and looked into his eyes. "Really?" she said with a sardonic smile. "You can say that, even after what you've gone through?"

"I'm here with you," he replied. "That's all that matters. That makes up for everything."

She buried her head in his chest again and held him tightly. "I love you," she said softly.

He felt hot tears forming, and he squeezed them back and sighed heavily.

After a long embrace, she pulled away from him and said,

"You've had a long journey. Come inside, all of you, for breakfast and a visit with my parents."

Louis and Bérenger exchanged nods, and Bérenger held up his hand.

"Thank you for your hospitality, my lady," he said, "but we will not impose. We have business in Ayr to which we must attend. Perhaps we should join you later."

"This evening, then" Colette said with a smile. "Bring an appetite."

Bérenger nodded genially, and the Templars turned to depart. Colette led Louis toward the house.

"Only *your* parents?" Louis said anxiously. "Are mine not here?"

She stopped and turned to him, her eyes solemn.

"They didn't come," she said. "Your father was too ill to travel. They insisted on staying behind. He said that if he was going to die, he would do it in his own home, on his own land."

Louis nodded. He had so looked forward to seeing them. He worried now that he might not get another opportunity.

"I'm sorry, Louis," she said. "It was best that they stayed."

He nodded again, and they went into the house.

Jacques Marti had grown older even in the short time they had been apart. He had never looked his age, and even now he didn't look seventy. But the years were catching up to him. Louis was certain the stress of their flight from Verzeille hadn't helped.

"You are here in Scotland for good," Jacques said somberly. "That much is clear. It will be a long time before you can go back to France, if ever. This is your new life. It will be quite an adjustment for you."

"Yes," Louis said. "I see that. In many ways."

"You will fight for King Robert?" Jacques asked.

"Do we have to discuss this now?" Colette asked with a sigh.

Jacques smiled sheepishly at his daughter. "No, my dear," he said. "We don't. But I would *like* to discuss it for a moment, and I'm sure Louis would, too."

Louis waved his hand and said, "No, it's all right. I'd rather not."

"You're on the right side of this, Louis," Jacques persisted. "It's all I'll say about it for now, but it's important that you know that."

"I'm glad you're finally here, and safe," Colette said. "It worried me to hear that you'd gone straight off to the north with King Robert. I feared that just when you were close enough to touch, I could lose you."

"You're not going to lose me," Louis said with resolve. Too many things had stood between him and his true destiny. He did not intend to allow that to happen again. "Not again," he said.

She didn't seem convinced.

"Have you heard no word from Willem?" Isabelle Marti asked.

Louis shook his head sadly. "Victor came to me at Mas Deu with news of Uncle Willem's death."

"In prison?" Colette asked.

Louis nodded.

Jacques crossed himself and glanced toward the heavens.

They stood in silence for a long moment before Isabelle threw her hands into the air and ushered Jacques toward the door.

"We've chores to tend," she said, "and those two are due for some time alone." She smiled and gave Jacques a playful shove.

When they were alone, they embraced as if their lives depended on it. Louis savored the scent of her hair, and the feel of her head cradled in his hand.

"What comes next?" she said softly. "How long are you here?"

"As long as I can be," he replied. "Until the king sends for me."

"To do what?"

"To help train his men for war with England."

"To train them?" she asked. "That's all?"

"I don't know," he said. "I don't expect to go into battle, but it's possible. Until the king needs me, I'll help to manage things here. I'll be here with you for as long and as much as I can."

She nodded and gazed into his eyes. "Will that make you happy?" she asked.

"There is nothing I want more," he said.

She lay her cheek on his chest. "How will you feel about

fighting for the king if he requires it?"

He thought for a moment, then said, "Torn. Never in my life did I imagine fighting against European Christians. I prepared my whole life to fight against the enemies of Christ, the adversaries of the Church. Now I find myself siding with an excommunicate king against a nation that championed the Crusades. I haven't fully reconciled myself to that fact."

She nodded and tightened her arms around him.

Louis wondered about the spiritual condition of a man who would murder another for political gain, particularly at the altar of a church. The idea of following such a man troubled him. It troubled him more, though, that his entire consecrated Order was betrayed and destroyed by men who would do no such thing. His beloved Uncle Willem was murdered by such men. Perhaps they would not have murdered a man like John Comyn in a house of God, but they held no qualms about burning frail, old men and women in village squares. In that light, Robert the Bruce's offense seemed the lesser evil.

Louis has always wanted to fight in the service of the God he loved. But he no longer knew which causes served God, and which served the devil.

He shivered.

"It's colder here," he said.

She glanced at him tentatively. "I'm used to it," she said. He sensed that she feared the cold would drive him away.

"I could get used to it, too," he said. "This land is beautiful. It's just colder, and more damp. I've never been more than a few days' ride from the Mediterranean Sea, and I've never been this far north. I'm accustomed to sand and sun and soft, dry breezes. Compared to that, this land is harsh."

"So much has changed for you," she said.

"One thing won't change," he said with a sly grin. He slid his hands from the small of her back to her waist, and he felt her shudder at his touch. "Wherever you are, I know I will find warmth."

She moaned softly and pressed her body against his. He

kissed her as if he had never kissed her before. She broke free and tugged at his hand, leading him to the stairs to the upper chamber. The passion that arose and consumed them surpassed any he had ever known.

Chapter 51

"WE NEED ONE DECISIVE BATTLE," King Robert's brother, Edward Bruce, fumed. He glared into the fire as pine logs crackled and sent glowing embers fluttering high up into the trees. "Ambushes and night raids are fine if we don't mind fighting for another hundred years. God knows we've done some damage to the English that way." He nodded and winked at James Douglas. "You've all done a right fine job of that, you have. I'm not saying you haven't."

Douglas shrugged and nodded, glancing at the faces of the Scottish and Templar commanders, bright with the glow of firelight.

"But this'll go on forever," Edward continued. "We need to force the English hand. Right now our men are afire for English blood. Wallace is still fresh and heavy on their minds. They'll fight like fiends in his memory, but I'm not sure for how long before they're weary of it."

"It's hard to say," Douglas agreed. "Our new friends have buoyed the spirits, as well. I'd say there's reason for cheer."

"Still," Edward said, "we need one decisive battle and an end to it once and for all."

"I believe we're getting to the point where that is possible," Douglas said. "The sting of Wallace's execution has dulled, and his most loyal followers seem ready once again to take up the fight...many of them with a burning vengeance."

"My brother has a lot to do with that," Edward Bruce said. "They needed to see decisiveness, and Robert showed them that, particular with regard to John Comyn."

"Comyn's murder appealed to them?" Louis asked.

"They'd seen enough of the nobles' squabbling over the last King Edward's favor," Douglas said. "Wallace's death disheartened them. The politics that followed repulsed them." He sketched a crude cross in the dirt with a stick, then peered at Louis and said, "Robert's actions may have horrified the pope and enraged the English king, but among Wallace's men, it made the Bruce a saint. They will follow him to the fires of hell to have their revenge."

Louis found himself admiring the passion of these Scots, and wanting them to rally. He had not expected to care one way or the other, but he grew more sympathetic to their cause the more he got to know them.

"If I may," he said to Edward Bruce. Edward nodded curtly for him to speak. "The Scots have been fighting the English for a very long time, for the most part with disappointing results." Edward stared at him coolly, and he hesitated.

"Speak freely," Edward said.

"Your men are brave, spirited fighters," Louis continued. "But on the battlefield, they have always faced stronger armies with superior cavalry, and superior weaponry. As a result of that, your men are most practiced at defensive tactics."

"Which is why we avoid the battlefield," Edward said dryly. "My brother, more than I, believes we would risk too much on the open field precisely because we cannot match English cavalry, and all we have left is defense."

"Perhaps that could be turned to your advantage," Louis said. All eyes turned to him. "The English would expect you to bring an inferior army to the field, and to remain in a defensive posture."

"Of course," James Douglas said.

"Anything else would surprise them," Louis said.

"Such as?" Edward said.

"An offense," Louis replied. "One that resembles a defense until it's too late to react to it."

"What do you have in mind," asked Walter Stewart, who had been elevated to commander at barely eighteen years of age. He was James Douglas's cousin, and a close confidant of Robert the Bruce. Stewart's reddish locks and closely cropped beard framed a narrow, boyish face and brown eyes that gleamed with a relish for mischief. His build promised to match James Douglas's in time.

Louis said, "Choose a battlefield that limits the English cavalry's ability to flank your lines, and place your armies so that they prevent that altogether." Edward and some of the others furrowed their brows. "The point is to make sure they can only charge head–on, and on a narrow field."

"And our offense?" James Douglas asked.

"Advance the schiltrons," Louis said.

Walter's face clouded with confusion, as did others' around the fire. The schiltron was purely defensive, based on the Roman *testudo*, or tortoise formation. A thousand swordsmen, heavily armed with maces and axes, clustered behind a wall of a thousand pike men who brandished heavy, twelve-foot spears. It was a devastating defense against the English army's heavy cavalry, but that was its only purpose.

"*Mobile* schiltrons?" James Douglas said with a dubious look.

Louis nodded. "The cavalry needs distance for the charge to gain momentum. The shorter the distance, the less effective the charge." Stewart's eyes brightened. "We wait for the first charge, as usual," Louis continued. "The English will think that the battle will go as all battles have gone until now: that they will pound your defenses, charge upon charge, until you break and run."

"We move the schiltrons forward!" Stewart exclaimed.

"Yes," Louis said. "After the first charge, instead of plundering the fallen English, we advance the schiltrons toward the English line before the second charge can begin. The second charge will be shorter, and less effective. We move closer after each charge, until the cavalry can charge no more. The English will have to stand and fight, and that's where the field is leveled."

Thomas Randolph, the king's nephew, spoke up. "King Robert will never agree to it. It would have to go exactly as planned, and if it didn't, we'd be finished. And the English will never allow themselves to be placed in such a position. How could we force them to line up with their backs to a wall? That will never happen."

"Not a wall," Edward said abruptly. Everyone turned to him. "A burn," he said mischievously, nodding. "Perhaps one like the Bannockburn."

The men fell silent. Randolph nodded his head thoughtfully. He had proven himself a masterful tactician, and the king would seek his advice regarding the field and the battle plan.

"It's perfect," Edward continued. "The question, though, is how to draw the English to Stirling Castle. I think that castle has been in English hands long enough. An attack on it could be just the thing to draw them north, and we would meet them at Bannockburn."

Randolph nodded excitedly then. "I see it now," he said. His face clouded, and he repeated, "The king will never agree to it."

"I'll see about that," Edward said.

James Douglas interjected, "We'll need to maneuver them precisely into position."

"We'll harass them with well–placed ambushes," Randolph replied. "In their rush to the castle, they won't waste time on small–scale assaults. They'll take them as evidence of our weakness, and change course to avoid the petty annoyance."

"We can manage all that when the time comes," James Douglas interjected. "The first thing will be to draw the English north. Until we do that, this is all conjecture.

"I'll handle that, too," Edward Bruce said with a wink and a grin.

Randolph clasped Louis's shoulder and said, "Tell me more

about these mobile schiltrons."

✠ ✠ ✠

King Robert the Bruce paced and fumed with fury. He kicked the ground and punched the air and muttered murderous oaths. "Fool!" he cried, turning to glare at his brother. "By God's eyes, what in hell were you thinking?"

Edward Bruce had convinced King Robert to allow him to besiege Stirling Castle. The siege had gone well, and by all accounts its governor was likely about to concede. Inexplicably, Edward offered him a curious deal, and inspired his brother's rage. He had just returned from Stirling to Ayr with the news, and to face that rage.

"How could you do such a thing?" the king bellowed. "One year! You gave the most powerful king with the mightiest army, the king of all but our small corner of these islands, an entire year to relieve a castle he should never have claimed? A *year*? Are you mad?"

"We'll need that year," Edward said curtly.

"What?" the king growled, his eyes ablaze.

Louis feared that Robert would kill his brother where he stood. He glanced nervously at James Douglas, who signaled him not to worry.

"We'll need that year to prepare," Edward said.

He sounded contrite, but Edward knew exactly what he had done. The only man in King Robert's court who could force his hand and survive it had done just that. He had made an agreement with the governor of Stirling Castle that unless King Edward II sent an army to relieve the castle, the castle would pass into Scottish hands.

There was only one possible result of that agreement, and it could not now be undone. The English would send an army, and Robert would face it head on.

The king glared hard at his brother. Commanders and Templars stood silent, waiting for the storm to pass. Finally, abruptly, it did.

The Bruce kicked a stone the size of a fist so that it sailed through the air for twenty yards before it skidded into the brush at the edge of the River Ayr.

"All right," he said with a huff. "We'll *need* a year to prepare."

It was then that Thomas Randolph revealed his thoughts about those preparations. It seemed to Louis a bit too obvious that he had given it so much thought in that brief moment. Surely the king had caught that, but he chose to let it go. In minutes, he had engrossed himself in the conflict he now faced, listening intently to the thoughts of his men, and offering quite a few of his own.

✠ ✠ ✠

Dawn rose on a muggy, misty battlefield alive with the tentative clinking and clanging of preparations for war. The Scots had camped among the thick–standing trees just south of Stirling Castle, between a massive hill to the west and the rutted, potholed field that sloped to the east toward a marshy carse at the junction of the Forth and the Bannockburn. The smoke of their fires hung heavy in the leafy canopy.

King Robert commanded a ready reserve of nearly six hundred infantry and men–at–arms, and eight hundred bowmen just inside the edges of the wood. In front of him, his brother Edward commanded the schiltron of the right flank, positioned atop the slope between the gurgling burn and Randolph's center schiltron. The three main schiltrons, center, left, and right, each numbered twelve hundred pike men and two hundred infantry.

Walter Stewart commanded the left flank, to the north and nearest to the castle.

James Douglas joined Robert Keith, who led five hundred knights and men–at–arms in a light cavalry force. They took position beside the king's reserves, under cover of the trees of the New Park.

From their position atop a hill that sloped from the New Park to the Bannockburn carse, the Scottish commanders surveyed the rolling valley that stretched from the castle to a single narrow ford across the burn.

The Scottish formations settled in to watch as the English approached from the southeast, advancing toward the burn on the ancient Falkirk road. The Romans had built that road nearly a dozen centuries before in their maddening bid to conquer the barbarian Picts. New conquerors followed it now, in a similar protracted bid to subjugate a tenacious people.

Louis and Bérenger Guifre accompanied the king, with the understanding that once the battle began they would retire to the rear of the hill that rose behind them, along with the rest of the Templars and the camp cooks, armigers, farriers, and other support.

It made sense, Louis thought, for the Templars to hang back. It would be one more element of surprise, which the king could draw at his choosing, most likely toward the end of the battle.

The commanders inspected their troops, and then rode back to the king while an abbot set about the blessing of the troops. The army knelt in prayer while the commanders reconvened.

They reviewed the main points of the battle plan while the English army picked its way along the road to the place where it crossed the burn. Randolph's men had dug deep pits along the edges of the road, and covered them over with brush. The pits caused occasional calamity for horsemen who strayed too far from the center of the ancient, narrow road. As a result, the cavalry pushed toward the center of the road, slowing and frustrating its advance. Angry cursing announced the misfortune of each of the fallen knights, to the mirth of the waiting Scots. The English commanders finally gave up and directed the cavalry onto the carse, precisely as the Scots had intended.

The pleased murmuring that arose among the Scots was cut short by frantic shouts from the south. A smaller English force had circled the swamps and attempted to cross the burn from the south, into the woods. Robert Keith's cavalry responded, along with archers and spearmen from among the reserves. They quickly repelled the expeditionary English assault.

"We thought they might do that," James Douglas said with a grin.

The king nodded. "They were counting on us to withdraw at the very sight of their massive host," he said. "They thought they'd catch us fleeing."

Another chorus of shouts rang out, this time from the direction of the castle. An English detachment of eight hundred men had used the distraction at the woods to cover their advance behind some hills and across the carse toward the castle. A successful attempt to relieve the castle and reinforce its exhausted ranks would give the English superior command of the field. It also would have satisfied the terms of Edward Bruce's bargain with Philip Mowbray, the governor of Stirling Castle, to cede the castle to the English if the English king relieved it within one year's time.

The king cursed, and Randolph ran off to counter the unexpected breach. He gathered three hundred of his pike men, and they flew down the slope as fast as their legs could take them, burdened with their blades and their heavy pikes.

"Shall I take some of the cavalry and join him?" Douglas asked the king.

Robert shook his head angrily. "No," he fumed. "He dropped the rose from his own cap; now he can retrieve it himself."

"We can't afford to lose him or his men," Douglas said.

The king set his jaw and said nothing.

After a moment, Douglas persisted. "We can't let them reach the castle," he said. The king did not reply. "They'll gain the upper hand," Douglas added.

The king sighed heavily, and then curtly said, "All right. Go see to it, then."

Louis followed James Douglas across the field to the hills overlooking the scene. Randolph's men had formed a schiltron between the English cavalry detachment and the castle. The cavalry had ground to a halt and prepared to charge.

Randolph was badly outnumbered. The English men-at-arms numbered nearly eight hundred, and now they spurred to a gallop toward the waiting schiltron.

Louis winced as the cavalry crashed against the sturdy formation, but the schiltron barely wavered as horsemen were thrown through the air and into a heaving swarm of Scottish blades. More than a fifth of the horsemen fell, and the remainder retreated to regroup.

The second charge was the same as the first. The English again took heavy losses, and then retreated to prepare the third charge. At that moment, Randolph ordered his men forward to close the distance between the sides. The English commander hesitated, startled by the unexpected tactic.

They charged again, but less effectively over the shorter distance. James Douglas smiled with satisfaction and nodded to Louis.

This time, though, the English did not withdraw. They continued to press hard against the schiltron, probing for vulnerabilities in the line. For a moment, it looked as though the heavy horse would break through and scatter the Scots. But suddenly, miraculously, the well-trained pike men began to advance against them.

Louis watched in awe as Randolph urged his men forward. The plan had been for the schiltrons to advance between clashes. Randolph had gone one better, and advanced against a full cavalry press. Knights fell to the pikes, to be cut to pieces by the merciless blades of Randolph's swords and axes.

Douglas signaled his troops to charge, and they galloped down the slope toward the battle. They had gone less than a dozen yards when, seeing them, the commander of the faltering English cavalry panicked and sounded retreat.

Nearly five hundred men, more than half the attacking force, lay in pieces on the blood-soaked ground. Randolph's men broke into a run and pursued the fleeing survivors, screaming for more English blood.

The pursuit was futile, and Randolph called it off and turned back toward the Scottish line. His face beamed grim satisfaction as he approached Douglas's men.

Douglas gaped in admiration as he turned to accompany the victors back to the line.

"You've reclaimed your rose!" Robert the Bruce called as the trio returned from the skirmish. Randolph's men rejoined the left flank to the laudatory roar of their countrymen.

"It was a distraction," Randolph said modestly. "It won't happen again."

"My lord!" a young, strident voice called from far off. Louis turned as a group of men–at–arms approached with the king's armigers. "Time to make ready," said one of the men–at–arms. He nodded for the squires to prepare the king's armor.

"Take your places," James Douglas said, and the commanders spurred their horses to disperse.

Louis watched for a moment as the English struggled with the rough terrain of the carse, cautiously negotiating brush–covered pits with hidden stakes, and sharp iron spikes set in position to maim horses that rode into them. He could sense the mounting exasperation of the English cavalry.

King Robert was about to exchange his palfrey for the powerful warhorse that trailed behind Robert Keith's steed when a shout arose from the carse. One of the English nobles had spotted the Bruce, and he appeared to be preparing to charge him.

Louis watched in disbelief as the noble couched his lance and broke from formation, moving toward them with his eyes fixed on the king. The Scottish commanders stopped in their tracks.

"Bohun," King Robert said with a growl. He spurred his palfrey and moved a dozen yards from where his commanders stood.

"My lord," James Douglas called after him. "Your armor."

The king sat stolidly astride the palfrey. He had removed his battle-axe from its sheath, and he held it loosely at his side.

"What's he doing?" Robert Keith said with a gasp. Louis's mouth dropped open.

"My lord?" James Douglas called.

The Englishman, Henry de Bohun, dropped his visor and spurred his warhorse into a charge against the Scottish king. English cavalry called after him, but de Bohun ignored them and gained speed.

King Robert remained impassive. The palfrey shuffled its hooves and flicked its tail, and the king cocked his head as if perplexed by de Bohun's actions.

"My lord!" James Douglas bellowed.

Louis's throat went dry. If the king were killed now, before the battle even began, all would be lost. The day would be a disaster, and the English would decimate the Scots.

De Bohun let out a cry of victory as he bore down on the king at full speed. The Scots let out a collective, anguished cry of their own. Still, King Robert sat quietly, unperturbed.

The Englishman's lance drove into the king, but before it made contact, he swiveled his palfrey and spun his torso deftly out of the way. The lance barely grazed his jacketed chest as the king rose up in his stirrups, raising the battle-axe high above his head. As de Bohun swept past him, he brought the axe down with all of his tremendous strength.

The axe cut through de Bohun's helmet with an awful, grinding thud, splitting the noble's head in two. Louis shuddered at the sound.

The axe slipped from the king's hand as the dead Englishman lurched sideways in the saddle. After a few yards, momentum carried the body awkwardly from the warhorse and into a twisted heap on the ground.

A resounding roar went up from the Scottish army, and the English stood in silent dismay. The king calmly dismounted to retrieve his axe.

Douglas, Keith, Stewart, and Randolph rushed to the king. They assailed him with elation at his victory, and horror at his recklessness. The king glared angrily at the axe, its ornate, polished handle badly broken by the force of the blow.

"By God's eyes, what were you thinking?" James Douglas yelled.

The king glanced at him, but did not admonish his impertinence.

The Bruce turned and gestured proudly toward the scene of his army's surging enthusiasm. "It's always a good idea," he said with a smirk, "to motivate the troops before a big battle." He walked to his armigers, handed them the broken battle-axe, and extended his arms to receive his chain mail coat.

The commanders exchanged glances and shook their heads in dismay.

The English had halted, stunned by de Bohun's recklessness, but they quickly resumed their movement into position on the marshy carse. It would take some time before enough had crossed and moved into positions from which they could engage the Scots.

Behind the English king and his commanders, a sea of burnished steel seethed and shimmered in the festering summer haze. Colored pennants fluttered in the meager breeze while the discordant murmur of ill–tempered soldiers wafted across the potholed field. The Scottish commanders watched in unconcealed awe.

"There won't be a battle today," James Douglas said. "It'll take them all night to place their troops."

"It'll take them until morning just to determine who's in charge," the king said with a laugh.

"There are so many," Walter Stewart said.

The king nodded reassuringly and said, "Numbers mean little to an army rife with discord."

"We know that better than any," Randolph said with a smirk.

"Not today," the king said. "Today we're as united as Wallace's men were at Stirling Bridge." He pointed toward the site of that momentous battle, to the north beyond the castle. "Today, we fight with the same spirit, the same unity, and by God's eyes, with the same result."

Louis's heart swelled with enthusiasm.

"And tomorrow," the king added, "we end this once and for all." He turned toward James Douglas. "It is our fate," he said through clenched teeth.

Chapter 52

THE NEXT MORNING DAWNED muggy and warm. Louis anticipated the familiar feel of chain mail, heavy cloak, and helmet in sweltering heat. He was well accustomed to discomfort in battle, but rarely had he worn full battle dress in such oppressive humidity.

He grinned at the thought of complaining about weather on the verge of mortal combat. He observed that the Scots barely seemed to notice it, and he wondered if he would ever grow accustomed to it.

"I remind you once again," came the richly baritone voice of King Robert the Bruce, "that there will be no breaking formation!"

The king's commanders gathered around the king. Louis put aside his hauberk and hurried to join them.

"The English have but one objective," the king continued. He pointed toward the north and said, "They come to relieve and reinforce Stirling Castle." He paused to look at each of the commanders. "We also have but one objective here today," he continued, "and that is to stop them. There is nothing before this day, and nothing beyond it. There is only this day, with a foreign tyrant in our land, and us here to crush that tyrant. At this moment, nothing else exists."

The Scots within earshot nodded. Louis admired the king's eloquence.

"They believe they will win this day, and take our castle," the king declared. "We will show them the futility of that hope, and that the road to their victory is closed. We will stop them where they stand, and we will send them home broken and empty handed!"

The king described once more the positions and formations the troops were to take, and their strategy for countering any English advance. He stressed the superiority of their position above the enemy, and the carse upon which they would meet them in battle. He emphasized the purpose of the new schiltron tactics, and ordered the pike men not to break ranks, even to plunder the fallen Englishmen, until they had thoroughly routed the cavalry.

"They will not break our lines!" the king thundered. "We will not falter, and we will not retreat!"

The king finished, and the abbot proceeded with the daily blessing of the troops.

Louis knelt and crossed himself along with the rest of the army. He wondered if the English were doing the same. If they were, he wondered briefly which side God would favor. More likely, he thought, God would simply abandon both to their fate. The futility of the ritual suddenly struck him, and he did not pray.

"Sir Louis," James Douglas called out. Louis looked up to see Douglas, Robert Keith, and the king hurrying toward him. The king wore a look of concern. Louis stood to meet them.

"Yes?" Louis said.

"Your armor," Douglas said, pointing to Louis's equipment. "It won't do."

"Why?" he asked.

"The king doesn't want you to wear it," Douglas said.

Louis raised his hands in dismay.

"Take mine," said Robert Keith. "I have enough for the both of us. My men will tend to you."

"I don't understand," Louis said. "Why would I not wear my own armor?"

"None of the Templars will wear their own dress," Douglas said. "We're replacing it from among our own."

"Why?" Louis repeated, mystified. Templar armor was the best available, and a significant advantage in battle. The quality of one's armor could be the difference between life and death.

"It must never be thought," the king said solemnly, "that the Templars won this day, or that without them we would have failed." Louis stared blankly at the king. "You see," the king continued, nodding toward his troops, "they are thinking only of the task that lies before them. They are not thinking of tomorrow, or what comes after." Louis nodded. The king placed a hand to his own chest and said, "But I must consider such things, always. For when tomorrow comes, they will all think back on what has happened here today. Poets and bards will tell of it for generations to come. This nation, and my rule, will be founded upon this day. It must always be known that it was won with Scottish blood, by Scottish men and Scottish might."

Louis understood, and he nodded fervently.

"I'm not ungrateful," the king added curtly. "I welcome the assistance you and your men have offered, the training you have provided, and your support for our noble cause."

"Of course," Louis said with a bow. "I'm pleased to honor your wish, my lord." In truth, he *was* pleased not to wear the crimson cross into this battle. He was, in fact, troubled by the very thought of doing so. He never would have believed that possible.

Above the intonation of the abbot's lengthy prayer, an eerie and familiar whispering filled the air, and Louis froze. A thick, dark cloud of arrows approached in an arc from the English line. King Edward's archers had launched into an army that yet knelt in prayer.

Louis cursed. *Perhaps I am on the right side of this thing,* he thought as he dove for the cover of his shield. What kind of warrior would loose a barrage upon praying men?

"Archers!" Edward Bruce screamed.

The Scottish archers scrambled to answer the English volley just as it slammed into their ranks. Nearly a hundred fell beneath the darts before they could nock their arrows. The remainder launched a volley in return.

The Scots snapped into formation with practiced precision as the English cavalry mobilized, and they set their pikes solidly into the ground. The front line pikes extended outward at the height of the sternum of a charging steed. The rear line leveled their own pikes over the front line, chest–high to the attacking knights. Encircled by the pike men, infantry brandished axes and swords and waited patiently for fallen prey.

A second wave of English arrows took an equally heavy toll. The battered Scottish archers disbanded and retreated to the rear of the infantry.

The heavy English cavalry gained speed. The thundering hooves of nearly a thousand heavy warhorses shook the ground as they bore down on the right flank of the Scottish line.

"Stand firm!" Robert the Bruce yelled as the pike men crouched into position.

The cavalry advanced despite scores of their number driving into pits or impaling themselves on steel traps. Edward Bruce's right flank braced itself for impact.

"Do not break rank!" Edward screamed above the galloping hooves.

"See to it that the Templars understand the king's orders," James Douglas yelled over his shoulder to Louis. Louis, transfixed by the unfolding clash, nodded his acknowledgement. "Sooner, rather than later!" Douglas shouted.

Louis waved Bérenger Guifre to his side.

"Get the Brothers to the rear of the hill," he said, pointing to the mound behind them, to the west. "Get them ready. But no surcoats, no crosses…and no beauséant," he added.

Guifre looked troubled. "No beauséant?" he said.

Louis shook his head and said, "Scottish arms. No beauséant. No Templar surcoats."

Guifre shrugged and nodded, and turned to go.

"Bérenger," Louis called after him, and Guifre turned back. "We hold back. We don't charge into battle until we're called, or unless things go very badly." Guifre nodded again. "This is not our fight," Louis said, "unless fate makes it so."

Guifre nodded more enthusiastically. "Yes, sir!" he called as he turned and rode to the rear.

Louis dressed in Robert Keith's spare armor and chose a heavy claymore from among a dozen swords stacked against a thick oak. One of Keith's men handed him a finely balanced, heavy-bladed axe and an onyx–handled dirk. Another placed a leather helm with inset steel plates on his head and laced it into position.

The light armor made Louis feel as though he were preparing for a sparring session with a Brother Templar, except that the blades he carried were real, and deadly.

The cavalry crashed with a roar into the right flank schiltron. Cries of agony rang out from both horses and men as they fell beneath the fury of axes, pikes, and blades. Louis turned from his preparations to watch the clash unfold. He was pleased that the schiltron held fast.

Englishmen fell by the hundreds beneath the piercing Scottish pikes. Those that survived turned back toward their line, leaving the fallen to their brutal fate. The schiltron broke formation, and the Scots fell upon the English knights with their axes, swords, and dirks. Screams rang out across the fields as the English fell to the slaughter.

The effectiveness of the Scottish schiltron surprised Louis. In a single charge, the English lost nearly four hundred knights.

Edward Bruce's pike men made quick work of the fallen, then quickly regrouped and marched forty yards toward the English line. They reset their pikes into the sod. The left and center divisions followed suit.

A second cavalry division formed to charge. They thundered across the field, again toward Bruce's right flank.

Again, the English fell. The second charge went as the first, and as it unfolded, a third cavalry division formed by the burn.

Louis mounted his warhorse and rode to the king's position behind the line. King Robert frowned inquisitively at his approach, glancing quickly to the hill that rose behind them.

"By your leave, my lord," Louis said, "I'd like to ride with Keith's cavalry."

"I said no Templars," the king snapped. "Where are your men?"

"They're behind the hill with the camp support, as you commanded," Louis replied.

"Go with them," the king said.

"My lord," Louis insisted, "but today I am no Templar." The king narrowed his eyes and peered at him. "Today, I'm just a man on a horse watching a valiant fight in which I would like to do my part."

"You're impetuous," the king declared.

Louis nodded toward Edward Bruce's schiltron, which was holding steady against the impact of a third cavalry charge. "They are my friends," he said with conviction, "and you are my king."

The king's eyes widened briefly, and his lips curled into a grin. He nodded and waved a hand. "With Keith, then," he said. As Louis rode off, the king called after him. "Louis," he yelled, "fight like a *Scottish* Templar!"

Louis bowed to the king and rode to meet Robert Keith. He motioned one of his squires to the rear to tell Guifre and the others of his position.

The third charge took a toll, but the schiltrons still held fast. A fourth charge began to advance. Edward's schiltron had so far gained nearly a hundred yards, while Randolph's center and Walter Stewart's left flank moved toward the right in support. Most of the Scottish forces were concentrated against the cavalry charges.

English bowmen reappeared to take advantage of that concentration. In the space between the English king and his cavalry stampede, they took their positions and loosed a succession of volleys.

Louis arrived at the light cavalry just as Robert Keith screamed to his men, jabbing a finger furiously in the direction of the archers.

Keith leaped into a gallop without waiting for acknowledgement, and his cavalry followed. Louis raced to catch up. The five hundred knights and men–at–arms skirted to the right of Edward Bruce's schiltron and raced down the steep slope toward the burn. At the bottom of the slope, a loop of the burn jutted into the carse, leaving less than a dozen yards between its banks and the English charge.

Keith did not slow his pace. Counting on good timing, he reached the edge of the loop just as the English cavalry passed, and an opening widened behind it. Keith led his men through that narrow space, behind the English charge, and into the exposed ranks of Welsh and English archers.

The Scots' war cry startled the archers. They turned and stumbled over one another in a futile bid to escape.

Louis swung his sword with a fury to which he had grown unaccustomed. His muscles screamed with the ache of sudden exertion. He knew that pain would subside as the battle wore on, but he was suddenly thankful for the lightness of his borrowed armor.

The first grinding thud of steel against bone refreshed his memory of battle. His sword cut deeply into the neck and sternum of an archer who had nocked a new arrow despite the crush of the cavalry. The blow resounded with the same dull thump and ringing blade that had accompanied his first battlefield kill. As then, and as every time since then, he shuddered at the feel of it.

He barely broke his momentum, drawing the sword from the body as it fell and swinging it around to the other side, taking off a second archer's head.

Louis jerked around to face a furious cry that came from behind him. A Welsh archer had drawn his dirk and was running at him in frenzy. Louis spun his horse and swung his sword in a wide, smooth arc.

The blade cut cleanly through the archer's left arm and halfway through his torso. The archer's eyes filled with fury and disbelief as the momentum of the blow threw him to the ground, where he lurched and rolled into a brush–covered pit.

The bowmen were no match for Robert Keith's light cavalry. The Scots cut them down like dry grass. Louis turned as they emerged at the northern end of the field to see nearly six hundred dead or dying men. The cavalry circled toward the northwest and ascended the slope to join Walter Stewart's left flank division.

The left flank and the center van had nearly merged with Edward Bruce's men, as the English cavalry had focused each of their assaults on that side, avoiding the widest expanse of the trapped and pitted carse. The schiltrons still held fast, and so far, Scottish casualties had been few.

Seeing the enemy archers decimated, King Robert's bowmen emerged from the New Park woods and fired with fury into the cavalry that pressed from the field. The cavalry pulled back, and the schiltrons advanced to push them farther still.

The Scots had moved their line nearly two hundred yards, and it had grown increasingly difficult for the English to mount an effective attack. The English commanders grew more exasperated with every setback, and many of the cavalry had turned to leave the field.

James Douglas yelled to Louis and pointed toward the Bannockburn ford, where several knights and their men were tediously picking their way through the muck of the marshy ground.

Douglas signaled the Bruce for permission to pursue the fleeing knights, but the king refused, pointing firmly toward the main English force, which was faltering now, and on the verge of retreat.

On the king's order, the bowmen shot out the remainder of their arrows. They then threw down their bows, took up swords and daggers, and ran into the midst of the melee. The king led his reserve of knights and men–at–arms into a charge down the New Park slope. Louis and Douglas rode to join the attack.

Scottish bowmen ducked out of reach of the mounted English knights' swords. Some crawled under horses and slit their bellies so that they threw their knights to the ground at the infantry's feet. Others swung claymores, which were much longer than the

English swords, into the mounted knights' feet and legs.

Curses and screams filled the air. The tide had turned decisively. The English infantry, trapped behind the retreating cavalry, could not make their way past the burn or through the marshes to the field. The press of their own knights, pursued by the swarming Scots, pushed them farther back until many fell into the burn and drowned under the weight of their weaponry. Bodies bobbed gently away from the banks, carried by the current toward the River Forth.

Louis rode into the teeming chaos. He rode hard toward an English knight, swinging his sword in a long low arc. As he reached him, the ground beneath the Englishman's horse shifted suddenly. The horse stumbled awkwardly, and hung for a moment poised at the edge of a pit, before it fell backward and disappeared into it. Horse and rider both screamed in agony as their momentum impaled them on the stakes concealed in the pit.

Louis turned as an enemy horseman bore down on him, swinging a heavy flanged mace. He moved reflexively, raising his sword to block the fatal blow and twisting barely out of harm's way. The Englishman brought the mace down with all his might and momentum.

Seizing a momentary vulnerability, Louis deftly turned the point of his blade into the knight's exposed ribs. The tip of his claymore disappeared into the crease of the knight's underarm, and momentum forced it through his heaving chest. The knight gurgled in shocked disbelief as blood erupted from his mouth and nose.

The mace, loosed from the knight's fierce grip, struck Louis's warhorse on the right flank. The horse reared in angry protest. Louis held tight, but they reeled perilously close to the pit into which his previous foe had fallen.

He reined hard and pulled the beast down. Blood trickled from a gaping wound on its side as it bucked and whinnied against the pain. He looked for an opening to return to the rear for a new mount.

Instead, Louis found himself trapped by the crush of the

retreating English cavalry. Horses of fallen knights ran panicked through the chaos, careening into combatants from both sides and adding to the mayhem.

A blood–soaked Scottish archer appeared on foot among the rampaging cavalry, with an axe in one hand and a dagger in the other. He glared at Louis through matted hair, his painted face twisted into a mask of fury. He curled his lips and shrieked a battle cry as he dove beneath the horse of an English knight.

The archer drove his dagger into the horse's belly. The horse reared up and threw the knight, spinning to kick at its attacker. The archer pounced on the fallen knight. As the horse ran screaming, the archer swung his axe into the knight's face. He reared up and drove the dagger into his chest, and followed with several more axe blows for good measure.

Louis turned to survey the course of the battle. The battle cries and bellowed commands were subsiding, giving way to labored groans and scattered final blows.

Most of the English cavalry had retreated, presumably to regroup. Scottish infantry harried them from behind, but only far enough to ensure they had ceded the field. The cavalry that remained mounted another charge.

Louis knew it would be ineffectual. The Scottish had shortened the field considerably, and frustration had eroded the cavalry's discipline. The English had neither the length of field nor the strength of will to execute a cohesive, thundering charge.

The final charge reached the Scottish lines in a ragged, lackluster stampede. There was no steady drumbeat of well–driven hooves, and no staggering crash against a strained and struggling schiltron. The impact was muted and feeble.

A great shout came from the hill as King Robert called his reserve into action. He must have sensed, as Louis had, that the tide of the battle had changed. The momentum had shifted decisively in favor of the Scots. The reserve forces streamed down the hill and into the dwindling melee.

At the sight of the reserves, the remaining English faltered and began to withdraw. A triumphant cry arose from the Scots, and the king bellowed a final order.

"On them!" he cried. "On them! They give way!"

Orders were bellowed from the other side, too, but they fell upon dispassionate ears. The English responded more to King Robert's cry, and they went into a general retreat.

Louis beamed at the turning tide. Battles such as this, where defenders of a noble cause realize victory over unjust aggressors, were the reason he had joined the Templars in the first place. It was ironic that he had not experienced such a thing until he found himself exiled to Scotland and fighting against English Christians.

A scream rang out behind him. He flinched at the sound and turned to face it. An English knight bore down on him at a gallop, his body rigid and listing precariously, a battle-axe wedged deep in his side below the bloody stump of his elbow.

Louis kicked his spurs and pulled the reins to avoid a collision, but too late. The heavy horse drove into him, throwing him and his horse flailing across the field. The gaping mouth of a staked pit, surrounded by the brush that had covered it, yawned before him. He and the horse slid headlong toward the sharpened stakes, and he screamed in horror just before his world went dark.

Chapter 53

THE VOICES OF ANGELS murmured to him in low, comforting tones. They spoke of his courage, his strength, and his skill. They whispered consolation and they lauded his devotion to God.

So, this is the Judgment, he thought to himself. But it was as though his thought was spoken, and the sound of it silenced their praise. He waited for them to resume.

One commanding voice came forth.

"Alas, it was all for naught," it declared. It was not the sound of judgment, but of simple observation. He wanted to dispute it, but he could not.

"Not for naught," said another, gentler, soothing voice. "The dream was noble."

"What is nobility, but well–appointed pride?" the first voice asked.

"Not pride," the soothing voice said, even as Louis also mouthed the words, trying to shake his head. "Not pride."

"Folly, then," other voices chimed in unison.

"Innocence," one said.

"Bravery," said others.

"No," Louis mouthed silently. His voice would not come. *"It was love...the love of God."*

"That love shall save you," the gentlest voice said.

Louis was drawn to that voice. It was familiar, and comforting. Was it the voice of his angel?

"Who are you?" Louis asked, peering into formlessness.

"It is I, my love," the angel said. "I am here."

A face took shape, with delicate lines and brilliant green eyes framed in chestnut hair that poked out from the edges of a nun's black coif.

"Mairead?" he tried to mumble, but his lips wouldn't move.

"We're here," the angel said in a warm, resonating voice.

A gentle hand caressed his cheek. The feel of it made him tingle, and a quickening arose inside him.

He tried to focus on Mairead, but he could not.

The voice came again, more clearly. It was a woman's voice.

"You were injured," the woman said softly, stroking his cheek. "You've been sleeping for a very long time."

His head suddenly filled with a pounding that drowned out all sound. Each beat, louder than the last, sent the rushing of blood to his ears, like the waves of a tempest. He grew aware of throbbing pain and a sickness that grew in his belly. He wanted to vomit.

"Rest," the woman whispered softly into his ear.

Darkness descended in a dizzying spiral, and peacefulness returned.

He awoke with a start. His right eye flew open, but his left remained closed, as if it had been sewn shut. He felt with his fingers the soft cloth that covered it, and his face throbbed at the pressure of his touch.

He looked around the best he could with one eye. He felt weighed down, but he could see nothing pressing him.

He called out weakly. A clattering sound and the rush of hurried footsteps answered his call. In a moment, his one eye focused upon the most angelic image he knew.

Colette's smile was weary and tense. The lines of anxiety hardened the contours of her face. Her skin was unusually pale.

He squinted to focus. "What happened?" he asked in a hoarse whisper.

"You were injured," she replied. "I thought—" Her lips trembled, and she paused.

"Badly?" he asked.

She nodded.

"How?"

A voice from across the room replied, "You were thrown into a pit."

He craned his head to see who spoke as Bérenger Guifre came into view. Behind Guifre, Robert Keith looked on with concern.

Louis nodded, remembering the fall from his horse, and the brief, terrible sight of the pit.

"We thought you were dead," Keith said.

"Even until now," Guifre added.

"You were nearly impaled," Keith said. "One of the stakes cut a cruel gash in your face. You're lucky to be alive...fortunate that an Englishman had preceded you into that pit."

"How are you feeling?" Guifre asked.

"Pain," Louis said. He touched the bandages on his face again, though more gingerly. "My eye?"

"You didn't lose it," Keith said, tracing the sign of the cross at his chest. "Not sure how much good it'll do you, though. It took quite a blow."

Louis's heart sank at the thought of blindness, even in one eye.

"You've got the best of care," Guifre said, nodding toward Colette. "She is the healing hand of God. The fact that we're talking to you is proof of that."

"We'll leave you to it," Keith said curtly. "I wanted to see you awake. But now you have to rest, and I must carry the good news to the king." He turned to go, touching Guifre's sleeve.

"Wait," Louis called. His voice was a raspy croak. Keith turned back toward him. Louis took a deep breath, and said, "Did we win?"

"Ah!" Keith exclaimed. He strode to Louis's side and placed a hand on his forearm, smiling broadly. "Famously," he said. "It was a total rout."

"It was glorious," Guifre agreed.

"Tell me what I missed," Louis said.

Guifre thought back for a moment. "Let's see'" he said, "you were thrown just about the time King Robert rode down the hill with the reserve forces. That shook the English badly enough. But when the Templars rode around from behind the hill along with late reinforcements from the Highlands, they lost all nerve. The retreat was so panicked that a good number of the English stumbled or were pushed into the burn to drown."

"Did they know there were Templars among them?" Louis asked, furrowing his brow. He recalled King Robert's command, and his vow to honor it.

"The wedge formation gave it away," Guifre said. "We executed the classic charge into the fray to divide what was left of the English forces. They recognized it and realized that the Bruce had us on his side."

Robert Keith glanced at both Templars and pursed his lips, saying nothing.

Louis shook his head. "No," he said, "that must never be repeated."

"What do you mean?" Guifre protested. "Everyone saw it."

Louis looked hard at Keith. "The English," he said deliberately, "had already begun to retreat. The battle was over before King Robert charged. I saw that myself, before I fell. If the English thought they saw Templars, it was in their panic and confusion, and of no consequence."

"I don't understand," Guifre said.

"Let it not be said that Templars carried the Scots to victory," Louis said. "We will forever deny that fable. For in truth, we did no such thing. Rather, we were blessed with Scottish hospitality, and the chance to witness Scotland's finest hour. It is of no consequence that we were there."

Guifre nodded, and Robert Keith beamed.

"See that everyone understands that," Louis said.

Guifre nodded again.

Louis smiled weakly. "So Scotland is free," he said.

"Aye," Keith said. He paused thoughtfully, and then added, "She is, more or less."

Keith turned to go, and he beckoned for Guifre to follow. Guifre hesitated, looking anxiously at Louis.

"Sir Louis," he said, his voice tense, "you…had a visitor."

Louis glanced quizzically at Colette.

"Victor," she said. "A week ago."

"Strange man," Keith observed.

"What did he want?" Louis asked.

Colette furrowed her brow. "I don't know," she said. "He didn't really say, and he wouldn't stay."

"Said he was checking on you," Guifre said, "to make sure you're alive. But in truth, he didn't seem genuinely concerned."

"That one's trouble, if you ask me," Keith said. "Said he was your friend, but I doubt that."

"Why do you say that?" Louis asked.

Keith shrugged. "Feel it in my bones," he said.

Louis could see that Colette shared the suspicion.

"I don't know what to make of it," Guifre said. "I just thought you should know."

Louis nodded.

Keith turned once more to go, and this time Guifre followed him, leaving Louis and Colette alone.

Colette sat on the edge of the bed.

"You look so worried," Louis said. With great effort, he touched her cheek.

She took his hand in hers. "I'd lost you," she said. "Again. I felt that I, too, had died."

"I'm here," he reassured her. "You haven't lost me." He touched the bandages again. "How bad is it?"

"It won't be pretty," she said. "I doubt you'll lose the sight in that eye, but the scar will draw stares." She smiled and added, "You're likely to frighten small children."

The gravity of the injury subdued him.

"Rest," she said. "I'll bring you food when you're ready."

He closed his eyes and exhaled.

✠ ✠ ✠

Louis was soon able to leave the bed, though the pain of his injuries lingered. He was relieved to discover his sight intact when Colette removed his bandages, but he avoided reflections of his face. He could see in her eyes that his wound was horrid, as much as she tried to hide it. His bruises had healed, but his gait was still stiff and unsteady.

They walked slowly across the field behind their stone house, toward the thickets that lined the edge of the woods. It pleased Louis that a gentle stream, much like the one on his father's estate in Verzeille, gurgled pleasantly not far from the field. They found a comfortable resting place and sat beside the stream.

"After all I have been through," he complained, as Colette sat attentively with her hands folded in her lap. "The fall of Acre. The end of the Crusade. The betrayal of my own sacred Order! After all of that, to be laid low, not by the mace or the blade of a superior foe, but by a careening corpse and the point of a Scottish pike."

In the moments when those dark thoughts tormented him, he was not easily consoled, though Colette always did her best.

"What matters is that you're alive, and healing," she said. "I'm thankful for that."

He forced a smile. He knew that in time, his bitterness would pass, and he would more readily share her thankfulness. Even now, in his better moments, he thanked God. He was not having one of those moments.

"You're feeling stronger," Colette observed. "It's good to see."

Louis nodded. "In a sense, I feel relief," he said. "I would be happy to never again raise a sword in battle, or see the shedding of any man's blood. I am content to be with you, here in Scotland, for the rest of my days. But it's an adjustment, to be sure. I'm not yet accustomed to the idea."

"It's good that you are finished with battle," she said. "You'll not likely be fit for that again, after the fall you took." She paused, and then said, "Do you think you'll miss it?"

"No," he said. "Not anymore." There was distance in his words.

"Are you truly content, then," she asked, "with the idea of staying here, tending to this estate, for the rest of your life? Is there anything that leaves you discontented?"

Louis could think of nothing, but he also could not shake an unsettled feeling in the pit of his stomach. He repressed it and forced a smile.

"Nothing, darling," he said. His arms encircled her in a warm embrace. "It's just us now. Everything else is finished, and gone."

"Louis," she said huskily, pushing away and gazing into his eyes. "I want a child, then. I have waited my whole life for the day we could be together, and now that we are, I want a child… before it's too late, and before some new malicious fate pushes its way into our lives."

"A child," Louis said with uncertainty. He never considered the possibility once he had vowed celibacy to the Templar Order. He had violated that vow with Mairead at Acre, and then renounced it so that he could be with Colette, but he had never gone so far as to think of children. The thought of it troubled him now, but it also carried the hint of a joy he had never imagined. To his dismay, he found himself pleased by the thought of a son.

"We'll need someone to carry on when we're gone," she said. "But more than that, it would be wrong to deprive the world of the progeny of so noble and so pretty a man."

She smiled seductively and pulled him to the ground. She pushed him onto his back and straddled him with a look of primal hunger. The aching in his joints was sharp, but fleeting, and soon enough forgotten.

He rode a sturdy, young palfrey through the fields, surveying the preparations for the spring planting. Months of healing had eased his pains, though stiffness still set in on the damp days. Even on the good days, his gait was still noticeably slowed. He was ever acutely aware of the ugly scar that ran jagged from his jaw to his forehead, passing perilously close to his left eye. A persistent twitch in that eye nagged at him.

The planting was ahead of schedule, and the weather promised a fruitful year. All was relatively well despite his injuries.

But in his heart, he was increasingly troubled. At first, the reason for his angst eluded him. When it finally came to him, it magnified rather than eased his distress. The worst thing of all was that he could not bring himself to confide in Colette.

She knew, though. He was aware of that. She had probably even sensed the reason for his turmoil, for she had yet to remark upon it. He knew he would have to broach the subject eventually.

He decided that sooner was better than later.

"There's a new pope," he announced as he came in from the fields. Colette turned to look at him as if his statement were as relevant as a passing cloud. "They call him John."

Colette nodded and furrowed her brow. "And?" she said.

"He sits at Avignon."

"That surprises you?"

"Well, no…it doesn't," he said in a faltering voice.

"So, then, what of this news?" she said. "How does it concern us?"

He moved gingerly to the heavy oak table that dominated the hall and sat down. He folded his arms and gazed at the floor, struggling with how to begin. Colette sat too, waiting expectantly.

"I've been thinking," he said. "I wonder if this pope will uphold the policies and proclamations of his predecessor."

"Which ones, precisely?" she asked with a new sharpness in her voice. She, too, folded her arms, and her face grew stern.

Louis knew this would not go easily. He decided not to pursue it. "Never mind," he said. "It doesn't matter. I was thinking, and nothing more."

"And it's been troubling you," she prodded. "So I think it's something more. And if it's something more, I suppose I'd rather know what it is than tiptoe around acting like I haven't caught on. Out with it, Louis. What's brewing inside your head?"

"I wonder if John would reconsider the question of the Templars," he finally said.

Colette's shoulders slumped and she dropped her head, burying her face in her hands.

"Never mind," Louis said, rising from the chair.

"No," Colette said. "Sit. Finish. What is it you want to do?"

He sat. "I'm not sure I want to do anything," he said unconvincingly. After a long pause, he continued, "The Order was never judged fairly, despite the worthy defense of influential jurists. The court was biased against them from the start, by the treachery of a bastard king and the impotence of a feeble pope."

"Yes, I know it was," she replied through pursed lips. "And you think this pope would have done something different?"

"Perhaps," he said.

"And what of it?" she asked. "It can't be undone. It's long past. Why even trouble yourself with it?"

"How could I not think of it?" he asked. "The Order was my ambition from my earliest days. I swore my life to it, only to see it destroyed."

"Do you think you can do something to change that?" she said sharply.

"I don't know," he said. "Perhaps. Maybe I need to try. I could go to John and plead the case one last time. It would not take long, and after I have done that I will return to you, and never look back."

"You really do think the Templar Order stands a chance of revival," she said. She was incredulous. "To what end, Louis?"

He said nothing.

She leaned toward him with growing intensity. "What then, if you succeed?" she said. Her voice had grown harsh. "Another Crusade? Is that what you want?"

"No," he said firmly. "I said I would not look back." War was the last thing he wanted, especially in Jerusalem, and especially if it meant leaving Colette. But he was feeling defensive, and he decided once again to drop it.

"What, then?" she asked. "What do you hope to accomplish besides changing this new pope's mind about events that cannot be undone?"

"Nothing," he said with a sigh.

"No," she said. There was fire in her eyes now. "You're not dropping this now."

He had never seen her this angry. They had had their spats from time to time, as all lovers do, but Louis sensed that this time he had crossed a dangerous line. He shook his head in resignation.

"I want to know what it is that you want. I want to know where this is leading." Her words were a sharp staccato, each with its own forceful impact. For a moment, he wished he were mute so that he might remain silent before their blinding judgment.

After a long moment, he sighed again. "Home," he said softly. "New Jerusalem. Where we belong."

"We belong here now," she said flatly.

"I always wanted to be with you – there," he replied. "I've always envisioned us in the place where we grew up together, talking, dreaming, and running through the fields on a quest to find our future." He looked deeply into her eyes and added, "In the place where I fell in love with you."

She shook her head forcefully and stood, her body rigid with rage. "That is no longer our home," she cried. "Why can't you accept that? I don't want to go back there. This is my home now. And you know why that is so, unless you never give it a thought! Do you even think about why we are here in the first place, Louis?"

A long, uncomfortable silence ensued.

"You and your dreams!" she shouted. "We would be in Verzeille if not for your dreams. Has that even occurred to you? Have you learned nothing?"

He began to protest, but a furious wave of her hand silenced him.

"It was *you* running through those fields, Louis! I was only trying to keep up. I ran behind you hoping that for just one moment you would stop and turn around and see that I was there, and that I was at least as important as those constant, wretched dreams." Tears flowed from her eyes, and she trembled with emotion.

"I...I'm—"

"It was you, Louis," she continued. "*You* running, *you* talking, and *you* dreaming. I listened. I understood. I supported you. And I *waited*."

"For what?" he asked.

"For you to listen. For you to understand." Her trembling stopped, and her face hardened. She leaned toward him with folded arms and added, "But you never, ever did. And you still can't, even now."

"I don't understand," he said feebly.

"Exactly!" she snapped. She shook her head and turned away. She stared into the fireplace while Louis searched fruitlessly for the proper words.

She heaved a heavy sigh and said, "I don't want to hear any more about your damned Templars. I don't want to hear about Verzeille, or New Jerusalem, or any more of your infernal hopes, or dreams, or selfish schemes."

"Selfish?" he said indignantly. "How have I been selfish?"

She turned and looked at him as if he were an imbecile.

"Do you really not know?" she asked.

"I have done nothing but sacrifice," he said. Indignation arose in him. He stood and smacked the back of one hand against the palm of the other. "I have sacrificed everything for my ideals! I sacrificed everything for God...for the Church. I gave my life to the Crusade, even when I saw the Crusade collapsing all around me. I have done nothing for myself, *nothing*, and everything for the greater glory of God!"

She peered at him through narrowed eyes. "And what is it that you sacrificed?" she asked.

He thought about the question for a moment, realizing that he had never completely defined the answer to it.

"An easier life," he said haltingly. "My own fortune as a powerful noble, in my father's right."

"Me!" she screamed, pounding her chest. "You sacrificed *me!* For so long you sacrificed our time together, the chance of a life together. You sacrificed *my* hopes and *my* dreams for yours."

"I didn't know that you had dreams," he said.

"Yes, that's right," she agreed. "You didn't. And *why* did you not?"

"I asked you once what you wanted," he reminded her.

"Yes, you did," she said. "You shouldn't have needed to ask that, and I should not have had to answer. A girl does not ask for what she wants. She hopes her God will send her someone wise enough to see it, and noble enough to provide it unbidden. A lady does not ask a man to love her. Either he does, or he doesn't, and she accepts her fate. You should not have had to ask. You should have known the answer, if not then, then not long after. And it did become clear to you later, Louis. I know it did, long before you set out on your Templar quest. But you refused to acknowledge it, because it conflicted with your dreams for yourself."

Again, he formed a protest, but he knew that she was right, and he chose to spare himself the indignity.

"I'm sorry," he offered softly. "I've always tried to do what I thought was right."

"I know," she said.

"Why do I feel so terrible about pursuing the highest ideals?" he said.

"Perhaps because you know in your heart that they were not the highest ideals, and that you could have chosen better."

He shook his head. She meant that last remark to sting him, and it did. But it did not diminish the task to which he felt compelled.

"The Order of the Knights of the Temple—"

"No!" she exclaimed, pressing her palms to her ears. "I said not one more word about them."

He moved toward her as if to embrace her, but he stopped short as she shrank from him. He reached for her shoulders, but she backed farther away.

"It's a matter of honor," he said.

"Is it…?"

"It is," he said. "The Templar Order deserves at least a passing effort at redemption." She turned abruptly away from him. "After all those noble men sacrificed, fighting and bleeding and dying for the Church and for all of Christendom, if there's the slimmest hope that I can do something now to redeem their memories, and their honor, how can I refuse to do it?"

"You can honor them by not going and getting yourself imprisoned in the pursuit of yet another futile ambition," she said. "Or at the least, you could so honor me."

"I want to stay here with you," he said.

"Then do it," she snapped.

"I need to make this right."

"You can't make it right," she said.

"I have to try," he insisted. "For their sake, I have to try."

"And for my sake, you must not." She paced the room, fuming.

She turned to face him again, and shouted, "If you can't do it for my sake, Louis, then for the love of God, give this up for your son!"

She let the words hang in a hollow, ringing silence as he absorbed their significance.

"My son?" he said weakly.

"Yes, your son." She stared hard at him. "I had hoped to give you that news to a happier tune, but alas, you've made that impossible. You've forced me to present it to you as a plea for you to do what you already know is right, to stay where you belong, and not to walk away from him the way you always have me."

Louis had trouble grasping the news, particularly while feeling compelled to defend himself. "I've walked away from you?" he said.

"You've spent your whole life walking away from me, Louis," she said, "leaving me to wonder every moment if or when I would see you again. Even when you finally came home, you didn't really come home to me. You came home to your new dream, your New

Jerusalem. If not for that, I don't know if I would have seen you again, aside from occasional and very brief visits. Well, you can walk away from me, Louis – that much is clear. But you *cannot* walk away from your unborn son and risk denying him the chance to know, to love, and to learn from his magnificent father."

Louis slumped into his chair.

"You think the Templars deserve your loyalty?" she continued. "Your child deserves your love. Your child deserves your presence. Your child deserves a place above your Templars, even if I do not."

I have always been loyal to you, he almost said in protest, but the image that had haunted him since Acre stopped his tongue. The lust–filled eyes of an ardent young nun still peered longingly through the shadows of time, summoning anew the shame he had carried since then. He stood and gazed remorsefully at Colette.

"I'm sorry to have upset you so," he said. "How long have you known?" The look on her face made him think she had read his thoughts about Acre, and he quickly added, "About the baby..."

After a moment's hesitation, she said, "Not long. I'm more certain every day."

"You don't know for sure, then?"

"I'm sure," she said firmly.

He sighed deeply and said, "I suppose that changes everything, then."

"You're displeased," she said flatly.

"No," he said. "Unprepared, with everything else on my mind."

She nodded again, reproachfully. "You should have gained more sense by now," she said. She ascended the stairway to the bedchamber without another word.

✠ ✠ ✠

"You don't think it's a worthy cause?" Louis asked.

He was disappointed. He had thought for sure that Bérenger Guifre and the other Templars would agree with him and rally to his support...perhaps even accompany him. He had called them together at the Templar hall at Ayr to discuss his thoughts of redemption for the Order.

"It's foolish," Guifre said. "And to what end?"

"There will be no new Crusade," added Mathieu Algais, a slender knight of short stature and a placid demeanor that belied his battlefield prowess.

"For a chance to finish what we started," Louis cried. "What else? New Jerusalem! A chance for an Occitan kingdom of our own." He could hardly believe they did not share his desire. "The Germans have Prussia," he said. "The Hospitallers have Rhodes. Even the Scots have their own kingdom now. Why should this not be our destiny, too?"

"Because," Guifre said, "for one thing, just as Philip would never have allowed it, neither will Louis X. And for another, because we are outlaws. Fugitives. Outside of Scotland, any common thief may murder us with impunity, and perhaps even for a bounty. Do you truly imagine that the son of the man who destroyed us would move aside and yield a region for which his forebears had so artfully schemed?"

Mathieu Algais grinned. He held a hand to his cheekbone, above a tangle of sparsely grown beard, and said, "I wonder if the fall didn't injure more than just your face. It appears you're not thinking very clearly."

Louis looked at Mathieu with exasperation. "Why?" he said. "Because I still embrace the dreams of our Order?"

Mathieu smiled kindly. "Because you think there's a chance you'd survive," he said.

"No one will accompany me, then?" he asked. He felt betrayed, and he allowed his expression to convey that.

"Louis," Guifre said, "no one believes it will ever happen. Every last one of us has long put off the hopes and dreams, or whatever else it was, that led us into the Order. None of us –

none but you, that is – expects any of that to ever again be real. It is dead. Long dead. And so will you be if you go back there."

"This pope is just like the last one," Mathieu added, "except for the name. What would he gain by reopening such a dreadful crypt? Why, in the name of God, would he entertain such a thing?"

"So we should just not try," Louis said somberly. "We turn our backs on justice, on honor, and on any chance for redemption. That's what we do now?"

"Yes," Guifre said firmly. "That's what we do now, if we have half the sense God gave us. If you had sense, you would heed our pleas and forget this scheme." He stood squarely in front of Louis and placed a hand on his shoulder. "Don't do this, Louis. Forget you ever conceived of it."

Louis shook his head and left the hall without another word. He could not believe how utterly the betrayal of the Order had crushed it. Its spirit was dead.

Their entreaties had not dissuaded him, but rather strengthened his resolve. If no one else cared enough to mount one last defense of two hundred years of bravery, dignity, and honor, then by God, he himself would compensate for that deficiency.

He ran his fingertips along the edges of his scar as he strode along the road toward home. It throbbed when his heart pounded faster, as blood coursed through the newly mended flesh.

Not thinking clearly, he scoffed. *Perhaps I'm the only one who is!*

Colette received the news in silence. He had prepared for another quarrel, but not for the haunting sadness into which she retreated. One last effort to win her understanding, if not her support, languished in the chasm that now yawned between them. Even his promise to return before the birth of his child hung vapid in that void. He recognized the futility of further efforts to win her support, and he decided to depart without further delay.

Chapter 54

Louis arrived at the Bishops' Palace as the sun reached its apex in the clear blue sky over Avignon. He approached the heavy front doors with foreboding, fighting the temptation to turn and walk as far and as quickly as he could away from this place.

He searched for the words that had come so readily to mind prior to his departure. They were so convincing then, and so sound in their wisdom. Weeks of anxious waiting had passed, and now those words cowered behind rising fears about that wisdom, and behind far more compelling words.

She's alone and carrying my child, he thought. He imagined that he would have a son.

He dismissed his instinctive, contrived protest that he was doing this precisely because of his son, to demonstrate for his benefit the essence of loyalty. He admitted that the lesson might be lost in the misery of his failure to return. He wished now that he had reconsidered for just one more moment, but he knew that it would not have made a difference. For Louis, wisdom had often come in hindsight, despite his fine intentions. Colette had all too often borne the heaviest price for that, and now perhaps his child would do the same.

Each day he had grown more convinced that he was making a terrible mistake. But now he was here, and he summoned the resolve to see his mission through.

Pope John XXII enjoyed a reputation for political agility. Many considered him a fair and thoughtful man who was willing to take contrary or unpopular positions. Louis would stand no chance with any pope, if not with John. Still, John's advanced age might render him fragile against the influences of powerful kings.

He hesitated for a moment, and then he brought the heavy, ornate knocker down hard upon the massive door. The sound echoed in the vestibule beyond.

An armed sentry appeared. He escorted Louis through the doors into a cold, spare vestibule that held a single wooden bench, where he motioned for Louis to sit.

Louis remained standing in the vestibule. After what seemed an eternity, the inner door opened, and a priest with a grave face gazed at him from the doorway. The priest was perhaps ten years his junior, and he carried himself with a haughty air. With a grunt, he turned and motioned for Louis to follow him.

The priest ordered Louis to wait outside the conference room until he was summoned. When he returned to call him in, he gave Louis a long look of disdain. He ushered him into the large and lavishly appointed room, occupied by the pope and four senior cardinals, and a bishop dressed in a black habit.

Pope John sat in a plush, high-backed chair on a raised platform along the back wall of the cavernous room. He appeared surprisingly young for seventy, with smooth skin, a narrow face with a longish nose, and deep-set opal eyes. He folded delicate hands on the massive table and gazed curiously at Louis.

The cardinals occupied lesser chairs on either side of the pope, and the stern-faced bishop sat to his far right.

The bishop's piercing stare seized Louis's attention. Of all the men in the room, that bishop conveyed the most palpable sense of danger. His gaze inspired the hollow dread of a fly trapped in the web of a deadly spider.

Louis's footsteps echoed as he moved to stand beside a lone wooden chair that faced the officials from the center of the vast stone chamber. It was a small and uncomfortable seat, with a badly tattered cushion. Deep gashes and dents in its legs suggested that the chair had been flung about, perhaps with some frequency.

A scribe took a seat at a writing table in a corner. He nodded toward the dour bishop as he dipped his pen into an inkwell.

The pope extended his hand toward Louis, to receive his kiss upon the papal ring. Louis genuflected, then braced himself against rising nausea and advanced to kiss the ring. He backed toward his seat, pleased that he had managed convincing reverence.

"Greetings, Brother de Garonne," one of the cardinals said. "Thank you for coming. I trust you've rested well from your journey." Louis nodded. "I am Bérenger Fredoli." Fredoli indicated his colleagues in turn: "Cardinal Guillaume de Mandagot, Cardinal Michel du Bec-Crespin, and Cardinal Arnaud de Pellegrue." Fredoli glanced at the bishop, whose curt glance indicated that he would prefer not to be introduced. "We're here to witness your appeal," Fredoli continued, "and to offer our judgment for the Holy Father's consideration as, in his preeminent wisdom, he decides your case."

My case, Louis thought, *or my fate?* He gazed at the dark bishop warily; the bishop did not break his icy stare. Louis turned his attention to Fredoli.

"Thank you, Your Eminence," he said. He sat in response to Fredoli's gesture. The chair groaned under his weight.

The pope leaned back in his chair and gazed appraisingly at Louis. "I admire your courage," he said. "Your conviction must be considerable for you to request counsel with me on the matter of an order that stands accused and convicted of heresy, and is accursed." The dark bishop smiled thinly as the pope spoke those words. "I am humbly flattered that you have spoken openly of your regard for my reasonableness and my spiritual wisdom. I encourage you to speak as openly here as you explain to me what truth it is that I have neglected to acknowledge until now."

The bishop's reptilian smile broadened.

"I intend you no disrespect, Your Holiness," Louis said. "I've come here only in humble reverence, to appeal to your Christian mercy in the name of good and decent men who sought only to do God's work. I have no personal knowledge of Templar transgressions against the Church; had I such knowledge, I would renounce the transgressors at once. I seek only a voice for those I know to have been faultless men of God."

"Do not heretics routinely deny knowledge of heresy?" the bishop interjected. Louis turned his attention to the bishop, as the pope raised a hand to silence him. The bishop did not entirely conceal his irritation with the pope's mild rebuke.

Louis began to suspect the bishop's identity. He spoke as only an inquisitor would speak. Of all the inquisitors who plied their passion in the vicinity of Avignon, the most likely to attend a papal council would be the Dominican, Bernard de Gui, the infamous inquisitor of Toulouse.

"How is it," the pope asked, "that faultless men came under suspicion, particularly of the highest crimes against God? If a man were truly pure, what would possibly cast a shadow of doubt?"

"Fear," Louis said with conviction.

"Fear? Fear of what?"

Louis glanced at de Gui, and said, "Fear of those faultless men, and their purity and strength."

Scorn twisted de Gui's expression into an ugly mask.

"Why would anyone fear a righteous man?" the pope asked.

"Men fear you," Louis countered.

"*Evil* men fear me."

"Yes," Louis said softly. He closed his eyes and nodded. "Precisely." He shifted his gaze to de Gui and said, "Evil men fear righteous men."

As the pope considered Louis's implication, Louis held the Inquisitor's gaze and shifted in his seat so that he sat a little taller.

"You claim that your brethren were pure to a fault," he said, "and that only evil, fear–driven men spoke against them?"

"I'm saying that the verdict against the Templar Order is in conflict with my personal experience, and my conscience compels me to bring that conflict to light. I am honor–bound to appeal to Your Holiness for reconsideration of that verdict."

"Your brethren confessed to the charges."

"As would most men under torture."

"Men who so proudly professed their willingness to die for their faith?" the pope asked.

"Death in battle is nothing like the pain of torture, Your Holiness"

"You know this because you have experienced both?"

"I know this because I have witnessed both. They are not the same thing. Each affects men differently. Death in battle against unbelievers glorifies God, while torture at the hands of believers is an affront to God. Such cruelty destroys the hope and resolve of the tortured, and it defiles the spirit of the torturer." Louis looked piercingly at de Gui. "Is this not why the Church delivers the heretic into secular hands for such things, closing its eyes to them…so as not to sully its holy spirit?"

"You question much of what your Church deems appropriate," the pope said sternly.

"I'm simply asserting that confessions gained by methods too base for the Church's tolerance are not credible."

"And what of the willing testimony of Templars who were *not* tortured, who insisted they had seen such things with their own eyes?"

"Men who were no longer Templars, for reasons they neglected to divulge?" Louis said. "I suppose I might question the credibility of such men."

"Then you also question the wisdom of this Church in accepting the veracity of their testimony."

"I do not question the zeal with which the Church has sought its own truth, or its determination to serve and glorify God. I question the evidence that was offered to the Church for consideration in that quest."

"What is *your* testimony?" the pope asked.

"Note," Cardinal Fredoli interjected, speaking to the scribe at the writing table, "that the witness is, and has been, in no way coerced by torture, or any other form of duress." The scribe nodded solemnly and complied.

The pope motioned for Louis to proceed.

"Since my earliest days," Louis said, "I have wanted only to serve God, and to do so as a knight of the Templar Order. I've dreamed only of seeing the Kingdom of God built finally and forevermore, and of giving my life, if necessary, to make that so." The Cardinals nodded, and de Gui smiled disingenuously, mimicking the doting of a father on a valiant son. "I found, upon entering the Order, that the conduct of its brethren truly reflected the ideals of my youth, and of the Church I loved. I found men who willingly sacrificed everything, even their lives, for the chance to promote and defend what each of us in this room holds precious."

"So, then," John said, "there was no errant or aberrant behavior among the brethren, ever?"

"Your Holiness, brethren were expelled because of aberrant behavior. I have already pointed out that such men formed the basis of the initial charges against the Order. The fact that they were expelled speaks, in and of itself, to the integrity of the Order, does it not?"

De Gui frowned at that, and glared fiercely at Louis.

The pope shook his head. "They claimed to have been expelled for refusing to participate in heresy," he said.

Louis resolved not to argue against the testimony of unworthy men, but rather to present his own testimony.

"The discipline of the Order was strict," Louis said. "There was errant behavior, as there is among any assembly of imperfect men. And there was punishment befitting every transgression, administered swiftly and without lenience, in accordance with the Rule of the Order. Had that not been so, Templar purity would not have become legendary, and I would not be here today making one last effort to defend it.

"I stand before you today to state unequivocally, before God and the Holy Spirit, that the Order of the Poor Fellow-Soldiers of Christ and the Temple of Solomon was comprised only of pious, noble men who swore their lives to the glory of God and Saint Mary. Those men did nothing but serve their pope from the day they swore until the day they died. They earned the reverence of the Church they suffered to defend, and not the contempt with which that Church rewarded them in the end."

Louis realized when he heard the echoing of his voice that he had spoken much more loudly than he had intended. The echo faded to a long and solemn silence.

Finally, Cardinal du Bec-Crespin, second to the right of the pope, cleared his throat and leaned forward in his seat.

"You would have us believe, then," he said, "that you have no knowledge whatsoever of any blasphemies, heresies, or any other mortal sins perpetrated among the brethren of your Order?"

"None," Louis answered. "None that were tolerated."

"Then there were some."

"As I've already said: there were some, but they were rare, and they were promptly punished."

"Name some of them," the cardinal said.

"Murder, defection to the enemy, unauthorized retreat: things such as these."

"Retreating in battle is not a mortal sin," the cardinal said with disdain.

"To a Templar, it is."

"You had your own rules, then."

"Of course we did. Do you not know our Rule? Life on the battlefield requires a stricter set of rules than life in the parish. Bernard of Clairvaux understood that, and he wrote the Rule accordingly. Facing death fighting infidels for the glory of God, sometimes without the support of those safe at home, requires extraordinary discipline, and harsher rules than those observed in monasteries."

"What else was extraordinary about life in your Order?"

"The inability of others to understand it," Louis said pointedly.

"You mean, to understand the Templar rituals?" de Gui said.

"The idols, the effigies, the cats, and the severed heads?"

"There were no idols, no cats, no effigies," Louis replied.

"But there were severed heads," the pope observed.

"Your Holiness, if you please...how many abbeys from England to Antioch possess among their reliquaries the remains of venerated saints? How many claim to possess the actual head of John the Baptist? I myself have visited monasteries and abbeys throughout Christendom that possess the remains of saints, the provenance of which consecrated men have confirmed. Yet, to accept that all such relics are authentic is to believe that John the Baptist was a grotesque human hydra. Everyone knows that the real head of Saint John the Baptist is in your own reliquary, here in Avignon. And yet, we do not chastise monks who venerate such false relics. Why? Is it not because even the likeness of a relic provides inspiration to a very real faith? Is it not because the relic's symbolism is more important than its substance?"

"What has this to do with severed heads in Templar halls?" Cardinal Fredoli asked.

"No Templar ever worshipped a severed head," Louis said flatly, "any more than any monk ever worshipped the bone fragment of a long dead saint. Rather, as the bone fragment conjures the remembrance of the martyr to whom it once belonged, every symbol and allegory of every priestly order commemorates a specific godly ideal or sanctified rule. But of course, you know this."

"And what, exactly, is the symbolism of the severed head of the Templars?" Fredoli asked.

"As is the case with all symbolism, Your Eminence, each symbol may have many meanings, depending upon the spiritual need to which it is applied. A severed head can represent, as it primarily does in the case of John the Baptist, the ultimate sacrifice for one's faith. It can represent wisdom in the pursuit of godliness. It can represent whatever precept or ideal is most profitable for the one who contemplates its meaning. Is this not so of many sanctified things? Why do you draw distinction with regard to Templar relics?"

The assembly mulled Louis's words for a moment before

Bérenger Fredoli continued. "And so," he said, "you would divulge it publicly if you knew of any heresy, or any heretics, among your brethren?"

"I cannot say that I have the wisdom or insight to discern a heretical heart. I lack the inquisitor's judgment of such things. I would surely divulge an agent of the devil, were I aware of such a thing, but I assure you that I am not now, nor have I ever been aware of such among the Templar brethren."

"Heresy was not discussed or debated among those brethren?"

"Heresy was discussed, of course," Louis said, "in much the same way that the faith and the military strategies of our Muslim enemy were discussed, at length. One cannot oppose a thing effectively without at least a cursory understanding of it."

"There were those among the brethren who sympathized with heretics, were there not?"

"I know of no one who openly sympathized with heretics."

"Secretly, then?"

De Gui interjected. "I've noticed, Brother de Garonne," he said with a smirk, "that you choose your words carefully. What is it that you guard?"

"I have heard," Louis answered calmly, "that imprecise speech, when misinterpreted, either intentionally or inadvertently, can carry the same weight as confession in some assemblies. I intend certainty of meaning, so that my words are neither distorted nor misconstrued."

"An innocent man would speak plainly," the pope said.

Louis stood and turned to face Bernard de Gui directly. He raised his right hand, his palm opened toward the bishop, and he spoke in a clear, unwavering voice.

"I swear before God and the Blessed Virgin Mary, and in the name of all the saints, that I believe, as I have always, and ever will believe, that Jesus Christ is my Savior, my God, born in the flesh and crucified on the cross to shed his blood in my stead, for my forgiveness and my salvation. I swear to Almighty God that I have never believed or considered any false preaching against Him, and that I would willingly give my life to defend the sanctity of His Name." Louis's eyes flashed as they remained locked with de Gui's. "Would any heretic swear in such a manner, Brother Bernard de Gui?"

De Gui's mouth hung slack for a brief moment before regaining its customary hardness. He lowered his eyes to the table and frowned. In one forcible statement, Louis had surmounted the trickery to which de Gui routinely resorted to prove heresy. The heretics de Gui pursued were forbidden by their faith to swear oaths; the willingness to swear proved innocence, while hesitation to do so confirmed guilt.

"I furthermore swear," Louis said, turning to the pope, "that never in all of my days as a Templar did I witness heresy, or a single offense against God or the Church, or even one of the charges that have been leveled against my Order. Upon this, I swear my life."

"Not only do you swear," said de Gui, recovering, "but you swear recklessly. The confessions of your brethren have been documented and sealed. They are a matter of record. Either they, or you, have lied."

"Your Holiness," Louis said to the pope, "I have already stated my position on confessions gained through torture. I humbly submit that such confessions should be regarded with suspicion, at best. Even the strongest of men are rendered frail by the heat of the inquisitor's flames. Anyone in this room would likely offer the most outlandish of confessions just to end such agony. The nature of such confessions is determined solely by the objectives of the inquisitor."

De Gui made no further effort to mask his contempt; he had championed those inquisitors' flames.

"You do speak plainly," Cardinal du Bec-Crespin said. It sounded like an accusation, rather than an observation. The pope motioned the cardinal to allow Louis to continue.

"Your Holiness," Louis insisted, "you know yourself that no confessions were gained, but by torture, or the promise of torture."

"In the absence of such encouragement," the pope asked, "why would the guilty confess? Is the heretic not a liar? Would not the heretic continue to lie, and claim his innocence forever, unless he were motivated by some means toward the truth?"

"Would not the innocent be likewise motivated to lie to stop the pain?" Louis countered.

The pope, the cardinals, and the bishop studied Louis.

"Your charge, then," the pope finally argued, "is that my predecessor erred in his dealings with your Order." He leaned toward Louis intently for the answer.

"He was given false information by a king with personal and political motives for destroying the Order," Louis answered. "That king engineered the destruction of an Order that answered solely to the pope, after he destroyed one of the popes to which it answered."

"And it is your belief that His Holiness Pope Clement was foolish enough, and weak enough, to be influenced and misled by a secular king?"

"His Holiness was given false evidence," Louis repeated.

"And he was incapable of discerning that fact," the pope pressed.

"I mean no disrespect to His Holiness the Pope," Louis said.

"No. But you do think yourself better able to discern the truth, and to determine what is and what is not just. You presume to be more qualified even than God, who alone ordains the pope to Peter's Throne, to determine whether my predecessor was fit for the investiture? You see clearly that which God cannot see, that Clement was a stupid, fallible man who could not perceive the lies of a secular king?"

Louis shook his head.

"Speak when you answer," the pope commanded.

"Your Holiness, I do believe that Philip placed undue pressures upon His Holiness Pope Clement, as he did upon Boniface during his reign. The attack on Pope Boniface at Agnani most certainly led to his death."

"That man...," John said with disgust, "Boniface, who dared to call himself pope, was a heretic."

Louis took a deep breath before he countered. He spoke in

an even, and carefully respectful tone.

"And God could not see that heresy when He ordained Boniface to Peter's Throne?" As tenderly as he formed the words, nothing could have softened their blow.

The pope stood suddenly in speechless, crimson rage. For a long and fearful moment, he clung tentatively to his composure. The cardinals stared in shocked amazement, while Bernard de Gui sat back contentedly, clasping his hands as if in thankful prayer.

Louis continued: "My point, Your Holiness, is this—"

The pope shot his finger toward Louis to silence him, his hand clenched so tightly that it quivered. He glared with withering condemnation, shaking his head.

After a long silence, Louis tried again.

"Your Holiness," he said, trying to sound contrite, "what I mean to say is that on one day, a man is holy, revered as the pope, but on the next, he is reviled and called heretic. It was the same for the Templars. For two hundred years, those pious soldiers of the faith committed their lives and their souls to their Church and their God, and then one day they were suddenly condemned, and called heretical by the Church they served. How do holy men of God fall so far from His grace? How could other holy men of God have been, for so very long, so terribly mistaken in their admiration for a priestly order that shared league with the devil? Is it not more likely that they were *not* mistaken, and that the true error took place not long ago, over the span of a few dark and hysterical years?"

"You are in no position to pass judgment on matters that pertain to God and His Church," the pope seethed. "It is not your place. You are on dangerous ground." John finally sat, almost reluctantly, throwing the lengths of his robes angrily to the sides so that they did not bunch on the chair beneath him.

"Your Holiness," Louis persisted, "surely, in your wisdom, you see how King Philip's schemes and manipulations damaged the Church. You have brought to your office great wisdom and piety. Wrongs have been done by others that only you can make right. I believe that those wrongs were perpetrated against God, as well as against His Holiness himself."

"You come here on my behalf, then, do you?" John said with contempt. "You presume to speak in my defense, too?"

"I only beg your mercy now, that you may look kindly upon the name of an Order that was devoted unto its death in the service of your office and your Church. I beg your mercy upon the souls of good men who sacrificed their lives to build God's Kingdom in Jerusalem."

"Your Order has been charged with heresy...and condemned," John said. "The men of your Order are damned."

"They were not guilty," Louis insisted. "Their conduct was above reproach."

"They ran to elude trial," Bérenger Fredoli said. "*You* ran. Why would an innocent man run? Their escape from justice attests to their guilt. What's more, fugitive knights crossed over to the Saracen side in Spain, and in other places, where they took up arms against Christian armies. How do you deny their obvious guilt, or attempt to explain their treason?"

"Pope Clement and King Philip made themselves enemies of the Order," Louis said. "The attack upon the Order was unprovoked, unfounded, and unjust. I submit that those brethren who escaped, and those who took up arms against forces that had declared war upon them and their Order, were doing only what is in the Templar nature to do: defending against attack."

The pope waved in annoyance, as if he were weary of the discussion.

"Tell me," Bernard de Gui said, "about the depravity, the homosexuality that was common among your brethren. Your former Grand Master William de Beaujeu both condoned and engaged in it himself, did he not? Tell me about the sodomy you witnessed during your time with the Order, and the lengths to which you went to rid the Order of that particular iniquity."

Louis carefully considered his answer. A lie would condemn him, but the truth would bring judgment upon good men he admired, men who had fought more valiantly than he, and who were now dead. He saw no profit in their condemnation. Furthermore, he realized that he held higher regard for Antonio Bollani and Richard Osborne than he would ever hold for these sanctimonious men. Between condemning his brethren and lying to the pope, he considered the lie the less egregious sin.

Still, a lie to the pope was no small thing. The weight of it briefly staggered him.

"I know of no illicit acts between any of the Brethren," he said firmly.

"You hesitated before answering," Fredoli said. "Why?"

"I prefer to consult my conscience carefully, Your Eminence, before answering such questions."

"To construct your defense of the wrongdoers?"

"To ensure that I have not overlooked some small thing, some evidence or indication of the existence of such things – to ensure the accuracy of my response."

"And?"

"There were none." Louis said. "I have no reason to believe any of the Brethren engaged in sodomy, or any other offense against God without being punished for it." He prayed silently for forgiveness for his lie.

"I have heard rumors," Cardinal Guillaume de Mandagot interjected, "of plans for a sovereign Templar state. What do you know of that?" Until that moment, de Mandagot had remained silent, pensive. His question was an abrupt change of direction. De Gui regarded him with a perplexed look.

Louis was disconcerted. He was not prepared to discuss New Jerusalem. He took a moment to gather his thoughts.

"It is common knowledge," he finally said, "that other crusading orders pursued that option as support for the Crusades diminished. As you well know, the Teutonic Knights established their own sovereignty long ago, as the Hospitaller Knights have, more recently. They've done so with papal blessing. It should astonish no one that the Templars considered a similar alternative to abandonment and annihilation in Outremer. It would have been reasonable for the Templars to expect comparable papal endorsement for such a plan, were they to present one."

"Tell us of the Templar plan."

"To what end?"

"To what end?" De Mandagot exclaimed. "You are here pleading for a Templar resurrection. How do you envision that resurrection? I'd like to understand what form the resurrected Templars might take."

Louis was surprised by the glimmer of hope de Mandagot's statement seemed to suggest.

"My plea is for the restoration of the Templar name, the removal of its undeserved stigma. The sanctity of the Order should be restored; it is that alone which I have come to seek. Rebuilding of the Order, I would think, is beyond the realm of possibility. One is unlikely to find twenty Templars who would desire such a thing."

"So," de Mandagot said, "you do not foresee a future Templar state?"

"If I did," Louis said, "would the Church consecrate the idea?" His question was met with silence, and Louis nodded. "I don't believe such a thing is possible," he said. "Even with the Church's blessing, kings would not allow it."

"What would be the structure of a Templar state, if it were possible?" de Mandagot asked. "I have heard talk of liberty, of individual freedom from the rule of kings and priests, of church and state."

At this, de Gui sniffed derisively. "That vile scheme is not dead," he said. "I have heard of it. It calls for a new social order founded upon anarchy, lawlessness, and reckless self-indulgence, unchecked by the proper authority of popes and kings. Such a scheme is a violation of God's will. It cannot be allowed to see the light of day."

"You've heard rumors and fabrications, Your Eminence," Louis said. "Some Templars envisioned a sovereign state, neutral and tolerant, vibrant and free, and committed to the support and defense of the Holy Church. It might have employed a parliamentary system such as those in England and Aragon, both of which have gained the support of nobles and commoners alike. In a peaceful, prosperous society governed by moral men both fervent and fair, tolerant of outsiders and non-believers, perhaps even godless pagans could be won to the love and service of our Christ."

"What place, specifically, would the Church occupy in such a system of governance?"

"The Church would enjoy the same welcome and protections of law that all citizens would enjoy. There would be no constraints upon fair and equitable enterprise. All would enjoy perfect security: each part defends the whole, and the whole defends each part."

"Equals," de Mandagot said, peering smugly at his colleagues. "Your secular state," he said, his lips curling as he enunciated the word *secular*, "would reduce the Holy Church, and His Holiness the pope, to the station of common men, equals among merchants and artisans, blacksmiths and farmers."

"Which is why I say the idea is inconceivable," Louis said, "and unworthy of further discussion."

"If you do not foresee a Templar state," the pope said dryly, "what shall become of the vast resources that went missing along with so many of your fugitive brethren, and for which the Holy See has yet to account?"

"Resources?"

"The greater part of your Order's wealth has yet to be brought to account."

"Of that, I know nothing," Louis said, shaking his head.

"Of course," de Mandagot said. "I'd have guessed as much."

"We will find it," said du Bec-Crespin. "In due time, of course. We won't stop until we do. That wealth belongs to the Church, for the support of its faithful and the poor. It does not belong to an order that swore a vow of poverty. But that is a discussion for another day."

The pope sat back and regarded Louis thoughtfully.

"Where are your brethren today, Brother de Garonne " he asked. He raised his hands questioningly. Louis said nothing. "Why do they hide in the shadows? Why is not even one of them here with you today, supporting you, at the very least with their presence? On that note, too – why are you here at all? Are you not the least bit afraid?"

"Of what should I be afraid?" Louis asked.

The pope turned toward de Gui, who leaned forward and cleared his throat.

"Did you not," de Gui asked, "submit to the initiation rites of the Templar Order?"

"Of course I did."

"And in that initiation, did you not deny the crucifix of Our Lord, Jesus Christ?"

Louis's heart sank. The discussion had ended, and his interrogation had begun. He hesitated, knowing that he could not answer that question truthfully without condemning himself. Even if he could make these cardinals understand, it was not understanding they sought, but rather burnt flesh, and nothing else.

He answered anyway. "The initiation rite is not what it might appear to one ignorant of its meaning," he said.

"Then enlighten this untutored fool," de Gui said, "that I may see the truth to which I have been, until now, blind." His lips tightened into a smug smile.

Louis worked carefully through his reply. "Many among the Templars were illiterate," he began. "The most effective way to convey ideas and concepts to illiterate men is through symbols and allegory. The initiation rite was designed to impart a clear and indelible understanding of the spiritual transition that the initiate had chosen to undertake."

De Gui peered curiously at him, and he continued.

"The initiate begins by taking upon himself the symbolic mantle of a base and ungodly man – Christ's own chief apostle in his moment of weakness and fear, when he thrice denied the Christ rather than standing to defend Him. Wearing that mantle, the initiate acts out the denial of Christ, three times, just as Peter did, so that he may experience in his heart the shame of such denial. This is nothing more than a reenactment of Peter's moment of faltering faith."

"A true Christian could not utter the words," de Gui said.

Louis ignored him and continued. "The initiate is symbolically slain for his transgression, so that he may be reborn into the love of Christ, to stand forevermore in adoration of the Christ. He then commits the remainder of his life to Christ."

The pope exchanged glances with his cardinals, and then leaned toward Louis.

"And the initiate kisses his commander on the anus," he said, "after he spits upon the cross."

"No!" Louis exclaimed, shuddering. He shook his head firmly. "No, he doesn't!"

"No?"

"No. The kiss is on the mouth. It was the kiss of love for the Christ, the kiss that sealed the union of the initiate with his Lord. It conquered Judas's kiss of betrayal at Gethsemane. It symbolized eternal love for our Holy Savior."

"It is homosexual, and it is blasphemy," the pope countered.

"It is no more homosexual than was Judas's kiss," Louis replied. "It was effective. No initiate ever forgot the significance of his vows, having acted out the allegories of the initiation."

"And yet, many forgot their vows under interrogation!" de Gui argued. He smirked triumphantly toward the cardinals, who laughed derisively. "Some of your brethren," he scoffed, "lied unto their death denying the very things that you now freely admit. And your confession comes without the benefit of an inquisitor's...encouragement."

"The inquisitors were unwilling to comprehend the concepts I've tried to explain to Your Holiness today. They took the explanations as confessions, as you are prepared to do now. I appeal to your greater wisdom, and to your goodness and mercy. I believed that you might better understand the hearts and the minds of my brothers, who were faithful from their glorious founding to their bitter end."

"I do understand," the pope said reassuringly. His stern demeanor changed to one of pity. "You have represented your brothers well. You shed light on questions that have plagued me since the accusations were first made. Others have suggested that perhaps the Templars should be pardoned, and its good name restored. Perhaps I may yet be further convinced." He turned to the bishop de Gui. "You see, I always maintained that torture was perhaps, more often than not, unnecessary. We needed simply to sit and talk openly, as men do."

Louis's heart sank further. The pope had taken his explanation as a confession, in the name of the whole Templar Order, to all of the charges of heresy.

The pope said to de Gui, "Have you documented this proceeding fully?"

"I've gotten it all," de Gui replied, nodding to the scribe.

The pope turned to the cardinals. "Have you further questions for the witness?" he asked.

The cardinals shook their heads smugly.

Witness, Louis thought to himself. *Witness?* His blood froze in his veins. He prepared for the entrance of guards who would haul him from the room in chains.

The pope turned to him. "Again, Sir Louis," he said, "I thank you for your courage in coming here today. I appreciate your regard for my wisdom in this matter. I will take it under advisement once again, along with your words of testimony. After prayerful consideration, I will inform you of my decision."

Louis was confused. These were not the words of impending arrest.

The pope continued: "The Church is in possession of your father's estate. It lies vacant. Retire there now, and await my judgment. If the Church's decision on the Order of the Temple is to be reversed, then your family's estates will revert to you. If the judgment stands, then the Church will retain those estates, and you may return to the refuge to which you fled, never to return. I understand that you turned from your Templar vows long ago; I will take that as repentance, and you will not be further punished."

A dizzying wave of relief washed over Louis. Despite the incongruence of the examination's tone and its conclusion, he thought that perhaps he had rightly judged the new pope. More than anything, he wanted to leave the palace and get to a place where he could sort through his confusion. His heart raced at the thought of going home.

With a start, the pope's remark about his father's estate registered. Why was it vacant, and in the Church's possession? What had become of his parents? Perhaps his father had died, but what had become of his mother?

He rose from his chair and bowed deeply. He stepped forward and genuflected, and then offered his kiss to the papal ring. The pope smiled thinly at the cardinals and extended his hand, but he quickly withdrew it as if another thought had come to mind.

"Sir Louis," he said with a curious look, "your friend… Guyot…"

"Victor?"

"Yes. Victor Guyot."

"Yes, Your Holiness?"

John glanced at the cardinals and said, "He remains fugitive."

Louis's eyes darkened, and he said nothing.

"We would very much like to talk with him."

"Why would that have anything to do with me?" Louis asked. The pope had crossed a line that Louis held sacred.

"Can you find him, and bring him here?" the pope asked.

Louis struggled to hide his contempt. "I don't know where he is," he said. "I haven't seen him in years."

"Try," the pope said. "Find him, and convince him to come with you to see me. We have some minor matters that we would like to discuss with him."

"If I see him," Louis said, "which is unlikely, I'll be sure to give him your message." He glared at the pope, who smiled wryly. Louis was certain that he saw amusement sparkling in the cardinals' eyes. *So much for cordiality*, he thought.

The pope extended his ring for Louis's kiss. Louis's lips barely grazed its golden bas-relief of Saint Peter in a fishing boat. He straightened and stepped backwards, nodding his farewell.

"Your Holiness," he said, "thank you for seeing me, and for

your consideration." The pope nodded absently. Louis turned to the cardinals. "Eminences," he said.

Cardinal Fredoli waved briskly, not so much in farewell as in dismissal. De Gui and the others ignored him.

Louis stopped at the door to glance back at the gathered ecclesiastics. Pope John had leaned toward Fredoli to whisper behind a cupped hand. The other three cardinals sat quietly. The scribe had carried his notes to de Gui, who had fixed his cold, reptilian gaze upon Louis's departure.

Louis shuddered as he pushed through the door.

The priest who had welcomed him rose from the wooden bench outside the door and silently escorted him out.

As they passed through the vestibule, a peasant sat huddled on a bench, his face lost in the shadowy folds of his cowl. Louis regarded him with curiosity, intrigued by the vague familiarity of the form beneath the cloak. He hesitated and instinctively placed his hand on the pommel of his sword, but the priest coughed impatiently and hurried him through the door.

He departed the Bishops' Palace in a fog. He tried to convince himself that the meeting had gone well. He was, after all, still free. But he feared that it had gone dreadfully.

He wondered about the man in the vestibule. Why would he hide his eyes? What fate would place a suspicious character at the palace at the time of his visit? His scalp tingled with apprehension, and he cast a glance behind him.

No one was following him. He shook his head and tried to calm his fear. He reasoned that if they had wanted to do him harm, they would not have let him leave. With a sigh of relief, he decided that his apprehension was unfounded.

He walked through the streets of Avignon slowly, lost in thought.

Chapter 55

Louis rounded the familiar curve in the road from Carcassonne. He was only minutes from home. He had run along this road a thousand times as a boy. He remembered it as a wide and well–traveled carriageway, brightly lit by shafts of sunlight streaming through the leaves of the beeches and oaks. But now it seemed to him dark and unfamiliar, haunted, and thick with foreboding.

Night was falling, and he was glad. The journey had drained him, and he needed sleep. He hungered for a tankard of wine, but as he pushed open the heavy oak door and peered into the darkened hall, he doubted he would find a drop of it in the old house.

He wondered if his parents had moved to Limoux, to the Marti estate. He wondered again if his father was still alive. He wondered when he would learn their fate.

He showed Alain, his squire since their flight from Mas Deu, to a bedchamber and bid him goodnight.

"Rest well," Louis said. "We'll be up early, and we'll leave for Scotland before noon."

"Tomorrow?" Alain said with a frown. "I thought we were to wait for word from the pope."

"Yes," Louis said with a nod. "That won't be necessary."

"I don't understand."

"I've done what I can do," Louis said. "There's nothing more for me to say, and the pope will make his decision whether or not I am here. He would have me wait for only one thing: my arrest, should he decide against me. I won't give him that."

Alain nodded with relief. "I think that's a good decision," he said.

"The first one I've made in a long time," Louis replied.

Alain shook his head as if to protest, but Louis stopped him with a wave of his hand.

"Good night," Louis said. "Up early."

He climbed the steps to the chamber his parents once shared. He spread his cloak over the pallet of straw and lay upon it. As badly as he wanted to sleep, he fretted over his audience with the pope.

He had lied to the pope. If anyone had told him years ago that he would one day lie to a pope, he would have vehemently denied the suggestion. For most of his life, he would have counted such a sin as mortal, and unthinkable.

He had lied in the defense of sodomites. Surely, God would demand a price for that. Or would he? *Why* would he?

He imagined the Great Orator of the Sermon on the Mount sitting in gold-hemmed, haughty judgment of flawed humanity, exacting the harshest penalties of Levitical law. *Let he who is without sin cast the first stone,* said the Christ who governed his heart. Surely, that Christ would embrace his fallen brethren, despite their human imperfection.

His sin with Mairead was a weakness, to be sure, a moment of passion in a sea of swirling chaos. Surely, that failure paled beside the supreme arrogance of gilded ecclesiastic judges. *Judge not, lest ye be judged,* the same voice echoed from the edges of his consciousness.

I fought for them, he answered to the voice. *I would have died for them.*

His Savior would embrace him, Louis decided. For all of his mistakes – and he knew now that there had been many – he had never intended malice. He had always acted in good faith, according to his conscience. He could be judged naïve, idealistic, and even proud, but never cruel or intolerant. He was willing to live with that truth.

Fitful sleep finally overtook him, but it was punctuated by anxious and troubling dreams.

He woke early in spite of the brevity of his sleep. Warm sunlight filtered through the windows, and he squinted against it as he rose. He wondered at the dream from which he had awoken.

He had dreamed that he sat with his back to a great, gnarled oak in a clearing atop a magnificent highland ridge. An apparition took shape before him, an ancient face with fiery eyes that pierced his troubled soul, and a voice that whispered like autumn winds through the trees.

Embrace the truth, the apparition had said to him, *and go home. They await you there, but time is short.*

He wondered about the meaning of the dream before he shrugged it off and rose to stoke the fire.

He heard Alain stirring about the hall. He descended the stairs to see him slinging his bow and a quiver over his shoulder, heading for the door. Alain turned as Louis appeared.

"I'll get us some food," Alain said.

Louis nodded and said, "I'll tend to the fire."

Alain gave half a smile and waved as he left.

The logs by the hearth were dry and cracked, and covered with dusty cobwebs. They caught quickly, and within minutes, Louis had coaxed the dying embers to a ferocious roar. He threw on his cloak and went outside.

His boyhood refuge by the stream was generally the same, if slightly overgrown with weeds and ferns. The cool water gurgled quietly over the rocks on its journey to the meandering Aude.

They had sat here together, he and Colette, so often and so happily, unaware that they would one day end up married, and she carrying his child. He grinned at the agony his feelings for her had caused him then.

He knelt at the water's edge and plunged his face into the icy current. The shock of it expelled his lingering drowsiness, and in a moment, the coldness numbed his face. When he could hold his breath no longer, he sat up, brushed his hair back, and wiped the water from his eyes.

He knelt gazing into the stream, straining to see his reflection. As the water calmed and the ripples faded, it shimmered into view. In a moment, it grew clear. The sight of his disfigurement jolted him. Even after the months that had passed, the dreadful scar was still alien to him. When spared the sight of it, he still imagined himself to be whole.

He remembered his reflections as a boy, when he imagined himself a man, a noble and powerful knight. That image never bore a blemish, let alone so deep a wound. In a sense, he had always expected his righteousness to keep him undefiled and whole. He knew then that God would be with him always, as long as his heart was pure. Now, he cursed his own naïveté.

He lost track of the time he spent sitting there on the rock at the edge of his stream playing out the memories of his youth, and marveling at the tortuous road that had led him from those days to this day.

Finally, he pushed himself up and strolled back to the house, hoping that Alain had been successful. He was famished.

When he got to the end of the overgrown path that led from the stream to the house, he stopped in alarm. A dark colored horse pawed at the ground where it was tethered outside the stable. As he quickened his pace, he wondered if Alain had returned yet from his hunt.

He turned the corner of the house and stopped short.

"Hello, brother," called a raspy voice. A familiar figure stood yards from the door, feet spread and arms crossed in a defiant posture.

Louis recognized the cloak.

"It *was* you," he said. He walked closer, his eyes fixed on his old, true friend.

"*What* was me?" Victor asked.

"At the palace," Louis replied. "That was you in the vestibule. You hid yourself." He stopped short at the sight of Alain by the corner of the house, prostrate in his own blood. His head was twisted at a gruesome angle, nearly severed. "What have you done?" Louis cried.

Victor grinned contemptuously. His hand moved to his sword, and Louis saw Alain's blood on its blade.

"What are you doing here?" Louis demanded.

"I was about to ask you the same thing," Victor replied.

"I belong here," Louis said.

Victor shook his head slowly. "No," he said. "You don't."

"Why did you kill him?" Louis said, pointing at Alain.

"We didn't need him in the way," Victor said casually.

"In the way of what?"

"This," Victor said, drawing his sword.

"What are you doing?" Louis growled as he placed his hand on the pommel of his own sword. "Do you really think you're going to kill me, too?"

Victor did not answer. He began to circle Louis.

"Why are you doing this?" Louis asked again, drawing his sword.

"Someone's going to do it," Victor said. "It might as well be me."

"Why?"

"You just don't get it, do you?" Victor said. "Even after all this time, you just don't get it. You're still so damned naïve." He spun around and swung his sword hard.

Louis parried and avoided the blade.

"What don't I get?" he asked.

"Did you think you could just come here," Victor said, "and say a few words to the pope, and everything would work out fine for you? All would be forgiven, and everything would just go your way?"

"No," Louis said. He deflected another swing of Victor's blade.

"No?" Victor said, sneering. "So, you came here prepared to die then." He swung again. "Good! Because you will."

"I tried to help you," Louis said. He brought his own sword around, not yet willing to kill Victor, but anxious to disarm him. Victor's deftness in avoiding the blade surprised him.

Victor stepped back and jabbed the tip of his sword into the stony ground. He laughed loudly and shook his head.

"You tried to help me?" he repeated. "Is that the best you can say? That you tried to help me?"

Louis was mystified. "How have I ever wronged you?" he asked.

"You still believe that everything that happens, happens to you, or for you, or because of you," Victor said. "How can one man be so infinitely and stubbornly blind?"

"I don't know what you're talking about!" Louis screamed.

"Why couldn't you just stay where you were?" Victor asked. "Why did you have to come back here, anyway?"

Louis did not answer. He had been flagellating himself over the same question for days. Besides, he was sure now that Victor would try to kill him, and suddenly nothing else mattered. He thought of his unborn child.

"You had everything," Victor said. "It was never enough for you." He circled about Louis, thrusting and jabbing. "You had Colette," he continued. "You had all this. But all you wanted was Crusade."

"Many men wanted Crusade," Louis said evenly. "It was a good cause."

"Then, when you had Crusade, all you could think about was Colette," Victor said. "Almost endlessly, I had to listen to your whining, pining for your darling Colette. And all that time I wondered why I followed you in the first place, why I didn't just stay here and take Colette for myself."

Louis raged. He spun and brought his sword down hard, wanting now to silence Victor for good.

"I loved her, too!" Victor shouted. "You never knew that, though, did you? You wouldn't notice such a thing."

"I suspected," Louis said with a snarl.

"And yet, you still subjected me to your lovesick whimpering," Victor shouted. "You see? It didn't matter to you." He jabbed his sword accusingly. "You suspected, but you didn't care that I might not want to hear it."

"You had no place caring for her," Louis said.

"And neither did you," Victor snapped. "You took a vow. You made a choice! Perhaps it was the wrong one, but you made it. You should have just left it at that. But as usual, it wasn't enough for you!" He lunged furiously at Louis, jabbing at him. His sword glanced off Louis's blade and struck Louis's thigh, cutting through his leggings and drawing blood. Louis winced and leapt backwards.

"Who are you to criticize my decisions?" Louis asked.

"Who am I?" Victor stared in disbelief. "I'm the fool who followed you, supported you, fought for you, and defended you! I'm the idiot who gave up everything just to pursue your dreams with you. Not my dreams; *your* dreams."

"What else were you going to do?" Louis asked.

"Yes," Victor agreed. "What was I going to do? Stay here and watch the woman I loved, the woman who loved you, brood endlessly over the fool who gave her up? Stay here and suffer that hell, all the while slaving for your insufferable father?"

"You had nothing!" Louis exclaimed. "You followed me because you had nothing, and you saw something in it for yourself."

"Yes, I had nothing," Victor said. He stopped circling and stood panting, holding his sword loosely at his side. "That is true. I've always had nothing. But now that's changed. Today, after I kill you, all of this will be mine...my reward for your death."

He lunged again, fiercely, but Louis sidestepped him and jabbed hard into his ribs. The sword pierced Victor's side, and he cried out.

"What will be yours?" Louis asked.

With his arm pressed tightly to his ribs, Victor waved his sword around. "All of this," he said. He brandished the sword then, pointing it at Louis, and added, "In exchange for this."

Victor had made a deal with the pope, Louis realized. He had made a deal with the devil in pope's clothing.

"This land belongs to my parents," Louis said, "and then to me."

"Your parents are dead," Victor said with a sneer.

"Dead!"

"They had the courage not to run," Victor said, "but they died because you didn't, and you ran. They paid your price, until you could pay it yourself."

"Who killed them?"

Victor grinned maliciously. "Who do you think?" he asked.

"You bastard!" Louis cried. His rage blinded him. He lashed out with his sword, but Victor easily deflected the blow.

"After all I did for you!" Louis growled. "This is how you repay me?"

"Think what you want," Victor said. "I don't care. You mean nothing to me now."

"I trusted you," Louis said. "How could I have been so foolish?"

"Finally!" Victor cried. "Finally, you ask yourself that! I thought the day would never come."

Louis wondered if everyone had thought him foolish all along. He certainly felt foolish now, but he could not believe he had been so all along. He tried to pinpoint the moment it had all gone wrong.

"Why didn't you just stay?" Victor asked. "Why didn't you just grow up and see that your life was here, and that your fantasies in the fields by the stream were nothing more than that?"

Louis dropped his sword to his side. His shoulders slumped as a voice inside him echoed Victor's taunt. It was Colette's voice. And in unison with it, he could hear the voices of his parents and his unborn child.

His thoughts raced to the pyres of the inquisition, to the persecution of Templars, and heretics, and anyone else who dared to challenge the Church. He thought of his mother as a little girl, running for her life as her own parents burned. He wondered what had driven him so fiercely to pledge his loyalty and his life to the men who had caused so much anguish.

He reassured himself that his loyalty had been to God, but even that felt hollow to him now.

"You have always amazed me," Victor said. His lips twisted into a snarl. "And I have always despised you. I never really knew how much I did until this moment."

Louis looked skyward and inhaled deeply. A breeze rustled through the trees and blew in waves across the grass. He held the breath for a moment, and then he whispered a prayer for strength. He knew he had to kill Victor if he were ever to see Colette again.

He thought again of his unborn child.

He would tell him one day, when he was old enough, how stupid his father had been, and how much he had risked for his foolish dreams. He would teach him to see past his own boyish dreams to the things that were precious and real. He would raise his son to cherish what he had, and not to sacrifice any of it for fruitless quests.

But first, he would have to kill Victor.

God, forgive me, he prayed as he hoisted his sword. He spun and swung in a sweeping arc, his blade a blur in the air. He braced for that awful sound of steel on bone.

Victor evaded the blow with surprising agility. Louis's blade sliced through air, and its momentum spun him around in an awkward lurch.

He cursed his mistake and prepared for another strike. He felt fleeting relief at not having killed Victor, but he pushed it away and lifted his sword.

Searing pain screamed in his chest, and he pitched forward as if he had been shoved. He gazed with horror at Victor's gleaming, blood–streaked blade protruding from his sternum. His eyes flew wide in stunned disbelief. As suddenly as the blade had appeared, it disappeared as Victor pulled it free.

He staggered and turned to face Victor. He clutched his

chest in a vain effort to stop the blood. His legs went limp, and he fell to his knees.

This is how it ends, he thought in dismay. He stretched a pleading hand toward his executioner, his lifelong friend, to whom he had entrusted his life. He gazed through a suffocating fog at Victor's contemptuous, twisted sneer and his bloody, upraised sword.

His heart screamed for Colette. He cried out to God to stop this madness, to make things right, and to take him home to the son he would never know. His horror faded, and he surrendered to the futility of his plea.

"You may take my life," he said between gasps. "You can take my land. But there's one thing. . .you can't take...and you will never have." He steadied himself with his sword and stifled a cough. "You cannot take my honor."

Kneeling in the place where his dreams had taken root, he closed his eyes and waited for the final blow.

Epilogue

"So, MY FATHER WAS BRAVE," young Willem said. He nodded slowly and picked at the sleeve of his cloak. His crystal blue eyes were doleful. "You never spoke of him like this."

Colette nodded and said, "You never really seemed to want to hear."

"He left us," Willem said. "I never knew him."

"You shouldn't be angry with him," she said. "He was a good man. There are few better."

"He should not have left," Willem replied. "He should have been here with us, if only for you."

Colette nodded sadly. Wisps of her graying chestnut hair framed a face still beautiful despite the rigors of a lifetime of longing and loss. She gazed lovingly at her son and wished that he had met his father.

The resemblance was striking. At twelve years old, Willem could have been his father's twin. When they spoke like this, she was often transported through the decades and the distance to the days she had shared with Louis.

"He did what he knew to be right," she said. "I wish he had been here, too, but more for you than for me. Had you known him, you could hardly be angry with him."

He nodded and said, "I'm still angry with him, but I'm beginning to understand more about the kind of man he was."

She couldn't blame him. Her own anger had nearly blinded her. It was that, really, and not Willem's disinterest that had kept her from these conversations. Over time, many of Louis's finest strengths and virtues grew evident in their son, and her resentment cooled.

"Did he really believe the pope would listen to him?" Willem asked. "Did he always believe that people would just do the right thing simply because he asked?"

"No," she said, "but he always believed in giving them the chance. He believed more than most in the goodness of men."

"To a fault," Willem said.

"Honor and nobility is never a fault, Willem," she replied. "I agree that he might have balanced his idealism with a measure of skepticism, but I would not fault a man for doing what he believes to be right."

He gazed thoughtfully at her for a moment, then said, "You loved him deeply."

She sighed and placed a hand to her mouth.

"So deeply," she said, "that I could have died whenever he turned to leave, and my heart stood still at his every return." She touched a fingertip to the corner of her eye and brushed away a tear. "He was my breath," she said.

Willem nodded and dropped his eyes. "I don't want to be like him," he said.

"I see much of him in you," she replied.

He shook his head and said, "I will not go through life like a wide-eyed lad thinking every man as noble as I. The one thing my father taught me is that lesser men will triumph over noble ideals."

"I suppose that depends on how you measure triumph," Colette countered.

"What do you mean?" Willem asked.

A small smile tugged at her lips. "I suspect," she said, "that had he exchanged his ideals for the comfort of indifference, his life might have seemed, to him, less worth living. I imagine he would have carried a sense of defeat for the rest of his days. He was the kind of man who saw triumph even in the failed defense of honor and truth, and defeat in the failure to act. He lived every day of his life in that manner. I never would have denied him that, even though I sometimes hated it. To do so would have made him less than what he was." She paused and gazed hard at her son. "He was a good man, Willem…the finest I ever knew. You would do well to embrace a measure of his character."

Willem stared at the table top. He bit his lip and tugged at his sleeve.

"The nobles speak highly of him," he said. "It makes me feel proud when they do. But some say he was a fool, when they think I don't hear. That makes me not want to be like him."

"Willem," she said gently, "the men who mattered admired him. What's more, they avenged him."

"What?"

"Your father's compatriots were humbled by his courage. His willingness to go alone to defend their honor in front of the pope inspired them to exact justice for him."

"What did they do?" Willem asked with heightened interest.

"Two of his closest friends, Bérenger Guifre and Ponç de Veneto, took six other knights and risked their lives to travel to Verzeille and find Victor Guyot. They found him living like a tyrant, gorging himself on the abundance of the de Garonne estate, without a care in the world."

"They killed him?"

"I suspect that Victor Guyot might have fared better in the hands of the Inquisition," she said. "Now, I do not revel in the death of any man, but I am pleased that those Templars found justice for your father."

"I have never heard that," Willem said.

"Nor will you ever speak of it," Colette said sternly. "The day may come when agents of the Templars will gain title to that land, and if they do, they will return it to its rightful owners."

Willem's mouth hung open.

"Your father did not die in vain," Colette added.

When he looked at her then, something shone in his eyes that she had never seen before. He was *proud* of his father, and his pride made her heart leap with joy.

Suddenly, his face clouded over again, and she caught her breath.

"I wanted to fight for the Bruce," he said, "just like my father did. But now I won't get the chance."

"It's all right, Willem," she said with a sigh of relief. "It's just as well. Peace will be good for Scotland. The Lord knows that thirty-two years of war have not done it a lot of good."

"But I won't get the chance to be a warrior like my father," he replied.

"So, you *do* want to be like him," she said.

He nodded.

"Well, my son, you *are* like him. Besides, something tells me that despite this peace with England, the clouds of war will long hang over this land. It would please me well to never see you off to battle, but it pleases me far more that you can be proud of your father. No father ever deserved that more, and if he could see it in your eyes as I do now, I know he would think it the finest thing he had ever seen."

Willem smiled widely. It was the smile of a boy who had finally come to know his father, and could love him.

Colette smiled too, but hers was the beam of a woman who, at long last, had caught in the eyes of her son a fleeting glimpse of the man she had always loved. No river of sadness could drown such boundless joy.

You may contact Jack Dixon and find out more about his books at his website:

www.jdixon.net

Also, please visit the Facebook pages for

The Pict
and
Jerusalem Falls

ISBNs

978-0-9817671-3-0	0-9817671-3-3	pbk
978-0-9817671-4-7	0-9817671-4-1	hc
978-0-9817671-5-4	0-9817671-5-X	ebk

3668701R00346

Printed in Great Britain
by Amazon.co.uk, Ltd.,
Marston Gate.